THURSDAY'S CHILD

An Epic Romance

by Joseph Wurtenbaugh

Thursday's Child
An Epic Romance

Joseph Wurtenbaugh

Cover Design by
Manoj Vijayan

The painting depicted on the right side of the cover is "The Last Judgment," painted by Jan van Eyck (approximately 1420-1425), on permanent display at the Metropolitan Museum of Art in New York.

Table of Contents

For Emily Ruth and Anne Jenet

PROLOGUE

The three men stood at the door of the board room.

"It's fool proof," said the one closest to the door, shaking hands. "You've done it again. I knew you would."

"Don't thank me too soon," said the other, smiling. "We've still got to find the lynch-pin. The mechanism." The third man moved silently away from the others.

"Oh, you will," the first responded, pulling a cigar out of his shirt pocket. "How long do you think before we'll be in play?"

"Four months. Six, tops."

"Great," said the first as he left. "Great. Congratulations again. Gotta go." He winked. "Got a date."

The third man had drifted toward a large window on the other side of the room. Now he gazed out at the dingy alley it faced, played idly with his key ring.

"Not my own favorite companion, either," said the other remaining man, coming away from the door frame. "But you've chosen well. You always do. He'll play his part." He looked at the other. "I hope nothing's the matter."

A long silence. "Do you need money? All you need to do is ask."

The man by the window half-closed his eyes, and shook his head side to side. Finally, he answered:

"I'm so tired of the shit," he said. "I'm getting so goddam tired of the shit."

"It won't be much longer," replied the other, trying to sound sympathetic, failing. "We're coming to the end of your own road. Only a few more winding turns, and we'll both have what we want," putting his hand on the third man's shoulder. "It's a promise. In writing. This is not the time to be anything less than unrelenting."

The man by the window did not move or turn, kept playing with his keys, continued looking out the window. A promise; in writing. Sure. Another long silence. "I'm just so god damned tired of the shit."

The other man pulled his hand away. "I understand," he said in a different tone. "But don't forget who you are and where you are; and where you came from; and what is at stake, particularly for you. I have great respect for your ability. But it's my destiny that interests me, not yours. If you are no longer interested in what was offered, just say so. We have an agreement; I intend to abide by it." Something flickered in the third man's eyes. "You'd better remember that."

The man by the window tried not to be intimidated, but he couldn't help himself. He was. "I'm not about to forget any of that," he said finally, hating himself.

"Are you sure?" The third man nodded. "Answer me out loud," the other insisted.

"Yes," he answered dully.

"Good. Good. Then I'll see you in the morning," clapping the other on the shoulder. With that, he was out the door and gone himself.

The remaining man lingered by the window. After a while he sighed, wondering about himself, about everything. What difference did it make, anyway? What was the difference?

Even so, he continued to look out the window. It was a long time before he left.

SEPTEMBER 1989

THE GLEE CLUB

I t was the morning of the autumnal equinox, 9:25 a.m. on a spring-like Tuesday in September in mid-town Manhattan. The only available elevator located on the first floor of the enormous Millroth building was fully loaded and ready to depart to the huge office complexes located on the upper floors. At least, it seemed fully loaded.

"Hold the door!" called out a young woman. Adele Jansen, all five foot, three inches, and 109 pounds of her, squeezed into the compartment. There was a collective sigh, then a grunt, and then somehow, she had wedged herself, nose to pectoral, against another one of the innumerable members of her species who were larger than she. She smiled at her fellow passengers as winsomely as she could. Glowering looks or not, she was too footsore this morning to stay one second longer in that lobby than she had to.

The elevator finally arrived at the twenty-eighth floor, the lowest of the four occupied by the law firm of Hapgood, Thurlow, Anderson, & Davis. Adele looked at her wristwatch – 9:29. On time. Pleased with herself, she squeezed out of the chamber and propelled herself toward the reception desk.

The other passengers in the compartment had already forgotten her. She was, after all, only one more small, pretty girl in a city that abounds with them.

"Any messages?" she asked Christina, the receptionist. The girl smiled back at her.

"Two, Ms. Jansen." Adele picked up the phone memos, glanced at them briefly, and then turned briskly down the hall. A long evenings' work done at home lay in her briefcase. Another long day was beginning.

The young woman striding purposefully toward her office made an interesting appearance. She was attractively dressed in a manner that masqueraded nicely as expensively fashionable. Only a perceptive and knowledgeable observer would have realized that the effect was an illusion, the combined result of simple materials, a superb sense of color, and an artist's flair for design. Her clothes were severely tailored, the lines deliberately ambiguous in places, effectively concealing her figure. All that was readily apparent was that she was not overweight. Her brown hair hung down just a bit closer to her shoulders than severe professionalism would dictate. She looked too small and young to be a member of a law firm. More than once she had been mistaken for someone's daughter or niece.

As Adele walked down the plushly carpeted corridor, deeply ingrained habits took over. She began to review her day's calendar, reminding herself of appointments and reconstructing the priorities of the files she had under review. The office was coming to life as partners, associates, and clerical staff emerged from the elevators, chattered and gossiped, and moved towards their workplaces.

The law offices of Hapgood, Thurlow, Anderson, & Davis were laid out in two rows of cubicles that girded the building. The outer row was occupied by partners and senior associates; generally, the higher the office and the larger the window, the more important the occupant. The inner row was the province of the junior associates. In the halcyon days of the mid-1950s, when the firm first took occupancy of the space, the idea was that every attorney would have his – very definitely "his" back then – own window. The inner row had been intended for the clerical staff. But five decades of relentless expansion had ended that dream. Now the secretaries and word processors were consigned to the center of the building, chained like galley slaves to their terminals. Junior associates occupied the old secretarial offices.

A few feet from her office door, she overheard the rumble of voices behind the closed door of an adjoining office – an inchoate mixture of baritone, bass, and the occasional tenor – chattering about something or other, probably sports. The Glee Club, as she called it privately, was meeting, as it did every morning. She could see them in her mind's eye – a half-dozen young men around the desk; Greg Steuer, the leader in his swivel chair, right leg up and over the desktop, foot dangling. One of the voices sounded louder than the rest.

"The ice maiden cometh," it said, followed by an appreciative group underchuckle.

"It was only one lousy memo," added another, also deliberately loud.

Referring to her, of course, and her famous look-and-feel memo. She stiffened for an instant, then kept going toward her own door, through it, and into her own space.

*

"It wasn't fair," said Willis Rutter, the one who'd spoken about the memo, after she passed. "It was all politics. I could have done what she did. Collishaw never even called me. I never had a chance. They didn't give me that kind of chance." He did not even look around. No one in the room knew enough truth about the actual event to give him the lie.

Right, thought the leader. He surveyed the group – all whining mediocrities or worse. Hapgood, Thurlow had a strict "up or out" policy. What everyone in the room had in common was that none was moving on the vertical axis.

"It wasn't your fault, Willis," someone said. "You don't suck up to the old farts the way she does." Everyone laughed.

"Plus she's under Hoffman's wing," snorted a third. "The ice queen and the ice maiden. Birds of a feather."

"They're going to put her on the Project, you know," someone else said. The whole room looked up, startled. An implicit rule had been broken. They gathered to complain of minor injustices. To articulate an injustice so major, so unspeakably unfair, was taboo.

"Who told you that?" . . . "No one, I'm just saying" . . ."No way" . . ."Not possible" . . . a chorus of disapproval ran around the room. The subject was closed by tacit agreement, the speaker in temporary disgrace.

"What I don't get," Willis added, "is how she gets them to fall for the line. I don't know how she does that."

"I'll tell you how she *doesn't*," another said, and everyone laughed again.

"Right," said the second speaker. "A mossy hymen, for sure."

"Naw. . . naw," said Greg, his foot still over the desk. "No one's a virgin anymore." He paused for emphasis. "Tried it once. . . and didn't like it," and everyone laughed again.

*

Four doors down, Adele sat down in the large judge's chair behind her desk and unpacked her briefcase systematically – laptop computer, the two floppy disks containing the last night's work, and six pages of neat, carefully organized notes. The office she occupied had the same tidy functionality as her briefcase. A large oak worktable stood on the left side of the cubicle, within easy reach of the desk. Approximately twelve large accordion files were placed in an orderly row upon it. Adele's undergraduate and law school diplomas hung three feet above in ordinary black frames. Underneath the diplomas were photographs of her family, standing in four small oval frames – her father and her three older brothers; Buck the eldest, the movie nut, with his children; Jack in the middle, the math teacher, childless and destined to remain so; and Michael the youngest, the stone mason, beside one of those amazing fireplaces that only he could create.

Her desk was organized with the same brisk practicality. The computer work station was on the right side, angled towards her chair. An in/out tray occupied the left corner. A vase – an outrageous porcelain blaze of pink and orange, with an outsized oval bulge at its base – sat in the center, with two white carnations protruding out. The bulge concealed a small clock that Adele kept on time to the second. Only someone with an exquisite sense of color and style could have seen beyond the superficial ugliness of the piece to realize how perfectly it set off the basic starkness of the functional decor. It was one of Adele's two concessions to her own individuality (not counting family pictures, which everyone had). The other hung on the right wall of her office opposite the photographs – a portrait of a middle-aged woman, oils on canvas.

She was still nettled as she sat down to begin her day. *Ice maiden.* So mean, so wrong – so dumb, so ordinary – they always say that. The Cuteness Factor again – the Glee Club members couldn't accept the fact that someone with her youthful looks, who seemed about as a harmless as a schoolgirl, had outdistanced them all. Tough. She had. But "ice maiden"? *Oh, do be serious.*

Grow up, stupid, she said to herself suddenly, adopting the normal harshness of tone she used with herself. *You're going to let it get to you? Boys will be boys, even when they're men.* Wonderful fuzzy animals, taken one at a time. Horrid in groups.

*

"Look, guys," someone said. "We spend too much time talking about her. She's only one more associate." *Oh, yeah, right*, thought Greg.

He'd started the same day she did – going obediently from one department to another, one floor to the next, lectures to the seventeen of them from all the biggies –excitement, curiosity, apprehension unevenly mixed, backgrounds cautiously explored, offers of friendship tentatively extended.

I'll give you the good news, Carolyn Hoffman, a dazzling blonde beauty in her early forties and the senior partner who headed up the intellectual property division, had said when they were all assembled in the conference room on the thirty-second floor. *This is a very prosperous law firm. We have something in the works that is going to ensure our prosperity – something very, very major.* This was the first intimation he, or any of them, had of the Project. *The most junior partner here earned over $600,000 last year. Senior partners earn twice to three times that – and you will be a partner within seven years or you won't be here at all.* She paused and smiled. *Which brings us to the bad news. Look to your right, now to your left. Only one out of every three of you is going to be here seven years from now. I know people have been saying similar things to you throughout your academic career, but this time it's true. Pay attention to me and I'll tell you how to maximize your chances.*

He'd paid little attention. He'd looked around the room, sized up the competition, and decided he was a mortal lock. That was when he first noticed her, with her cutish, almost innocent good looks. *Scratch that one*, he thought. *No way*. Throughout the balance of the day, she asked no questions, said little; the only thing at all distinctive was her habit of taking notes on a laptop computer, inputting so quietly and unobtrusively that no one was disturbed. But she was the only talent in the group of new associates. The other females were dogs.

Long day, he smiled. *Like to go to dinner?* He was tense. Girls had always been a valuable means of relaxation, soft and accommodating, the occasional tears and recriminations notwithstanding.

Sure, she answered. The dinner was light and pleasant. She proved to be a surprisingly lively, cheerful girl. Too bad she didn't have a chance at Hapgood. Later, she offered no resistance when he took her into his arms in the backseat of a taxi, in fact, showed an encouraging amount of enthusiasm. *This*, he thought, *is going to be easy*. He was disappointed, but not discouraged, when she refused to allow him to see her up to the East 60s apartment she shared with another young woman. *Some of them are like that. Even some of the good ones.*

She accepted again when he asked her out three weeks later. But this time it did not go well; a definite coolness, no progress at all, in fact nothing. He was irritated at the little fool. Didn't she understand anything? Didn't she know yet how it all worked? Perhaps she was angry that he'd waited too long, perhaps she wondered if he'd found a little action in the meantime. *But they all have to get used to that.*

After that, zero. *I'm sorry, Greg. I can't, Greg. I don't have the time, Greg.* Finally, he'd gone to her office, confronted her. *What's going on?* She'd looked up from the keyboard on her desk with those big green eyes – they had been so lively that first night, they were so cool now – and met his gaze calmly. *I don't owe you any explanations, Greg. I'm sorry you think I do. We had a good time that one night, but that's all.* He stormed out, burning with resentment, angrier than he'd ever been with a woman. Somehow, some way, the little bitch had judged *him*, found *him* wanting. Who the hell did she think she was?

By then she'd written the look–and–feel memo, as it had immediately become known. The triumph had been complete, style as well as substance. *You think you're biting into a cream puff*, Baxter had said to Richard Collishaw over drinks when it was all over, *and you break your teeth on granite*. If it had been left to him, Collishaw, discreet senior partner that he was, might not have repeated the remark. But there were others present and they were not discreet. The word spread like wildfire. Then came a series of small but noticeable successes; everywhere he went he seemed to be hearing about her. Everything she did seemed to create a ripple. *I don't think she spends any more on clothes than we do*, he heard one secretary say to another, *but there's always something – ya know?* He did know. He knew instantly whom they were talking about.

She was clearly on her way. He was still treading water – sinking, as a matter of cruel fact. *Please rewrite the second section of the brief, Mr. Steuer. It is not up to the standards of the firm. Please put more effort into the answers to these interrogatories, Mr. Steuer. Work of this slipshod character may draw sanctions from the court.* No one used to hand him this crap. He was becoming frightened.

Meanwhile, she came to work every day with that same cheerful smile, the same perpetual good humor, as if nothing set her apart, as if their tracks weren't diverging. He got the same chirpy hello, *Hi, Greg,* she gave everyone else – Willis the Whiner, Josh the Moron, senior partners and junior partners, the rest, as if he'd never kissed her in the backseat of a taxi, as if he were no different than any of the others. And the biggies ate it up. Were they all blind? Couldn't any of them *see?* He could. It was all phony, all a manipulation. Beneath the sparkling facade, the winsome demeanor, Adele Jansen was a cold, ruthless bitch, the kind who'd do anything to get ahead. He'd heard about that kind of woman. Now he'd met one. She'd used him, he felt, though he was unable to say exactly how.

By that time, a few of the younger associates were meeting every morning in his office to gossip and complain. A Whiffenpoof society, they all knew, though no one said that out loud. Out loud they complained about firm politics, bad luck, opportunities handed to others. Greg had nicknamed her "Ice Maiden" one day. It fit in with Carolyn Hoffman as Ice Queen. They all laughed. He discovered that he was not the only one who was sick with envy of her.

*

Cut it out, dummy, she thought suddenly. *Forget it.* What did any of them matter? She was wasting time on them she did not have to waste. Time instead to get on with the day and construct her schedule.

She laid out the contents of her briefcase on the desk. First, the program and booth map of the Webmaster Arts Expo, now in full session at the Garden. She had spent the better part of the last two evenings there, walking, making notes, introducing herself, doing more walking, on rare occasions passing out business cards – in general, hoping lightning would strike, and, in the meantime, walking her feet off.

What a waste. What a big, dumb waste.

Well, what did you expect, stupid?

*

This is one bad night, the young man standing in the deserted booth had thought at about 10:45 the night before.

At least, if you struck out at COMDEX or CES, the Consumer Electric Show, you were spending a week in the winter in Las Vegas, surrounded by sex and glitz. You could walk down the aisle and watch the junior executives standing in line for autographs – Miss January, Miss June – sometimes the whole damn calendar. Get an autograph yourself, if you liked. Spangled booths all around, major players, big money. You had a feeling you'd arrived. If you failed there, you were at least striking out in the big leagues. Here – a large, drafty hall, sawdust underfoot for traction, a million struggling start-ups, only a few of the big publishers in evidence showing off their futuristic stuff, more for political than business reasons. No centerfolds.

But even that was not the worst. The worst was to wind up, by sheer chance, across the aisle from the hit of the show, probably the last twenty years' shows, the all-star, the future actualizing itself in an 8 x 10 booth. He looked sadly at that booth. Still thronging, still twelve deep, the crowd growing even though it was only fifteen minutes until the close for this evening. It had been that way all week long. Definitely not the right place to be, across the aisle from that.

Only one consolation this evening. He wasn't the only one having a bad night.

He'd been watching the girl for over forty minutes now. At first, she'd been waiting patiently on the left side of the crowd; it took her a few minutes to realize that the line was getting larger, not smaller, that she was making no progress. Then she circled around to the right, but had no better luck. No one was making room this evening, at least not around that booth. She didn't give up – back to the left, then the right again, like a little terrier repetitively trying the front and back doors of its master's house.

He had her pegged for a college freshman or sophomore. Kind of interesting, really; jeans and a loose-fitting sweatshirt. Finally, she tried elbowing herself through the crowd. *No way*, he thought, smiling. One of the men standing ahead of her turned around, said something, scowling. *Hey, c'mon, fella, give her a break*, he thought to himself.

Now she was standing in the middle of the floor, the most eloquent look of total exasperation on her face, cute in spite of herself. Suddenly, she turned and caught him watching her. He smiled and shrugged. She grinned herself, shrugged herself, and started over to the booth. As she neared, he realized that she was a bit older than he'd thought at first.

"Not having much luck tonight, are you?" he said consolingly.

"No," she agreed. "I knew it would be crowded, but not like this." She fell silent; the two of them gazed at the throng at the next booth. "Is it really that good?" she asked.

"Yes," he answered without any hesitation. "I went over two mornings ago before the doors opened. Fantastic. I've never seen anything like it."

"Oh, well," she said, noticing the wistfulness in his eyes, looking around at the empty booth, thinking of something kind to say, "maybe they're just lucky."

"Indeed they are," he answered quietly, "lucky to be geniuses." Her head swivelled in surprise; he met her eyes directly. "Nice guys. Maybe a little nerdy, but then that's true of most of us engineers."

She smiled again; then, "Well, let's make the best of it. Can I see what you guys brought? I mean," she went on, her eyes dancing, "even though I didn't make a reservation."

"Oh, yeah, right, exactly. You're supposed to take a number and wait your turn, but I'll let it go this time. I'll just clear all the corporate spies out of here and boot it up." Grinning, he did just that. "Everything you want in a graphics package," he said. "Fairly conventional, but with some wrinkles of our own." He explained a few of them to her, working the keyboard as he did.

"Can I try something?" she asked.

"Sure."

She bent over the keyboard, frowning in concentration. Her fingers flew over the keyboard. *Wow*, he thought, *she's good*. Lost in thought, bending over the counter into the booth, she was oblivious to her clothing, pinched against her waist. He wasn't. There was a nice, compact little body underneath the baggy clothes, with some interesting, well-proportioned curves. The bad night was getting better by the second.

"Oh. . . I see," she said, looking at the display. "That's some subroutine. Now. . ." – frowning – ". . . let me try this."

"You really know what you're doing," he said, in a different tone. "Are you majoring in engineering? Or computer science?"

She looked up, her eyes dancing again. "Neither. Actually, I *had* a double major – political science and art history. At Syracuse." She paused. "I'm a lawyer on Wall Street. I'm twenty-five years old."

"Oh," he said, his surprise apparent, "I'm sorry."

"Don't be. It happens all the time. Anyway, it's my own fault. I came dressed in the uniform you guys wear. Tomorrow," she said, looking at the adjacent booth, her face set with determination, "it's going to be a cocktail dress and pearls."

"You may come tomorrow, but you won't see that."

"*What?*" she cried.

"Yeah. Sorry," he said. "They're going public. Didn't you know? This is part of the road show. A lot of those guys in line are financial managers. They're packing it up a day early and going to the Midwest."

"Rats! Damn it!" she exclaimed.

"Look. . .if it's that important, you could talk to their investment manager." He pointed to a middle-aged man standing off to one side. As if on cue, the man turned his head and met her eyes, held them for a moment. "Do you know him?" the young man in the booth asked. It had seemed as if she did.

"No," she said, shaking her head, her face a picture of frustration, "and I can't really justify any priority, either. If it's going to be a public company, it's already got lawyers. The ones that haven't are the reason I'm here." She stared at it for another long moment.

"Oh, well," she sighed, then turned back towards him. The program he'd demonstrated was still on the screen. "That's really good," she said quietly, then looked up at him, shrugged, and made a small moue. He grimaced in return. *She understands*, he thought.

"Look," he said, acting on impulse, "this isn't a great night for either one of us. Could I buy you a drink?"

"It's tempting," she said, "but I have to work tomorrow." She studied him, thinking. "But. . . if you called me at my office some time, we could work something out."

"I can't," he said. "I'm going back to California the day after tomorrow."

"Oh," she answered, lifting an eyebrow, "*oh*. I see." The young man went red. "Kind of a fast worker, aren't you?" she added softly.

"Not at all," he said, still embarrassed. "I only wanted some company."

She closed her eyes and put her hand in front of her prayerfully. "Oh, wow! One guy like you in the whole wide world and you're standing in front of me! What a lucky, lucky day!" She opened her eyes and cocked her head, smiling, sliding her lower lip flirtatiously under her teeth.

"All right, all *right*," he admitted. It was fun to be regarded as a womanizer, particularly because he wasn't. His romances occurred as most do in real life: after a slow process of mutual recognition. "There's no harm in trying, is there?"

"Absolutely not. That's what makes it interesting." She looked around one more time. "But I do have to go." She gave him a small wave with her fingers, pulled a business card out of her jeans, dropped it on the counter, picked up some of the slicks from the counter, and turned to leave.

"Hey! You! You!" He glanced at the card – *Adele Elizabeth Jansen,*

Associate, Hapgood, Thurlow, Anderson, & Davis – "Adele! Wait!" he called.

"Yes?" she asked.

"Thanks for the time. I'll call you if I come back to the town. And who knows? Maybe the company. . ."

She nodded, smiling. "Right. Maybe the company. . ."

*

A nice guy, she thought the next morning, sitting at her desk, scanning the slicks. But she hadn't gone to the Software Arts Expo to meet nice guys. *Face facts, dummy. It was a disaster.* She'd squandered three nights and 150 dollars and missed the only exhibit there that was important.

That poor guy in the empty booth. She'd almost accepted the invitation to the drink (if not the other implied one). As the program ran, a rush of sympathy had poured through her. She could envision the hundreds of man-hours that had gone into devising those small improvements, the subtle twists – and it was all for nothing. Dealer's shelves were crowded with established products. There were hundreds of thousands more in use. No way that their little program could penetrate that barrier. No way – she could tell he knew that – and he'd had to stand there and watch the future stampede by him.

All the more amazing, then, what he'd said. *Indeed they are, lucky to be geniuses.* Genuine compliments between software gurus are as rare as they are between opera singers. *It must really have been something*, she thought. *And you missed it. You idiot.*

Oh, well, she sighed, folding over the program. *Other days will come. Better days. Johnson and Jansen; we don't quit and we don't lose.* She checked her calendar on the laptop for the next one – two and a half weeks, the IEEE conference on nanochips. Much harder than this one; software she knew, she'd been computer literate for a decade. She didn't know beans about circuit engineering. She'd written Jack for an elementary book. But she'd be there anyway, listening, visible, charming – this time in a cocktail dress and pearls.

She shook her head, thought of the little group four doors down the hall. What hilarity there'd be, what scorn, if they knew how many of these conferences, seminars, trade shows she attended. The idea of a second-year associate doing practice development on her own; it really was ludicrous, stupid – she could see that herself.

But still she went. Let the Glee Club gossip and stew, worry and sweat, about the politics of the Project, who's in, who's out. Adele Elizabeth Jansen was looking for projects of her own.

*

Four doors down the hall, the morning session was breaking up. Two guys had to go up to the thirty-first floor for a closing. Outside, Josh the Moron drifted down the hall towards Adele's office, carrying the same old torch he'd been toting for over two years now. Josh wasn't going to get even as far as the backseat of a taxi. Anyone could see that.

Greg became momentarily reflective before his own day started. When had he actively begun to hate her? He could not be sure. He only knew when the last straw had dropped. About two months before. He'd finally wangled an invitation to one of the parties Carolyn Hoffman threw every Friday night when she was in town. Well, not exactly "wangled;" she'd passed him in the corridor, eyed him, suggested he come by. He'd become excited. Gossip about those parties was the first gossip anyone heard when they joined the firm. Everyone who was anyone, financially, theatrically, or politically showed up there sooner or later – so the story went. Make the right connection there and you were set. Finally, his chance had come.

It was as advertised. The penthouse was massive. It seemed as if every showgirl and model in New York was there; also, visiting hotshots on the Project, and a host of other biggies. Muted light, soft music, the best to eat and drink. It was irritating as hell to see Adele there – she'd got someplace first again – but satisfying to see how outclassed she was by the competition (not that it seemed to bother her, the little fool).

He'd stayed later and later. Finally, he was the only one left. He realized the invitation had not been coincidental. He departed the next morning, completely elated.

He'd always known how to handle women, had handled this one perfectly, at the same time committing to memory every one of Carolyn Hoffman's glorious curves. A great night, a breakthrough. Maybe even his passport to the Project. The failure of the firm to realize that that's where he had belonged all along was (in his opinion) the whole problem. He was a big-picture guy, a builder, a doer. It was all this petty detail, the morass of minutiae, that had mired him down.

Two days later, first thing on a bright Monday morning, he received a memorandum from Carolyn Hoffman. Along with two other associates, he was going to be reporting to – supervised by – Adele Elizabeth Jansen. Incredible; the scratches on his back were still fresh. He couldn't believe it. She'd been anointed – *anointed!* – no question any longer – and at his expense.

He went up to the thirty-second floor, asked for an interview, and was admitted at once. *Why did you want to see me?* she asked from behind her desk.

This memorandum, he answered.

What's that to you? she said, in a cold, neutral voice without any of the reaction he'd expected. Ice Queen, for real. Coming up here had been a mistake, he knew already, but there was no going back.

Because I don't like reporting to Rebecca of Sunnybrook Farm, he answered, trying to match her evenness of tone. She smirked in response.

Oh, I agree she's naïve, Greg. Very naïve. I know that. But she'll learn. Believe me, I have plans for her, which was satisfying to some extent. The little bitch would not have liked at all the tone in Carolyn's voice if she'd been able to hear it.

Then why have you done this?

Don't you know? Don't you really know? she asked, and now she was smirking at him.

The thought came unbidden to his mind – *because she's brilliant.* He would never repeat it out loud, never think it again if he could possibly avoid it. *No,* was what he did say out loud.

Because she proves she can handle it, day by day, Carolyn answered, going in for the kill. *And you prove you can't – day by day.*

Didn't Friday night mean anything to you? he asked, hating himself as he did so. He sounded like too many girls he'd known, when the time had come to give them the bad news, to kiss them off and move on.

Friday was Friday, Greg, she answered, the contempt evident in her voice. *Today is today. Even Rebecca would know that.* She turned down to her desk.

He went back to his own floor completely humiliated, his mind made up. This was no place for a guy with his kind of moxie, that was the whole problem. Carolyn didn't know it, but he'd had a long talk with someone he'd met at her party. The moment he was back in the office, he picked up the phone. In a quarter hour, his plans were set. He was getting out.

*

Enough of this; onto the current files. Lawton, the truly dreadful divorce case that she was stuck with because one of the particularly antiquated old farts on the thirty-second floor thought that it needed a "woman's" touch, God damn his eyes; the really interesting Italian DVD piracy claim; and the others. Set the priorities.

O.K., do it first; force yourself – review and transmit the Lawton affidavits as soon as the express delivery arrived from Bermuda. Because of all the files on the desk, that was the only one she truly hated. If she left it to last, she might not do anything at all, and that poor maid she'd confronted yesterday deserved that much attention, even if the rest of them did not. Sighing, she picked up Lawton and was ready to begin when a large shadow darkened her doorway.

She looked up at Josh Palmdale looking gravely down. The tea tray had arrived at the same time he did.

"Coffee?" he asked.

One of H. T. A. and D.s' (as the associates referred to it) quainter and more popular customs was the formal service of coffee, tea, and related beverages twice a day, at ten and four. "Formal" was perhaps too strong a word. The tray came around with real (stainless-steel) silverware and polyurethane china cups.

"A diet cola, thanks," said Adele. In over two years, Josh had not yet noticed that she was almost a cola-holic, taking her caffeine sweet. She neither liked nor disliked him. Tolerance was the right word. She had made her feelings – or more accurately, the absence thereof – clear enough, but still he came into her office nearly every morning. Did he know that people he thought were his friends called him Josh the Moron? Would it make any difference to him if he did know?

"Where were you last night?" he asked without more formality.

"Over at the Webmaster Arts Expo," she answered, concealing a flash of annoyance. *As if it's any of your business. One of these days, Josh . . .*

He grunted. He was one of those people who project such absolute self-assurance, such an unshakable sense of self-importance, that people tend to accept them initially at their own evaluation. She had been mildly taken in by him at first. So had many of the others. But it soon became evident his capabilities were markedly inferior to any of the other young lawyers' in the firm. For a time, Adele had been privately puzzled as to how he had obtained the job in the first place. Finally, she learned that he was a legacy of a sort, that his father, a much more capable man, was a major practitioner in the Washington, D.C. area, that the old boy network had arranged this opportunity for Josh, in the hope that his breeding would tell, sooner or later – if not, alternatively, his connections. Josh had apparently accepted all this largess as the natural order of the world.

Worse. He had been assigned the office next to Adele's when they first began practice. Worse yet: he evidently had a yen for women like her. After his initial direct approaches had been rebuffed, he had developed, in lieu of an acceptance of the reality, a concerned, solicitous manner towards her that he rationalized as a protective, unselfish attitude. He pictured himself as noble and altruistic; he was either unaware, or indifferent to, the childish possessiveness that lay at its heart. She was fully aware of it.

"Why'd you go there?" he continued.

"It had some interesting exhibits," she lied casually. Even if she had confided in Josh, he would not have understood.

Because the Glee Club is right about one thing. It is − was − only one memo. Because if nothing else happens, that's all it'll ever be. I'll be right back on the same escalator as everyone else. Because too much time has already gone by.

"What else is up?" he continued. He had settled into the chair across from her desk without being invited.

"Nothing much," she said. As usual, it was more trouble than it was worth to shoo him off. "Typical day. Not enough time and too much to do in it. I've got to get the Lawton affidavits out today, time's running. I hate that case."

"I don't know why," shrugged Josh. "One billable hour's the same as another. If I were you −"

The phone rang. Adele picked it up.

"Ms. Jansen?" said the switchboard operator. "Stand by for Ms. Hoffman."

A VIEW OF THE HARBOR

"**A**dele." Carolyn Hoffman's phone voice was, as always, firm and inflectionless.

"Yes, Carolyn?"

"Who's that?" asked Josh.

"It's the Ice Qu– it's Carolyn Hoffman," Adele answered, her hand over the speaker. "You'd better leave."

He did, reluctantly. His only contact with the senior partners of the firm came in the form of interoffice memos attached to files sent to him by junior partners.

In the meantime, Carolyn had gone on: "Are you available about 10:30 this morning? For a conference in my office? Adele?"

"I'm here, Carolyn. And I am available." Of course, she was available. The interrogative form of the command was a polite fiction. The million-and-one other things she had to do would have to wait.

"Good. I'll see you then. The conference is with Jenet Furston." The receiver went abruptly dead.

Adele glanced at the clock in the oval vase. It was already 9:50. She arose from her chair and closed the door; no more uninvited visitors. When the express mail arrived from Bermuda ten minutes later, she reviewed the affidavits and dictated a brief cover letter to the deputy district attorney.

By then, it was 10:25. She logged the time, picked up her laptop, and rode the elevator four flights up to Carolyn Hoffman's office.

*

Carolyn Hoffman's office was one of the prerogatives of power, located on one of the corners of the thirty-second floor of the Millroth building, with a magnificent view of two sides of the harbor. The two inner walls were wood panelled. One was covered with various autographed photographs of Carolyn with politicians and show business celebrities. In front of one window stood a small round conference table, filled to the point of overflowing with files, binders, stapled documents in mild disarray – the visible embodiment of the Project. An overlarge mahogany desk in the center of the room faced a small alcove in which a leather-covered sofa sat, with an oak-and-glass coffee table in front of it. An ornate tea service stood on the coffee table – large, monumental furniture, mildly oppressive.

Carolyn Hoffman and Jenet Furston, a gray-haired, late-sixtiesh woman only three or four inches taller than Adele, were seated on the couch, teacups and saucers in front of them. Two of the most important women in New York City.

"...do not intend to postpone or cancel my trip," Jenet was saying. "Of course, I'm going to go."

"But this is *NATPE*," Carolyn explained, in the deliberate, patient tones of a teacher lecturing a backward child. "NATPE. It hasn't been in New York forever. It's never been in November. It is too important to you. You are too important to it. You can't–"

"I can and I will, Carolyn," Jenet answered primly. "I've attended enough of these conventions. My presence or absence isn't going to make any difference to anyone. There will be tents and circuses enough without me."

"Some really major events are going to happen that week," said Carolyn. She knocked on the table. "If all goes well. There are people I think you should meet. There are definitely people who want to meet you. I'd urge you to reconsider this."

"I have considered it. I'm not going to change my plans," Jenet replied. "I believe we've talked more than enough about this, Carolyn." She looked up, saw Adele, and smiled broadly. "Ah, the ubiquitous Adele, with her even more ubiquitous laptop. It's a pleasure to see you again, dear."

Adele smiled back. "It's nice to see you, too, Jenet." A completely genuine smile; she liked Jenet Furston, knew that Jenet liked her.

They had more in common than friendship, though Adele had never found the right occasion to mention it. Their families had actually crossed paths. She had heard of the Furston name long before she had come to New York City. The fortune which Jenet had inherited had been founded in the timberland and along the early railroads that ran through the same upstate country from which Adele came. There was still plenty of Furston property there, plenty of rich people with the Furston name.

In fact, when she had casually mentioned meeting Jenet to her father, he had recalled that her mother had done a portrait on commission for a Furston sometime in the long, long ago. Adele had been curious enough to rummage through the meticulous catalogues her mother had kept on one of the rare weekends when she was home, in the off-chance that the subject had been Jenet herself. It turned out that there had indeed been a commission, but the only description of the painting her mother had left was its title, "Mother and

Child," so it obviously wasn't Jenet. For all her warmth and graciousness, Jenet Furston was childless.

Carolyn only nodded. "Sit down, Adele." She turned again to Jenet. "Perhaps I haven't made myself clear. This is extremely important. The opportunity will not come again. The Furston Press has a lot of prestige in this industry. It may not have worked out the way you planned, but –"

"Enough, Carolyn," Jenet interrupted genteelly. "I understand what you are saying. I appreciate your advice. But since I pay you well enough for it, I don't feel obligated to take it always." She picked up her tea, sipped. "*Please*, Carolyn," she said, softly.

"I don't mean to go on and on about this," Carolyn answered, in the same soft tone, "but this is a unique occasion. I know what you think of your execs, but –"

"I think the world of the two of them, they do as well as I do most years, and there were popping corks and shouts to high heaven when I told them I wouldn't be there and they'd have some freedom of action. Carolyn," she said, with the slightest inflection of steel, "I really appreciate your concern. But I have made my decision. Adele," she went on, somehow addressing both of them, "I'd like us to talk about why Adele is here."

Carolyn opened her mouth, closed it, then sighed and spoke. "There's something Jenet would like you to do," she said wearily. "What was the agenda number, Jenet?"

"Number 6." Jenet paused. "Thomas Bryant Newcombe."

"Who is he?" asked Adele.

"That's a much harder question to answer than you'd think, Adele. In a word, he's a writer. He works for us on a fairly regular basis as an independent contractor – editing on assignment, screenplays, that sort of thing. He's become one of our most important resources."

"There are a lot of people like that," Carolyn said, impatience in her voice. "They hang around the fringes of the industry. They do a little of this, a little of that; somehow they get by. Not much more. Intellectual riff-raff, in a phrase. Hardly worth the time of a chief executive." She smiled and sighed. "Jenet has the largest collection in the City."

Jenet looked sharply at Carolyn, then turned her head to Adele. "Carolyn's right, of course, generally speaking," she said, "but this man is different. It's not too much to say that he's unique. He does things no one else can do."

She went on in explanatory fashion. "For example, what he's doing right now. We have had a long, very successful association with a person – I have to be discreet. Let us say, the author of one of the better-known series of

Joseph Wurtenbaugh

character mysteries written in the last two decades. They're not precisely to my own taste. But the public can't seem to get enough of the sleuth. Unfortunately, this person's invention seems to be dried up. That's hardly unique. When it happens, we hire – if the name writer lets us – someone to carry on – if we can find one good enough. We call him an outside editor, but that's a euphemism. Basically, it's a ghost writer for a professional. It's a sensitive subject, for obvious reasons.

"That's one example. It's not a cut and dried thing; there are all kinds of little emergencies all the time. Of course, in television and film production it's almost a constant; we always need a screenplay or a teleplay doctored. You get the idea."

"So, this Thomas Newcombe is that type," Adele said.

"Tom Newcombe, to be precise. He goes by Tom. Yes – not just another one, but definitely our best – in fact, the best we've ever had, probably the best anyone has ever had. I said unique and I meant it. He seems to be able to pick up anyone's style in mid-paragraph and write it better than they can themselves and twice as fast. And yet always with his own originality, no matter what the format. It seems to come as naturally to him as breathing."

She took a sip of tea and went on: "He's not just the best contract writer we have, actually. He's probably the best writer we work with, period."

"That's odd," said Adele. There was the obvious question. "Then why – "

"–doesn't he publish his own work under his own name and become rich and famous?" Jenet shook her head; her hands fluttered up to her shoulders in a gesture of helplessness. "Or simply work more and become rich? I don't know, Adele. He does just enough to get by – and he actually seems to prefer the anonymity. It's a real help with screenplays. There's no problem at all with the Guild."

"The problem is that we are wasting time on an individual like this when there is so much to do," Carolyn said with unfeigned exasperation. "Jenet, really."

"Has he ever done anything in his own name?" Adele asked before Jenet could answer Carolyn. She was becoming curious.

A cloud passed over Jenet Furston's face. "Yes. Four volumes of poetry. We've published them all, the last one four years ago. It was the first of them that brought him to my attention."

"Were they any good?" Adele asked.

"One woman's opinion? I think all four were superb. I think he should have won four Pulitzer Prizes. I think it's the best stuff anyone's done in several decades. If he paid the slightest attention to self-promotion or to promoting his

27

work, he'd have a national reputation by now. But he doesn't do anything." She put her teacup down.

"Three years ago, someone noticed his second book at the MacArthur Foundation. They got very excited. They didn't know how to contact him, so they wrote to me. I got very excited." Frustration was seeping into her voice. "Something like that – a genius award – the publicity – it would do wonders for him. I sent on the material and the application." She paused. "He never bothered to write them back." A small bitter smile pursed her lips. "Of course, that only made them more interested. The director phoned me. They set up an interview in our offices. Two people made a special trip. They waited three hours. He didn't come."

She shook her head. "He doesn't review books, he doesn't give readings, he doesn't have an agent, he has no interest in literary politics. I respect him for that last, actually. But you must do something – and he doesn't do anything. He could get all the support he needs, but. . ." Her voice trailed off. The room was silent for a moment. "That's what he should be doing instead of all this contract writing nonsense," Jenet added softly, speaking almost to herself.

"What do you want from me?" asked Adele, slightly bewildered.

The small, gray-haired woman remained lost in her thoughts for a few moments longer. "As I said, he owes us a manuscript," she said finally. "A mystery. And I want to be sure it's delivered on time. In fact, I'd like to have it two weeks early if that's at all possible."

"That, Adele, is the only reason you have been asked up here this morning," Carolyn sighed.

"Has he ever been late performing?" asked Adele.

"No," said Jenet. "He's never late. That's almost the problem." She was half-musing, thinking out loud.

Adele was becoming puzzled. "I'm not sure what it is you want me to do, Jenet."

Jenet Furston sighed, then straightened her shoulders and sat up. "I'm sorry, Adele. I'm not being at all clear. From an ordinary business perspective, I want the book early because I'm getting pressure from the name author about it. It isn't due according to the contract for another three weeks, but he's planned a vacation in Bermuda about that time and he'd like to get started on the rewrite before he leaves. You can probably guess I'm dealing with a pretty spoiled person.

"By the way, by the time he's done rewriting he'll have convinced himself that he wrote every word – and the material will be in considerably worse shape than when Tom turns it over to us. *C'est la vie.* That's my problem." She continued. "But I do have an ulterior motive here. There's more going on than just business."

She sighed. "It's foolish to hide my opinion. Tom is an extraordinarily talented man – the one in a generation, maybe even the one in a century type. He is also, unfortunately, an extraordinarily unhappy, troubled person. It's a very difficult thing to explain; he conceals it well; most people don't notice at first. But there's a darkness that's always with him, a sadness of some kind. It bothers me very much."

Carolyn rolled her eyes toward the ceiling. "Is this a recent thing?" Adele asked.

"No. He's been that way for as long as I've known him. I've never seen him smile – not really smile – or open up, or laugh at anything."

"I think someone is conning you with a little display of theatrical melancholy, Jenet," said Carolyn. "It wouldn't be the first time. Come on."

"No, Carolyn, there are other things. The way he works, for instance. At least the way he used to work: monstrous 17 and 20-hour days, day after day, that go on and on and on until he's exhausted. It's as if he's driven."

"What's wrong with that?" remarked Carolyn. "Sounds like we could use some associates around here with the same problem." She smiled a completely artificial, toothpaste smile at Adele. "Present company excepted."

"No, you couldn't, Carolyn, at least not for long. This is some sort of compulsion, very unhealthy. At any rate, I heard about it and I said something about it. He used to use one of our vacant offices. Now he never does. That's another reason I want Adele to talk about this. Then he'll be gone for days, weeks, incommunicado. With a different person, I wouldn't think much of that, but it bothers me with Tom."

"Just another bewildered young man in search of his sexual identity, I'll bet," said Carolyn.

Jenet looked over her glasses at her. "He has no doubts whatsoever about his sexual identity, Carolyn. He's seduced too many of my junior editors for there to be any question of that."

"Wine, women, and song?" asked Carolyn, raising an eyebrow.

"Perhaps. Some people think so; there are extraordinary rumors. But I doubt it; I can't see Tom carousing or roistering ever, he's not that type."

"Drugs?" asked Adele.

"No. That's another thing. He's almost compulsive about his commitments. He honors them to the letter. Including contracts. That's why I can count on the book being on time. I think."

"So Jenet. . . Jenet," said Carolyn, exasperated, "what precisely is the problem here? Why are we spending time on this?"

Jenet put down her teacup and looked at directly at her. "The same old story, Carolyn; nothing I can describe in so many words, nothing I can quantify. Instinct." Carolyn smiled a sad, patient smile; Jenet turned her head toward Adele.

"I am very concerned about Tom. Something in his personality is stealing his life; whatever private war he's fighting with himself, he's losing. When he first came to New York, he spent a lot of time in our offices. He hardly ever comes in anymore. He hasn't brought us any work of his own in over four years now; all he does for publication are these contract jobs and he seems to do less of that all the time. He's out of touch more. I worry about him; I worry quite a lot. It's hard not to."

"Jenet," said Carolyn Hoffman, her impatience veiled only by thinnest cloth, "this is another one of your projects, isn't it? There have been so many one-in-a-centuries. Tom Newcombe is probably another young fool who thinks he's Dylan Thomas or John Berryman reborn. I am sympathetic, Jenet – I truly am – but I have to be concerned about the amount of the time this is consuming when time has become so scarce. And I have heard this so often before.

"With NATPE coming up and you not being there, there isn't –"

*

The same old story, Adele thought. The view here was magnificent. From one large window, the George Washington Bridge was visible in the distance, the sun silvering the water in back; in the other direction, the Statue of Liberty. As Adele watched, a large, weather-beaten freighter was coming up the channel, home from the sea, probably bound for New Jersey. Everything bright and glowing – the view was a postcard. And then, suddenly, it was with her again – a feeling of distance, estrangement – something that came over her every once in a while, during the rare intermissions from running. It had nothing to do with the impostor's syndrome, for she knew by now she was no impostor. But what was she doing here? How could she possibly–?

Small town dads have been doing this for a century, I guess. You put your little girl on the train for the big city. Then you kneel and pray. . . that heaven will, indeed, protect the working girl, her father had toasted at the party the night before she left. Everyone laughed – her older brothers, high school friends that were still in town, everyone who mattered to her (except Bri and his wife, posted to Zaire and unable to attend) – everyone. The bar exam was behind her. Her last summer in the town where she'd been born.

The next day she boarded the train – it seemed more thematic than flying – and rode into the Big City to start her life. The job was sensational, but she knew no one; a half-day's acquaintance with the young woman to whom a roommate matching service had introduced her, a few family friends of a different generation to call when she was settled. The City was bigger, faster, somehow more solid, heavier, than anything she had anticipated.

And colder. And lonelier.

She'd first seen this view, first visited this office twenty months before, shortly after the impact of the look-and-feel memo. When she'd left, she'd had a mentor, Carolyn Sims Hoffman – a big step forward. It had been nine o'clock on a January morning nineteen months before; the rising sun burnished everything in the room. *Room decor by Midas & Co.*, she'd thought that day, not unkindly. Not furnished exactly to her own taste, but what potential! What possibilities! The things her mother could have done had she sat behind that desk, the person she could have been had she had these prerogatives! *Thursday's child*, her mother had said so often as she brushed Adele's hair and braided it for school. *You were born on a Thursday, pumpkin. You have far to go.* Yes. Although her mother had not taken that advice herself.

How odd, how very odd it was to be standing here looking over the great city. To have come so far.

And not know exactly why.

*

The irrevocable self-commitment that had led her to this place of large horizons had been made on one momentous day during her twelfth year. Most such resolutions thaw and melt in the heat of adolescence. Hers had gelled and hardened. In the common ways, she was no different than any other high school girl, a little more attractive than most, a lot brighter than almost everyone. She had one special boyfriend, but dated others, sighed over popular idols like all the rest. Her closest friends were aware of the persistence with which she pursued her goals. The other students, most of whom had known her since childhood, paid her no special attention, took her for granted. But even then, she always finished what she started. She became indispensable to the yearbook editors and dance planners, and a terror in field hockey despite her size.

Although she had inherited her mother's gift in close to full measure – the same eye, the same hand, the same flair for color, a genuine talent of undetermined size – she rejected absolutely the choice of lifestyle artistry represented, reducing it instead to the status of avocation. Objective, quantifiable accomplishments – grades, test scores, field hockey wins – were what mattered. She won the Art Prize three years running – she was not permitted to compete in the fourth – but it was the utility of the achievement as resume material that she valued, not the prizes. By the time she was a senior, she had made more than a little impression – *cool, calm, super bright Adele Jansen* was what the editor (Bri, of course, also her boyfriend, also her debate partner) had printed underneath her picture in her senior yearbook. No one jeered. The description accurately reflected the opinion of most of her classmates. She had been embarrassed, but pleased.

That same year she won a major Regents scholarship and decided to enrol at Syracuse. Her father, a gentle, bookish man, had long been of two minds about Adele. He loved her and took enormous pride in her achievements. He was also terribly, terribly afraid for her.

"Pumpkin," he said softly over a restaurant table on the night before she left for school, "it's not hard to get ahead in this world, if all you want to do is get ahead. Your mother and I wanted so much more than that for you."

She was touched, moved to her depths. But her commitment had become unalterable. Anyway, her father did not fully understand either the extent or the precise nature of her ambitions.

*

The freighter had glided silently to the right of the frame. The entire harbor bathed in the last rich light of summer, an inspiration to verse. *The City now doth like a garment wear the beauty of the morning.* She wondered idly about the contents of the ship's hold. Unlikely vessels, unlikely cargoes.

"I am so pressed for time these days, Jenet. I feel a responsibility to you and to the Furston Press, to take care of your needs. But I need your help – at least for the next few weeks. So much is happening, there is so much I have – "

The pace of the Project had accelerated dramatically in the past few months. Everyone in the office could feel it, even a spectator like Adele – anxiety building, heightened tension in the corridors, a now-or-never sense that the time had come, that if all the effort did not culminate in a result soon, it would all have been for naught. The pressure showed in the dark circles under Carolyn's eyes (which makeup could not quite conceal), the disarray on her conference table (formerly so uncharacteristic), and in her steadily growing impatience.

"I take some pride in your accomplishments, too. You have been an inspiration to so many – "

Adele glanced at Carolyn – silk dress, matching shoes and belt, emerald necklace, matching brooch, two bracelets on each wrist, and three rings – *always too much, Carolyn* – found herself listening with the mild annoyance that had become a constant when she met with Carolyn.

To want or not to want – that's not the question at all. Who wouldn't want to live like this? The real question is the price. What is it? Do you ever find out exactly? If you do, would you be willing to pay? Inconsistent ambitions, irreconcilable dreams – no one has only one dream. How much to seek of this, how much to surrender of that? To dream, perchance to vacillate; maybe the vacillation, the wobble of the heart, is the dream destroyer itself. Maybe the whole trick is the willingness to pay the price, whatever it is, without knowing, without asking first. Maybe that was Carolyn's trick.

Not one Adele particularly wanted to learn. But how else?

*

After somehow surviving the catastrophe of her first year, she was done with Syracuse in six semesters, taking full course loads during both summers, finding time to start for the varsity field hockey team in the first two autumns. In a quixotic act of homage to her mother's memory, she doubled her poli-sci major into art history and practical art. Then it was on to law school, this time at a prestigious Ivy League university, again on a substantial scholarship. She found to her satisfaction – but not surprise – that she could excel even at that rarefied level. She qualified for law review academically in her first year and became an articles editor at the end of her second. In her third, she co-authored an article for the review on issues of copyright pertaining to computerized reproductions of old masters' paintings. The quixotic act of filial homage had paid practical dividends, as so many quixotic acts do. With it also surfaced the first intimations of how hard and cold the life she had chosen for herself could be. Nonetheless, that article, and a superb academic record, led her to downtown Manhattan and the intellectual property department of the law firm of Hapgood, Thurlow, Anderson, & Davis.

Adele Jansen had been only twenty-three years old that first day at Hapgood. By that time, neither the pleasantness of her manner nor the basic sweetness of her disposition could conceal any longer the strength of her character and the magnitude of her talent. She had become formidable, whether she liked it or not. (She didn't.)

And now, two years later, she stood before the magnificent vista and wondered what exactly it was she wanted, why she was there, how she could sometimes feel completely detached from everything around her. How odd that so many essential things remained mysterious. The only thing she truly knew for certain was when it had all started. On a day in her twelfth year, which thirteen years later still remained the most significant one of her life.

The day of her mother's funeral.

*

All she could remember now was a blurry confusion of candles, flowers, and tears. Sobs all around her – her father, her brothers, Buck's wife, an enormous outpouring from the school. She sat beside them stony faced, refusing to give in to her grief. More than one resolution was born that day.

Adele was the only girl and the youngest of the four by a good margin. Buck was nearly fifteen years her senior. Michael was already in second grade when she was born. By then her mother had finally found a small space to pursue the hobby that should have been her life's work. Days brightened with the unique sunlight filtered through the cramped attic that doubled as her mother's studio, days filled with art and the best kind of wisdom, the joyful kind. Days that she now knew would remain among the most special of her life. . . but she hadn't known that then, had discovered it too late, foolish child, only when they were gone, abruptly, permanently, unjustly. In death, her mother had become ordinary, another schoolteacher's wife. She was gone. Everything was gone, disappeared as if it had never been.

Her mother had flourished in too confined an arena. Adele knew consciously even as the thought arose, as she knelt there, eyes dry, that factually it was not so, that the cancer which had blasted her mother's life had nothing to do with the way in which she had lived. But she would not surrender the intuition to the fact. Something solid took hold out of the emotional chaos. With a precocious grimness, her daughter resolved then and there that she would not repeat her mother's mistake, would rectify it, in fact – that she would live, strive and succeed in the larger world, the world of weighty affairs, into which neither of her parents nor any of her brothers had ever ventured. Her course in life had been set from that day forward.

It was no childish caprice. It did not disappear the next day. Through all the tumult of the intervening years, she had never deviated, never wavered.

And now she stood where she always planned to be. Adele Jansen had arrived.

*

The freighter was almost out of sight now. She wondered if it had limped in from the South Atlantic, where another unseasonable tropical storm was raging. No longer correct to call them unseasonable; nowadays, they seemed to rage with greater ferocity every autumn. The weather was changing, the world was changing, the straight way not nearly so easy to find as once it had been.

Really, just another version of the same old story – how to shape a life out of this raw material without being shaped by it yourself at the same time. Adele wished she could be certain of exactly how her version would turn out.

Get with it, stupid. She turned back from the window.

"A penny for your thoughts, Adele," Jenet said, interrupting Carolyn, curious.

"Oh," Adele answered in her chirpy, schoolgirl voice, smiling brightly, "I'd be swindling you. Nothing important."

Jenet turned back to Carolyn. "I understand what you mean, dear," she said gently, but with a hint of iron in her voice. "And I thank you for the concern. But you must let me set my own priorities. This is important to me."

"I still don't understand what you want, Jenet," said Adele. "I mean, what can a lawyer do? Shouldn't he be seeing a therapist?"

"He probably should, but he won't. Tom isn't stupid, Adele. In fact, he's astonishingly perceptive in a kind of an I-am-a-camera way. He amazes people when they first meet him, they think he's psychic. It's really part of the same pattern. He's always on the outside looking in, in a way, and he misses nothing. It can become unnerving. But therapy? He'll never do that. I think he lives in despair most of the time." She picked up her teacup. "I mean the word literally: Despair, from the Latin de and spero, without hope. That's supposed to be the one unforgivable sin because the sinner has stopped believing in forgiveness." She looked out into space. "I think he doesn't believe anything could ever be different. I think somewhere along the line he abandoned all his hope."

Jenet took a sip of tea, and then went on, more business-like. "Well. Let's get off the subject of Tom per se; I can go on for about three days about that.

"The reason I've brought all this to your attention is this: I am afraid the association of this man with the Furston Press is weakening. That disturbs me. Quite apart from the personal factors, this man is a valuable asset. If he's going to waste his time on this nonsense, I'd just as soon it be with us. He takes his obligations seriously. I want to be certain that he understands what they are. He accepted our advance about ten weeks ago. I told you his disappearances have gotten longer over the years. He was out of touch for about seven weeks, until yesterday. That's much longer than it's ever been. There's still three weeks to go, but I'm worried that he won't deliver." Jenet paused, and glanced at Carolyn – then stiffened. "Perhaps for his own sake as much as ours. It's occurred to me that he may be using these commitments like a crutch – the same way that some alcoholics won't start drinking until after 5:00. I worry if he ever missed one of those deadlines he'd fall apart completely. I want to be sure that doesn't happen."

Carolyn shook her head.

Jenet ignored her. "When either I, or someone from my staff talks to him, it always seems as if we end up nagging. We'd love to have a closer relationship with him. It's a trap I've fallen into too often. I could give him all the work he could handle. If he'd let me – and if I were certain it wouldn't interfere unduly with his real work. It must become tiresome for him, and perhaps that's the reason he's become less communicative with us. So I thought –"

"–that if a professional instead of –" said Adele. She saw the point now.

Jenet smiled at her. "Precisely. I want him to be counselled, firmly and effectively, as to what his obligations are." Her hands fluttered up in that same helpless gesture. "To be certain he's aware of them. But I don't want it to be at all oppressive or threatening – least of all, patronizing. Someone with a light touch. His own age. I want you to talk to him, Adele. I don't want to be offensive, Carolyn, but I think Adele is more suitable for this task than yourself."

"I'm not at all offended," said Carolyn equably. "I'm a lawyer. Nursing wounded babies is not my cup of tea. And I don't have the time anyway."

"There is something else I need," Jenet continued, a bit more briskly. "What I mentioned earlier. We really could use the manuscript at least ten days early. We're willing to pay him a five thousand dollar bonus if he can do that."

"O.K.," said Adele.

"But don't proselytize on my behalf, Adele. About other things he could do or that sort of thing. Keep what I've said to you to yourself. I don't want you to sound –" Jenet stopped suddenly, as if a thought had struck her, then resumed. "I am certainly not expecting any missionary work here, my dear," she said emphatically. "It wouldn't be useful. Certainly no hand-holding. And" – she spoke even more deliberately – "all I'm expecting from you is your skill as lawyer. All I want is good legal counsel for Tom."

"I understand," Adele answered.

"I'll messenger down a copy of the contract and you can draft a little amendment," said Jenet. She paused. "I know you don't agree with my views on this, Carolyn, but it is what I want. You can spend as much time as you need to get the point across, Adele. As far as I'm concerned, it's all billable time."

She smiled wryly at Adele and made a comic face. Carolyn and Adele smiled back. Jenet Furston knew the rules.

*

What business is it we're in? Carolyn Hoffman had asked a little less than two years earlier, speaking at the first training meeting to the seventeen recent law school graduates who had become associates with Hapgood, Thurlow, Anderson, & Davis. Adele had been one of seven women among them.

The practice of law? some brave soul had finally volunteered.

Wrong, Ms. Hoffman answered flatly. *We are in the profession of practicing law. We are in the business of buying and selling time.* With that, she went on to explain the elaborate accounting methods and procedures by which the time of the partners and associates was measured, recorded, analyzed, and billed. Always, always, always, the critical element in any project was billable time – how much would it cost, how much would it generate.

Adele could feel heads sagging and spirits drooping all around her. But the lecture was music to her ears. She had been managing and budgeting time expertly most of her adult life. *This,* she thought, is *going to be duck soup.* Thus far it had proved to be exactly that.

*

"We have things to do, Jenet," Carolyn reminded her.

"When do you want me to see him?" asked Adele.

"I'm supposed to meet him at the reception this afternoon. If he does come, I'm going to have him call you." It was the custom of the Furston Press to hold an informal cocktail reception toward the end of each month in honor of those authors whose books were being released the next.

An idea struck Jenet. "Why don't you come? If he is there, you can make your own appointment."

Adele looked at Carolyn. "Do you have anything on then?" asked Carolyn.

"No."

"Then go. It'll be good background for you – and I know you're good for the time."

There was no need for additional directions. The Furston Press occupied the top five floors of the Millroth Building, some ten stories above the floor on which the women were speaking.

"Is that all about this, Jenet?" said Carolyn. "Can we get back to the important things?"

"I suppose so."

"I'm going to be sending you something today or tomorrow," said Carolyn, addressing Adele.

"Something to do with the Project?" Adele blurted out, then became irritated with herself. She did not want the Project to dominate her thoughts the way it dominated everyone else's.

"No," Carolyn smiled. "A sideshow. But I think you'll find it interesting."

What to say? Adele nodded.

"Are you coming Friday night?" asked Carolyn, again addressing Adele.

"Yes, of course," said Adele. *Of course*, always, when she was asked in front of Jenet. Truth be told, that was Carolyn's little needle. Adele was becoming extremely impatient with those Friday night gatherings. Carolyn knew that; Adele was sure of it. Carolyn had adopted her, she acknowledged the favor, but they were both becoming increasingly aware that they did not, at the most basic level, care for each other – in fact, had reached a stage of passive, covertly acknowledged dislike. Nothing came easily in the City, least of all the simple things.

Carolyn gave Adele a private look that said clearly, *you're excused*. Adele picked up her computer by the handle, said good morning, and began to leave, realized she had overlooked a courtesy, turned around.

"Jenet, why do you think so much of his poetry? What kind is it?" Ignoring Carolyn's quick glare.

Jenet perked up. "It's excellent. Terse, extremely compact, very controlled in the older forms, ottava rima, iambic pentameter; you know I don't appreciate the other kind." Carolyn shot Adele a warning glance. "His subjects are varied, anything and everything, but he writes a lot about mathematical theory."

"What? Mathematics? Arithmetic? *Numbers?*" said Adele incredulously.

"Yes, I know. How anybody could find poetry in that sort of thing, I don't know, but he does. It's surprisingly accessible, too. He's only written one lyric poem that we've published, but it's long and extraordinarily lovely. I have often wondered about the person to whom it's addressed.

"Anyway, I find something new every time I read them. He's one of the few writers we publish that I reread for my own pleasure. He truly has a unique voice. There's real talent there, probably more than talent. And now it's been over three years.

"He's genuinely gifted," she added softly. "Contract writing. Mystery stories. Teleplays. What a shame. What a waste of time. What a colossal waste of time."

She was talking mostly to herself again.

THE RECEPTION

When Adele got back to the twenty-eighth floor, she found a message from Walter Greenfield, the junior partner to whom she reported on the Lawton case. *Stupid*; meeting him was the only silver lining in the whole benighted Lawton mess and – of course – he was the one person she'd forgotten to call this morning. She phoned him at once.

"Any progress?" he asked, without more formality, with none of his usual theatricality.

"Yes," said Adele. "Breakthrough. Yesterday. The maid finally talked to me. That's off the record, if we can keep it off the record. She's worried. . . about her job." Adele fell silent. He said nothing. There was no such thing as "off the record" in a case like this. Both knew that.

"And said?"

And said? – easy enough for him to ask. It had been hard enough for her, the one-and-a-half hours she'd held her on the phone, improvising, backing up, going forward, now stern, now cute, *please, senora, I have the floors to do, there are so many other things to do, please, please, leave me alone*, ignoring the inevitable pangs of guilt, pressing on, flattering, lying, until finally the other gave up. She'd hung up the phone successful, awash with remorse and anger. That poor maid. *Damn* Lawton. *Double damn* Murdoch.

"She didn't know the island, but she had a rough idea of the itinerary – and she had a guess about the travel agent. We lucked out. Her guess was right."

A fierce explosion of breath. "And the agent told you? Where they are? I'm surprised."

"Antigua. It did take a little persuasion." Another hour, in fact, until another individual finally realized that, as improbable as it seemed at first, the charming young woman with the chirpy girlish voice on the other end of the line was not going to relent, not going to retreat, not going to back off, until she'd learned what she had to know. *Johnson and Jansen.*

"Very good. You'd better get on the ph –"

"I already have. I talked to Jameson yesterday. He wasn't thrilled to hear from me, but he came around. He'll sign an affidavit. So will his son. I went over the contents with him."

"Great. You should get it down to him Fed-Ex ASAP."

"I'm a little ahead of you," said Adele. "I did it late yesterday. I located a secretarial service near the hotel with a fax machine and a notary. They Xeroxed the fax and took it over to Jameson, got it signed, then expressed it back. I expect it back today. The docs won't look pretty, but they should do for the deputy D.A. I'll get him fair copies later in the week."

There was a silence on the other end of the line. "I'm beginning to understand why you have the reputation you do," said Walt Greenfield, in a strange, unnatural voice. She guessed it was his Jimmy Stewart. He had zillions of them, alike only in that they were all terrible. But at least he'd relaxed. "I sure as hell don't have any other ideas. Keep me posted."

"Will do," said Adele, and began to hang up.

"Er – Adele?" Walt said in his natural voice. A bad sign.

"Yes?" she asked cautiously.

"Er – there's something else." He paused; she could feel his discomfort; she tensed herself. "Er – Ralph asked me yesterday to have you do a log. For billing purposes."

"Log?" she said, bewildered. "Billing purposes? I don't understand." She filled out her time slips on the Lawton case the same way she'd been doing them for two years, the way Carolyn Hoffman and the others had taught. No one had ever complained.

"Yes. Murdoch's afraid he'll have to justify your time to Lawton. He wants more detail."

"But I don't –" *understand*, she was about to finish, but then stopped – because all at once she *did* understand. She understood all too well. A wave of pure fury swept over her. One more stupid, useless task – and the only reason she'd been stuck with the thing in the beginning, she was certain, was because she stuck out, because an absolute useless, old fart moron like Murdoch needed to brag to the other useless old farts that the best recruit they'd had in ten years was on assignment to him – and now he did this –

"Walt," she asked, trying unsuccessfully to keep the anger out of her voice, "has he ever needed a log from one of the guys? One of the men? About anything?"

"O.K.," Walt answered after a moment, "I know what you're saying. I'm hearing you loud and clear. This isn't my idea. I think – I know – your time reports are more than adequate. I told Ralph that yesterday, but he's got his own ideas. Just go along with it, O.K.? It's not worth it to argue. Right? I apologize to you on behalf of the whole firm. I'll make it up to you. But please don't draw the line on this one. It's easier just to go along with it. Right?"

"Right," Adele acknowledged, after a moment, still seething. Because he was right: it wasn't worth it to make waves on something so trivial, and in any case, it wasn't Walt's fault. "I'll have it for you this afternoon."

"Good. Good," he replied. "This, too, shall pass," he added in a tone too strange to be even remotely recognizable. "Good bye."

"Good bye," Adele answered, and hung up. She looked down at the Lawton file, open in front of her, with complete, unadulterated loathing.

*

Another morning passing in a blur; another day of more to do than time to do it in. Adele sometimes hoped that a day would come when she would discover anew again what it was like to have a life not lived on the dead run. Moving up in a firm like Hapgood meant more and more minutiae, less and less time for the truly significant. Simply proofing ordinary correspondence and redrafts of memos and contracts took up an astounding proportion of her working hours. She gritted her teeth and did Ralph Murdoch's log for him, recording the keystrokes for the column structure as a template so that some good might come of it. A template of that type might be useful if she ever found time to refine it.

The Lawton case continued to drain her time in all sorts of ways. Shortly before noon, the elder Jameson phoned directly from Antigua. Adele held her breath. He did not renege on the promised affidavit. . . exactly. Knowing full well that the district attorney expected affidavits from both him and his son, he merely said that his son did not remember the outing in the detail the father did, that conscientiously he could not expose his son to the slightest risk, that the boy could not sign the statement in its present form. Fine, no problem; simply make a photocopy, strike through the parts the eight-year-old couldn't remember, and have him sign that. *Oh, no,* answered the conscientious father, playing the game, *not good enough,* he had to have a revised version for the lad. Adele knew exactly the game he was playing, and knew he knew she knew. But confronting him would be was a fool's errand. In the calmest, most professional voice she possessed, she assured him she understood his concerns, hung up the phone, revised the double damned affidavit to his specification, and had it on its way within the hour. *You're not getting away that easy, buster.*

The usual small irritations. In mid-afternoon, in his habitual surly fashion – glowering in the doorway for a moment, muttering something inaudible, and disappearing as soon as he possibly could – Greg Steuer delivered a brief for her review, points and authorities concerning an evidentiary dispute in a litigation pending in a federal district court. She watched him retreat down the hall.

Hasn't he figured out yet I don't like this any better than he does? Or was it

41

that it didn't matter to him anymore? She glanced rapidly over his brief, sighed again – dreadful work, unproofed. Some of the sentences didn't parse. She was all but certain the citation was inaccurate, perhaps some even fictitious. What exactly did Carolyn expect her to *do* about this, anyway?

All in all, a day not that much different from all those that had immediately preceded it. At least there'd be a party at the end of this one, no matter how trivial and mundane the assignment that brought her there, no matter how pure a business function. With that brightening thought, Adele glanced at the vase clock and noted with some astonishment that it was 3:55. Another afternoon had vanished without a trace.

*

Five minutes later, she stood in the entryway to the reception room of the Furston Press. She had seen it twice before, but it was always a pleasure to view it again. Her eyes feasted for a long moment before she entered.

A wonderful room. A superb achievement. She could only marvel at how many man – *no, be accurate* – woman hours had gone into its creation. It was no more than an expanded foyer, furnished in subtle, unpretentious style. But what style! One of the largest, thickest Persian rugs Adele had ever seen – a bit over twenty feet in diameter – covered a floor of richest cherrywood. The draperies were hand-woven, relating to, but not matching, the rug, and permanently drawn so as not to obscure the view of the harbor, the same as Carolyn's office, only from a much higher, wider angle. A medieval tapestry on one of the interior walls faced two large, modern paintings on the other, one a blue-period Picasso. Had it not been for the exquisite taste with which everything had been chosen, the room would have failed completely.

Instead, it was superb. Somehow everything fit. In some way, everything stood in communion. A living, breathing masterpiece, a marvel – which almost no one these days noticed.

Now the decor was dominated by a serving table placed four feet in front of the tapestry. Hot hors-d'oeuvres lay under three chafing dishes on the right. Champagne, white wine, and sparkling water were placed on the left. Two sideboards and a placard on a tripod stood in front of the other wall. The placard identified all the new titles that the Press would be issuing in the next four weeks. Copies of five major releases were attractively arranged on the card sideboards. In their case, the reception marked the beginning of the promotional campaign.

At four o'clock, the reception was sparsely populated. Twenty or so early arrivals stood conversing animatedly in small numbers around the room.

Jenet spoke to one gathering of three, moved to the next. Adele watched for a moment, then looked around and began to circulate. She saw no sign of any person who might be Thomas Newcombe. No one there remotely fit the description. It would be a shame if he didn't show up. Truth be told, she'd come to the reception as cynical as Carolyn, if a bit more close-mouthed about it. She'd known a few "poets" in college and graduate school. Always a self-designation, almost always an excuse for some kind of affectation. But Jenet had excited her curiosity. A talented author who prefers ghost writing to his own work – that definitely lay off the beaten path.

A small, tingly excitement began to build out of her stomach. A tangible mood of quiet celebration pervaded the room, contagious, impossible to resist. A good party might just be in the offing, and Adele had no objection whatsoever to good parties. She might have come there on business, but it would not exactly have broken her heart if someone interesting also showed up. Six people came through the door at once, led by a short, bearded man whose face sparkled with high spirits. She watched, enjoying him, enjoying his exhilaration. Obviously one of the authors; *I hope it goes well for you*, she thought, not unkindly.

"Ah, Adele!" said Jenet from behind her. "Welcome." Lowering her voice just a trifle, she added, "He isn't here yet. Just circulate, dear, enjoy yourself, and I'll introduce you when he arrives. If he arrives." With that, she moved on to another guest.

Adele walked slowly toward the tables and looked over the titles – two mysteries, two popular novels, and a semi-scholarly book about various problems in dysfunctional families. It was an all-too-typical month for the Furston Press. She recognized the hero of one of the mysteries – a crime--fighting veterinarian in one of a series of novels with a strong animal rights theme. The others were new to her.

Jenet circulated by her again. "I know," she said quietly as she passed, "but I do try. Petrosian's book is very good. It won't sell 2,000 copies but it's very good." Adele shrugged her shoulders and smiled. Jenet looked towards the entry, brightened automatically as another party of four appeared, and stepped forward as gracious hostess. As always.

Adele watched her move on, her heart touched. She'd learnt more about Jenet and the Famous Story in the last year. The Big Joke. The Furston Press was a true labor of love, founded when Jenet was still in her mid-twenties, to promote the literary tradition with which she'd fallen in love in college. She had expected to lose money in the cause of something she regarded as more important. Instead, to her own astonishment as much as anyone else's, she discovered executive abilities that had apparently been lost to the Furston family since the fortune had been founded – a gift for delegating responsibility, an exquisite sense of the capabilities of different persons. Even the most obscure publisher is deluged with manuscripts. When she examined them more out of kindness than interest, a superb editorial sense came to light. An even more impressive talent for maximizing production values was uncovered when the sheer quantity of material for which she was responsible led her into television and film. In both cases, success resulted more from an abhorrence of waste and a sense of responsibility to others than any real belief in the worth of the material.

Nowadays, book publishing accounted for less than ten percent of gross revenues, and the divisions that really mattered to her – the ones that published what was important to her – only an infinitesimal fraction of that. For reasons of her own, Jenet had retained its original name. Nowadays, too, her PR people spent nearly two working days a month answering letters from television viewers curious as to why such a notable production company carried the name "Press."

The room was filling rapidly now, swirling with hubbub and chatter. Jenet Furston was one of those few people in the media business with no real enemies. Adele saw her move to another guest, take his hand, chat warmly, an apparently serene gray-haired widow in her late 60s. In its allocation of rewards and deprivations, life had played one of its little jokes on Jenet Furston. She had wanted art; she had craved children; she had been denied both. At early middle-age, she had resigned herself to a comfortable old age with a husband she treasured (a mild, slightly eccentric expert in Irish Renaissance literature, ultimately a full professor at Barnard, with an ordinary, unpublicized career – even some of Jenet's closest friends did not realize that it was she who envied him, rather than the other way around). She had been consigned to widowhood instead.

The Big Joke was obvious. Jenet had been showered with money she didn't need and fame for which she had no use whatsoever. She had been deprived of everything that truly mattered to her. Even so, there was never in her manner any trace of bitterness or complaint about the capriciousness of fate.

Some of the people who knew the whole story thought it was hilarious. Adele Elizabeth Jansen was not one of them. Oh, she got the point of the joke, all right; it was just that it didn't seem all that funny.

*

Forlorn thoughts for such a lovely afternoon. In spite of herself, Adele's mood was darkening. *This is a* party, *Jansen.* Perhaps the disappointment from the night before was still with her. She glanced at her watch. It was close to five, and less and less likely Jenet's project would show. More time lost.

She circulated towards a livelier gathering.

"*–already know what you are*, he says to the girl," a crudish looking man was saying. "*What we're doing now is negotiating.*" His companion smiled faintly.

Oh, really. Give me a break. Adele had always hated that joke. Not only was it as old as the Seven Hills of Rome, the woman in it is such a patsy. What the woman should say is, *We know what you are, too, and it only took one question.* Come to think of it, maybe that's what she really did say and no one wrote it down. An old memory of Adele's own, the darkest, and one never recalled voluntarily, nudged into her consciousness. Automatically, she pushed it out. A bit nettled, she felt her mood deteriorating further.

With the idea of diverting herself, she drifted towards one of the small groups that had formed about the room. In its center was the bearded, middle-aged man she'd seen earlier, speaking animatedly to two men and a woman. He was the shortest person in the group, only three or four inches taller than Adele, but he was dominating the conversation. She moved closer.

". . . more of this than you would ever suppose," he was saying in a voice with a slight Slavic accent. According to the tag he wore on his lapel, he was Dr. Armen Petrosian. Adele recognized the name from the jacket of the book on family problems. "The victims are not conscious enough of their anger to protest. As for the perpetrators. . ." He waved his left hand in the air, a gesture of dismissal, and shrugged. His audience nodded passively.

And that did it. Murdoch, the stupid, sexist log, Henrietta Lawton's shameless manipulation of truth that had created the whole mess, the frustrations of the last three weeks – it all came boiling up.

*

"Isn't it becoming somewhat faddish?" Adele asked lightly. Even when on the boil, her manner was open and pleasant. All the heads turned towards her.

"What do you mean?" replied Dr. Petrosian mildly.

"Faddish. I mean faddish. I'm thinking of a case I'm involved in – I'm a lawyer in this building – a divorce case. The wife thought she was losing so she apparently made up this story about her husband fondling their youngest son." In fact, two days before the hearing on child custody and spousal support. It was all so *obvious*.

"Made up? Can you be sure?" Raised eyebrows.

"I think so. It turned out that the boy and his father had spent the entire day with two friends of the dad's and their sons. He wasn't out of sight

45

for a second. The wife didn't know that when she went to the police. But that hasn't seemed to make any difference to the D. A."

Petrosian shrugged. "I would think such a matter would be easily resolved."

"These days perhaps it isn't as easy as it should be," Adele rejoined, a bit unfairly. Walt Greenfield had warned her – *Fasten your seat-belt, look-and-feel lady, sit back in your seat. You are about to follow the white rabbit down the hole to the other side of the looking glass. You are about to enter the world of New York's super rich.* He paused and changed his voice. *They make money the old-fashioned way –* pausing again – *they inherit it.* (The first time she heard one of Walt's trick voices; she'd deduced John Houseman, but he snorted that Houseman was too easy, that it was Houseman as done by Barry Fitzgerald. Truth be told, it hadn't sounded like anything at all, only weirdness.)

Walt had been right. It wasn't easy at all. The Lawton divorce figured to make waves in those circles for a long time to come. James and Henrietta Lawton were both victims of severely overprivileged childhoods. Whoever lost was going to be childishly, petulantly bitter for decades. Adele had tried for these people, she really had. The old advice of making the best of things had in her opinion become a cliché because of its wisdom. But no one else had tried. For three solid weeks, all they'd all done was do their best to waste her time. The world was turning, clocks were ticking, great things were happening, the Project was heating up – and there she had been hopelessly mired in an assignment that had not the slightest connection with anything in which she was remotely interested. All because the old fart Ralph Murdoch, to whom Walt Greenfield reported, wanted to brag that he could command the attention of any associate and thought the case needed the "woman's touch" – whatever on Earth that was.

"Perhaps there is more to the accusation than you think."

"No. No, there isn't." She had the affidavits in hand now. Plus James Lawton's homosexual tendencies, if any, were deeply concealed; the divorce proceeding had originally begun because he was evidently one of the top ten womanizers on the East Coast, a fact which he partially corroborated during the first conference she and Walt had with him by propositioning Adele at the first opportunity as directly and unartfully as anyone ever had in her life.

"I think the problem is that it has all become topical. I think the District Attorney knows that there's nothing there, but he can't do anything about it. And that's why I asked if maybe it wasn't faddish."

Dr. Petrosian cleared his throat and swayed slightly; he had obviously had more than a little to drink in celebration of the publication. "It is true, of course, that any genuine problem or situation can be manipulated by unscrupulous individuals. But it is the object of human society to distinguish between those that are unfounded and those which rest on some genuine factual bases, is it not? Before they can be distinguished, they must at least be identified. In my opinion, silence, and the tradition of silence, is by far the greater evil with respect to these situations."

"Is silence really that well-established a tradition?" asked Adele. "These days it's more honored in the breach than the observance, isn't it? Maybe the number of these situations has remained constant over time. Maybe it's just that the noise level is higher."

"Perhaps." His voice had a slight edge. "But that does not affect my thesis. This increased noise level, as you put it, in my opinion is a progressive development, one which should be applauded and encouraged. It is infinitely preferable to the alternative."

She was becoming sorry now this had started, but it was not and had never been her habit to back down. "I don't know. Samuel Johnson once defined patriotism as the last refuge of scoundrels. Maybe that isn't true anymore. Maybe it's been replaced by stories about dysfunctional families, about lost childhoods. Listen to NPR and you think it's universal. Isn't it possible that losing your childhood is a normal part of growing up?" she added in conclusion.

And knew instantly that she had said too much – much too much. Petrosian closed his eyes for an instant and let his breath out in the manner of a man who has just heard once again some patent nonsense that he has heard many, many times before. His irritation was now evident. "My dear young lady, the problem with such statements is not their truth or falsity as such, but the convenience with which they can so easily become a rationalization for dismissing –"

He had more to say, but some friend tapped his shoulder. The doctor turned, composed himself, smiled, and extended his hand.

"I didn't mean –" Adele tried to interject, but the doctor's attention was now engaged elsewhere.

Damn it, she thought, annoyed, deeply annoyed, at herself, not him. Her recent frustrations; Lawton; the crude jokester a minute or so earlier; she'd let them all get the best of her. It wasn't fair. Those were her problems, not his. She didn't know Dr. Petrosian from Adam, but he didn't deserve that. He was at least twice her age. It was his book. It was his party. He'd come in such a good mood it had been a pleasure to watch, and she'd ruined it for him. This was probably one of the most important days of his life. He shouldn't have had to confront some little snip blowing off steam. Above all, Jenet would not want her guests to behave in that way. She circled the fringes of the group for an opportunity to say something, to apologize.

She felt a presence at her shoulder through the din. The reception had become crowded and noisy. The wine was disappearing.

"Adele," said Jenet Furston, "there's someone I'd like you to meet."

Oh, well. His anger seemed to be dissipating as he chatted on with the man who had interrupted them. She'd speak to Dr. Petrosian another time. Jenet took her sleeve gently and led Adele though the throng to the other end of the room. The crowd was a little thinner there, but no less noisy.

"Adele," said Jenet, "this is Tom Newcombe."

"Hello," he said and shook her hand. Although she had to strain to hear him over the din, the sound of his voice was exceptionally pleasant – deep, soft, with a subtle, almost musical lilt. His hand was strong, but his grip was light and gentle.

*

He was not at all what she'd expected from Jenet's description. She had thought – if she had thought at all – she'd be meeting a grim, brooding Byronesque figure, bristling with anger, or perhaps someone slightly dazed, spacey, like an over-tranquilized mental patient. She had no intimation that he would be so. . . arresting.

He stood about six foot three, over a foot taller than she, well-proportioned and big-boned, with large hands. His hair was light brown, combed, but not too well. A sense of strength, not entirely graceful – someone you had to warn when you asked him to lift a door, because he could tear off the door jamb if he weren't careful, strong like that. He was wearing a coat and slacks, neat and clean, but somewhat worn, presentable rather than fashionable; but the look seemed right for him. No one would ever confuse him with a movie star, but there was also no question that he was an attractive man.

"Adele is a lawyer, Tom," Jenet went on, "an associate with Hapgood, Thurlow, Anderson, & Davis. I'm very much impressed with her ability."

"I'm impressed with your courage," Tom said to Adele. "I'm scared to death of courts and law myself."

"I'm not that kind of lawyer," said Adele, and smiled because the remark had a chance resemblance to one sometimes made in an entirely different context. His eyes twinkled for a moment and the corners of his mouth turned up. Good; better; at least there was a sense of humor clanking around in there somewhere.

Other than his voice, the most striking thing about him were his eyes: large, deep blue, alert, and intelligent. She would have guessed he was a perceptive person even if Jenet hadn't already told her so. Now they reflected a natural curiosity, as to who she was and why they were being introduced. She could feel a certain warmth in them as well.

But he also seemed careworn, in the sense that Jenet had described that morning. He was paler than he really should have been, with noticeable circles under his eyes; either he hadn't been sleeping well or he'd been engaging in some type of dissipation. *Wine, women, and song,* Carolyn had speculated; maybe, but it didn't seem to fit at all – except for the "women," *that* part she could instantly believe. He rarely raised his hands above his chest; most of his gestures trailed off into vagueness. The overall impression was one of weariness, of fatigue.

Jenet had described him well. There was a sense in which he stood apart, in the midst of the gathering, a perpetual observer; a darkness, too, as if he beheld some distant, sad thing that no one else could see. When she made her inadvertent joke, his eyes had flashed, the corners of his mouth had turned slightly up, a half-smile; she felt intuitively certain that was as far as it went, as far as it ever went. *I've never seen him smile – not really smile – or open up,* Jenet had said. *Yes* – and it was impossible even on first impression to imagine him laughing out loud at anything – and yet he did have a sense of humor.

"I've asked Adele to meet with you and go over the contract," said Jenet.

"Why?" He was not alarmed, simply puzzled. "It's clear enough, isn't it? I owe you a book sometime in the next three weeks."

"It's more complicated than that, Tom," said Jenet. "I want you to know your rights and obligations, and I don't want to always be the one to have to tell you. Anyway, the Press wants to renegotiate the arrangement. We're prepared to offer you a bonus. And –" Adele watched, fascinated, at the spectacle of another human being visibly struggling with temptation and losing – "if you have some time, there's anoth –"

"That's all right," he interrupted gently, clearly refusing. "But why review the contract?"

"Adele can go over all that tomorrow," Jenet answered, retreating. Someone was trying to catch her eye across the room. "Tom, please indulge me."

He shrugged, and turned towards Adele. "O.K. What time?"

Adele had checked her calendar before she left her office. "About 10:00?"

"Fine. I'll see you then." That same faint half-smile flickered across his face. She shook hands with him again, then turned to Jenet.

"I'd better be going, Jenet. Thank you for the invitation."

"You're always welcome at these functions, dear. You needn't wait on the formality of an invitation."

"Thank you." Adele circled back towards the center of the room. She wanted to say something to Dr. Petrosian before she left; she would not feel right about herself until she had. But he was still deep in conversation with the person who had interrupted him. She'd drop him a note, instead. A psychologist of his stature must be easily reachable. Then she made for the elevator.

*

The compartment crept back towards the twenty-eighth floor. An interesting evening: the authors, the excitement, the *faux pas* with Petrosian, the tall, quiet man with the blue eyes. *Maybe one in a century,* Jenet had said. High praise, the type of hyperbole Adele discounted automatically – more than that, he hadn't done anything that should have impressed anyone, one way or another – and yet. . . and yet. . . he did have presence, no question.

He had seemed entirely natural, without any of the theater she had expected. The thought crossed her mind that her expectations reflected Carolyn's attitudes as well as Jenet's. She had little doubt that she had experienced in that brief encounter the reality of Tom Newcombe, that the sense of weariness, of sadness that enclosed him, was genuine. It troubled her slightly. She couldn't help thinking about it. But not to dwell upon; it was also evident, both from what she had seen and from what Jenet had said, that the type of problems he had were problems only he could solve.

The elevator arrived at her floor. Still, what a pleasant voice, what striking eyes; no question, an interesting person. She was looking forward to the meeting in the morning.

Then, with a self-discipline that had become routine over the years, she shifted her mental focus abruptly, cutting off all thoughts of the reception upstairs, switching to the evening ahead. Tom Newcombe would have to wait until the next day. She checked her slot for messages – nothing from the district attorney – retrieved her briefcase and computer. The clock read 6:05; there was plenty of time left in the evening to log a few more billable hours. Time was money. She put the computer in her briefcase; then, briefcase in hand, left the office.

✳ ✳ ✳

PARLOR TRICKS

The vase clock read 9:57 the next morning when the intercom line on her phone buzzed.

"Yes?" said Adele into the receiver.

"There's a Mr. Newcombe here to see you, Ms. Jansen," said Christina at the front desk.

"I'll be right out." She closed the file on which she'd been working, opened the one with the Newcombe contracts, and walked out to the reception area.

He was standing, reading something, when she greeted him. He half-smiled in response. His eyes were bright and alert, but the circles underneath them were darker than they were the day before.

"Thank you for being on time," said Adele. "Coffee or tea? A soft drink?"

He closed his book. "None, thanks. I always am. On time, that is."

"Let's go down to my office, then." He turned, put down the book, and picked up a three-ring notebook. They walked past the reception desk and turned left down the hall, Adele leading.

They went through the door of her office. She moved behind her desk and sat down in the overstuffed judicial chair, a small self-indulgence of hers. The chair was leather and stuffed, designed for a much larger person than her. She looked ridiculously small in it. The incongruity amused her; a little private joke. She gestured at the more comfortable of the two client chairs in front.

But he did not take a seat. He stood immobile for a long moment, apparently forgetful of himself and her, only his eyes and head moving, taking in everything. His manner was too natural to be at all sinister. Her sense was of an open, artless interest in new surroundings. After a short while, he stepped in front of the desk and touched the top of the hideous vase lightly with his right forefinger. Slowly, he traced its rim around. His face brightened for an instant. He said nothing.

Then he took two strides past her desk and became still again, taking in the oil painting – then another long moment. Adele swivelled her chair and watched in silence. All this was much too interesting to interrupt. After a few seconds, he turned to face her. At last he spoke:

"That's your mother in the painting, isn't it? You must be the artist. And she was an artist, too, wasn't she?"

*

Her eyes widened, and her mouth dropped open. She was too astonished to conceal her astonishment. He stepped back in front of her desk and sat down in the chair at which she had pointed, without acknowledging her reaction (though she thought she spied the hint of a twinkle in the corner of his eye).

"It's really excellent," he said quietly. "You must be very proud of it."

She was still dazed. Most of the people who came into her office didn't notice the portrait. Of those who did, only a few had guessed the identity of the artist, even fewer that of the subject. But no one had ever come remotely close to discerning the ultimate hidden secret.

Until now.

"I am," said Adele. "But how –"

He shrugged. "It's unsigned. If it were in anyone else's possession besides the person who painted it, it certainly would be. There's a family resemblance. I wasn't sure it was your mother. It could have been a favorite aunt – that was just a good guess. I was puzzled at first by the expression on her face. Then I realized you'd portrayed her looking at a subject. An artist."

She was amazed. He was exactly right. She didn't particularly advertise the fact these days, but she herself was indeed the painter. The portrait had been done to complete her coursework in an upper-division class. The instructor had been impressed, had spent half the semester trying to convince her that she had a real future in whatever field of commercial art she chose. (Adele would have been even more flattered if he had not spent the other half trying to seduce her.) She'd used an old photograph as a reference, but altered the expression to the one she cherished most, her favorite, her mother contemplating something that lay just beyond her easel. No one, not the instructor, not her brothers, not even her father, had ever divined the real point.

"You're very perceptive," she said shakily. "No one – that is – I mean, no one has asked." She paused, smiled weakly. "I'm not sure myself the reasons it's there." Something showed in his face; he had understood at once what she meant, perhaps more completely than she would have liked.

He paused. "It's also highly idealized," he said, softly and gently, with a note of genuine warmth. "A bit elegiac. That's why I used the past tense. If that's right, too, I'm sorry."

"Thanks," she answered, "it's O.K. It was a long time ago." She smoothed her dress and partly regained her composure. "We should get started now."

The review of the existing contract was short and perfunctory, an embarrassment. Tom Newcombe was fully aware of all the substantive provisions and particularly his obligation to deliver a finished first draft of the manuscript in standard form within three weeks, in consideration for the receipt of a prepaid fee of some twenty-five thousand dollars, etc., etc. Adele felt compelled to explain.

"This was Jenet Furston's idea. I guess it really wasn't necessary."

He nodded. "I'd thought as much. She's worried if I blow one of these things it'll all fall apart. But I'll be on time. She needn't worry." He looked away from her, with the oddest, blankest expression. "About that, anyway," he added vaguely.

"But this isn't a complete waste of time," Adele went on, quickly. The expression on his face unnerved her. She wanted to see it change. "Jenet said it last night. The Furston Press would like to renegotiate." She told him about the circumstances and handed him a one-page modification of the contract. "Jenet is willing to pay you an additional five thousand dollars if you can deliver the ms. in a week."

He scanned the page quickly, shrugged, and flipped it back onto her desk. "No matter. Jenet's always been a good friend to me. If she needs it early, she can have it early. I don't need the bonus. I've got my own reasons for getting finished with this."

The second major surprise of the morning. She had become acquainted with the life-styles of a number of writers, artists, and musicians in her short career, a few personally, most indirectly through incidental involvement with legal problems they either had or had caused. Generally speaking, they had as little in common with each other as any other fair cross-section of the population. But one thing common to all in her observation was a deep, pure, untroubled love of money.

Except this one.

"Mr. Newcombe, are you sure?" she asked. "Are you positive? This would be a bonus fairly earned. There's nothing dishonorable about it."

"Yes." He was gazing from his seat at her mother's portrait again, answered without looking back towards her. "I'm sure."

"I really don't understand." *You must be either crazy or stupid*, she thought.

"Actually, I'm neither crazy *nor* stupid, Ms. Jansen." He had emphasized the word "nor" slightly. She started again, knocking over the contents of her tray. He paid no attention. "But sometimes I do do things my own way."

She was trying to reconstruct her desk, with darting, flustered movements. "But how –"

"It's only a parlor trick," he said softly, turning towards her. "The phrase is a common enough one in a situation like this. If you hadn't been thinking something like that, you wouldn't have even noticed when I used it." He handed her back something that had fallen on his side of the desk. "It produced a little bigger effect than I thought. I'm sorry, I didn't intend that."

She was doing a miserable job of reconstruction. She was not used to having her poise so completely shattered. Her eyes kept examining papers she neglected to read.

He looked on to her desk. "It's right there."

"What?"

"The contract amendment. That's what you're looking for, isn't it?"

She put her hands palm down on the desk lightly, then lifted them up at him in a placatory gesture, as if she were a dam holding back a river.

"Mr. Newcombe, *please*," she said, and he said nothing more. She finished reconstructing the files, her way, in silence, then looked up at him. His eyes were twinkling in earnest now. She could not stop hers from sparkling back – how not, it *had* been funny.

"You're quite sure?"

He nodded his head and spoke with only the slightest additional emphasis.

"Yes. Jenet's generous, but not that generous. Jorgensen – that's the name author – is pretty well written out – I've done his last two books. But I've heard he owns a lot of good properties. My sense is that Jenet may have committed a deal on one before she had him nailed down. Producers do things like that, don't they?"

"Yes," Adele said. "They do."

"I don't want to gang up on her if that's right. If I ever do need the money, she'll pay me; she's like that." He paused. "So, for right now, no, I'm not crazy and yes, I am sure."

She looked at him, then shrugged herself. "If you say so, then." She was grateful for the explanation, realized it had been tendered by way of indirect apology.

"There is one thing, though," he said as she closed the file.

"What is that?"

"It's more convenient for me to finish up in the next two or three days than in seven. Maybe your law firm could give me some help?"

Adele was puzzled. "I'm sure we can, but wouldn't you rather work at home? Or up in Jenet's offices?"

He shook his head. "They make too big a deal out of me up there," he said quietly. "I don't like the attention. My place would be O.K., but I'm not good enough on my word processor to go as fast as I'd like. To do this quickly I'll need some stenographic help."

"You use a word processor?" she blurted. An idiot thing to say, she realized the moment the words were out.

"Sure." His eyes sparkled for a moment and the half-smile played on his face. "I don't think quills are legal anymore, Ms. Jansen. Aren't geese an endangered species? You'd know." His tone was good-natured, not sarcastic.

"I'm not that kind of –" she began automatically, then reddened, realizing she was repeating herself from the afternoon before – realized, too, as his eyes flashed again, that tricking her into that repetition had been the real point of his little joke. Games within games. She grinned broadly. The fun was too good natured not to enjoy, even if all the jokes so far had been at her expense. Beneath her smile, wonderment. The last thing on Earth she would have expected was that this brooding presence of a man would be playful.

"Anyway," he continued, "you need ten good fingers to be really quick and I've only got seven." He held up his left hand beside his face.

The hand was badly deformed. His ring, index and fourth fingers were grey, twisted, useless stumps. The only normal digits were his thumb and little finger. She had not seen that in the dimly-lit room the night before; the book had concealed it this morning.

"Ouch," said Adele. "How did that happen?"

"No big deal. An accident I don't even remember. I think I'm probably the best seven-fingered typist in the world, but that's not much of an honor. Something like being the best one-legged Tarzan in Hollywood, if you know that old Cook-and-Moore routine."

She smiled again. "What do you need, then?"

"A tape recorder. Two transcribers in relays. A place to dictate that's reasonably quiet. A sandwich for lunch; if you're one of those law firms that has round-the-clock secretaries, a sandwich for dinner. I can move awfully quickly; the story's mostly blocked out in my notebook. The rest is in my head."

"I'll see what I can do." She picked up the phone and punched Carolyn Hoffman's number, fighting temptation all the while. Some time would be necessary for Carolyn to settle this with Jenet. It would be pleasant, so pleasant, to let him stay in here, to talk to him, to find out more about him, listen longer to that soft, mellifluent voice, until some decision upstairs was made.

But it would not be a good use of firm time.

He made it easy for her: "I'll wait in the lobby until you hear back. I know you have other things to do. I brought something along of my own."

Adele nodded. She should have been relieved, her conscience now clear. She was surprised to find herself annoyed instead. He nodded back, stood up, and left.

She looked at the door behind him for a long moment after he was gone. He had for sure turned out to be interesting, in fact, much more than interesting. There was a sense of largeness about Thomas Bryant Newcombe that had nothing whatever to do with his height. He had made quite an impression on her and that was no longer an easy thing for a man to do.

Impression? said a little voice. *Speak truth, stupid. He all but blew you out of the building and he wasn't even trying.*

She looked up, reproving her own inner thoughts.

All right, conceded the voice. *Maybe he was trying a little.*

*

After Carolyn Hoffman's secretary connected her, Adele briefly described the events of the morning.

Carolyn grunted. "It sounds feasible if Furston is willing to pay for the secretarial. Did he really say he wasn't interested in the bonus?"

"Yes."

"Great. It's always nice to save Jenet some money. You'd better write up a release, though. He may claim later he had an oral contract for a larger bonus. These artistic flakes can be awfully fickle."

"Are you sure, Carolyn? I mean –" she began reluctantly. A good thing they were not face to face; Carolyn would never know the way she had reacted to the word "flakes."

"Don't argue, Adele, I don't have time for it today. Just do it, O.K.? Meanwhile, I'll phone Jenet about the other thing and get back to you. Damn it, I knew I'd get dragged into this. Why she has to micromanage something this trivial is beyond me." The phone went abruptly dead on the last word, as it always did at the end of a call with Carolyn.

She pulled out a yellow legal pad and slowly started to draft the release. There was something about this task she didn't care for. She had barely begun when the phone rang.

"Stand by for Ms. Hoffman," said the secretary, and Carolyn Hoffman came on the line.

"I couldn't reach Jenet – but I'm going to authorize this on my own. I'm sure she'd approve, particularly with the savings. Just go ahead."

"O.K.," said Adele, but the line was already dead.

She buzzed the head of the secretarial pool – the floor manager – and arranged for the transcribers and workspace in a small conference room. Then she went back to the lobby.

He was making notes in the margin of the book, which was in German. "Mr. Newcombe, everything's all set."

"Great." He closed the book, stood up, and followed her back into the office. She strode briskly down the corridor; he ambled along, one stride to her two.

"Would you like to know something about the mystery?" he asked as they walked.

"I am a little curious," she said, truthfully.

"Nothing unusual. But I don't doubt the assistant editor'd like the story early. I left the heroine locked in a closet, poisoned, with the antidote on a table outside. She'll die in an hour if she can't get out."

She looked back over her shoulder. His eyes were sparkling above the dark circles. "Can you tell me how?"

"Sure. She has her pet white rat in her pocket. It gets out through a hole in the wall, jumps on the latch, and unlocks the door. I forgot to tell you about the rat."

He's playing again, she thought. There was a game going on here, some sort of catch. Her own eyes flashed as she thought about it.

"How is it the rat knows that precise trick?"

"Oh, she trains it in the closet. I forgot to tell you, this particular rat escaped from another novel. It was irradiated at this medical lab where it became super intelligent and –"

She looked again over her shoulder. She felt a perceptible pleasure in looking straight up at him. "There's not one word of truth in any of this, is there?"

"Not one," he agreed, his voice quiet, his eyes dancing, and then they were at the door of the small conference room the floor manager had set aside for him. A cassette tape recorder and a half dozen tapes were placed on a small table.

"That was the worst story I ever heard in my life," she said, smiling.

"You've lived a sheltered life. You should have read what I started with," he said, gesturing towards the table, eyes alive, voice still so soft, so controlled. She wished him good luck, then left.

Her spirits and her head were high as she returned to her office. It had been a good day already.

*

All at once, without any notice, it seemed as if she had entered the Zone, one of those rare, wonderful interludes when everything seemed to fall naturally, inevitably into place. When she checked for messages at the front desk, there was one there from the deputy district attorney considering the Lawton situation. He'd read the affidavits, wanted to talk to her. She tried to call him back, but he was in court for the rest of the day. He'd left another message – *Don't worry; will call tomorrow.* Her heart leapt with hope.

In the office, in her inbox, was an interoffice envelope from Carolyn, the new thing she'd mentioned. Adele opened it with no special expectation. . . and. . . mouth dropped open, eyes widened, breath became short. It almost seemed too good to be–

But it wasn't. She had *it*. She was looking at *it*, holding *it*. It couldn't be, but it was.

The start-up, Artificial Intelligence, Inc., the superstar company that had exhibited at the Software Arts Expo, the one whose booth she hadn't even been able to approach – now she was looking at the preliminary prospectus for its initial public offering. She looked at the note from Carolyn. It read:

These guys are looking for new counsel when the IPO's completed. We have to get the business. Can you help? Read this and get back to me. /s/ C. Hoffman

Artificial Intelligence, Inc., or AI Squared. She could have done without the mathematical pun, but what's in a name? The excitement around that booth had been palpable – the sense that those who saw the demo had seen a once-in-a-lifetime event, something that would not come twice. It had been a crowd of hard-bitten professionals, too, not easily impressed. She'd tried to fight her way through, simply for the opportunity to see it. A wall of obnoxious human flesh had prevented her. . . and now the company had just dropped, as doth the gentle rain from heaven, from the thirty-second floor into her inbox.

Control yourself, dummy. You've only been waiting for this break for eighteen months, not forever. Well, maybe forever. All the work, the time, the money she'd spent –and it had happened so easily! She noted the date on the cover of the prospectus – October, date left blank, as it always is on a red herring. It was closing soon. Could she help? Could she *help*? Oh, do be *serious*, Carolyn, could she ever! *Pinch yourself – look before you leap* – but it looked like finally the break might have come. Associate or not, no one else in the firm could handle this, and the partners who mattered knew it. Maybe, just maybe. . .

*

She reviewed the prospectus with a giddy, reeling happiness, made some preliminary notes; all the disappointment she'd felt two nights before was erased. She had her secretary find the address of Armen Petrosian and scribbled a quick note to him, as sincerely apologetic as she could make it. The perfect day for it; a day to make everything right.

Adele swivelled back in her chair for a moment, reveling in her mood. Today, it all felt like duck soup, candy from a baby, easy as pie, everything's comin' up roses. It all might happen. It all might be more than a daydream. A nice way to feel, if only for a moment, and all because of the delivery of one little prospectus.

Really? All because of that? She had to smile at herself again. *Mostly* because of that. Her thoughts drifted towards the east conference room. Somehow it had begun with the unnerving, yet exhilarating, encounter she'd had with that unusual man. Somehow all the good news seemed related to that; for some reason, she did not believe in the coincidence.

She forced herself to focus on her other work, her heart dancing. When the release she'd prepared for Thomas Newcombe came back from word processing in its final form, she took it across the building. She felt a happy, tingling anticipation as she left her office, the source of which she did not wish to examine. But her mood dampened step by step. This task, alone of all, was not right, did not fit the pattern of the day.

He was deeply involved in dictation, working on the third cassette, as she entered the room. His eyes flickered up, his semi-smile rippled across his features in recognition. "I have a release for you," she said. "To formalize what we agreed."

He shrugged – "No such word," he remarked offhand, "'formalize,' I mean" –glanced at the release, shrugged again, and picked up the pen. She felt his presence again, the same sense of stature as before. The pen all but disappeared into his right hand. He had enormous, fascinating hands. She stole a glance at the floor. Enormous feet, too. Probably has an enor–

Stop it. Stop it this instant.

He signed it without comment, handed the pen back to her. She was more than a little shaken – supposing he really could read minds? It had been a long time since she'd had such a direct, physical reaction to a man. He turned back to his notes. She left hurriedly. It seemed inappropriate, even dangerous somehow, to interrupt, not even to express her misgivings about all this.

*

Shortly after lunch, the phone rang.

"Adele?" It was Jenet Furston, with a tone in her voice that Adele had never heard before. "I tried to reach Carolyn, but she isn't available. I'm due now at two meetings, but I've got a note on my desk that's very disturbing. About Tom Newcombe."

"Oh. He said he preferred to finish quickly, and that if we provided him transcribers –"

"No, no, no. Not that. That's trivial. What's this about a release?"

Her heart sank. "Well, he said he wasn't interested in the bonus and –"

"*Damn* it, Adele!" Adele was startled. Jenet almost never used profanity. "*God* damn it! Don't protect me from myself! I want him to have the money if he earns it. Frankly, it wouldn't bother me all that much if he got it and he didn't earn it. How dare you interfere!"

"We just thought –"

"Well, please *don't* think. Would you please leave my business to me? I've done all right so far. I pay people fair value for their work and I don't expect anything for nothing. I have no need of charity, thank you. I might have expected this from Carolyn, but I counted on better sense from you. This isn't like you."

"Jenet, he was worried that you'd been out-maneuvered somehow. By the man he's ghost writing for. He wondered if you were hesitant to say that to Carolyn and me, and he didn't want to hold you up if that were so."

There was a short, significant silence on the line. "Damn that man," whispered Jenet, finally, speaking to herself. Then she went on, brisk again:

"But that doesn't change anything. Whatever the reason, it's worth $5,000 to me to have that book next Thursday. It wasn't your business to interfere with that – and this preposterous release! In the face of such a generous gesture!"

Adele sighed; time to bite the bullet. "I'm sorry, Jenet. It won't happen again. It was my fault, not Carolyn's. I knew it was a bad idea when she first mentioned it." Then suddenly, she felt relieved. The one thing that had been out of the order of this glorious day was about to be rectified. And it was interesting that Jenet perceived such a sharp distinction between her and Carolyn. Jenet had almost sounded personally disappointed in her.

There was silence on the other end; then Jenet resumed in her normal voice: "Well, I'm sorry, too, dear, I probably shouldn't have spoken so harshly – and I'll blame who I want to blame; it won't be the first time. But Adele, don't be such a *lawyer* all the time.

"Anyway," Jenet went on, all business now, "I've no more time for this. I'm taking no more chances. I'm sending a personal check down by messenger. Give it to him now. If he says he's going to deliver on time, he will. He always does. As for the secretaries and things, just provide them. And keep an eye on him, Adele; I don't mind paying for your time to do that. Trust me, it's worth it to me."

"All right," said Adele.

"Goodbye, dear. Don't be too upset by all this." With that, Jenet rang off.

A messenger arrived with the check ten minutes later.

*

"Who's the fellow in the conference room?" asked Josh Palmdale as he slid into one of her client chairs.

A surge of pure territorial annoyance had to be suppressed. As usual, it would cost more time to take him on than it would to answer the question. "A writer; a poet, in fact. He's doing a project for the Furston press."

He sniffed. "Oh, *that* type."

"That's more or less what Carolyn Hoffman said." More and more irritated; rhetorical agreement was the fastest and easiest way to end this. She was not going to let the likes of him ruin this fabulous day.

"Watch out for him, Adele," he said pontifically.

Enough; it all blossomed into full-fledged anger. It was tempting to set the record entirely straight – *Who the hell do you think you are?* – except that somehow it didn't feel seemly even to discuss a person like Thomas Newcombe with a person like Joshua Palmdale. A half-measure would have to do.

"Thank you for the advice, Josh," she said, icily. "Now, will you please leave me alone? Please? I'm very busy."

He was momentarily startled; then rose and left the room stiffly. *No ointment without its fly*, she thought, but she would not let him spoil her mood. She picked up the AI Squared prospectus and reread it for the tenth time. Most of the good material she had on it was at home. She could hardly wait to dive into it. The hands on her vase clock seemed to be moving so slowly today.

*

Just after 4:00, there was a soft tapping on her door frame.

"May I come in?" said Tom Newcombe. "I've got both stenos transcribing. I could use the break."

"Sure. Want to share a coke with me? How's it going?" she said, smoothing her dress and straightening her hair.

"Well. I'm going to be done for sure tomorrow or the next day. I'll be here a long time tonight."

He looked drawn and pale, the fatigue apparent, although his eyes still shone bright and alert. She reacted to it in spite of herself. Yes, his problems were personal problems, yes, he alone could solve them – even so, it was hard not to worry a little about this strange, peculiarly likable man.

"Mr. Newcombe, you don't have to work that hard. You shouldn't."

He held up his right hand. "First names? `Tom'? `Adele'?"

Adele smiled. "Of course. Tom, you should take care of yourself."

He regarded her for a moment. "It's better this way," he said softly. "Believe me."

"Well," she said. "At least you're going to get your bonus." She handed him the check. "Jenet sent me the check and told me to tear the release up." Her smile became larger. "Don't embarrass me by negotiating how not to accept it. I don't know how to negotiate like that."

He thought about it. She could see his mind working with the same acuity as it had that morning. "I'm sorry. I got you into trouble, didn't I?"

"No. I got myself into trouble. I should have known better. I think I knew better at the time. Don't worry, it all blew over soon enough. Jenet told me to pay you now and keep an eye on you until you're done. That's all."

She handed him the check; he shrugged, folded it, and put it in his shirt pocket. Then he looked up at her mother's portrait. She followed his gaze.

"Most people who find out I can do art wonder why I gave it up," she said. "You haven't asked."

"It's fairly obvious, isn't it? You have to be both very, very good and very, very lucky to succeed there.

Here all you have to be is very, very good. You made a sensible decision."

She hardly needed to tell him he was correct. "It's not advice you've taken yourself."

"I didn't have your range of alternatives," he said, quietly, and Adele was at once sorry she'd spoken, for he was thinking again of something far, far away with that same awful expression on his face.

"A lot of people ask me about my name," she said, deliberately changing the subject.

She was relieved to see him become lively and curious again. "Oh? Why?"

"It's a little old-fashioned. There is a story."

His eyes were sparkling now, interested in the game. "Family name?"

"No."

"Hmmh." He was silent for only a moment. "Is there a movie lover or theatre buff in your family? Because the only Adele I can think of is Adele

Astaire, Fred's sister – the more talented of the two, everybody said."

She shook her head in wonderment. "My brother James – everybody calls him Buck. He's fifteen years older than I am. He's been a movie nut all his life. He suggested the name, and no one had a better idea. Actually, I have three brothers," she found herself gushing, "Jack's twelve years older and Michael's eight. I was dead last by a big stretch. Jack is a –" She caught herself. "My goodness, I'm going on."

"You're not boring me."

"That's good. But even so. . . my goodness. You've found out a lot about me in a short time," she added, a bit nervously

His eyes became really animated then. "Have I? I don't think so. No more than what you want me to know. I think your secrets are important to you, Adele, and you're pretty good at protecting them. The few things you've got here are all very private. The picture, with its secret. That vase looks like it's pretty, but you know it isn't, that it's ugly, that it only works in context. You really don't show much of yourself here, only enough to get by. I've barely scratched the surface. I'm sure of that. I think you're the sort of person who's got some safe private place where you keep what really signifies, what's really important to you – all the ingenious, lovely things that are too mysterious for the multitude here."

She could only look at him, lift an eyebrow, and smile an enigmatic smile. No need to say anything – she was not even surprised anymore. The lower right-hand drawer of her desk at the apartment was what he was talking about. Her treasure drawer.

"You don't succeed entirely, though," he went on. "A little bit of you peeks out even in these small things. The same way that handkerchief sticks out of your pocket." She was wearing a reddish-brown, rust-colored pleated business suit, from the pocket of which a bright orange handkerchief protruded. It was the kind of color coordination that appealed to her – impossibly daring for most women, because it would fail catastrophically if it weren't perfect. It didn't, because it was.

"Maybe that's as it should be," he continued. He rolled the oval vase slowly between his hands and contemplated it. "It's the flowers that grow between the bricks that are the most memorable. Maybe they're also the most important."

"That's high praise for an ugly vase," she said, smiling.

He stopped toying with the vase and looked up, directly into her eyes. "I wasn't talking about the vase, Adele."

"But then wha – Oh. *Oh.*" She blushed. "Thank you," she said, and meant it.

There was a short, awkward silence. Then he rose. "I'd better get back to work. I'll see you in a while."

"Good luck," she said.

But you have your secrets, too, don't you, Mr. Newcombe? her thoughts trailed after him as he left. *I wonder what they are.*

At 6:30, before she left the office, Adele looked in on him, still hard at work, transcriber in hand. The AI prospectus was under her arm. Most of her notes and information were at home, in her apartment. She'd authorized overtime for Helen Wilder, one of the transcribers, who had actually been willing to work at her ordinary hourly rate because she was dying to know how the story turned out. No way; she'd be paid her overtime. Adele wasn't about to make the same mistake twice in one day.

"The sandwich is in the small locker in the lounge," she said. "In fact, two of them." Their eyes met in amused, mutual recognition of another inadvertent joke. She sounded more like a housewife than a lawyer. She was in a fever to get home and dive into that prospectus. Even so, she found herself lingering for a moment longer.

"Good night now, Tom. Remember you've got plenty of time. Don't kill yourself."

"Good night, Adele," he answered. "It'll be all right."

✳ ✳ ✳

Joseph Wurtenbaugh

NIGHT THOUGHTS

A dele got home at about 7:00. Home was an apartment she shared in the East 60s with the young woman to whom she'd been introduced through a tenant matching service. It was a match made in heaven. Joan was the perfect roommate. She was never there. After dinner, Adele worked until 9:00, reviewing the prospectus of AI Squared, pulling out references in the computer magazines to which she subscribed, going over the notes she'd taken at the Software Arts Expo. Her excitement grew. If even a portion of the preliminary evaluations were accurate, Carolyn had hooked a whale.

According to the reviewers, the young founders of AI Squared had come up with a method of generalizing expert systems from any field of expertise into one simple, easily modified program. Better, it was written in Linux, not LISP, not Prolog. Best – this was hard to believe – it was compact enough to run on an ordinary microprocessor, on any of the installed base of billions. It was still experimental, still very much in the development stage, only barely in beta test, but if the accounts were even slightly accurate...

Stay calm, dummy, she told herself as she closed the last of the journals. *Sure, this could be it, this could really be it. But there's a long way to go. First get the client, then get happy.* She pulled her nightdress out of the bureau.

Then it was calisthenics; then a half-hour's dogged labor on the Russian novel she was forcing herself to read; then time for bed.

After ten restless minutes, she sat up in her bed. On the rare nights when she did not go straight to sleep, it was nearly always because she was uncomfortable about something or other. Not so this evening – a pleasant, tingly, wholly irrational anticipation was the reason. She felt too good to sleep.

Because of AI Squared? Oh, yes, by any objective standard, definitely the big news of the day. But – *be real, girl!* – not the reason you can't sleep.

What an interesting person. What an unusual man.

What was he doing this very moment? Still at work? She hoped not. That reminded her. She rose from bed, went to her desk, and wrote a note to herself to ask about the title of the book, so she could read it when it came out. In fact, it would be interesting to find out the titles of all the books he'd ghosted, fun to see if she could determine what was his and what was someone else's – as a purely academic exercise, of course.

She sat at her desk. She still wasn't at all sleepy. How long had it been? Long enough, anyway – three or four weeks at least. Without bothering to turn on the overhead light, she slipped out of the chair onto the floor, lotus-style, and opened the large drawer in the lower right-hand corner – the treasure drawer.

Its only contents were a half-dozen artist's sketchbooks.

She reached for her favorites first, the second oldest ones in the collection – the two dream house books, the first one now more than eleven years old. The dream house was actually not one, but four alternative houses – exactly which one was the real one kept changing. That was part of the fun. Each was sketched out room by room, interiors and exteriors, with cut-outs and notes from catalogues, shop addresses, fabric patterns, and furniture designs, everything. She had been daydreaming about her house since she was fourteen. She had ideas in mind for the decor that no one else would even dare to try, subtle combinations of color, perspective, pattern that would glow without dazzling, delight the eye without any of the mechanisms being visible.

She wanted her house more than she wanted anything else in the world. Her mother had never had an opportunity like that. For her, it had been a simple three-and-two her whole life, the only private space being the little attic upstairs.

She leafed through those sketchbooks quickly – she didn't need light to see their contents – then put them both down and picked up the most foolish, silly one of all, not coincidentally the oldest, begun when she was little more than nine – the wedding book, inspired by Buck's marriage. The first sketches were the ones she'd done that day, a small, extremely inept, extremely excited bridesmaid. They were followed by the ones done five years later, at Jack's wedding. The sketches impressed her even now – not bad for a girl of those ages. Her favorite brother Jack – no one could have foreseen the pain that lay ahead for him. Not something she wanted to dwell upon tonight. In the pages beyond lay her own dreams – wedding plans laid out in detail, bridal gowns in all sorts of fashions, bridesmaid's dresses, tuxedos of all kinds, floral arrangements, designs, decorations for the reception, even a suit for the minister. It was a foolish book because she'd known since the middle of high school that all that would have to be postponed indefinitely, in all probability to a time when she was too old for such a ceremony to be sensible aesthetically. It was silly in any case because neither she nor her family could possibly have afforded a tenth of what she had in mind. Still, she kept adding to it. Adele never quit on any project once she had begun it. Mostly, it was fun.

She shook her head in the darkness. She was right to keep this private. What raucous laughter, what condescension, maybe even disbelief, if that small group of lads in the adjoining office this morning could see her now – cool, calm, super-bright Adele Jansen, sitting cross-legged in the darkness, mired in adolescent dreams and visions. Greg Steuer had made her such a point of controversy, some unfathomable mystery, as if she was some surrealistically fiendish combination of Dragon Lady and Little Mary Sunshine. Tough-minded, yes; ambitious, true; she was those things, she had to be. But she was also the squishy soft sentimentalist sitting here, sketchbook open, flannel nightgown, legs folded lotus style beneath. *It's really so much simpler, Greg; I act sweet because I am sweet; and I go for things because I am ambitious.* Both aspects of her personality were equally real, equally important to her.

He'd seen that, hadn't he? she suddenly thought. *Both sides right away.* Remarkable. She would have thought she'd be frightened to be that transparent, that open, to anyone. But she wasn't frightened.

Adele picked up another, older book. *Ice Maiden*, the Glee Club called her. Resentment tickled her for a moment, followed by a flash of self-irritation. She was too old, too mature, to take that sort of nonsense seriously. But still. . . so unfair. So stupid. True, she did her best to maintain her poise in professional situations, no question about that. But in no other way was she a solemn person. She had never made any attempt to disguise the natural liveliness of her personality, her sense of fun. The Ninotchka, padded-shoulders image of a career woman was such a bore. In any case, it wasn't her and she didn't try to pretend that it was.

Ice Maiden. Back at Syracuse, some of her classmates had said something similar in different words. *What you are, Adele, is a control freak*, someone announced authoritatively to her face during her last year there. *You're afraid to let go.* Same epithet as the Glee Club, right? Two synonymous phrases – seemingly.

Not quite. She *was* a control freak. She was *not* an ice maiden. The truth of the first was directly related to the falsity of the second. The plain fact was that she happened to be about as icy in personal reality as your average, everyday active volcano.

Did the people who used labels like that know what it was like to be hyper-emotional? *Did* they? She could tell them stories. There was the morning she was supposed to give a paper on the Hagia Sophia, the great temple in Istanbul. She'd done her usual thorough job, borrowing slides from one of the graduate instructors and working up a solid presentation. The room had become dark, the projector was on, she'd started in, when suddenly she'd lost her breath entirely – it was so *beautiful!* – and stopped, red, speechless, trembling. It was only the fact that the assistant professor was both sensitive and sympathetic that had saved her from a major public humiliation. Incidents like that used to occur all the time. These days she was wiser to herself, could head off the storms when she felt them coming. But still they came.

Sometimes it was funny. Classic works of art were hardly the only occasion. Buck's second rerun theater was going down for the third time during her senior year in high school. Among his other desperate moves was a series of Saturday matinées aimed at the family trade. Everyone in the family helped out. Adele's job was to provide free childcare for the ones whose parents couldn't attend. One Saturday attendance was unusually good. The reason was a clown and a magic show, not the movie. Even Buck, the ultimate cinema enthusiast, of whom it was almost literally true that he had never seen a film he didn't like, could find little good to say about it. It proved to be a very poorly made three-hankie weeper, a sort of third class *Lassie, Go Home* knockoff, only with a little girl and a pony. The script was horrible, the actors were execrable – even the pony was unappealing. The plot contrivances were obvious, the story absurd and banal – the little kids themselves were jeering and throwing things at the screen. Everyone in the theater was laughing at it – everyone, that is, except the theoretically super-bright Adele Elizabeth Jansen, Regent's Scholar and soon-to-be co-valedictorian, who sat through the awful thing, fully aware she was being manipulated, fully aware of how dreadfully superficial the manipulations were, even so clutching her handkerchief, biting her lower lip – *the poor little pony!* – to keep from sobbing along. Dear God.

Or the horror movies that everyone thought were so funny while her hair stood on end; or the news shows with famine reports that other people endured, but made her physically ill. Memories like those could make her wince even now, years afterward; no point in dredging up more of them. But the worst, the most potent thing of all, was sex.

Sex was the worst because sex was the best. Sex had the power to destroy her.

*

The prosaic fact, which none of the members of the Glee Club knew, or at least understood, was that cool, calm Adele Jansen, the Ice Maiden, was about as hard to turn on as your average, everyday table lamp. She had found out early in adolescence that she was not the type of girl who could remain poised and unruffled in a boy's arms. She was the type who became hot and flustered and lost her composure almost at once. And she became fully engaged so quickly! On more than one occasion in high school, the only thing that had saved her virtue from an undoubtedly premature demise was that the boy had been even more frightened of what he had wrought than she was.

Then she had gone to Syracuse. These were not boys anymore, they were men, albeit callow and immature, and they did not become alarmed when a girl became unexpectedly passionate. She lost her virginity almost immediately. There were coed dorms and fraternity parties every weekend. She'd had some initiation. No reason, really, why any of that should have bothered her – this was the modern age, wasn't it? She was the modern single woman; she kept up with her classes. If she wanted to be a party girl during her downtime, that was her business – wasn't it? Finally there had come Rush Week before spring break, the final Friday night, when events had occurred that couldn't be rationalized, that had to be addressed – and when she came home for break that April, five days later, she couldn't look her father in the face.

Sitting here on the floor of her New York apartment eight years later, it was easy to sympathize with the stone-faced girl who had returned home that holiday. She had only been seventeen, was far more naïve than she realized at the time. The men who exploited her had all been much more experienced. In a sense, her scarlet sins had been committed in all innocence. It really was understanda–

No. She broke in on her own thoughts. *No rationalizations, stupid. It was your doing, your fault. What you learned then, you are never going to forget. You know what you'd become.*

At first, she'd done no more than go to a few parties, the same as many others, and she'd the same things that the others did there – some of the others. At least, that's how it had begun. But she'd lost control almost at once, discovered aspects of herself that she had never dreamed existed, became engulfed in a tidal wave of experience with which she had not been prepared to cope. It had seemed dangerous – it *was* dangerous – but for a long time that had been part of the fun, part of the excitement, the roller coaster barely on track, the exhilaration of recklessness.

And then came the week of Spring Rush, ending on the last Friday night, when it had – when it – well, whatever you had to say – when the whole insane life style had bottomed out into one squalid, unspeakable, ultimately humiliating and degrading scene. . .that afterwards she had ever been. . . that she could possibly have felt gra – gra – gr – She choked on the word, like she always did.

No. Don't go there.

She had helped her sisters-in-law with the meal that Easter, while the children around her bustled and played and the men in her family sank to their annual nadir of uselessness. But the remainder of that week she spent in her room, thinking. *I'm a little behind,* she smiled. *You know how it is.* No one believed her. *Delly?* Jack asked, knocking softly at her door; Michael persisted with his blunt questions until it was obviously useless. Buck made discrete inquiries in the form of movie allusions. Her father fretted – so unlike his daughter to keep secrets from him. They had become unusually close during her adolescence, so much so that he sometimes felt guilty, as that could not have happened if her mother had lived. Now he worried, sensing the worst, knowing all too well what can happen in the first flush of independence. She sensed his anxiety and twisted deeper into guilt and shame. It would have been wonderful to say something. But the worst was so much worse than anything he could have guessed. Smiling, determined, she held him at bay as she did her brothers.

Something had to be done. The discoveries she'd made about herself had to be addressed. Even then, she had a wry, self-critical sense of humor when it came to the Adele who actually was. But the Adele-who-could-be, the person she intended to become, was someone she took very seriously. That person would never have permitted herself to. . . would never, ever have participated in the final. . . her cheeks burned red with shame, and she could not bear even to bring to mind the final recollection. Stiffly, conscientiously, in tight-lipped solitude, she drew her own conclusions, made her decisions. Instinctively, she buried – as best she could – the details of the memory. That she had ever, in her life, allowed herself. . .

Then the memory was locked away, never to be re-examined voluntarily. There was nothing more to be gained there. With an act of sheer will, she deafened herself to the clamorous voice of the demented, reckless beast within her that craved resumption of the same lifestyle. By the time she left for school Sunday night, the fundamental decisions had been made. Her social life, which she had regarded in those first few weeks as a holiday from her larger ambitions, was going to be subjected to the same rigorous self-discipline she enforced in other areas of her life. She returned to campus braced for one major confrontation, which never occurred – the non-occurrence confirming, in its own way, the wisdom of her decisions.

Afterwards, she was true to the promises she'd made to herself. Perhaps the scale of the trauma helped. For a long, long time she was unwilling to trust herself in any way, with anyone. Her nascent reputation faded as the persons who remembered her first few months graduated or moved on. The one-time party girl was forgotten. The controls were in place and they stayed there, whatever anyone might say, no matter how the body rebelled. Although the lifestyle she required of herself never was an easy one for her – at times one that seemed unendurable – with one pardonable exception she had stuck to it.

She was and always would be a girl who could burst into flames on the slightest provocation. Greg Steuer, experienced womanizer that he was, had not been mistaken about the heat he felt in the backseat of a taxi, had not misperceived the pure physical joy she experienced in his arms, her fierce delight in his touch and embrace, the shortening of breath, the quickening of pulse. But Greg Steuer, a very shallow young man, in assuming those reactions provided the keys to her solution, had completely misunderstood the woman he was holding. The controls were in place and they stayed there, flames or not. The lessons of the Spring Rush night were never to be forgotten, however much the memory might be.

Control freak? They thought they were insulting her, but nothing could have been more flattering. She was controlled because she had to be. She knew why. Besides, she had some opinions of her own, which were best kept discreetly to her. People who ranted about the superiority of feelings? People who glorified the awful daring of a moment's surrender which an age of prudence could not erase?? They had to be pretty cold fish if they needed all that help.

Enough. This was too good a night for such thoughts. For this night, anyway, leave all that for another day.

*

Bri. He had a book all to himself.

The yearbook editor, her debate partner, her first boyfriend, and the one pardonable exception to the Spring Break rules – about which she felt no guilt at all. When your oldest friend in the world comes back from Harvard with his heart broken by some frigid bitch at Northeastern, worried he's becoming impotent, there's only one thing any self-respecting girl can do – particularly when she had been in love with him once (and wonders if she still is). Besides, he really should have been the first – would have been if he hadn't been gentleman enough to let a hooked fish off the line more than once.

There were at least two dozen sketches of him, beginning when he was fourteen. She didn't have the best; she'd framed that and given it to him on the day he left for college. It still hung over the mantle in his mother's home. The problem two summers later had been that they were no longer lovers, just best friends, although that explanation sometimes seemed to her to be too simple. At any rate, it didn't click. They both recognized it at about the same time, but he'd said it first and best.

"Delly," he'd said, as she lay naked in his arms, "we're not making love. We're having sex, and that's not good enough for either one of us," and that had been that; they never went to bed together again.

Brian Johnson and Adele Jansen. *Johnson and Jansen. We don't quit and we don't lose.* They'd slapped hands and whispered that before the start of each debate; silly adolescents. She adopted it as her own motto, brought it over to field hockey, except that the Roosevelt Tigresses did lose every once in a while. Johnson and Jansen didn't, not in their senior year. They would have won State, too, if it hadn't been for that male chauvinist pig from Oneonta.

The regionals had been going on for three days, a double elimination system – lose twice and you're out. They hadn't lost at all; there were only two teams left, them and two boys from Schenectady who had lost once. They were being judged by all of the judges in the competition, thirty-four of them. The room was packed, and they were winning.

The only problem was the judge who actually conducted the debate. The rules that year permitted questioning by him. Few of the judges exercised the option, but this one couldn't shut up. He was an older man who apparently could not get over her size and look – the Cuteness Factor in its essence. The first questions he'd asked her were so patronizing it was embarrassing; it got worse from there. Every woman in the room was looking at her, some cringing, some contemptuous, none supportive, as if she'd brought all this on herself.

"What do I do, Bri?" she'd whispered as she sat down after the penultimate round of questioning.

"You've got to do something, Delly," he'd hissed back; he was seething on her behalf. "This is going to be the story of your life if you let it." He'd named it first. *The Cuteness Factor, Delly,* he'd said, during one of their planning sessions. *In any given room, you are the front runner for the Most Likely to Be Disregarded award.* He'd spoken semi-facetiously, kindly, in that way of his. But she'd taken what he said to heart. No getting around the truth of it; she looked cute – worse yet, sounded cute. Her larynx was in the same proportion as everything else so that her voice, while pleasant, was light and high-pitched. There is no point in even trying to adopt a formidable manner when you're doomed to chirp or twitter. She had to find other ways. The Cuteness Factor – often frustrating, sometimes useful, but never, never to be disregarded.

She had been the last to speak at the debate final. Time was almost gone when the judge asked his last question: "Just what does a pretty little thing like you do for fun when you're not winning debates?" He thought he was being funny.

Something fundamental snapped. She beamed her brightest, most winsome smile. "Well, I like to cook and do needlepoint, of course, and there's always quilting," she chirped. The room became tense then, but she paused only for dramatic effect, and plunged on: "But if you must know, my favorite hobby is sucking cock." She'd never even said the words before, let alone done the deed. There was an audible gasp from the hall. She looked him directly in the eye. "I particularly like old, withered ones," she added sweetly.

"And she's terrific at it, too!" Brian, who knew first hand she was still a Pure Thing, had shouted, standing up behind her and for her. Bri was a stand-up guy in general. If they were going down in flames – and they were – they were going down together.

They'd been there till after midnight. They'd won the debate, all right, thirty-one to three, no problem about that. The problem was that the geezer had turned out to be the president of the regional forensics society, the principal of a high school in Oneonta, a lay minister in his church, humorless, and a close personal friend of the principal at Roosevelt, equally humorless. After an interminable time, they'd been disqualified on the basis of an ancient rule that prohibited rude and vulgar speech. The comments on the ballots of some of the judges who did have a sense of humor – mostly women – were their only consolation.

The detention system at Roosevelt was intended primarily for freshmen and sophomores. No one could remember the last time two seniors had earned ten days' worth in the last two months of school. They must have been the only co-valedictorians in the history of the state who spent the week before graduation cleaning erasers.

*

He was in Zaire now, a member of the Foreign Service, with his wife, the one-time frigid bitch from Northeastern. Brian had evidently found some method of warming her up that fall. Adele was both pleased and disappointed. She was sure she had something to do with the warming up; on the other hand, he'd married too soon, and – and – truth be told – she did not like Linda one bit better than Linda liked her. Not nearly worthy of Bri.

Impotent? That was a joke. Of course, he'd been so demoralized at first that she'd had to do quite a bit of work. That little episode at the debate had proved to be prophetic. ("I *knew* you'd be terrific at that," he said.) But once he was aroused she had no complaints at all. Friends or whatever, it had been glorious when he'd taken her into his arms, run his hands over her body, and–

Thinking quite a bit about sex tonight, aren't you, dummy? Her smile expanded in the darkness. Three guesses why – no, she only needed one if she could use two words, both proper names. Best to call off that train of thought; whatever else, it wasn't likely to make her drowsy. She started to put the sketchbooks away.

The first dreamhouse book went back second to last. Money – that's a surefire cure for romantic dreaming. *Why dream about love when you can worry about money?* She was on the fast track, sure, but the track of what she wanted seemed to be moving so much faster. Another Same Old Story; the Rube Comes to the Big City. You think you're ready for it, but you find out you're not. The velocity with which money travelled here! The inertia it acquired when it came to rest! Hapgood, Thurlow paid her five times what her father had made in the best year he ever had – and yet. . . and yet. . . compared to the ultra-rich – say, the horrible Lawtons – she had a sense she was losing ground. *They make money the old-fashioned way.* Scary.

She owed a fortune to her law school. Worse: there were other debts, debts of honor. Her father had made up the whole difference between her expenses and her scholarship and savings while she had been at Syracuse. *Your brothers are grown and gone, your mother's not with me, and I don't need that much anymore. You worked all through high school; you're going to work the rest of your life. I want at least one of my kids to use the college years for what they should be.* He'd never asked, she wasn't able yet to volunteer, but she knew how much he'd spent to the penny, and it was money that would be repaid if it were her last act on Earth.

So much money she needed. It could be all it was, really, was a dream, unattainable. The world was filling in so quickly. Everyone wanted what she wanted. She was no racist, but she was a card carrying, unapologetic currencist – deeply prejudiced against Eurodollars, Hong Kong dollars, British pounds, Swiss francs, Japanese yen. She had no capital, no family resources, no contacts; how was she ever going to catch up? And do all the normal female things – not having children of her own was unthinkable – at the same time? Her mother had been an undiscovered genius – how might that heritage be exemplified in her own life? Without being transformed and debased by her own ambition? How? *How??*

Enough. Normally, demoralizing thoughts – but nothing was going to demoralize her tonight. She was still on a roll. Tonight was one of those glorious nights when everything seemed possible, easy; reach up and pluck the fruit off the tree when the summer's night breeze blows the branch towards your hand. After all, $1,000,000 a year if she just kept going. Sometimes it didn't seem that hard.

She put the last book away, the one with the most recent sketches. There were things in there that would surprise some people who thought butter didn't melt in her mouth – a wicked sketch of Carolyn Hoffman in the manner of Grosz, depicting her as *truly* bejeweled – toe rings, ankle bracelets, calf bracelets, thigh bracelets, navel stone, and so forth, ending with a ridiculously large pearl nose-pin. She had done a flattering caricature of Jenet Furston, portrayed as a lighthouse. There was also a drawing of a lapdog, unmistakably a lapdog, but also unmistakably Josh Palmdale, wagging its tail as a big hand stretched down holding a biscuit.

With the drawer closed, she sat for a moment in the darkness, her thoughts traveling to the root cause of all this good feeling. *Seduced too many of my junior editors for me to have any doubt of that*, Jenet had said. She could believe it. He was fascinating in a wonderfully mysterious way. But not for her – too far out of her orbit, leading a life that might as well be led on another planet. She was grateful to him for this nice erotic pulse and the delicious flavor of the moment. But no more would come of it than that.

She stood up abruptly, directly out of the lotus position. *Enough, dummy; it's time to sleep.* Another mountain of billable time was waiting to be mined in the morning. She slid under the covers.

She still felt great, but she had finally become sleepy. Thoughts were becoming random. Drowsily, she realized she'd been wrong about one thing right from the start; time to admit it.

He was much, much better looking than she had realized at first.

A DAY LIKE ANY OTHER

"**I** have good news for you, Ms. Jansen." The deputy district attorney handling the Lawton matter was on the line.

"Yes?"

"I'm not going to file charges against James Lawton. In fact, I'll support a petition to expunge the record of the arrest if you file one."

Adele let out a deep breath. "That is good news. Are the affidavits the reason?"

"Yes and no. They were very impressive – really excellent work. But I don't know whether they would have been enough to tip the scale all by themselves. They were enough to make me send my investigator back to re-interview Mrs. Lawton.

"I've got an awfully good investigator. She takes these things seriously and she gets as angry over the phony cases as the real ones. Angrier. At any rate, she really grilled Henrietta Lawton. It helped that Mrs. Lawton had heard about you, about how thorough you were. She finally broke down and admitted she made the whole thing up – what you guys thought, the divorce hearing. We've got it all on tape."

Adele pricked up her ears. "On tape? Can you turn a copy of it over to me?"

"Sure. You could always subpoena my investigator to the hearing if I didn't. Just send me proof that you've notified her attorneys about your request."

"Done," said Adele. There was a short silence on the other end of the line.

"Ms. Jansen," said the deputy district attorney, "I know you were a little impatient with us for going on with this after all the evidence you accumulated. But we take this stuff awfully seriously these days – maybe because of all the years we didn't. If you have any other domestic clients, you should warn them to be careful. This is an area where an innocent person can get hurt pretty easily by their spouse. The presumption of innocence isn't what it used to be with child abuse."

Adele thought of Dr. Petrosian. She had regretted that conversation, but not because she thought she'd been wrong. "Thanks. This happens to be my first and last domestic case, but I'll pass the word along. And thanks for everything else."

They hung up. Adele sat back in her chair for a moment, exulting. This was going to turn out to be as good a day as the last, maybe better. There was only one small cloud on the horizon, one which should clear up momentarily.

Her first stop when she arrived at the office punctually at 9:30 was the small conference room where Tom Newcombe had been dictating the night before. It was for purely professional reasons, of course. Jenet had asked her to keep an eye on him. But he hadn't come in yet. That wasn't the end of the world. It was still quite early. But it was enough to create that small cloud.

She dialed Greenfield. The rescheduled property hearing was now only three days away.

"*Tape?*" She could hear the excitement in his voice. "Henny Lawton confessed on tape?"

"Yes."

"Boy! Boy oh boy!" Greenfield laughed out loud. "That changes everything. We've got her behind the eight ball now. I'd bet Mrs. Lawton just talked herself out of at least twenty million bucks and exclusive custody of the kids. Murdoch's going to think you walk on water."

"Thanks, but no thanks. I'd rather not have the by-line on this story. I might get drafted again."

"Well, you're going to get it. My days of glory-hogging are over. You're the man – that's not right, the heroine – of the hour, Adele. Put in for a bonus, if you want, take the rest of the day off; it's fine with me and it'll be fine with Murdoch."

"The only thing I really want," said Adele, "is to be sure I don't get any more assignments like this. Something big happened yesterday."

He laughed again. "Carolyn Hoffman's already taken care of that. Her comments at the last partners' meeting about the misuse of your time were – shall we say – forceful? I wish you'd been a fly on the ceiling. You'd have enjoyed it. Carolyn has plans for you.

"As for this," – he switched into one of his voices – "get a letter over to the D. A., copy to Henny's lawyer, send the file back to me, and you're off the hook. I promise. You have seen the last of Mr. Lawton."

"Jack Lemon?" she asked politely. "I mean, the young Jack Lemon? Ensign Pulver?"

"Pee Wee Herman," he said. "Really. You're losing your ear. But my word's still good."

"Thank God," said Adele.

This should be a great day. She was finished with Lawton; she'd learned she was considered important enough to be discussed at a partners' meeting. But there was still that small cloud – getting larger.

She glanced at the vase clock: 10:25. She wondered if any of the eagle-eyed secretarial gossips would notice if she revisited the small conference room. She decided to chance it and go anyway.

The room was still empty except for the tape recorder. *Damn.*

She went back to her office impatient with herself. She was old enough to know all about the non-boiling characteristics of watched kettles. She dictated the letter to the deputy D.A. (copy to opposing counsel), a general memo to the family law people summarizing his informal advice, and started on the first of the million-and-one other things she had to do.

There was a soft knock on the door frame

"Good morning," said Tom.

*

Adele felt a pleasant tightening of her stomach, the same combination of shyness and breathlessness as when she was thirteen and a boy she secretly fancied asked her to dance. The sensation surprised her. She had not known exactly how much she liked him until right then.

"Hi," she said. "I was expecting you a little earlier."

He looked much better than he had the day before. The circles under his eyes were reduced and there was some color in his face. His mild blue pupils were bright and sparkling.

"I worked until nearly 3:45 last night."

She was surprised. Work obviously agreed with him; but she felt compelled to disapprove. "Tom, you shouldn't have."

He shook his head. "I sleep better when I'm exhausted. Besides, I had another reason."

"What was that?" said Adele.

He hesitated. "I'm hoping that you'll take the afternoon off and come away with me."

"I'd love to, but I can't," she responded automatically.

The half-smile appeared on his face. "Yes, you can," he said softly. "That's the whole point." He reached into his pocket and pulled out a handful of micro cassette tapes. "This is what I did last night – things I would otherwise have been doing this afternoon. If I had, it would have been on your time and you'd be billing it to Jenet Furston. As it is, the time's already over and the day is yours. You're trading the evening behind for the afternoon ahead."

"I wasn't here."

"You might as well have been. You were in spirit. The only reason I was working was to free you up today. It's the same time whether it's then or now." He paused; the shadow smile flickered across his face. "If you put in the time again, that's the time times two, less the time already done, and that makes the two of us negative, and that can't be right."

"You're too intelligent not to know that's a rationalization."

"I'm intelligent enough to know that there's not that much difference between rationalizations and rationales. You're going to bill the time to Jenet, aren't you? Whether it's then or now."

He was absolutely right, of course. "You're very cynical."

"Realistic. If it was done then, you're free now."

"I owe the firm the time," she said desperately.

"No, you don't. I've already put it in for you. It's my gift to you. Accept it. Please." His tone was light, but there was a serious element as well.

She looked away from him and down at her hands, smiling. She was surprised to discover she was tempted. He cocked his head to one side to meet her eye, in the manner of a curious dog looking through a doorway.

"I can't, Tom," she said as she looked up. "I'd love to, but I can't. It's pointless even to talk about it." She paused. "Where were you going to take me?"

"The Metropolitan Museum. The Prado show. If you haven't been to it."

She slapped her hand to her forehead. "Oh, God! Get thee behind me, Satan! I haven't been, and I'd *love* to go."

About eleven months earlier, the Prado, the great museum in Madrid, and the Metropolitan Museum of Art had exchanged one-year loans on substantial portions of their respective catalogues. The Met now had on exhibit a large number of priceless canvases by Velásquez, Goya, and others. Adele had meant to view it, but the exhibit had been constantly mobbed at the beginning – it still was, on weekends – and it gradually slipped off her calendar. Now the time was almost gone.

She might have known he would pick the one thing in the City that was well-nigh irresistible.

His eyes gleamed for an instant. "Then come away with me."

"I can't, Tom," she said, with the distinct feeling she was losing this argument, an even stronger sense that she didn't want to win. "I can't. I wish I could, but I can't. These are my nose-to-the-grindstone years. They have to be. I thought you understood that," she added, a bit reproachfully.

"I do," he replied, "and you're right. But you can't make any rule that absolute. You have to test it. The only thing worth buying with money is time.

Give up all your time to make money and you've made a bad deal. It's only one afternoon. The time's accounted for. Please."

She paused; it would have been apparent to a much less observant person than Thomas Newcombe that she was teetering. She had the unusual (for her) urge to do exactly as she pleased. Impulses of delight were lonely things in her life.

"You can take one day off," he said. "Jenet asked you to keep an eye on me."

Jenet *had* asked her to look after him – Walter Greenfield *had* mentioned taking the day off. There was nothing immediate to do on AI Squared. She'd done what she could the night before. She had no appointments today, nothing pressing now that Lawton was finally behind. It had been a long time since she had taken any vacation time. It was possible.

She appraised him, feigning exasperation, turning the possibility over in her mind. He spread his arms out beside his hips, palms up, half-smile on his face. *Please.* His eyes were alert and alive. It was wonderful to see him like this, free from his afflictions – if only for a moment – flattering to think that she might be the cause.

It was only one day, after all.

All at once, she decided. With a look of mock anger, she picked up the phone and buzzed Carolyn Hoffman's office. "I really shouldn't be doing this," she said to him. "I've never done anything like this before."

"In conference?" Something to do with the Project. "Then –" she gulped, took a deep breath, and gushed on – "leave her word that I've left the office. Jenet Furston asked me to look after the contract writer and he wants to check the physical details of two sites. I'm going with him." She was certain she was completely transparent to Carolyn's secretary.

The secretary took the message without comment. Adele hung up.

"Well –" she said, but Tom was no longer seated. He was standing to the side of the desk, holding out her purse. As she shouldered it, he took her elbow with his bad hand and helped her out of the chair. In another quick stride, he moved to the door to escort her out. Adele was amused.

"If I didn't know better, Mr. Newcombe, I'd think I was being hustled."

There was quiet laughter in his face. "You are. I don't want you to change your mind. I especially don't want the phone to ring."

Three short steps took Adele out the door. They stopped at the word processing department where he left the tapes for transcription. Then they were into the elevator and gone.

*

During the long years to come, whenever she was asked the same inevitable and invariable questions, she always felt a small, private frustration that she herself did not know exactly how or when. It had all begun slowly, so slowly. There were so many ways in which it was a day like any other.

"I think that's the hardest thing in the world to do," said Tom. "Portraiture. History, prophecy – in real time, and not, both at once. Chasing the bubble."

"What?" said Adele. They were standing on the third floor of the museum, in the hall which exhibited paintings from the tenth through the fourteenth centuries, naïve but oddly compelling windows into different realities, times long past.

"Portrait painting. You. Velásquez."

"I can now die happy," said Adele, "having been mentioned in the same breath as Velásquez. Only don't say that to anyone else or you're liable to be committed. The thing about chasing the bubble won't exactly help, either. I don't follow that myself."

They were alone. The day was one of those perfect autumnal days that God and nature give to New York every once in a long while by way of apology for so many of the others. Most of the City had decided it was a day better spent in places other than museums. Those who had come to the Met had come to see the Prado exhibit. Tom and Adele had also gone through that before doing anything else. It had always been her practice to view an exhibit quickly, allow the initial impressions to settle, and then review it thoroughly. They did just that – anything she wanted to do was apparently fine with him – then went to the third floor, which amazingly turned out to be deserted.

"I remember watching the little kids blowing soap bubbles. Every once in a while, there'd be one different from the rest, or refracting light peculiarly, or something, and the kid would want to keep it, play with it, understand it. But they couldn't; it was too delicate, too evanescent, gone too quickly."

He paused. "The moment. An instant here, now, then – see, this one's gone already – to capture it, solidify it, what is, what was, what could be. In a face, in a person, in a portrait. Fragile as the kid's bubble, but infinitely more complex. Time bubbles. It doesn't seem possible."

She listened then with two minds. On the one hand, it was marvelous to hear him creating work-in-process. He was trying out ideas, she could tell. On the other, sooner or later she would have to tell him that the only conclusion she had reached about aesthetic theory, after three years of study, was that it was utterly worthless.

Beneath it all, she could feel events beginning to rustle, the first faint stirrings of a crescendo, a summing up of the last two days. Something was going to happen. All this was leading someplace. He'd begun in a low key, deliberately pedantic. Even so, she felt a subtle, glimmering excitement.

"Or –" his eyes brightened momentarily – "give it a math spin. A Cartesian framework. The horizontal axis describes the person as they are, the vertical as they could be, the potential, their character; actually, character is potential, the sense of what someone is or is not capable. Then you find the one angle where the two intersect, actuality, potential, zero-zero," – here, he brought his bad left hand down on his good right one, forming a ninety-degree angle – "An artistic adz? He bisects the bubble, displays the person who is, the person who could be."

What a dreadful way to approach art, Adele thought. She tried to be diplomatic. "I think –" she began carefully.

" – that the trope is terrible?" His eyes sparkled. "You're right. Just awful. Still, you play with it, spin it a little, twist it around. Every once in a while, you toy with an ugly duckling long enough, something works out. Other times, it stays ugly. We'll see." The half-smile flickered across his face. "But you fearless portrait-painters go on chasing them anyway. I admire that."

Her own eyes sparkled in reply. "Actually, the comparison of art to snake hunting had eluded me until this exact second," she said. "But I do think I'm in the large majority on that one."

"Or –" he began again, but enough was enough. It would be bad if he embarrassed himself. She had to tell him that art theory, no matter how brightened by metaphoric language, was of no interest whatsoever to her.

"Tom –" she started.

"If you're about to tell me that theorizing about art bores you to tears," he said softly, "don't bother. It's obvious."

"But how –"

"You were a practicing artist. You'd be extremely unusual if you had any use at all for theory. *Am Anfang war die Tat.*"

"I wasn't going to say anything about theory, exactly," she lied, stony-faced. "I was actually going to ask you just how you'd managed to live as long as you have."

"With great difficulty," he answered, without missing a beat. His voice was as soft as ever, always with the same slight lilt. But his eyes were alight, the half-smile that came and went was dancing about his face, and he had clearly begun to play.

"Anyway, I wasn't talking about art, really. I was talking about time, about the monumentality of a single second."

They took another few steps. The air was becoming stiller; their complete isolation remained unbroken. There was an eerie, positive excitement astir today. Something marvelous was coming into being, but she had no idea what.

"But why painters only?" she asked. "Don't you do the same thing when you write a poem?"

"Oh, no, no, no – not at all. Painters are hunters of time. Writers are architects. A poem exists outside of real time, in a world of its own, in its own structure. It is what it is, once it's been written, and the world of real events doesn't affect it at all. The first line is always first, the second is always second, and always will be. Even if you read it backwards or from the middle, you don't change it. You just make a fool of yourself. It is the way it is from the first second it comes into full existence, and events don't alter it.

"It's not in real time. Actually, nothing important exists there. An artist takes an ordinary moment out of real time into its own, that's the glory of it."

They moved along towards the next painting. Suddenly, he stopped and looked up towards the ceiling, the half-smile playing on his face. It was as if he'd just heard the faint strains of a sweet, mysterious music, coming from a great distance.

She held her breath for a moment. The sense of the marvelous she'd been groping for was now almost tangible. Something eerily magnificent was poised on the verge.

He spoke: "Nothing important." He looked around, looked at her. "And neither are we, Adele. We're not in real time anymore; it disappeared somewhere along the way, I can feel it. Can't you? Outside, in the real world, there's a direct relation; when you move a few feet, you move a few seconds. In here, there's no relation at all. You move a foot either way, a yard up or down, and you might move several centuries. When the direct relation is gone, so are all the limitations.

"We're not in real time here. What's possible between us is too important to exist there. This is some time out of time that we've created, you and I, that's ours alone. Anything is possible, here, today. Anything can happen." His voice was no louder than a whisper, but the hall echoed with it.

So that was it; this is where it had been leading. Time out of time, a reality of their own. Yes.

She knew there was a sense in which it was only another metaphor. She could see it in the sparkle of his eyes, feel it in the light touch on her shoulder. Even so, even knowing that, he'd conjured up a powerful spell. The world she knew wavered and became hazy. She was sharing his world now, the largeness in which he existed, a delicious universe of limitless, undifferentiated possibility. The still air had become tingly and alive. Everything was possible. Anything could happen, here, today.

There was still no one else on the floor. The two of them remained entirely alone. A pervasive sense of deep mystery emanated from the carpeted floors, the walls, the stillness itself. The Christs and Madonnas of a different millennium looked down upon her, with their odd postures and eerie, gentle eyes. She felt suddenly that everything around her lived. She had fully caught his mood. There was a special wonder in these dark rooms, where history gathers and thickens, the only places on Earth where the dead in reality speak to the living.

She gazed around in the same manner he had and touched his sleeve.

*

A great shimmering magic had overtaken them and the afternoon. She was not sure – she never would be sure – when or how it had begun, or of its precise dimensions. The only thing of which she was completely certain was the identity of the magician.

It was a day for wandering, through hollow lands and hilly lands, through a timescape large to the point of immeasurability. It was a time for speaking, of many things: shoes, sealing wax and coronets, kind hearts and great sailing ships, old, sad tales of the death of kings, newer, stranger ones of the birth of galaxies, the Incompleteness Theorem, fashion and feminism in the fourteenth century, verticals and horizontals – he would not give that up – object code. It was no day for introspection, questions, second thoughts; instead, a day for deeds, the simple acts of doing with which (as he'd said) everything begins.

The museum itself was territory that was far more hers than his, where her mastery was so instinctive as to be unconscious. She was the guide, seer, medium of information; he the student and receptor. But it was her sense that in all this she served a wizard, playing Ariel to his Prospero.

They wandered from room to room, floor to floor. Now and then, they encountered others, but the enchantment now had grown too strong to be dispelled so easily. Something on the wall would catch his eye and he would touch her arm and ask a question, or she would point out something she thought he should see. Adele experienced the common frustration of persons five years out of school at the disappearance of so much undergraduate knowledge she had assumed would be hers forever. But she was delighted to discover that her eye and her instincts were as sound as ever. She would tell him what she saw; mostly he would only nod and listen. Having defined the territory, having created the spell, he was content to retreat for the large part into his preferred role of watcher, listener, quite willing to observe her as she mapped it out. Occasionally, he would transmute her insight effortlessly into something uniquely his own, strange and rich.

It was fascinating simply to watch him lose himself in his own thoughts. She would never have believed that it could be pleasurable simply to watch another human being in contemplation, but it turned out to be so.

*

"You know, I was never with the people who left it all to instinct. You know, let it flow, let it just happen, that sort of thing," said Adele. "Analyzing a work of art always made it better for me. But maybe you do over-quantify." This last said with a little timidity; she was unaccustomed to talking so personally so soon, but they had reached a level of intimacy in a short period that was unprecedented for her.

"It must sound that way," he said, "and maybe you're right. But I think I'm not articulating it well. Wholes and sums, to try to say the same thing another way. It's not quantification as such that interests me. It's the randomness of the correlation. It's easy to say quantification doesn't quantify, 'All I'm certain of is uncertainty,' easy juvenile paradoxes. But the randomness is a genuine mystery. Sometimes the numbers define the entire reality, often they don't." They were in front of the Rembrandt painting of Aristotle and the bust of Homer.

"What about something like that? It could be broken down, bit by bit, digitized – and there are beings in the world, or shortly will be, for which the digitized version and that are the same. You couldn't really argue with such a being if – when – it obtained speech and claimed that both versions are identical. And yet. . . and yet. . . those cases where the whole equals the sum, those cases where the whole is so much greater, and no easy, calculable rule to distinguish the two. Magic, perhaps, except that there is no such thing." He looked more closely at her. "You're smiling. You've thought about these things, too, haven't you? Tell me."

"It really is funny. Funny, odd. That's exactly what I wrote my law review article about. I said –"

"Wait a minute. Wait a minute. Let me guess." He closed his eyes for a long moment, thinking, then spoke as he opened them. "You're an intellectual property lawyer, right? You must have written about who owns the rights if someone does write such a program, because on the one hand he's copying the painting, but on the other, every line of the source code is new. Is that right?"

She nodded slowly, smiling. "Exactly. It's become a fairly pressing problem. In theory, anyway."

"What did you decide?" He seemed genuinely curious.

"It's very, very complex. The issue really becomes complicated if the programmer uses some compression technique – because if it's compressed enough you can argue that it's not a work of art any more, which is protectible, but merely highly compressed information, which theoretically isn't. I thought I'd be writing about law, but I ended up over at the general library, reading about people like Shannon and Norbert Weiner. I got enough out of it to finish my article, but I can't say I understand it in depth; I'm not a mathematician." She stopped briefly. "I'm sure you know that work."

It was humorous; he actually blushed. "Oh, yes. Shannon's Information Theory. An old friend. That stuff comes pretty easily to me. It's just a knack."

Right, she thought, *just a knack*. "I don't want to pretend to you. I'm not philosophically inclined. I'm a nuts-and-bolts person. I wouldn't have gotten into that stuff if I hadn't had to. Anyway, I said that programs like that were unique items of intellectual property. That ownership and copyright protection depended on the medium you used to run the program. Like a DVD program before there were DVD players. It really was a good article. It really was." She bit her lower lip; a very painful memory had returned.

He noticed, stopped, looked hard at her. Useless to attempt to keep secrets from him. "But something went wrong, didn't it?" He eyed her more closely. "You did the work, but for some reason you didn't get the credit for it. Is that right?"

She nodded and forced a smile. "Sexism and alphabetism, no one can beat 'em both. I had a coauthor, a man named Dawson. He was absolutely useless after the first draft when we began to realize how hard the subject really was. All he did was check cites and he wasn't even good at that. But –" she sighed – "when it came out his name was first on the title and he was male. After all, girls aren't even supposed to have heard of Claude Shannon. He got most of the calls back and he took all the credit. The editor-in-chief of the review could have helped, but he was worse. He said a lot of things about me and the article that weren't true – also not very nice. He went out of his way to discredit me. So. Dawson is an instructor at Harvard now and everyone thinks he's a real expert – on the strength of my article. He never even sent me a Christmas card."

Now the memory had returned with unrelenting force. One of the emotional storms that swept over her so easily; she went white with rage and frustration, as if it were all happening now, instead of three years ago. She made her eyes focus stiffly on the painting in front of them. She was certain she'd said too much.

From high above and behind her she heard his voice. "I can understand the co-author, but not your editor. That's real malice. What was in it for him? Why?" Silence; she knew he was thinking it through, could feel him appraising her, was certain he'd get it right.

"Because you wouldn't sleep with him," he said flatly, after a moment.

Her eyes were stinging. There was a lump in her throat the size of a cantaloupe. She nodded her head miserably up and down. She said nothing. *Are you going to make a fool of yourself and cry, you big baby? You knew they were both bastards from day one. It's your own stupid fault you didn't take care of yourself.* If she had tried to speak, she would have burst into tears. It had been a point of honor with her her entire adult life to resist that.

He laid his hand gently on her back. "We've talked much too much about this." His tone changed: "Tell me, does it ever become frustrating being constantly underestimated?"

The color came back into her face and she smiled. She felt momentarily shy and embarrassed. She had never revealed that incident to anyone – too shameful, too humiliating. Even so, she did not know him well enough to tell him that the sense of bearish, protective warmth he'd conveyed when he touched her more than compensated for the pain of the recollection – that she had suddenly become glad she'd confided in him. "No. I've sort of developed it into a style – and I've become pretty good myself since then at setting the record straight when the time arrives. I like being who I am. Cute's part of it. But I'll never let what happened happen again." She smiled more broadly, fully herself again, met his eyes. "You didn't underestimate me for a second, did you, Tom?"

His own eyes sparkled in reply. "No," he said quietly. "Not for a second."

And as for you, Mr. Newcombe – is it possible to overestimate you? I'm beginning to wonder.

*

In everything he said, in the way he expressed it, a pure muscularity, an impression of extraordinary wingspan. She had no doubt that he was as near as makes no difference to a full-fledged polymath. There was a feeling of liberation, a sense of open-ended freedom, simply in being with someone who moved between different modes of thought and expression so easily, so gracefully.

Her sense was that he was opening up to her in a way he seldom did, that she was experiencing a Tom Newcombe that very, very few people ever encountered. There was a little pride in that thought, also in the evident enjoyment he was taking in her company, although that only leaked out through his eyes and the constant quick turn to understated humor. The fire burned brightly in this man, she was certain, but it was fire under ice. It occurred to her all at once that the two of them were much alike in that respect, a very pleasing thought.

It was odd; the topics they discussed were so often so abstruse, so serious, and he played so quietly. But she could not remember when she had played so hard or had more fun.

*

But more was beginning to happen between them than ordinary conversation, no matter how magical. A different type of dialog had also begun, the oldest type, somatic rather than verbal, and magical in its own way for all its familiarity. A powerful physical pulse was beginning to beat underneath the surface of the afternoon.

Adele was not aware of it until it was in a sense too late. He'd been rather clever; he had not laid hands on her in any way that was at all unseemly or indiscreet – a touch on her shoulder here, the slightest pressure on the small of her back there, nothing to which any modern young woman could sensibly object. But the cumulative effect of all this incidental contact was devastating. She had become physically aroused to no small extent – and she had little doubt that that was exactly what he had intended.

There was a moment, when she first realized what had happened, when she could have called it to a halt. She rejected that idea immediately. That there would be a day of reckoning for this, she knew. No holiday lasts forever. But she shifted the thought resolutely to the back of her mind. That day was that day; this was this. For now, the mental and physical rapport that she had had with Tom from the beginning, which was deepening second by second, was too rich to interrupt.

At the start of their journey, she had stood discreetly eighteen inches away from him. Now she stood at his side, so close that her skirt brushed his trouser leg. At the start, they had both faced the paintings as they talked. Now she turned to face him as often as it seemed natural; it was so pleasant to look straight up into his mild, blue eyes. The question came unbidden into her mind as to what it would be like to be in his arms, and her body answered at once that it would be good, a very nice thing indeed.

It was not merely the quantum of his touch. It was the quality as well, the combination of strength and gentleness he conveyed. He was an enormously strong man physically, she was certain of it – and yet the pressure of those large, interesting hands was always so very light.

All in all, he was the most attractive man she'd met since – since – since – she couldn't remember. It could even be that the combination of all those qualities made him irresistible. She was next to certain of one thing: that he intended to find that out before this was all over.

She weighed that prospect and came almost at once to her own tentative decision.

*

A little after 2:00, they both realized at the same time that they hadn't had lunch. Adele became aware that she was very tired; Tom looked weary, too. The level of stimulation they had maintained was exhausting in itself.

There was a cafeteria on the first floor. They each had a small salad and a diet soft drink. Adele was surprised to see that he did not eat much more than she did.

"If I had to describe you in two words, I'd say `number mystic'," said Adele.

He made a subtle face, no more than a twitch of the right corner of his mouth. "Pythagoras reborn? I hope not." He paused. "Still, I have to admit I personalized them when I was younger. I saw three as very personable, but a little eccentric, five as a type of stuffed shirt because it's only a divisor of fives and tens. Things like that."

"I read a short story once about the number seven coming alive to a young scientist," Adele remarked, taking a sip of diet cola. "Seven was a pretty young girl."

He nodded. "Yes. By Fritz Lieber. A real jewel." His eyes sparkled. "What are you saying, Adele? Are you trying to inform me that I have the honor to be lunching with a cardinal numeral?" and she could only let her own eyes dance back in reply.

An older Midwestern couple was sitting at the table just behind them. When Tom left to fill the cups with water, the man tapped Adele on the shoulder.

"We couldn't help but overhear some of your talk upstairs. You two are better than a tour guide. Your friend has to be the best talker I've ever heard."

"Thank you," said Adele. "I'll tell him that."

Then, as she turned, from behind her, she heard the woman whisper in a tone she was not intended to overhear: "Fred! For Heaven's sake! They didn't come here to entertain you. They're lovers, probably secret lovers. Leave them be."

Her ears turned red. She was only grateful that Tom, who was just then returning, hadn't been there.

"What'd they say?" he asked as he put the water down.

"Oh, the man just complimented you on your conversation is all."

He regarded her. "It's you and me, Adele, not just me. I hope you don't think I'm this good all the time," which was the nicest thing he could possibly have said.

"But I didn't mean the man," he went on as he took a sip of water. "I meant the woman, the one who called us lovers."

He took another sip and looked innocently past her shoulder. "You really shouldn't blush like that, Adele," he said mildly. "It's unbecoming."

*

They were back on the third floor with the old religious tableaux. He had talked less and less all afternoon; for the last hour, it had been only monosyllables. It seemed as if he'd been content to listen to her, lost in his own thought processes. Suddenly her curiosity about what they were became overwhelming.

"Most people think of this as real connoisseurs' stuff," she said. "For art historians. Why do you like them so much?"

"I like the collective, impersonal faith that's there," he said slowly, after a moment, realizing he was being drawn out. "Later on, that gets marginalized by individuality."

"I wouldn't have thought of you as particularly religious."

"I don't know whether I am or not," he answered, after another moment. "I am a believer in the commonplace mysteries of the world. Theistic, of course: if there were no God, pi would be a rational number. But not this –" he gestured towards the Christ in front of them – "not any longer. I genuinely wish I could believe. It was fine in its day, but the day is done. It's too solar now.

"But that doesn't mean the commonplace mysteries are dead or the pure faith that's in those paintings," he went on, just a bit hesitantly. There was a shyness in his manner that was completely charming. "That's always the same, whether it's at Babylon, Peking, Rome, or –" he rolled his head upward – "Alpha Centauri. It's only that particular iconography that's finished. Someone's going to find the symbols to replace the Sun-God with the Star-Scatterer, maybe in our lifetimes, certainly in your children's. The great beast is slouching forward again. Some people have been hearing its footsteps for a century now. Pretty soon, you're going to have to be deaf not to."

They moved down the hall. She touched his shoulder softly. She was having a terrible time keeping her hands to herself.

"Commonplace mysteries? You mean Mandlebrot sets and strange attractors? Things like that?" Adele asked, straining her memory.

"No. That's wonderful work – work of genius. But not at all mysterious or counterintuitive. Confirming intuition, in fact. I mean the mysteries you encounter everyday."

"Maybe the computers will resolve that, too," she said, prompting again.

"Not the fundamental stuff," he said more firmly, now definitely opening up. "They've only made the dark glass darker. Sixty years ago, it was plausible to wonder if all the real questions were all only language on holiday. Now the babies on the island are all around, Turing machines, pure tabulae rasae, the experiment everyone always wanted to do, happening everywhere. They think, but they don't know they are. They speak a fine, serviceable language with none of these confusions. That's the language that should have evolved if all there was was blind matter and howling force. Only it didn't, that's the major problem, that's the most commonplace wonder of them all. The flesh of the language turns out to be so much different than the skeleton it hangs on. The existence of the question is proof of the answer."

And now he was voyaging alone through seas of thought too strange for her to want to follow. An image of herself calling to him from the shore flickered through her mind as she spoke.

"Just what are these fundamental mysteries?" she said.

He shrugged, and spoke now without any hesitation: "What you'd think. What human beings are, why they are. Why intelligence is. Time – always changing, but always now. Self distinct from identity – somehow you know you'd still be you, even if you were someone else. You know some things are right, and some are wrong; it doesn't matter whether they're useful to you or not, and you know that, but you don't know why. Dreams about the measureless when everything you experience is measurable – infinity arising out of finitude. Quantity and quality, wholes and sums, that they correlate randomly, we talked about that. That such things can be, black holes in rationality itself, mirrors of the ones in the sky."

"Oh," she said airily, "*those* mysteries," waving her hand dismissively, her green eyes flashing so he'd know he'd been set up, and was rewarded with the half-smile and brightening glance that were his substitute for laughter. He put his hand on her back and they took a few more steps.

"Cynic," he murmured.

"It serves you right for that trick in the cafeteria," she said, poker-faced, without looking back. "And you were too talking about that vase yesterday. Hell hath no fury like a woman scammed." He half-closed his eyes in reproach.

"Anyway, you sound more like a philosopher than a poet," she went on.

He shrugged. "One coin, two sides," then stopped abruptly.

He stood, transfixed, in front of a glass case that housed a small oil-on-wood painting.

It was the famous Gothic depiction of the Last Judgment, painted by one of the Van Eycks in the mid-fifteenth century. In the top half, the saints are assembled in heaven, a literal heavenly choir, painted in the colors of the first morning of creation. At the bottom, the sinners are driven into hell, cast down by a blond cherubim – a child – with a sword, the damned writhing in torment, their bodies twisting unnaturally in their agony, fear and despair in their faces, some half devoured by toothy, bestial demons.

It was the bottom half of the picture that had absorbed him.

"Yes," he said, mostly to himself, "I forgot that one. Too good a day. The soul; salvation and damnation. Predestination; destiny. Not literally like that, of course, but still. . . " His voice trailed off. He had the same dead, faraway expression that she had seen twice the other day. She hated that look. All the joy of the afternoon disappeared in an instant.

She touched his sleeve; she wanted to get away from there, quickly. "Tom, please. I'd like to show you my favorite things here. And then if we could go through the Prado show again? Please? Tom? Tom, listen to me."

He gazed at the damned for an instant longer, then tore his eyes away, was back with her again, to her considerable relief. "Sure."

He turned back at the Van Eyck a last time. "You look like that angel, except for the blond hair."

"So does every other woman in the building." She looked at the picture herself, shuddered, and went on without thinking. "I'd never be that kind of angel. I'd be the kind that he didn't paint, that looks after little children."

*

"These are your favorites?" They were standing in front of *The Triumph of Marius*, one of three huge panels by Tiepolo of scenes of ancient Rome.

"Yes. The reasons are personal. It's not the art as such." She paused. "My mother painted like that, the same balance, the same – I don't know – brightness. She was every bit that good." She paused again, and then looked up at him. "You're the first person in my whole life I told that to," she said quietly. "Not even my own family." Not her father, not her brothers; she was the legatee of that gift, no one else. And now she had confided a sense of it to a comparative stranger. The extraordinary intimacy she'd developed with this man, so quickly! Exhilarating and frightening.

"Thank you," he said quietly. "Why not any others?"

She shrugged. "Afraid I'd be committed to the loony bin, I guess, or that someone would laugh." She turned and looked up at him again. "But it's true."

"Why isn't she here?" He was not challenging, simply asking.

"She lived on too small a scale, horizons too narrow. She had quite a local reputation; she still does, I suppose, but it didn't travel. Maybe there's a little sexism. At any rate, it didn't happen. Not that that's all bad. She was a happy woman, probably a lot happier than most of the artists who are here."

"A desert rose. Tell me about her," he said quietly, and Adele did – the art shows, the excitement, the long, lovely Saturday afternoons they had shared when she was a child. He listened until it was apparent that she was about to make herself unhappy, then stopped her with the lightest touch of her shoulder.

"Let's go back through the Prado now."

*

They walked through the exhibit again, slowly, past the masterpieces of El Greco, Goya, and Velásquez. There was little said. They were largely talked out; and Adele felt a bit shy, since she had become almost maudlin – for the second time that day – in front of the Tiepolo. She was not sorry she'd spoken, but wondered about herself. She had said things to him that she'd never said to anyone – and yet it felt right, even if she was a bit anxious. She was nearer to him in the direct physical sense than she had been anytime that day and that was good, too; it seemed natural.

They stood at last in front of the great parody-portrait by Goya, *The Family of Charles IV*, which has bequeathed a small, but enduring riddle to history, namely, why Goya wasn't executed immediately after it was unveiled. The only conceivable explanation is that the members of the royal Hapsburg family really were as stupid as he portrayed them to be.

"Some vertical," she said. "It's frightening."

"I suppose they can go down as well as up," he said, almost sadly.

"I'm still not sure I agree with that Cartesian thing – it's too analytical – but it is a useful point of departure," she conceded.

He said nothing for a moment, then put his hand lightly on her right shoulder. Without turning back, she covered the huge expanse with hers, small and delicate, and squeezed his gently, the first time either of them had directly acknowledged the other's touch. It was not a politic thing to do. Even if Jenet hadn't told her, she knew by this time that he was not a man who needed encouragement about romance or sex, whatever his other problems. But it was what she wanted to do, and she did.

Then the most intense and unusual afternoon of her entire life was over.

*

"Well," he said, on the steps outside.

"Well?" she asked. The spell was still intact.

"I'd like to take you to dinner. If you don't have other plans."

"I don't." *Even if I did, I'd change them*, she thought, though not for worlds would she have said that out loud. "That would be very nice."

"There's a place I know near Greenwich. Italian, red-checkered tablecloths, that sort of thing. It's not very fancy, but I like it."

"That sounds fine, but I'll bet I'm a little overdressed. Can I go home and change and meet you there in an hour?"

"Sure." He took her hand, held it for a few long seconds, and looked in her eyes. She felt a small but perceptible rush of blood, very pleasant. They stood that way for a moment, then went down the stairs where he hailed a cab for her.

She had told him a half-truth. She probably was overdressed, but not seriously so. The real reason she wanted to go home was to pick up her diaphragm and spermicide, and a change of clothes. She wasn't on the pill or patch anymore, not sexually active enough to justify the gynecological risk. But what had been tentative a few hours ago had become a dead cert now. Something was almost certainly going to happen tonight, something almost had to happen. With that tingling anticipation came an undertone of danger, one she chose to ignore. The ancient misgivings were going to have to yield to the wonder of the moment, never mind that she knew already what had to happen the morning after. She felt her blood begin to rise.

How long has it been? Much too long.

She had also decided to bring along a small spray bottle, filled with one of her stronger scents. She did not care for such perfumes herself, but most men did. Lastly, she wanted to change into lingerie he would find a bit more interesting than what she wore to the office on an ordinary workday. It was the same as anything else in her life: if you decide to do something, you do it *right*.

*

It was twenty minutes to six when she got to the restaurant. There were only a few people seated. Tom was by himself at a table for two by the wall. He brightened when he saw her.

She looked around her, decided she liked his taste in restaurants. The atmosphere was open, informal, cheerful, not ersatz intimate or ostentatiously romantic. It matched her mood perfectly.

"Hi," she said.

"Hello. It's nice to know you're a woman who means an hour when you say so. I ordered a glass of white wine for you."

She looked: he had a glass of mineral water. "None for you?"

He shook his head. "I don't drink when I'm not drinking," he said, very quietly.

She was puzzled. "It's just that I'd assumed from things I heard Jenet say that you were the wine, women, and song type."

She'd meant to flatter. Most of the young men she knew and had known would enjoy hearing themselves described that way. Not this one; he was as subtle about that as about everything, no more than the slightest darkening of his eyes. But it was apparent that it bothered him considerably, that she'd hurt him.

"I'm sorry. I meant to please you."

He took a sip of water. "I know. But it's not the way I'd like you to think of me."

Questions she would have liked to ask: *Why not? What do you mean by that? What did you mean, 'I don't drink when I'm not drinking'?* But she felt nervous in pursuing these subjects; besides, there was no point. "I'm sorry. That was unforgivable. You must forgive me."

His eyes flashed in recognition of the joke. "I have to forgive anyone who hands me a paradox by way of apology. But it's all right. That's the way it must look to the outside. It's not like that on the inside at all, Adele, not at all.

"It's got to stop," he said almost to himself. "And it will." He had that same damned blank, faraway look again, and it was her fault.

She did not understand anything he was saying, only knew it was a subject she wanted to change quickly.

"It could be worse," she said. "You could have commissioned Goya to do your portrait."

She didn't fool him, of course; he knew what she was doing. But he reached out, squeezed her hand, re-entered the conversation, and things returned to normal.

The meal passed as quickly as the afternoon had. She noticed again he was a surprisingly light eater. Their talk now was small talk – the book he was just finishing, personalities at her firm, recollections of Jenet Furston.

The waiter finally cleared the table. They simply sat facing each other for a moment, not saying anything.

"I don't want to take you home just yet," he said finally. "It's been too good a day. We could go someplace. There's all kinds of places we could go." He was choosing his words carefully. She wondered if he was as nervous as she was.

He cleared his throat. "But what I'd really like to do is take you back to where I live. I'd like to be alone with you for a little while."

Well, there it was. She felt the muscles in her abdomen tighten slightly. But she wasn't seventeen any more, she was twenty-five, single and independent, and there was no reason to be coy.

"I'd like that, too, Tom," she answered softly. Then she became self-conscious that she'd been too easy. As he rose and took her hand to help her up, she made a nervous little joke. "But you have to promise me you won't seduce me, though."

The half-smile flitted across his face; he shook his head slightly side-to-side, negatively. "I can't promise you anything of the sort, Adele.

"I already have."

Her stomach turned to ice and her knees loosened. It was not merely the expression of confidence, which always had an aphrodisial effect on her. It was more the near certainty that he had intuited her darker secrets, the things that had concerned her most in her bedroom since that long spring break eight years before.

He pulled his chair out, and extended his hand. She took it instantly, and rose. *You made rules for yourself about this sort of thing*, an ancient, distant voice warned. But this was not a day for rules. There was no way she was going to deny the monumentality of this moment. The morning after would inevitably dawn, but an infinity of night lay before. For now, all the questions had the same, one-word answer:

Yes.

***

NIGHT SONG

His apartment was much as she expected it: one-bedroom and kitchen, surprisingly neat, surprisingly small, and close to the restaurant, which did not surprise her. Twilight had become dusk by the time they got there.

He turned on a small reading lamp on a desk that stood by the wall. "Excuse me," he said and vanished into the bathroom. She heard running water and realized he was shaving.

She looked around. A small computer sat on the desk. Above it were three short bookshelves with a surprisingly few volumes on them. Tacked to the lowest shelf was a small, hand-lettered sign with one word on it: "WHY?" Two stereo speakers were placed on each end of the top shelf, attached to a simple sound system that was about level with the desktop. It stood on top of a two-drawer metal filing cabinet. She noticed the system was all but an antique. An old-fashioned guy.

Across the room, under the only window, was his bed, queen-size and neatly made. An end table was beside it, with a table lamp on top. On the other wall facing the kitchen entrance was a small three-drawer chest next to a tiny closet. A large stuffed reading chair stood on the other side of the closet. Beside it were two hand weights, twenty or twenty-five pounds each. He did not appear to own a television.

All in all, it felt comfortable. The room seemed to suit him, the same way his clothes did when they first met. It was a male affect, somewhat Spartan. Somehow, she had expected that.

Her blood was rising faster. The old familiar excitement was coming over her. *Stay calm, dummy. The time will come – he'll see to that – and try and be a little ladylike about this for once in your life.* That last wasn't going to be easy. He'd done a good job during the afternoon; she was keenly anticipating his touch. He was becoming more attractive to her with each passing second.

She remained standing by the desk. The only places to sit were the desk and reading chairs, or the bed, all of which seemed inappropriate for one reason or another. Among the books was the German one he'd had the other day and another title in Italian – Dante, as she looked closer. Both were library books. The CDs standing on the file between the desk and the system were an eclectic collection, except that they were all words and music – songs, popular shows, lieder and opera, nothing instrumental. Few of the titles meant anything to her. She was a visual person, had never been particularly musical. Music was something to shake to on Saturday night.

He emerged from the bathroom. "May I?" she said, and went in.

She was relieved to find it as neat and clean as everything else. She took care of the contraceptive and sprayed on enough perfume to please him (she hoped) without overpowering herself. As she turned to leave, she noticed a new, unwrapped toothbrush in the glass. There had obviously been more than a little advanced planning going on here. Her excitement grew.

He was standing by the window when she came out. He had adjusted the little lamp so that it backlit the room. The light was almost sacramental, like candlelight in a church. The silence was absolute. It was much like the third floor of the museum had been earlier in the day.

She suddenly felt shy and stepped over to his desk.

"How many languages do you speak, Tom?"

"Two. But I read six."

She moved towards his desk and studied his books as if memorizing their titles meant the difference between life and death. She knew he was watching her. She sensed that he was a trifle hesitant, and that endeared him to her a little further. She could feel him summoning up the moment.

"Come here, Adele," he said finally.

She waited for a second. Control was becoming difficult; she wanted to maintain her dignity for as long as possible. Then she stepped towards him, slowly and deliberately. He gathered her up against him with his bad left hand, then the other came around.

Her body had been right. It was good, wonderful in fact, finally to be in his arms, to feel small and fragile against his immensity. He did nothing immediately, simply held her against him and lifted her hair up, again and then again. The surge of blood began to reach the flood.

"I've wanted to do that from the first moment I saw you," he said.

He raised her chin and kissed her slightly, a little hello kiss, over before she could react to it. Then he kissed her again, and this one was a lot more than hello, but still very gentle.

The hell with that noise! Did he really think he was going to get away with *that?!* The afterburners blazed on, full blast, all the systems fired into action, and here it came, screaming in like a jet, the way it always did with her. He was so big and delicious she had to eat him up, now, right now! She put her arms behind his neck and pulled him savagely down to her, kissed him, *really* kissed him, teeth, tongue, lips and mouth, as much biting and gnawing as anything else, grinding into him, hands clutching and pulling at his hair, ears, shirt, she couldn't stand it he was so luscious, it wasn't her fault, how could anyone stand it! Eyes mostly closed, open every now and then, like reading by lightning; she could see that he had not been at all surprised. She saw a hint of amusement in his eyes, and of course he liked it.

Great going, idiot, said the voice, contemptuously, now from a great distance. *Typical. About as ladylike as a forest fire.*

He let it go on for a while and then gradually quieted her, took everything under control. She swayed against him, her head resting on his chest, her body slightly trembling. Her heart was beating like a sparrow's. She was panting. The room seemed to have a lot less oxygen in it than it had a moment before. Anyone looking for cool, calm Adele Jansen had better look somewhere else. The stopper was out of the bottle, the genie was completely free. No point in even pretending anymore.

"Tom," she said, rolling her head on the point of her nose against his chest, her voice low and thick, quavering slightly, "I hope you're going to take me to bed. Because if you're not, I think I'm just going to die."

He stroked her hair for a moment or two, then put his hand under her chin and lifted her head up. For some reason, she was reluctant to meet his eyes.

"Look at me," he commanded gently. "Look at me, Adele." She raised her head a bit more and did meet his eyes.

"Good," he said, softly, "I am going to make love to you. But let's get this straight. This isn't a democracy. You don't have a vote. For a little while you're not going to be making suggestions, or jokes, or saying much of anything. You're going to do what you're told when you're told to do it. All I want from you is body language. Do you understand?"

Oh, God! How she *loved* talk like that! Adele could give herself all the lectures she wanted, but it electrified her blood, and that was that. Her instinct at the restaurant had been right; he did know, he had figured her out completely. That last speech was so totally out of character for Tom she was certain he was playacting. But knowing that didn't make any difference. It worked anyway. Every member of the Glee Club would have bet long money at short odds that she was either going to hand him his head back on a platter, or else collapse into a heap of gelid horror. Instead. . .

"Yes, sir," she answered, in the smallest, meekest voice she had, relishing the tingly delight that suffused her entire body as she spoke. Loose delicious notions of taking and conquest flooded her consciousness. Her core sexual being emerged, the essential Adele. She never felt more completely female, more real and alive, than at these moments, when a confident, capable man took command of the situation and of her. Complete surrender, acquiescence to the most primitive male territoriality, was as feverishly, deliriously enthralling as it always had been.

And as scary.

*

What she had been mortified to discover in her first year at Syracuse was that at her core, when all the layers of civilization had been stripped off, she possessed instincts, responses, needs that would have made an houri blush. She reacted to blunt male aggressiveness the way a kitten does to catnip. Whether she liked it or not, the aura of a confident, assertive man, determined to do what he was created to do, brushing aside all resistance, aroused a fierce response of her own, a primal authenticating satisfaction in surrender, grounded in the most basic roots of her being. *Like* it or not? Too tame. She did not merely like it. She loved it.

It had been some year. All the old notions, all the old beliefs she'd had about herself – everything was whirled into confusion, the trivial and the important, the trite and the meaningful, laced throughout with fevered explorations in one bed after another, with misgivings and vertiginous uncertainty. All the values she'd learned, all the ambitions she had, all the new experiences, tumbled over and over in loose chaos, like clothes in a dryer. Underlining everything was the pleasure, delightful, irresistible, and a growing fascination with morbid, titillating fantasies.

But finally the end came – the Friday night at the end of Rush Week. Titillating fantasy became a squalid, horrific reality. She reeled back in disbelief at herself, of the depths to which she was capable of sinking. The next few days were the most frightening of her young life. The sordidness of her acts threatened every large goal, every vibrant dream in her life. It produced one unendurable memory – that after it was over she had felt gr. . . she had even felt gra. . . that she had actually been gr. . . gr. . . gr. . . the word always stuck in her throat. She could not even complete the first syllable.

But the worst, the very worst, the capper, was that even afterwards some demented part of her being still insisted that she define herself in that way. Something inside her wanted to crawl back and continue.

Don't panic, Adele told herself again and again, alone in her old bedroom over the Spring Break. *Face facts*. Although at first it was difficult to do either, she finally managed to do both. She hoped she had learned the lesson. A cold, steely discipline was imposed. Cautiousness entered her life, where before she'd been fearless. She now knew herself for a fact to be the natural prey of the worst sort of predatory male, a born conquest. There were men in the world, she was certain, much more clever than the one she strained to forget, who were entirely capable of exploiting her vulnerability cynically and ruthlessly. If she weren't careful, she could easily destroy her prospects in a senseless marriage, or squander years of her life in a pointless affair.

As the years went by, she saw that fate overtake too many women, women she esteemed and respected, much less vulnerable than she, nonetheless unable to cope with a fever in the blood generated by men whose desirable characteristics were apparent only to them. What she had been through conferred no special immunity upon her. She knew herself too well. The notion of losing possession of herself sexually to a man confident and experienced enough to crown himself her lord and master, was, and always would be, tinged with a deep, enthralling eroticism, a sick, tingly allure. The only reason she'd gotten away as easily as she had was that she'd been lucky.

Involvements had become frustratingly rare, and celibacy (which she hated) the norm. The best ones had to have an element of macho to be interesting to Adele, but the worst could also do that number – and, once the blood rose, it didn't make any difference. The power he gained over her arose out of the delicious tingle of her own sexual authenticity, and had nothing to do with merit. Once done, it was terribly difficult to undo. So trust had become essential – an unusually high degree of confidence in a man, before she was willing to entrust, and thereby endanger, her one and only self with him. It had only been three days since she met Tom. They had really only become intimate that afternoon; there was more intuition in it than she would have liked – but whatever the reason, her confidence in Thomas Newcombe and the rightness of what was happening, was absolute.

Deliberately, Adele discarded the fragility of the past. Wilfully, she blinded herself to knowledge of the future. Freely and voluntarily, she gave herself up completely to the man and the moment.

*

He raised her head and kissed her, tenderly at first, then gradually becoming more intense, very slow, and very nice. The fires blazed up again, but she held herself in check. It would no longer do to let it all go – he was in charge now, not her. She glanced up at him, met his eyes for a moment, then dropped hers again, simple and unmistakable body language. *I'm yours.*

"Lift your hands over your head, Adele," he said, gently but firmly. "I'm going to undress you. Make it easy for me." She obeyed him instantly. He reached around her and began to unbutton her blouse and skirt – surprisingly clumsily, but then she remembered he did not have two good hands. Even so, the garments came off in due time and she stood naked before him, except for the briefest of black, bikini-style panties. She blushed every time she came across them in her bureau drawer, but they were completely appropriate for this occasion.

She had expected anytime about now that he would make a rather pleasant discovery. Her nude figure was much, much better than anyone could guess through her clothes. She had always been reluctant to dress provocatively. Since she had joined the firm, her everyday apparel had been chosen with particular attention to the severity of the line, its concealing quality, as much as color coordination and style. It was hard enough to practice law with the Glee Club all day long without being ogled by them as well.

Concealment had been easy. She was not that big on top measured simply in inches. But because she was so short, she was actually somewhat full-breasted, viewed in perspective. Her body swerved in from her chest to her waist and then flared out again at the hip in the best coke bottle tradition. All the athletics had flattened and tightened her muscles. She was one of the rare women whose desirability increased as her clothes came off, a fact of which she was secretly (and extremely) proud.

Her sense of humor temporarily overrode her more primitive instincts. He was trying to be impassive about it, but he couldn't help himself. His eyes went from her shoulders to her toes, back up, then down again, his appreciation visibly growing. She met his glance as his eyes were coming up the second time, just so he would know he hadn't gotten away with anything. It was fun to see him look sheepish. Finally, finally she'd managed to one-up him.

She smiled slightly.

"Surprise," she said lightly, her eyes dancing with mischief. "Sometimes what you see isn't everything you get."

His eyes were twinkling, too. It was a relief to see how quickly and easily he could let go the macho posture. "Evidently," he said. "Are we even for the vase now, Adele?" he went on, caressing her left cheek, and she smiled and nodded.

"Now step forward," he growled, "and don't speak again unless you're spoken to." Her blood sang again, and she complied at once.

Now she was entirely undressed. His arm came down again behind her knees and he lifted her up. Her body had been right, too, about his physical strength; though she weighed a little less than 120 pounds, she felt feather-light in his arms. She put her head on his shoulder and breathed against his chest.

"You smell nice," he said. She was sure she did. She was sure that the people in China who were inhaling the scent this very second also thought she did. Why the powers-that-be had given most men entirely defective noses was a complete mystery to her.

He stepped to the bed and laid her delicately down upon it. Then he sat to remove the rest of his clothing. A surprise: he had an enormous, spectacular birthmark, large concentric red and purple rings extending from under his neck to the midpoint of his back. She ran her hand over it as he pulled down his trousers.

"That's some birthmark," she said. "You're lucky it's not on your front."

"Yes," he said as he turned to her. She was lying on her right side with her head on the pillow. He stood for a moment in profile, and she took in his body; could not help feeling smug. *I did that.* Once again her sense of humor came striding forward.

"You're a little Cartesian right now yourself, aren't you?" she said. "Horizontal and vertical axes, both," and was rewarded again with that faint half-smile.

"Shhhh," he said, and lay down beside her on his left side, caressed her cheek for a long moment, lifted her hair up again and then again. For a time, he did nothing besides that. The semi-darkness took on the warm, living quality she'd felt in the museum. The arousal play was over. It suddenly occurred to her that Tom never used words casually or inaccurately, that when he had said he was going to make love to her he'd meant to do exactly that. A very pleasant thought; without losing any of its intensity, her excitement softened into a tenderness that was only partly sexual, maybe only a small part.

He waited until the stillness had ripened and then spoke, softly, next to her ear:

"I've been thinking about *your* portrait, Adele," emphasizing "your" ever so slightly, and the magic began again. No; the magic continued; she realized it had never lapsed.

In a low, musical voice, he took her back to the museum, fully poet this time, the other side of the coin. He went from one quicksilver image to another, a collage of impressions, observations, snapshot memories – the light on the third floor as it shone on her hair; the quick flush of color in her cheeks when she blushed in the cafeteria; the way her hands fluttered like doves when she described the Tiepolo.

Time bubbles, she realized dreamily, and so they were, airy and delicate, strung together like sunlit dewdrops on the thread of a spider's web or the bubble nests that the most beautiful of all tropical fish construct for their mates, gossamer stuff of ethereally subtle engineering, castles of light, that the smallest breeze can scatter. She did not interrupt, she hardly dared to breathe. She sensed how ephemeral the spell was. It wouldn't have worked at all in real time, she would have had to interrupt or laugh or *something* out of sheer self-consciousness. But he had isolated her again on that same little island of reality, all their own, and in this place everything worked.

"Wholes and sums, Adele," he whispered. "You and me. No correlation." Had he been planning this when he said that? It hardly seemed possible, but. . .

Can such things be? she thought. *There are still men alive who do it this way? And I'm with one of them? Can this be happening?*

Now the paintings themselves were his subject, and how she would appear in each if she were painted into it – her face profiled against the Tiepolo sky, the slight curve of her waist as Velásquez would have shown it, the guardian angel Van Eyck didn't paint, but should have. There was an Adele in his words that she knew and an Adele that she barely knew, the Adele who could be. *Am I really thus?* she thought. *Is that why he loves me?* (Not aware in the trance in which he had enveloped her that she had used the word.) *Could this person actually be me? I hope so.*

Of course, she thought, then suddenly, *the Cartesian thing, the vertical. Was he thinking of this all day long? He must have been.* Despite the hazy, romantic spell he had cast upon her, she grasped the quality of the improvised nightsong he was creating for her – amazing, all of a kind, all the random elements of the day united into a coherent organic whole, the inevitable imperfections notwithstanding; a marvelous verbal tapestry in celebration of her person, woven together of all the different threads of their experience, vanishing in the same instant of its creation, intended only for an audience of one. He was exercising the full, awesome power of his gift to create a unique love offering for her. What was it Jenet said? *Maybe one in a century.* Yes.

Please don't let this end, she prayed to something. *Let this moment last forever; it's so beautiful. Please.* He was in fact doing what he'd said, making love to her, in the oldest and best of all possible ways:

Rendering her beautiful in her own eyes.

He paused finally and the quiet returned, lengthened while he stroked her slowly. The poetry was over, she was sure. All things have to end, but she would remember this as long as she lived. Then he suggested her portrait by Titian. She knew at once how she was supposed to respond, that he had set another of his little traps. But it was a pleasure to play her own role well.

"Tom, you know I'm not a redhead."

He touched her hair. "If Titian had been with you today, it wouldn't be Titian red. It might be Titian brown, if he stood behind you when you talked about your mother; or Titian green, if he saw your eyes flash when you made a joke. Or Titian pink, if he was lucky enough to see you like this."

He cupped her breast with his good hand – the pink to which he'd referred was there – and now things became directly, immediately, and joyously physical. Her body reacted with its usual wild enthusiasm, but the wave of sensuality did not dissipate the magic that he'd created, that somehow still sparkled in the background of her consciousness. *This is different*, she thought. *It's the same, but it's completely different.*

"Time out," he said, suddenly, rolled off the bed, and pulled open the drawer on the nightstand. She felt acutely disappointed. Normally, a condom was an absolute requirement of hers. Not tonight; her confidence in him was complete, and there wasn't enough time. Big Bill was right on the money this evening – the consummation was indeed one devoutly to be wished.

"I've taken care of birth control, Tom."

He nodded. "I'd guessed. But –" a sudden flash of that dead, far-off look – "a lot of things happen to me that really shouldn't. I can't take a chance with someone like you."

The passivity of the first phrase puzzled her, the look troubled her more than ever before, but she was not going to repeat the mistake she'd made at the restaurant. Now he was back with her and everything was beginning again. He brought her back to where she'd been in no time, but he took no chances, proceeded slowly, as he'd promised, at his own pace.

"I hope you don't mind," he drawled, slowly, wonderfully, "but I'm going to send that high IQ of yours on a little vacation," and then proceeded to do exactly that.

Rationality began to fade, thought processes unraveled. He was so slow – better than too fast – maybe too slow – there had to be a happy medium – this man has no mercy at all! – just does what he wants! This was like being cooked slowly, slowly over low heat – a quick random joke, never again would she dine on lobster, too much sympathy for their plight – was this ever going to *end*? – this man is absolutely without pity! – a sudden realization, he was not going to finish this until he really had driven her completely out of her mind – not to worry, she was three-quarters there already. . .

But now at last he had pulled her into his arms and the embrace was strong and purposeful. In complete control now, irresistible force, a lion, slowly, deliberately, he rolled her onto her back.

"I think, Adele," he said, looking down at her from what seemed to be a great height, his own voice now a little husky, "it's time you and I became better acquainted."

Good. Great. *Finally!*

*

A few minutes later she was lying on his shoulder, looking into his eyes, playing with the hair on his chest. He was curling the hair on the back of her neck with his right hand. Neither one of them had spoken for some little while. The calmness of the night had returned as if it had never been broken.

"I don't think you're the kind of man who cares about that sort of thing," Adele said finally, "and I hope you're not, but if it matters at all to you, all that was on the level."

It was both familiar and strange. As usual, beneath the riot of sensation she did not have a completely accurate memory of all that had happened. A sense that she had been beautifully, magnificently conquered; a finish that made her feel like a piano would, if someone hit all of its keys in unison and then unstrung them all, slowly, shudderingly, a couple of seconds later. She felt that it was the best thing that had ever happened in her life, but then she always felt that way. All that she had experienced before, though rarely at this magnitude. How she managed to live without this, how she could go for days and weeks, months, without the touch of a man's hand, the feel of male solidity – at times like this it seemed unimaginable.

What was new and strange was the depth of feeling in the room. Somehow she'd been cherished, glorified at the same time. She could not remember when she had felt more content.

However, there was, as also happened with some frequency, when she was with a man she trusted completely, who had done a reasonable job of working her up, the realization that, without being entirely aware, she'd put on quite a show – Dolby Digital sound, visual effects by Industrial Light and Magic – that had from time to time in the past been greeted by polite and not-so-polite expressions of disbelief. It was that last realization that had prompted her to speak.

It was a minute or two before he answered. "Right the first time. It isn't an ego thing with me. Too many variables. Besides, I think all that comes pretty naturally to you; forgive the play on words. You're not exactly what I'd call inhibited."

"No," she blushed, and pulled his maimed left hand over to her – that one had become her favorite – kissed the palm softly. He had cast off the Neanderthal persona entirely, but some of the harem girl was still left in her, fading gradually away with the afterglow. "Do you dominate all your women in bed as completely as that? Or just me?"

"I don't like sentences with words like `men' or `women' in them. Which man? Which woman? The point is, I thought you'd like it."

"Not always," she said, not altogether truthfully, "but definitely with you. I love the way you took me. How did you know?"

"The way you said the word 'seduce' in the restaurant, sort of rolling it around in your mind. Your body language right then. Also –" he paused, a little uncomfortable – "I haven't been with that many women" – (*I'll bet*, she thought) – "so I don't know whether the generalization is all that accurate. But generally, the more intelligent the woman, the more primitive she is sexually. You're the most intelligent woman I've ever met. It was a good guess you'd be the most primitive. Which indeed you are."

An old, dark memory – her worst – intruded for just an instant before she squelched it firmly. She pulled herself up at that and looked at him. "Am I? Am I that unusual, Tom? Is there something wrong with me?" She was not so completely self-accepting as not to wonder about such things, to worry from time to time that beneath all the high blown rhetoric about houri instincts lay the humdrum fact that she was a closet masochist. There had never been a man she could ask about this before. Even Bri became shy and embarrassed. It was useless to talk to her girlfriends. They either envied her these problems or were appalled by them.

He studied her for a moment. "Don't go fishing, Adele," he said at last, "you know there isn't. Lots of people have that sort of thing kicking around inside them to some degree. Lots of women. That's no secret. You're just a little closer to yourself than most. You're an exceptionally intelligent person. When your higher brain functions that well, why should it surprise you that your lower brain does, too? It doesn't seem to me that you let it get out of hand. You make it work for you." He touched her lightly. "You're awfully good in bed, you know."

She blushed again and lay back down on his shoulder. "Yes. Thank you. I do know." Another silence. "That's very reassuring if you're right. I hope you are."

*

A minute or two later, she ran her hand over his chest. "That thing you improvised, that poem. It was wonderful. I've known lots of people who call themselves poets, but you really are one, aren't you?"

"I don't think of myself like that. The label seems silly and pretentious, artificial, somehow. I don't really like it." She turned her head to look at him; it was odd, but beneath the softness of his voice she could have sworn he'd become agitated. Why?

"What would you call yourself?"

"I don't know – writer, wordsmith, hack, something like that."

"You're no hack. You must know that. Are you still writing poetry? Jenet hopes you are."

"Yes. I never really stop working." She hadn't been mistaken; for some reason this whole topic really bothered him. "But I don't really do it for publication. It's got nothing to do with that. It's just doing numbers." His voice trailed off into silence, an eerie verbal echo of those vague gestures at the reception where they'd first met. So strange.

Suddenly her mind was alive with questions. *Why should any of this upset you? Why do you write poems that you don't publish? Why do you write other peoples' books? Why don't you write your own? Why did the Van Eyck disturb you so much? What are you thinking of when that awful look comes over you? Where do you go when Jenet can't find you? What is it that makes you so sad? Where do you come from? Where are you going? What do you want? Do you want anything?*

Who are you, Tom?

The questions trembled on her lips and. . . and. . . died there. No point in upsetting him, no point in destroying the evening. The morning would come soon enough; she already knew what had to happen then, had known before she came here. That thought, too, she buried. She wanted to savor every last second of this night before the dreary day arrived.

"Will you stay the night?" he asked, very, very shyly, as if it were a major thing. "I'd like that." Again, she was surprised. Of course, she'd spend the night. She would have been affronted if he hadn't asked.

"Sure. But I've got nothing to sleep in."

He got up out of bed. "I've got a pyjama top for you." He opened the top drawer.

"Recently laundered, I'll bet. I do believe you were expecting company tonight, Mr. Newcombe." His eyes sparkled as he tossed it over to her.

It occurred to her then they might not be finished. "Should I put this on right now?" she asked, with feigned innocence. "Are you going to do me again?" Deliberately provocative, eyes half-lidded, sitting up bare-breasted – her best men's' magazine look.

Tom shook his head side to side. "How you do talk. To answer you a different way, yes, I was planning to make love to you again." He sat down on the bed. "But not if you're not up for it. You're moving a bit awkwardly. Tell me the truth, Adele. Are you a little sore?"

She was surprised to realize that she was. It had indeed been quite a while and he'd turned out to be a very vigorous male. "I am, a little. But not so much it should bother you. You can do what you like with me."

He shook his head again. "Forget all the conquering hero nonsense. I'm not going to do anything to you if I can't bring you off. It'll wait till morning.

I'm not fifteen anymore."

"All right," she said in a more normal tone of voice. "Anyway, it must be pretty late."

"No. Only 9:15."

"9:15?" She looked at the clock, saw he was right. "But it seemed to go on for so long."

Tom turned out the light, pulled the sheets back for her, and then climbed into bed beside her. "It didn't happen in real time, Adele. Nothing that happened to us all day long happened in real time." She smiled in the darkness. It was the perfect curtain line.

*

He pulled her to him. The discovery of a genuine compatibility; he slept on his back, she on her stomach. She settled onto his right shoulder, the safest place in the universe, as if it had been created for her head. Her hand smoothed over his chest, again and again. It was wonderful to touch him.

She remembered then the only thing that wasn't perfect. It still annoyed her. "I wish I was yours right now. I mean, *really* yours. You know what I mean." He did not reply.

The darkness surrounded them with a warmth and serenity, the same as the other rich silences of the day. She had never experienced such a thing with anyone else. He ran his left hand over her hair again and again. The rhythms were slowing, rhythms of sleep. Unconsciousness was close. From out of the darkness, he spoke:

"I love you, Adele."

"I love you, too, Tom," she answered, from the heart, before she could think to exercise caution. Instantly, she tried to suppress the thought; it was too dangerous, much too dangerous. Too late, because for a thousand-millionth of a second – a nanosecond –she knew that it had not been empty rhetoric, not a goodnight wish, that he had meant what he said, and so had she. The baby snake had bitten. It had all gone much, much further than she had ever imagined it could.

"Good night, now," he said.

"Good night," she answered, *my beloved*, she added in thought, barely able to stop herself from vocalizing that as well.

They slept.

Time began again.

✳ ✳ ✳

DREAMSCAPE

It was not the stirring that first awakened her. It was the stiffness. His muscles had become rigid and hard underneath her head. She could feel a pool of sweat there, too.

For a moment she did not know where she was. Then she remembered.

"Tom?" she said, and straightened up off his shoulder. The digital clock on the nightstand showed 1:55 a.m. "Tom?" she repeated.

His forehead shone in the dimness of the night, beaded with perspiration. His lips were moving soundlessly. As she watched, his right arm came up to his head unnaturally, a stiff, broken clockwork parody of a shipboard goodbye, totally unlike the soft, controlled gestures of the waking person.

In one large, convulsive, amazingly quick maneuver, he flopped from his back to his stomach, pulling the pillow over his head. The two good fingers of his left hand dug so deeply into the pillow that they disappeared from view in the pillowcase. His legs kicked spasmodically once, then again.

"Wake up," said Adele. She was becoming frightened. "Wake up, Tom, you're having a nightmare."

He did not respond in any way. His hand continued to clutch at the pillow, which twisted and curled in his grasp. His breathing became labored and heavy, like an athlete's at the end of a long workout. The spasmodic kicks of his legs went on, every few seconds.

"Wake up," demanded Adele desperately. She knew little of sleep, nothing of sleep disorders, but it was obvious this was no ordinary dream, that a fearsome nightmare had ridden into his sleep. The sweat, the heavy breathing, the tension in his body – he was in a state of full-adrenaline panic.

He was still holding the pillow down over his head, but now he began to clutch at the air with his right hand, over and over. His breathing became even more labored. Then suddenly he flopped again from his stomach onto his back. He arched his back up, weight on his shoulders and heels, then dropped to the mattress. His eyes opened.

For a moment she was relieved, but for a moment only. Then she had to stifle a scream. His eyes were glassy marbles, set in a blind, taxidermical stare. He was still asleep; he was still dreaming.

A torrent of violent emotions poured over his face: fear, anger, hatred, frustration, fury, panic, rage, mixed in a changing mélange as she watched. His features were incredibly volatile, altered several times every second in response to the underlying vision. His lips were moving, too, no longer soundlessly, but with a mumble too low to make out.

She ached to hold him, to take him into her arms and exorcise the night vision that had taken him prisoner. But fear held her back. The gentle masculinity that had lured her to his bed was gone. The person beside her was traveling over a fearsome nightscape of primitive violence and fear. She was a strong, athletic woman for her size, but her size was five foot, three inches and 119 pounds. He was a foot taller, at least ninety pounds heavier, inconceivably stronger and, at the moment, unaware of anything except a dreadful inner vision.

So she did nothing.

His eyes finally closed, but he kept on mumbling. His arms came down to the mattress, spread out wide. His left hand grazed her pyjama top; she moved it carefully out of the way of the fingers that clutched and unclutched convulsively. It seemed as if this had gone on forever; she looked at the clock. 2:20, twenty-five minutes.

Now he rolled back onto his stomach. It seemed to Adele that the movement was a little less quick. His breathing was a bit less labored, and then returned gradually to sleep rhythm. She dared to touch his forearm; his muscles had begun to relax. She felt a wave of relief and tiredness sweep over her. It had been exhausting merely to watch this.

He shifted gradually back onto his back, his normal sleeping position. He moved his right arm, the one she'd been sleeping under, in the same manner as when he was awake. It was searching.

"Adele?" he said, still three-quarters asleep.

"It's all right," she answered. "I'm here," not because she meant it. She did not want him to wake with that horrible dream near to consciousness. She was very, very tired herself. She did not have the energy right this moment to wonder what all this meant. Instead, it was the work of an instant to slip back onto his shoulder and pull the blanket up over her own shoulder. His arm dropped over her. In another minute, she herself was asleep again.

It seemed as if the dark time of the night was past.

* * *

THE MORNING AFTER

It was only slightly past dawn when Adele's eyelids fluttered open. She was still on his shoulder, his arm still around her, and he was still fast asleep.

She slipped out from under his arm and got noiselessly out of bed. In the cold light of day, the events of the night seemed unreal and phantasmal. Even so, she still felt shaky. She padded silently into the kitchen to inspect the refrigerator. It was in the back of her mind that she would make breakfast for them.

Morning. Here. *Damn.* The day had come too soon. *What do you mean, stupid?* Regrets about what has to be? *Yes − lots of them.* Put the thought to one side. Make the best of what time is left.

Eggs, milk, and bacon were there − diet cola as well, her own, slightly off-center morning caffeine preference. Tom had observed her well in every respect. She hesitated, and then closed the door. None of those things was what he was going to want for breakfast. She had something else in mind herself. She tiptoed to the bathroom, went through her morning rituals (including the contraceptive, fresh spermicide), returned to his side, and pretended to sleep.

Pretended only for a moment − it was only a little after six and she was soon catnapping for real. She did not hear him rise, she did not hear him return. When next she opened her eyes, the pyjama top was gone and he was gently nuzzling her neck just under her chin.

Gently nuzzling? Did he really think he was going to get away with that?! Didn't he know *yet* how yummy he was!? Wonderful to start the day in a man's arms! Here it came. . .

He let it go on for a while, then pulled her towards him. "I'm sorry," said Adele, half-apologetically, as she felt her body pulled forward as if by the tide. "You make me feel so romantic."

His eyes swept over her. "I'm going to make you," he growled, his voice heavy with sleep. "Period." Impeccable timing as usual, even when groggy, setting her blood on fire − then, as good as his word, irresistibly, but somehow sweetly, he overwhelmed her, exactly as she wanted. He went more quickly this morning, but by no means hastily. Her blood raced faster in her veins until the world overflowed in the same wonderful way as it had the night before.

She felt a trickle on her thigh.

"Damn," he said. "Damn it to hell." He was holding up the condom, split in two at the top. It was empty.

She understood at once. Pure elation, pure exhilaration. "Fate, Tom. That's exactly what I wanted. Nothing happens by chance, you know. I knew I was meant for you." At least for a little while.

He still looked vexed. "It's all right," she went on. "I've got my diaphragm in and my period was only four days ago. Unless you're worried –" The hair on the back of her neck stood up.

He caught her meaning. "No, no, no STD problem. I'm sure that's O.K. I have to get an insurance physical every time I sign one of those contracts with Jenet. I was all right three months ago and there hasn't been that much –" he hesitated – "everyone else is safe even when –" he mumbled something she could not make out – "down. But I wanted to be ultra-safe about everything." His voice had an odd, forced tone to it. His rate of speech was noticeably slower than it had been the night before.

She relaxed again and brought his bad hand to her lips. "Well, if that's all, then I'm glad. I – I wanted this to happen." Suddenly shy – odd, how easy it was to discuss the pleasure, what worked, what didn't, and how difficult, the primal satisfaction of the biological union. "It wouldn't have been right otherwise."

"Are you sure it's all right?" he asked, with the same odd deliberation.

"Yes." She was positive.

But now the haze of sex and sleep began to disappear, and she could see and think clearly. For a moment, Adele thought her heart would stop beating. She had to stop herself from covering her mouth with her hands. The sense of darkness, the miasma, the distance – all of it was tangibly in evidence this morning, blanketing him, surrounding him. All the stray glimpses of yesterday now coalesced into a single point, a horrible, vague dissociation, as if he had lost completely the way to his center.

Finally, with what seemed to be enormous effort, the slight smile appeared on his face. "Then so am I."

*

As they ate their scrambled eggs on a small table in the kitchen, she observed him carefully, her heart aching in her breast. His face was drawn and haggard, the same dark circles under his eyes as when they had first met. His movements were slow and deliberate, his voice softer than she had ever heard it. An image formed: an archaeologist slowly, painstakingly reassembling the shards of some precious item of pottery that had fragmented into a thousand pieces. For a time, he was utterly lost to her, the prisoner of his own thoughts, that terrible vacant look his only expression, slowly recomposing himself.

Gradually, thank God, it became better, as if he was journeying back to life from the awful, far-off place of those looks. The sparkle began to return to his eyes. The man of the day before slowly reappeared.

"Did you sleep well?" he asked after a while.

"Yes, thank you. Your shoulder makes a wonderful pillow."

"It's not a rhetorical question," he said, meeting her eyes. "Did you sleep *well?*"

Oh. "I really did. But you did have a nightmare. A doozy. About 2:00 a. m."

He sighed. "I was afraid of that. I hope you weren't upset."

She reached across the table and touched his hand. "No, Tom, I wasn't. I was worried about you. What do you mean, you were afraid of that?"

He looked away. "It's a recurring dream. It happens – a lot. I've been told it's fairly disturbing to watch."

"It wasn't at all pleasant. But it must be much worse to experience it. What's the dream about, anyway?"

"I don't know." He shook his head and his hands drifted up in one of those vague gestures. "I can never remember it. There's something about a door – not even an image of a door, more like the concept of a door – and something terrible if it opens. And that's about all."

"But what –" He signaled a stop with his good hand.

"I'd rather not talk about it. It's very embarrassing to me. I'm sorry it disturbed you. In fact, that's why – never mind why." He fell silent. She could not think of anything else to say.

A silence descended on the table – not the warm enveloping kind of the day before, but the awkward, embarrassing type. Behind them, the table radio squawked out the morning news. The half-smile appeared and he began to provide his own commentary, laconic, quietly spoken, but very, very funny. She was surprised that he knew so much about current events. She was certain he had no real interest in them.

He seemed to be growing stronger and livelier as the morning wore on. *Maybe it's just that he's not a morning person, maybe it's only that he's slow to rise.* But she knew it was much, much more than that. So much dignity, so much nobility – so much pain. She laughed lightly over the rim of the diet soda at something he said. Underneath the laughter, once again questions flooded her mind.

Who are you?

Why are you so wonderful? Why aren't you as happy as you deserve to be? What's the source of the darkness? What's the reason?

114

Do you know yet how deeply I've fallen in love with you? I'll bet you do. You know more about me than I do about myself.

Do you know yet that after I walk out that door I'm never coming back? That when we say goodbye at my office that I'm never going to see you again? That I don't dare let myself? I hope you don't know that. Please. Not yet.

But she said nothing, her heart breaking, only laughed again at another witticism. He looked up at the microwave clock.

"You know, it's still pretty early," he said. "Only 7:15. What time do you have to be at work?"

"9:30."

"Are you still feeling sore?" he asked, gently.

"No. Not at all." Her mood was becoming steadily more dismal. Their time together was almost up. It had been too short, it wasn't fair. Suddenly all she wanted to do was hold him for a while, make love to him, let him know how precious he had become to her.

He took her hand and they walked hand-in-hand back into his small bedroom, a little overdramatic since the distance was all of fifteen feet. He scooped her up, threshold style, at the last step and laid her down on the bed.

He really was marvelous in bed himself, never used the same arousal technique twice. But this time she stopped his hand with hers. "No, thank you, Tom. I'm all climaxed out for now. That's not what I want. I want to be with you."

"I'll hold you for a while if that's all you want."

She grimaced – *are you kidding?* – put her arms around his neck and interlocked her fingers, then grinned broadly up at him. "That isn't what I meant at all. I'm really a very selfish woman about sperm, you know. I want all you've got, all of it, nothing left over for anybody else." She became serious: "And I want to be as close to you as I possibly can; and to give you pleasure. Sometimes I like that even better than my own thing. So, please, no, don't just hold me. Never just that."

He put the back of his right hand against her face. "Pretty civilized this morning, aren't you? What happened to the cave girl?"

"She's around," Adele smiled. "She's never far away."

He reached toward his table drawer and she stayed his hand again. "Tom, it's already happened, hasn't it? It couldn't get any worse, could it? You don't have to get all dressed up for me."

*

Fifty minutes later, Adele Jansen stood in the doorway of the apartment, showered and dressed. Tom had pulled on slacks and shirt while she was in the shower.

"Well?" she asked.

"Well," he said, and took her into his arms. She interlocked her fingers behind his neck.

"Are you coming?" A quick spasm of pain at the thought he might not. She realized then how hard this was actually going to be, so much harder than she had thought at first.

He nodded. "Look for me about a half an hour behind you. I'm going to finish the damned thing today."

She was looking up into his eyes. The last time she was ever going to see them from this angle. Suddenly it was on her again. She pulled him towards her, not quite as savage as when she was anticipating sex, but still very intense. After a while he lifted his head. The faint smile was on his face.

"How you do go on."

"It's not my fault. It's yours. You're yummy."

"Yummy?"

"Yummy. Don't ask me to explain. I could never explain yumminess to a man." *Too cute by half, idiot. You're not feeling cute.* Anyway, he'd never bought the cute act. Not for a second.

"I won't, then." Another short silence. She didn't want to go. A sudden intuitive crunch, that it would be all wrong to leave. All wrong. But she had to. Suddenly she had to say important things – now, when it had nothing to do with sex, before or after, when it meant everything.

"Tom, I – I – that is, I –" *(Don't! Don't say it out loud again! What's the point?)* – "I guess I'd better be going."

He released her as her arms came down. His left hand came up, her favorite, and he caressed her briefly, softly. She turned her face into his hand to kiss it; as she did, their eyes met for only an instant.

He knows.

The faint smile once, and then he moved towards the bed and began to make it up. A stronger impulse, a crazier impulse came over her – to close the door softly and remain there, inside, with him, smile when he finally turned around. *Did you really think you could get rid of me that easily?*

No. Not possible.

She turned and went down the hall. The last thing she remembered was Tom making the bed, surprisingly neat, hospital corners.

*

116

That lovely smell, a combination of machine oil, stale breakfast carbohydrates, electricity, and five generations of body odor. She liked the convenience of the subway; nothing else. She had some luck this morning. She found an aisle seat. Adele would have stood before she'd take a seat by the window. One of her thousand little tricks; the creeps do not usually show themselves on the commuter runs, but if one did make his presence felt, at least he wouldn't trap her against the side of the car.

She looked around at the other travelers amongst whom she sat – each with a destination, a journey's end, a place somewhere in the caverns in lower Manhattan; a collective sense that means existed there by which ends could be shaped, ambitions and goals mutually definable, congruent and reciprocal; finite purposes, the bedrock actuality of the doable. Secretaries rode beside her, junior executives, brokers, associates, and accountants – even an older financier, somewhat out of place in this milieu – maybe the limo was in the shop today – in every case, the horizon of the day circumscribed by the ultimate constraint of the practical, the possible.

What can you say? she thought. A mountain lion, a gazelle. He dwells on some mountaintop of thought where the air's too thin for almost anyone else. No – better – a large magnificent sea eagle, wings across the horizon, flying for days without sight of land or the need to see it. Yes. *Wonderful.* What flights! And how totally unselfconscious about it – humorous, playful, and always with that little dose of common sense to keep it in perspective. With all the theory, such a keen sense of reality.

But what can you do? Respect him, sure. Admire him, easy. Even – no, especially – say the word – love him, love him a lot, care about him, treasure him and the memory of everything that happened between you. No regrets, and don't ever deny you lost your heart to him, because you did.

But what you can't do, what you can't ever do, is build together, achieve anything together, share dreams of large houses and measured public success. This world of means and ends, this workaday universe, was her realm, where she meant to strive and thrive and succeed, someday, on her own terms. She liked this life; she was good at it; ultimately, she was not interested in seafaring, however much she might be dazzled by people who did. Ultimately, he had no interest in this arena of hers, the reality with which she grappled on a daily basis. Ultimately – it was so brutally unfair, so wrong! – there was neither a long- nor short-term future for them together. That was truth, brutal or not, fair or not.

No capital, no connections, so far to go – the only resources she had were talent and time, her own time, too precious to waste. Carolyn was right about that – she was in the business of selling time, as is everyone else, and no one who expects to accomplish anything can give it away. Deviate for a few moments in the back of a taxi and you make an enemy for life. The day before had to have been, had to have happened; it was unthinkable that it would not – but to dally further, to tarry longer. . . the City was unforgiving. In the profoundest sense, an involvement with Tom would be a waste of time, stealing away her hours, worse, usurping the place of someone who – while he might not be as wonderful – could share the life she intended to lead.

Which means – you know what it means – *say it, coward!* – say it and accept it. Look it in the face.

Never.

She felt a spasm of the purest, most intense pain, as if her soul had been cut in two; image of knife slashing curtain. Never. In spite of herself, she twitched in her seat and winced. The businessman who had taken the seat beside her looked over his glasses and copy of the Times.

"Are you all right, miss?"

She smiled somehow and nodded. "Yes, thanks. Just thinking."

Because no one in her entire life had got to her like that was

why. Bri was close, but she'd been a girl then. That was puppy love. It was as if Tom had a set of tuning forks adjusted to every last pitch in her being. Every corpuscle in her soul was vibrating.

You can't do this, something inside her insisted. *You are reducing everything that happened to the status of. . .of. . .*

One-night stand? Yes. (*No!* It hadn't been like that at all.) She'd deliberately ignored the main rule the day before – that there was no chance of permanence here, no chance for anything lasting. Perhaps a reason for holding back? To have not made love, to have left it all unconsummated? *No!* Out of the question; what had happened had to happen – even as what was happening now had to happen.

She put her hands on her elbows and held herself in, rocking slightly, only one more inconspicuous person in a car on the Eighth Avenue local, her anguish the most private type. The same impulse came to the top of her consciousness as earlier in the morning. Get off the train, go back the other way, *I love you, I must have been crazy to leave here, I'll never do that again, can you forgive me?* (That was a puzzle – *for what?* – and yet she knew she'd say it), and he'd lay the little finger of that bad hand down on her lips, shushing her, and. . . and. . . not possible. No. Forget it.

She felt her stomach turn, almost heave, something claw at her consciousness. She drew herself up slightly in her seat. Somehow, in some way, the deepest part of her being was fighting back, furious – her lower brain, as Tom would have said. She folded her arms, realizing then that she was at total war with herself. The recent memories pounded into her: quiet, good natured private jokes; the strength, the gentleness; that whispered, improvised nightsong; the ecstasy; the sense of being treasured; all of it. She folded her arms, rolled back in the seat; her seatmate glanced at her again and she managed a small, don't-worry-about-it smile.

No. I am not going to give into myself. I no longer let the emotions hold sway; what happened once is not going to happen again. Yes, it is love, and God! He is magnificent, but it can't work and it won't work and it doesn't outweigh everything else I am and can be. No.

Coward. Admit it.

Yes.

That, too, had to be acknowledged for that, too, was the truth – in fact, that was the bottom line. Despite all his attractiveness, despite all his gentle charm, it was overwhelmingly apparent that Thomas Bryant Newcombe was a very troubled man. The constant weariness; those far-off looks; the scene in front of the Van Eyck; that dream; those first terrible moments upon waking. Her heart had ached for him this morning. Her desire to remain had had not the slightest element of the erotic in it. It had been a simple longing to stay and give comfort. But to become involved further was to wade into a quicksand of pain and frustration, without any solution for him, with only misery for her. They were problems that only he could solve. Nothing she had learned of him had changed her mind about that – and it would be madness to go further.

In one sense, he was the most dangerous kind of man there was, one who could break her heart over and over again – not maliciously like some callous womanizer, but without even knowing what he was doing, like a blind elephant that doesn't know where it's stepping.

Another puzzle, interesting enough to break momentarily the bleakness of her mood. Why did she find him so attractive in view of all that? She had always been tender-hearted towards people with problems, moved easily to pity and sympathy. But those qualities were without any sexual appeal whatsoever to her. Even as an adolescent, she had never found the quivering chin, sensitive type of teen idol at all attractive. She liked her men strong and confident – gentle, too, of course, but out of instinctive grace and kindness, not necessity. Tom was different from the norm in so many ways, and yet she had never found anyone more attractive in her life. Why? How?

That train of thought ended; the local had reached her destination. *Never,* said one voice. *You can't do this,* said another. Head erect, mind clear, heart heavy, Adele Jansen emerged from the train. There was no question at all what had to happen. But for the first time in a long time she wondered whether she had the strength to go through with it.

119

*

Her office looked the same as when she had left. She was surprised at first, then amused at her surprise. There were a few phone messages, but nothing earth-shattering. The clock in the oval vase was still keeping accurate time. The world had evidently gone on turning quite nicely on its own during her impromptu holiday.

She had only a little quiet time in which to catch up. She filled out her time report for the day before; she recorded it as vacation time. She had never intended to cheat Jenet. Her mind was a blank, apart from basic functions. Minutes passed quickly as she organized her files, made notes on her calendar. The tea tray came by. She took a diet cola for herself, a Danish, napkin, knife, fork, and pat of butter for Tom.

"Where were you last night?"

It was Josh Palmdale at the door, more agitated than she had ever seen him. He entered her office without saying anything more.

Adele was too startled to react. She looked back at him, an expression of surprise and ridiculous guilt on her face.

"Where were you?" he repeated, and it was apparent that he was angry. "The girl at the reception desk said you left with that writer. I tried –"

"She isn't a girl, Josh, she's a woman," said Adele, stalling for time, trying to collect her thoughts, "and her name's Christina. After two years, you should –"

"Never mind that crap. I tried to call you until 11:00. I wanted to talk about Lawton. They reassigned the file to me."

That figured. With the heat off, it wouldn't matter who worked on the case. She was becoming angry herself. "Working. But that's none –"

"Where?" he demanded. "You weren't here. You weren't at your place. Where?"

"She was with me," said Tom. Neither Adele nor Josh had heard his soft knock. "I owe the Furston Press a book. Jenet Furston asked for someone to keep after me until they get it. The someone turned out to be Adele. It's no big deal."

Josh looked at him for a second, then turned back to Adele. "This is the fellow in the east conference room that you left with, isn't it? The writer?" Without waiting for her to answer, he turned again to Tom.

"Look, you. Adele may have been working, but I'll wager you're a little more ambitious. I know all about your type. You have too beautiful a soul to muck around in these things, don't you? Can't soil your hands with all this sordid money stuff. The best things in life are free, right? Now you're finding out what you did to yourself, what a mess you've made of your life, and it would be so nice, wouldn't it, to have a pretty, million-dollar-a-year girlfriend around while you work on the next Ode to a Grecian Urn."

"'On a Grecian Urn,' actually," said Tom. It was apparent to Adele that he had taken the full measure of Josh Palmdale and had no more interest in him. He looked away, picked up the fork with his right hand, and dropped it out of sight.

Josh Palmdale, her self-anointed protector – she should have done something about this *months* ago – went on:

"Let me clue you in on the facts of life, fella. You're not going to make it. She is. You've blown it. She's a full-blown superstar. You don't fit in here or anywhere else. Adele does. Everywhere. So you're going to go back to whatever hovel you came from. Understand? And you're going to forget all about her. I'm not going to let your stupid daydreams get in her way. Look in the mirror and all you'll see is an anchor. That's all you ever were or ever going to be. Whether it's 'on' a Grecian Urn or 'to' a Grecian Urn."

He continued relentlessly. "Not that you have any real chance. Adele is all business. She wouldn't have been with you at all if it weren't billable time. Guys like you," he finished, "don't really know anything." Josh said this last with a smug, triumphant tone in his voice, as if it were a devastating revelation, the throwing of a large bucket of water on a child's sand castle. He did not notice Adele roll her eyes up. If ever there was a human being who understood the various uses of time, it was Tom. That was how the whole thing got started.

"The best you're ever going to do is to waste her time. But I'm not even going to let you do that. Are you going to go back to the conference room by yourself – or am I going to have to take you?"

He was finally, mercifully silent.

Suddenly it dawned on Adele that this was it, the crossroads, the time for an absolute decision. It had arrived as they all do, unexpectedly, Appointment-in-Samara style, from the opposite direction, the way an express train roars into a station when the passengers are looking the other way.

She sat paralyzed for a moment, immobilized by the only certainty of this whole preposterous farce – that, despite all the immaturity of his tantrum, Josh Palmdale was right, had echoed in his own pea-brained way her thoughts on the subway. She could not decide what to do or say. Her indecision lengthened for one instant too long, an eternity – it was the small intervals that were the most poisonous, wasn't that what he'd said? – and she realized then that the decision had been made as she hesitated, determined by her indecision itself, by default.

She looked at Tom, feeling guilty and helpless. There was an expression on his face, a look in his eyes that she couldn't read. All at once, she understood one thing more.

He had *known* – he had foreseen from the start – that this was inevitable. He had known when he met her, when he flirted, when he lured her out of her office, during the long hours at the Met, when he took her back to his apartment, even while he improvised his long, marvelous nightsong for her, that this moment would come, and that it would come now. He had known from the beginning, from before the first deed was done. Had he hoped? Despite knowing? She could not bear the thought.

Suddenly, without warning, a different image formed, as startling as it was abrupt.

It was the painting of the Last Judgment again, the Van Eyck from yesterday, only this time she was not in front of it, she was inside and a part of it. She was standing underneath the throne of God, looking across the river, to the other side of the throne, at Tom, standing among the damned – tall, noble, dignified, faultless even, but still utterly and remorselessly damned, without hope. He gazed back at her, close but infinitely far away, without anger or sadness, and only the barest hint of longing.

Now she recognized the look on his face. It was resignation, complete resignation, a stoic, weary acceptance of that fate. Now, too – insights piling onto each other now that it was too late – now she found the solution to the puzzle of his attractiveness. It was. . . courage. It was the way he endured and persevered in the face of. . . of. . . she didn't know what. Whatever his burdens – and she doubted neither their reality nor their magnitude – he carried them without any discernible self-pity or neurotic cries for help. It was odd to regard a man in the ordinary toils of civilization as courageous, but at that moment she realized that she did.

"Tom?" she said uncertainly; for a moment, all the cold analyses on the subway had disappeared, she had forgotten entirely the existence of Josh Palmdale. The strongest impulse yet: to go to him, move to his side, and let whatever happened happen. *Do it.* But her practical sense stifled that, too, she hesitated again – and then that chance as well was lost forever.

Tom moved towards the door. "I just stopped by to check in, Adele," he said softly. "I'll be finishing up in the conference room." Then he turned towards Josh.

"I wouldn't take you on, friend, even if you started something. I've never done anything violent in my life; I don't believe in it. The first move in any game is deciding to play. That's not a game I play. I don't even fight back. But if ever it did happen, you might not have liked the outcome."

He lifted his right hand from below his waist and dropped the fork on Adele's work table. He had twisted the stainless-steel implement not merely into an "O" (hard enough) but into a type of "Q," the top of the handle now touching the handle bottom just below the tines, the tail of the letter. He smiled his faint half-smile at Josh.

Then he was gone, vanished through the doorway.

Adele felt a momentary exultation of the Neanderthal, my-boyfriend's-back variety. The look on Josh Palmdale's face – a Disney cartoon version of an ancient Egyptian on the river bank who thinks to pluck a pussy willow and finds himself holding a lion's tail instead – was going into her sketchbook at the earliest opportunity.

She closed her eyes and let the time extend, the silence build. She did not want to do or say anything until her rage had come to full boil. Josh became uneasy as the adrenaline left his bloodstream.

"Adele," he began in a forced avuncular tone, "perhaps you think I was a little –"

"Get out," hissed Adele, through clenched teeth. In a way, it was unfair. He'd only articulated the conclusions she'd already reached; he was merely the messenger bringing bad news.

But she didn't feel like being fair. She would never have imagined a day would come when she would empathize with the monarchs of the ancient world who executed the messenger, but now she did, wholeheartedly. Stupid messengers stupid enough to announce bad news deserved every ounce of stupid hot lead poured down their stupid throats.

"Adele, I know that type," he said, shocked. "How they get their hooks into you. I only meant –"

"I said OUT!" hissed Adele. "And don't come in again unless you're invited." For an instant, it crossed her mind to tell him that Tom had been lying to protect her, that she had spent the night with him, and that he had made wonderful love to her. But that would be cruel and she had never done a deliberately cruel thing in her life. Then she realized that Tom had in his own way taken his revenge – that for the briefest instant Josh Palmdale had confronted the real Joshua Palmdale, had seen himself as the pompous, ineffectual, silly fool he actually was; that that particular insight was etched unforgettably, unforgivably, indelibly in his memory. So she said nothing, contented herself instead with burning two holes in his chest with her eyes.

Josh left hurriedly without another word.

*

She waited until 11:30 to go over to the conference room. There was plenty to do to make up for the lost day. Also, she was too embarrassed to face him easily.

But finally she did go. It was not that her decision had changed. She knew the right outcome had occurred, however messily. But she wanted to buy him lunch to make up for the dinner he'd bought her; it was important to her to give him a proper farewell. It wasn't that she didn't care for him or wasn't going to go right on caring for him. She wanted him to know that.

"He's gone," said Christina.

"Gone?" echoed Adele blankly.

"Yes. He said that all that was left was proofing and he could do that easily enough at the library."

"He left you a note," the receptionist continued, and handed it to Adele. There was a gleam in her eye.

Fully aware now that anything she said or did would be grist for the office rumor mill, Adele only nodded and walked back down the hall. She did not open the envelope until she was back in her office and the door was safely shut.

The note read:

Dearest Adele,

I can't say that I think too much of your colleague's manners, but we both know he had a point. It would have come to that sooner or later; we have very different lives. It's just as well it's now for a lot of different reasons.

As it is, we've had just the one day and night. I never thought of you as just a one-night girl — I'm sure you know that — but perhaps you want me to write it anyway. (He was right twice.)

Whatever you might hear of me later, I want you to know that you made me very, very happy while I was with you. I meant everything I said to you last night.

I wish I could wax a little poetic for you, but right now all I have is truthful prose.

Love,
T.

He hadn't written out his name; just a T with a curlicue that came up over the letter and then pierced it like an arrow.

For thirteen years, she'd trained herself not to cry. She didn't now. But she could not prevent her eyes from misting.

Damn.

She dried her eyes with a Kleenex; then, as casually as she could, she sauntered over to the elevator area. Maybe he'd forgotten something, maybe he'd come back for a second. Then they could still have that lunch.

She lingered until it was becoming ridiculous and obvious, then left. It had been easy to make her resolutions about him when he was nearby, when leave-taking lay in the future, when time remained to be lived through before. But now the time had all disappeared with devastating suddenness, the way the last sands in an hourglass run faster than the rest.

You knew it would be like this, moron, she thought, and slowly started to reconstruct her mental discipline. *It's stupid to regret what you can't change. Better get used to it. Never.*

She sat back down at her desk. Lunch was forgotten; she had no interest in food whatsoever.

He had disappeared completely.

Damn.

✳ ✳ ✳

THE WAGES OF SIN

It was bound to be a dreary day, but Adele had suffered through dreary days before. She forced herself to go down two floors to the cafeteria and eat a tuna-fish sandwich. Afterwards she returned and buried herself in her files.

Concentration on the task at hand had been her refuge most of her adult life. It was helpful now. Resolutely she barred any thought of the last two days. There would come a time in the not-too-distant future when she would bring everything into perspective. Right this moment, it was all too recent, too immense.

The ordinary routine was with her again. Greg Steuer stalked down the hall during the middle of the afternoon later, dropped off the revised pleading which he should have done two days before, glowered, then left without a word. She had other things to do, but took a moment to glance at it. He'd made the first two changes she suggested, left everything else the same. She shook her head. He was so bitter. The other two Carolyn had her supervise were fawning and obsequious – and Josh with his smugness, and the rest. She didn't want to have to do with any of them – or any of this. Particularly today. *Tom* – the name reverberated in her mind for a moment, before she slammed the door on it.

At 4:30, Carolyn Hoffman's secretary rang to confirm her attendance at the party that night. Her first impulse was to cancel. The last thing in the world she felt like was one of those parties. Then she realized that that was exactly backward. The one thing she should not do was sit home alone tonight with her own thoughts.

She confirmed her original plans.

"Oh, one other thing," said the secretary. "Carolyn said to tell you that the guy managing the underwriting on that company – what is it?"

"AI Squared," said Adele, her stomach turning over.

"Yes. He stopped by while you were gone with that writer yesterday. He was disappointed he missed you. He'll be at the party tonight."

She looked at the desktop for a long minute after the call. Great. Perfect. Opportunity comes to call and you're not in. Yesterday Tom had asked her if she was an ordinal number come to life. Today she would have responded that what she really was, was Murphy's Law incarnate.

*

The George Washington Bridge, lit up like a Ferris wheel at a county fair, dominated the larger picture window of Carolyn's townhouse. The penthouse apartment had almost the same view as her office, transposed twenty city blocks to the north and four to the east. The decor was modern, Danish, blacks and whites, glass and mobiles, a conversation pit in front of a white brick fireplace. Opulent; tasteless – the same effect as Carolyn Hoffman's office.

Adele stood in front of it, silent, alone. The party was becoming lively all around her; she remained lost in her own thoughts.

"You're kind of poky tonight, aren't you?" said Carolyn from behind her.

"It was a long week," said Adele, without looking back.

Carolyn lowered her voice. "I hope you're not worried about that little snafu with Jenet Furston. We did what we're supposed to do. She understands that."

She understands more than you think, Carolyn. "I know. I'm still not sure it was the right thing."

Carolyn shook her head. "That's the only thing that worries me about you, Adele. You've got it all – except I'm not sure you can do what's necessary. That bothers me about you. It's a concern."

Adele answered again without turning her head: "Don't worry about that, Carolyn. I can do what I have to. Believe me."

Carolyn looked puzzled, then shrugged, turned, and joined her other guests. Adele continued looking out the window for another long moment, at the great illuminated bridge and the stars shining beyond it. Then she turned away herself.

You didn't come here to brood, stupid. You could have done that all by yourself. Now circulate. Which she did.

*

Groups of people in twos to fives stood in front of the fireplace, about forty persons altogether, but hardly the only guests who would attend that evening. The party was actually more of an open house, people coming and going until about 2:00a. m., when everyone went home – or away, at least – with the exception of one visitor, invariably young, invariably male, different nearly every week.

Like most of the other new associates at Hapgood, Thurlow, the first genuine gossip Adele heard was gossip about Carolyn's parties; in fact, she had a distant recollection of having read something about them years before in one of the celebrity magazines. *Atop the cloud-capped tower... the glittering city below... gorgeous Carolyn Hoffman, one of the pre-eminent entertainment attorneys in New York, presides over a regal... sooner or later, everyone who is anyone...*

She'd been thrilled when she received her first invitation to a "soirée" (as Carolyn grandiloquently entitled them), about a week after the look-and-feel memo impacted. Major progress. Her first impressions had seemed to confirm everything. The view was spectacular; no better food and drink could be found in the city; all sorts of notable people, from politics, from finance, from Broadway chatted comfortably in the living room. She'd circulated, a small girl only eight months away from the university, pretending (successfully?) that she wasn't overawed.

Lately it had begun to pall – too much glitz, too little substance. Too many rich, famous men, too many young, voluptuous women – everyone after trophies, no one exactly sure who was collecting whom. At first, she'd dressed for these occasions. Lately, she'd made herself deliberately inconspicuous, wishing that she could break the string. For some reason, her presence there had become important to Carolyn, reassuring in some inarticulable way – and every once in a while Adele did meet someone interesting. But that was rare.

The worst to date had been the night some three weeks earlier when Greg Steuer came. So proud, such an arriviste. Something in his manner touched her deeply – so pathetic, completely out of touch with where he was, naïve really. He cut her dead. She already had the memo, that he was to begin reporting to her. He wouldn't have it until Monday. She said nothing about it. Later, when he stayed on and on and on, she wanted to warn him that Carolyn used young men the way some men use young women, that the road he was on led to a dead-end.

Then she became angry at herself. He hated her, would destroy her if he could, for no better reason than she had capabilities that he didn't – a complete male chauvinist pig, worse still, one who had fully rationalized his pugnacity. What goody two-shoe instinct of her own prompted kindness towards him? She couldn't keep playing little sister to the whole world. Still, she'd kissed him once. He was still there when she left that night.

That had been the worst of the parties. Until this.

*

What a bore. What a colossal bore. How flat and unprofitable, how stale and weary, all the uses of this world. *Sea air is fresher*, intruded the thought, and she grimaced with the unexpected pain. How completely he overmatched everyone here. *Tom.* She reined herself in. She was close to tears, and that would not do, especially here.

"Did you get the message from my secretary?" said Carolyn, suddenly appearing at her right elbow. "George Sorenson is here. He's – I mean, he's the underwriter on that deal." It flashed through Adele's mind that Carolyn was holding something back. "He's here. He'd like to meet you."

"Of course," said Adele, suddenly alert. Carolyn led Adele in the direction of a well-dressed, middle-aged man. Two or three well-known heads turned as he passed; someone running for Congress stepped out of his way. He seemed immediately familiar, but she could not place – *oh, of course* – the financier who'd been at the Software Arts Expo – the small spark she felt that night. Even the nice young man she'd been standing beside had recognized it. But nothing was possible tonight.

"Adele, this is George Sorenson. George, this is Adele Jansen. She has quite a reputation in our firm. We call her the 'look and feel' girl." Carolyn, who on this as on most Friday nights was vacationing in a fifth of Stolichnaya, giggled and moved off.

"'Look and feel'?" said George, quizzically, a flat outer-Burroughs accent.

"It's not what you think. It's the name of a memo I wrote in a software copyright case during my first year at Hapgood. It had an impact all out of proportion to its quality." She was more than a little annoyed at the drunken, condescending double entendre. No one on Friday night would mistake Carolyn for an ice queen.

He nodded and looked around. The volume level of the party talk was becoming louder in direct proportion to the lessening volumes of the decanters. The music seemed louder, too. There was no quiet place to talk.

"I'm sorry I missed you yesterday," said Adele, her voice raised.

"No matter," he semi-yelled. "I dropped in on my own. I have to talk to you, though. Franklin Fischer really wants Hapgood, Thurlow to have this deal. You seem to be the key." He paused. "Were you the girl at –?"

"Yes," she shouted back.

He started to say something else, then gave up. "This is no place for this. I'll call you at work and set up an appointment. The deal isn't closed yet, anyway. It's nice to meet you." He handed her his business card: George Sorenson. Partner, Consolidated Financial Services.

She nodded again and extended her hand. A brief shake – mild, surprising electricity – and then he was gone, prowling back towards the middle of the room.

But now it was 10:30 and she had done enough. Time to leave, time to be alone. Adele thanked Carolyn – a raised eyebrow at such an early departure – and left.

*

The form of it surprised her, nothing else, now, as she stood before the mirror brushing her hair, alone in her apartment. That there was going to be heartache, that there was going to be a world of sexual frustration, that it would be intense – these things she had known. But the form surprised her.

It took on the sense of a profound feeling that everything was wrong – the angles of reality askew, crooked, acute or obtuse where they should be right, sides not joined properly, a feeling she sometimes had when she was premenstrual, but now many times stronger. She should not be here, in this desolate, lonely apartment, in this barren bed. She should be with her lover, with Tom, heart to heart, body to body. It wasn't right. Everything was all wrong. Everything in the universe was slightly off-center.

Nothing happens by chance. For some reason, the sentence, spoken so casually that morning, echoed again and again through her mind. She closed her mind to it as best she could and prepared for bed. An hour or two with that miserable Russian novel might do the trick. Suddenly, as she looked at herself in the mirror, the inner voice addressed her in a different way, as if all the unconscious, inarticulate elements of her being had, in their fury over the decision she had made that morning, clambered into her consciousness and acquired speech.

You have done an awful thing this day. You have made a horrible mistake.

It startled her for a moment. But this was only sex and irrationality talking, and she was not going to give in to it. She had learned her lesson about that long ago. Determinedly, she turned on the bed lamp and reached for the book.

*

She woke up groggily at about 2:00 a.m., an unusual occurrence; she almost always slept through until morning. But something was nagging at her subconscious this night, strongly enough to wake her. She was almost fully roused before she realized what it was.

It was the dream, that awful dream, that he'd had the night before. Somewhere in the world he was writhing in that terrible nightmare this very second, imprisoned in sleep with no one near to help.

Then again, maybe he wasn't alone. She wondered why she would have assumed he was. At any rate, she did not find the latter thought any happier than the former. *He's mine, damn it, and no one else had better be with him.* The sudden articulation and the emotional force that accompanied it startled her. Stupid; foolish; she knew how silly it was, but for a moment could not check the feeling.

Something else, too, a small itch at the back of her mind – a gnawing sense that something had been left unfinished, the same way she felt at the end of a day when something important on the agenda had been left undone. It was associated with Tom – but what? She turned the day over and over – enduring the heartbreak – that last look – but could not find it.

Once conscious, she found it surprisingly difficult to return to sleep. It was odd, but the memory of the dream bothered her this night more than the actual observation of it had the night before. It was a while before she was sleeping again, and even then her sleep was lighter and more broken than was customary.

It so happened that the impression had been even stronger than she had first thought. She woke up at 2:00 the next night, and the night after that, troubled by the same nagging underthoughts. Only then did her sleep pattern revert to normal.

*

It was her habit to work until noon on Saturday. On this day, she worked until five. She had an invite to a party that evening, a combination celebration and commiseration, hostessed by Irene, her best friend in the City, another hockey player, to mark the beginning of Irene's first year residency in oncology. The presence of all sorts of interesting guys had been guaranteed. Irene swore she'd performed the inhumanly difficult task of weeding out the gigantic egos to the maximum extent humanly possible. Adele'd been looking forward to it. . . but it was not to be. She had to be by herself. She phoned her regrets. Her friend instantly suspected an affair of the heart, but was wise enough not to press the matter.

On her way home, Adele stopped at a video store with an unusually large selection. Thank God for the DVD, God's gift to the lovelorn. There was any number of mindless movies that she'd never got around to seeing. No romantic comedies tonight – horror was the thing. Dumb horror, of course, too stupid to be scary, but with enough cinematic tweaks to provide some visual white noise. Buck would be aghast if he ever found out, but he was never going to. Total running time, eight and one half hours. 5:00? 1:30. A little popcorn. Perfect. Take care of some correspondence, too, at the same time; she was way behind with girlfriends scattered all over the country, and she owed her brother Jack a letter as well.

She wrote and addressed nine e-mails, the longest one to Jack and Becky. In none of them did she say anything about Tom. Slashers slashed and doors creaked in the background, providing enough distraction to numb without requiring intelligence to watch. That part of her mind that never stopped working noticed that the art direction in one of the films was unusually good. She made a mental note to look up the art director on one of the databases and check him out.

One couple finally faced down the demented assassin in a burning farmhouse in the country. Faced with what appeared to certain death, they bid their final farewells to each other. On any other night, in any other frame of mind, Adele would have found it maudlin to the point of being sickening, if not out-and-out hilarious. Tonight, she leaped to the machine and skipped the chapter.

By then it was 1:00 a.m. and almost time for bed. Sunday would be easier. The morning challenge to get through the entire Times before noon; she never had, but she would someday. In the afternoon, she had a date for a club game of field hockey in the Park with Irene and the others. Sunday would be O.K. By Monday, she was certain she'd have the psychological element back in control. The other thing would take longer, but that was merely physical. She'd been there before.

*

The wages of sin. In theory, they're supposed to be paid either in the afterlife or the next reincarnation. Adele Jansen paid them here and now, almost immediately. If she had paid any sooner, it would have been withholding at the source.

The end of any affair for her inevitably meant a few days of climbing the walls and cold showers (literally) until her body grudgingly accepted the fact that the celibate regime had been reimposed. It became almost an articulate argument. *What's wrong with a little healthy animal fun?* every nerve ending whined. *Everyone else does it.* But she knew what was wrong in her case, she had found out by experience, and the body could not be permitted to have its way.

Which did not mean there wasn't going to be a lot of sweating and restlessness, exactly what was occurring this particular Wednesday evening. The television was on, but she wasn't watching. She was pacing up and down the large living room of the apartment like a caged panther. Thank God Joan wasn't there to ask embarrassing questions.

The easy remedies had been exhausted. The Russian novel had been closed two nights earlier, with a fervent prayer that someday the critical community would realize that a novel can be controversial and still be trash, particularly in a leaden translation. On this evening, she had already tried distracting herself with the most unsexy thing to do she could think of, in this case, teaching herself to program in "LISP." It hadn't worked. She hadn't expected that it would.

She had lived through this frustration before, but seldom to this degree. His mouth, his hands, all of the places he'd touched. In the immediate aftermath, everything had been so hazy. Now, a week later, she seemed to recall it all microsecond by microsecond, fingertip by fingertip. It was always thus.

I think, Adele, it's time we got better acquainted, after which they certainly had. So confident, so completely in charge. . . so quintessentially male. Decides he's going to bed you, and just does it. *God!* Simply remembering that low seductive drawl, the confidence, produced a delicious pleasure. Where does that kind of guy learn to talk that way, anyway? Is there a school someplace? It was hard to believe it came entirely naturally. She reached one end of the room, looked skyward at the wall, and turned.

Hands, mouth – not to overlook the obvious – how had one of her college friends put it? *The closest encounter of the nicest kind with fully engorged, prime time, grade A erectile tissue,* she'd said, in the course of announcing too coyly that a period of celibacy had ended. *Right.* No matter how many times Adele encountered that particular anatomical phenomenon, it still seemed miraculous. He'd felt like something sculpted by Michelangelo, damn him. It was useless trying not to think about it; she could feel him even when she wasn't thinking about him, as if it were happening now. She turned at the other end of the room, arms folded.

"God," she said aloud, the air hissing out of both sides of her mouth, her eyes rolling toward the ceiling, "did that man know how to fuck!" Her public vocabulary was free of any Anglo-Saxonisms. They didn't wear well with 'cute'. But she was alone now, and spoke the way she thought. Then she paced the room back the other way.

She had no other choice. Mechanical devices or self-manipulation made her romantic soul shudder. She gave some passing thought to phoning her last lover. She had broken off with him eight months before. He'd been an art director at one of the Madison Avenue ad agencies, young, talented, lively, and fun. He'd come to one of Carolyn's parties, they'd shared some cynicism. She'd liked him a lot, enough to try it out. His expressions of approval when he found out what she was actually like in bed had been extremely vocal – too vocal, really. It should have been a warning. As he gradually discovered the full extent of the emotional and intellectual resources she had at her disposal, he'd become more and more withdrawn and diffident, almost dysfunctional sexually.

Baby, he'd said one night, at the time when they'd usually go to his place or hers, *this isn't working.* Her eyes flooded automatically, but the predominant emotion was relief – if he hadn't said something, she was going to have to. *We'll always be friends*, he'd said, taking her hand, meaning it, proving it in various small ways afterward. Then he'd gone back to women who were no less accessible and much less challenging.

She'd been disappointed and more than a little hurt. She hadn't done anything wrong, had simply been herself. She was also a bit frightened. That was not the first time she'd lived through that particular story. It might turn out that it was the basic story of her life.

Her last lover? That was a joke. The English language was much too kind to men. She'd been to bed with one old friend; there were a few men (like the art director) for whom she'd tried and who had tried for her and it hadn't worked; and there was a much larger number who could truthfully say – and undoubtedly had said – that they'd screwed her.

But she'd had only *one* lover.

*

Her blood surged in her veins one evening coming home on the subway. She was seated. Useless to fight with sexual fantasies when she was in this state; more practical to go with it, save her strength for more important battles. She closed her eyes and let it sweep over her.

Some women have faceless stranger fantasies. Adele's were Nameless Stranger. All right, let's have him get on the train, attractive, of course, well dressed and well off. Let's make it instantly apparent that he's fundamentally trustworthy, too; after all, this is a fantasy. He sits down on the seat beside her, replacing in her mind's eye the pear shaped, middle-aged executive who actually occupies it. He appraises her, calmly and confidently. He speaks:

You may have fooled everyone on this car, but you're not fooling me. You're ripe for the taking. Pick up your purse. You're coming with me.

She's helpless, of course, picks up the purse. *Do I have any choice?*

No. This isn't a democracy, Ms. Jansen. You don't have a vote. I'm going to do it my –

Hold it. Her eyes popped open. *What kind of Nameless Stranger fantasy is this, for heaven's sake?* She shook her head from side to side, smiling at herself. It was almost like the punch line to an old joke.

That was no Nameless Stranger, that was my...

Then, suddenly, it became frightening. Nothing like this had ever happened to her before. She had expected she would miss him, would have been disappointed in herself if she had not. But to have her own sleep disturbed by his dreams, to have her fantasies invaded so easily?

Tom had evidently found and pushed some buttons she hadn't known existed.

*

George Sorenson phoned twice. The road show for AI Squared was in full swing; he expected to be in Europe and then in the Midwest with the company officers. After checking her calendar and Carolyn's with his the second time he called, they settled on a day to meet, Friday, October 15th, three weeks and a day after her day with Tom.

She marked it down in her desktop organizer, resident in the laptop. References to AI Squared's expert system kept appearing in the trade journals; the more she read, the more excited she became. She could hardly wait to lay her hands on the program itself.

She also did a bit of discrete checking on Consolidated Financial Services. Although it had little public presence, it was very well known among New York's super rich by its initials, CFS. Despite a small clientèle, it had a reputation as an extremely large, extremely successful, extremely aggressive hedge fund, active in all trading arenas. Rarely did it undertake its own syndications, but the ones it managed were nearly always successful. George Sorenson was one of its two partners.

The pattern fit. Everything was falling into place.

*

The sexual fever subsided as it always did. The strange new emotions disturbingly lingered on. Every once in a while she would be overcome by the peculiar feeling of something left undone she'd felt the first night afterwards. But, gradually, order returned to her life. The small pleasures of her daily routine became gratifying again. Those stray memories which did pierce her guard produced only a distant ache, not the acute pain that they had at first.

She ordered the Prado catalogue which, when it arrived, went straight into the treasure drawer, where the farewell note he had written already resided. She also purchased a new sketchbook. On the first page she drew him the way she had first encountered him, the afternoon of the reception at the Press. The work pleased her greatly. She could not determine whether it was because the drawing was good or because of her feeling for the subject. There were, she knew, going to be many other drawings.

In a different book, she also did the sketch of Josh Palmdale she'd promised herself, the moment of horror at the discovery of the lion. She drew the lion naturalistically. The thought of caricaturing Tom, even in a flattering way, was anathema.

She put the sketchbooks away. Then suddenly, impulsively, she pulled out one of the dreamhouse books and paged through it. Spanish Colonial, willows along the driveway, at least one room with a truly unique Moorish decor, sketched, because she'd never seen anything in any catalogue remotely like what she had conceived in her mind's eye. It would fail utterly if anyone else tried, but she could do it, she knew it. She studied it for a moment, and then put it back, thinking other thoughts.

Very nice, but eagles do not make their homes there. It hurt less and less with each passing day. The great winged being was flying west towards the setting sun, far out to sea, miles and miles and miles now from any of the everyday reality where she dwelt. It has no need of land, it follows no ship; it makes its own paths through pathlessness. The great wings that had filled her entire horizon for such a brief, glorious time had dwindled into a black, distant speck, silhouetted against the sunset. *Farewell, my beloved. Part of me goes with you. I will never forget you.*

It could never have worked, not for a second. Except for that strange bonded feeling, the occasional spark of weird urgency, everything was over, the pain, the hurt, all done, all gone – that in itself made her sad and wistful.

*

The connection was scratchy and distant, as if it originated from the moon. But she'd know that voice anywhere.

"Bri!" she said.

"I hope I didn't wake you up."

"No, it's only eleven. How is everything?"

"Great. I'd better make this quick. These connections break down all the time. Linda and I are coming home in about two weeks."

"Your incompetence has been uncovered and you've been cashiered?"

"Close. My incompetence has been uncovered and I've been promoted. That's the way it works in the Foreign Service. We're on our way to Bogota. Anyway, Linda's got to go up to her family" – she recognized tension in his voice; he moved on quickly – "and I'm going to come to New York. I'm scheduled for a briefing from some guys at the U.N. delegation. I'd like to see you."

"When?"

"Plane gets in Monday the 18th. Thursday that week?"

"Done. I'll take the afternoon off. Wanna have lunch and get drunk? Then maybe a show?"

"Perfect. I've got all kinds of things to tell you. I'm really looking forward to seeing you, Delly."

"Me, too." There was a pause. Then he began. "Johnson and –"

"–Jansen," they said in unison. "We don't quit and we don't lose."

"'Bye now," said Bri. "I'd love to talk, but I've got other calls."

The timing could hardly have been better. When you've had to give up a new lover, there is nothing so useful for perspective as an old friend. She definitely intended to discuss all that had happened between herself and Thomas Bryant Newcombe with Brian Johnson.

*

A small package arrived at her office on Monday morning eighteen days after she had been to the Met. She glanced at it casually, and then not so casually when she saw the characteristic 'T' pierced by the curlicue. Her pulse began to race; she could feel herself breathing faster. She did her best to maintain control, but her hands trembled as she tore open the wrapping.

The package contained a small jewelry box. Inside was a pendant on a gold chain. The base figure, in gold, was a small cherub. Its hair was brown, made of crushed topaz, divided by a thin gold band as halo. Two tiny emeralds made up its eyes; and the pinkest of tiny pink rubies was in its navel.

She smiled as she turned it over. She got it; a private joke – Titian brown, Titian green, and Titian pink. She could see his eyes twinkling as he'd instructed the jeweler about the navel stone. Sensible of him to cheat like that; she might have blushed to wear it if he'd had the stone(s) placed where the pink really was.

He'd had the piece engraved. It read:

To A. E. J.

One of the angels he didn't paint

T. B. N. 9/23

Momentarily, she couldn't place that, then recollected her spontaneous self-description in front of the Van Eyck. Tom evidently had remembered all along. She put it in her pocket and went down to the washroom to see how it looked.

She fastened it around her neck and looked at it carefully. Well, maybe it wasn't the greatest – it didn't exactly – but she was sure that she had something – that there was somewhere she could – I mean, surely it isn't that–

Face facts, stupid. It's hideous. A writer he is. An artist he ain't.

She loved it. She examined her neck again. There was no question that she would wear it often. The inscription, more important the source, meant a great deal to her. All she had to do was remember to wear something over it so that no one else could see.

The sense of loss, which had entirely subsided, became for an instant acute again. Why couldn't it have been possible? *Damn it.* In the same instant, that same feeling as the first night afterward, that this was all wrong, that leaving him had set the base of the world askew. But then it was gone – and maybe this time it was premenstrual; that time was near.

Back in the office, she noticed he'd enclosed a note. It read:

Had my blood tested. All is well.

T.

She'd forgotten all about that, but was glad he hadn't. There was a second of intense, irrational disappointment that he hadn't written more. But there was wisdom in that restraint, the same wisdom that she had enforced on herself.

She sighed, put the note back into the box, and the box on the side of her desk by the computer where she wouldn't forget to take it home. Then she gathered herself and returned to the task at hand – with some difficulty.

Idiot, don't waste your time on regrets for what had to be. And yet, in spite of herself, she did.

*

Four days later, on the Friday morning before the big meeting with George Sorensen and Carolyn, she began to sip her morning diet cola as she always did.

Suddenly, the thought, just the thought alone, of taking anything like that into her body made her literally sick to her stomach.

She put the drink down. She thought nothing more of it at the time.

END, PART I

CHOICES

"**Y**ou guys are right on schedule," said the man seated at the side of the conference table. He unrolled a cigar. "You're more reliable than the railroad."

"Thank you," said the man at the head of the table. "It usually works out."

"When do we move?" asked the first.

"November 26th," answered the man standing by the window without looking back. "Day after Thanksgiving. When all the honchos are watching ballgames or sweating at racquetball."

"So long?"

The man at the window shrugged. "Gotta develop cause. Do a shelf reg. No need to rush."

Interesting, thought the man seated at the side of the table, the odd man out. Most of the two-bit hustlers and Wall Street sharpies would give their eyeteeth to know more of the inner workings of these two. He had his own share of street smarts, and then some, but all he'd observed so far was that the deferential one seemed to make all the executive decisions. Many people had observed that. But perhaps it was rehearsed. He lit the cigar and glanced towards the man at the window. What was he thinking of? Revising the plan? Devising alternatives?

In point of fact, the man at the window had long since become bored with the plan. While it was not fool proof, the risks had been calculated and recalculated so often he had lost interest.

He was thinking in fact of coincidences – that the girl at the party would turn out to be the same one as at the software show; that her hands would be light and graceful as they fluttered over that Velásquez thing; that, miraculously, she'd accept the lunch invite.

That she'd be unforgettable.

The coincidence had begun to bother him. It bothered him more the longer he thought about it.

*

"You're pregnant," said Alice Marshall, Adele's gynecologist. It was Thursday, six days after the attack of nausea. "There's no doubt."

"I can't be," answered Adele automatically. Since morning, she'd been hoping against hope that the drugstore test had been wrong.

"If you can look me dead in the eye and tell me you haven't had sexual relations with a man sometime in the last six weeks," said Dr. Marshall, "I'll phone the Pope and tell him the good news."

"That's not very funny, Alice," said Adele, still numb. She was sitting in the doctor's private office across the desk from her.

"I have to tell you, you're the last of my patients I would have thought would be careless about this," went on Dr. Marshall, a little more kindly.

"But that's *it*, that's exactly *it*, that's why I'm so mad," said Adele. "I *did* take care. So did the man. And look what's happened."

"You'd better tell me everything," said Alice.

Adele did just that, reporting only the clinical facts, not the romantic detail, and not the last incident of love-making. It was embarrassing to relate and Tom'd been all but tapped out anyway, to put it bluntly. The doctor's expression grew more and more sympathetic.

"I don't blame you for feeling exasperated. You really are unlucky. Two devices, the fourth day of your cycle – and if he had an ejaculation without intromission within twelve hours of the actual insemination, his sperm count couldn't have been all that high." Alice gestured towards Adele's abdomen. "That's one tough critter you've got there – better than a 10,000 to one shot, I'd say. In fact, considerably higher odds."

Adele shrugged and looked away, out the window.

"Have you told the father yet? That you're worried, anyway?"

"No." Adele looked back. "I was really only with him the one day. Don't look at me like that. It wasn't like that at all. He's a wonderful man, he's – he's – he's very difficult to describe. But by the time it was over, we both knew there was no way anything realistically could work. Our lives are too different. So it ended almost as soon as it began."

Both women were silent for a moment.

"Well," said Dr. Marshall, "this isn't necessarily the end of the world. This is the twenty-first century, not the nineteenth. I think you know what your options are. What do you want to do?"

"What do I *want* to do? What do I want to *do*?" said Adele, the numbness exploding into anger. "What do you *think* I want to do?! I want to get into a time machine, go back two months and get back on the pill, that's what I want to do! But I can't do that, can I, Alice? For heaven's sake," she went on, subsiding into mutters, "what do I want to do, what do I want to do, what kind of foolish question is that?"

The room became silent again. "That's not you, Adele," said Dr.

Marshall, gently. "And this isn't my fault."

"I know," said Adele, recomposing herself. "I'm sorry. But this is the worst thing that could possibly have happened. The very worst."

"That, too, I have heard before. I don't have many patients who regard abortion as a form of alternative birth control. If misery does love company, you have a lot of company."

Adele shrugged. She knew it was selfish, but right at that moment she didn't particularly care how or what Dr. Marshall's other patients felt. "There's only one thing I can do, I suppose. Where are these things done, anyway?"

"All over. But I send most of my patients in this situation to a little clinic over in the East 60s. Very nice, very discrete. You can be in in the morning and out that evening. Not that there should be any difficulty," added the doctor. "It's really only an ordinary D-and-C."

"Yes, I know," said Adele tonelessly. "It's all so very ordinary, isn't it? Well. Let's get it over with. Can you do it right now? Can we get it over with now?"

"No," Alice answered soberly. "We can't."

Adele's skin began to crawl. "Well, then later this week. Whenever you say."

"No, not later this week, Adele," Dr. Marshall answered even more soberly. "You're of a type that's very high risk for any office procedure. You're as tightly muscled down there as any patient I have ever had. It's hard enough to give you an ordinary pelvic. I want you have to have a D-and-C. Under a general."

"All right, Alice," Adele replied, her heart sinking. "Give it to me, then. When?"

"In about four weeks," Alice said, looking her directly in the eye. Adele's eyes widened. *No! Not four weeks!* "You'll still be well within the first trimester. I can't in good conscience ask for any priority. You came in to see me far more quickly than a lot of women."

Oh, God, no! Not four weeks! "Alice, that is completely unacceptable. I'm not going to accept that. I can't. There must be some way –"

"The City is full of women from places where they don't have this alternative. Bed space is scarce. Four weeks is the best I can do, Adele."

"Alice," she said, infuriated, "maybe I should find someone who can do it."

Her doctor did not even react. "Seek a second opinion by all means. But anyone who's medically responsible will give you the same advice I have." It occurred to Adele that Alice had not even reacted to her spleen, had treated her like a child in mid-tantrum (perhaps correctly). "I know what you're thinking. I know why you want it done quickly. But it's not appropriate. I want to be certain that when you look back at this – incident – that it's only that. An incident, not a turning point or a tragedy. Not something to be regretted always. Four weeks. You do athletics. You noticed your condition far sooner than most. I can't realistically jump you over others in more need." She shrugged. "So that's what it should be. Now," she went on promptly, crisply, "I'd like you not to make any other plans for that weekend, though, in case there's some complication, or you're feeling bluesy, or whatever. Be in by eight in the morning – and absolutely nothing to eat or drink after midnight. I have a list of printed instructions."

Adele glared at her fiercely for a moment and then – gave up. No escape – the piper was obviously going to have to be paid to the very last penny. She could only nod and turn to the window again. Another few seconds passed. "I'm sorry for getting angry. I guess you'd better have your nurse make the appointment."

"No," said Alice. "These are appointments I make myself."

She picked up her phone and hit an automatic dial code. The dialog was short and perfunctory, then she put the receiver down. Adele looked out the window and tried not to listen. "That's done," said the doctor.

"You meant what you said?" Adele suddenly turned and asked. "Ten thousand to one?"

Dr. Marshall appraised her. "Yes. I meant it. Each device has about a one percent failure rate. One hundred times one hundred – why are you smiling?"

"No good reason. It's that the father would like this. He thinks like that."

"Then you consider the timing of the intercourse, the day in your cycle – they're high odds any way you look at it. Why? Does that make a difference to you?"

"No. Not at all. Just curious." She continued looking out the window. *Nothing happens by chance*, she'd said that morning.

Then she spoke: "Alice, do you need this office right now? Can I sit here by myself for a while?"

"Sure. Absolutely. I've got patients in the examining rooms, as a matter of fact. Four weeks from Saturday. The Saturday before Thanksgiving. You'll have the weekend to recover. Remember to pick up the appointment information before you leave."

"Thank you. I will."

*

No, God no, not this, anything but this. On the short list of the problems she had never wanted to confront, never wanted to have anything to do with, this one stood at the very, very top.

The timing could not have been worse. The public offering of AI Squared had closed only two days earlier. As perplexed and confusing as she found some aspects of what had transpired when she met George Sorenson, she knew for certain now that it was a major opportunity, one which not reoccur for a long, long time, if ever.

Now this.

She got out of her chair and stood by the ninth-floor window. There was a small view of Central Park in the distance. *I wish I were yours right now. I mean, really yours.* Yeah, yeah. *I'm a very selfish woman about sperm, Tom, I want all you've got. You don't have to get all dressed up for me.* Sez Irene Dunne to Cary Grant. Ha, ha. She flopped her right wrist up in a mincing gesture of mock sophistication.

You complete, fucking I D I O T!!

It wasn't the politics. The politics were easy – a snap. That someone, anyone could tell her what to do with her own life, with her own body, after an unlucky or unwise act of sexual intercourse – no how, no way, nowhere, absolutely out of the question, un-unh, forget it.

But it was different at the personal level. She'd known many women for whom all of this would be like rolling off a log. She had always known she wasn't one of them. And four weeks! If only it could be done this weekend! Right now it was only a gynecological problem, a late period. In four weeks, given time to think – no way not to think – her imagination coming into play, the rush of sympathy she always felt towards anything small and helpless. . . four weeks!

Nothing happens by chance. Ten thousand to one. She was starting in on herself already.

Not that there was any real choice. For a moment, she gave herself over to thoughts of the unthinkable. Was it at all possible. . .? No. There was more involved than the shame, more than the loneliness, more than the discomfort and the ultimate pain. The bottom line was the complete abandonment of the fast track, the absolute derailment of her ambition, the expense of time. She'd given up Tom for that reason. Now she was going to have to give up his baby, too.

Besides, even if she went ahead with it, what would the aftermath be? She'd only have to abandon–

Suddenly, her mouth dropped open and her eyes widened. She reasoned through an entirely new train of thought, a new possibility, even as her shoulders drooped and her spirits sagged. It could work; it could definitely work. The realization brought her no joy whatsoever.

Great. Absolutely great, moron. Way to go. You just cut off your retreat. Now you can't even rationalize it. You are a real prize.

She sighed and turned away from the window. The clock on the doctor's desk showed ten to twelve. She was going to be late for the lunch date with Bri if she didn't hurry. A moment to jot the appointment down in her laptop – better plan to spend the entire weekend. There was no question she was going to feel a lot more than bluesy. She had to keep this from Bri, somehow – too humiliating to her, not fair to burden him with this when he was on holiday.

It had seemed at first that he'd come home at the best time. It had turned out to be the worst.

*

She had chosen a restaurant famous for a cafe terrace, so they could eat outside, Parisian style. But the weather was changing. That wasn't going to be possible. She arrived about five minutes after the reservation. Bri was nowhere in sight. Good; every once in a while that famous tardiness of his came in handy. She had herself seated and waited for him, toying with her water glass and thinking.

Then all at once he was through the door. He didn't look like he'd changed, still as kind on her eyes as ever. Adele didn't know anymore whether he really was as good-looking as she'd thought. She cared about him too much to be certain.

She waved her hand and called out lightly, "Bri!" and he saw her and came over.

"God, but it's good to see you, Delly," he said, taking her hand as she stood; by tacit understanding, they spared each other the perfunctory kiss on the cheek.

"Exactly mutual, Bri," she said as they sat. "What's new in the world?"

He proceeded to tell her what was new, in Africa ("Don't call me Mistah Kurtz. I liked it. I'm happy to be home, but I liked it"), Zaire, the last three years. The wine came and he poured her a glass. He was too animated to notice immediately that she didn't drink any.

"But I've saved the best news for last," he said.

"Which is?" Bri took a sip of wine and looked suddenly shy. Then he looked at her glass. "No wine?"

"It's all right. It just doesn't taste very good," which was the truth as far as it went.

"Well –" he paused. "No simple way to say it. In about six and a half months, Linda and I are going to make you a godmother."

"Bri! Oh, Bri, that's wonderful! Congratulations! Do you really want me to stand in for you? I didn't think Linda liked me." She was being polite. They both knew Linda hated her. She was puzzled as to the reasons. He was fully aware of them.

"Yes. It did take some friendly persuasion, but she agreed. Anyway, that's why she's not with me. She's up with her own folks." A shadow darkened his face. He had been wrestling with her parents for the soul of their only child ever since he met her. Then suddenly he was appraising Adele more carefully. "Delly? Delly, this is good news. Delly? What's the matter? You look like a piano is about to fall on you and you can't move out of the way."

It was too much of a coincidence. No use to try; besides, now all at once she wanted to tell him. She permitted herself a small sip of wine. "Because, Bri, unless I do something about it, I'm going to become a mother myself about that time. The real kind. I only found out for sure an hour ago."

He went white himself. "Oh, my God, Delly."

"What am I going to do, Bri? What am I going to do?" She put her head in her hands. "This is the worst thing that could ever have happened."

He took a big drink of wine and became thoughtful. "I don't know what to say. I don't know what to tell you. You remember when you were in that radical feminist stage and you ran around saying you didn't think men should even have a vote on the abortion thing?"

"I still believe that."

"Well, I guess that's the point. I thought that was pretty wild at the time, but do you know I've come around to agreeing with you? You'd be surprised how many men think the same way. I don't know what's going on in your body or what you should think about it or do about it. I have no idea. Two months with Linda has convinced me of that."

He reached across the table and gripped her shoulder lightly. "I do know that you're going to take it pretty hard. You were always so child-oriented, from as far back as I can remember. If there is anything I can do, let me know."

She patted his hand and managed a weak smile. "Thanks, Bri, but it does happen to lots of girls. They get through it, so I guess I will, too."

He smiled back. "I hope so." He searched for something to say. "But. . . jeez, Delly, you with kids. That night when we were sophomores and I came over to your house in a fever? I knew you were going to let me take your blouse off; I was finally going to get to second base. And I found you trying to teach your nieces Parcheesi, and it was obvious they were too young, but you wouldn't quit, you went on and on, while I waited for you in heat. Or –"

"Brian *Johnson*," she said in mock indignation, thankful. She knew what he was doing. "That's *not* fair. As I recall, the blouse did come off and you slurped all over me. Furthermore, I went with you for three-plus years and there was not one time I didn't come across for you when you asked. If more didn't happen than did, don't blame *me*. You knew what was possible."

"Touché," he grinned. "Agreed." He refilled his wine glass. "You know, Delly, when I think of all that, the funny thing is, it's never about the stuff we did when we were twenty. It's the stuff we didn't do when we were eighteen that gets to me." She nodded in understanding, if not necessarily agreement. "I still don't know why you didn't go skiing with me that Spring Break week."

"Stuff came up, Bri," she said, with the slightest trace of agitation. He knew there had been more to it than that, but he also knew she was never going to tell him exactly what.

Then he became serious again.

"I do want to help," he said softly. "I know you, Delly. We go back a ways." He grinned slyly. "All those parties – all the times someone's kid brother woke up, I'd look around and you'd be gone, and I'd find you upstairs, reading a story or drawing a picture. . ." He studied his wine. "I didn't mind as much as I let on, you know."

"Well, my goodness, Bri," she answered lightly. "Confession time. You seemed pretty impatient at the time."

"No," he said, telling her the truth. "I was only playing the game. Those sorts of things were part of what made you special. That's what I really thought." She blushed; his mind drifted back. "The parties. Or –"

*

The Cuteness Factor – he had been the one who gave it its name. The Most Likely to Be Disregarded Award – he was the one who'd invented it. But he'd never succumbed himself to that illusion – or so he liked to think.

Johnson and Jansen. He was a good high school debater, one of the best, good enough to win eighty or ninety percent of the time, with anybody as his partner. But the reason they never lost was because Delly was an absolute Terminator. The opponents rarely figured the program out until the play was all but over. They'd be reacting viscerally to him, the six-foot male, while the petite girl, the real enemy, was jabbing away in that cheerful, good-natured manner. The balloon would be leaking air out of a dozen holes before it even knew what hit it. She was somehow able to play off the difference between her appearance and her skill level, exploit it, without ever falling into the alternative traps of coyness or false dignity – a real tightrope act. That was why the fool from Oneonta, who kept ruining her balance with that patronizing drivel, had been so exasperating.

But there was another Delly, too, warm and alive and passionate like no one else. She'd been the most exasperating girl at times. *I know I said I'd go, but I can't, Bri; Jimmy won't let anyone sit with him but me. Delly, you promised me. You promised me this would never happen again. I know I did, but I can't. Even if I did go, all I'd think about is him crying in his room. Small people have to stick together, Bri. I'm sorry, but I can't. You can take someone else. Bri? No one too pretty.*

It wasn't hard to see then why little kids blackmailed their parents emotionally about her. As impatient as he'd be to sit down on the couch, turn out the light, and do some damage, it was beautiful to watch her. She invented games for them, made up stories, did things no one else could do. *What is this? It's an oval! No, it's a – Horse's face! No, it's a – Viking boat? Don't draw so fast, Delly, let me guess first, Delly. It's – it's – it's me!* And she would smile and tear out the sketch and hand it to whomever.

Later, when mothers and fathers had gained unlimited confidence in her, he had discovered the silver lining that comes with having a girlfriend who does a lot of baby-sitting. *Sure, you can come over. They said it was okay. They trust me, the fools.* She giggled. *They don't know you're a sex maniac.* Then she would be in his arms, body pressed hard against his, mouth against his and wide-open, looking up at him from time to time, with wide, imploring green eyes.

Other girls got along well with kids. Other girls could draw. Other girls liked to kiss open-mouthed. It wasn't that Delly was different than any of them; it was only that she was so much more – so much more – so much –

More.

*

Now the woman that girl had become was looking out the window of the restaurant at the dreary overcast day. "I don't have any relation like that at all to it now, Bri. Right now, it's only a little blot, a maddening useless excrescence. But I won't have the – I don't even want to say the word – the procedure for four weeks. And all that will change, won't it?"

Yes, it will, Delly, he silently agreed. *I know you too well. Every time you see a small child on the streets, every time you walk by a pregnant woman, every time you pass a happy family, something's going to click. You're going to create an identity for this little thing whether you want to or not, you're like that, too imaginative, too emotional (in this case) for your own good. By the time this is over, you'll have lived through a special misery all your own – and you won't let one bit of it crack through to anyone else, will you? You wouldn't even have told me if my own news hadn't hit the bull's eye.*

"Tell me about the father," he said, deliberately breaking the mood.

"It's funny," she answered. "Before I found out about this, I was looking forward to doing exactly that. I was looking forward to telling you all about him. His name's Tom – Thomas Newcombe. I met him at a publisher's reception."

She told him everything, through and including the dinner they'd shared. "Then we went back to his apartment –" All at once he held up his hand and turned to the left.

"Hi, guys," he said, all smiling affability, to the four businessmen seated at the adjacent table, who had inconspicuously terminated their own conversation and were now listening intently to theirs. She hadn't noticed, but he had. For as long as she had known him, friends or lovers, Bri had always taken good care of her.

She smiled to herself. She'd seen this performance many, many times before. Not that it was an act – if it had been an act, it wouldn't have worked. He was entirely genuine; the curiosity, the real interest he had in other people, was entirely natural. Remarkable; in two minutes, the four businessmen had become his friends, in five minutes, friends for life; if he'd gone on for fifteen minutes, he'd have been the principal beneficiary in all their wills. But he quit after five – *you don't wanna eavesdrop on a lady, do you, fellas?* after which they ostentatiously turned their attention to the business plans they'd brought with them.

"Not bad," she said, very softly, grinning.

Grinning himself, he held his right forefinger up to his lips. "You were saying? You did what?"

"We went back to his apartment," she said, and then suddenly became very shy.

"To go to bed," Bri prompted. "Where you went crazy like you always do."

She nodded. "Where I went crazy like I always do. In fact, crazier than usual. But not so crazy that I didn't use my diaphragm. And he used a condom." Bri looked puzzled and she finished off the story as clinically as she could. They might be more friends than lovers these days, or so he said, but no way was she going to parade the details of a physical involvement with another man.

"My doctor says it's a ten thousand to one shot – more, because neither one of us should have been that fertile. I guess it's not my lucky month."

"Wow." What else could he say? "Wow. What's he like, anyway? You didn't say."

He felt a sharp pang of jealousy at the look on her face. She noticed. "Bri, don't be like that. You'd like him. He was a wonderful person – a sort of combination poet, mathematician, and philosopher, but so sweet. I thought at the time he was a genuine polymath. Intelligent without being at all intellectual or pretentious."

"What's he look like?"

"Very big – about three inches taller than you – he's not bad looking, but not nearly as handsome as you, Bri. Lean, not muscular, but very strong, very gentle, and very –" She suddenly blushed beet red.

"–good in bed," he finished for her.

"Yes," she said, almost inaudibly, and touched him lightly across the table.

"Then why was it over so soon?"

"A lot of reasons. Good reasons." She paused. "His life is so different from mine and he wants different things. We had a lot in common as people, but nothing at all in terms of ambitions or goals or things like that. And this is not a guy I could ever be casual about. It came on so strong, it was definitely an all or nothing thing. So it had to be nothing – and if that was so, the sooner, the better.

"Besides –" should she say this? – "I didn't tell you this, but he has problems. Real problems. I don't know what they are, the time was too short to ask. But something bothers him. I mean, he handles it well, you don't see it all the time, but it's there. He's got a good sense of humor, but he never smiles or laughs. And he has these terrible dreams" – she blushed again. "I didn't want to take all that on. I don't have time for that." She did not at all like the look on Bri's face; it had not sounded very pretty to her, either, the way she said it.

"Sounds pretty cold, Delly," he said softly.

"Damn it, Bri, that's not fair!" she exploded. "It's easy for you to say! You've got what you want – the Foreign Service, and Linda, and everything. I don't have anything yet! Do you know how hard it is to live in this place? How petty and mean everyone is? How expensive? And all I've got is me and my time and what I can do and I've got so far to go! I haven't even started on the family things and they're so much harder for a woman than a man! People don't take me seriously like they do you; I'm not tall and male and with a deep voice. I have to prove myself every day, every time, before I can make any progress at all! I don't have contacts, my family isn't rich –"

"Neither is mine, Delly," he said evenly. He was becoming angry.

"Comparatively it is. There is so little time, and – and –" Then he saw at once he had goofed it. Another of the emotional storms she was subject to had overtaken her. She'd lost color, she was biting her lower lip. The look on her face he knew – had known – forever, a combination of hurt and anger. *How could you do this to me, you of all people?* He was always putty in her hands after seeing that look. In a way, it was flattering. She let her guard down for so very few people. It was almost a privilege to be one who knew her as she really was.

And she's pregnant, too; don't let yourself forget that. He'd wanted to help and he'd hurt her. He took her hand.

"I'm sorry," he said softly. "I didn't realize. It must have been very difficult."

She shook her head up and down, the way she always did when she was too choked up to speak and waiting to recover her voice. He said nothing until she was ready.

"I'm sorry, too. I guess I didn't make it clear. I wanted this guy, Bri. I wanted him so badly. I wanted to stay with him more than anything. I didn't kid myself. It embarrasses me, it all happened so fast, but –" she swallowed – "I cared about him; I loved him then; I – I love him now. He was so magnificent. But –" she took a swallow of water, shaking her head from side to side.

"I'm like anyone else. Love's more important to me than anything. But it's not more important than *everything*. It's not infinite, it doesn't outweigh everything else, and I'm not going to pretend it does. I am not going to live small. I'm not going to narrow my horizons or lower my sights. I am not going to make the same mistake my mother did." Her eyes blazed with determination. This, too, he had heard before, seen before – and never failed to be moved and intimidated, both at once. She turned her head towards the window.

"But I wanted him so much," she added plaintively. "I wanted so for it to be possible. But it wasn't. So maybe it was cold. It had to be." Another pause, then she went on:

"Don't be jealous again, but he replaced you at the top of my if-it-has-to-be-anyone list. You know." Abruptly her look darkened. "Maybe I've got it backwards. Maybe you and he should be at the bottom, the men I most don't want it to happen with. Because. . ."

A long silence before he spoke: "I don't see where you have much practical alternative."

"No." Then she scowled. "Still, it bothers me that I'd do anything simply because it's easier. I've never been easy on myself." A contemplative pause. "Other women do it, you know."

He did not at all like this turn in the dialog. "Sure, when the biological clock is running and not much else is happening for them, and even then most of them have a screw loose. But not –"

"I could do it, you know," she said, her eyes narrowing, clearly now contemplating alternatives. *Jesus Christ, no; Delly, don't even think it, don't hurt yourself any more than you have to.*

"And what then? You couldn't raise it –"

"Him or her," she said absently. *Damn it*, he thought, *it's started already.*

"–I can't see you letting any stranger adopt him or her. Really, what could you do?"

"I thought of that in the doctor's office this morning. Let Jack and Becky adopt my baby is what. I trust them and I'd always be close to – him or her. It would solve a lot of their problems, too. Adopting a blood relation. They'd think it was a miracle."

He was not only her boyfriend, but a Jansen family friend, close enough to be aware of Jack's childlessness and the reason for it, the sterility that was slowly but surely poisoning his marriage, his life, his soul, a compost heap of depression and guilt from which bitterness and alcoholism were beginning to sprout like weeds. It was a sound idea, like all of Delly's – good for Jack, Becky, the unborn child, good for everyone except the only person he cared about in this whole ridiculous fandango.

"I still don't think it's very practical," he said desperately.

"You're right," she said suddenly, tossing her head and snapping back to the here and now, to his immense relief. "It isn't. I don't really have much choice, do I? Bri –" she looked up at him – "do you have any advice for me? Is there anything you think I should do?"

He thought about it. "Actually, there is. I think you should talk to Tom about this. If he's anything like you say, he'll have something positive to add. If it was me, I'd want to know – mind you, it would still be your decision – but I'd want to know that I'd fathered a child. And if there is even the teeniest, tiniest outside chance that you're going to bring his child into the world – and the way you're talking, Delly, there's at least that; if you ever decide that's what you want to do or you should do, you'll do it, and the sky can fall into the ocean before you'll back off, I know you – if there is that chance, he should know that, too. Why are you frowning? Is it that dumb an idea?"

"No. I'm frowning because it's obvious and if I weren't such a ninny, I would have thought of it myself."

"My God, Delly, have mercy on yourself. It's only been an hour and you're still reeling." He was secretly very pleased. *If this Tom fellow cares about you at all and has the influence that I don't, he'll talk you out of any hare-brained scheme you might come up with.*

The waiter had arrived with the check. "I'm taking care of this, Delly. After news like that," and for once she didn't argue.

She was fumbling in her purse. "Here are the theater tickets, Bri. I don't feel up to it tonight. I want to go back to the office and make some calls. Then I'm going to go home." She paused.

"You know, there's one thing I didn't mention. When the condom broke, I was pleased. You can guess why. I said then that nothing happens by chance. It was a throwaway remark, but it's stayed with me. And now this is all so wildly improbable. I can't shake the feeling that all of this means something, that something is going on here."

"You mean that the baby is destined?" *I hope to God you don't mean that.*

She shook her head emphatically from side to side. "No. Not that at all. Something else, something I can't put my finger on. Something I haven't figured out. Only that there's a reason for this I don't know yet. It's weird." Abruptly she closed her purse.

"I've got to go. Bri, I've been terrible. What a selfish toad I am! I didn't ask at all about Linda or her pregnancy or – "

"Quite understandable."

"Even so, will you phone me later and fill me in? Please?" He nodded. "God, it's been good to see you!" She was standing now and he extended his hand. "Un-unh," she grinned, moved past his arm; put her arm around his neck, and kissed him hard, and open-mouthed on his mouth, held it until he responded. Then she stepped back, smiled, waved, turned, and was gone. The crowd of jostling reservees, focused only on the availability of the table, did not pay her more than a second's glance.

She was, after all, only one more small, pretty girl in a city that abounds with them.

*

He'd done well, very well; he knew that. She'd come in low spirits, left in high; Brian Johnson, your ordinary, everyday mood altering agent. Johnson and Jansen. Delly. He had never underestimated her. That had not at all been the nature of his mistake.

So stupid when you're eighteen. His motives were so tangled then it was hard to reconstruct them now. The wide world beckoning; a small town he itched to leave; a great girl, but too much a part of a too familiar landscape. Perhaps then – and perhaps even now – he was a bit in awe. Mutual (he believed) agreement that it was time to separate, time to cultivate actively others. *We'll always be friends, Delly,* he'd said. She'd nodded, eager (she maintained) in her own way to be off – but then without warning had come a storm – lips trembling, pale, swallowing her breath, *I'm going to miss you so much, Bri* – and he'd had to hold her, tight, afraid to look at her or she'd get him going, too. Such an idiot he'd been.

He'd known well enough what those big green eyes were imploring him to do. Even a high school sophomore can recognize a "take me" look when he sees one. But he also knew full well that he lacked both the psychological and physical experience to do justice to the matter. It was not until midway through his freshman year at Harvard that he found himself sufficiently. They had made the date for spring break, both knowing full well what was implied – and then, without warning, without explanation, she had cancelled on him and gone back home instead. He had puzzled over the reasons, worried about them even – but she had never elaborated. After that, what with one thing and another, he was not back in town at the same time as Delly until the summer after his junior year. (Were all the mischances really that accidental?)

They'd had their long overdue affair then, rationalized by mild anxiety he'd developed about sexual inadequacy. Delly and a more relaxed attitude took care of that soon enough (although he realized he was stuck with the not-thinking-about-onions problem for life). But in the larger sense, it didn't work. They both realized it, but he sooner than she. It was not the culmination of dawn-fresh, shining passion they'd once shared, but a monument to its passing. A gravestone.

The crowd was glaring at him from behind the rope. So what. Tough. He wasn't moving until the erection the table cloth was concealing had fully subsided. That last kiss, as only Delly could kiss. The desire had never died entirely.

The mistake – for whatever idiotic reason, he had assumed that the wide world he planned to enter teemed with Dellys, improved, sophisticated, non-provincial Dellys. What a fool. He had seen enough now of that wide world to know fully that what he'd left behind him at eighteen was priceless, unique. The knowledge clawed at him constantly these days.

It's what we didn't do when we were eighteen I regret, he'd said. That was partly true – but regret was a mild word for the wild yearning that would seize him from time to time. Memories of warm spring nights and bundled winter evenings would overwhelm him, with recollections of Delly the Terminator and wide, green, beseeching eyes mixed together. A rueful smile, a shake of his head – in his salad days, he'd managed simultaneously to take her for granted and be overawed by her. Pretty dumb for the rising young star of the State Department.

Now, when it was much, much too late, he appreciated fully the enormous gulf between what he had lost and what he'd won. He could not free himself from that awareness. That was the reason Linda hated her, a reason he would never voice aloud. Occasionally, when they would argue, the point would be made by Linda. *Admit it, Brian, what's really bothering you is that I'm not Adele*

Jansen. Never, so long as he lived, would he admit any such thing, not because she was wrong, but because too often she was right.

You live with what you've done, he reminded himself, *the choices you've made. You are what you are.* The clock can't be reset to zero. The Big Lie – that these days he felt only friendly towards Delly. He'd been selling it long enough and hard enough that he believed she'd bought it. She was dead wrong about one thing, though. He didn't have all he wanted. Linda? He loved her well enough – he believed – she loved him – he hoped. It would work for them. He would see to it that it did. To do otherwise was to compound the error. But it wasn't what he wanted.

Now, finally, he did stand up to leave, far too late to placate the cannibals. He pushed his way through the crowd. Still. . . still. . . a good test for the afterlife. If there was an eternity, and if he'd made the cut, he'd know it at once. He'd be eighteen again, with Delly in his arms, the night before he left for school, the night he broke with her. The second time around he wouldn't blow it; this time he'd say what he should have said, do what he should have done, now that he knew better.

Because if he hadn't blown it, he would never have lost her. Or so he liked to think.

THE LOOK AND FEEL GIRL

"**I** thought you were taking a half-vacation day, Ms. Jansen."

"I am, Christina. Don't put through any calls or messages. I'm going to make a few calls of my own and then be out of here."

Not a bad kiss. *You really forgot yourself back there; he may be your old boyfriend, but he's a married man now, soon-to be-father.* Oh, well; he'd been so sweet, she had to do it. Besides, every once in a while, it was fun to remind him that she'd never bought entirely into that we're-just-friends nonsense.

Her mood had changed 180 degrees. She was feeling gay to the point of giddiness – silly, really, because she was certainly no less pregnant than she'd been this morning. Part of the reason was Bri. She couldn't help but feel better about anything after she'd talked to him about it. But she sensed there was another reason as well, one she had to hunt for. She thought for a moment.

There it is. Yes. She was going to see Tom again – talk to him, be with him, look into his blue eyes – have that lunch, say some things that should never have been left unsaid – and not for any reason for which she was blameworthy. She hadn't weakened. But what could she do? Bri was right, it was only fair, the only right thing to do. The fact that it would also be an unadulterated pleasure was a side benefit. No cloud without its silver lining. For a moment, all the shock of the morning, all the sadness about what had to be, faded.

She had no worry that their brief affair would be resumed. On Tuesday, at the moment when the formula in the vial turned pink, when her stomach dropped through the floor, at that instant every ounce of sexuality in the world had vanished. She had felt about as physical since then as your average, everyday dust mop. In her present frame of mind, it would be a hundred thousand years before she even shook hands with a man again (teasing kisses with old boyfriends didn't count). It had evidently finally dawned on her subconscious that the p.e. teachers and biology textbooks had been right all along, that it was really true, that sexual intercourse is indeed the means by which babies get made. Nothing romantic was conceivable – so to speak.

But, God, it was going to be good to see him again!

Then she punched in Jenet Furston's number.

*

Jenet's secretary did not have Tom's phone number. Before Adele could say another word, the call was transferred.

"Adele, my dear. I'm overscheduled already. But why did you call?"

"I'm sorry to disturb you, Jenet. I was asking your secretary for To – Mr. Newcombe's phone number."

"No, she wouldn't have that. Just a moment" – Adele could hear Jenet riffling through an old-fashioned Rolodex, and then she gave Adele that information. "Not that it will do you any good if you're trying to reach him. He's not there. I tried to contact him yesterday about another of our problems, and he was gone."

Damn. "Do you have any idea where he is? Or when he'll be back?"

Jenet sighed. "I'm afraid I don't. This is Tom's standard operating procedure; it's the way he lives. He disappears for days, sometimes weeks. He'll surface again when he needs money or he wants to work for some other reason. He could be anywhere."

"How does he manage to keep the apartment?"

"He has an arrangement with the owner. The landlord sublets by the day to commercial travelers who want to save some money over a hotel. There are quite a few of them as it turns out. Someone like that will answer the phone if you call."

Adele was becoming increasingly puzzled. "But how does he live? Where does he stay?"

"I don't know, Adele, I really don't," said Jenet. "I do know that once when he was on one of those work binges, he slept through at the library. But other than that, I don't know."

Slept through at the library? she thought. *How weird.* "What about family? Or –" her blood ran cold, she hadn't even considered the possibility before, but she choked out the word somehow – "a wife?"

"He doesn't talk about his family – and he's never been married – that I do know. It's come up from time to time." Adele heard a deepening thoughtfulness in Jenet's tone that she did not particularly care for.

"What about these rumors you mentioned? Wine, women – that sort of thing?"

"Oh, those," Jenet snorted. "They're too incredible to be true – and the sources are hardly reliable. You know, a lot of my staff have ambitions of their own. There is more than a little jealousy of some of my "projects". It doesn't bother me. I do try with all of them. I reward my little fellowships, I spend some money, I publish some truly execrable things. But we all know it's largely an exercise in futility. Carolyn doesn't have to tell me that."

She sighed. It had not been an easy life. "Tom's the prize. Everyone here knows that. Occasionally someone can't stand it anymore and tries to poison the well. It's nothing I take very seriously. It's only human nature."

"What do they say, anyway?" persisted Adele.

"Nothing worth repeating, Adele," Jenet answered, with a firmness in her voice that stated unequivocally that the subject was closed. "Anyway, nothing factual, nothing that would help you contact him."

"But there must be some way to reach him. There must be."

"None that I know of offhand. Believe me, I have experienced this frustration myself often before. Adele," Jenet went on suddenly, "Tom Newcombe is one of the most – no, he's *the* – most private person I have ever met. He evades direct questions. He ignores indirect ones. He says nothing at all about himself. Nothing. Ever."

This was odd – bewildering, in fact – although somehow she was not surprised. "But if he's on contract with you all the time you must have some sort of personnel file on him – for taxes and withholding, that sort of thing. Don't you?"

"Yes, we have something like that. I'll have his file pulled and get back to you. But I doubt very much it will be at all helpful."

Adele hung up the phone and sat uneasily back in her chair. Her good mood had vanished – one of Tom's shorter-lived time bubbles. Something was out of order here, something was radically out of whack – the same feeling of dislocation she'd had on that first Friday night afterward, but focalized now.

The phone rang and it was Jenet. "I have the file, but I'm afraid I was right. It's not very useful. There's nothing here about his family or background."

"Place of birth? Date of birth?"

Jenet chuckled. "He wrote 'n/a' in both spaces."

"Education? School?"

"He wrote one word: 'none.' We also ask for nearest living relative. He wrote 'none' in that blank, too."

She was going to try something else, then was silent, recognizing the uselessness. Jenet filled in the void. "There's not a particle of information here, Adele."

This was well past the point of the ridiculous. "Does he have any friends on the staff? Anyone with whom he was – you know – intimate?"

Jenet snorted. "I think I mentioned that he's had affairs with a few of the available young women on the editorial staff. But all of the relationships were casual as far as I know. I don't think any of his amours ever became truly intimate with him. Rather sad, really."

Another unpleasant surprise; she felt a sharp, intense, completely unexpected pang of jealousy and possessiveness. Somehow she kept the rhythm going: "Hasn't there been anyone who was more serious?"

Jenet thought. "Well, there was one who claimed she did, Georgia Flaherty – no, her name would be Richmond now; she's married. I don't think anyone really believed her. She's hardly his type. Not someone he'd open up to. She's bright, but a committed lightweight, if you know the type. She didn't do well here. Of course I heard about this long after it happened, ninth-hand. Nobody gossips with me. I don't really know."

There was quiet on both sides of the line; Adele was deciding what to do next. Jenet spoke:

"My turn, now, Adele. Why do you want to find him?"

"Oh," lied Adele glibly, "some personal legal business he asked me to take care of."

"What business would that be?" asked Jenet.

"You know I can't answer that, Jenet. Attorney-client privilege."

"Of course," said Jenet, thoughtfully, "although your client could have made it a little easier for you to communicate with him, couldn't he?" Silence hung in the air.

"Be that as it may," Adele said, after a moment, "I'll find him." She decided it would be indiscreet to ask for Georgia Richmond's address just then. "But I did get interested in his poetry. Do you have any of the volumes on hand?"

Obviously, Jenet had not been convinced – of anything – but at last she subsided. "Yes, I do, as a matter of fact. The name authors he writes for often want to see his work before they commit." Jenet's voice took on the enthusiasm it always did when the topic became literature. "They're still in print, you know; we don't sell more than a few dozen copies each year, but they do sell. It gives me hope. I'll send over a set."

"Thank you," said Adele. "Er – Jenet?" She writhed, but had to say it: "Please don't mention any of this to Carolyn."

There was another silence on the other end of the line. "Of course not," said Jenet, finally. "Goodbye, dear," and she disconnected.

What's going on here? Place of birth, not applicable? And it was inconceivable that Tom did not have some exposure to higher education – if not a degree, then at least a place at which he'd been enrolled. She felt anew the one thing she had not told Bri, not because it was any big secret, but because it seemed so irrelevant, so dumb. That was the peculiar sense of urgency she felt about all this, that whatever was to be done had to be done quickly. There was no reason for it, no rational explanation. That's why it was dumb. Yet she felt it now more intensely than ever.

You've lost three weeks. You have got to catch up. Yes. She felt all of that was true – but why? It made no sense whatsoever.

She sighed. Some half-vacation day. Now she'd marooned herself here waiting for Jenet's messenger. Maybe she'd better give it up, settle down, and bill some time. She put down her purse, was about to settle in, when the phone rang.

"I know you said no calls, Ms. Jansen, but this man says it's personal. He wouldn't tell me what his name was."

The coincidence would really be too incredible, but a girl can always hope. Maybe he really was psychic. She pressed down the blinking light. "Tom?" she said, unable to keep the anxiety wholly out of her voice.

"No," said the voice at the other end, after a moment.

It was George Sorensen.

*

Six days before, she had sat in the chair to the left of Carolyn's desk, listening to Carolyn describe the services that Hapgood, Thurlow could provide to AI Squared, the soon-to-be newly-fledged public corporation, to George Sorenson. She could only hope her state of adrenaline nerves was not visible. *You've only prepared for this for three weeks, dummy. Or maybe all your life. Pull yourself together. Johnson and Jansen.*

She kept her mind focused on the two of them, but with an effort. For the second time that morning, when Carolyn offered, the thought of a cola drink had almost made her sick to her stomach. She felt so – strange – in an indefinable way. A touch of the flu? But an alternative hypothesis, based on the fact that her period was now three or four days late, was beginning to beat in the recesses of her brain like a distant tom-tom. She put it off to one side. That possibility was too horrible and unfair to be taken seriously. Besides, she had never been terribly regular menstrually.

Anyway, everything today seemed peculiar, not merely her own body. In their preparatory meetings, Adele had been mildly baffled at the urgency, the importance Carolyn attached to obtaining this client. But now, listening to her, she seemed almost perfunctory, literally walking through the script. Strange.

And George Sorenson? Seen now in a clear light, he was not at all what she would have expected from a man of his station. The edginess, the sharpness surprised her. It was the vibration of a street hustler on the make rather than an investment banker who'd arrived. He strove for a genteel, cultured quality when he spoke. But the nasalisms of the outer Burroughs, where he had almost certainly been raised, crept into his voice despite all his efforts. She found it oddly affecting.

Most puzzling of all, he was a self-confessed technological ignoramus. All he had talked of so far was the placement of the stock, the aftermarket problems, the takedown CFS could expect, the great pitch he'd made in Brussels to a group of Eurobankers. Sure, these were things about which a managing underwriter should be concerned. But he appeared to have no perception – no, stronger than that – no interest even, in the technological miracle the company had supposedly created. How strange.

"We did terrific dog and pony shows in London and Chicago last week," George was saying. "I'm going to close the deal on Tuesday. We're oversubscribed."

"Congratulations," beamed Carolyn.

"Thanks," answered George, standing up and changing chairs. "I'll tell you, this was a rough one. These guys are O.K., but real naïve, as green as the grass. What they don't know about everything would knock your eyes out. It's been six weeks of hustling them on the stage, hustling them off, and putting the hook out before any of them stuffs his foot in his mouth. They're going to need lots of help."

"I've told you already about the help we can provide," said Carolyn, still smiling.

George sat down. "I know that." He turned to Adele. "Hapgood does 95 percent of our legal work. But I don't know about this," shaking his head. "The main thing the guys are interested in is protecting their products. This firm has never had a reputation as a specialist in high-tech companies. You had that little ripple with the Parallax case last year, but it's not an area you've ever developed."

"That's why I wanted you to meet Adele," said Carolyn. "She gives us a capability we haven't had before. She actually made the major contribution in Parallax."

"The look and feel memo, right?" said George. He turned to Adele. "Carolyn told me a little. I'd like you to tell me the rest."

The muscles in her stomach tightened. She was on.

"Well," said Adele, smiling, "actually it starts like a children's story. It was the day before Christmas two years ago. . ."

*

The call had come out of the blue at about 10:00 from one of the junior partners assisting Richard Collishaw. Could she come to the large conference room on the twenty-second floor at once? Of course she could.

It's about Parallax, Collishaw had said, seated at the head of the large table, surrounded by associates and officers of Parallax. *You all know the case?* He was addressing eighteen associates and junior partners. Indeed, she did know. They all did. Parallax Systems, Inc., one of the largest software publishers in the world, had recently brought to market a desktop publishing program with astonishing advanced features. In order to penetrate the installed base of users as quickly as possible, the program had been designed to have the same "look and feel" on the screen as the most popular current product, one sold by Ohwanee Corporation. The contents of the Parallax program were different in innumerable ways and provided far more features. But the basic menu presentation, the form ("look") – and order – ("feel") – of the screen display, was similar.

Eight weeks before, in mid-October, Ohwanee had brought suit against Parallax, claiming that the look and feel was an element of its copyright and that Parallax had infringed upon it. It had obtained a temporary restraining order in federal court. Collishaw had been retained by Parallax on the strength of his general reputation as a trial lawyer. He knew nothing of high-tech. Now he was involved in an endless hearing concerning the granting of a preliminary injunction which would effectively resolve the case.

It is no secret that I am not happy with the progress of this litigation, Collishaw had said. It certainly wasn't; the entire firm knew of it. The hearing was before an able, conscientious judge, but of the old school, hopelessly lost in the technical jargon and concepts involved in the case. It was becoming more and more likely that his decision would be largely intuitive, unacceptable in a case involving hundreds of millions of dollars.

We are now recessed until after New Year's. I have asked you all here frankly in a spirit of desperation. I had my staff cull through the resumes of everyone in the firm. All of you have some unusual feature in your background – he glanced quizzically at Adele *– that may provide the means by which we can give the court some perspective on the real issues before it. I have prepared a copy of the major pleadings and p's and a's for each of you. Over the next few days, I'd like each of you to give the matter your best, most creative shot. At this point, we are receptive to any idea, no matter how unorthodox. I will summon you all again on January 3rd.* He grinned. *Have a nice Christmas.*

*

"I went home to my dad's house for the holiday," Adele recounted to

George, "and I thought about it. It occurred to me – I remember I was about to take a bite of ham – that a computer interface is only a method of communication between two human beings, the programmer and the user – and so is a painting – and they're both two-dimensional in a regular plane." She was into the style now that Bri had so admired when they debated. She accented ever so slightly the delicacy and femininity of her manner. Her voice had its normal lightness of tone. There was no pretentiousness at all about her – and yet her intelligence and purposefulness were unmistakable. It was as if an actress were auditioning for the ingenue's position in the company with a reading of Hamlet, and a perfect reading at that. George Sorenson was looking at her in an entirely different way. Carolyn was attentive, too, smiling, encouraging.

So she was doing O.K., wasn't she? Adele could not shake the feeling that something was out of order. The rhythm seemed wrong, somehow.

"Once I thought of a painting as an interface," she said, with a quick self-deprecating grin at George, "then the trick was to think of something that was equivalent to 'look and feel'. But that actually was the easiest part. Maybe the most notable change in Western art, at least representational art, in the last thousand years is the development of what's called point-of-station – the way deepening perspectives have enabled artists to position an imaginary observer of the scene – the creation of a fourth wall, and framing the action from that theoretical viewpoint. Back in the Romanesque era, the religious tableaux that were done then, there are only three dimensions at best. Artists didn't even consider the observer. He's here, there, and everywhere, not at all a part of the canvas. For instance, if you were to go up to the third floor of the Metropolitan Museum, you'd see – you'd see – the third floor –" She stopped dead.

"Adele, are you all right?" said Carolyn, prompting her.

Adele shook her head, clearing cobwebs. "Yes. Sorry. I lost my train of thought for a moment. Anyway, you'd see these flat plane pictures from back then. The imaginary spectator has no position with respect to any of them. But as you followed the history through the museum, as you saw perspectives get more and more complex, you'd see later painters creating the composition from the particular perspective of that imaginary person – as fixed in space as anything on the canvas. The fourth wall becomes more and more open and the position of the observer more and more clearly defined. In the last examples I used, you know exactly where you, the spectator, are in relation to the action" (turning the page for him) "*The Wreck of the Medusa, Death of Marat*, above all, *Las Menninas*, paintings that everyone knows –" (*very, very dumb, stupid, he obviously doesn't know them*) – "at least, everyone that majored in art history." Another self-deprecating smile. "Here, let me show you."

She moved to the table as George stood up. He stood behind her; she analyzed the plates quickly and deftly: "You see, you're standing where the Emperor and Empress must have been standing." Normally, she would have felt uncomfortable with anyone standing that close, but today she didn't mind; in fact, found it reassuring.

"That opening up of the fourth wall as a type of artistic device seemed to me to be a good analogy, for all practical purposes the equivalent of 'look and feel' on a computer screen. And the evolution of the imaginary observer, I thought, would provide anyone with a real solid insight into what was wrong with Ohwanee's case. Because you can't – you shouldn't be – able to copyright – to own outright – anything that fundamental." She smiled winsomely at George Sorenson as she returned to her seat. No question any longer that she was going to succeed.

Was there ever any question? In an odd way, she was certain there had never been. Then what was the real point of this exercise?

*

Much to the disappointment of her family, she left Christmas dinner early that year and caught the first train back to New York. The size of the city helped; there were several bookstores that were open Christmas night. It took her a while to find the coffee table thing she wanted. Then she was up most of the night making her selections. There were many difficulties; she wanted the plates to be in color, she wanted names famous enough to be recognizable to a federal trial judge presumably ignorant of art history, and she wanted them to be immediately illustrative of the point.

She had gone back to the bookstore the day after Christmas and bought all eleven other copies of the book. The manual labor she did herself. ("I'm better with scissors and paste than anyone else I know," she said to George.) In the nine days before January 3, she rewrote the text of the memorandum endlessly. It had to be perfect – clear and concise, but interesting and humorous. On the night of January 2nd, she was up until 3:30 a.m. working on the final revisions.

The next day everyone reassembled. Only three of the other associates had come up with anything; their ideas were so dreadful that Collishaw kindly, but firmly, interrupted them in mid-presentation.

She distributed her memo, some sixty pages long with illustrations, and began to talk. On that morning, she looked no older than a high school junior. She'd had no time to wash her hair the night before, was too tired in the morning, could do no better than tie it up in a ponytail with a ribbon. Everyone was slumped down when she started.

Lightly and easily, with a considerable dusting of humor, she launched into it. They began to straighten up almost immediately. By the time she was finished the ambiance of the room had changed completely.

Do you think this will work? asked Frederick Harrison, the chief executive officer of Parallax, not bothering to hide his excitement.

Absolutely, said Richard Collishaw, absolutely. *It works on me.* He turned to Adele. *Ms. Jansen – Adele, this is completely brilliant work. I cannot remember when I have been more impressed with anything an associate has done.*

I'll second that, said Harrison, ridiculously. He had no way of knowing what other associates did and what they didn't.

Had to, Adele answered. *We couldn't let Ohwanee win – and let that overpriced piece of shit rule the market?* The shock value was perfectly timed; the entire table – except for Willis Rutter, scowling, bitter – broke into a roar of laughter, probably the first any of them had experienced in weeks.

Tactical decisions were made quickly. It was decided that the best use of the memo was as an exhibit to the testimony of Harrison. Collishaw laid his partner's ego aside; there was unanimous agreement that the only attorney who could realistically handle the direct examination was Adele. The rest of the day was spent coaching the witness – and the lawyer.

*

"Of course, I really was too wet behind the ears to do it all by myself. I probably still am. Mr. Collishaw coached me for two days and he was right at my elbow when we went to court. I was too much into it to know how it went; I could only tell that Mr. Harrison did great. But when we were done, everyone said it was the first thing that had made an impression on the court in six weeks."

Five days later it was a matter of historical fact how well it had gone. *Mr. Baxter,* the judge said, interrupting counsel for Ohwanee during his final argument, as he held up Adele's memo, *if I understand you correctly, you are saying that Raphael, had he obtained counsel as competent and eloquent as yourself, could have enjoined Velásquez from executing this magnificent painting.*

Three days later the order came down, dissolving the temporary restraining order, denying the preliminary injunction. Ohwanee's case had collapsed and Adele Elizabeth Jansen had become an instant legend between the twenty-eighth and thirty-second floors of the Millroth building: the "Look and Feel" Girl. The break that others wait years for, the opportunity to distinguish themselves from the legions of equally bright, ambitious young professionals, had come her way within five months after she started the practice of law.

*

"We won the case. I got a five thousand-dollar bonus. And that's my story," Adele concluded. Then she changed tones entirely: "Mr. Sorenson," she said, looking him directly in the eye, "it wasn't only one case. I've been programming my own computer since I was fif – "

"You don't have to sell me," George interrupted, much to Adele's astonishment – *so quickly!* "I'm sold. I'm going to arrange a meeting for this firm with AI Squared. You'll get my vote, but that's not the key one." He looked at his watch. "I've got to run. I'm late for another meeting." He nodded significantly to Carolyn. "You'll be hearing from me." Once again, as at the party, Adele could have sworn something passed between them.

"You did great," whispered Carolyn to an increasingly puzzled Adele, as George Sorenson moved to the door.

"Can I walk you to the elevator?" asked George.

Once in the compartment, the two of them the only passengers, he turned to her. "I'd kinda like to see you," he asked, with a slight hesitation. "I mean you and me. Is that O.K.?"

She turned her head sharply, caught completely off guard. Thoughts raced through her mind – lesser of two evils, need to break out – still – what a surprise! He looked to be early 40's, older, but not absurdly older . . . still . . . . she'd never even contemplated an involvement with a man that age, let alone had one–and apparently nothing in common – still – not good to alienate him with so much at stake – still – unwise to encourage if there was no possibility. Was there? She eyed him. Yes, actually, (surprise, surprise), he was interesting in a way, and she felt comfortable with him.

"Sure," she said.

"What's your phone number?" he said, as the elevator stopped at her floor,

"I never give out my home number to someone I've just met," she said with a smile. "Call me at work and we'll talk."

"O.K.," he nodded as the door began to close. "See you around."

Back in her office she pondered for a few moments over all the bewilderment of the morning. George Sorenson had made the decision so quickly – too quickly. She was next to positive it had been made before she ever opened her mouth. Why the need to perform? Why the formality?

For that matter, why did it matter? Plenty of companies use one law firm for their corporate work, another for their patent work, and so on. George

Sorenson had to know that. So why did he care whether Hapgood, Thurlow could do the work adequately? He could always go elsewhere. The more she thought about it, the odder it seemed.

And Carolyn – Adele had her own reasons for wanting Hapgood to acquire high-tech clients. There was a gap in the firm's practice a mile wide, and she knew exactly the right small, young, female lawyer to fill it. She could make a reputation for herself as a specialist in that area, first as an associate, later as a partner. But to get the reputation you have to get the work; to get the work, you have to get the clients. So today was a banner day for Adele, personally and professionally.

But Carolyn? Carolyn's practice had evolved into entertainment law, books and plays into movies, clients such as the Furston Press and many much larger. She had an international reputation in those fields, and she deserved it. To a certain extent, the indifference to high technology at Hapgood was a direct result of that. Associates had been hired to fill the needs that her practice required; other areas had been ignored.

So why did she want AI Squared so badly? It wasn't a practice expander for her. The annual fees from a corporation that size wouldn't pay one month's rent in this building. So why? And what was the significance of those quick little looks between them? Or was she just imagining things?

She thought of George Sorenson again and suddenly regretted very much that she had invited him to call. *Get wise to yourself, stupid; you're not going to be getting involved with anyone.* She couldn't deal with George Sorenson or anyone right now. Not for a while.

Oh, well. She probably wasn't his type. Maybe he was only being cordial. Maybe he never would call.

She hoped not.

*

Now he was on the phone, four days later. He might as well have been calling from a different solar system. Everything had changed that morning in her doctor's office.

"Adele? How are you? I'm calling about that get-together we talked about."

"Yes," she said, wondering what to say.

"Say lunch? Lutece's? Or 21? Friday?"

"No," she said firmly, searching desperately for a way out. "That's too formal. How about plain brown bags in the lunchroom here – where we can just sit and talk?" She was fervently hoping he'd decline.

There was a silence on the other end. It was evident he did not at all appreciate the suggestion. Finally, he sighed.

"Well, anything you say, I guess." *Damn it.* "Can I meet you there about noon?"

"Fine," Adele answered, her heart sinking. They said their goodbyes and she was left holding the receiver, thinking.

More than ever, she did not want to have lunch with George, or anyone for that matter. But she was going to be working with him. Also, he could be a valuable referral source. It would be stupid to offend him. Besides, he was not without interest. In different circumstances, he might have been quite appealing.

She sighed in her turn and noted the date in her PDA.

*

It was 9:45 that evening. Bri had phoned to be certain she hadn't changed her mind about the show. She hadn't. Adele had put the last task of the day off as long as she could. The problem was not Jenet's messenger. The books had arrived at about 2:00 that afternoon. Later, she found all manner of small chores to do.

But now she was in her bed with this task alone still before her, and she could no longer conceal from herself the fact that she was nervous about this. The wounds from that brief encounter were still fresh – easily reopened. Worse: suppose when she read his work she found him to be a poseur, Josh's version of him? That would be awful. Still. . . she opened the first volume of Tom's poems and began to read.

Her initial misgivings faded quickly as she began to scan the text, skimming as rapidly as she could. Although she had respected Jenet's opinion about his work, she had naturally reserved her own judgment. It was a relief to decide for herself that Jenet was right, Josh – of course – wrong, that Tom was by any standard an extraordinarily gifted man.

His subjects were almost invariably ideas: historical ironies, aspects of philosophy, quirks in natural science, above all, mathematics. She would have guessed at that from the way he talked at the Met, even if Jenet hadn't said. The verses bristled with allusions and references, so much so that the editor had appended more than a few footnotes. Despite that, they were easily accessible. What came through was that there was a jungle of hidden sub-context underneath, if a conscientious reader chose to explore it.

Jenet had not described the poems he wrote on mathematical themes with absolute accuracy. They were not really about numbers. They were actually speculations and ruminations about the tensions between various different levels of reality, realms of pure thought and worlds of turbulent matter, all their paradoxes, incongruities, and correlations, as to which he stood as priest and sceptic both at once – a rational mystic. The poetry was not hard for her to follow. He had a real talent for turning abstract ideas into concrete images.

The poems contained a surprising amount of humor. She would not have thought anyone could write a thirty-line dialog between the whole number "2," characterized as schizophrenic, and its irrational square root, but he had, and it was truly funny. If she had had time to look into the Pythagorean number theory referenced in the footnote, it would probably have been funnier yet.

In a different volume, he had written four obituaries, Shakespearean sonnets, for Fermat, the seventeenth century mathematician. This particular footnote Adele did not need, as she knew the story. Fermat had written in the margin of a book that he had discovered some marvelous proof about the sums of exponential powers above two. But he left no description of it other than that. The joke was that no mathematician, no matter how talented, had been able to rediscover the proof in the three centuries that had passed.

Tom had written him four obituaries. In the first, Fermat was a laughing, taunting ghost thumbing his nose at posterity; in the second, a ghoul, reaching back from the grave to steal the time of the living; an explorer in the third, pointing the way to a distant point that never would be accurately defined – and in the last, a forlorn ghost, a sort of mathematical Flying Dutchman, as bewildered by the marginalia as everyone else, explaining to anyone who would listen that he'd made a mistake, but condemned to wander until the world believed him. You didn't have to know anything about the sums of cubes or Fermat's Last Theorem to laugh out loud, which she did.

His old friend Shannon appeared in the third volume. This poem took the form of a playful retelling of Hansel and Gretel in about seventy lines. In Tom's version, Hansel is clever enough to drop white stones every few steps in addition to bread crumbs. Amusing; she recognized Shannon's second theorem instantly. But the stepmother has poisoned the bread. A flock of ravens eats the crumbs and then falls out of the sky, dead, creating an entirely different pattern in a different part of the forest. A wolf eats the birds and follows the pattern towards the children. A hunter tracks the wolf by its droppings and kills it before it can do harm. The witch normally finds her way to her gingerbread house by following the ravens on her broomstick. Without that guidance, she becomes hopelessly lost and never does get home. Hansel and Gretel go into the forest and come out again without ever knowing how close they came to an adventure.

She remembered enough of her law review article to know he was having some sly fun with Shannon and some of those who had subsequently elaborated on information theory. But on the surface it was simply a light, witty retelling of an old story, written in smooth, metered *ottava rima*. Odd and a bit unsettling – not one single nuance in the text gave the underlying theme away. There was not even a footnote. If it hadn't been for a chance happening in her own life, like any other casual reader, she would never have realized that there was a sub-text. The only faint clue Tom had provided was the peculiar title: "Breadcrumbs and Entropy."

So clever – yet he hadn't made any effort at all to display the cleverness, there, or in the mathematicians' obituaries, or in many, many other places. It was as if showing it off didn't matter at all to him. *If he paid the slightest attention to promoting his own work. . . but he doesn't do anything.* Why? This was wonderful material. It deserved a large audience. Why didn't he bother? If he could do things like this, why did he do anything else? No wonder Jenet was frustrated. If Adele could believe what he'd implied on the night she'd spent with him, he was even indifferent to publication. Why?

Who are you, Tom?

Suddenly, then, the wounds did reopen. A wave of sadness engulfed her. This was such strong, thorough literature – witty, elegant, meticulously crafted, high-spirited, and lively. It occurred to her she was an all but unique reader. She had met and known the man before becoming acquainted with his work. No one reading his poetry could possibly have guessed at the actual personality who had created them – the tall, quiet man with the deep blue eyes who never smiled. *My Tom*, she thought, uncontrollably, with a mixture of vicarious pride and regret, eyes misting, on the verge for a moment or two, before she recovered herself.

But in terms of her ultimate objective, the project was a complete bust. She remembered a professor in an English survey class making the distinction between public and private literature, the former based on topics that were accessible to everyone, the latter focusing on the personality and subjectivity of the author. In terms of that classification, Tom wrote the most public kind of poetry imaginable. The voice was impersonal, the subject matter open and available. Whatever personal references there might have been were buried far below the surface.

There was one exception – a poem of some two hundred lines entitled "To a Cloistered Nun," contained in the second collection – the one lyric poem Jenet had mentioned. The central image was a comparison between the cell the nun now occupied and a room the writer had once shared with her. The verse was lovely, alternately charged with the memory of a once-fierce sensuality, the melancholy of time forever lost, and the conviction that the beauty that had been born then was imperishable. In Adele's opinion, it was by far the most beautiful piece in the combined collection.

It was like nothing else in the four volumes. It was, however, much like the thing that he had improvised for her as she lay in his arms that night – although that had been raw and unfinished and she had been too sensually gone to remember it clearly. That work and this were alike in one particular, that the natural warmth she sensed in him peeped through – not so much different from what he'd said about her and the orange-trimmed handkerchief she'd worn that first day.

She read the nun poem through twice, carefully, with mixed feelings. She could not avoid a trace of raw jealousy. Tom had clearly cared deeply for the unknown woman at the center of the piece. But curiosity predominated. *I wonder what she's like. I wonder if she's at all like me.*

However, with respect to facts, it was no different than any of the others. It yielded nothing. The four books had come to nothing. *He says nothing at all about himself,* Jenet had told her.

She looked at her clock-radio – five minutes after midnight. Time to quit for this day. She reached for the bedside lamp. Suddenly the uneasiness she had felt that afternoon returned, several times magnified. There was something wrong here, something terribly, terribly out of order. The reclusivity, the indifference to the product compared to the care that clearly went into its making, the depth of secrecy that seemed to surround Tom – it was out of all proportion, unnatural, not right.

There was also that strange urgency. *You've wasted another day, stupid. You can't afford to do that.*

Quiet, she said to herself. It had only been one day, and a long one at that – the doctor's office, Bri, these poems. She'd do better tomorrow. The major event revisited her as consciousness departed.

Pregnant. Dear God. Why me?

THE MONEY GUY

The law library of Hapgood, Thurlow, Anderson, & Davis was situated on the thirty-first floor. The room was a monument to functionality. Ten-foot metal bookstands, with ridiculously narrow bases, stood about thirty inches apart from each other, filling ninety percent of the space. Two long, narrow worktables had been squeezed tightly into the remainder, in front of the shelves that towered over them. There was no natural light. It was not a room for the fainthearted or particularly the claustrophobic.

Adele spent the first two hours of the next morning there, putting out a fire. One of the litigators in trial on a copyright infringement case needed a memorandum on fair use to support a jury instruction he intended to request. Never mind that he should have asked six weeks ago (*Sorry, I thought I was O.K. but anyway, I need it now*). Volumes of the Federal Reporter piled up on either side of her as she worked quickly and efficiently. She enjoyed research when she could do it without interruption. Time flew. Before she knew it, it was 11:30.

Time for a break. Time to make an awkward phone call.

She asked to be put through to Jenet Furston directly.

"Jenet, could you give me Georgia Richmond's address and phone number, please? If you still have them." She tried to sound as nonchalant as possible.

"I do. But. . . Adele, there's no way in which the Richmond person could put you in touch with Tom. It was at least three and a half years ago."

"Jenet, *please*. Just give me the information."

"Adele, I – that is, I – it's not that I mean to – oh, very well." Adele copied down the address of an affluent bedroom community in Connecticut and a phone number as Jenet dictated.

There was a short, clumsy silence, and then Adele spoke:

"Thank you." She paused again. "You've guessed so I might as well admit that there is something personal in this. But I can assure you there's no need for concern about Tom."

"It's not Tom who concerns me," Jenet answered, to Adele's considerable surprise. "But I suppose it's none of my business." The two women said their goodbyes.

The phone rang less than a minute later.

"Adele," said Jenet rapidly, "I'm badly overscheduled today, but I have to take time for this. You're going to think I'm a meddlesome old busybody, and I know I am, but this whole thing is preying on my conscience. I must be getting on in years faster than I realized. When I first thought of asking you to speak to Tom, it never occurred to me – no, that's not true – for a second in Carolyn's office – but you're so serious minded –"

"What never occurred to you?" Adele asked, a bit shakily.

"That you're both young, you're both attractive, you're both exceptionally bright. That you might find each other attractive."

"Why would that upset you? You said how talen –"

"Adele, you mustn't become involved with him," Jenet interrupted.

She felt a chill, then, on that sunny Thursday morning. "What are you trying to tell me, Jenet? That he's a – a" – she groped for words – "a bad person in some way?"

"No, not at all. I personally think he's as sweet as he seems to be. I think. I really don't know at all. I guess that's what I'm trying to say," Jenet went on. "I don't know; nobody knows. Sometimes I wonder if he knows. Tom Newcombe is a labyrinth, Adele. He's the type of personality you could wander around inside for years and years and not know one thing more than on the first day you started. There are caves within caves and tunnels within tunnels in that man. I don't think it ever ends.

"It's not that I don't like him. I do. You know how concerned I am about him. But I know how easy it is to become obsessed with him – first hand, because it happened to me. When he first came here, he was so promising and so unassuming, so sweet – I will not hide from you, if I had been a younger woman and if I'd had my freedom, I would probably have had an affair with him myself, which is not something I have ever done lightly. But he was that fascinating to me.

"But I'm glad now I wasn't that young. I'm not saying that it's his fault because I'm not at all sure it is – I don't know, that's the whole problem, don't you see – but I am certain that there is no winning with him. For a few weeks – no, it was even months – I did all I could to unriddle him. All I could think of was how to solve the mystery. It was the only thing I talked to my staff about. I think they actually began to wonder about me. But I got nowhere. I lost sleep and weight, and I got nowhere. Finally, I gave it up; I had too much else to do; I'd spent too much time on it. Now I think I was lucky. I think if I'd been younger I would have lost a lot more than time in those caves. I might have wandered around in there forever. I might even have lost my self."

"You didn't talk this way when we were with Carolyn," remarked Adele, hoping the upset was not audible in her tone.

"No, I didn't," said Jenet primly. "There are a great many things I don't say in front of Carolyn. The world has come to a pretty pass when a person is intimidated by her own counselor." She paused. "Carolyn's changed a great deal in the last three years," she added pensively.

"But I regret the omission now," she continued. "If I hadn't been blind to the implications of what I was doing, I would have said a great deal more."

"Jenet, I didn't get involved with Tom, if that puts your mind at rest," lied Adele, in the service of a higher good. It was not fair to inflict Jenet with problems that were purely of her own making. "I do want to see him, but that's not the reason."

"That's good to hear," said Jenet in a doubtful voice. "You needn't tell me I've spoken out of turn," she continued. "I know I have. But I develop protective feelings sometimes towards the younger people around me – with you in particular because – because – oh, for a number of other reasons that are too silly and foolish to share. Perhaps it's because I'm childless. At any rate, I can't tell you how bad I'd feel if anything I did caused you harm."

"Thank you," said Adele. She was touched. She wondered if Jenet Furston knew that she was motherless. She was curious about the foolish, silly reasons Jenet mentioned, but now was not the time.

"You will be careful with him, won't you, Adele?"

"Yes, I will. I promise," said Adele. "Goodbye now."

The chill had not vanished from the warm morning. She realized it had nothing to do with the temperature. Despite that, she was grinning from ear to ear. The joke was simply too rich not to appreciate, even if she wasn't exactly sure whom it was upon.

You mustn't get involved with him, Adele.

Thanks for the advice, Jenet, she thought, looking at the telephone. *Thanks a lot. It comes just a little bit late.*

*

Now it was time for another call, one she was for some reason quite reluctant to make. Why? She didn't know, only that there was a strong temptation to go back to the library and finish what looked to be a long memo before she did it. No – can't waste any more time. Resolutely, she picked up the phone and punched in the number.

"Hello," drawled a female voice on the other end.

She swallowed hard and plunged in. "Hi. Is this Georgia Richmond?"

"Yes, it is. And who is this, please?" in a slightly petulant tone.

"My name is Adele Jansen. We haven't met; you don't know me. Jenet

Furston gave me your name. I'm hoping you can help me locate someone I'm trying to find."

"And who might that be, pray tell?"

"Tom Newcombe. Thomas Bryant Newcombe."

There was a forcible expulsion of breath. "*That* bastard. And just what is your interest in the dear boy?"

She kept her temper, but she could not remember when she had taken such an intense, instant dislike to anyone. "I'm a lawyer. He's a client of mine. But he's also a friend." The indiscretion was deliberate; to have said nothing would have been an act of disloyalty to Tom in a way that silence with Jenet earlier had not been.

Georgia Richmond laughed a short, brittle laugh. "Oh, I see – a *friend*. Probably a new enough 'friend' not to know that Tom Newcombe doesn't have friends. It's only the new ones that think he does. But," she went on, "I'd be happy to talk to you, Adele dear, about your – friend. If I can warn someone else about that snake, it'll be my pleasure. Would you like to get into it right now?"

"No," said Adele promptly, "I'd like to meet you face to face, if I could." *Where it won't be so easy for you to leave until I find out all I want to know.* "Are you coming into the City soon?"

"Yes. Monday. Holiday shopping."

"I'm an associate with the Hapgood firm. It's in the same building as where you used to work. Could I meet you somewhere for lunch, or a glass of wine after work?"

"Oh, poor working girl. I remember the days. The glass of wine will be all right; I'm meeting my husband for dinner later." They agreed on a place, a restaurant up the street with a bar.

*

The memorandum was hard and difficult; between researching, dictating, and revising she ended up working until nine o'clock that night.

Cut it out; you could have knocked this out before dinner if you'd really wanted to. You're killing time. True, as she thought about it. She looked back at her log, considered for a moment, then erased the entries for the last two hours. There was no way she could justify that as client time. The plain fact was that she did not want to go home any earlier than she had to, to a place where her thoughts would be her only company.

Jenet and Georgia Richmond had unsettled her. That was the simple truth of the matter. *What's going on here? Something is very wrong.* That sense of portentousness she'd mentioned to Bri; the sense of urgency she hadn't; to both

175

was added now an undertone of ominousness, as if the darkness that lay behind Tom's eyes was slowly but inexorably leaking out into her own life. Ridiculous; irrational; stupid – but incorrect? She couldn't be sure; more to the point, she didn't even want to consider the possibility, which is why she had stayed so late.

Maybe it was nothing. Maybe it was only the change in seasons and the ba – *the pregnancy, damn it!* The days were perceptibly shorter now; daylight savings ended this weekend. At this time of year, it always seemed to Adele that the world was becoming darker second by second.

She pulled herself up. *All pretty silly, meathead; not your normal style. Anyway, you have to go home.* So home she went, where she discovered she'd been right the first time. Thoughts of all kinds indeed pursued her well into the night.

*

11:45 a.m. on a Friday for which she would in truth thank God, since it marked the end of one of the longest, most traumatic weeks of her entire life.

"Mr. Greenfield's on the line for you, Ms. Jansen," said the receptionist as she swooped past the front desk, on her way back from a conference with Carolyn.

"Hi, Walt," she said when she picked up the phone. "What's up? Nothing about Lawton, I hope."

"Not at all, my little chickadee," he drawled back, doing a dreadful Fields. "In fact, no one has to worry about the Lawton family – until the next time."

"Oh, Walt, you settled! Congratulations."

"This morning. I'm celebrating by taking a few of the troops out for a big Friday lunch, where they will be regaled by wine, linguine with clam sauce, and war stories from my days with the D.A." He paused. "Did I ever tell you they used to call me 'The Man of a Thousand Voices'?"

"I wouldn't be a bit surprised," she answered tactfully, smiling into the receiver.

"Wanna come?"

"What a wonderful idea!" said Adele. "Suddenly I appreciate anew that special brilliance that separates the partners here from the rest of us plebeians. Count me in."

"Make all the proletarian jokes you can while there's still time, Miss Fast Track," Walt responded. "You're a short-timer down there and you know it. I'll see you in five minutes by the elevator."

"Wait a minute," said Adele, in a different tone of voice. "Who else is coming?" Walt named some names and she relaxed. Josh Palmdale was not among them. Three weeks of martyred looks, three weeks of at-least-I-still-have-my honor posturing – she'd had to endure them in these narrow corridors, but not over a tablecloth.

"Only a few fellas beginning the weekend early," continued Walt. "Southern Cal's at Notre Dame, the Giants are at Philly, the Jets are at Miami, beer's in the refrigerator, potato chips are in the pantry, God's in His heaven, and all's right with the world. Come along."

"I have to," said Adele. "I sense a moral duty to history here. Someone has to remember you all the way you were before your brains melted. See you in five," and hung up, feeling great. Walt wouldn't tease about anything as serious as partnership. Short-timer wasn't all that short; fast track at Hapgood, Thurlow was a minimum of five years, of which only two had passed. Still, if it all happened as Walt implied it would, if she didn't blow it, a partner in a major Wall Street firm at age 28. Not bad. Not bad at all.

If she didn't blow it; suddenly, the realization of what that implied crushed down upon her. All the end-of-the-week lightheartedness vanished in an instant. *It's not your time now, little one*, she thought. *I'm sorry. I really am.*

She picked up her purse and started for the door, when the buzzer on the phone sounded.

"There's a Mr. Sorenson here to see you," said the receptionist.

She had forgotten completely. "Tell him I'm in conference; I'll be a moment." She hung up the receiver, shot through the door, down the corridor, and the two flights of stairs that separated the twenty-eighth floor from a small cafeteria on the twenty-sixth. There she purchased a tuna fish sandwich, an apple, and a half-pint of whole milk. Her body was still not permitting her previously customary diet soft drink. Then it was back the same route – a quick check in her pocket mirror to be sure she was presentable – and out into the lobby.

"Hello, George," she said brightly. "I've been expecting you."

He was easily deceived. He smiled a gleaming, surprisingly nervous smile, put down the financial journal he'd been scanning, rose to his feet, and they went together towards the lunchroom.

They passed the front desk and the elevator bank where Walt and four others were standing. His eyes opened wide when he saw whom she was with. *I'm sorry*, she mouthed as she passed, *I forgot*. Walt understood at once.

"Premature senility," she could hear him say from behind her as the group stepped into the elevator. "Tragic. Strikes the most unlikely people."

*

177

Like everything else at Hapgood, Thurlow, the lunchroom was furnished expensively, even though used almost exclusively by the clerical staff. Four round oak tables, salvaged from an earlier remodeling of the conference rooms on the upper floors, each of which could sit six or seven easily, were placed at comfortable intervals throughout the room. Each was surrounded by four to six padded folding chairs. A large mural print depicting the signing of the Declaration of Independence covered one wall. Facing it was a tiled countertop that ran the length of the other wall, broken only by a sink, and a water and soft drink dispenser. Three vending machines and a refrigerator stood against one of the narrow sides. The entrance to the room, a doorway on either side, was at the other end. There were no windows. The lunchroom was in the middle of the building.

She entered the lunchroom with George a pace behind her. It was dawning on her that she was not entertaining any ordinary guest. Walt's reaction to start with – then another partner had nodded approvingly at Adele. A third had stepped aside. Even Mr. Collishaw, down on the twenty-eighth floor for God knows what reason, had given a mini-salute, forefinger to forehead.

"George."

"Dick."

She was duly impressed in spite of herself. *Dick.* Richard Collishaw, the only person she had ever met to whom the adjective "presidential" could be fairly applied, was not a man who encouraged easy informality. Nineteen months after the famous memo bailed him out of a pickle, he was still "Mr. Collishaw"; she was still "Ms. Jansen."

Eight or nine of the clerical staff were seated at two of the tables. At another, a bridge game that had been going on at noon for at least fifteen years was in progress. All the heads turned as George Sorenson went by. On the basis of appearances alone, he was the type who could turn heads. He had middleweight good looks, five feet ten inches tall, one hundred and sixty, pale, but healthy looking – a man who worked out, but spent a lot of time indoors. The only thing that marred the impression was a definite agitation, almost a nervousness, oddly out of place in a man of his age.

He carried his own brown bag. They took seats at one of the two vacant tables; with what was supposed to be a comically elaborate flourish, he extracted a delicatessen roast beef sandwich ("Government choice Grade A, right?"), then a small slice of chocolate decadent ("Sugar for the afternoon, natch"), and a half bottle of Gamay Beaujolais. He smiled awkwardly.

"Well," he said, taking a deep breath, "wanna have lunch?" She could only smile and nod.

The brown bag rattled; he really was ill at ease. "Why are you so nervous?" she asked, genuinely curious.

"Why?" he asked, surprised. "Do I seem that way?"

"Yes."

"Oh," he said, "I'm always nervous with people when I meet 'em."

"That surprises me," answered Adele, seizing the opportunity to ask some questions that had been troubling her. "I can't think of any reason why you have to get along with me. I mean, I can do the job for you and AI Squared – and I do think I'm going to make a name for myself in the field in a few years. But for right now I'm the beggar, not the chooser. You don't have to bring everything under one roof; I know that; you must know it, too. So I am surprised."

He shrugged. "These are pretty green guys. I mean, they're computer whiz kids, but they got a lot to learn about everything else. I want 'em dealing with only one law firm, one set of accountants, people they can learn to trust. Keep it simple."

"I see," said Adele, actually not seeing at all, actually thinking that three mathematicians competent enough to write object code of that quality could probably handle the complexity involved in a corporation doing business with more than one law firm. She was more baffled, not less.

"Besides," he added, "I don't know if you know this. Franklin Fischer, my partner, and Carolyn Hoffman – have sort of an understanding. We like to throw work your way when we can."

"I didn't know that," Adele answered reflectively, then went on boldly while the time was right. "I was surprised at how quickly you made your mind up about me. It was as if you knew what I was going to say before I said it."

"Not at all, not a bit," George said hurriedly. "I'm always a quick decision maker. At any rate, don't worry about it," he continued. "You sounded great. We know what we're doing. I think these guys are going to get along with you. I set up a meeting with Carolyn and one of your corporate types next Wednesday at 11:00 over at our place. Can you make that?"

"Of course," said Adele, taking out her PDA and entering the date. Once again, the politeness was a pure fiction; if Carolyn had arranged it, she had to be there.

"Look," he said, running his hand through his hair, "I really didn't come here to talk business."

"What, then?" she asked openly.

He shrugged, and moved uncomfortably in his seat.

"Not business," he said, with a nervous little smile.

*

Thus began a long, awkward, groping hour, punctuated by one missed connection after another. Most of it was her fault, she decided later – the tension, the uneasiness. Nothing was possible for her with anyone at the moment – a big mistake to have acceded to this, to be sitting here at all, pretending in any way that something might be.

"You're a financier?" she asked, clumsily, making conversation.

"Nope," he answered quickly. "A money guy is what I am. I've been on the Street for the better part of twenty years."

"You don't look –" she blurted out. "I mean, you don't seem like –" *the type*, she'd intended to finish. *Idiot. Big mouth. Remember how important this man is to you!* "I meant –" she continued lamely.

"I know what you meant," he said. ("What you meant" sounded like "wadyamen" in his accent.) "Don't worry about it." He shook his head from side to side. "I told you, I'm a money guy. From the South Bronx. The Ivy League types are financiers. The MBAs." He paused. "I've been eating financiers for breakfast for twenty years," he added quietly.

His diffidence evaporated temporarily as he talked. Once he'd believed talent was all it took, skill was all that mattered. He'd come out of the Bronx on the dead run, never mind an MBA. He already knew how to do a discounted cash flow and what an organization chart should look like. But the doors slammed so hard in his face his nose was bloodied. The contents of the book didn't matter; it was sufficient that the cover was a "dese, dem, and dose" guy from somewhere in New York or New Jersey. After six months of complete frustration, he finally ended up stuck in the same brokerage job he'd had part-time during college. With a wife and a thirty-thousand dollar debt, and now a baby on the way.

"Back with idiots," he said. "Back with guys who could barely pass their Series 7. All the big financiers couldn't tell the difference between me and them. I started all over. I started with cold calls, with no one to make a break for me but me. I hustled twenty hours a day, seven days a week. In seven years, I was making more money than the other guys on the floor put together. I didn't make any friends, I walked all over those other clowns, but I brought in the bread."

A shadow hurried up behind him. "Mr. Sorenson?" said Carolyn's secretary. "Mr. Collishaw mentioned to Ms. Hoffman that you were in the building. She'd like to see you" – a quick glance at Adele; dawning realization that he was occupied – the expected *as soon as possible* became "as soon as it's convenient."

"Right. Right," he answered, impatience barely concealed. "When I'm done with lunch."

He faced Adele again, resumed: "But I still wanted in – here, where the real action is. This is the big game. I didn't care what anyone said, I knew I could be a player. Know what I mean?"

I know exactly what you mean, she thought. In spite of himself, George Sorenson had begun to make an impression.

"I tried it again. I figured if I could pick winners in the secondary markets, out in the sticks, someone would figure out I could put my own deals together. And you know what happened? Nothing. I had success, you see, but I still didn't have class. And I knew that as far as the financiers could see, I never would.

"So I went back to trading. About four months later a headhunter called for Franklin Fischer." That name rang a distant bell. "He was running a little reinsurance company, with family money, but he had big ideas. You could see right away he was going to make it. That's when I finally got my break. Franklin said, `I don't give a damn how you talk or where you came from. What I like is that you're smarter and greedier than anyone else.'"

And angrier, thought Adele, but said nothing.

"We shook hands and teamed up," he said simply. "CFS – Consolidated Financial Services – was born. And here I am."

She nodded, smiling, not sure how to react.

He shrugged. "Started managing money. We did O.K. – better'n O.K. – we got a lot of managed accounts. Then our own trading set up. A few years ago we acquired a little brokerage boutique. We've done a lot of financings, venture, mostly in-house. Nothing big until recently."

"What happened to your wife?" she asked, curious. "Or has anything?"

"Divorced," he said flatly. "Twice."

"What happened?"

"My first wife?" he said. "Loved spending money, wasn't willing to pay the price. We split up – I don't know – how long has it been? Eleven years, now? Good riddance. She wasn't a player. The second time – hell, that only lasted six months. I thought I was in love, but I wasn't. I was in heat."

"Any children?"

"Two from the first one. I haven't seen 'em in seven – no, eight – no, nine years now. It doesn't matter to me. They hate my guts. Look," he said, realizing too late from her expression that he had totally misunderstood the point of her questions, that she had not been asking about possible obstructions, "don't get me wrong. I take good care of 'em. They get half of everything I make. Hell, they see more of it than I do." He grinned uneasily. She smiled weakly. It wasn't working.

"O.K.," he said suddenly, "All right. O.K." He paused. "I said what I thought you wanted. Mistake, right? The way it really was, when Linda divorced me, I let her have exclusive custody. I didn't have the time anyway. I was too busy. I figured I'd make my pile and then make up the time." He paused. "I thought they'd be grateful. It didn't work out. It was too late. You can't make up that time. They wanted nothing to do with me." He looked her directly in the eye. "That's what really happened."

Another uncomfortable silence. She smiled helplessly, stupidly at him, touched, but speechless. He groped for words.

"What's that?" he asked, searching for a change of subject.

He was looking at the necklace Tom had given her. She had neglected this morning to wear anything over it. "It's an angel," she answered. Without her being consciously aware of it, her hand fluttered up to her neck and fingered it protectively.

"It's cute," he said, in a manner that implied that it was anything but. "But something nicer really could be there."

"I own prettier things myself," she said, somewhat defensively. "But this is my favorite. Someone gave it to me." There was something she did not at all like in this turn in their colloquy.

"Someone. . . special?"

"Someone very, very special," she murmured, "but very far away." More or less true, but mostly convenient – the same as with Josh Palmdale, she did not want to talk about Tom with this man.

Another shadow appeared behind George. "Mr. Sorenson? I heard you were in the building. We have another new problem with those assholes in Dallas. Could you come up –"

"Yeah. Right. O.K.," he said, his irritation now visible. "Right now, I'm having lunch with a lady. If you *please*. . .?"

"Oh," said the other, surprised. "Sure. O.K. I'm sorry." George Sorenson turned back to her.

"It must be nice to be so important," she said lightly.

"Sometimes," he sighed. "Right now I'd just like to be a guy with a girl." He straightened up. "That is – I didn't mean –"

"It's all right," she said, surprising herself, because it was all right and usually the word "girl" on these premises was most definitely not. "We're being social. It's O.K."

"Yeah," he muttered. Another awkward silence.

"What's this about Dallas?" she asked uncomfortably.

"That's part of the big deal," he responded. "Run, run, run. Fischer Communications Systems. This media conglomerate thing."

She stared at him. "Fischer Communications Systems? *That* Fischer?"

Now she remembered where she'd heard the name. "You're involved in that?"

He nodded matter-of-factly. "Yeah. Doing it in fact. Heard of it?"

"*Of course* I've heard of it!" She could not help herself from gushing. "It's all everybody talks about! Everyone calls it the Project; it's what everyone wants to work on. I had no idea that you –"

Beneath the gush, she was reeling. Neither George nor Carolyn had said a word about it, at the soirée, at the briefings, at the meeting – *nothing* – there hadn't been any clue at all, not a word. Her mind buzzed with confusion. How? *Why?*

"It's me, all right," he answered nonchalantly.

"But Carolyn – you – neither of you said anything," she went on. "I mean, forgive me for being astonished, but –"

He rubbed the back of his neck with his hand. "Oh, hell. You mention it and everyone gets all hot and bothered. This deal – it's got nothing to do with anything. And I don't think Carolyn thought we'd be eating lunch." He shrugged. "So."

"Everyone says it's the largest acquisition ever!" she continued, still amazed. "That there's never been anything like it."

He waved a hand. "See what I mean? Jeez. People. Gossip – even in a law firm with clout. There's been lotsa deals bigger'n this, or same size. RJR Nabisco was half again the size." He paused. "Does involve more entities. Probably the largest reorg ever. That's true." He shrugged and grinned. "I'll tell you all about it if you want." His smiled narrowed to diffidence again. "But I don' really wanna talk business."

"I did go on," she said half-apologetically, "but you're so offhand about it."

"It's more something I'm doing for Franklin than something for myself."

"But didn't you say –?" she looked puzzled.

"That we were partners? Yeah." He grimaced; a shadow flitted over his face. "But that got old a long time ago. Too long a story for now, but there was no easy out. Then this media thing came along. The Project. Franklin wants it bad. My end is when it's finally complete, we dissolve the partnership, he goes his way and I go mine. I'm on my own. Finally." He shrugged. "If it's ever done. I've been at it four years now, I put all my time into it." He held his hand up. "Keep that part about the split on the q.t., huh?"

She nodded. Something prickled in the back of her brain. Something didn't add up. *I've been baby-sitting them for three months now.* "But then. . . if it's so important, if it takes all your time. . . why – how does AI Squared fit in?"

"What?" he said, startled. "AI – oh. Nothing. A chance too good to pass up no matter what else is happening. That's all. Same as other deals we've done all this time." He smiled. "Gotta keep the brokers busy."

It still bothered her. "But this one is so small compared to the Project. And – George, I hope you don't mind if I say something – I got the impression the other day you don't care at all about the technology, the software. You didn't say anything about it when we met. I don't understand."

"Jeez! You ask the damnedest questions," he answered, shifting his weight completely around in his seat. "I'm a money guy. I push the paper, I get the guys in the trenches to write the tickets. I don't pretend to be a software honcho. But – but –" he shrugged – "I can hear what people tell me. It's hot." He looked at his watch and sighed.

"I'm off to Dallas today at four. And I really got to see Greube before I go," leaving her with more questions than answers.

"Greube?"

"The guy who interrupted us." He smiled suddenly. "You don't know him?"

She smiled in response. "There are a lot of lawyers in this firm."

He stood up. "Gotta go." They moved together towards the door. She could see Greube waiting for him, hovering in the hall outside.

"Adele – ah – you goin' with anybody? Seein' anyone? I mean, besides –" he asked, gauchely, gesturing at the necklace. She looked at him, disconcerted by the directness of the question.

"God," he said, seeing her expression, running his fingers through his hair, "I've never been a smoothie at this. Franklin's a smoothie. I wish to God just once I could be a smoothie."

"I'm not dating anyone," she said, because that last had done it. Something had finally worked for him. Somehow the awkward courtship, the totally anomalous insecurity in a man of such importance, had become endearing, at least momentarily. "And I've never cared for smoothies." He grinned at that, relaxing. "But –" she owed him at least partial truth, disclosure of the enormous shadow that hung over her life at this moment, the great wings – "I am sort of on the shelf right now. I'm getting over someone."

"Right," he said, gesturing with sudden intuition. "The guy who gave you the angel."

"Yes," she answered.

He had enough sense not to press it. "Well, I guess I'll be seeing you at the AI Squared meetings," he concluded, moving away. "Maybe we'll talk. I'll look forward to it."

"So will I," she answered, and he brightened again, waved in an offhand way, and went with Greube down the hall.

She was surprised at herself. She'd meant what she said.

SWEET MEMORIES

O*h, no*, Adele thought as she entered the restaurant. *This can't be happening. Not again.*

Stay cool. Don't go near that. Don't – but, like an iron filing drawn by a magnet, she was already moving towards the perambulator that stood between the two young women and their shopping bags. It was 4:45 p.m. on Monday afternoon.

"My goodness, she's cute," said Adele. "How old is she, anyway? Six months?"

"Very good," said the taller one. "Seven, but she's a little small for her age."

"Not too small to learn to shop," said her friend, and all three laughed.

"She's precious," Adele said, shifting her briefcase and moving off.

"Thank you," said the mother. "Do you have any of your own?" Adele's left hand had been concealed by the briefcase handle.

"No," she answered, smiling, "I'm not married. Someday, maybe. Good luck with her," turned, and left the two to their iced tea and conversation.

I'd never dress a girl in pink, she thought as she sat down. *Or a boy in blue. Come on! Everyone does that; be a little original.* The color would depend on what the baby looked like. With a girl as cute and pink as that, a certain shade of off-white muslin – she could see it as she thought of it – pastel blue trim, fabulous. *Of course, you don't have that kind of flexibility with a boy, you could never dress him in pi –*

Stop it. Stop it at once. Guiltily, almost furtively, she opened her briefcase and pulled out the files she had brought with her.

*

Georgia Richmond turned out to be one of those rare individuals whose appearance matches their voice. She came through the door of the bar at Wesley's at about 5:05, carrying a number of irregularly sized packages, and approached the table where Adele was sitting.

"You must be Adele Jansen," she said. It was not a difficult deduction. The bar was uncrowded and Adele was the only single woman there.

"Let me help you with those," said Adele. The packages went onto one chair and Georgia Richmond on another, across the table from Adele. She was at least six inches taller and a totally different physical type: pale, blonde, with a thin face, aquiline nose, a slender, boyish figure, and long slim legs, accented today by an off-white skirt that was cut short. Her hair was piled bouffant style on top of her head, completing the impression of verticality.

"That looks delicious," she said to the waitress, eying the drink beside Adele. "I think I'll have a vodka-and-tonic, too."

Adele's drink was in fact tonic only (one of her little tricks in drinking situations), but she said nothing.

"How do you come to be living in Connecticut?" she asked.

Drawing Georgia Richmond out about herself proved to be about as difficult as getting water from a faucet. Before the waitress had returned, Adele learned that she was a graduate of a fashionable girl's prep school in Virginia, that she had gone to Barnard ("I was accepted at Wellesley and Holyoke too, but I wanted to live in Manhattan"), that she had done well enough in comparative literature there to begin course work at Columbia for a master's degree at the time she started at the Press, and that she had given it all up when she married Robert ("Robby"), an orthopedic surgeon in his late 30s with the means to support her in a style to which she had always intended to become accustomed.

"I mean, what really was the point of going on?" she asked rhetorically, taking a swallow of the drink that had just been served. "It's a good life without any of the aggravation. I've got a maid and a big house and the rest – and a husband who likes providing for me. Most of my classmates would give their eye teeth to trade places with me. All I'd really been doing at the Furston Press was killing time. I mean, what was the point, anyway?"

Adele smile and nodded. *This is the enemy*, she was thinking behind the smile. The accommodating models and would-be starlets at Carolyn's parties were no threat to her. The girls in men's' magazines did things their way. She did things hers. Adele and that type were like planets in totally different orbits, concentric circles with no points in common. But to have the ability, to have the means, to obtain the training and seize the opportunity – and then to lack seriousness – that was unforgivable. Greg Steuer, the other Glee Clubbers – most of the resentment could be traced to simple sexism and she was not shy to say so. But on those occasions when one of them complained about the absence of basic purposefulness of too many women professionals – "Another la-dee-da lady lawyer," as Walt Greenfield, no chauvinist, had once described an embarrassment to her sex at a different firm – Adele remained silent. There was too much truth to it.

*

"But enough about me," said Georgia, more accurately than she would ever know. She finished her drink and signaled the waitress for another. "You want to talk about darling Tom, don't you?"

"Yes," said Adele, "For both personal and professional reasons. I can't say more than that. I hope you understand – attorney-client privilege, you know."

Georgia snorted as the waitress placed the second vodka tonic in front of her. "The professional is your business, but if you take my advice you'll give up the personal right now. Tom Newcombe is a bastard's bastard and that's all there is to it.

"I know how it looks at first. He's tall, he's good-looking, he's got all this talent, he's terrific in bed – but I'll bet you already know that, don't you, Adele dear?" she smirked and leaned forward. "Let me clue you in, sister: when he's in that steam piston mood of his, he doesn't even know your name. You're only one more warm female body, no matter what you think. It took me a while to figure that out."

Adele had expected she would have to cope with anger, listening to a person whom she didn't like at all say unpleasant things about someone for whom she cared deeply. But she had not anticipated this. *Steam-piston mood?* She could give her own testimonials to Tom's virility, no question about that. But it had all been done with such tenderness, such deep feeling, there was nothing mechanical about it – and *of course* he had known her name. Was Georgia kidding? He'd known it every second.

"Jenet said you knew him a little better than most of the others he worked with. That he had some affairs. But no one got close to him."

Georgia snorted again and took a large swallow of her drink. "Jenet's a naïve old biddy. He had affairs with everyone who was available and quite a few who shouldn't have been. We all thought he was really going to be a major superstar someday. Everyone wanted –" she shrugged – "you know."

Literary groupies, Adele thought, her blood rising. *Keep calm, Jansen*, she told herself, for the second time in thirty minutes.

"And I'm not going to play innocent. I was no different than any of the others. I'm one more notch on his belt. Of course I hadn't met Robby then. And I did make one mistake none of the others did. The biggest one you can make with a man like that." Georgia finished her drink.

"I fell in love with him."

"How did it happen?" Adele asked

"Jenet assigned me to work with him on this screenplay we had to complete. It was one of his first projects. I think she was hoping it wouldn't go well; she was very disappointed he wasn't submitting poetry. Of course I'd heard of him. When I started at Furston, everyone said Tom was the cream of the crop, a real prize. He was all Jenet talked about. And then I met him." She sighed. "It wasn't hard to be attracted to him. He was so quiet and interesting, so sexy. He really got to me even though he was so solemn. And a dream to work with; he was as talented as everyone said. But I knew his reputation and I didn't want anything to do with him. I didn't want to be like all the others."

"What happened?"

Georgia snorted. "What do you think happened? He got me anyway. It was late one afternoon. We'd done some good work. Then it began to get personal. He was so sensitive. He had so much insight into me; I was amazed. I'd heard about men that have you in bed before you know what's happened, but I never thought I'd meet one. But one minute I was behind my desk and the next I was in his arms on my couch and we were making love. At least, I thought we were making love. What we were really doing was fucking. He doesn't know anything about love.

"It was great sex, I'll say that for him. But I should have left it at that, quit while I was ahead. Instead, I . . . I . . . took him seriously. I couldn't believe that a man who understood me so well didn't care for me. Of course I should have known. That's the way he seduces all his women. Tells them a thing or two about themselves they thought no one knew, then touches them, and – oh, that perked you up!" Georgia smirked. "Did you think *you* were any different?"

It can't be, Adele thought. *It can't.*

"But I wasn't willing to let it end there. I went after him after that. I dressed for him. I made up excuses why we should work over at my apartment. I did it all. And what did it all add up to? He came over to my place a half-dozen times. He ate dinner once, and he stayed over twice. That's the sum total of my big affair. I never visited him. I never even found out where he lived –" Again, Adele straightened upright in her seat. Georgia appraised her coolly.

"I didn't do *that* badly. Darling Tom doesn't pay return calls very often – in fact, not to anyone but me at the Press. Definitely the first bite of the apple type." She paused. "I hope you're not waiting by the phone these nights."

"Not at all," said Adele evenly. "My interest in him is different."

"*Really?* Purely platonic, I'm sure," said Georgia, smirking again.

Adele was now seething behind her neutral mask. The ambiance was growing darker. Georgia Richmond was rolling a large ball toward the edge of a big cliff. Revelations were coming she did not want to hear, but knew she had to know.

The waitress put a third drink on the table.

"I know he's mysterious. Jenet Furston called him a labyrinth," said Adele.

Georgia's eyes narrowed. "Labyrinth? Not bad. But in the old myth, there was a monster at the bottom of the cave, wasn't there? There's a monster in this cave, too, Adele dear," she went on. "I should have realized there was a reason for all that silence. Let me tell you how it ended. What I found out about your – friend.

"I told you the big mistake I made. He didn't come often, but –" suddenly, wondrously, her entire demeanor changed, softened. "They were lovely evenings. He really has such – insight." She fell silent for a moment, lost in the memory. For an instant – for only a second – Adele thought she caught a glimpse of what he might have seen in her. "I began to care about him, and I began to kid myself. Then one weekend, about six weeks after I'd begun with Tom, my sister – my twin sister, from North Carolina – came to visit. We were always competitive. I had lorded it up a little about him, how great he was, and how he'd picked me over the others. Tom and I were supposed to have a working session that evening. I hadn't told him about the visit. I was hoping to introduce them naturally, but he didn't show up. Finally we went out to dinner, with cocktails and wine, and I *really* went on – how-I've-finally-found-the-guy, now-I-know-what-love-is. All that crap. My sister was fascinated. But the next day – the very next day –"

Georgia picked up the drink and swallowed it in a gulp. Her face was quivering with rage and frustration. She signaled the waitress. "I'm going to need one more of these, please.

"It was Saturday, about 1:00. . . I got a call out of the blue. It was this laughing bitch who told me if I wanted Tom, I'd better come get him. Then she gives me an address of some fleabag hotel on Eight Avenue and a room number. Fourth floor. I went over there with my twin. The clerk at the desk sneered at us like we were – we were –

"The condition of the room was indescribable. The beds and the bedding had been tossed apart to make more use of them. Do you get the idea? There was every kind of stain you can think of, everywhere, and all these empty liquor bottles, and the whole place stank to high heaven. My sister turned to me like she couldn't believe her eyes. `An orgy!' she said. `A real one!' She looked at me like. . . " Georgia Richmond shook her head again. "And that's exactly what it was.

"There in one corner, totally passed out, looking like any wino on any street corner you've ever seen, is the great love of my life, Thomas Bryant Newcombe. But he's not alone in the room. There are these three –" she closed her eyes – "sluts. Two of them, about in their forties, watching the third, some teenager, pull a blanket around his head. The girl wasn't even completely dressed. One of the older ones nudges the other and says –" Georgia Richmond made a face, an expression of mock surprise – "'Ooooh, twins! Could we have used you last night!' Then the other one steps up to my sister – my *sister* – pinches her on the cheek and says 'You're a little too late, dearie. He's all used up for now.' They both laugh like banshees, and my sister laughs right along with them." The waitress put the next drink down in front of her.

She closed her eyes, and shook her head slowly from side to side again. "Even that wasn't the worst. The young one finishes doing what she's doing with the bedding, puts on a halter-top and a little skirt, and starts to leave. She'd found a note I left him at work, with my number in his clothes and made the others call. She was afraid he was going to kill himself drinking. They'd thought from the note I was his – that Tom and I were – they *laughed* at me. And I knew then I'd made a complete, utter ass of myself." All the sophistication had left her voice.

"Anyway, the little one looks at me with these large brown eyes, and then this little streetwalker – this stupid little whore! – says, in this solemn voice, southern accent, 'You be good to him now. Let him sleep for a while. You got to take care of him.' To me! She says this to me! In front of my sister! After all I'd said! As if we were the strangers, as if I was the bad one! That –" Georgia Richmond intoned it formally – "was the single most humiliating moment of my entire life."

*

The table was silent for a moment: Georgia was gathering strength, Adele digesting what she'd heard.

"I found out more later. I had to. I couldn't leave it at that. I pretended to the hotel clerk – absolute vermin – that I wanted to be in on the next party. He gave me some names and numbers. Then I made some calls."

She took a deep breath. "I was always curious where he goes when he's not around. What he's doing that makes him miss all his appointments. Aren't you? Do you know what your friend does when he's not around, Adele dear? Why he's so secret? When he's not working, he goes on these colossal binges of alcohol and sex. If he can't find anything better to do, he'll hole up in some cheap hotel with a lot of hard liquor, a couple of his miserable friends, and however many sluts and whores they can round up – that can be quite a few; he knows how to get hookers, too – and then they'll just – just –" She searched for the word. "Do I have to paint you a picture?"

"No," said Adele. All this was cutting into the quick of her soul; a flood

191

tide of grief and horror was cresting within her. She had intended to preserve the memories of her moments with him as among the most treasured of her life, but now – but no, no, NO, Georgia Richmond must never know that.

"But he can nearly always find something better to do. You see, your friend is very seldom alone in his secret life. He's very, very popular in the swingers' scene. At parties. The anything–goes type."

"Swingers' scene? I would have thought –"

"So would I, but it still goes on. It's still alive. The gatherings are as ridiculous and disgusting as you might imagine – except when Thomas Newcombe participates. He makes all the difference. He brings everything to life. When the word gets out that the darling boy is around and available, all the rats come scurrying out of the walls. They find a place, the shades come down, they buy their booze, the music starts. Then, Adele dear, all hell breaks loose."

"I can't imagine Tom ever becoming raucous," said Adele, aware that the mask was now slipping badly, that this terrible blond harpy saw full well that her soul was naked and defenceless.

"Oh, *he* never loses his head. But everyone else around him does. He sees to it. He's the enabler, the center, the master of all he surveys. You know how he is, he can almost read minds. Sometimes it seems as if he knows what you're thinking before you've thought it yourself. He sees into everyone's secret little garden and all sorts of interesting little things grow. Things people never thought they'd do, never thought they could do, sometimes things they won't forget until the day they die, won't ever forgive themselves for –because he makes it all seem possible and even natural. There are people who've been to those parties who say he's the Devil himself. Believe me about that; I've talked to some of them."

Georgia Richmond sipped her drink. "I know him to be the biggest sonuvabitch who ever lived, but I'd never deny his power. I've felt it myself. He's better than anybody I've ever met getting people all wound up, you know. He really knows how." She looked Adele dead in the eye. "You *do* know that, don't you?" she added softly.

A long moment, while their eyes met, then Adele nodded slowly herself, affirmatively. *Live through these minutes, get through this time, then go home, think.*

"I rather thought you did," said Georgia, softly. "Let me guess some more. You were with him for a while, and for a few days, or hours, he was everything you could possibly have wanted." She clasped her hands together. "He was *perfect*. He was *wonderful*. Have I got it right?" Slowly, painfully swallowing her protest, Adele nodded. Georgia leaned forward. "He's a sociopath, Adele dear," she said softly, almost a hiss. "He has the one great advantage they all do over a real man. He can be whatever you want him to be.

Your romantic ideal. And he's much, much worse than most. Because he *is* a genius, darling, and he isn't just interested in sex. That's much too easy for the great Tom Newcombe. He's after the most precious part of you – the place where you're most open and vulnerable – your soul, if you want to call it that. He goes after it with his genius, and he always gets it. Always." Then she straightened up.

"What was I saying about his parties? Oh, yes, he's in control there, like Satan on his throne, with everything going on around him, getting crazier and crazier, prompting everyone and anyone. 'Anything is possible' is his motto – and before it's all over, everything that could happen does happen. He makes it possible."

Anything is possible, here, today. Anything could happen, he'd said. That day.

"And of course the Prince of Darkness, his Highness himself, Thomas Newcombe, is available to anyone who wants him, and they all want him. He will be with this one, and that one, and whatever sluts and whores are around until –" she stirred the ice again and looked down – "how did the lady so delicately put it? Until he's all used up. And he's too drunk and exhausted to do anything more and he collapses the way I found him. And the big party is over, and all the rats go home, back to their petty, pathetic lives . . .except for a few who'll never forgive Tom or themselves for what happened. It's all over . . . until the next time. That's why he never has any money. It's all gone on whiskey and whores. And that's why he always looks so tired; it's not because of any high-minded problem in his soul. It's just plain old, everyday, garden variety dissipation."

"Liquor only? Not drugs?" Adele asked, numb, groping, still trying to go forward somehow.

Georgia snorted. "No drugs, no underage girls, nothing illegal. If you need your Ecstasy, you take it before you get there. But don't award him any merit badges for civic virtue, Adele dear. It's only that he's a coward about the law. It's not that he's inhibited. He isn't inhibited about anything, not really."

She noticed now the expression on Adele's face. "What's the matter?" she sneered, twisting the knife. "You thought when he blew off steam he had two beers and said hello to a blonde? So that's your friend," she continued. "That's his secret life. Everything he does, he does so he can afford that. He loves it. It's what he lives for.

"Forget all Jenet's prattling about him, all the soft soap. He's an alcoholic, amoral, hedonistic womanizing bastard and the only thing that makes him different from any other jerk is that he's better at it. Plus he prostitutes himself and a real gift to make it possible."

Her blood had turned to ice. Georgia Richmond was no longer in front of her. Instead, an image had formed:

A dimly-lit room, music without cadence, sex without joy, shadowy bodies twisting sinuously in the background, Tom in the foreground with that slight smile on his face – no. . . no . . . no smile, that didn't fit, and no sparkle in his eyes, either. The Van Eyck Hell it was, re-enacted from time to time, in small, sordid rooms around the City where the sun neither rises nor sets, and anything is possible.

If you're that kind of man, if you want to enjoy all the possibilities, she thought dazedly, *all the women, you wind some up with alcohol and sexual variations. Others you wind up in a museum. It doesn't matter to you; it's all the same just so they all wind up horizontal. If you're that kind of man.*

If.

It can't be. I couldn't have been that far wrong about anyone. Especially him. I couldn't have. Not again.

Could I?

*

She wrenched herself back to the present. "Maybe the people who told you all this don't like him," she said desperately. "Or they're jealous. That's what Jenet thinks."

Georgia snorted. "Jenet believes what Jenet wants to believe. He's had her tied up in knots for years. If she wanted to find out the truth, she could have done what I did, which was just get some names, answer a few ads, and make some phone calls." She stirred the drink again. "What I've told you is true, Adele dear. I know you know that."

She knew it was. She also knew she had heard enough, and did not want to hear anymore. "How did it end between you?" she asked.

Georgia laughed bitterly. "Sandra and I shook him awake. He was soaked with sweat. He smelled terrible. When he finally came around, I didn't have to tell him we were through. He knew it the second he woke up. I had some stupid idea that he could explain. I hoped, anyway. But he didn't. My Sir Galahad looked at me and my sister. Then he shook his head – and he went straight back to sleep, and I knew that was all the apology or explanation I was ever going to get from him.

"And that's all. My sister still makes big ha-ha jokes about it."

*

There was a long moment of dead silence. Then, with difficulty, Adele recollected why she was there:

"During the time you were together, didn't he ever say anything about where he came from? His parents, whether he had brothers and sisters, things like that?" asked Adele, with falling spirit.

Georgia stirred the ice again, took a sip, and spoke: "No. I tried to draw him out a few times, but he doesn't draw out. After I found out the truth, I decided he must be some sort of black sheep from somewhere. They probably like talking about him about as much as he likes talking about them."

The worst case was materializing. "*Think*, Georgia, please," said Adele, desperately. "You were more intimate with him than anyone. He slept with you. He must have said something."

Georgia looked at her. "I don't think I was ever intimate with him, if you want to be accurate, Adele dear. And if you mean it literally, I didn't sleep with him. That was another one of my – never mind. What happened was twice he fell asleep by accident on my couch. After that, I didn't want to sleep with him."

"Why not?" Adele breathed, but she already knew the answer.

"You must be one of his pop tarts," Georgia sneered again, "or you'd know. He has these dreams, dear. Nightmares. Both times. He thrashed around and scared the hell out of me. The second time, he broke my table lamp."

"Did he say what he dreamt about?"

"No, but do you wonder? With a conscience as bad as his must be?"

"But he must have told you something sometime," Adele persisted. "Something about his childhood, where he was born, games he played, something like that." Georgia shrugged and shook her head. "He must have. Think. Damn it, *think*!"

The taller woman began to become indignant, noticed Adele's expression, thought better of it. She was silent for a moment. "Once, I mentioned how lovely upstate New York is and he told me he'd been born someplace up there. But that's all."

Adele took that in. The two women were silent for a moment, then Georgia Richmond began to speak in a low, bitter voice. Her s's and t's were no longer crisp; the vodka was having its effect. In vino, perhaps, finally a little veritas.

"I was sure he cared about me. He did find me alluring" – she looked up, drunken anger in her eyes – "there is *no* man who wouldn't find me alluring! I wasn't just someone to fuck! I felt different with him, special, and that was because – because – listen to me, there I go again! He gets to you like that, he's so damn subtle! I don't like womanizers. I never wanted to be a name on anybody's list. All I know is he let me care for him, he let me trust him – and he knew what he was and how he lived. I will never forgive him for that. Never!"

She lifted the glass again. "What the hell. I should have known he's a bastard. He seems warm, because of all that insight, but it's just a trick. He never really opens up to anyone. Eight weeks and he never even took me home. He never once said directly he cared about me. He just let me pretend. I wonder if he even likes women. We're just bodies to en– what are you smiling about? It's not at all funny."

"No, no, it isn't," Adele answered quickly. "It was just something about the way you said it." This was a lie. The truth was she had been unable to react quickly enough to the unexpected wave of pure happiness that had just washed over her. He *had* taken her to his home that night. *I love you, Adele,* he'd said – directly, out loud.

Maybe I know him better. In one day. Maybe. Just maybe.

But the dark thoughts returned almost at once. *Or maybe he played one more mind game with me he didn't with her. After all, with her, who'd bother?*

"Maybe there's a reason for it all," Adele said, musingly. "Maybe there's an explanation."

Georgia Richmond shook the cobwebs out of her head, stood up, and began to gather the packages together. "You think you're pretty smart, but you're really just a little fool. You really are naïve, Adele dear." She moved towards the door.

"You're going to do what I did. You're going to do what Jenet still does, what they all do. You're going to go right on making excuses and apologizing for him until you've given him enough rope to hang you with. You poor, stupid little shit." She looked down at the tab.

"The drinks are on you, you know."

"Of course," answered Adele, calmly.

She moved away from the table without any pretense of a fond farewell. Suddenly, she turned around and faced Adele. In her off-white dress, with her pale face, framed by the cavernous darkness of the dimly lit bar, she looked like a visitation from another world.

"I don't like you any better than you like me, Adele dear; let's be honest with each other. But I'm going to give you better advice than any your mother or your big sister ever gave you:

"Get out. Get out now before it's too late. Don't go near him, don't have anything to do with him. I'm glad now I never really got near him. I was lucky. I could have been hurt much, much worse. Get too close to him, and he will destroy you.

"Forget the poetry, forget the soft voice, forget all Jenet's pretty rationalizations. Thomas Newcombe is evil, Adele, evil. He finds the best part of you, he makes you believe in it, then he turns it into shit. You can believe me or not, but you're going to find out for yourself. I can see that already. Perhaps that's for the best. Maybe that's what you deserve, anyway."

With that, she turned rapidly and was gone, as if she could walk away from times past by walking out of the building.

It was only a little after 6:00, way too early to go home. She considered a glass of white wine, but her body instantly vetoed it with a flash of nausea. After a few more moments, Adele got up and went back to the office.

✳ ✳ ✳

INSOMNIA

The next morning, as soon as she had finished organizing her day, Adele phoned Walt Greenfield's secretary and arranged a time to meet. She was in luck. He was not in trial or deposition, but available most of the day.

"Greetings, deserter," he said, cheerfully, as she entered his office. "What brings you to the thirtieth floor?"

"I need a favor," said Adele. "A personal favor."

"Why I should do you any favors at all after being inflicted with young Palmdale, I don't know," answered Walt, "but go ahead, shoot," he went on, more somberly. No jokes or voices – he could see she was in a very serious mood.

"You spent a few years in the district attorney's office before you came here, didn't you?" He nodded. "I need an investigator. A private investigator. Discrete. Reliable."

"Give me a dollar, Adele," he said, now as serious as she. She complied; fortuitously, she had brought her purse along. "Now I am retained as your counsel and you are fully entitled to avail yourself entirely of the attorney-client privilege. You should also know that I like you quite a bit. What's the problem?"

She liked him, too, but now wasn't the time. "No, Walt; leave me be on this. I will tell you it's nothing illegal."

He continued to observe her. "You look a little piqued this morning."

"I didn't sleep very well last night. Nothing to do with anything – a little insomnia is all."

He continued to look at her sharply for a moment, then broke off his glance and sighed. "O.K. What kind of investigator do you want?"

"Someone who's good with computers. Someone with access to a lot of databases. Someone –"

"–who can find out a great deal about someone else in a hurry without the someone else being any the wiser."

There was silence for a moment. "Yes," said Adele, folding her arms. "Exactly."

"All right," he said, finally. "A guy named Bill Abercrombie will call you sometime this afternoon or tomorrow. Don't ask him for his address or phone number. That's my only rule. Don't break it."

Puzzlement showed on her face.

"Oh, he's kosher. Don't worry about that. I'm not protecting you from him or vice-versa. The thing is, I don't want any of the creeps who call themselves my partners to get the chance to bribe or strong-arm him into doing something he shouldn't."

Her surprise at his vehemence was too large to be concealed. He took note of it. "Did I shock you? One of these days we have to talk. But for now Abercrombie will be in touch with you today or tomorrow – and don't forget where to find me if you really need me."

"Thank you, Walt," she said, the sincerity evident in her voice, then turned and left.

*

Customarily she had slept long and sound, the length of the night. No longer. Now she pitched from one side of her bed to the other, a small boat on the large ocean, buffeted by wave after wave of thought, gusts of emotion. She *couldn't* have gone that far wrong about anyone. She *couldn't* have. It wasn't possible – and Tom, of all the people in the world. It *couldn't* be.

A great storm had broken out in her life. She knew that for a certainty now. The winds were already howling at gale force, and they were going to get far stronger before the storm blew out. Her little bark was far out at sea, tempest-tossed, and it would be a long, long time before it saw calm water again.

The first few hours afterward had been the hardest, dragon-ridden as well as stormy. *Satan on his throne, the Prince of Darkness – could such things be?* For a time, she was afflicted with all sorts of fantastic, Rosemary's-baby type notions. *Don't be ridiculous, nincompoop,* she finally told herself. Georgia had been speaking figuratively, not literally. (Besides, if he really were the Devil and seeking a suitable mother for his child, he would have chosen Georgia Richmond, not her.)

Even so, the thought of Tom in those dreadful scenes, the focal point and instigator of all the senseless, dehumanizing activity she had visualized as Georgia spoke – a feeling of vertiginous deadfall, dizziness in a falling elevator, ultimate nausea. She felt herself trembling all over.

Get hold of yourself, idiot, she told herself, sitting again lotus style on the floor of her dark bedroom. *Think. Define the problem. Johnson and Jansen. Don't react, think. Think!* Thinking was like walking a tightrope between two masts over a roiling sea. But slowly, painfully, the rational processes began.

Tom corrupt? Thomas Newcombe evil? *No* – and this involved more than Tom, much more, she realized that at once. She'd made her mistakes about men, plenty of them, she'd be the first to admit it – but she'd prided herself on the fact that she'd *learned* from them, left all that behind. Not so, if what Georgia Richmond said was the truth, even the partial truth. She could never trust herself again, never again have full confidence in her own judgment. She wouldn't let the matter rest there. She could not.

Think.

*

On the one hand, he didn't look the part. He didn't act the part. Dress was neat, not flashy – living quarters, modest and quiet. So *small.* He was no epicure. He'd showed no interest whatsoever in expensive food or drink. In fact, he'd had nothing at all to drink with dinner when a glass or two of wine would certainly not have been out of place. The day before they went to the museum, he turned his back on $5,000 that was honorably his. Libertines don't do that; they need money all the time.

Then there was *him,* the affect of the man, that marvelous combination of strength and gentleness she'd felt throughout all her time with him. Could that really have been only an act? The overall effect had been one of enrichment, liberation, large space, and larger possibilities – love, not to avoid the word. There had been no affectation in that bed. She was sure of it. He couldn't be a sociopath. She knew the type, after all; she'd been there before – the last week, Rush Week Friday night. She cringed as the memory involuntarily surfaced, would not allow herself to remember the name. Tom wasn't like that. No sociopath is that good.

Or is he? On the other hand. . . *damn it, stupid,* she thought, twisting, twisting, in an agony of doubt – she *hated* this. The man who'd caused the Rush Week disaster had been a boy really, a silly, shallow youth. Maybe all she'd learned was how to cope with that juvenile type. Maybe she'd met the mature kind this time, the big-league version. Maybe the mature Adele was no better at coping with that type than the girl Adele had been with the junior variety. The thought was deadening, sickening. She had to force herself again. *Think.*

So. On the other hand. Maybe he was that ultimate predator. He'd read her like an open book. *Roger* – there it was, the name of the vermin who had engineered the sordid debacle of Rush Week, and the awful memory, popped into her consciousness, vivid in all its squalor despite all the years passed. It had reappeared that night with Tom, too. Perhaps subconsciously she'd detected a resemblance. *Is there something wrong with me, Tom?* She winced at the bare possibility she might have asked that question to that kind of man. Would a day come when that remembered sentence would be in the same category as the word she always choked upon?

Perhaps the woman Adele *was* no match for the grown-up variety. Perhaps she was doomed. Maybe everything that had happened was a matter of Tom knowing how to get to her, *really* get to her, putting on exactly the right act. She became more anxious. Maybe he was that type. Maybe he enjoyed the confusion and distress he had engendered, felt a sick kind of pleasure in reaching into her mind and tinkering with the controls. Maybe that was his notion of conquest. Maybe all she was to him now was a line in one of his little black books with a certain number of stars beside it.

No (she smiled in the dark), Tom would never use a star system; he'd be the scale-of-ten type for sure. She felt a quick moment of wistful longing. That she found any humor at all in this situation was a good sign.

But bottom line, get to the worst. Damn it, although she wished she didn't, she *believed* Georgia Richmond. Her story had had a basic authenticity. The emotional tone of what she'd said – the anger, the frustration, and – yes – the attraction Georgia still felt for him – all of it felt genuine. Worse: There were those rumors Jenet had refused to discuss. Worst of all. . . Adele herself could picture Tom in those awful scenes, dark and brooding, but still central, controlling all the events around him, though taking no pleasure in any of them. In a basic intuitive way, it fit him exactly.

Taking no pleasure – yes, exactly, very significant. That set her off on a new tack. What was it that he'd said at dinner that night? *I don't drink when I'm not drinking* – and the way he'd reacted when she made the remark about wine, women, and song, wincing, as if he'd been cut to the marrow of the bone. So what is he, anyway? A swinger who doesn't like to swing? A playboy who doesn't like to play? Some weird, third-millennium neurotic? She'd never heard of such a neurosis.

Did that make him a victim? Jenet might have thought so. It would have been easy to agree. But her tentative conclusion was that that was impossible. Tom was gentle, not passive, too powerful a being, too strong a personality in his own quiet way, to be anyone's tool. Even people demented enough to think there was something to be gained from endless, aimless rutting would sense that. Georgia was probably right. He was the enabler, the big generator that all the foolish little mechanical people relied on for power.

But there was that hand-lettered sign on his bookcase – "WHY?" And that curiously passive way he'd referred to himself when he was putting the condom on – *things happen to me that really shouldn't*. And the other thing at the restaurant – *It's got to stop, and it will.*

The weariness – she brought up his image from back when she first met him, compared it to that of the next morning. He'd been more tired – but also more alert, and he produced a prodigious amount of work that day. The affect wasn't that of someone recuperating from a night of debauch. It was. . . it was. . . different. He'd looked more tired the morning after with her, too, even though he'd had nothing to drink, and they'd gone to sleep about 9:30 and only two acts of sexual intercourse had occurred, hardly enough to exhaust a young man.

The most important thing – she returned to it again and again – most important of all – the dream. That horrible, horrible dream. That was more, much more, than simple bad conscience; in fact, she was certain that that held the whole key. If Georgia was right, if there were a monster in the cave, it was there it could be found. For sure. No doubt. But how? She shook her head in the darkness.

Who are you, Tom?

She had felt an unease from the beginning about not asking those questions, a small frog gnawing at the roots of a large ash tree. Now the unease was deepening into guilt. The frog was larger and had grown teeth. She should have found out more about a man who had touched her so deeply, who he was, what troubled him. She should have asked those questions. But she hadn't.

It was getting late. She climbed back into her bed. No way could she ever get to the bottom of this by evaluating the outward show; she was going to have to rely on the inward, her sense of the man, her instincts – yes, the very ones she had distrusted for so many years. Even so – better hers, no matter how untrustworthy, than Georgia Richmond's.

Then a different thought, a fantasy, a longing, this one not volitional – that Tom be here, with her, right now. He'd lift her hair. Their eyes would meet. He'd bring her head to his shoulder, talk to her in that soft, deep voice, and explain everything. It would all go away, she would never have to think of this again, never again have to confront any of it.

If Tom were here, said the contemptuous inner voice, *he'd have you undressed and bedded in thirty seconds and when he was done with you, you'd believe every stupid thing he told you and you'd never know whether it was because it was true or because you wanted to believe it. You know I'm right. Which is, sister, the whole dilemma.*

Because maybe that's what's already happened.

So.

She pulled up the covers, closed her eyes, and willed sleep upon herself. But unconsciousness was, and was going to remain, elusive this night. Instead, her thoughts veered off in an entirely different direction.

For other forces were also at work. The mental process that she had anticipated in her doctor's office, that she had dreaded then, was now in full swing.

It's not your time, little one. I'm sorry. I'm truly sorry.

*

"Thank you for meeting me so quickly, Mr. Abercrombie." It was 3:00 p. m. on Tuesday.

"No problem. I'm only a couple of blocks away. Most of my clients are white-collar. Walt Greenfield told me it might be urgent."

He put away a crossword puzzle (Sunday London Times, she noticed) that was all but solved. Except for the conservatively tailored cut of his suit, Bill Abercrombie, now seated in her office in the same chair Tom had occupied, would have been perfectly cast as Nicely-Nicely Johnson in *Guys and Dolls.* He opened his notebook and began writing.

"His full name is Thomas Bryant Newcombe," she said. "His address and phone number are on the paper I gave you. He's between 25 and 35. I was told he's 28, but I'm not sure the information was correct. He was born somewhere in upstate New York. He's the author of four books of poetry –" she reached behind her, picked them up – "here they are. They're my only copies, I'm very fond of them, and I'd like them back."

She paused, put her tongue against her teeth. "He evidently attends gatherings on a fairly regular basis that are notorious in some quarters for the amount of alcohol consumed and –" *just say it, stupid*, she thought, *just spit it out!* – "indiscriminate sexual activity on the part of all participants." Abercrombie stopped writing and looked up at her, startled. She went on: "People with known patterns of sexual promiscuity, sometimes even street women, attend. He may be known in the hotels and places where such – goings-on – take place. He may also have frequent commerce with prostitutes. If the police or health officials keep a registry of such persons, he may be on that."

Abercrombie cleared his throat. "Ms. Jansen, it's none of my business, but is this the sort of man in whom you should be interested?"

Her face became a wooden mask, her eyes turned to stone. She said nothing, simply continued to look at him, letting the silence lengthen. He began to smile.

"You mean, it is none of my business."

"Exactly right, Mr. Abercrombie," she said evenly. "Exactly right. You have chosen your profession well. It is obvious to me that you are blessed with considerable deductive powers." He was not offended, actually smiled more broadly.

"I didn't think I'd been amusing."

"It's not that. It's that you're just like Greenfield said you'd be."

"Which is?" She loosened slightly.

"He said, `She's cute as a button and sweet as apple pie, but don't let her fool you. She's a stone cold killer zombie from outer space.'"

She began to smile. "In which voice? His Bogart or his Cagney?"

"Couldn't tell," he answered deadpan. "They're both so terrible. They sound alike. I have never met anyone," he went on, "who couldn't do a decent Bogart. Until Walt."

She was grinning broadly now. "Such a *nice* thing to say in any case. I'll have to thank him properly the very next time I see him. But. . ." She became serious again.

He nodded. "It's your business."

"Even from Walt Greenfield. Maybe especially from him."

He nodded again. "What do you want to know about this guy?"

She thought for only a moment. "Everything. And by Friday."

*

Adele Jansen had been living in Manhattan for just over two years now, commuting daily from the East 70s to the offices of Hapgood, Thurlow in Midtown. Out of bed in the morning, dress, into the tube, emerge at the other end, into the elevator, into the office, then back into the tube nine, ten, or twelve hours later. Her social life consisted mostly of weekends with other people her own age (except for Carolyn Hoffman's "soirées"), all trying to make their way in the city.

There had been weeks – months, sometimes – when she could have sworn there wasn't one person under fifteen left in Manhattan, that all the children there had either been deported to New Jersey or followed the Pied Piper to Connecticut. Now, suddenly, they seemed to be materializing everywhere – highchairs in restaurants, carriages and baby carriers, precious little boys in sailor suits holding their mothers' hands, lovely little girls in pinafores riding on their fathers' shoulders, all races, all nationalities, all beautiful, everywhere.

The process was inevitable, irresistible. In spite of all her admonitions to herself, the process had begun. *A boy, most likely*, she would muse before she could catch herself. How odd, how strange, to think that if she did nothing she might give birth to a son! She had always been mildly annoyed at the cultural prejudice that decreed all firstborn children should be male. To find herself as much the victim of it as anyone else afforded her a certain bitter amusement.

And if he had his father's strength. . . and if he had his father's softness. . . all at once, lying there in her bed, everything would be so breathtakingly, heart-stoppingly possible! She felt an enormously strong emotional pulse beating right underneath the surface. If she wasn't careful, if she relaxed her guard for only a moment, she found herself swept into a daydream in the manner of one of the old 1930s movies she'd watched at Buck's theater.

*

In the lobby of the Grand Hotel:

[Adele] *Tom! Thomas Newcombe!*

[Tom] *Adele? Adele Jansen?? It must be thirty years.* (He has become a sixty-year old, smiling, public man.)

[Adele] *My, it's good to see looking so well and happy.* (gushing a bit) *I'm a big fan, you know. I read all your books.* (shy) *I was afraid you'd forgotten me.*

[Tom] (earnestly) *I couldn't forget you. The time we spent together changed everything for me. I became a whole man. I never saw you again. I never had the opportunity to thank you.*

[Adele] (mysteriously) *Tom, do you remember the morning after? When the condom broke?* (very softly) *When we made love in that wonderful way, we... made a baby.*

(He goes pale.) [Tom] *Adele, you should have told me! You should have let me help!*

[Adele]*I am telling you, my darling* (taking his sleeve). *I am telling you that the man we are here to honor tonight... is your son.*

(Fade to black. Music rises – mostly strings, Eric Korngold or Max Steiner, of course.)

Hollywood-style daydream – all the misery, all of the pain, all of the give-ups, the big, the little – all left easily, painlessly, on the cutting room floor.

*

Her eyes had moistened, head on the pillow as she looked up into the darkness.

That was sickening, said the inner voice disgustedly. *I don't believe you. You are hopeless. Everyone thinks you're so smart. But there is nothing so sweet and gooey you won't eat it right up, is there?*

No. Nothing.

But not only her imagination afflicted her; her rationality had joined in. She did not like to think of it that way – in the nature/nurture controversy, she was solidly on the side of nurture – also, the one place where everyone should be, must be, equal, in her opinion, is *in utero* – but still. . . still. She wasn't exactly dumb. Neither was Tom. Other people would state both propositions much, much more emphatically. The baby might be special, very special, a real contributor. Look how he had fought his way into existence! And Jack and what this would mean to him – there was absolutely no fantasy about that.

Jack, second in sibling order, her favorite brother, because he was the one with whom she could always talk. He could have had a career every bit the equal of hers, and then some, but he'd turned his back on it to become something she privately thought was worth all the lawyers in Manhattan – a superb, dedicated high school math teacher. He'd been blessed with a wonderful wife as well, Becky, whom Adele adored. But the children that were a necessary part of the equation had not arrived. Finally, he'd bitten his lip and seen an internist. The verdict was stark and final – exceptionally low sperm count, less motility, no hope. The cause was almost certainly an accident he'd had while playing varsity baseball in high school. Jack got drunk that night for the first time since his undergraduate years.

Now, three years later, he drank more, both more than he should and more every day – and Becky tried to forgive him for that and (yes) for being sterile. She was only human, only female. At base she could not understand how her husband, so masculine in every other way, could fail her in such a fundamental manner. They had applied to adopt, but the waiting list seemed endless. Adele had looked into an off-the-books adoption for them a year earlier and been forced to counsel them against it. If Jack's drinking problem continued to get worse, they wouldn't be suitable candidates in any case.

*

She lay in bed, staring at the ceiling, her hands folded across her lower abdomen, where a partial solution to all that misery lay nestled. Her marvelous brother; a solution also for maybe a very, very special child. There would be only one person hurt, perhaps not all that badly. Other single women seemed to live to tell about it. Three minus one equals plus two. Bri hadn't thought too much of that arithmetic. What would her numbers mystic think of it if he knew? Not much more than Bri, she was almost certain of that. But ultimately hers was the only opinion that mattered. *This isn't a democracy*, he'd said. Neither was this. It was one decision about which she had all the votes – and rather wished she did not.

Bri was probably right – no, *was* right. The sneers, the gibes, the fall from grace, the look on Carolyn Hoffman's face – and all this at a time when the major break might finally have arrived. No; impossible. She shook her head.

It's not your time, little one.

She willed sleep, hard, but still it wouldn't come. There was no mystery at all about the reason.

She did not want to do what she knew she had to.

*

Abercrombie smiled.

"Friday? Everything? I can't do both, Ms. Jansen, they're mutually exclusive. Which do you want?"

She looked at him. "Friday, then. As much as you have by then." She could not tell him – it was too embarrassing – that she would have preferred that afternoon, that she regretted the loss of even two days, that the itchy sense of something left undone she'd felt all along had become many times stronger the evening before, had taken on a definite urgency.

*

Get a hold of yourself, she told herself over and over again, and by Thursday evening she had. The emotional swell still boiled and seethed underneath her. Occasionally, some random thought, some visualization of the revelations of Georgia Richmond, would pierce her guard, and the entire universe would lurch sickeningly, nauseatingly to one side. But by and large, the cool, calm girl had everything back in control.

There was no reason why she had to go on with this. She could see that now. Bri had originally suggested she talk to Tom in the hope he could bring some comfort to her situation, assuage the pain of confrontation with the inevitable. Tom could undoubtedly have done that if he were available. But he wasn't available, *damn it*, and by the time she made contact with him all the pain would be historical. Plus the search for him, though hardly begun, had proved to be an enormously complicating factor.

More than that, there were many reasons not to go forward. Jenet Furston and Georgia Richmond had both warned her about him in their different ways, from their different motives. Warning signs had been posted everywhere when she was with him. This was very dangerous territory, at the minimum from the emotional perspective, maybe in other contexts as well. It was obvious she was going into the swamp, barelegged. Snakes were everywhere.

So. What, then – quit? Give it up? The answer came to her simultaneously with the articulation of that possibility.

207

*

No way. Not a chance.

No way but forward. *Nothing happens by chance.* None of this was an accident. All the signs that had been intended to scare her off – by whom? by what? – were drawing her onward. She was going to find out the answers to the questions, all of them, somehow, and find out why it was important that she do so. Until then, until it was over, she would keep faith in herself and in the tall, quiet man she could only hope she knew better than any of the others.

11:00 now. Tomorrow, Friday, was a big day. AI Squared – this was it, *don't blow it,* she must not let this quest interfere with that – and Abercrombie, almost more important to her, the next step on the journey. Resolutely, she closed in on sleep; as she did, one last memory stole into her consciousness, her favorite, lingering on for a long moment, too sweet to evict at once.

I cannot believe this. You're going to do it again? Dissolve into melted butter like the heroine of a romance novel? When it might have been – probably was - just another sexual illusion? And at the best all it was, was pillow talk, his way of wrapping you around his little finger – can't you see that?

No. It hadn't been only pillow talk. Even if it had only been in the moment, he had meant it in that moment and so had she. So bring the moment back, and if she melted, like so many other foolish, silly women, so what. She just happened to be that exact kind of critter.

I love you, Adele, he'd whispered out of the darkness, the one thing she knew for certain Georgia Richmond had never heard him say.

"I love you, too, Tom," she whispered aloud this night, into a darkness that was deepening with each passing hour. Wherever you are. Whoever you are. Whatever you are.

Joseph Wurtenbaugh

WAVE OF THE FUTURE

"**A**re we all set?" asked Carolyn, looking around her office.

"Yes," said Harry Greube, the junior partner and corporate specialist who had interrupted Adele's lunch with George a week before.

"I'm all right," Adele answered, truthfully. She was focused entirely on the task at hand. The firm's three file copies of her famous memo were in her briefcase. The door had been closed and firmly locked – for a while, anyway – on the long, rambling trains of thought that were bedeviling her nights.

"Then let's go," said George Sorenson. "It's not a good idea to keep Franklin waiting. On any of his deals."

They set off. Since the offices of Consolidated Financial Services were only three short blocks away, they had decided to walk. The day was overcast, lowering – all the days had become overcast and muggy, unnaturally prolonged tropical weather. Normally a brisk walker, Adele lagged behind this day, mentally rehearsing her presentation one last time.

"Nervous?" asked George Sorenson, suddenly beside her.

"A little," she nodded. "This is pretty important to me."

"You'll do fine," he answered, taking her elbow to escort her around a patch of torn-up sidewalk. It felt so natural, she turned her head up in surprise. Then he turned his head away from her. His hand came up in one of those hesitant gestures; he spoke without looking. "I'm hoping you'll have lunch with me, again, today – afterwards. We have quite a lunchroom."

She looked up at him, said nothing, waited until he met her eyes, still said nothing. There was something that had to be settled right now, at once, before the meeting.

"Of course not," he said, finally understanding. "Not related at all. I got all kindsa faults, but with me, business is business. Trust me on that. It's got nothing to do with the company. I'd – just like to have lunch with you." He looked more pointedly at her.

"You're wearing that angel again today, aren't you?"

"Yes," she said, her hand coming up to her throat in the same unconscious defensive gesture as when he'd first noticed it. "It's become kind of a good luck charm to me."

"I see," he said, a bit more significantly than she would have liked, and turned into a small alley. "So how about that lunch?"

"All right," she answered. "Sure." A few paces ahead, Carolyn, walking beside Harry Greube, stopped and turned around.

"We're here," she said.

*

The building came as a considerable surprise. For whatever reason, she had assumed that the offices of CFS would be located in some confabulation of glass-and-steel, the most modern available. Instead, she found herself standing in front of a pleasant, four-story structure made entirely of red brick with old-fashioned, doubled-paned windows, on either side of a broad porch that led to a white double-door with a brass knocker on it. The buildings on either side of it were in a state of normal brown dilapidation. Probably at one time the living testament of some landowner's victory over an urban developer, it had been carefully and painstakingly renovated. The red brick shone, the result (she could tell) of an extensive acid cleaning. A small black sign with gold letters reading "CONSOLIDATED FINANCIAL SERVICES" hung to the left side of the door. The structure would have fit right in to the most picturesque part of Church Street.

"Let's go in," said George. "Party's waiting."

Behind the doors was a reception area, equally quaint and old-fashioned. An attractive girl sat behind a broad walnut desk with a raised front edge. Two massive red leather couches faced the desk. Behind the girl, on the wall, was an antique blackboard with the names (presumably) of all the members of the firm, marked in or out. A mahogany roll-top desk, clearly intended for ornamental purposes only, stood to the right of the reception desk. The rest of the furnishings matched perfectly.

"Sorenson party," said George, crisply, to the receptionist. "AI Squared."

"They just arrived themselves," she answered. "They're just setting up."

"Good," he replied, then turned to the other three with a slight smile. "We've got a minute. Let me show you where the action is before we go up." She found it interesting to see his confidence build as he neared his own territory. He pushed opened one of the doors and the other three followed him into the interior.

The contrast was so abrupt and startling that she had to stop herself from gasping. All the light disappeared at once. Adele felt a sharp, momentary panic, something that happened often when she was suddenly plunged into darkness. A reeling vertigo that shot into the pit of her stomach, a disorientation no less terrifying because it was familiar. Bri had learned that early on. As habitually tardy as he was, he was never late when he was taking her to a play or movie, always allowing for plenty of time in the theater beforehand for her eyes to adjust.

She resisted the impulse to reach for George in the darkness. She could make out a dim illumination ahead. They moved a few feet forward, passed through a curtain she hadn't seen before in the darkness, and then they were there, in another large room, the source of the dim light.

"This is the trading room," George said, calmly. Harry Greube looked around, fascinated. Carolyn had obviously been there before. Adele bit her lower lip and took it all in.

They stood at the entrance of a large, dark room. The illumination was provided by tiered layers of video display monitors, covering all four walls, at least two hundred of them altogether, obviously a quotation system, doubtless covering every market in the world. In the interior were row upon row of desks, each in its own small cubicle, each with a tiny VDT on the its top, as if the spawn of a sea monster had spattered out around the room. At the center, on a platform, the only raised point in the room, inside a circular desk as much countertop as desk, rolling from one theater of action to the next in a swivel chair, sat Franklin Fischer, the center of so much rumor, hope, and anxiety in her own offices, and the center of the chaos here.

None of the traders remained seated for long at any particular desk; instead, there was a constant scurrying chaos, hunched figures scrambling insanely between monitors and telephones, frenzied movement back and forth, pencils scrabbling on paper, red tongues of light on telephones blinking patternlessly throughout the room, all the individual whisperings merging into one collective gibbering hiss.

"Come," said George, "I'll introduce you." He moved calmly through the madness on every side, up an aisle that had not been readily visible, to the center of the room, to Franklin Fischer's desk. The ceiling was not finished; wires and cables tangled and coiled; impressionistic notions of spider webs, serpents on branches, flitted through her mind. George caught sight of the group out of the corner of his eye, interrupted a conversation with a young broker, and rolled over to the other side of the platform.

"Carolyn," he nodded, not waiting for the introductions. "Mr. Greube. And Ms. Jansen, the look and feel memo writer," surprising Adele considerably. He smiled a hurried, patrician smile. "Hello." His attention focused immediately on George. "George, an excellent meeting yesterday. I received a call from Alan Smith not twenty minutes ago. I doubt very much Salt Lake City is going to be a problem any longer." Adele studied him as he spoke. He had the same kind of leonine good looks as Richard Collishaw, the same type of aristocratic bearing. Yet while she had always found Collishaw attractive if a bit distant, there was something about Franklin Fischer that was off-putting. He cleared his throat. "There are one or two points you have to clarify."

"No sweat," George shrugged. "I'll get to it later this afternoon."

"Good. Good." Fischer looked at the others and smiled again. "My apologies for this distraction. Good luck. I hope you can succeed with these young men. No one else has." A significant look passed between George and Franklin. "See you, George." With that, he sat back in his chair and rolled away; one of the phones on the other side of the desk had begun to blink; somehow he'd seen it. It took Adele a moment to realize that they'd been dismissed, that the meeting was over.

*

"What did you think?" George asked her, standing again in the lobby, waiting for the elevator.

"Fascinating," she lied. Tell him the truth? That it had been a small ordeal, that she could hardly wait to get out of that room? No way. Her true first impression? A thousand-eyed monster devouring its worshipers, gorging itself on their souls. A good thing in one way they had been in the dark – the cool, calm girl had her hands full staving off one surge of adrenaline panic after another. *Get me out of here!*

She was more than a little annoyed with herself, *such a baby*. After all, it was nothing more than a display of communications technology, something with which she was quite familiar. All it was was a trading pit. The ceiling had been deliberately unfinished to facilitate repairs and upgrades. A lot of people would have given anything to be there. A cataract of money thundered into that room, drenching everyone. But still – still – the darkness, the chaos, the sense of madness, that dreadful hissing undertone.

"Good. I thought it bugged you a little bit." His sensitivity surprised her – not, she recollected, for the first time.

"I assumed it was a quotation system. I mean, the monitors on the wall," she went on politely.

He held his thumb up affirmatively. "NYSE, Amex, NASDAQ, BOT, the works. All over the world as well; we got two satellite dishes on the roof of a skyscraper, cabled over to here. We trade everything – currencies, futures, options, everything. It's a twenty-four hour operation. I set it up, but Franklin likes to manage it on the floor. It used to be all he wanted to do."

"What's keeping the elevator?" asked Carolyn impatiently. It had been stuck at the third floor for some time. Harry Greube pressed the button again, as useless as that was. Finally it started down.

"'Used to be?' What does he do now?" Adele asked conversationally.

"Now?" He smiled faintly. "He wants to be a communications mogul," said George. "Which is good news for me," he added, almost as an aside. The elevator arrived and the door opened. The lone occupants, in defiance of all probability, were a young mother, struggling with an open briefcase and a pile of market charts, and her baby.

"I'm sorry," she gushed and struggled. The two men and Carolyn stepped past her into the elevator. Adele grabbed the charts, folded them expertly in one movement, and somehow got the briefcase closed over their bulk.

"Thanks," said the woman.

"My pleasure," said Adele, as she stepped into the car herself. "How old is he, anyway?"

"Eight months," said the mother as the door closed. The elevator started up.

"You'd think she'd have enough sense to leave the little poop machine at home," said Carolyn to no one in particular.

"We were stuck with her on the merger," George replied by way of explanation. "But not for much longer."

*

The boardroom was a gracious paneled room that faced the street. It was dominated by a large conference table with sixteen wooden chairs, an Oriental rug underneath. This day a small personal computer sat on the right side of the table. The three young men who had been seated around it stood up irregularly as Adele and the others entered the room.

"Hi ya, geniuses," George said, with completely unconvincing camaraderie. "These are the people I'd like you to meet. Lem Michaels. . . Peter Steinitz. . . Hsen-Chiang, damn it, I never get that right. . . Carolyn Hoffman. . . Harry Greube. . . Adele Jansen. Adele's the woman lawyer I told you about."

Hand shaking all around, shuffling of feet, the usual hesitancy while everyone figures out who's in charge. She studied them quickly during the interim, smiling to herself. Newly hatched nerds, no doubt about it – remnants of shell still clung to them. Sports coats that didn't quite fit were worn over ties that didn't quite match. The Chinese fellow was wearing white socks and running shoes. All three were bespectacled, all three were smiling shyly, diffidently, clearly because she and Carolyn were attractive women. None was much older than she – classics of a kind, Hollywood typecast.

She liked them.

The leader was evidently Lem Michaels, the tallest, at least six-two, slender and rather nice looking, except for a pronounced, disfiguring overbite. A flash of annoyance at that, a small thing not done right. She came from a relatively poor family. She knew what it was like not to be able to do everything you want for your children, but what could have been so important that they didn't get those buck teeth fixed? He had every right to be a handsome man, except he wasn't. He was now looking at her, eyes bright with interest

"Where do you want to start?" he asked finally.

"I want to see the program," Adele said immediately, not letting anyone else answer. "I want to play with it."

"Sure," he grinned.

"I was at the Software Arts Expo, but I couldn't get near your booth," she added. The crowd around the booth had been ten deep. It seemed as if they were all six-foot men with three-foot behinds. She'd tried to wait her turn until she realized there weren't going to be any turns this time out. She started to push and elbow herself, not exactly what she was best at, until finally one of the cordon turned around. *Why don't you go back to the playground and leave this stuff for big people?* At which point she had given up – for then – and gone over to the deserted booth with the nice young man in it.

But today it was her turn.

"The basic program is on the CD," said Peter Steinitz, a shortish, rotund man. "A simplified medical protocol is in the B. Type in – "

"Why aren't you using the hard disk?" asked Adele, puzzled.

A ripple of stiffness ran through the room. "There are only four copies of the program in existence," said Lem softly. "This one, and one each of us has in a safe place. We won't let *anyone* copy it."

"Oh," said Adele. *Idiot*, she thought to herself. *Obvious.*

"Anyway, input this onto the B drive," Steinitz went on, handing her a sheet headed APPENDICITIS, with a definition obviously copied from a medical dictionary. Obediently, she began the input.

All at once, doubt swept like a whirlwind through her mind. She knew a ton of dummy-dopey expert programs in medicine, law, and the like. It couldn't be that this was just one more. Could it? And yet all those people, all that excitement . . .

"You know, there are a lot of home doctor programs out there already," she said, as casually as she could.

Lem grinned. "This is no home doctor. The results may be the same, but it works on totally different principles. Look, test it. Fracture the language, muddy up the input – see for yourself."

"O.K.," she said, and finished the entry.

"Now switch to A," Steinitz said, "and direct the unit to read B, and begin however you like." ALLO, she began. HI. . . ALLO, it responded. HELLO

MUY OK, she answered, deliberately fracturing languages.

BUENO, came back. TIENE USTED DOLOR? DO YOU HAVE DOLOR? TIENE USTED PAIN? DO YOU HAVE PAIN?

It's querying in all the language variants, she thought. *Wow.*

YES, she typed.

"Giving up the polyglot approach?" Lem smiled.

"Yes," Adele said, still dead serious at the keyboard approach. "I can't compete."

WHERE IS THE PAIN? the screen showed.

"You're a patient with appendicitis," said Lem, calmly. "Give it back those symptoms – take a look at the definition if you need to – but don't make it too easy. Make it work."

She decided to play the part of a child. She typed in:

NO, SAMANTHA DOES.

Instantly the computer responded: WHO IS SAMANTHA?

MY DOLLY, she input. She could sense great silent hilarity behind her. Another instantaneous response:

HOW OLD ARE YOU?

Amazing, she thought. *It's going to adjust the vocabulary.* She answered:

8.

The video display showed:

WHERE IS THE PAIN IN YOUR DOLLY?

IN HER TUMMY, Adele answered.

DO YOU KNOW YOUR RIGHT HAND FROM YOUR LEFT?

"Say yes," said Steinitz quickly. "We haven't worked out a protocol for that with a child yet."

Adele wheeled around. "Are you cheating at all with this program?"

"A little," answered Lem calmly. "I'll tell you how in a while. Run it for now." At this moment, he didn't sound nerdish in the least little bit. His answer didn't bother Adele in the slightest, but she could feel Carolyn and Greube exchanging glances.

She typed in YES, and the program continued to run. It asked its questions of her in words that a normal eight-year-old child should have been able to understand. She responded in kind. She was coy and guarded about localizing the pain, but it was no use. It was as if she were playing twenty questions with the all-time world champ. After a remarkably short interaction, the screen read:

TELL YOUR MOMMY OR DADDY OR BABY-SITTER THAT YOU PROBABLY HAVE APPENDICITIS. YOU MUST SEE A DOCTOR IMMEDIATELY. IF YOU ARE HOME ALONE, GO TO THE PHONE. DIAL 911 AND ASK FOR THE POLICE. DO IT NOW!

"Very good," nodded Lem, approvingly. "Very few people think to play the part of a child. Particularly one who speaks fractured English. You pulled up a couple of tricks we have that are buried pretty deep."

"What if the child didn't have appendicitis?"

"At the moment it would come to the end of the decision tree and quit," said Peter. "Because it doesn't have any other definition. But when it's fully loaded it would proceed down the alternative path until it reached finality."

"And the base program will read any protocol? Go through the same decision analysis with any field of expertise?"

"So far," said Lem, now sounding presidential. "It always seems to be a matter of shaded levels of discrimination" – he suddenly became uncomfortable; Chiang had looked up at him – "or, as someone else might say, `finer points, finer pens, finitude.'"

She knew the quote, but could not immediately identify it, smiled instead. *Wow*, she was thinking, *wow*.

Beware of the one-in-every-kitchen syndrome, a speaker at one of the many seminars she had attended in the last two years had said. *Even if the technology does succeed at that level, it may not do it in your timeframe. Take television. These days everyone owns one, many people have two or three or four, not to mention video displays. But if you'd bought in in the mid or late 30s you might have died waiting. Or your horse might not have won, even though it was running in the right race.*

Good advice, but even so. . . *wow*.

"How did you cheat?" she asked.

"For the purposes of this demonstration, we greased the decision paths," said Peter Steinitz. "Not that it wouldn't go through the exact same process, but a hell of a lot slower."

"It's still very experimental," Lem added. "We've got a lot of work to do. Right now, if you were suffering, say, from dehydration, it would take ten or twelve hours to tell you you needed a drink of water. We're a long way from where we want to be. But we'll get there," he finished, with a quiet, non-swaggering confidence that was more eloquent than anything else he could have said. Everyone was silent for a moment.

"One thing that's bothered me," said George. "I can't see anyone taking its opinion instead of a doctor's, no matter how smart it is. I don't know about the sell." Lem gave him a sharp, surprised look.

"That's not how you'd use it at first," answered Adele, without looking back, before anyone else could speak. "You'd use it for a second opinion, a backup. Maybe even a doctor in his office would like that."

"Exactly right," nodded Lem, approvingly.

All right, beware, be cautious, that expert at the seminar had been right. But good God! A universal intelligence, expert on any subject, available to anyone, right at one's fingertips, capable of running on an ordinary black box. Who wouldn't want one? A home doctor, a home lawyer, an expert chef, an expert companion in any hobby you could name. . . *good God!* She looked around at the three young founders with new respect. They were going to be rich and famous, soon, and so was everyone associated with them.

It was true. It was real. This was indeed it. *Don't blow it, stupid.*

"One more thing," said Lem. "You haven't seen the best. Run the directory on the CD. See for yourself how much active code there is."

She did; a chill literally went down her spine, and her mouth dropped open. "I don't believe it," she said.

Only nine files, only 380K of code. The rest of the CD was full of cyber gibberish, clearly for camouflage purposes. She had assumed the disk was one of the new hyper-dense type, storing five or ten megabytes. She had never heard of an artificial intelligence program that needed any less. The program had only needed half the capacity of an antique floppy disk, one-fifteenth of the amount of code of the next smallest experimental program, but performing as effectively or more than any of them on less than seven percent of the space.

The goose bumps persisted. This was more, much more, than a business opportunity, even an extraordinary business opportunity; this was a revolution she was witness to. . . she thought rapidly, tapping her fingers slowly on the table. Her own problems were completely forgotten. Lem smiled at her through his buck teeth. Then, suddenly, she was certain she knew everything; maybe she'd picked up a trick or two from Tom. After a moment, she looked up, surveyed the entire room, and then spoke with great deliberation.

"The source code's only secondary, isn't it?" she said slowly. "What you really want to protect is the algorithm. It's a whole new method of quantifying rational processes – isn't it?" She looked around again. "Only one or two of you are master programmers. The others –" she paused for dramatic effect and looked carefully at each of them in turn – "the other one or two are one or two of the greatest mathematicians in the world. Maybe who have ever lived."

"Well, I don't know about *that*," said Lem, blushing, for a moment very much the ex-nerd. "But you're right about the math. It started with Chiang and me, a couple of years ago. We were both on fellowship at Cornell, doctoral candidates, and the head of the department introduced us because we were thinking down the same lines. There was a lot of talk, and a lot of ideas, and then all at once we decided to write a joint doctoral thesis. But we wanted to illustrate what we were doing. It was so heterodox, so revolutionary, we didn't think anyone would buy it unless we developed an application. Chiang knew Pete – he was in computer science, the best – and he was going to write a program for us. He had some ideas of his own, then suddenly we all knew we really had something. And here we are."

"A little application of fractal theory," Pete grinned. "Constantly reiterated. I can't say more."

Lem took charge again. "I don't know about the greatest in the world, Ms. Jansen. But we're pretty good. I do know that." Confident enough now to be self-deprecating, the master in his own field – and one of the movers and shakers of the world, buck teeth, shyness.

*

Do any of them know? she thought, thinking in her mind's eye of Carolyn, George, and Harry Greube. No, they didn't. She could tell.

There had been a day in real time within the last few years. On that day heads of state had nodded to other heads of state, the stock market had gone up or down, some people had won at games played for money and some had lost, babies had been born in hope and old men had died in despair. But the most important thing that happened in the world that day had happened in a small, nondescript room in Ithaca, New York, where these three shy men had met and talked, and done great things, and the human race had wobbled one more giant step forward in the same improbable manner of all its giant steps.

Don't they know? If intelligence could be crowded into that small a space, what wasn't possible? Even the small RAM's these days had more capacity. Visual and tactile recognition systems, genuine, affordable robotics, genuine discriminating ability in the most commonplace appliances – vacuum cleaners that could steer themselves around objects, collision avoidance devices, real ones, planes, trains, and automobiles – real, discriminating intelligence everywhere, a world so different from this it could barely be imagined. She felt chills again.

"Lem's the dreamer of dreams," Peter Steinitz was saying as she returned from her vision to the here and now. "Chen's just an all-around genius. And me? I'm fun to know. Keep the distinction in mind," he added, deadpan, "since most people have trouble telling us apart." She had to smile at him. The others were silent.

"I guess it's time we heard from you," George said, a little awkwardly. Adele realized she'd been contemplative a bit too long. She smiled sheepishly at all of them, stood up from the chair, moved back to Carolyn and Harry, and took a seat with them.

*

It went well.

The three young men listened politely, if indifferently, to Carolyn's description of the law firm, her introduction of Harry Greube, and his discussion of the nuances of corporate and securities law that would affect AI Squared. But they made no comments, asked no questions. It was clear that the focus of their attention was on Adele. They shifted forward in their seats as her part of the presentation began, barely fifteen minutes after Carolyn had begun. The indifference vanished.

She smiled, opened her briefcase, and distributed the three copies of the memo she'd brought with her. *Do it with schmaltz, stupid*, she told herself. *Johnson and Jansen.* The Glee Club would never have believed it, but she was more in agreement with them than they would ever know. It *was* only one memo, and she had long since become bored by it and the Junior Miss act that always had to accompany the telling of the story. But this was not the time for second thoughts. If she could pull this off, she'd have a lot more to talk about over the next few years than one memo.

So she told her story, told it with even more than the usual grace, and they enjoyed it. Apart from everything else, it was great fun for anyone to look at the paintings while listening to them analyzed by someone who knew what she was talking about. When she was finished, she could tell she had made an impression, perhaps even an impact. There was reason for hope.

Chiang leaned over to Lem Michaels and whispered something, then straightened up and grinned at the room.

"Chiang understands English perfectly, but his accent's so thick he's embarrassed to speak," said Lem, by way of explanation. "But he has the same question that I do. How do you know so much about software, Ms. Jansen?"

"Oh," Adele answered, "it's really pretty simple. When I was a sophomore in high school, someone donated some used Macs to the school. I was – well, I guess this is no time for false modesty – I am pretty good at art. The graphics capability interested me and I wanted to learn how to do it myself. I had some ideas for a project. I have three older brothers. One's a math teacher who's *really* good with computers. He taught me how to program. Then when I went to college my dad gave me a laptop as a graduation present and I had to learn – *really* learn Windows, and then Linux. And – I guess like you said – here I am."

Lem nodded. "I didn't mean to probe – but so few women –"

"I know," Adele answered. "Jack – my brother – taught me as if it were a language. It was really so easy that way. I think more girls would get into it if it were presented that way."

"We wish they would, too," said Steinitz, with deliberately overstated lechery, and everyone laughed, Adele included, though the immaturity of the joke troubled her. "You didn't seem at all nonplussed by the program. It scares a lot of people."

Adele smiled. "Something else my brother Jack once told me: `Never be afraid of intelligence, no matter what form it takes. Frankenstein's monster is a monster because it's stupid, not for any other reason.'"

"Some brother," remarked Lem, without any cynicism. "But –" he gestured towards the computer – "tell us how you would protect this."

"Obviously you put the common-law copyright on it," said Adele. "Carolyn or I can explain what that means later. But I don't think you register with the Copyright Office. You'd have to file the source code, and I don't think you want to do that. If I understood you correctly, someone can code the same formula a little differently" – all three nodded – "and you can't copyright the formula, any more than Newton could copyright the theory of gravitation or Einstein could copyright $E=MC^2$. You're going to have to protect it with some sort of internally coded protection."

"Could we do that?" asked Lem. "Could we add some crash mechanism if anyone tries to crack the code? Is that legal?"

"Sure," said Adele. "It's your program. You have to warn your customers that it's there, of course, and you'd have to replace the program if someone crashed it inadvertently. But those things aren't a problem. The danger –"

"There'd be a problem if it screwed up other files in the CPU, wouldn't there?" asked Steinitz. "Or – God forbid – the network."

Adele nodded. "Exactly. That's what I was going to say. The danger, if you have any kind of file management system – and I suspect you must – is that it'll mess up other resident files. Customers who lost data might sue you for megadamages. You'd have to be extremely careful about how you designed the mechanism, and you'd have to tell them all about the risk in the warranty."

"You know," said Peter Steinitz, "we could. . . ", and it was fasten-your-seatbelt time, the three of them shot off into the stratosphere, Chiang forgetting his accent and his shyness, as one idea after another took wing. Occasionally, one of them asked a legal question, which she answered as best she could. Adele herself could barely hang on. The others in the room were completely lost. She was privately quite pleased with herself. She had not anticipated any of the issues that the AI Squared founders had raised this morning, but she'd still been able to cope. The seminars which she'd attended on her own time, the journals she'd spent her evenings reading – it had all paid off.

"Hold it," George finally said, intervening after about ten minutes. "This is supposed to be an interview, not a brainstorming session. You're choosing a lawyer here. I think you've heard enough. Do you have any more questions?"

The three sat, chastened, for a moment, then Chiang leaned over to Lem, who smiled. "Chiang wants to know, if we retain your law firm, can we be sure we will be working with Ms. Jansen?"

"Of course," smiled Carolyn toothily.

Mixed emotions. Exhilaration, because she was clearly on the downhill slope; this was working out. At the same time, she writhed slightly in her seat. They were green; she wished they knew one percent as much about human nature as they knew about software design. The look on Carolyn's face was not exactly one for the scrapbook.

"Anything else?" asked George. "Good. Then thank you all very much. We'll –" The phone rang in front of him. "Yes – yes – O.K.

"That was Franklin," George told the room. "He wants to see you, Carolyn and Harry, about that communications deal. Something else has come up. Me, too. Guys," he said, turning to the others, "you'll have to excuse us." He pressed a buzzer on the phone. "Debbie? I have to leave the AI Squared group for a while. Show them down to the trading room. They'll find it interesting." He replaced his files in a leather briefcase and stood up abruptly. The three of them went through the door at the same time as a woman, evidently named Debbie, came through it.

"Guys?" said Lem. "Will you go on with Debbie? I want to talk to Ms. Jansen for a minute." George Sorenson's assistant smiled and the three of them left. Adele and Lem were alone in the conference room.

"Anyway, I've seen it before and it gives me the willies," he added. Internally, she registered pleasant surprise – another point of agreement. "Step out into the corridor, will you?"

"Why?" she said, when they were out there.

"Because I think that room is bugged is why," he answered. "And that's what I want to talk to you about – that, and a lot of other things. Something weird is going on here. There's something screwy about this whole deal, and I don't know what it is. What I wanted to ask you, that I couldn't ask you in there, is this." He paused and took a deep breath.

"If we do this, can we trust you? I mean, you personally?"

*

It hadn't made any sense to them from the beginning, he told her. They had known from the start that the experimental model they had developed was exciting, exciting enough to make them decide (at Lem's urging) collectively to quit academic mathematics and go out into the business world. They had organized a company and applied for a research grant from EBS, number one in the world in the manufacture of business and computer equipment, though it had developed huge corporate inertia. To compensate, EBS had begun a policy of co-investment in promising new companies with products that had potential value to the giant. Lem was certain they qualified.

"But we never heard from them," he said, bafflement in his voice. "Instead, about eight weeks later, we got a call from George Sorenson on behalf of this CFS. First, he arranges this venture capital financing, much more than we need. That was about a year ago. Then, suddenly, he's taking us public and parading us around in all these bank boardrooms. Two years back, I didn't know what an institutional investor was. Now I've met a couple hundred of them."

"What's wrong with that? You've become rich, haven't you?" asked Adele, deliberately drawing him out.

"Oh sure, no problem there, but it doesn't make sense. You see –" he scrunched up his face and thought – "you mentioned $E=MC^2$ in there. Well, if I could use that as an analogy, we're at that stage of where we want to be eventually, and they're treating us as if we'd already built the A-bomb. We're still in basic alpha testing, Ms. Jansen. We're years and years away from an off-the-shelf product. And then there's all the application programs that have to be written, and we'll have to teach the programmers from scratch. We're a long way from any kind of payback."

"I get the idea," said Adele, thoughtfully.

"And George Sorenson – did you see the way I looked at him in there when he said that about the sell? That was because that was the first thing he'd said in eight weeks that showed any interest at all in what we're doing. He introduces us like we're three gold nuggets when we're doing our dog-and-pony stuff and ignores us every place else. He doesn't know a damn thing, really, about what this is all about – you got there faster in an afternoon – so why? It seemed like he ran off every free moment he had to do some giant communication deal he's working on, about a thousand times bigger than this. So what's up? What's going on?"

"Have you asked him?"

"Yeah – and I get this kind of shuck-and-jive. He reminds me of how rich we're all going to be, how young we are all that stuff. And it's true, and it's great, but –" he shook his head.

He faced her squarely. "I'm no great shakes at this stuff, I realize that, but I'm J. Pierpont Morgan compared to Chiang or Pete. I'm the guy that started all this. They're counting on me, believe it or not. So that's why I have to ask you – can we trust you?"

"I'm only a second-year associate," Adele equivocated. "I'm not a partner. I report to Carolyn Hoffman."

"I know *that*," Lem answered. "But you're different. That's obvious. That was apparent from the way they all reacted to you. And you're good – I could tell that. I feel good about you, I'll tell you that, too. You have no idea how many law firms George has run by us, and I've turned 'em down because I couldn't ask this question. But I want an answer from you. I want to hear you promise me, Ms. Jansen."

"Adele," said Adele, thinking. *Tell him*, her instincts told her. Tell him that there was a lot about this that she'd found pretty damned strange herself, that there was a very peculiar feel to much of what had happened.

No, her rational judgment said, and it was that judgment that prevailed. This type of distrust between the founders of a start-up and its financial backers was common. She had heard numerous speakers say that. They were members of two different tribes, perceived two different realities. She had no hard evidence that anything was out of the ordinary, only a feeling. The situation would not be improved for anyone if she nudged an unfounded suspicion into paranoia.

Most of all, this was not the time to be upsetting apple carts. What George Sorenson had given George Sorenson could take away. A chance like this might not reoccur in a hundred thousand years. So – no, definitely not. *NO!*

"You can trust me," she said, smiling. "Not that I really think you have anything to worry about in all this." They went back into the boardroom. The PC was still on, giving the Windows screen. She studied it, then looked back at him.

"Wow," was all she said. "Wow. I'd heard about it, but I didn't believe it. To think it's for real." She looked up at him. "Wow."

He smiled suddenly at her. "We might do it, mightn't we? It could be it all will happen," and she smiled back at him, *yes, it just might be, and thank you for the first person plural*, two people looking towards an entirely new age, entirely new beginnings, standing in a blissful dawn in the very heaven of youth.

"I think so," she said. "I want so much to be a part of it."

*

He nodded thoughtfully, and then smiled himself, very shyly. "I wanted to say something personal, too. Er – ah – er – I noticed you weren't wearing any rings, I mean, I didn't mean to pry. It's not that I mean – I mean, what I mean – is – if you're not seeing anyone steady – what I mean to say – I wonder if I could see you – of course, I'll see you if you're our lawyer, I didn't mean that – I mean, socially. If that were possible. If you know what I mean."

Not exactly the most polished line I've ever heard, she thought fondly, *but very sweet.* Lem Michaels was clearly not a man who was used to asking women out on dates. Maybe this was the first time in his life he'd tried to pick up a girl he'd just met. Then, suddenly, the trace of annoyance she'd felt earlier hardened into real anger. This was a nice guy. She was sure of that by the way he'd looked after his friends, a math wizard to boot, an important person, someone who was going to change the world. He shouldn't have to be diffident with her or anyone. *What was so awfully important they didn't take care of his teeth?* she thought. *So help me, if my boy has that problem he'll see an orthodontist if I have to go without a new outfit for twenty years.* (She was sufficiently distracted not to notice the implications of what she had just thought.)

The most frustrating thing is that under normal circumstances she would have accepted the invitation instantly. She just didn't feel the click. Her instinct was that she never would, that it plain wasn't there. But she would have found out. She would never have turned him down flat. He was definitely a possible – smart, decent, and it had been a long time since looks had mattered all that much to her. If it weren't – if it were not for – she would have found out. But voluntarily beginning a dating relationship was impossible at the moment.

"I'd love to, Lem," she said, smiling and sincere – to that point – "but I am sort of involved with someone right now."

"Oh," Lem said, unable to hide completely his disappointment. "I see. I hope you didn't think I got out of line."

"Of course not," said Adele. "You shouldn't say things like that. Or think them. You're kind of a catch, in my opinion."

"A lot of girls say that to me," Lem smiled, semi-bitterly, "while they're recommending I date other girls." He switched subjects abruptly, deliberately, avoiding further embarrassment. "That was some paper you put together – the history of western art compared to software interfaces. I admire people that can put two different disciplines side by side like that. It's a gift." He looked at her more closely. "That started you thinking. What about?"

"Oh," Adele answered, who had indeed pursued a new train of thought, "I have a – friend – who does the same thing – lays disciplines side by side, I mean. I hadn't realized he and I had that in common until you spoke."

"Is the – friend – the one you're involved with?"

"Yes," answered Adele, trapped, unable to invent a lie quickly enough.

"What's his name?" asked Lem.

"Tom," she said, now really trapped. "A writer. Thomas Newcombe."

Lem looked at her. "The guy who writes the poems about math?"

"Yes," she said, the astonishment evident in her voice. "But you surprise me, Lem. He doesn't have a very large readership."

"Maybe not, but my prof at Cornell in topology was nuts about that stuff. He got us all hooked on it. That was him I was quoting, you know. Pens and points. I guess you knew that." He peered at her. "You're his girl?"

"Yes," said Adele, treading water, lying, and yet the lie gave her immense pleasure. She basked in the phrase, the thought, for a moment. *Tom's girl.* Bri had always introduced her in the same old fashioned way – *This is my girl, Adele* – and she had known, committed feminist that she was, that she should reprove him, both for the "girl" and the possessive pronoun. The only problem was that she melted, every time he did it, too quickly to do anything. It is useless to try to raise anyone's consciousness when your own has just stepped on the elevator to the subbasement.

Chiang and Peter Steinitz came through the door. Lem turned to them. "Hey, you guys," he said. "Do you know what? She goes with Thomas Newcombe."

Peter eyed her with additional respect. "Really!? That must be something. He's very clever. He must be fun to know."

"Oh, yes," said Adele, dazed, the exhilaration fading in the confusion of feeling, "a barrel of laughs." It was dawning on her that the lie she'd told for personal reasons might very probably be turning into the deal clincher – a very unsettling thought.

"I can see I was out of my league," Lem remarked, which was almost the last straw. Anger on his behalf – *no one is out of your league!* – came crowding into her consciousness; she suddenly realized the implication of what she'd thought earlier, about her mythical son, and then the night thoughts broke open the locked door and came roaring in. The residue of the panic she'd felt in that hellish trading room, the excitement of the meeting and what she was certain was her triumph – all of these jostling in her mind, elbowing each other for room, a huge, clamorous cacophony of raw emotion. A good thing Lem hadn't said anything that required an immediate response, because she was momentarily too internally bewildered to have replied coherently.

Get focused, stupid. Concentrate on one thing. She did, on Lem, on all the things he'd said about himself that she hadn't liked hearing. *If I were a free woman, so help me, I'd take him on in a–*

Oh, my dear God. If she were free, which in fact she was. She'd been almost over Tom – and then these last few days – she had obviously taken some giant steps backward. Oh, well. Another day would come. Maybe when it was all resolved, when it was all behind her – *don't let yourself think of what that implies,* she thought, now with almost a lump in her throat – maybe something could work out. After all, if she had sold Lem on a phony romance, she could as easily sell him on a phony breakup. When the time was right.

George, Carolyn, and Harry Greube came back into the room, not a moment too soon. "I guess we're all finished," George said. "Thanks for coming. The four of us will meet this afternoon and let you know."

The three young men shook hands all around and left. Adele put the memo copies back into her briefcase and locked it.

"Have you forgotten we're having lunch?" asked George.

"Of course not," she answered, looking up brightly. "Just putting these in a safe place." He bought it. Either she was becoming a more accomplished liar or she was on a roll. She had, in fact, forgotten completely. Again.

*

She was surprised again to find herself enjoying his company. A slight hint of awkwardness remained in his manner, but without question things were warmer.

"I bought a book on Velásquez, you know," he remarked. "You got me interested the first time."

"A coffee table book?"

"Well," he said, "I always thought of a coffee table book as one that sat on a coffee table. This one is about as *big* as a coffee table." She smiled. "I don't know. But it's not as good without a – a – what's the word?"

"Docent," she said.

"Docent." He looked at her shyly. "Any volunteers?"

"Well," she grinned, enjoying the flirtation, "there are tons of them at the museums."

"Not exactly what I had in mind," he answered, enjoying himself. "I had in mind something more personal." Adele colored slightly. He grinned kindly, and sensibly moved on.

The lunchroom was as George had promised – dazzling, if somewhat small. The petite filet he'd suggested for her was cooked to perfection. There was no one else at any of the four tables; it was well after 1:00.

"I'm very surprised at this building," she said, making conversation.

"How so?" he asked.

"Oh, I guess I was expecting something a bit more modern."

"It used to be. We've only been here eighteen months. The building used to belong to –" he named one of the old established brokerage boutiques – "the type that wouldn't give me a job." He smiled. "But they ended up with a heavy short position on one of our takeovers. Deeding this building over was one of the ways they covered. We had to agree to keep some of their old staff on. With the chef, it was a pleasure."

A memory from the morning returned; all at once, the sauce lost its entire savor. "That's what you meant about that woman with the baby, wasn't it? What you said to Carolyn? She's going to lose her job when the contract expires."

He was completely taken aback; hesitated; then nodded. "She was a stock analyst for the other firm – a specialist in retail chains. Pretty good, from what I hear. But the track's too fast here for that kind of thing. Babies don't fit in. Look," he said, fully aware that this was now not going the way he'd hoped, "she'll catch on somewhere where it's a little less intense. It'll be all right. Look –" he was becoming urgent – "they tried to run a little trading boutique here, with liberty and justice for all. But they blew it. Not enough toughness, not enough smarts. Now they're all gone and we're still here. They made promises they couldn't keep. So what good are the promises now?" (The Bronx inflections came back into his voice when he got excited.) "I didn't make these rules. I only live by them. That's the way the world is. It's the way it's always been. It's nothing any one can help."

Adele sat silent, thinking. He watched her uneasily. All at once, it seemed unreal, alien, to be here, now, talking about art and software and high finance, and all the while keeping the little secret in her abdomen. *What would he think if he knew?* she thought. *What would any of them think?* The cool, calm girl had done her thing, and done it well that morning. They'd all watched and applauded and approved – what little they knew of the underlying reality. What would they think if they did know? With all these thoughts came, all at once, the crushing, desolate loneliness she had known often in Manhattan in the last two years, a premonition that she was destined always to be a stranger in this strange, cold land, everything that she wanted perpetually out of reach.

"George," she suddenly asked, "there's no hidden purpose to this AI Squared thing, is there? Something I should know about that I don't?"

"Why?" he asked, startled. "Why do you always ask that?"

"I know you're doing the Project. I have an idea how big that is. This whole thing must be such a distraction to you. I don't understand."

"No," he answered, looking startled. "There's nothing funny going on.

It's a financing, pure and simple. Pretty exciting company, isn't it?" He glanced at his watch. "Damn it. I've got to get moving. I got to get up on that Atlanta stuff. I don't –" want to end on this note, she was certain he wanted to say.

"You really did well today, you know," he said desperately. "You knocked me over. Again. You're really special," he muttered, with an obvious sincerity that touched her to the core.

"Thank you," she answered.

He looked at his watch again and grimaced. "1:45. I wish I had more time today. I'd like to talk more." She nodded, surprised again to find herself sharing the sentiment. Suddenly she wondered at herself, why she hadn't told this man the same lie she'd told Lem, that she was still involved.

Two o'clock. Her own meeting with Abercrombie, the news about Tom. Her focus shifted abruptly.

"I've got to get back to the office, too. Thank you so much for the lunch. And everything."

By the time she was out on the street, her concentration was solely on the appointment back at the office – so much so that she forgot, for the moment, her initial reaction to the way George Sorenson had answered her question about AI Squared.

That she had been virtually certain that he was lying.

A RETURN TO THE MET

She arrived five minutes before two o'clock. Abercrombie was already in the lobby, knocking off another crossword. They nodded, exchanged a glance; she had a sudden intimation. *Prepare thyself for the worst.*

"Marjorie," she said. "Could you hold my calls?" She forced a grin. "Such as they are. Bill," she gestured towards Abercrombie, "I guess I'm ready."

*

"You know, I'm good at what I do," said Bill Abercrombie. "I went from the NYPD to EBS to the FBI to my own shop because I'm that good. I've got a collection of passwords, keys, contacts, backdoor entries, the works, that it's taken me twenty-five years to put together. I don't think there's anyone else in the business––" he paused – "in the world – who could have even promised you a report in three-and-a-half days, let alone delivered."

He fell silent. He was definitely not a happy man.

"Maybe you'd better just give me the news," said Adele, heart sinking.

"Maybe." Abercrombie looked around her office and sighed. "The headline is there isn't any news. I'll get to the text in a moment."

He looked around again and met her eyes. "There was no person named Thomas Bryant Newcombe born in upstate New York twenty-five to thirty-five years ago."

Adele's eyes widened with astonishment; worst case, yes, but she had expected at least some reality, some something. "You're kidding."

He shook his head slowly. "No. Let me go on. There was no person with that name born anywhere in New York, in fact. Or Vermont, Massachusetts, Connecticut, New Hampshire, Maine, Pennsylvania, New Jersey – I know they're west and south, but I thought you'd want me to check –"

She nodded.

"–or the provinces of Ontario or Quebec. There's been no one adopted by that name. There's been no one who changed his name to that. And there's been no one married or divorced by that name. Or appearing as the father on anyone else's birth certificate."

She took some consolation in those last tidbits – but why would anyone lie about where they were born? Especially about the region; he hadn't even named the town to Georgia. What could there possibly have been worth hiding that deeply? Adele nodded dumbly. "Go on."

Bill Abercrombie had been holding a notebook, a stenographer's wire pad, in his right hand, which he now opened and through which he began to flip.

"You've probably heard of a false identity trick that involves using the birth certificate of a dead infant or child. A lot of con artists use it to start credit scams. It's not so effective anymore because the credit bureaus have the resources on the Net to match up birth and death certificates. But I wondered if maybe this guy started early or was way behind the times."

"Yes," said Adele glumly. This was becoming a very depressing report, and she sensed that Abercrombie was only getting started.

He nodded negatively and clicked his teeth. "But I've never heard of a con like that that didn't turn on phony credit. Only he doesn't have any credit. He doesn't have a Visa Card, not with any major bank. They all use the same clearinghouses. That's an easy check. He never has had one. He's never had a Master card. Ditto American Express, Discovery, or Diner's Club. There are a few others, so small you've never heard of them. He's never had any of those cards, either.

"Which means, by the way, that he doesn't travel much, because no one could get that far without plastic money without paying a lot of big expenses with cash, which would get such a person listed in the FBI file of suspect terrorists, drug traffickers, and the like, which file he is not in. I double-verified with the Federal Reserve list of persons who've made cash deposits in chartered banks of more than ten thousand dollars. He's never done that. He's not on that list."

"Wait a minute," she said, anxiously. "I didn't mean for you to do anything illegal." Everything he'd mentioned before the FBI and the Federal Reserve had obviously been open to the public or available by inquiry. Exploring government files made her nervous.

He grinned. "Relax. I'm still an independent contractor for the Feds. I've got legal access to those files. I didn't have to backdoor anything."

He cleared his throat. "Back to the main thing: There are four major credit bureaus that provide credit information to retailers and banks. He isn't in any of their bases. Which means he's never asked for any kind of credit. Also, he's never bought a car, at least not on credit. He's never applied at GMAC, or Chrysler, or Ford, or any of the acceptance companies that the dealers in foreign cars use. Which means, Ms. Jansen, that in his entire life he has never bought one single thing that he couldn't pay cash for. If he ever uses personal checks, whoever accepts them has never bothered to run a credit check on him. And he's obviously never bounced one, even by accident."

She called up her memories of his small apartment. The stereo system had been an ancient boom-box with detachable speakers. It couldn't have cost more than one hundred fifty dollars new. The books had been library books. It was a fair assumption the disks were as well. The computer was a clone of one of the older IBM models. With so many Manhattan businesses constantly upgrading their networks and office equipment, it could have been purchased for a song, might even have been abandoned. There was nothing special about that bed, except what had happened in it. It could easily have been second-hand. No new appliances in the kitchen or elsewhere.

When he had last come to the office, he'd had on the same comfortable, neat looking, but somewhat worn jacket that he'd been wearing the first time she'd seen him. At the time, she'd thought nothing of it. He was obviously one of those men who are disinterested in dress, an attractive quality in some personalities. Now it occurred to her that the two coats she'd seen were probably the only ones he owned.

A sudden insight; the net worth of all the material goods he possessed in the world couldn't be more than $2,000, probably less than half the cost of the big desk in Carolyn Hoffman's office. Maybe Georgia Richmond was right; maybe all his money was spent –elsewhere.

Maybe not.

Abercrombie cleared his throat. "I was surprised his name wasn't in the file of any tenant evaluation service."

Adele thought for a moment. "He has some sort of deal with the landlord. The guy sublets to commercial travelers. It's not my field of expertise, but I'll bet that's a violation of some rent control or zoning ordinance. That's probably it."

Abercrombie nodded glumly and made a note. "Back to what I do know. I thought, maybe some cutey-pie con I've never heard of before, though without meaning to brag, that would have to be pretty cute, believe me. But he's never even been booked, let alone arrested. In fact, he's never been fingerprinted – which means he's never applied for a civil service job, or the bar exam –" Abercrombie smiled "–or about a hundred other things. The FBI keeps a separate file on known aliases. The name Thomas Bryant Newcombe isn't on it. Nor any variant.

"He doesn't have a brokerage account, at least not with Schwab, E*Trade, Paine-Webber, Merrill, Witter, Pru-Bache, or Shearson-Lehman, or the other majors. He doesn't own stock in any Fortune 500 company, at least none that he's traded. He hasn't been involved in any stock transactions that have cleared through the New York Stock Exchange or the American. NASDAQ's too big to check in this period of time. He doesn't have an account with the Chicago Board of Trade, the Mercantile Exchange, or any of the smaller options exchanges. So I'll tell you if it's some new cute con, it's awfully new and awfully cute."

He closed the notebook for a moment. "I'll tell you, Ms. Jansen, I'd been running these checks for about a day and a half, and" – the phone on her desk rang.

She picked it up, irritated. "Marjorie, I thought I asked you –"

"It's Ms. Hoffman on the line, Ms. Jansen. She wanted me to interrupt you."

"Very well."

*

Carolyn came on to the line. "Adele? I got the word. It's ours. Unanimous vote. We're expected at their board meeting, next Wednesday at 10:00 a.m. Also, they want a report from you as soon as possible. About what you talked about, putting some protective mechanism and the problem of consequential damages." This was not the phone Carolyn she knew; the usually inflectionless voice had an edginess that was unfamiliar. "Get right on it."

"Sure," she said, but the line was already dead. Funny – it should have been one of the high spots in the year, if not her entire life, but at this moment in time, the events of the morning seemed to have happened a long, long time before, to someone else.

"Sorry for the interruption, Mr. Abercrombie. Go on."

*

He cleared his throat. "I began to wonder whether all this wasn't some practical joke you and Walt cooked up. I don't know about you, but I wouldn't put it past Walt."

She smoothed her hair. "It's no joke, Mr. Abercrombie," she said evenly. "You haven't wandered into the Twilight Zone or a Stephen King novel by mistake. He exists. Believe me."

Abercrombie opened the notebook and went on. "He's a writer so I checked those files, too. He's not a member of ASCAP, or of the Writer's Guild, or any of the other semi-unions. There are at least two dozen literary societies in this city, some pretty major; he doesn't belong to any of them. He doesn't have an agent, but I didn't expect he would."

He shifted in his chair. "He's never been admitted to any hospital in this city, no patient records −" he shifted again − "including Bellevue. He's never been the subject of a commitment proceeding here or any other place in the state.

"You'd guessed right about one thing the civil liberties people aren't supposed to know: the Department of Health does keep a confidential file on potential transmitters of sexually communicable diseases. But he's not on it.

"He's not on any of the mailing lists that any of major mail advertisers use −" Abercrombie looked up − "Ms. Jansen, I can't begin to tell you how invisible you have to be not to show up on any of those lists. Every membership organization you could think of, big or small, profit or not, sells its membership and mailing lists to one of 'em, sooner or later. He's never applied for a driver's license or a personal identity card. He's not registered to vote, anywhere in the state. He's never received welfare, not general assistance or any of the FICA stuff. He doesn't have any insurance policies, life, health, disability, or casualty, with any of the five major carriers in New York. He's never been registered at either NYU or CCNY. He doesn't −"

She held up her hand; she had heard enough. "Mr. Abercrombie, I get the picture. Did you find out anything positive? Anything at all?"

He looked at her for a long moment, and then sighed. "Yes. He files tax returns, Federal, state, and city. I didn't have them retrieved. In the first place, that's really tough. In the second, I doubt they'd show that much − but most important, it's a major, major league felony." She nodded in agreement.

He continued: "Not that I think there's anything there. The returns are always on time and none of the revenue agencies has an audit going on him. The only other thing is −" he shrugged and went on.

"He has a New York public library card. Stated address, care of the Furston Press. And that, Ms. Jansen, is about all there is on this guy in about 500 databases that I have had searched. If I haven't said it in these words before, this is incredible to me, completely incredible. Derelicts, winos, people you'd think have dropped out of society for good − even people like that show up on some computer file someplace. They get arrested sooner or later. Bag ladies end up in public shelters. They all end up in somebody's database somewhere − except this guy. If you had told me before I started that there was any adult this invisible living on the planet Earth, let alone Manhattan, let alone a published author, I wouldn't have believed you. But that appears to be the case."

"What about the telephone?"

"Paid cash for it when it was installed. Pays his bill promptly every month. No credit." He looked up. "I took a peek at last month's bill. You should know that is crossing over the line a little. Nothing. Not one long distance call. Not even a toll call."

The small office was completely silent for another moment. She felt frustrated and disappointed – but oddly, not at all surprised. She was beginning to develop a feel for the problem now; somehow, in a curious way, in the back of her mind, she had expected this outcome.

He handed the four volumes of poetry back to her. "That was a surprise, too. I'd got a completely different impression of the guy from what you'd first said. I usually don't like that kind of thing, but that stuff's pretty good, even the math junk. You should know I bought my own copies. I wondered who the nun is. Do you know?"

"No," she answered shortly. There was a short silence.

"Well," she said at last, I guess you've come to the end of your report." He nodded in assent. "Do you have any overall impression you can give me? Apart from what you've found out?"

"Good question," he said, looking back at her. "But no good answer." Then he sighed and tapped the books. "These; the way you described him on Tuesday; what I found out about him, or maybe what I didn't. I don't feel a pattern here; I don't have any feel at all, to tell you the truth; and normally I can do that sort of thing in my sleep. But nothing seems to make sense with this guy. Nothing adds up the way you'd expect. I have the feeling that the more you find out, the less sense it's all going to make. I don't know who he is, or who he isn't, but I can tell you this for sure, Ms. Jansen –" he paused for dramatic effect – "he don't compute. He just don't compute."

*

The bad grammar was for emphasis. She smiled palely and shook her own head up and down.

"Thank you, Mr. Abercrombie. But that," she sighed, "I already knew. How much do I owe you?"

"Costs only. About two hundred and fifty, telephone tolls and log time." Her eyes widened with curiosity. "I don't bill fees when I don't produce. I'm not a lawyer." They smiled at each other across the desk. "I'm not the gumshoe type of P. I., but if you give me the leads – you know, who gave you the dirt on him – I'm sure I could have him traced."

She shook her head. "No. That would take too long. Besides, I don't want so much to find him as to find out about him." Also, she would have to take up the matter again either with Georgia Richmond or Jenet – absolutely out of the question, for different reasons with respect to each.

He nodded. "Well, then, is there anything else you want me to do? Are you going to give up on this?"

She looked up at him sharply, startled – then grinned from ear to ear. "Oh, my goodness, no, Mr. Abercrombie, not a chance, not the slightest chance. What you've told me has been disappointing, obviously, but it hasn't changed anything. I am not going to quit on this. I am going to find out about this man – somehow. I have to. I'll think of something – and when I do, I'll be in touch, I promise you."

"Then I have a question, Ms. Jansen, a variation on the one you asked me," he said. "And that is. . . why? I don't want to become involved in anything illegal any more than you do. If this is some exercise in vindictiveness or for some petty revenge. . ." – his voice trailed off for a moment – "or major revenge. In confidence, of course," he added.

Fair enough. She considered what to say. Suddenly, she didn't want to lie anymore. There'd been enough of that, with Jenet, with Georgia, with Lem Michaels, and she was sick of it.

"Thomas Newcombe was my lover, Mr. Abercrombie," she said, to his complete unsurprise. "The only one I've ever had, though there have been other men. I'm sure you understand the distinction. We didn't make each other any promises. I was the one who broke with him, actually. This isn't a vendetta, nothing like that. I didn't know anything of what I told you Monday when I was with him, about his – other life. I can't believe a man like that, even slightly like that, could affect me so deeply. There has got to be an explanation. Our relationship was short-lived –" she was embarrassed to tell him exactly how short – "and he doesn't talk much about himself. I should have found out more about him while I was with him, but I didn't. And that's why I'm employing you. No other reason. I am not going to quit on this until I find out what I have to know. Because –"

Storm warning; an intense morning had come before. As she let herself talk, she could feel a much larger emotional tempest brewing now. She had been about to tell him that her feelings about Tom were still very much alive, to mention that mysterious sense of urgency. *Take care, dumbo* – if she didn't slow down, if she wasn't careful, it would be full upon her, she would be fighting back tears, lips quivering, swallowing hard – humiliating enough when it happened in front of someone who knew and cared for her, but intolerable in front of a comparative stranger. She checked herself.

"–I have to know why. I have to know the truth about this man." Her eyes misted slightly as she forced a smile. "I bet you hear stories like this all the time from all kinds of naïve young women. Don't you?"

"You're anything but a naïve young woman," he said suddenly, "and I've never heard a story like this in my life. But I have to tell you – maybe it's an occupational hazard – I stopped believing a long time ago that the truth sets anyone free. In my business, usually it hurts. Often it hurts a lot more than most people ever guess it will. Suppose it all turns out like that?"

"Then I'll have to be hurt by it," said Adele, swiveling in her judicial chair, "and I'll have to live with the hurt and I'll have to think about what all of it means – and that does scare me, of course it does; how could it not? But I'm not going to call this off. I'm not going to quit on it."

"Fair enough," Abercrombie replied. "Call me if – when – you need me."

*

The phone woke Adele at about 8:30 the next morning, much later than her normal rising hour, after another weary, bleary rolling night. "Hello, this is Robert," said the voice. "Is Joan there?"

After twenty months, she had this down to a science. "Yes, Bob," she lied. "But she's in the shower. Wait a sec." Silently, she depressed the hold button and dialed the number of the apartment where Joan (according to the note on the refrigerator) had actually slept.

"Hi, Denny," she said cheerfully to the sleepy male voice that answered. "Can Joan speak to her roomie?" One moment later, lowering her voice, "Joan, I've got Robbie for you on the other line. I'm going to forward the call in a moment. I told him you were in the shower."

She sensed Joan turn away. "Denny. . . a little privacy? Girl talk. O.K.?" meaning, *O.K., connect him.* Adele hit the button again, waited for her to speak – "Hi, Robbie. How's it hittin'?", then gently depressed the receiver.

No question, it was not easy to conduct a triple affair. It never had been, but call forwarding for sure had made it a lot easier. Adele had first met Joan, an aspiring young actress blessed with an ample private income, in the offices of a tenant location agency. They'd liked each other on two minutes' acquaintance. It had been obvious they could share an apartment without coming to violence. Later, she had listened with sympathy to Joan's tales of the city, to the general effect that the casting couch was alive and well and living on Broadway – listened sympathetically, in fact, long after it became apparent that Joan had an affinity with couches of all kinds.

Her ostensible roommate had come to New York with a fiancé and an independent income. She still had the fiancé, still had the money, but she had also managed to acquire two married lovers in the interim. None of the men knew about each other, nor did either of the wives know about Joan. Adele had derived much quiet amusement in less turbulent days from the perpetual juggling act, some performances of which were truly amazing.

She soft-boiled an egg for herself and poured a glass of low fat milk. She stared longingly at one of the cans of diet cola still sitting in the refrigerator. Normally, she went through three six-packs a week, but this one – purchased in the same drugstore and at the same time as the home pregnancy kit – was still unused. She shook her head. *When are you going to let me have a cola, you little beast?*

The practical outcome of the elevation of her roommate's lifestyle was that Joan had four different places to sleep, and both the motivation and the means to maintain the pretense that she had no more than two. Adele had the apartment to herself nearly all the time. Right at the moment, the arrangement was perfect. She had no interest in the social pyrotechnics of someone else. She had problems of her own.

She drifted out of the kitchen and into the living room, slowly eating the boiled egg. Without really thinking about it, she switched on the television. Some good luck there, for a change – amid the desert of Saturday morning, one of the networks was broadcasting one of her favorite cartoons, the Chuck Jones masterpiece about the singing frog in the cornerstone. She watched it with affection for a few moments, all the while wondering about the problems of people who know secrets they can't share with anyone else. These days everything seemed to be significant.

On a normal Saturday, she'd have been dressed and on her way to work by this hour. It was not that she didn't have anything to do. The report that Lem Michaels and his friends had requested was going to require some time and considerable effort. But not on this day – not that this was going to be a day of leisure. It was going to be devoted to work, for sure, but to her personal work, the most pressing thing in her life – the Problem.

I'll think of something, she'd told Abercrombie the day before. *O.K., genius, what?* The time has come, the walrus said. Mentally, she went over the report Abercrombie had given her, becoming more and more depressed and frustrated. A good detective – the number of doors he'd tried and found locked was amazing. A true work of imagination, to think of any stone he'd left unturned. *I'll think of something*, she'd told him. Easy to say then.

As she finished the toast, it struck her. Not here, of course not here – back to the source. Not entirely rational, but – a sudden certainty – this was not a day for rationality, but for intuition; not for rumination, but for action; not for thoughts, but for deeds.

The decision made, she moved quickly. A shower, change into Levi's, a loose-fitting blouse, and an oversized leather jacket Michael had handed down to her – the day was grey and bitter – then out the door, lock the door, and gone. She had decided to walk. It wasn't that far from the East 70s and she often thought best as she walked.

*

It was much the same, yet so much different. The Prado exhibit had closed nearly three weeks before. The next major show was not nearly so interesting. She paid her admission, walked through the entrance and into places at once familiar and strange, and went up one flight of stairs.

Prior to accepting the job at Hapgood, Thurlow, she had been to New York City three times in her life. She had toured the Metropolitan Museum of Art on all three occasions. This, the way it was today, was the way she remembered it. Raucous humanity – schoolchildren and tourists, families of four, babies in strollers (of course), a continual hubbub; more the atmosphere of a high school homecoming game or a Fourth of July picnic grounds than a cathedral of art, a marvelously nonchalant ambiance for one of the great institutions in the world.

Motes of dust danced in the gray sunlight reflected through the windows; morning light had always been her favorite. She browsed by the Tiepolos, a short woman, hands in pockets, lost in the flood of humanity, thinking of many things and remembering magic. There was no enchantment here today. It was an ordinary morning, noisy and confused. No immediate brainstorm; but, even so, she'd done right to come, she could feel it – a good place to be, here, in front of the Tiepolos.

We're not in real time anymore, Adele. Sometimes, late at night, she wondered. If there were real magic – but there isn't, of course – but suppose there were, it would be like that, wouldn't it? It wouldn't be something that happened with a formal incantation, pentagrams and a recipe of owl feathers, eye of newt. That's cooking, not magic. Because if you can understand it, if it could be quantified, then it can't be magic, right? It would have to be something that you couldn't quite identify, something you were never entirely sure had happened or not, the thing at the corner of your eye that always skitters away as you turn your head. Or something ordinary becoming extraordinary without your knowing when or how.

Scary, that thought – because it would change you, too, wouldn't it? If it were magic – if there were such a thing, which of course there isn't. But you wouldn't ever know exactly how, because – if you did – it wouldn't be what it was – magic. You wouldn't ever know. A very – *very* – disturbing thought, that last.

Sometimes, late at night, she wondered. Now, on this ordinary Saturday morning, standing amidst all the everyday reality, magic so distant, she wondered again.

*

The same basic exhibit, as it had been for at least twenty-five years. What had Tom said? *I like the collective, impersonal faith.* Yes; exactly. Outdated, but still glorious in its way. She wished she could take some pleasure in it, feel and enjoy its full restorative power. Someday soon, when all this bedevilment was behind her, she would have to return.

Of course. One small piece drew her forward, that she had to see again, had to confront; she knew exactly which among all. She turned the corner and there it was – "The Last Judgment," painted by Jan Van Eyck, housed in the same innocuous glass case. The pleasure of the morning disappeared.

She sat down on a small black leather bench across the hall from it. The distance was too far to study the detail of the small triptych, but she had neither the need nor the desire to go closer. She could see it in her mind's eye as if it were only six inches away.

She had always disliked that painting. Now she hated it. It was not that it was bad art. On the contrary, it was by any standard a work of genius. The wealth of detail, in a piece of such small dimension, would have been extraordinary even with CAD techniques; in the context of the resources available in the mid-fifteenth century, it was an astonishing achievement, worthy of its place in history.

She loathed it.

It was a work of malignant hatred, misanthropic to its core, vicious, sadistic blood lust masquerading as divine justice. There was no place for mercy, no place for compassion in that universe – the damned in their torments, the hypocrites in heaven, the middle ground – the only place where real human understanding, kindness, gentility can take root – the middle ground, utterly absent. The most frightening thing of all was its sincerity. There was not the slightest trace of cynicism or second thought anywhere in it. Worse. Tom perceived something special in that vision; it held some power over his being. Worse yet. She hadn't the slightest idea what the relationship was, what any of it meant. She pondered the question for a moment or two without any result.

Think, stupid. She felt like the hero of an old fairy tale, the prince who has to ride up the glass mountain to win the princess. This was exactly like a mountain of glass, no break, no foothold, no place to take a stand. Try as she might, she could not think of anything that Abercrombie had missed. *Damn it, think!* She looked up at the triptych; she could almost imagine it sneering at her, smug in the knowledge of the secret, daring her to do her best – *What business is this of yours, you pregnant slut?*

"Is everything O.K., miss?" Startled, she looked up. The speaker was one of the museum security guards.

"Yes," answered Adele. "Why do you ask?"

"You've been sitting there for nearly forty-five minutes."

"Oh," said Adele, surprised. "I was lost in my own thoughts. I had no idea."

The guard nodded, understanding. "That's all right. It's easy to lose track of time in here."

"Yes," said Adele, picking up her purse, looking up at him. "I know."

*

So this avenue, too, the path of intuition, had led to a dead end, like all the others. Perhaps it had been foolish to have thought it would be any different. No point in wasting more time; she stood to leave, gathered her purse. Then, all at once, the strangest impulse of her life struck her. She moved towards the Van Eyck, studied it through the glass case, and then, again on impulse, spoke aloud in a level tone:

"I'm going to beat you. No matter what this is about, no matter what you do, I'm going to win. This is one you're not going to get. I don't quit and I don't lose. Especially not on this. I'm Adele Jansen," she added, "just so you don't forget." She had not spoken loudly and yet the corridor, the floor, the building, the city, the universe, seemed to resonate with her voice.

She had little understanding of why she had said what she'd said. She had even less of what precisely the challenge that she had made meant. But she felt better; she had the sense, whatever the off-the-wall reason, that she had finally accomplished something. The guard was looking at her, she noticed all at once, and she felt a rush of embarrassed blood. Then he whistled softly, lifted his two fingers to his cap and snapped them down, a casual but genuine salute. She smiled sheepishly at him as she moved towards the stairs.

*

Lunch was a tuna salad at a luncheonette and another glass of milk. She would have preferred a diet cola, but her body was still having none of it. Culturism aside, she had as yet no intuition as to whether the child was a boy or a girl, but she was absolutely certain that she was bearing a future health food addict. A tofu and bean sprout eater, for sure, she thought, enjoying the joke momentarily, then becoming overwhelmingly sad.

If.

The city swirled around her, the ebbs and flows of the ordinary currents of human life as she sat, one small person at a lunch counter. She reviewed the whole day she'd spent with him, minute by minute. A little erotic glow – absolutely lovely to be swept off her feet like that, without even knowing it's happening until it's too late. She had thought she was too sophisticated for any man to accomplish such a thing, but as she looked back, there was no question the outcome had been a foregone conclusion before she even knew the game had begun. A man who knew what he was doing; he had definitely deserved his conquest. Of course, the fact that they'd fallen rather deeply in love that day hadn't exactly hurt his chances. Odd – after all that she had learned since, with all the doubts she had, with all the misery that she knew lay in front of her, she regretted nothing, particularly not that they'd made love, only wished that she'd somehow been more careful.

She went on thinking, deliberately randomizing, thoughts rattling around in her mind like loose change in pants pockets – Tom, the baby, George Sorenson, AI Squared, everything. She took another bite of tuna salad and turned it over again. There had to be a solution to this. There had to be. Randomize again – thoughts of Lem Michaels, the problems with protecting the source code, the prob–

Source code. Source. Copyright. Back to the source.

She stopped chewing. Copyright; Tom; source; manuscripts. The Furston Press would have retained the first manuscripts Tom submitted, the originals. It had to, if for no other reason than to defend against any infringement claim. The books were still in print. That first submission had to be in some file somewhere. He would have had to provide a return address. No communication would have been possible otherwise. The cover letter must surely be still in the file – with luck, the original envelope, with a postmark, as well. That should be enough – the break in the glass mountain, the foothold, all she needed. Give her just one whiff of the scent, one crack in the glass, and she would be through in a shot, gone down the trail, and she didn't give a damn that the metaphor was mixed.

Excited now, she gulped down the remainder of the salad. It was going to have to wait; there was no one at the offices of the Press on the weekend who would know how to retrieve that file. First thing Monday, she would phone Jenet's secretary. It was irritating to her that she hadn't thought of this earlier. Losing even thirty-six hours over a weekend was annoying. She had ceased trying to understand the mysterious urgency she felt, simply accepted it as one of the background elements of the strange scenes through which she was unexpectedly living.

She slid off the luncheonette stool, paid the bill, and started for home. Only one thing left on her list now – to put together some sort of costume for the Halloween party on Sunday evening to which Carolyn had invited her. (It was for that reason she had been spared the normal Friday night soirée this weekend.) But that wouldn't take long. She already had an idea.

But what else? She was unexpectedly the possessor of far more free time than she either needed or wanted. There was nothing she really wanted to do, including attend that party, except live until Monday morning and dive into the task. But if she didn't fill the time somehow, she was going to spend the whole weekend brooding. Not good; there was a fine line here between justification of her faith in her judgment (the goal, definitely desirable) and erotic obsession (definitely not) which she did not intend to cross if she could possibly avoid it.

Oh, well. Phone a girlfriend and go antiquing; maybe even Joan, if she could roust her out of bed. There's no such thing as an apartment that can't use a decor upgrade. Get the materials for the costume. Glitter and be gay – and for heaven's sake, don't let anyone perceive that your teeth are on edge, that you are regretting every precious second you're forced to squander.

THE PROJECT

"Sit down," said Carolyn, gesturing towards one of the empty chairs in front of her desk. "We have to talk."

Adele sat, concealing her impatience. This was not at all the way she had wanted to begin the week, here on the thirty-second floor, in this small palace. She had intended to go straight into her office and place a call to the Furston Press. But the message in the phone slot from Carolyn had been too clear, too peremptory. *See me first thing Monday morning. Urgent.* Now Carolyn sat across the desk from her, frowning and tapping a pencil.

"I suppose congratulations are in order," she said dubiously. "It went very well on Friday. Better than you would have ever dreamed. George Sorenson was extremely impressed. They talked about it. That's what the meeting was about, when we were called away. They want you to be a part of the Project. I said all right, but not until I'd talked to you." She smiled sourly. "I suppose you've heard some of the rumors about it?"

"That it involves all sorts of media and Internet companies. That it's very massive. George told me a little more about what he's doing," Adele responded automatically.

Carolyn looked up sharply. "*Franklin Fischer's* the one doing it. You'd better get the program straight right now. This was Franklin's inspiration, Franklin's vision from day one. George Sorenson's an errand boy."

"It doesn't seem that way," Adele answered, perplexed.

"It's nearly four years old now," Carolyn went on, ignoring her, with only faintly concealed bitterness. "You cannot imagine the work, the money, the sacrifices that have been poured into this. Our plans are firm. However –" she sighed – "be that as it may, I guess you're part of the A-team now. One could say you have arrived." She stopped, and continued looking at Adele, as the silence lengthened.

"Is there a problem?" Adele asked finally. This was not going well. She had been hoping it would be a short conference; *these are the things I want you to do.* It wasn't working out like that. The day was gray and smuggy outside. The beautiful view was gone.

"Not necessarily," Carolyn answered in the same dubious tone. "I sincerely hope not – for your sake, Adele, for your sake mostly. That is what I wanted to see you about." She paused again. "I'm very worried you're not ready. I don't mean you're not capable. That's not what I mean."

"What do you mean?" Adele said.

"I mean, I wonder whether you're tough enough. Whether you really know how much is required."

"What are you talking about?" Adele responded, with the faintest hint of exasperation.

"A lot of things," she answered. "Greg Steuer, for one."

"What about Greg Steuer?" Adele asked.

"He quit Friday. I guess you didn't hear. Something of a coincidence – he's gone off to CFS. To do investment banking." She smiled to herself. "If he thinks that's going to be easier, he's got another think coming. But what I really meant was the way you supervised him."

"What?"

She paused. "He didn't cooperate with you for a second, did he? You rewrote his work for him. You redid it, not him. Don't deny it. I know. I checked."

Adele reddened. "It didn't seem like a fair test to me. We've never gotten along. Besides, it was billable time no matter which of us did it."

"Except that we bill your time out at $240 per hour and his at $120," Carolyn answered calmly. "He didn't have it, Adele, and he couldn't stand it that you do. That was the reason you didn't get along. Good body, though," she added softly.

Suddenly Adele understood why Greg had been invited to the Friday night party that particular Friday night. Carolyn had had some very practical reasons. Poor Greg, whatever his faults. *Maybe I am naïve.*

"You spent your own time – overtime, I'll bet – doing his work for him, didn't you? And he wouldn't spit on your grave. But the main thing, Adele," Carolyn went on, "is that it wasn't a test of him. We'd already made our minds up about him here on the thirty-second floor." She paused. "It was a test of you."

"Me?"

"You. How you'd cope with a supervisory task. What you'd do when you had to be tough." She paused. "You didn't do well."

"What should I have done, Carolyn?" she said, embarrassed and irritated.

"Come to me the very first time he wouldn't play ball," Carolyn said promptly. "He would have been out on his keester that very day. That's the way I was hoping you'd handle it. But you did what I expected. You can't afford sentimentality, Adele. Not if you want to be a partner here. Not if you want to succeed at this level. There's no space for that. You have to let the chips fall where they may. That's what I meant about doing what's necessary the other night."

She stood up and paced out from behind her desk. "Now I'm requested to put you on the mainline of the largest, most important thing this firm has undertaken in a century. The futures of several tens of thousands of people are directly involved. Millions, indirectly. The destiny of Hapgood, Thurlow. And I have to tell you: I don't know. I have the strongest possible reservations about this." She picked up a folder and stepped over to the table in her alcove, where she had entertained Jenet. She sat down on her couch, crossed her legs, sighed heavily, and handed Adele a large, glossy accordion file with a gold seal on it. Four cartons filled with other files stood beside the couch.

"What I have to know, Adele, what I have to be certain of. . . is. . . can we trust you? If you are entrusted with responsibility here, after all that has been done, after all the effort, can you be trusted?" She appraised her for a long moment, did not wait for an answer, went back behind her desk.

"You can read it at your leisure," Carolyn said. "With all the free time you'll have now that Steuer has left. I've dictated a couple of notes. This is the summary. Everything –" she gestured at the cartons – "is in there – the whole plan. Forty-one files. Four years in the making. The Project."

Adele scanned the summary quickly – a plan to acquire various media companies – newspapers, radio, television broadcasters, cable systems, independent ISP's – all across the United States. "I don't understand. This is all about corporate acquisitions. This is stuff for our securities and M & A people. I don't know what I have to offer."

"Neither do I," Carolyn remarked, shaking her head. "Neither do I. But someone wants you included in. Even if it is the eleventh hour. You don't have to ask who." She shook her head in disgust. "Franklin would never be so sentimental, so foolish."

*

She'd stood there the night before, dressed in her improbable costume, watching the festivities, watching the clock. Halloween had become a major singles event in the City. Carolyn had far too many guests to accommodate in her townhouse; she'd rented the entire community room in an adjacent complex. It was festooned tonight with black balloons, all manner of art decor hobgoblins, outlandish jack-o'-lanterns. Mannequins dressed in a variety of old-fashioned costumes hung from gibbets scattered around the floor. A third of the room had been tented off; underneath was an incredibly detailed haunted house. It was likely that one of Carolyn's Broadway art director friends had done it. The exit was concealed. A guest emerging found himself unexpectedly enmeshed in a thick webbing of rope and nylon, as the eye of a sea monster rolled up – a momentary thrill, a good effect. Carolyn had sensibly stationed someone to stand guard in case anyone got seriously trapped. Adele had been one of the first to go through it, an early arrival because she intended to be one of the earliest departees. Monday was beckoning.

A six-piece band played on a raised platform, light rock and pop in deference to the age span of the guests. Adele watched the dancers swaying in the center of the room, costumes ranging from garish to truly appalling – all the while eying the door, planning her exit. Suddenly George Sorenson was beside her.

"Would you like to dance?"

"Ah – oh – er – sure," she finally said. "But I should warn you, I'm an absolutely terrible dancer."

"Don't worry about it," he said, leading her to the floor. "I'm terrific. We'll do fine," and – surprise, surprise – he was as good as his word, guiding her expertly through a number of complex steps, leading her firmly, not too intimately. He noticed the expression on her face.

"Fooled you, huh?" he smiled slyly. "Didn't think a money guy had any social graces."

"I didn't imagine this was in your repertoire," she admitted.

"Had to learn in my mid-twenties," he said. "Necessary. Got to like it. You're not as bad as you think," he added, whirling her expertly around. "A helluva lot better than most businessmen's wives."

She looked up at him, grateful for the momentary respite from the burden of care. The dance ended; she thanked him and returned to the edge of the floor. A few moments later, when he asked again, she accepted at once.

Again they glided easily around the floor. It felt natural and comfortable to be in his arms. Like many young women her age, she had never danced with a truly expert ballroom dancer. It was wonderful. Her feet seemed to find the rhythm and the right steps effortlessly. He did in fact possess the tight, hard, middleweight muscularity she'd sensed when they had lunch, and it was pleasantly diverting to be held by him. To her amazement, she found a tiny spark of party mood glowing within her. She was actually on the verge of having a good time. Maybe she'd stay later. Why not? Nothing could be done tonight. Maybe–

"This is the devil's special night," a man dancing by dressed in a ridiculously ordinary red costume, with horns on a cap and a pointed tail, remarked. "You have to make it special for me." His strikingly underdressed partner giggled.

Satan on his throne, she remembered. *The Prince of Darkness.* His special night. What was he doing? Someone on the other side of the room bumped into a cord. With an eerie, insane languor, one of the dummies hung around the room turned on its gibbet –a gruesomely realistic re-creation of the Hanged Man, the Tarot Card. She could see its death's head leer over George's shoulder.

She stopped dancing. "Anything wrong?" he said. "Anything I did?"

"I don't feel well," she said, shaking her head, then looking up and managing a smile. "I was going to go home before you asked me to dance. You changed my mind. You're a wonderful dancer."

That seemed to assuage him. They edged off the floor; people stepped aside for him again. She gathered her things.

"Before you go, there's something I'd like to ask," he said.

*

"Franklin'd never let his head get turned by a pretty face. Not at this stage. Not with plans so firm, and the end so close. But George. . . are you two an item?" Carolyn asked, with exaggerated nonchalance.

"No," she answered, stiffening slightly. The question was natural enough, but still over the line, too personal. "All it was was a couple of dances. He did ask me last night to go to with him to this dinner that CFS is holding next Monday, and I said yes. But that's because they're celebrating all their latest deals, including AI Squared. Lem and the others'll be there."

"Good," said Carolyn, without much enthusiasm. "Excellent. It'll be a little bit like the NATPE banquet. It's a good trial run."

"NATPE?" Adele asked. "What's that got to do with–?"

"The Project?" answered Carolyn. "The completion date. We scheduled it a year ago when we learned the convention would be here. It's the natural time. All the execs'll be in town. The contracts have to be executed by the 19th. It's all in the file. You'd better read it. That, Adele, is going to be the longest, most hectic week of my life. And now yours. There's a great deal more I want to accomplish at NATPE. Plus get the Project finally done. It'll be madness all week long and then – and then –" Carolyn sighed as if she were summing everything up – "then a banquet. A monster dinner. Everyone will be there – and if we've succeeded, a press conference directly afterwards. An announcement – I've been planning that and looking forward to it for four years – and it will all be over for a while. Don't plan on any personal time that week or the weekend before. It's going to require *everything*." She sighed. "For three years now, ever since we began the negotiations, it's been like organizing a dog food commercial. If one jumps up, they all jump up. Nothing stays in place."

"The 19th?" Adele asked, with a sickening realization.

"Yes," Carolyn reiterated, annoyed. "Monday the 15th to Friday the 19th. What's so hard? Why do I have to repeat myself?"

Because I have an appointment with a doctor on the 20th is why. Because this isn't a coincidence. The sense of ominous foreboding had sharply accentuated. *Stay the weekend if you're feeling bluesy.* Right. *Nothing happens by chance.*

"No reason," Adele replied. "I'll read the file." Impatient, she turned to leave.

"Wait a minute," said Carolyn. "We're not finished yet. You won a prize last night."

*

"Of course I'll go," Adele had answered. "It sounds like something I should go to." His features settled into disappointment for an instant. "I do have to leave now."

"You're still thinking about that guy, aren't you?" he said.

"Yes," she answered quietly, after a moment. "How did –"

He laughed quietly. "Did you think you could wear that costume and not have me. . . ?" She blushed. "Maybe our time will come," he finished.

She looked up at him. "Maybe," she said softly, astonishing herself again, because she meant it.

*

"Don't ask me why," said Carolyn, echoing her thoughts. "I personally didn't agree. Only you, Adele, only you, would come to a Manhattan Halloween party dressed as an angel. Good grief. I'll admit you looked cute enough in it. You got all the male votes. I guess the spoiled bastards are bored with bare midriffs. Still. . . " Carolyn shook her head – "an *angel*. Adele, really."

Adele held the cut glass decanter – not bad, she could do something with it – and shook her head inwardly. Carolyn wasn't being entirely fair. She had actually been a rather sexy angel, if she did say so herself – but then Carolyn knew so much and understood so little. As if any ordinary woman in her right mind would willingly join a tits-and-ass competition on a track that fast! She had modified an old white shift of Joan's, applied some gold paint to the cords of some old sandals, cinched an aged glittery belt of her own tight to give some dimension to her body, created two tiny decorous wings with stiffened terrycloth, and pinned a gold-plated necklace chain around her scalp and through her hair by way of halo – borrowing a trick from Tom's jeweler.

It wasn't much of a costume, but the party had been as she expected – acres of flesh, boulders of cleavage. She was one of the few women there with any kind of allure. She'd known when she arrived it would be O.K. But it was embarrassing to have done this well – and hardly worth the palpable increase in the tension between Carolyn and her.

"I suppose we're finished," Carolyn went on. She tapped the file. "I hope I've made my point. This –" she tapped it again – "is a great opportunity for you, Adele. Everyone in the firm wants in on this. You're the only associate who's going to participate. But it is also very dangerous for you. You can't blow this. You can't be weak or foolish. You can't –" she paused for emphasis – "fuck up – or there will be consequences." Her eyes narrowed. "I guarantee it. It's too important."

Adele nodded absently. *Tom.* She stole a glance at the clock – 11:15. *Damn.* The morning shot. "I guess we're done, then, Carolyn," she said, breaking an unwritten rule by speaking first, and stood up to leave.

The doorway was blocked suddenly. It was Richard Collishaw, the only member of the firm prestigious enough to enter Carolyn Hoffman's office without knocking.

"Carolyn, there's something – ah, Ms. Jansen, my old look-and-feel companion. I was a bit distressed that I couldn't join you and Mr. Sorenson for lunch the other day. Good morning."

"Good morning, Mr. Collishaw," she replied.

"Carolyn, there are a few matters I'd like to discuss with you. My calendar's overloaded. Lunch is the only time. Can you join me?"

"Of course," said Carolyn, reaching for her purse.

He turned to Adele. "Ms. Jansen, I understand that you did good work on our behalf again last Friday, that you were instrumental in our being retained by a new corporate client. Congratulations."

"Thank you," Adele replied. She suddenly suspected that Collishaw's appearance may not have been coincidental.

"Would you care to join us for lunch?"

No! I absolutely would not! "I'd be delighted," she said.

"I've been explaining to Adele how important the Project is to this firm," Carolyn said, and now Adele knew for a certainty that Collishaw's appearance was no accident. Trapped.

She did her best to enjoy the lunch, without looking at her watch too often.

*

Willis Rutter glowered at her as she came down the hall after lunch. *I told you so*, he'd said to two furious, green-eyed members of the Glee Club an hour or so earlier. The rumor mill had wasted no time. Adele barely noticed them as she walked past, or the stacks of new boxed files in her office. She was as curious about the Project as any of the others, but curiosity had to wait. The first call she made that afternoon was to Jenet Furston's assistant. Once again, although she did not mean to bother Jenet herself, she was put through to her directly as soon as she identified herself, before she had any time to react.

"Hello, Jenet," said Adele uneasily. "I didn't want to bother you. Your secretary connected us before I could stop her."

"My secretary has instructions about your calls, dear," answered Jenet calmly. "Why have you called?"

No hope for it now; she sucked in her breath and went on: "I've become very curious about Tom's manuscripts, how he came to submit them to you, things like that. Do you recall anything about it?"

Jenet sighed. "It's like everything else about him, Adele. What I don't know is so much more than what I do. He's always been reluctant to publish. It was like pulling teeth to get him to show us anything – and now he's stopped altogether, of course. Then when he'd produce his work, it was so extraordinary, it didn't make sense he'd be shy. It wasn't that he didn't know its quality. He knows. At the time, I thought it was only a kind of author's stage fright. That's more frequent than you might be aware. Nowadays I'm not sure what the reason is or was."

"But you must be talking about the second, third, and fourth volumes. Do you remember how he submitted the first?"

"No," said Jenet thoughtfully, "I don't. It would have had to be a blind submission, I suppose, but I don't review those for obvious reasons. All I remember is an assistant editor coming to me and saying she had really found something – which she had."

"Would you have kept a file on it? Would you still have the original submission?" asked Adele, regretting, but unable to avoid, a certain eagerness in her tone.

"Oh, yes, of course, we'd never discard that if it ended up in print. Let me think. It's been nearly seven years; I suppose all of that would be in storage. But that's not far from here. Would you like me to have the files pulled and sent over to you? It won't take more than an hour or two."

"Yes, thank you, Jenet, I'd appreciate that a lot." Finally, finally, some progress – but she forgot her relief in the awkward silence that followed. Finally, she spoke herself: "Jenet, I can guess what you're thinking. I didn't think you were a busybody the other day; I was grateful for your advice, I'd be grateful for any more you have. I did listen to it, I thought about it, but I've made up my own mind about some things I have to do. I know you can tell that. Please don't be angry with me."

"It's not that at all, Adele, I'm not at all angry," said Jenet with the slightest trace of wistful sadness. "It's that there's nothing more to say, is there? You've crossed over the line. You've gone into the cave." Adele felt the quick chill again. "And now you're at risk and it's my fault. It's too late to give you any more warnings. All I can do is wish you well and hope nothing happens that makes me feel even guiltier than I already do."

"You have nothing to feel guilty about."

"Yes, I do, dear. I'm not the sort of person to set wheels in motion and then pretend I didn't turn the key." Another silence. "In any event, Adele, take care of yourself. There is terrible, terrible danger for anyone who becomes involved with this man. I know that sounds melodramatic, but I am absolutely sure I'm right. And there are other reasons – there are some things – you in particular – I'd like –" She stopped.

"Jenet, is there anything more you want to say?" Adele asked.

"No. Not really," Jenet answered, after a pause.

She did not say anything more.

*

Nothing more to do now, until the Furston delivery arrived. Perhaps it was time to start earning her salary. She undid the tie on the accordion file and pulled out the first of the manila folders inside. So this was the Project. The caption read:

FISCHER COMMUNICATIONS COMPANY ACQUISITION PROJECT.
FILE #1 (OF 41)

By the metonymical processes common to all organizations, the long title had been shortened to the single word "Project." The first page of the first file was a roster. Eighteen copies of this file had been distributed; her roster, recently typed, showed hers as the eighteenth. Innumerable lawyers had worked on elements of it, but these were the only ones who had possession of it in its entirety. All the others were partners. In fact, only two others were even junior partners, one of whom was Harry Greube. She was the only associate.

She read on. In overview, the Project consisted of a plan to acquire no fewer than twenty-five, no more than thirty-five, media companies, Internet service providers, software publishers, cable television systems, and the like. To that end, a Delaware corporation had been formed, Fischer Communications

Acquisition Corporation; negotiations with all the candidate targets, originally sixty-seven, had begun three years previously. The sheer size of the total anticipated acquisition price was staggering – approximately 250 billion dollars, of which, however, only approximately five percent was cash. The balance of the payment was in the form of common shares of the acquisition company. A condition precedent as to all acquisitions was the procurement of a minimum of twenty-five companies or divisions, with a service base of no less than 65 million customers or subscribers, by December 31 of that year.

She read with mounting excitement and perplexity. The introduction spelled everything out. Although there had been massive consolidation in the media industry, particularly in cable television, both satellite and Internet distribution systems provided a huge ongoing business opportunity. Significant economies of scale would result if enough different systems could be unified in a single structure. At least twenty-five companies were essential. Thirty-five stretched existing financial resources to the limit.

Acquisition of that number of systems was a practical possibility, she read. Fischer Communications Acquisition Company could afford to offer earnings multiples many times in excess of the value of the enterprises as private companies, because of (a) the additional value of scale, (b) plans to bring the acquisition company public within twelve months after completion of the acquisition, and (c) the technological value that VINUX would add. Pro forma financial...

(Adele stopped. *VINUX? What was that?* Obviously, an operating system of some sort, but she had never heard of it – a fact surprising in itself. She noted it for future reference and went on.)

...statements were referenced in the second file. She picked that up. Even with conservative assumptions, potential income and cash flow were staggering.

Because of the wide geographical spread and the absence of a coherent federal regulatory policy, FCC and Department of Justice problems were expected to be minimal. However, the newly organized system would constitute the largest single integrated population base of cable viewers/Internet users in the country. It would be able to negotiate directly with broadcast networks and pay-per-view services, possibly even influence program content. It could do its own production and program origination. It would also be able to influence strongly the development of HDTV; VINUX – there it was again – would enable it to offer massively expanded digital music and video, of superb quality, with ironclad copy protection, to anyone with an adequate receiver.

The next files contained evaluations of the other major cable operating companies and Internet service providers with which the new company would be competing, with detailed evaluations of the possibilities of alliance or takeover, hostile or not; an analysis of the present state of network television; a discussion of the threat of competition from the other major players; and an eleven-page conclusion.

Wow, she thought. The last file in the master folder consisted of a form acquisition contract, some 111 pages in length. She opened one carton and pulled out a file. It consisted entirely of notes and memoranda on the progress of one of the negotiations. She checked another; more of the same. Even from a comparatively small sample, it was apparent what Carolyn meant by a dog food commercial. The notes described false start after false start, one firm understanding after another unraveling, then re-knit. Some of the targets were divisions of public companies, whose management fretted about the effect of a major divestiture on stock valuation and public relations. Others were concerned they would be if word of their interest leaked out. Some prospects worried about regulation, others about deregulation, a few about reregulation. Endless wrangling had taken place about the inclusion of "most favorite acquisition" clauses, firmly rejected in all instances, out of the question in negotiations of this scope. Nine of the companies had withdrawn on that ground alone.

The problems presented by the cable television systems alone were staggering.. The targeted cable systems were spread across the entire 50 states, subject to a crazy quilt of state and municipal regulation. Some were considered public utilities. Others were regulated under one or more municipal ordinances. Some cities had a right of repurchase of the system if the management or ownership of the operating company changed significantly. Others had retained the right to cancel or modify the franchise in that eventuality. The problems had multiplied from the dozens into the hundreds, each one with its unique nuances, each one containing the potential of a messy, deal-breaking litigation. Adele shook her head almost in disbelief. *That anyone would even try this.* But try it someone had, and apparently solved each of the problems with a relentless, dogged persistence.

The progress notes were terse, occasionally humorous, always with an undertone of purposeful ruthlessness that was somewhat disconcerting. They were the writings of a money guy, not a financier. Of that she was all but certain. George an errand boy? It didn't seem to fit. She leafed briefly through the mass of paper, then carefully replaced the files in the cartons. There were only forty, though the log said forty-one. She contacted Carolyn's secretary, pointed out the omission, was told it would be remedied when she had time to do the Xeroxing. Adele shrugged mentally. One more accumulation of correspondence on one more negotiation couldn't make any difference.

Finally, she returned to the master set and skimmed the contract. No wonder all the other associates had wanted to work on this; it was an encyclopedia of acquisition and securities law, a crash course on the Deal and How to Do It. She felt a little surge of pleasure. She was going to learn a new skill. There was certainly no harm in that.

But her misgivings, her bewilderment, outweighed the excitement. What on earth was she expected to *do*? Why had she been invited to sit at this particular table? For her decorative value? At least one of the players thought she had some. She had often discussed that issue, as to which the opinion of everyone she valued – fathers, brothers, male friends, girlfriends, her own – was unanimous. *It doesn't matter how you get through the door, it's what you do when you get there.* A rational enough thought in the abstract. Rather depressing in the concrete.

She had to do something. She would not permit herself to a free ride on anything. Work on the Project might do for an apprenticeship in corporate law, but she could never become expert in three weeks. The only possibility was finding out more about the technical background, VINUX in particular. The contract mentioned it; its implementation was one of the major conditions subsequent of the acquisition. If it weren't available or online within six months after the close of the deal, anyone who wanted had the right to rescind, unwind the transaction. The technical specifications were set out in an Exhibit D to the contract. She could barely parse them.

Oh well, she shrugged, closing the file. She made a note to call the president of the cable company that serviced her apartment building, sweet-talk him, get a crash course in how it all worked. VINUX? She'd do what she could. With that she returned the manila folders into the files and bound them up.

Now, finally, off to the library. It was time to get going on AI Squared, something on which she did know what was expected of her. She stopped as she rose from her chair.

It was all so strange, wasn't it? Six weeks ago she'd been spending her own money, prowling up and down the aisles of an obscure technology show, hoping against hope for a key to the future. The next day she met Tom; then AI Squared; now this. She could not escape the sense that somewhere out of sight a switch had been pulled that night, that large, invisible gears had been set in motion, that all of it – Tom, AI Squared, the ba – *pregnancy, damn it!* – now the Project, all of it – were parts of the same distant machinery, wheels within wheels turning someplace just out of sight. She felt a pervasive sense of distant menace, the same feeling she'd had when Jenet spoke about Tom – that a web was slowly dropping around her, no less genuine for all its ethereal, gossamer quality, a net no less a net for the fact that its parameters were unknown. Adele shivered slightly as she packed her briefcase. *Not a good feeling for a control freak,* she thought. *Not at all.*

Nonsense, she told herself firmly. *Knock it off, stupid.* She remembered a happier superstition as she moved towards the elevator. Good things, bad things, both come in threes. AI Squared, now the Project – she wondered what the third would be.

*

A welcome sight greeted her when she returned, a second delivery. The files from the Furston Press were stacked neatly on her desk in an accordion file of their own.

Her impulse was to burrow into them immediately. No. Smarter to clear the decks first. A few calls to return, a few notes for the files. She forced herself; when she finally set to work, the work would be unimpeded.

Now – that done – finally – to Tom's files.

There were five of them, one for each of the books he had published, one general file. The general one was the thickest; she opened that one first without any real expectations.

It proved to be the file that Jenet had had with her when Adele first heard his name – a bafflingly vague curriculum vitae, various trivial miscellany, copies of all the contracts Tom had signed with the Furston Press, some twenty-six in all over a five year period. Four covered his own books. Four had to do with work on screenplays. The others related to popular novels. The work he had undertaken had progressed rapidly from relatively simple editing tasks to major ghost writing.

She'd heard of all four films and, surprisingly, many of the novels. They were all mainstream entertainments, ranging from moderately to highly successful in the commercial sense. She had a vague recollection that one of the screenplays had been nominated for a Golden Globe or People's Choice Award. But none had any lasting artistic or literary value. Most of all, there was no insight into Tom to be gained here; the subjects were too eclectic, the tasks too diverse to shed any light on his own personality. He'd simply performed wordsmithing at a very high level of skill.

Sadness all at once – she hadn't read his poetry when Jenet had first mentioned his name, but now Adele understood what Jenet had meant. These projects were a complete waste of time for a man of his gifts; Rembrandt killing time doing postcards. It was a shame. Still, it gave her pleasure to go through the file to the end; each time she saw that scrawled signature with the arrow through the T her pulse quickened happily; she momentarily felt a little closer to him. She shook her head at herself as she closed it finally. *You've got it bad, moron.*

She went to the next one, the last in chronological order, the last volume published. This file also was not useful. There was the original manuscript in neat, word-processor form. The file contained a series of notes between Tom and the editors without much content. Not surprisingly, it was not possible to suggest many meaningful revisions of poems that were so well-wrought and densely coherent from the outset. Most of the correspondence dealt with the footnotes. Adele was also not surprised to learn that Tom had supplied all of them, even though they were attributed to the editor in the final published text. Jenet hadn't been exaggerating his reluctance to publish. It appeared he responded only after four or five requests. (*Why?*) There were also some internal memos between Jenet and the editors, a royalty contract, and a copy of an advance check, the latter typical of Jenet's generosity – Adele knew enough about the economics of bookselling to doubt that it would ever be fully recouped.

But of the stuff she was hoping to find, there was nothing – no discussion of dedications, no list of persons to whom author's copies should be sent, not the smallest crumb of personal information. She was no longer surprised.

The third and second volumes were more of the same. One note in particular caught her attention, about the poem to the nun:

Tom,

This is really a marvelous piece. I think it would be wonderful if you identified the dedicatee.

Bobbi

Roberta,

Thanks for the kind words, but I don't think so. What happened was traumatic both for me and my friend. She'll know who she is. That's enough.

T.

It was frustrating that that was all, but at least it was something – there had been a trauma of some kind. Tom did not use words imprecisely; something serious had happened. Was that when the nightmares had started? And the other horrible things? Was it the consequences thereof that he was hiding from?

She picked up the last file, the earliest, nearly seven years old, hoping that at least some of the answers could be found there. In addition to being the oldest, it was also the thickest. She opened it with some trepidation; if there was nothing here, this try, too, would have come to a dead end.

It made for interesting, pleasant reading, albeit with a little sadness now at seven years' distance. Most of it was interoffice correspondence between associate editors, senior editors, and (finally) Jenet. The sequence of events emerged vividly from the memos – the cursory review of a blind submission no different than thousands, even tens of thousands, the Press received every year, nearly all of them junk; the realization that this was different; the growing sense of wonder and excitement as the discovery was passed to ever higher levels of editorial authority until it reached Jenet. Tom's initial product had generated a contagious enthusiasm, even a sense of reborn purpose. It was this type of project for which the Furston Press had been created.

Oh no, she was suddenly thinking, *it can't be*. None of the documents contained any return address, any reference whatsoever to his whereabouts. He had evidently already been in the City by the time all this had begun in earnest. Back, back, back, further, further into the file she went, despair quietly stealing over her. She pushed the feeling back, biting her lower lip and plowing further back. It's got to be here. It's got to. Since it's got to, it is.

Finally, she reached the end – the original manuscript, neatly presented. There was no envelope or return address included. She leafed through them with an icy, stoic calmness; her thoughts were already turning to what she might do next.

The last document in the massive file was the cover letter that had accompanied the poems – handwritten, she noted with some surprise, and not by Tom. The script was right-handed and feminine. It read:

To whom it might concern:
The poems submitted herewith were written by Thomas Bryant Newcombe, a friend of mine. Although I may not be an unprejudiced judge, I think they are worthy of your attention. Any response to this letter should be returned to me.
Thank you for your consideration.
Sincerely,
Millicent Peters

The letter had the conventional heading for a business letter on the left side. The upper left hand corner was obscured by the sheer weight of the paper in front of it. Hoping against hope, she shoved the other contents of the file as far up as they would go. Thank God, thank God, there was something there. It read:

Box 1291
Student Union
Harpur College
Binghamton, New York

Binghamton. Harpur College. Student Union.

SUNY, State University of New York. He must have been a student there – and if he had been a student there, he must have filed an application, high school transcripts, the works.

"Yippee!" she shouted, completely elated, punching her right hand in the air the same way she did when she scored a goal in field hockey.

Breakthrough!

Try and stop me now.

DISCOVERIES

I t proved to be one of the shortest-lived elations of her entire life.

Everything started out well enough. She obtained the general switchboard number for SUNY at Binghamton, dialed the number, and was put through at once to the student records division.

"Did a student named Thomas Bryant Newcombe attend the University in the year 19--?" Adele asked.

"Just a minute," said the clerk. There was a brief delay. "I can confirm that a person by that name was enrolled here from 190- to 19--."

Great. "Can you tell me what home address he provided when he first enrolled? Or whom he wanted notified in case of an emergency?"

"I can't do that, madam," the answer came back, a feminine voice filled with schoolteacher primness. "I can't divulge any confidential information in a student's transcript without appropriate authorization from the student. I am only authorized to confirm enrolment."

"A residence address that's over ten years old would hardly be considered confidential, I should think."

"It's a matter of university regulations and Federal law, madam. I cannot release any such information without the consent of the student."

"Look," Adele said, "if I was in contact with the student, I wouldn't have had to call you. I don't need the street address. His hometown will do."

"I'm sorry, madam. Rules are rules."

"They obviously are," said Adele, and hung the receiver up abruptly. Immature, unfair, she knew, but her disappointment had turned to rage instantaneously.

Gradually her anger faded into frustration. Every occasion seemed to be informed against her. Once, when she was an undergrad, she had attended a performance given by a brilliant European mime on a Hurok tour of the United States. The most memorable pantomime he had performed was that of a man trapped in a glass cage who frees himself with great effort only to discover another, slightly larger glass cage right outside. Now she knew exactly how the character in that sketch felt at the moment he discovered the second cage.

However, there was no point in sitting here brooding over the senselessness of the world. It was necessary to get going again. *Think.* An idea struck her; she picked up the phone.

"Could I speak to Mr. Greenfield, please?" she asked his secretary. When Walt came on the line, she asked if he would have Bill Abercrombie phone her as soon as it was convenient.

Ten minutes later, the phone rang: "Ms. Jansen, what can I do for you today?"

"I found out where Mr. Newcombe went to college – SUNY at Binghamton – but they won't tell me anything about where he lived or anything like that. I want to get a copy of his student records as soon as I can. Can you tell me if that's possible? And how fast you could do it if it is?"

"First tell me how you found that out." She did and heard him grunt, making a mental note of the lead. "It's possible to retrieve that kind of information. I'll get back to you a little later in the afternoon. There's something else we'll have to discuss before I do anything."

The phone rang fifteen minutes later.

"Ms. Jansen? Bill Abercrombie. It's a piece of cake. A couple of years ago, the University transferred all of the old records from microfilm to a new digital system."

"I doubt if that part of the LAN is accessible from the Net."

"It isn't, but don't ask foolish questions. I can access it easily enough. The password's got to be on some electronic bulletin board somewhere, with all the hackers on campus, and records that old can't be sensitive enough for any really sophisticated protection. Once I'm in, I can have 'em printed out on a laser printer, so I can get you what you want." He paused. "But –"

"But what?"

"That's what I wanted to talk to you about. This time, what you want me to do is illegal," he said. "Not big-league stuff, because we're not planning to defraud anybody or steal anyone's identity - but very definitely illegal – a misdemeanor according to both federal and state law."

"Which we're conspiring to commit," she remarked, thinking aloud. "A Class E felony."

"Right."

"Does that bother you?" she asked.

"No," he answered. "I make my living beating this nickel-and-dime stuff. It's not too risky; with a good password, I'll be into the system and out without anyone even knowing. But I'm not a member of the New York bar. You might not want to take the chance."

Adele thought about it for a long, long moment. When she finally spoke, she spoke slowly and deliberately: "Thank you for the warning, but no. . . no. I meant what I said Friday. I can't let this stop me. It may not be legal, and I don't

like that, but this is more important than legal red tape. I'm sure that's true."
Just don't ask me why.

"All right, then. I'll go ahead. Unless there's some problem I can't foresee at the moment, I should have the file to you Wednesday afternoon at the latest."

Damn and double damn! She wondered if the lunch with Collishaw had cost her another day. "Thank you. I'll look forward to hearing from you," Adele said aloud, and they hung up.

She wondered again about herself. A law-abiding person – some of her friends thought excessively so – she'd just agreed to commit a genuine felony. And her only regret was a lost day.

*

"Congratulations," said Franklin Fischer the next morning, with an easy smile, surprising her. "Welcome aboard. Now you're one of us."

"Thank you," Adele answered. "I know these guys have a long way to go, but –"

"No, no," he said, smiling more broadly, dropping his voice. "I meant the other thing."

"Oh," she said, understanding. "Yes." The sheer scope of the Project continued to stagger her. In less than twenty-four hours, she'd been routed enough correspondence to fill another thick manila folder. Legal fees must amount to several hundred thousand dollars a month; travel expenses alone ran well into five figures. "I'm not at all sure what I'm supposed to contribute."

"I suppose only George knows the answer to that," he said, with the same smile, in the same low tones. "As far as I'm concerned, it's enough if you keep him happy." Anger surged through her. He took no notice. "Just so it happens," he continued, his eyes fixed on a distant point. "Just so it gets done."

"I understand," Adele replied, smiling fixedly. They were standing in the boardroom of Fischer's offices, the same room where she'd met Lem and the others five days before. Lem and Peter Steinitz were also there, chatting with Carolyn, Harry Greube, George Sorenson, and another man named Victor Podgorny ("Call me Vic"). Podgorny was the oldest person in the room, a short, cigar-smoking man in his mid-sixties whom Adele learned had played some part in the initial venture financing.

"Good," he answered, and moved towards the larger group. Adele stood alone, until George Sorenson edged away from the larger group.

"Hello again, dancing girl," he said.

"Hello," she answered coolly.

"What's the matter?" he said. "Everything O.K.?"

"I don't know," she answered, with a small private glare. "I guess you know I'm supposed to be working on the Project now. Carolyn told me it was your idea."

"Yeah?" he said. "So? I thought you'd like that."

"So I don't know what I'm supposed to do is 'so'. Mr. Fischer told me a minute ago it was enough if I kept you happy. Is that why you want me involved?"

"*Oh*," he said, understanding, turning to Franklin Fischer's back with his own glare. "No. Shit. No way. Let me explain it to you Monday night, when we have a little time. This isn't the place."

"I was reconsidering the whole idea of Monday night."

"Hey, look, Adele, don't do that," he answered. "Come with me. O.K.? I'll see you at a quarter to six. It'll be all right, I promise. Cut me a little slack, huh?"

She thought. A recollection of the dance they'd shared.

"All right," she said. "5:45."

"O.K., gentle people, shape up, we're wasting time," Franklin Fischer said suddenly, sharply. "We must begin." George Sorenson didn't react at all; Carolyn and Victor Podgorny immediately sat down; Lem, Harry Greube, and Peter showed approximately equal degrees of startled guilt. Adele felt a flash of irritation. It wasn't as if Fischer hadn't been socializing himself.

*

The board consisted of five members: Franklin, George, Victor Podgorny, and the two founders who were present, Lem Michaels and Peter Steinitz. Franklin Fischer was the chairman. Lem was the CEO; Peter vice-president of engineering. Adele had been mildly bothered the day before when she learned that the founders were not a majority of the board, but Harry Greube had assured her it was a perfectly ordinary structure in a venture capital financing of that type, normal contractual provision, standard operating procedure. Still.

Franklin Fischer called the meeting to order. Most of the business was routine –perfunctory resolutions ratifying the actions the officers had undertaken in the last few weeks to close the public offering, authorizing the issuance of certain shares of common stock, approving a stock option plan, and so forth. They all had been prepared by Harry Greube several days in advance of the meeting, and they were passed quickly and unanimously, without comment. Among them was one appointing the law firm of Hapgood, Thurlow, Davis, &

Anderson counsel to the corporation. Not exactly news, but nonetheless Adele felt a small frisson down her spine. Although she was not yet a partner, the company was hers now for all practical purposes. The way was finally clear. Out of the corner of her eye she saw Lem smile broadly at her and she couldn't help but smile back.

"I believe that completes the first order of business," Franklin Fischer said formally; he presided over the meeting with a gravity suitable for a meeting of the board of General Motors. "Thanks, Mr. Greube, for handling all the formalities so capably," and for a moment Adele liked him, too, the best of all chairmen in this best of all possible worlds. "Let's move to the business part of the meeting. Let's hear the reports from our executive officers."

*

It was not going well. In fact, it was going abysmally. After a baffling, irritating hour, Adele fully understood Lem's frustration, his anxiety. The sense of expectancy, of momentous happenings, that had been redolent in the hall where the Software Arts Expo was held, that she'd felt acutely when the program ran in this very room, the world renewing itself – all that was absent entirely today.

Every decision that Lem made – the important, the trivial equally – was called into question. Had he signed a commercial lease for offices in New Jersey? It was a matter of the gravest concern. Why had he not brought such a serious matter to the attention of the board? Because the space wasn't all that large, the rental not that great, the term was only for a year; it didn't seem that important. *Not important!* Significant looks were exchanged around the room.

Adele bit her lip. The item of highest urgency to Franklin Fischer and Victor Podgorny seemed to be the question of the rental per square foot of a temporarily vacant office in the suite. Bored and restless, she did some mental arithmetic. Based on the differential Podgorny was talking about ("I know the values there"), the board was expending its time and energy on a matter worth about $1,100 per annum. The collective fees of the three lawyers present were close to matching that on the time spent already. She looked around the room, unavoidably met Peter Steinitz's eye, and realized he had done the same calculation much earlier.

Then the board took up the question of officers' salaries ("You have to think of the public perception, Lem"), even though the three founders were paying themselves no more than two-thirds of what Hapgood paid Adele. After the salaries had been reluctantly approved came the question of ratification of the lease of certain computer equipment items. Now Franklin Fischer and Victor

Podgorny had a different concern. Was this all they needed? Mightn't development proceed faster if they had a DEC mainframe or a Cray? No, Lem explained patiently, the specified equipment was all they needed.

Throughout it all, Lem persisted admirably, the dreamer of dreams, attempting to convey the vision Adele had seen when the program ran. He failed utterly. Worse: Underlying everything was a quiet taunting, a subtle but definite bullying. The two of them ganged up; Franklin Fischer turned to Podgorny, Podgorny turned to Fischer, always in tandem. Adele became convinced that the decisions Lem made in truth didn't matter. If the offices Lem had rented had been less expensive, Franklin Fischer would have been concerned that the company wasn't presenting itself effectively. If the computers had been more expensive, Victor Podgorny would have suggested they could get by with less. All this really was, was an exercise in territoriality.

Another Glee Club, she thought suddenly. *Men in groups. Spare me.* Boredom and exasperation were congealing into anger. Lem Michaels might have been young and inexperienced, but he was the world shaker, not these middle-aged businessmen. What was the point of this hazing? She regretted that she had ever felt one second's liking for Franklin Fischer.

Relax, she tried to tell herself. *Two different tribes.* But something intervened from her subconscious. *Don't kid yourself, stupid. It's more than that. Something is wrong here. Something is very, very wrong.*

Nonsense, she told herself firmly, as Franklin Fischer launched into another condescending homily about business practice. Suddenly, in a place, at a time, where she least expected it, she found herself thinking of her lover. What would Tom see if he were here now? What things would lie open to him that lay hidden from her? And yet she was glad simultaneously that he was not present, that he had never seen and never would see this aspect of her life. Why would that be?

Foolish fool. Because you're a child is why. She straightened up and surveyed the room again. Harry Greube, the secretary, took notes. Carolyn seemed to enjoy watching the exercise of power by a man who was evidently more than a friend. (How did she rationalize her Friday night flings?) George had remained inscrutable the entire time, occasionally prompting the other two to move on, reminding them he had an afternoon flight. The one time his eyes met hers, he gave a slight, almost imperceptible shrug. She had hoped for a time that he'd intervene, but that was too much to ask. Right or wrong, Franklin Fischer was his partner, not Lem.

"I'd like to get to something that should really interest you," Lem said carefully. "We've finished the first draft of our five-year projections. I think you'll find some pretty exciting things."

"Why didn't you furnish this with the agenda?" Victor Podgorny asked as he leafed through it.

"We only got it done last night," Lem answered.

"Next time a little sooner," Podgorny grunted.

Adele found her own copy underneath the other materials. She perused it rapidly. A faint aura of the spring morning feeling returned. Pete and Chiang had made a small breakthrough in the coding. The program now operated perceptibly faster, though still not nearly fast enough. An offshore chip manufacturer had contacted Lem with the idea of negotiating a license for certain limited applications. Inquiries from mathematicians and computer experts were pouring in from all over the world. As she read, she could hear Lem, with the proficiency of a movie voiceover, explaining to Victor Podgorny and Franklin Fischer what all this implied, how far they'd already come.

She finished skimming at the same time he did talking. She looked up, expecting, hoping that some sort of breakthrough had occurred. *No.* Franklin Fischer had the amused smile of a benevolent, but worldly-wise grandfather, listening to the misplaced enthusiasm of a small child.

"Commendable goals, Lem," he said condescendingly. "A bit visionary – I do believe you're still spending most of the time in the ivory tower – but commendable."

Adele saw Lem's knuckles tighten on the table. "Mr. Fischer," he said slowly, "there's nothing visionary about this. All this is entirely practical. Long range, to be sure, but practical. Probable, in fact."

"Without a finished product?" Podgorny said. "Without a marketing plan? With only a concept?"

"Yes," said Lem. "The concept's that good."

Franklin Fischer's smile became even more patronizing. "I know what visions are, Lem. I have one of my own. We have no objection to daydreams – only that they be accompanied by some common sense. Sometimes you idealists with your castles in the air forget there's a real world. We're trying to help you mature faster. That's what this is all about."

Peter Steinitz looked around, furious, saw the same anger in Adele's face and turned back to the table. *Oh, no,* she thought, *I hope he doesn't think I was cuing... oh, God... he does.*

"Maturity? Who's kidding who? This hasn't been about the real world at all," Peter said, the first words he'd spoken at the meeting. "This has been a series of putdowns. All morning long."

"Pete," Lem said.

"Let me talk," Pete went on, shaking off Lem's hand, his voice rising. "You spent forty-five minutes talking about the amount of rent in a lease that's less in a year than the lawyers will charge us for the same forty-five minutes. That's the real world? You gabbed and gabbed about our salaries. You know damn well they're less than half what the big shops would pay us to knock down code on accounting packages. Then you worry about the computers leased, which you don't know anything about. And you couldn't or wouldn't understand the only important thing that Lem told you!" He looked around. "You guys are more interested in putting us in our place than listening to anything we say. Who's kidding who!?"

Right into their hands, Adele thought dismally. *Green as the grass.*

Franklin Fischer turned to Podgorny, the look of innocent concern on his face marred by a tinge of theatricality. "Vic, did you get that impression?"

"Not at all, Franklin," Podgorny answered firmly, shaking his head. "I didn't hear anything like that. I think you've been giving excellent advice to some young men who are badly in need of it."

"That's what I meant about maturity." Fischer turned back to the head of the table. "Perhaps you don't understand the function of a board of directors, Mr. Steinitz. The board should supervise –"

"Bullshit," Peter interrupted. "Cut the crap."

"You ungrateful little snot," Podgorny said. "We've made you rich."

Peter glared at him; Lem struggled for a reply. Things were coming rapidly unglued. Adele realized abruptly that the person who had the most to lose if everything fell apart was sitting in her seat.

"Gentlemen," she said lightly and easily. "Gentlemen." All heads turned to her. "Don't you think it's more a matter of two different styles? Two different tribes? I've been listening all morning, Pete. I'm sure no one meant any offense," she went on, deliberately hypocritical. "We can all understand why you're upset, but you did speak somewhat strongly."

"Good advice," George interjected.

"O.K.," Peter muttered, comprehending, after a moment. "I guess I was out of line. Sorry."

"Thank you," Franklin Fischer said formally. "What's the next item on the agenda? The question of copyright?" Her turn; she felt a quick surge of adrenaline.

George looked at his watch. "I'm sorry," he said, genuinely apologetic. "School's out. I've got to go."

"This is material that is better presented to the executives first in any case," Franklin Fischer remarked, glancing over the memorandum she'd circulated.

Adele swallowed her disappointment. She had looked forward to presenting it. "There are some pretty unorthodox suggestions in there," she said. "I think the board will find them interesting."

"Next time," George smiled. All around her the meeting was breaking up. Victor Podgorny had already packed his briefcase. He pulled out a cigar, looking from time to time at Lem and Peter, shaking his head, contempt written on his face. Franklin Fischer turned to chat with him.

Lem motioned Peter Steinitz, and the two of them stepped into the hall. Adele watched them depart. All at once, an enormous, intense foreboding swept over her, a genuine fear for Lem and Pete, in their earnestness, their innocence. *There is evil here. Those men are bad. They mean to do them harm.* She shook her head, but the feeling persisted. *Oh, do be serious, Jansen.* It was just a bad board meeting. Such things happen. Calm down. *It'll get better,* she told herself, and tried to believe it.

Then she stepped out into the hall.

*

She found the two of them, standing where she and Lem had talked five days before.

"*–can't* do that, for God's sake, Pete," Lem was whispering. "We have got to get along with these guys."

"He started it, Lem," Pete all but whined back. "All that captain of industry crap! He was baiting us from the start. Couldn't you see that?"

"I know he started it," said Lem, "but you can't let yourself react. It's the Golden Rule joke – he's got the gold, you know the rest."

"I know," Peter answered. "Maybe I should resign. Maybe Chiang should be on the board."

"No way," said Lem. "He's still too shy – and I need you, Pete. We're outnumbered as it is. What do you think?" he asked Adele suddenly, turning.

"I think you're both right," Adele said. "He was baiting you, Pete. But you can't let it get to you."

"She's right, guys," George said, coming up behind them. "Gotta get used to it. It's a heat-kitchen proposition. Comes with the territory." There was the same distance in his manner towards them that she'd noticed at the first meeting. "Be a good idea to make nice with him Monday night."

"Oh, yeah, right," Lem said. "There's this dinner Monday night, Adele. It's only for people who've done deals with CFS, not the sort of thing your boyfriend could take you to, so I was wondering –"

"She's going with me," George replied, before she could say anything, much more proprietorially than she would have liked. Lem appeared crestfallen.

"Lem, it's mostly business – the other deal Franklin Fischer's doing.

My boss is making me go," Adele explained, and now it was George's turn to look a little crestfallen, which also did not please her, but what in heaven's name could she *do*?

"O.K., Monday night, then," he waved, and then hurried down the hall. "Wait for me, guys," she asked, then stepped back into the boardroom to pick up her things. Lem, Pete, Carolyn, and Harry had taken their copies of her memorandum with them. George's was there on the table, with copious notes. Franklin's copy was open to the second page. Podgorny hadn't opened his.

"Nice going, Adele," Carolyn said. "Sometimes that goody two-shoes style of yours comes in handy. Did you ever see two bigger assholes? First meeting and they get into a fight with their backers." Harry Greube chuckled.

"I'd like to take them to lunch, Carolyn," Adele said. "I've got to go over the memo with them and they could use some cheering up."

"Sure," Carolyn shrugged.

George came rushing in. "Forgot your thing," he said as he went by. He picked it up, then stopped.

"Boyfriend?" he asked, eyebrow raised.

Oh, what a tangled web we weave

*

"It's not simply business," Lem said disconsolately. "You like him."

"Yes," she said, after a moment. They were alone at the table; Peter Steinitz had gone to the bathroom.

"I don't understand. He must be fifteen years older than you, he's not –"

"I don't want to discuss it," she said.

"What does Tom say? I mean, he can't be too happy that –"

"I *don't* want to discuss it, Lem," she said, annoyed with him, because she didn't want to be firm with him, but he'd forced her to. He subsided, looked away. Very, very gently she touched his arm.

"It doesn't happen with everyone."

"For some people, it doesn't happen with anyone," and she bit her lip. He had not the slightest idea of how to court her. She had lost all interest in him at the personal level. She had never had any use for men who traded on their vulnerability – and he had no sense of how dangerous vulnerability could be in the City. Green as the grass. *Grow up, Lem,* she implored silently. *Soon.*

"While Pete's away," he said, mercifully moving on, "what did you think? You saw what I was talking about the other day. Why all the hostility? If he doesn't understand what we're doing, why'd he buy in?" He was so much more attractive when he presented himself in this way, rather than with his heart on his sleeve. She hoped he'd learn that, too, soon.

She'd expected the question, had prepared her answer. "I don't think you have anything to worry about," she said. "I'll tell you the truth. I didn't at all care for the way Fischer and Podgorny behaved. I don't think they'll ever understand the technology, but I think they will understand the business opportunity. I think it will work out." She prayed she was right.

"Maybe," Lem answered. Just then Peter Steinitz returned to the table.

She performed then as she knew how: light, graceful, amusing. Peter perked up at once. Together, they pulled Lem out of the glums. The lunch became a solid working lunch, but also funny, hilarious, at times even raucous. Gradually the vision returned and filled the booth, a sense of new worlds being born. Together they worked and laughed, three young people playing in the first light of a new age, indifferent to the gray, somber clouds outside.

Adele did not return to the office until 3:00. When she did, she found a thick package from Bill Abercrombie in the middle of her desk.

✳ ✳ ✳

EXPLORATIONS

A dele had restrained her impatience until after the workday was over. If she had opened it at the office, she doubted that she would have recorded any more billable time. Given the secrecy with which it had been obtained, it was highly unlikely that there was anything she could do during working hours anyway. But now it was 7:30, she was home, changed, fed, and showered, and there was no longer reason for restraint. She sat down at the small desk in her bedroom and turned on the light. The apartment was silent. Joan, as usual, was elsewhere.

Abercrombie had done it the way he had promised. The pages consisted of a clean, crisp, printed text, even the handwriting clear (if not necessarily legible). There were a surprising number of pages in the folder, more than 50, a good sign. Tom's transcript, the bloodless, unadorned record of fundamental aspirations and accomplishments in those years, was on top, followed by a number of letters from various members of the faculty. Even at a glance, it was clear they were more than a little unusual. But a glance was all she spared for now. It was the material at the back of the file that she craved, the high school transcript, references, everything else that would be in a normal college application. It might itself contain the solution to the mystery of Thomas Bryant Newcombe. If not, it must, it had to, point the way to the place where the ultimate answers could be found.

A document marked "APPLICATION," the laser printer's rendering of what had once been a manila envelope, at the very rear of the folder. The next few pages were the core. She flipped the page back.

There was no transcript. There were no references, no application, not one thing she had expected. His application had consisted of only three items. The first was a GED. The second was the computer record of his SAT scores. The third was a letter. The letter read:

Herbert Reinfeld
Director of Admissions
Harpur College, SUNY, Binghamton

Dear Herb;

Enclosed are the SAT scores and GED of Thomas B. Newcombe, the young man I mentioned to you. I want to thank you for the confidence you have reposed in me. I am truly sorry to have had been so mysterious; there will come a day, I trust, when professional confidentiality will not be such an obstacle to open communication - and when that time comes you will be the first in whom I confide. This is an extraordinary applicant and an extraordinary story, and thanks to you we have both become a part of it.

In the meantime, I hope these test scores give you some reassurance that my former student knows whereof she speaks, and that we haven't all taken leave of our senses. I daresay that most of the Ivies would take a chance on this boy on the scores alone. If I could impart to you today the information I someday will, relative to the circumstances under which Mr. Newcombe attained this level of achievement, you would realize how truly remarkable the achievement actually is.

Finally, I will reconfirm no financial aid application will be made at this time. There are sufficient resources elsewhere.

Once again, thanks for the effort and the trust.

Sincerely,

Dr. James A. Lambeth

Professor, Clinical Psychology

And that was all.

*

Her fist came down on her desk with all her strength. The quiet room reverberated from the force. It *couldn't* be, it simply couldn't *be*. She read it again, but that was indeed all – the test score, the GED, and the letter. For a few moments, the riot of emotion – mingled disappointment, anger, frustration, even the smallest dollop of fear – was so intense that it disabled all her thinking processes. Gradually, with an effort that by this time had become all too familiar, she reined herself in.

Who is this guy? she asked herself.

The more she learned about Tom, the darker the mystery became. *Caves within caves,* Jenet had said. Nonetheless, the evening had only begun and there was a lot that could be done. She began by rereading Lambeth's letter. Not much there – the good professor could give lessons to almost anyone with respect to maintaining professional privilege. "Extraordinary circumstances" – but he hadn't said whether they were extraordinarily comic or tragic, or even if the circumstances were Tom's or someone else's. *Very good, Professor, God damn your eyes.*

Even so, there were a few things to be gleaned. He'd used the female pronoun. Therefore, the former student was a woman, a psychologist, and young, if still in communication with her professor. An extraordinary story that could not be fully told because of a professional relationship, sufficient money somehow – that last really surprised her, everything about Tom bespoke impoverished circumstances. Besides – the question suddenly struck her – how had he become as financially invisible since then as Abercrombie had found him? Above all, achievement under remarkable circumstances.

However, any deduction beyond the bare bones was hopeless. Based on the Tom she had encountered five weeks before, it was a fairly good inference that the person whose privacy Lambeth had so assiduously protected was Tom himself. But that was hardly a certainty. It might be a parent, near relative, distant relative, teacher, even a friend or Lambeth's student. A probability, yes, but no conclusion possible. *Damn.*

She spared a glance at the SAT scores – superb, as she would have expected – then took a long look at the letter. *Information relative to the circumstances under which Mr. Newcombe obtained that level of achievement.* She reread the words, pondered them. *How truly remarkable it is.*

Then the insight struck her. *Of course, silly.* Professor Lambeth could not have been referring to positive or even neutral circumstances. An upbeat background wouldn't be significant relative to that kind of performance on the boards. The circumstances had to be adverse, so adverse, in fact, that the adversity probably had some relation to the absence of a transcript. For a moment – only an instant – she had an intuition so acute that it was almost visual, the certainty that she had caught a glimpse of it, the monster in the cave, red obelisk eyes glowering back at her from the darkness. Then the image faded. She tried to shake the thought, did not entirely succeed.

The file was still open to Lambeth's letter. Was there anything more to be gained here? No. She sighed, opened the folder back to the first page, and went to work. The first thing to check was the address he'd given, at the beginning of the document; and check she did, expecting nothing. She was not disappointed. It was an apartment address in Binghamton, clearly useless at this distance in time.

The transcript was four pages long, one page each for freshman year through senior. She glanced through it once, then turned back again to the beginning and began to pore over it.

There was no discernible direction of study, let alone an identifiable major. Most of the courses Tom had taken were either in foreign languages and literature, or mathematical theory – no surprise there. There was also a smattering of survey classes in the physical sciences, and a fair sampling of history of all kinds. He'd taken nothing related to English literature (a big surprise), philosophy, or the social sciences. He'd stayed on campus all three summers. He must have accumulated much more coursework than he needed in order to graduate.

The first odd thing she noticed was his grades. There were only two kinds – A's and incompletes, mixed in relatively equal proportions from his freshman year on. The incompletes all had an asterisk beside them. The footnote to which the asterisks referred was at the end of the transcript. It read:

* - *altered to passing grade by vote of Academic Senate, 5/22/--*

There was a double asterisk right below that. The note read:

** - *diploma as Bachelor of Arts, major defined as comparative literature, awarded by vote of Academic Senate, 5/22/- -*

She looked, found the double asterisk on the first page of the transcript, in the box that indicated whether he had graduated.

Curiouser and curiouser. Some of the incompletes had been more than three years old when they were altered to passing marks. She was also certain that the faculty of Harpur College did not award degrees in such an unorthodox manner every day of the week. It was even more unusual than the initial application.

The record of his progress was also strange. He'd taken elementary classes in three languages – French, German, and Russian – and then advanced classes in the literature of each. But if she understood the numbering system correctly, he had never enrolled in any of the intermediate courses. He had gone straight from the most elementary level to the most advanced. Even more impressive, when he was a junior, he'd enrolled directly into a graduate survey course on Italian literature. There was no indication whatsoever in the transcript that he had ever studied that language formally.

(A minor mystery suddenly struck her. *How many languages do you speak?* she'd asked that night. *Two,* he'd replied. English was obviously one of them. But it seemed as if he'd given all languages he studied the same amount of attention. All right then, which one was the second?)

The same pattern held true for the academic work he'd done in mathematics. After completing the barest prerequisites, he'd apparently enrolled in whatever courses interested him without regard to how they fit together. Very little was practical, computational stuff. It appeared he'd headed from the start towards the deepest swamps of theory – set theory, games theory, number theory, an upper level seminar on symbolic logic, a graduate survey of modal logic. The objective difficulty of the class work had made little or no impression on him. The mix of A's and incompletes seemed to be utterly random, regardless of a given course's difficulty.

Preliminary conclusions danced in her mind, tempting her to jump. But the time for analyzing all this would come later; right now, there was still much more data to acquire. She turned the page back and moved on.

A page of typewritten notes followed on a transcript page marked "Miscellaneous," evidently summarized from other files by someone in the registrar's office. His academic counselor all four years had been an associate professor named John Goodson. Tom had not been involved in any extracurricular activities of any kind in any year. He'd never joined a fraternity. There were no disciplinary proceedings of any kind.

As a freshman, he had been excused from a prepaid contract involving room and board in a campus dormitory only three weeks into the first semester. He evidently lived off campus from that time on. Also as a freshman, he had won first prize in a college playwriting contest, then declined it for some reason not set forth in the brief note. At the beginning of the second semester of his sophomore year, he'd sought alcohol counseling and treatment and completed a program designed for undergraduates with a dependency problem. Adele felt a quick, sharp pang as she read that.

I don't drink when I'm not drinking, he'd said. The pain in his eyes that night; something for which he'd sought help when he was only nineteen. Evidently, it hadn't worked out.

In his junior year, he'd been nominated for Phi Beta Kappa, but rejected, probably – she guessed – because of all the incompletes. Not a big deal, anyway – her own key had never opened any special doors for her. At the beginning of his senior year, he'd re-enrolled in the student alcohol program and completed it again. (Another quick pang.) In April of that last year, he'd been admitted to the infirmary for three days. There was nothing else.

Interesting, all of it. Now she turned to the letters at which she had glanced so casually the first time through. There were twenty-one of them. The first one was typical. Handwritten, it read:

Harpur College
Binghamton, New York
May 26, 19--
To whom it may concern:

> *I am confident that this letter is being read by either the executioner or the biographer of Thomas B. Newcombe. In either case, the circumstances under which he left the University will already be known to you and I will not recount them here. My purpose is simply to document the reality of his academic achievements in light of the unusual circumstances under which his*

degree was awarded. To put the matter succinctly in so many words, in plain fact Mr. Newcombe was the most gifted student of language I have encountered in over fifty years of study and teaching. He is the only human being I have ever met for whom the concept 'second language' had neither meaning nor application.

This alone should suffice; however, since I am certain many of my colleagues will comment on the character of Mr. Newcombe, I will add my own opinion. Despite everything, I remain convinced of the essential integrity of Thomas, indeed of the underlying beauty of his character. There is much that needs to be explained, but I am certain adequate explanations exist. I must in truth confess that these last are statements of faith, not fact, but in making them I am also fully aware of the risk I face of the ridicule of posterity as personified by you, my reader. Nonetheless, I consider myself still his friend as well as professor, and I hope that whoever is reading this letter is reading it in the same spirit.

Sincerely,

Stefan A. Riesenberg
Professor, German Literature

*

My God, thought Adele. *What's going on?* In spite of herself, the last paragraph had produced a lump in her throat. A nice person, this Riesenberg, whatever else he might be.

The ones that followed were similar. They were all from faculty members. They were all addressed to the file itself; "to whom it may concern" or the like. They were all quick to praise his academic ability in phrases such as "extraordinarily gifted," "unique in my experience," "unprecedented intuitive grasp," and others of the same type – and they were all either silent, puzzled, or condemnatory about the human being who was Thomas Newcombe. The kinder ones said nothing or admitted how little they actually knew of him. The harsher ones were unreserved. Three of those writers mentioned an incident involving someone named Peters:

Harpur College
State University of New York
Binghamton, New York
5/28/19--
To whom it may concern;

In accordance with the conditions of the resolution of the Academic Senate, I am adding this letter to the transcript of Thomas B. Newcombe. I will confirm the truth that he was one of the most gifted students of mathematical logic I have ever taught. While his analytical abilities were exceptional, I have had others as adept. However, in his intuitive grasp of systemic proofs, he stands without peer in my experience. For this reason, in the interests of justice, I concurred in the Senate resolutions of 5/22.

However, also in the interests of justice, I must record my personal opinion that Mr. Newcombe is in fact a cold, calculating psychopath as cunning as he is intelligent. The Peters incident was only the most public of many that have been rumored. (It is not beyond the realm of possibility that this entire denouement, concluding with the vote of the Senate, is the result of Mr. Newcombe's conscious manipulation.) He has not been a useful addition to this academic community and I personally view his departure as a blessing. For this reason, I do not include any personal reference.

Very truly yours,

Richard Aherne
Assistant Professor, Mathematics

*

Pompous ass, she thought, then had to smile at herself. On the subject of Tom, something inside her took no prisoners. Any enemy of his automatically became an enemy of hers; no applications for clemency accepted. Aherne in reality was probably a sensible person, undoubtedly more so than she at this point in time.

That was the last of the letters. She was back at the end, with the application. She had been through everything. It was time to begin taking stock.

*

She rose from the chair, walked slowly into her kitchen, poured herself a glass of milk, and then sat down on the couch in the living room. What on earth to make of all this? What could anyone make of it?

Begin with the obvious. That was no ordinary transcript. There probably had never been another one like it in the history of the State University system, maybe in the entire country. No question that Tom had left a mark at Harpur College – all the incompletes, the jumps to upper division work, the strange method by which the degree was granted, the letters – taken all for all, the whole story had to be unique.

She sipped the milk more slowly. Despite her disappointment about the absence of hard biographical information there, some tentative conclusions could be drawn. She had the strong impression that Tom at eighteen was as mysterious a person as he was ten years later – striking in a way, unforgettable, but then as now extraordinarily (almost unnaturally) private. Some of the faculty members, most notably Riesenberg, had evidently liked him quite a bit. Others had detested him. But none had indicated that he or she really had known him.

Mysterious in exactly the same way then was now? For precisely the same reasons? It seemed likely, but she was not yet ready to come to any definite conclusion.

Three of the letters had mentioned an incident, evidently a scandal, involving someone named Peters. Others had alluded to it. Even Riesenberg, who offered him friendship, had begun the sentence *"Despite everything"* and worried about the ridicule of posterity. *Peters, Peters* – the name had come up before in this. She closed her eyes and concentrated, going back over the territory she had covered in the last few days.

Of course, Millicent Peters, the girl who had submitted the poems to the Furston Press – in November of 19--, come to think of it, a few months after the votes of the Academic Senate. A fairly good inference that she was the Peters, then. But how? Why? The letter she'd included was so sweet, almost loving (a spasm of irrational jealousy) – what could have happened? Did he abuse her publicly or do something else equally reprehensible? Adele couldn't imagine Tom becoming actively angry or openly abusing anyone. Even Aherne, the pompous ass, who disliked him as much as anyone, called him "cold" and "cunning," as if he had done whatever he did by stealth. More than that, the cover letter from Millicent Peters was dated five months after the Senate resolution – in November of the next academic year. What sort of young woman would have submitted the poems after a major public incident? If all had been forgiven, why wasn't there some mention in the file?

Maybe the occurrence had something to do with alcohol. Not likely – if faculty members took offense at every silly thing done by undergraduates while they were under the influence, the good professors would do nothing all day long but take offense. Besides, even Georgia Richmond said he never got raucous even when he was – drunk. She consciously abandoned the line of thought. Insufficient data to go further – for now, it would remain a mystery.

Another sip of milk as she pulled her feet up underneath her. She glanced at the clock – only 8:45; she had used her time efficiently tonight. There was no question at all in her mind as to what she had to do next, and plenty of time left this very evening to begin doing it. She swigged down the milk.

The area code for Binghamton was 607. Was there a James or J. Lambeth listed in the city or the immediate environs? Yes, there was, one only. She memorized the number as the recording played, disconnected, then paused for a moment to collect herself and think of something. It was necessary to do this with a little discretion. Abercrombie's warning was uppermost in her mind. She did not want Lambeth to wonder whether she had obtained his name from a confidential file.

The phone rang twice. "Hello?" said an adult male voice.

"Hello, my name is Adele Jansen. Is this Professor Lambeth? Professor James A. Lambeth?"

The voice hesitated. "Well, I am James A. Lambeth, but I'm a junior and not a professor. I think you're asking for my father. But he's been dead nearly five years now."

"Oh," said Adele, "I'm sorry," entirely truthfully for more reasons than one.

"Why did you want to speak to my father?"

Her heart sinking, she recited the legend that she had decided upon. She was an attorney retained by the Furston Press. One of its authors was working on a book of case studies of bright children with unusual backgrounds. The name of Professor Lambeth had come up in that context, and she had been assigned to do the preliminary legwork because of the subtle issues of legal privilege involved.

Lambeth did not question the story and seemed sympathetic, but quickly confirmed her worst suspicions. His father had said little to his family about his practice, and his private papers had long since been destroyed. There was no way he or anyone in his family could really help. She thanked him and hung up.

Damn. Another surge of frustration; every time, *every time*, the obvious avenue was blocked. There was never an easy path. Only one try left – for this evening, anyway. She phoned information again, obtained the number, and punched it in.

"Hello?" A child's voice.

"Hello. Could I speak to your father?"

The child dropped the receiver without another word. The patter of feet, the sound of voices in another room. Then a man came onto the line. "Yes?"

"Professor Goodson? My name is Adele Jansen. I'm a lawyer in New York. I'm trying to locate a student whose academic counselor you were about ten years ago. I hope you'll understand if I can't be any more specific than that. There's professional discretion involved."

"Of course," said the voice, though sounding a bit puzzled. "But I doubt I can be of any help. I must have acted as counselor to hundreds of kids over the years. Most of them I barely remember, if that. How did you get my name?"

"He's mentioned you on occasion."

"Oh? What's his name?"

"Newcombe. Thomas Bryant Newcombe."

There was a noticeable hesitation, then a short, low laugh. "Well, well, well. Ms. Jansen, you would mention the rule proving exception. The absolute, all-time, rule-proving exception." He laughed again.

"Of course I remember Tom. Nobody, but nobody, forgets Tom Newcombe."

*

She set up an appointment with him. This was someone she definitely wanted to meet face-to-face. What with one thing and another on Goodson's schedule, the earliest possible time was Saturday morning at his office. They agreed to meet at 10:30 a.m.

Adele went back into her room, closed the folder, and carefully put it into her treasure drawer. It was not yet 9:30, but she was exhausted, already ready for bed. It occurred to her that she was beginning to become very, very weary. All her life she had been blessed with superabundant energy, but now, what with the demands of her normal office routine, the constant emotional turmoil, the difficulty sleeping, and the changes that were beginning to occur in her body, she seemed to be running short.

She slipped a flannel nightgown over her head. A sudden thought, a smile; one glimpse of her in that and George Sorenson as well as Lem Michaels would almost certainly look elsewhere. Then she turned out the overhead light.

She realized at once she was not going straight to sleep, as tired as she was. The same ruminations as every night, the same unavoidable thoughts, relentless, unresolvable speculation about the nature of her unborn, never-to-be-born child and the real identity of his or her – *its, damn it!* – father, a twin haunting, an inescapable infliction of self.

This evening she had made two phone calls, either of which could provide demonstrable proof that she was guilty of a serious misdemeanor. But her only regret as sleep finally began to descend was the four days that had to pass before she could meet Goodson. Another four days wasted – Saturday would be only two weeks before the appointment Alice Marshall had made for her – and NATPE filling the week before that. Meanwhile, the days were becoming perceptibly darker, it was still a long time till the winter solstice, and time was racing faster now, truly beginning to fly.

Joseph Wurtenbaugh

SCHOOL DAYS

The city of Binghamton lies about 150 miles due west of New York City. These days it is still a pretty drive, but it has changed. Once, not long ago, the hills en route rose wild and there were deep woods which no axe had ever cut. Now little is rural and too much is blighted. It was the sort of trip that made Adele wistful for times and places that had disappeared generations before she had been born. The world was filling in now so quickly, much, much too quickly. Everyone wanted what she wanted. So little was left. The great forest has all but disappeared here. It vanished from Europe three centuries ago. It will be gone in another century from Asia and the southern hemisphere. A mercy that she wouldn't be there to see it.

The day was grey, in an odd, diffuse way, without the crisp cold edge that presages winter – more strange, unseasonable weather. The trees were blazing with autumnal glory, but with the definite feeling that this was the last show before the curtain. She had picked up the rental car on the outskirts of the City. Once free of the metropolis, the trip went easily and she was alone with her thoughts.

After some of the ugliness she had passed, the campus of SUNY at Binghamton came as an exceedingly pleasant surprise. It was large, several hundred acres, the countryside around it lovely. A surprising amount of surface water, a large pond, even a game preserve – altogether a treasure. The only negative was the tasteless functionality of the buildings, a major, glaring architectural mistake. Adele felt a surge of false melancholy. She had strongly considered Harpur College off the catalogue, been accepted, might have attended if it hadn't been farther away than she wanted to travel, what with the family situation, the money problems, the rest. Everything would have been different if she'd come here, wouldn't it? It wasn't so much regret for the actual reality that had in fact become her history as a brief mourning for all the potential pasts ineluctably lost.

The university itself was one of those secrets of American higher education that for some reason, year after year, remain well-kept. One of the crown jewels of the SUNY system, it prided itself on providing a public alternative to the Ivy League and Sister Seven schools and could legitimately claim to have succeeded in the main. Yet it remained almost unknown outside of

New York State.

It was 10:05 before she found the central administration building. She took a second to shift the car seat back as far as it would go. Another one of her thousand little tricks; any creep who came prowling around in search of a victim would get the impression that a large male had been driving the car, rather than a small woman. That kind of world.

*

Goodson's office was on the second floor of one of those overly utilitarian buildings. The door was half-open.

There was a moment of indecision; she felt a surprising hesitancy toward knocking and identifying herself. So far, everything she had learned about Tom had either been unsettling or unpleasant. Perhaps when she was finished with this meeting she would find that the storm which had engulfed her little boat three weeks before had become even fiercer. But there was too much distance traveled, too much further still to go, to hesitate for long. She forced herself to knock on the door. "Professor Goodson?" The door swung open on the second knock.

It revealed a scene totally out of keeping with the austere efficiency of the building. Books, papers, boxes of papers, boxes of books, boxes of boxes were stacked in apparently random piles around the room. Two eight-foot bookshelves stood on either side of the room, filled to overflowing. A number of children's drawings were taped to the top shelf of each bookcase, a charming incongruity. In the center of the room was a large desk, also overflowing. The desk, in fact, seemed to be the fountainhead of the clutter, the source of the paper Nile. Behind the desk, a man was slowly standing from an upholstered swivel chair, extending his hand.

"You'd be Adele Jansen?" asked Professor Goodson. His voice was crisp, syllables clipped, neat, totally at variance with the decor of the room.

"Indeed I would, professor. Thank you for seeing me." Goodson was about five foot ten, thinning hair, a slender man in his mid-fifties, dressed today in corduroy trousers and a patched cardigan sweater. He might be in the mainstream now, but she doubted he'd been there forever. She'd have bet money he'd been sunburnt at Woodstock or the like. His smile seemed genuine. His eyes were definitely curious.

"I'm John Goodson. You can spare me the professor," he said. They shook hands and both sat down. For a moment, neither could meet the other's eye – the normal awkwardness of two strangers about to discuss a third person whom both know intimately in different ways.

"Well, you want to talk about Tom Newcombe," he said at last. "What do you want to know?"

She smiled, resisting the temptation to answer, *everything*. "I guess I'd start where you did, profes– Mr. Goodson. You said on the phone that he was the rule-proving exception, that he was unforgettable in some way. What did you mean?"

He smiled in turn, opened his mouth, stopped, then tapped his fingers on the desk in the way a pipe-smoker empties a pipe. His head turned towards the window. "It's not easy to answer that question," he said, almost to himself. Suddenly he seemed much older; the room seemed larger. This was not to be talk of small stuff. He went on, in the manner of a person speaking of long ago times, faraway lands, distant, bittersweet memories. His voice took on a singsong quality:

"All I can tell you is that I've known for a long time that people were going to come to talk to me about Tom. You're either the first or second, depends on how you count, but there are going to be others. I was always sure of that. I didn't know whether it would be because of his past or his future, because of his accomplishments or his crimes, because of his talents or his demons. I didn't know – still don't –" he smiled – "exactly what you'd want to know about him. But I was certain that people would come. I've never felt that way about any other student. I doubt I'll ever think that about another. But Tom –" here his hands fluttered up towards his head, an uncanny resemblance to Jenet's gesture of helplessness on the day Adele had asked Jenet why Tom didn't publish his own work – "what can you say?"

He continued in his own way. She tried to interrupt him as infrequently as possible, because he was, as it happened, telling her everything.

*

"He didn't make a particularly overwhelming first impression. In fact, I can't remember the first time I met him. He sure as hell didn't stand out in the crowd of freshmen."

Goodson shifted around. "The play was the thing, the first time I remember hearing about him – the play. The artsy-craftsy crowd over at Purchase runs this little competition for one-act plays every spring. It's open to the whole University system, but they take a little pride over there that someone at Purchase usually wins – usually a graduate student. So it made more than a little ripple when one of our people walked off with first prize – and when it turned out to be a freshman, it was big news, at least around here. It turned out to be one of my group. That's the first time I remember hearing Tom's name."

"What was the play about?" Adele asked.

Goodson was shaking his head. "I got a hold of a copy. I still have it. It was one of those ideas that are so obvious you wonder why no one ever thought of it before. What he'd done was dramatize that dream that everyone has – you know, that you've forgotten a class, or didn't buy the book and now it's time for the final and you're not ready? In his version, the hero oversleeps and knows he's running way late, that he's got to get to the exam. But he can't get started. He keeps meeting people, all kinds, that interrupt him and delay him. He never does get out the door. He calls the professor, but that makes it even worse. Finally, at the end, he realizes that they were all manifestations of his own Self, different aspects of his own being, that it wasn't meant to be, that the problem was some inner flaw in himself all along."

"It sounds like something Kafka wrote."

His eyes widened with acknowledgment. "Yes, a vignette in *The Castle*. Only" – he whispered conspiratorially – "don't quote me on this or anything, but I think Tom did it a lot better. It all sounded pretty grim just now, didn't it? But it was a comedy. The dialog was very funny, and it was all fresh and natural. Each new visitor was a big surprise. The professor starts to call him back with his own comments on the visitors. It was funny as hell. It seemed clever as the dickens even on those terms."

"Seemed?"

He nodded. "Yes –'seemed'. I haven't told you the half. Let me skip ahead. A couple of years after Tom left, I got to talking about it, I don't know why, at a dinner party Katie and I were throwing. One of our guests became curious and I loaned my copy to him. The next night he phoned me in a fever. It seems that underneath it all, what the play really was, was a commentary on certain sections of Calvin's *Institutes of the Christian Religion*. Tom had shaken up the order of the argument and done some other things to conceal the point, but it was all there – all anyone had to do was compare it with the original."

Goodson was shaking his head. "And, this guy says, there are other things – parodies on Augustine and all the other Christian theologians who theorized about predestination. In fact, that's what Tom called the play – *Predestination*. I suppose that should have given us all a clue. Our guest –"

"What?" said Adele. "What did you say was the title?"

"*Predestination* – a really charming thought, that God, for reasons of his own, has created some souls expressly for hell – that they're bound there no matter what they do. Those were the sections of the *Institutes* the play referenced. I didn't know much about it at the time, but rest assured, I found out in the next few weeks. I got curious –" he suddenly smiled – "I wonder how many of the people who watch that watered down Calvinism they preach on

Sunday mornings know they're saying amen to infant damnation."

"Go on," said Adele, still taking it in. *Oh, yes*, he'd said, standing in front of the Van Eyck hell. *I forgot that one. Destiny. Predestination.*

"At any rate, our guest wanted to meet him as soon as he could, but that wasn't possible, of course. Tom was long, long gone. Still, the whole thing was the quintessence of Tom."

"Why? That the play was that good, that subtle?"

The pipe cleaning gesture again. "Well. . . it's very good, but also very much the work of an eighteen-year-old boy. I don't mean to overdo it. But what I meant was that he hadn't said anything about that aspect of it. All he'd had to have done is write a cover letter, or even a footnote, and they'd have gone off like Roman candles over at Purchase, maybe even in New York. He knew that. He must have. But he didn't bother, or he didn't want to, or – or" – the hands fluttered up again – "I don't know.

"And, for that matter, what's an eighteen-year-old boy doing all boned up on that obscene junk? Infant damnation? I mean, Calvin? Augustine? Who reads that stuff outside of graduate school, for Christ's sake? But of course I didn't wonder about it at the time I first met him. I didn't know."

He stood up suddenly and stepped to the left book case. "Here, I'll show you something." He pulled out a book and handed it to her. "Read the dedication on the flyleaf."

It was Tom's fourth volume of poetry; she didn't know why it should have surprised her that Goodson owned a copy, but it did. The dedication read:

To Professor Goodson, my mentor – the least Calvinistic man I know – with apologies for all the frustration

T.

She handed it back. "Did he give this to you?"

"It arrived in the mail about three years ago. No return address. Of course, I already owned a copy. You may not have known it, but Tom's a very popular writer around here. The math guys are really into it." He looked down at the dedication. "He'd guessed by that time someone would have clued me in to the second meaning in the play so he let me in on the joke. As for the rest –" his voice became very soft, very gentle – "I only wish I had been his mentor, or someone else was, and he didn't owe me an apology for that or anything." He turned to replace the book, but not before she could see that his eyes had moistened. Adele felt an empathetic lump in her throat.

"Why has he stopped writing verse?" Goodson asked suddenly, tapping the book. "This stuff is fabulous."

"I don't know," Adele said. The room became silent.

It was a moment before he spoke again: "Well. Onward and upward. Then he made more news by declining the prize. It turned out he hadn't entered the play. An assistant in a writing seminar had done it for him – and Tom hadn't known when he entered it that the winners would be produced – it's a condition of the contest – you wouldn't think that would bother anybody, but he pulled it. Don't ask me why."

Goodson shifted again in his chair. "By this time, it was late spring, I was beginning to hear his name a lot from other faculty. You know, it's not easy for a freshman to make an impression around here, no matter how bright he is. The lower division classes are large, the kids are smart and awfully intense. But that year everyone seemed to be talking about Tom Newcombe and asking me questions since I'm supposedly his academic counselor. That was embarrassing because I couldn't remember meeting him. I dropped him a note and asked him to come around. I had reason enough to talk to him. I'd taken a look at his class schedule and it was a complete mishmash; math and languages, no declared major, nothing that seemed to be leading anywhere. Some counseling made sense."

He smiled to himself. "I'd read the play by then, so I was expecting a machine gun quipster – some short, motor-mouth nerd with glasses, Woody Allen or Mel Brooks redux. We academics have our preconceptions, too. Instead, in walks this big, tall kid with clear vision. Quiet. Controlled."

"He didn't smile, back then? Or laugh?" Adele asked, her pulse quickening.

His eyes were focused at a point behind her in space, his mind on a time even further away. He spoke slowly. "Oh, no, no, no, never, out of the question, you couldn't even imagine it, the most serious kid you ever saw. I thought, I really thought it might happen the day he came over with Milly, but – "

"Milly?"

"Millicent Peters. I'll get to that," said Goodson, straightening up, shaking his head, shaking off the past the way a dog dries itself. "Anyway, he came in that first time and we talked. I didn't make any progress at all with the major – hell, I never did, we finally had to declare one for him – but he asked me to do him a favor. He wanted to skip the intermediate language classes and go straight to the upper division level. He wasn't interested in speaking proficiency, only reading. I told him that was impossible, but he asked me to give it a shot and I thought, what the hell. I sent him over to Stefan Riesenberg – he was acting as head of the Modern Languages department – and asked him as a favor to give Tom some informal proficiency test. Stefan owed me a couple of favors.

"Riesenberg was a pretty crusty old bird. He'd been through a lot. I thought if Tom was getting ahead of himself, Stefan would take care of it quick, bim, bam, bop. But he phones me back about three days later, more excited than I'd ever heard him, and tells me we've got a prodigy on our hands, a genuine wunderkind, he said. Evidently he'd given Tom something to translate – some light verse of Heine's, I think – and Tom just knocked him flat."

He put his feet up on the desk. "He got waivers from all the other department heads, too – Riesenberg helped – later, it was the same thing in math – and that, Ms. Jansen was the way it went for the next three years – Tom going pretty much where he wanted to, doing what he liked, and going through the curriculum like a hot knife through butter, if you'll forgive the cliché. He made quite an impact here, Ms. Jansen. Quite an impact."

"What about –" *the incompletes*, she was about to say unguardedly. *Watch yourself, fool; you're not supposed to know about that.* "Then he was a straight-A student?" she asked instead, carefully.

"No," he shook his head. "No. I guess that's where we start to get to the other part." A bewildered, perplexed look came over his face. Like with Georgia Richmond, strong emotions were returning with the memories.

*

"He kept missing exams," he said, bemused. "Started at the end of his first year. He'd do all the coursework, come on like a supernova, then he wouldn't be there for a midterm or the final. It didn't make any sense at all. Profs kept giving him incompletes. I got a lot of calls about that."

"I wouldn't have thought that would be allowed," she said.

"It isn't. But what can you do when your superstar student doesn't show up to take his final? You can fail him on the final and give him a C – but that's not right. You could give him an A anyway – but that's not fair to the others, even if they're not in his league – or you can rate him incomplete and defer the decision, and get into a battle royal with the administration. Which is what most of them did. My advice."

He stood up. "But it didn't make any sense. You know, Ms. Jansen, when you meet a capable kid, they all have some kind of ambition – maybe to be President, maybe to run Wall Street, maybe to know more about Alexander Pope than anyone who ever lived. But they all want *something* – and they go for it. No one ever does all the work and then throws it away for the hell of it. But Tom. . ." He shook his head. "And meticulous in every other way – ask him for a thousand words and you got something between 996 and 1004. It made no sense." His voice trailed away.

"Do you know what ambitions he had?"

"No. Not then, not now," he answered, his voice flat and dead. "In my honest opinion, he didn't have any. I really think he went on his way, day to day, without knowing why himself. But that doesn't seem possible, does it?" He seemed puzzled and thoughtful, as if all this was happening now, as if he had to find a solution to a dilemma he faced at this very moment.

"How did he get along with the other students? Did he have any close friends?"

He shook his head slowly from side to side. "No. Not that he was unlikable; I think the other kids generally liked him, even if they were mostly afraid to approach him. A few of them made fun – he wasn't at all in the mainstream – but he got along, by and large. But to make a close friend you have to have shared experiences, and I don't think Tom shared much with anybody."

"What about girlfriends?" she asked, her heart in her mouth.

A slight, melancholy smile creased his face. "A long story, Ms. Jansen; a long, long story. I guess it's time to talk about Milly Peters."

*

"Milly Peters was two years behind Tom. I wasn't her counselor, but I had her in a couple of classes. She was an awfully pretty girl, so pretty it was easy to overlook how capable she was." He looked over at her. "I have a feeling you may know a little what I'm talking about."

She smiled in acknowledgment of the compliment. A nice man, this James Goodson. She liked him.

"At any rate, she was one of my better American lit students and I can make the going fairly tough. At a different school, she would probably have been the sorority queen, cheerleader type – that's the type of good looks she had – but we don't go in much for that stuff here. She did like acting. She won the lead in the spring play her second year. She was a hell of a Rosalind. She seemed to have everything going for her – brains, beauty, the works. She was engaged; her fiancé was a senior at Columbia. He was going off to med school the next year."

He sighed and put his hands behind his head. "She was the last girl I would have thought would get involved with Tom – not the type at all, you'd think – but then it happened and God! – I was happy for them." He paused. "Not very professional, I know, but he'd begun to get to me, you see, too damned quiet, too damned tired all the time, and I'd started to wonder what the hell he was going to do when he graduated. That's the sort of thinking you try to avoid – I mean, it's hard enough to live one life, it's a big mistake to get involved with other people's late adolescent crises – but still, it was hard not to worry about him. I guess it came with the territory."

A thoughtful moment, and then he went on: "But then the lilacs were in bloom, and Tom and Milly were going together. It surprised me when it happened, but when you saw them together it seemed so natural. Milly glowed and Tom – Tom was as content as I'd ever seen him.

"Katie – that's my wife – had been after me a long time to bring him home. She'd heard enough faculty chatter about this young titan striding over the Binghamton campus, she wanted to meet him. I'd actually made him a few invitations, but he never accepted, always very polite, but he never came. But this time he took me up on it, and he brought Milly."

The sweetest expression of reminiscence came over Goodson's face. "That was a day. They were good together, you know?" – he was lost in his memories, did not notice Adele gnawing her lower lip – "it made the world seem right to be around them. It was a perfect April day – you know the type? – everything was perfect. I'd been counseling Tom for four years, I'd been taking calls about him forever, it seemed, I'd read his play, but I'd never really seen him in action, if you know what I mean. I hadn't had him in class. I only knew what the big story was secondhand." He wheeled around. "Have you ever heard him improvise? I mean, just *do* it?"

"Yes," said Adele calmly. "Once. But I was the only other person there."

Goodson was lost in his own recollections, missed the implication. "The four of us ended up in the living room, Katie and me, Tom and Millie, about 7:00. Laura, my oldest, was there. She was five. It had been a pretty boring day for her, and it showed. She got a little whiny. She liked to play with stuffed animals back then; there must have been about a dozen scattered around the room. At any rate, Tom started to make up a story for her; he picked up a couple of the dolls and just started to roll."

He sighed again. "I forgot the details a long time ago. It was a story about a little girl – named Laura, of course – and a lot of her animal friends, some good, and some bad. But some of the good ones needed to hide from the bad, so Laura went to the store and got invisible pills – two kinds, ones that would make them disappear, and others that would make them reappear again. Only when she was coming home, she tripped and the pills got all mixed up. Then one of the bad ones stole some. So the good animals kept disappearing right when she wanted them around, and the bad ones showed up when she least expected them. You get the idea.

"I didn't notice, but he gradually got all the stuffed animals together behind a chair, and they'd pop up, and go down, regular Punch-and-Judy stuff.

But it went on and on and on, at least thirty minutes, about ten characters and the little girl, in and out, thrills, spills – I don't think he ever raised his voice – hilarious. Milly, Katie, and I listened. Laura was in stitches – and then when he could see she was becoming tired, he knotted up all of the stories and finished it up.

"I'd had a little wine – more than a little – I really didn't know what was going on, but it was all Katie could talk about the next day – she's an elementary school teacher, she knows that stuff – the way all the stories came together, all of the little characters were different, all of the little plot twists. He'd created the elements of a first-rate children's story and he'd done it on the spot, just to entertain Laura.

"You know, Ms. Jansen, if I'd had a tape recorder going that night, I could have made us a fortune" – he paused – "I mean us, I'm no thief. Tom could do it himself, of course, any time he wants to. But it's the same thing as the play. He doesn't bother. I don't know. My daughter Laura's twelve now, it's been seven years, we've had other students over, but he's the only one she ever asks about. She's going to ask me all about you tonight.

"He made a believer out of Katie that night, too. I'll tell you how. We were at the door, he was leaving with Milly, and he turns to Katie and out of the blue asks her how her pregnancy was going. She almost fainted; she hadn't even told me yet. He'd figured it out from the way she'd reacted to some stuff in the story, things she'd said and some things she didn't say. I should have warned her. He was always doing tricks like that. Scary as hell if you weren't ready for it."

Adele sat up a little straighter, poker-faced. *That* was an interesting thing to know.

He folded his arms down on the desk. "I can still see them that night: Tom with the toys, Milly's eyes shining while he did his number. I really thought he had a chance then. I really hoped it would work out for them."

"And then?" said Adele, her heart in her mouth.

The hands fluttered up again. "And then ten days later she was in the hospital with her wrists slashed, and he was in complete disgrace – and it was all over."

*

"What happened?"

He shrugged; all the pleasure of the memory was gone. "I got the story secondhand, of course, but. . . evidently Tom was supposed to go to be interviewed by some scholarship committee Riesenberg had set up, some fellowship at Heidelberg. But he never showed up. Instead – evidently – he holed up in the town with a lot of gin and a couple of – of – let's say floozies. And the floozies turned out to be great pals in every way. Her fiancé had heard about Tom and Milly. Some friend of his tipped the fiancé off to where Tom was – at least, that's how the story went. The bastard got photos, the works, and brought one of the girls Tom'd been with around to see Milly. The idea was probably to get her to drop Tom and come back to the future doc. But she took it a little further than they all expected. She slashed her wrists."

Adele struggled for words. "Did she–?"

"No. She lost a lot of blood, but she pulled through. But Tom came to visit her in the infirmary and she staged quite a scene – threw an IV bottle at him, yelled to everybody that he was the Devil himself. You'd better believe it was all anyone talked about around here for quite a while. Seemed forever." Goodson looked over at her. "You look a little pale. Is this getting to you?"

"No," Adele said, not entirely truthfully. "It's just that it's a lot like something that happened later in the city."

Goodson shrugged again. "I wouldn't be surprised. After that, it all came out – liquor, girls, not like the other kids get girls, you know, but these. . . scenes. Unreal; it was hard to believe then – I'm not sure I believe it now. Katie for sure doesn't believe it. She's always said there had to be something more going on. Then someone at the Psych Center told me that he'd been in for alcohol rehab twice. That really floored me. He didn't look the type at all; he'd kept it awfully well hidden.

"It went from bad to worse. A couple of Milly's admirers jumped him a day later, knocked him around and broke a couple of his ribs. He went to the hospital; he was supposed to be there for a few days. But he signed himself out the next morning. And that morning, Ms. Jansen" – he made a horizontal motion with the flat of his hand against his throat – "that morning was the last time anyone at this school ever saw him. He was gone just like that. Kaput. Finito."

"Then he never graduated?" Adele prompted.

"Don't jump to conclusions," Goodson smiled. "Nothing with Tom is like anybody else. When it was clear he'd left for good, Riesenberg made the faculty senate convene for a special meeting. I can still hear him: 'I have been teaching shopkeeper's children this *verdammt sprache* for forty-five years,'" Goodson quoted, "'I am not going to have the most talented student of my career leave me without a degree.' He was only a year or two from retirement. He persuaded everyone in the last semester to give him a pass credit, and all the others to change the incompletes to passes. There was a giant reaction from the administration, but Riesenberg pushed them around, too. They finally caved in, but everyone who'd changed a grade had to file a letter explaining why.

"So Tom has his degree, the goddamndest thing you ever saw, in comparative lit – I picked his major for him; he never did declare one. His diploma's sitting over in the registrar's office for him, if he ever comes back to pick it up. Which he never will. I'm certain of that."

The room was silent then for a moment. She thought he was finished, but then he spoke again: "You know, there were so many screwy things. The guys who beat him up – he was a strong kid. I ran into him a couple of times working out. But he didn't do anything to defend himself. He had the bad hand, but even so. . ." His voice trailed off.

That's not a game I play, he'd said. *I don't even fight back,* he'd told Josh Palmdale.

Goodson sighed heavily. "But that's about it." Her perplexity hung heavily in the air. Goodson noticed, and smiled, not unkindly. "Join the club," he said softly. "When you ask questions about Thomas Newcombe, Ms. Jansen, you don't get answers. What you get is more questions." And now he was finished; he looked at her, waiting.

*

"What happened to Millicent Peters?" Adele asked finally.

"She finished the semester, came back the next fall." He shook his head. "She wasn't the same person. She never got over him. She even took out an ad. In the school paper, asking him to call, saying something about the poems he'd left with her." Goodson gnawed on his lip. "It was quite a comedown. Quite a humiliation. She came to see me, too – gee, it's almost seven years ago to the day. She asked pretty much the same things you're asking. That's why I said you might count as the second one."

He sighed heavily. "All the vitality was gone, all the pep. She must have lost twenty or twenty-five pounds, and she didn't have all that much to lose in the first place. She was like a zombie. Basically, I was on Tom's side throughout all of it, but that day, if he'd been in my office, I would have wrung his neck with my bare hands. I didn't think she'd stay till the end of the term and she didn't. Where she went, I don't know." He paused. "Her father came down in the spring – with a loaded shotgun. He got stopped by the police for speeding, someone saw the gun and turned him around. He said he was hunting pheasant. There were a few people around here who didn't believe that."

"Are you sure he didn't have any close friends? Any other girlfriends?" she asked, desperately.

He could only smile sadly and shake his head. "I'm sure he had other girls besides Milly, but no one I could name. He was never a part of dorm life. He lived off campus almost from the start. The college let him out of the boarding contract after all of three weeks."

"Why?" she breathed, but the question turned out to be rhetorical. She already knew the answer.

"He kept waking everybody up. He was a restless sleeper. They couldn't even single him. The walls are too thin."

Adele digested that for a moment, then smiled sheepishly at Goodson. "A real dumb one: Did he ever talk to you about his family? His parents? His hometown?"

Goodson smiled back. "You already know the answer, don't you? No. He didn't say anything at all. I didn't even wonder about it until his junior year. I ran into him over the Christmas break and it became fairly clear he wasn't going anywhere – never went anywhere. It bothered me enough to check his file." He sighed heavily. "More great weirdness. No transcript, no nuttin'. He'd been one of Jack Lambeth's projects, but Jack was a good secret keeper and two years dead. All there was a fantabulous SAT score, a GED, of all things, and a letter. I can't help you at all there."

"The death had nothing to do with Tom, did it?"

"Oh, no, no. Bone cancer metastasized in his liver; Jack was gone before he knew what hit him." He smiled. "It doesn't surprise me you'd ask, though."

"Did you ever talk about personal philosophy? What's the meaning of it all, that sort of thing?" she asked, trying a different tack.

He pondered. "No. Once I asked him why he hadn't enrolled in Reisenberg's seminar on German idealistic philosophy – you know, Hegel, Marx, the existentialists – and he told me he'd looked into it and decided the whole of it, line for line, word for word, was worthless. I didn't pursue it. I happen to agree with him." He sighed. "But generally, the type of discussion you're talking about – it doesn't happen with him. He simply won't participate in it."

But he did with me, she thought. She was coming to the end of the line. *Think, stupid.* She caught his eye and held it. "Professor, what do you think of him? You, personally?"

He blew out a slow breath. "Personally? When I think of Tom, I think of the day he came over with Milly, the way he entertained Laura. I think I met the real Tom that day. But there are plenty of people here who think he was a con artist, plain and simple – a real bright one, but still a con man. And if he was that, and I was only another victim, I wouldn't know the difference, would I?"

Her own central question stated directly. She smiled at him and he went on. "But I'll tell you. I think that quietude of his is deceptive. I don't mean that he's deliberately deceitful. I don't believe that. But he's like the eye of a hurricane. Wherever he goes, the wind swirls around his heels and everyone near him gets blown to kingdom come. There was no one here who got close to him who didn't get bloodied somehow."

He threw up his hands again. "But who can say? Riesenberg got mauled the worst. He had a rough career – Jewish refugee from the Nazis, then he goes on teaching German in the States, worships Goethe. The other German scholars distrusted him and the Jewish faculty thought he was nuts. He could get pretty bitter about it. He thought he got caught in the crossfire and it kept him out of the big leagues. He really built Tom up around the circuit. He finally had a student who could outdo anyone of theirs.

"Then his prize pupil not only doesn't show up for the big interview, but God! When the word got around as to where he'd actually been. . . Some of those bastards even implied Stefan had ponied up Tom's submission himself, that the whole thing was a phony. Academics can be so charitable. It was a total humiliation for the old guy.

"But – but" – Goodson raised his hand significantly – "Riesenberg retired five years ago. At the dinner, he listed the four proudest moments of his career, and the fourth was having the privilege of instructing Thomas Newcombe in German literature. We had a drink afterwards and he took me aside – `Jim' he said, `I was lucky, he came along so late in my career. You will wait your whole lifetime for this to happen again, but it never will.' I knew what he meant." Goodson did a German accent that Walt Greenfield would have died for.

He looked out the window, slapped the desk with his hand, and straightened up. "So! Anything else?"

"Can you give me Milly Peters' home address?" she asked. "And send me a copy of that play?"

"She left her family address with me way back when, but I don't think she lives there anymore." He riffled through the debris on his desk, found an older Rolodex and passed it over. Adele copied down address and phone number rapidly. "The other thing's no problem if you'll tell me where to mail it."

"Thank you," she said, and did.

He stopped her as she was rising. "Can I ask you one question?" he said. "An important question. Why do you want to find Tom?"

"Well –" she began, hesitantly, about to go into the usual attorney-client charade, when he interrupted:

"I know an attorney can't say too much. But I'm not asking too much – just the basics. Does someone want to sue him? Or have him arrested? Has he inherited money? Is he in trouble? What?"

She hesitated again, thinking, when her intuition unexpectedly intervened. *Level with this man. Tell him the truth.*

"It's partly professional," she said, going with that. "My firm is counsel to the Furston Press, Tom's publisher. But I'll be honest – it's mostly personal. I met Tom not long ago. I – I – I came to care for him very deeply. It was obvious our lives didn't match at all, so we left each other. Now I feel I have to find out who he is, why he moved me so much. I'd rather not explain exactly why. It's extremely personal."

He looked at her appraisingly for a moment. "O.K.," he finally muttered.

"Why do you ask?"

"Oh," he said, "nothing much. A few years ago, we computerized all of the old student records. There's some sort of password system that's supposed to be very secure. But a lot of the technical people worried about it anyway. The administration refused to put in a top notch security system; it was too expensive. Instead, they sent around this form so that faculty could flag a file if they wanted to be notified if it was pulled. So at least the sensitive ones would be identified and we'd know if any hanky-panky was going on. You could do as many as you liked. I only flagged one."

Adele's heart had stopped beating. He was holding a short computer printout, almost certainly containing an ISP address that could trace back to Abercrombie.

"Tuesday late someone broke in and retrieved Tom's records. Wednesday you called, and here you are. You said he'd mentioned me as his counselor, but unless he's changed a lot, he doesn't talk much about that sort of thing. I wondered if it might be more than coincidence. If someone took those files who wanted to make trouble for Tom, if anyone ever takes them for that purpose, I intend to make a lot of trouble for that person." He was dead serious.

The room was quiet and still. Goodson looked at Adele. Adele met his eyes as calmly as she could.

"I don't know what you're talking about," she said evenly. He continued studying her.

"You more than care about him, don't you?" he asked after a long, long pause.

"Yes," she answered, very, very quietly. The room was still.

Another few seconds – then he'd made up his mind. She watched as he crumpled the paper and threw it in the wastebasket. "Obviously a coincidence," he said definitively. "It would be pointless to waste time doing anything more about it. Besides, I don't know what the Keystone Cops we have around here could do."

She nodded and rose. It was time to go. He stood to shake her hand. "Ms. Jansen – Adele – you can tell that I like Tom, but I hope you paid attention to what I said about the hurricane. I don't think Tom means to be dangerous, but he is, somehow. I'd hate to see you or anyone hurt as badly as Millicent Peters was."

They all finish that way, don't they? Georgia, Jenet, this man; no matter how they feel about him, like or dislike, hate or admire, they all end with a warning. "Thank you. I appreciate the advice. But I have to finish this; I have to. You've been very helpful. Thanks again." She gave no sign of how unnerving his advice had been.

He showed her to the door. "What's true for professors is true for certain women, I guess. You're not going to meet two of him, are you?"

"No," said Adele. "I'm not."

Then she shook his hand, turned, and walked down the corridor. It was 2:30 p.m. and time to leave.

A good day, the best in a long time; real progress. Now she knew the answers lay further back; disappointing, yes, but at least she knew that for certain. She circled by his old apartment just in case, finding nothing, which is what she expected. Her thoughts were already turning to Millicent Peters as she drove away.

✳ ✳ ✳

CHEMISTRY

As far as Adele Elizabeth Jansen was concerned, professional football had one, and only one, virtue, and that not nearly significant enough to be redeeming. It provided a reliable method for fixing the whereabouts of a large percentage of American males on Sunday afternoons in the fall. If you knew which team a particular man followed and when its Big Game would be on television, you stood a good chance of being able to reach the critter at home by telephone, with luck before his brain had entirely melted. Only always call at half-time – kid sisters learn that lesson early on. Based on the city in which he lived, it seemed likely that James Peters was a Buffalo Bills follower, like the men in her own family. It was for that reason that the radio was tuned to that broadcast as she sat at her desk in her bedroom, at 1:45 on Sunday.

She was in a better frame of mind this day than she had been in in some time. She had slept past 9:00. The day before had been long and exhausting – but worth it. Progress, finally.

The announcers droned on behind her, their voices rising occasionally with the crowd noise. She amused herself while she waited for the intermission by sketching Professor Goodson – in addition to everything else, he had an interesting face – seated on a throne amidst all the clutter, holding a cornucopia spewing paper.

Most of the questions still remained – certainly all of the major ones. But at last she could reach some firm conclusions. For one thing, she could finally reject Georgia Richmond's ridiculous notion that Tom was an ordinary reprobate, concealing a double life because it was an embarrassment to him. *No way* – he'd been much the same person ten years before that he was now. Boys of eighteen, even boys as unusual as Tom must have been, neither have the resources nor feel the need to lead an underground life. The whole idea had been, as she had suspected at the outset, absurdly simple-minded, which figured, because Georgia Richmond was an absurdly simple-minded person.

So you are excused, Georgia dear, finally, and thanks for nothing. Whatever's going on here is complicated beyond anything you ever understood or tried to understand. She looked up from the sketchbook; her lighthearted mood turned serious for a moment. Complicated, yes, and more than that – there were inferences based on what Goodson said that she did not want to draw just yet, impressions she would not let form – potentially too sad, too painful.

Back to work. The noise of the crowd swelled behind her. Another thought struck her; if she was going to do an album about this whole adventure, it should be done right. *No, damn it. Yes,* something responded. Sighing and giving in, she began a sketch of Georgia Richmond. There was only one possible time bubble she wanted to bisect, of course – and a short while later she studied her work. She'd got all of the petty spite in the expression, as well as the incipient intoxication, Georgia Richmond as she had been that evening. *Not bad, Jansen.*

Something was missing. Of course – a witch had to have a familiar. Without any hesitation, she added a mangy cat to the portrait, curled behind the neck and peering over the right shoulder with the exact same spiteful expression as her mistress. Now she was really pleased with herself. *Pretty petty revenge,* something whispered inside her. Tough. The pettier the better. *Talk like that about Tom, will you? Go to bed with him?* If Georgia Richmond had a sketchbook, she could draw her, Adele, any way she liked. Pop tart indeed.

*

After about four centuries, the first half finally ended and it was time to do some real work. She stifled the hesitant anxiety she felt, picked up the phone, and punched in the Peters' number. The call was answered on the second ring.

"Yes?" said an abrupt male voice. She had guessed well; she could hear the half-time in the background.

"Hello, Mr. Peters? Mr. James Peters" – he grunted in acknowledgment – "my name is Adele Jansen. I'm a lawyer in Manhattan. I'm trying to locate your daughter Millicent. I'm hoping she can help me find someone else."

"Who?" he demanded, even more abruptly. The coldth in his voice had become palpable. She took a deep breath; he had intuited whom she was going to name.

"His name is Newcombe. Thomas Newcombe."

"Why?" The phone receiver iced over.

Forgive me, Tom, she thought. *You, too, God.* "He's made big trouble for a client of mine, a woman publisher. She wants to really nail him to the wall. But he's ducking process. He's dropped out of sight. I'm trying to run him down."

"What'd he do?" demanded Peters. "Screw her over and then skip town?"

"Something like that," Adele went on brazenly. "I'm not exactly sure. The rumor is she caught him red-handed with another woman. But I don't know that for a fact."

"Yeah, that's Newcombe, all right," he almost spat. "He's a real sweetheart." Then he was silent.

"Well," said Adele, after a time, "can you help me? Can you tell me how to get in touch with Millicent?"

"I don't know what good it would do. She won't talk to you. She doesn't talk to me, or her family, or anyone. And I don't know how she'd know where Newcombe is hiding out."

"They were close once. Maybe they're still in touch."

"Why?" he said, suddenly suspicious. "What makes you say that?"

"My client's heard him speak of her."

"I can bet how," he snorted.

"No" – enough playing along was enough – "not like that. With a lot of regret."

"I'll bet. The only regret Newcombe has is that he didn't put her all the way into her grave. Then he could have taken a little picture of the headstone and put it in his trophy case. Same as with your gal, if he gets a chance."

"It sounds as if you really don't like him," said Adele, a little shaken, trying to joke it off.

"Like *him?* If you find him, tell me where and I'll *kill* him," snarled Peters. "I drove down once to Binghamton to do it. I'm still sorry the cops stopped me. Do you know what he did? Do you know what he did? I've got five kids. Four of 'em aren't worth a hill of beans, worthless trash their whole lives. But Milly – God, Milly! It was like someone touched a wand to her forehead the day she was born. She was beautiful, she was funny, she was smart – top of her high school class, you know, prom queen, the lead in the school play. First Peters kid to go to college. She had everything; hell, sometimes I had to pinch myself to be sure she was my kid. Then she gets engaged to Bill Clarkson, this future doctor at Columbia. God, I was so proud!

"Then – then –" his voice became infinitely bitter – "she meets the great Thomas Newcombe. Maybe I protected her too much, maybe I didn't tell her enough about what men can really be like. Because all she is to the great Mr. Newcombe is a couple of weeks' fun and then he's off to the next girl. He took her the way I drink a can of beer. He broke her heart for the hell of it. Do you know what happened?"

"No," said Adele. It was better to let him get through this his way.

"She tried to kill herself, is what happened. She slashed her wrists. She was lucky she didn't die."

"Did she get over it?" Adele asked.

"No," said Peters, real anguish in his voice. "She's never going to get over it. She doesn't talk to anybody, she doesn't answer letters, she won't take visitors, she's never going to get over it, if you want to know. Look it," Peters went on, a little calmer, "this is getting to me. I don't know how I can help you. I don't want to talk about this anymore."

"Please," said Adele, the desperation in her voice entirely real, "please let me at least try. If I can just get in touch with her, I know it'll help me do the right thing," with the ambiguity deliberately intended. The sheer pain in Peters' voice had touched her. She did not want to lie to him anymore than she already had.

There was a long, long silence on the line.

"All right," he said, at last. "What's the difference? She's not going to say anything to you anyway." He left the phone briefly, then returned.

When he first began to recite, Adele was so startled she almost gasped in surprise. Then she picked up a pencil and followed him as quickly as she could. Finally, she had found out something significant. When he was finished, there was an awkward silence. The second half of the game had started.

"Thanks a lot," she said uncomfortably. "I don't want to take you away from the game."

"The hell with that," he snarled. "Did you think I always spent my Sunday afternoons with this crap?"

She stood by the phone for a long few seconds after the call was over. All at once she felt small, in a way that had nothing to do with her height.

*

"Good evening." The voice on the line was soft and feminine.

"Good evening to you. I'd like to speak to −" she suddenly realized Peters had not given her all the information she needed − "to Millicent Peters, if I could."

"I'm sorry," the voice said pleasantly. "That's not permitted at this time."

"Oh," said Adele. "Can I leave her a message? Can she return a call?"

"Oh, yes. Though she almost never does − I can't remember the last time she has; she's the most distant of all of us − and the privilege lapses when it's not exercised. I don't know when it's available to her again."

"I understand. Even so, my name is Adele Jansen. I'm a lawyer in New York." She gave the voice her office and home phone numbers. "Please tell her − "

It was then 8:30 p. m. Adele had spent nearly six hours deciding what she would say if something like this happened. *She doesn't talk to anyone,* Peters had said. Adele believed him. Millicent Peters. . . Adele had no feel for the person, none for the personal reality, only the barest sense of who she was, what might be important to her. Only the hint her father had inadvertently dropped. So the message – it had to be perfect, something that would make her curious, draw her out. But nothing too sensational, nothing that gave scandal, or. . . it had to be perfect.

She had mulled over the difficulty all afternoon. Then, as she brooded at her desk, her eye had landed on the sketch of Georgia Richmond – and she had known, she had known at once, what her best chance was.

"–I met a man named Tom Newcombe about six weeks ago. He took me back to his apartment. He took me to his home. I've seen his home, where he lives. And he told me he loved me. He used those exact words. I care about him very much. I've lost touch with him, and I'm hoping Millicent can help me find out more about him."

*

Because that was the one thing she knew for certain that had never happened with Georgia Richmond. Because her hunch was that that almost never happened with anybody. Because, while she didn't know what would cause Millicent Peters to return the call, she was certain what wouldn't – the possibility, even the bare possibility, that she would find herself sharing the most intimate secrets of her life with someone like Georgia Richmond.

Because she couldn't think of anything better.

*

"I hope I haven't offended you," said Adele, a bit defensively. Necessary or not, it was embarrassing to reveal so much to the complete stranger taking the message.

The voice laughed. "Oh, no. Of course not. People have the strangest notions. It would take a lot more than that. Let me see if I got this right." She read the message back, and she had. "You do understand I can't give you any assurances that Millicent will return your call. She never does."

"Yes, I do. Thank you for your help. Good evening."

The phone didn't ring before she went to bed, although she was hoping – listening, truth be told. It was ironic. Through most of her adult life, she had gone out of her way to avoid falling into the worst of all the social clichés, Girl Waiting Anxiously by Phone. Despite everything, it had finally happened, only the caller for whom she was hoping was a woman. There are clichés in this life, Adele decided, that are simply unavoidable.

*

"I have to admit I'm impressed," said Adele, truthfully.

"Waddaya `spect?" smiled George Sorenson. "Me to hold an umbrella and whistle for a taxi?"

"I – I don't know what I expected," Adele answered, truthfully again. "Certainly not this." Certainly not the twenty-five-foot white stretch limousine with a uniformed chauffeur, facing seats in the passenger compartment and a wet bar, in which George Sorenson had called for her this Monday evening. She was ensconced now on one of the brown, deeply contoured back seats, her back to the driver, facing George. His satisfaction in the impact of his little surprise was readily apparent.

"You sort of implied this dinner wasn't all that big a deal," Adele went on.

"It isn't," he responded. "But it's not the event. It's who you're taking."

What a sweet thing to say! she thought giddily. Another long day, concentrating doggedly on her tasks, jumping in spite of herself every time the phone rang or she heard a page. . . and nothing had happened. Nothing. It seemed as if it had gone on that way forever. Now, all at once, the limousine, the glamor, the prospect of spending an evening with a man who was openly interested in her – a wonderful, exhilarating feeling, a simple good time for a change, the expectation of ordinary fun as intoxicating as fine wine. *I need this*, she thought.

Even the heavy cross-town traffic, normally a postcard from purgatory, made no dent on the ambiance The ride could take as long as it had to. Tonight, that was the driver's problem, not hers.

"You're not the only one surprised," he added. "You can really fill an evening gown when you put your –" he paused, deliberately lowered his eyes and smiled – "mind to it," and she smiled back, not a bad joke. Adele owned two formal gowns, the one she was wearing, a light, peach-colored thing which showed off a modest but interesting décolletage with the collar unbuttoned, and a white creamy off-shoulder model considerably more daring. Both were much slinkier than her everyday wardrobe. She'd chosen the more sedate of the two on program – she *always* kept something in reserve – but things were happening anyhow.

"Thank you," she answered. "I guess it's a question of mind over matter."

"I doubt that," he grinned again, arms folded, again surveying her body, not bothering to conceal his admiration.

"Champagne?" he asked, grasping the throat of a bottle in an ice bucket she hadn't noticed.

"No, thank you. I'm trying to keep my weight down."

"I guess it's time to talk," he said good-naturedly. "Who goes first? Me or you?"

"You," she said, not entirely understanding.

He grinned and raised an eyebrow. "'Boyfriend'?" She looked at him oddly. "What you said the other day," he continued. "At the board."

"Oh," she said, comprehending now. "It's a very, very difficult relationship to describe. A writer – a poet – I knew some time ago. Lem remembers him because he knows the poetry," actually grateful for once to be able to say something about herself and Tom that had a slight resemblance to the truth. "But it's not a commitment and I'm not playing games with you," surprised to realize, as she said that last, that that, too, was the truth. It occurred to her that every time she was with George Sorenson she surprised herself. "I didn't tell Lem everything."

He peered at her suddenly and smiled knowingly. "You've got your angel on tonight, haven't you?"

"Yes," she said, suddenly defensive. "You have sharp eyes," which indeed he did, since the necklace was buried underneath a triple strand of artificial pearls. She'd thought it was concealed well enough. The occasional gleam of gold added to the overall effect. *Stupid*, she realized then. *It's got nothing to do with his eyesight. It's become the first thing he looks for.*

He gestured towards the necklace.

"Yes," she said. "He's the one – and the memory is important to me. But it is a memory."

He sat back in his seat, happy, relaxed. "Good enough. Your turn."

"The Project," she said simply, in turn. "Why me?"

He waited a moment. "It's the most important thing I've ever done," he said. "It's my ticket out." His voice was cold, impersonal, the same distance she'd observed when he was with Lem and Pete; she was meeting for the first time the man who ate financiers for breakfast. "I'm going to get it done no matter what." He paused. "It's got problems –"

"I know. I read about Atlanta this morning." Every day, an avalanche of paper arrived in her office, lawyers all over the country reporting. She had started filling her sixth carton that morning and no end in sight.

"Right. The city council. The problems are never the same. What I do then –" he looked at her, his eyes cold and expressionless – she felt a delicious ripple go through her, with a definite sexual undertone; she was being escorted by a very formidable man – "is stockpile brains. Smart people solve problems, you don't know how, but they do. Honest to God, I don't know how you'll fit in. But I want you around. Insurance. Satisfied?" His look was calculating, not challenging; he was telling the truth. Carolyn was an idiot.

She nodded. He grinned and changed tone, now the man who wooed her with such touching, persistent awkwardness at lunch. "It's also true that I think the brains are very well packaged. And it's true that I like having you around. That bother you?"

She thought for only a moment, then shook her head from side to side. "No. Not the way you put it. Not at all. Thank you."

"You're quite a girl," he went on softly. "You told the lie to Michaels to let him off easy, didn't you?"

"Yes."

He shook his head. "I watched him chase women over all the U.S. and half of Europe. Most of 'em weren't even polite. You could see 'em laughing at him. Those teeth, and he comes on like a kid. I wish I could have felt sorry for him."

"Why not?" she said, alarmed by the odd coldness of his last phrase.

His face was hard. "Because it's business. He's a business guy now. Michaels has to take care of himself, same as everyone."

"You know. . . Lem and Pete. . . Chiang. . . they're geniuses, George. Every word you've heard about them. It's all for real." Suddenly it was urgent, critically important, that he know that – more than know – understand, comprehend. Suddenly it had to be said.

"I know," he said, in the same impersonal voice. "I believe you. Look, let's not talk any more business." She started to say something – there was so much more she wanted him to say – but he looked up, through the front windshield.

"We're here," he said.

*

The reception was another pleasant surprise. She was no great admirer of pyramids of inner space, but whoever had staged this reception shared her opinion. A mock courtyard in the center of the lobby was enclosed by a canopy from which Japanese lanterns in all sorts of festive designs and colors hung, glowing on the black marble floor. Iridescent colors shone on the splashing water of a fountain that stood outside the entrance. Inside, a buffet was spread that was anything anyone could wish; she'd restricted herself to a light lunch on that hopeful idea, was delighted to see that her intuition had been correct. A spectacular ice sculpture – a recreation of Cellini's *Perseus Holding the Head of Medusa*; it must have taken forever to do the carving – graced the center of the serving board, overlooking an array of crab legs, mussels, cherrystone clams on the half-shell. Roast beef, leg of lamb, lobster tails dominated one end; marinated mushrooms, artichoke hearts, every conceivable kind of salad, were laid out at the other. A little thrill of excitement; this was a routine dinner function of CFS organization? She'd love to see a special one.

"Not bad, is it?" George remarked, a bit smug. Adele looked up at him, widened her eyes in acknowledgment. "The Project isn't the only thing going on. Most of our operation is trading, but we did about 750 mil in stock issues this last quarter. AI Squared wasn't the biggest by a mile. All of 'em deserve some kind of celebration."

"Evidently," said Adele. They moved to the buffet line and picked up plates.

Seventy to a hundred people stood in various places under the canopy or moved through the buffet line. Placards showing enlarged covers of eleven prospectuses (AI Squared among them) ringed the entrance. Lem, Pete, and Chiang were there, standing in a larger group. Lem turned his head, noticed her, and nodded in recognition. She risked a small wave in return; George wasn't looking. Victor Podgorny was already seated at another table. Adele did not try to catch his eye, and he did not see her. Not all of the guests were financial; Adele recognized more than a few faces from the Arts and Letters section of the Times. A giddy sense of having arrived began to suffuse her. Not even the sight of Greg Steuer, gliding aloofly by, resplendent in a rented tuxedo, could diminish it.

"Hello, George," said a tall, stately, middle-aged man, in his early to mid-fifties standing a bit ahead of them. A coldness in his manner was apparent. "How is your business progressing?"

"Hello, Jake," said George, with the same notable lack of enthusiasm. "I'm doin' O.K."

The man waited for a second, then bowed stiffly, awkwardly from the waist towards Adele. "Jacob Rothenberg. My wife, Ruth. Pleased." His wife, a woman only a bit taller than Adele, as dignified as her husband, had been screened from view.

"Adele Jansen. Thank you, good evening."

"Oh," said George, embarrassed. "I goofed it. Jake and Ruth, this is Adele Jansen. Adele, this is –"

"We've met," interrupted Adele, as much to break the tension that crackled between the two men as for any other reason. All four of them laughed, the men somewhat uneasily.

"How's it with you, Jake?" said George, after a long, silent moment, as the group moved down the buffet line.

"Well. My little projects are gradually picking up some momentum. I'm satisfied."

"We really should get together. Maybe I could help you out."

Rothenberg looked up sharply. "I doubt that, George," he said with an all but icy contempt. "I doubt that very much." They were near the end of the line. Thank God.

"Whatever you say, Jake," George answered, cold on cold. Before the couples could mercifully separate, another joined them, certainly the oddest at the dinner. The man was four or five years older than Adele, no more than three or four inches taller, but weighed at least two hundred and seventy pounds, with thinning hair and gold granny spectacles. Adele had a vague idea she might have seen him in the CFS trading room. His companion towered over him, tall and voluptuous. Adele, with her artist's eye for faces, recognized her from frequent appearances in lingerie ads in the Times Sunday Magazine. The situation reeked of something bought and paid for.

The fat man was Ralph Something-or-other (another botched introduction), a CFS colleague. She could sense George becoming restless, impatient, but the other rambled on about the pressure, the difficulty of the Street. ("I don't think I had five minutes for lunch all last week," said Ralph, a statement the truth of which Adele strongly doubted.) The model oohed and aahed. Adele, Jacob, and Ruth Rothenberg were silent, Jacob conspicuously.

Finally, Ralph Something put his hand familiarly on his companion's waist and the odd couple moved off. Ruth Rothenberg turned to her husband. "My God," she said, shaking her head. George stirred uneasily and bit his lip. Adele felt his embarrassment. They, too, were an unlikely couple. She looked up, deliberately caught Mrs. Rothenberg's eye.

"It's what I call a *quid pro quo* date," she chirped brightly. "The man lays out quid all night, and the girl lays out a little quo later on."

Ruth Rothenberg nodded automatically, then did a double take. "That's really rather clever. What did you say your name – "

Franklin Fischer was suddenly in the group between George and Jacob Rothenberg. "George. . . Jake, Ruth." He stole a glance at Adele. "Ms. Jansen, welcome to our party. What a charming dress," he murmured, "George has always had excellent taste in his choice of friends. George, a problem has come up. With Atlanta. Their attorneys are concerned that the reorganization will not be tax free. They – "

"I thought this was supposed to be a social occasion, Franklin. . . George," Rothenberg interjected, with something of the same iciness he'd shown to George. . . and yet it seemed to Adele that most of the tactile bitterness was missing.

"I don't believe that distinction is meaningful these days, Jake," Franklin Fischer answered easily. Jacob Rothenberg ignored him. Fischer turned to George. "Their lawyers advise applying for an IRS ruling."

George waved his hand. "That'd set us back eighteen months," he said, a faint note of exasperation in his voice. "We been over that ground. Tons of times. They're the ones with the stock repurchase option if a founder leaves. They're O.K. It's a holdup, plain and simple. Continuity of interest. Remember?" There was a blank look on Fischer's face. "They say they got a problem if they have to buy back more than seventeen points, but it's no worry. If –"

Recognition dawned on Fischer. "Yes, yes, of course. I recall now. In any case, I committed you to a meeting in Atlanta tomorrow. To clarify any problems."

"Not necessary, Franklin," George spoke flatly. "We got more to deal with in the Midwest. I had plans."

"I think you should alter them," Fischer answered. "There is so little time. We cannot afford a snafu here." George shrugged. "I'd like to brief you on the call." Fischer smiled ingratiatingly at Adele. "If I can borrow your escort for just a moment?"

She could almost feel George's thoughts – the briefest moment of turmoil, rebellion, followed by a realization that there was no sensible choice but acquiescence. He turned to Adele. "I've got to leave you for a sec," he said.

"It's all right," she answered quietly. The two men left. Adele, Jacob, and Ruth Rothenberg were left alone.

"It's what I've told you. That's what the style is going to be from now on, Ruth," said Jacob, ignoring Adele. "Monomania. Unlimited greed as the only virtue. Nothing matters but money for money's sake, power for power's sake. Every second not spent in the accumulation of one or the other is a second wasted. No sense of anything else. No appreciation for the responsibility that must accompany it."

Ruth touched his arm tenderly. "Darling, you don't have to go on with this. You've done well. We have more than enough."

He shook his head. "And leave the world for those vermin to inhabit alone? Never. That's the mistake the Romans made with the Visigoths, that the Chinese made with the Mongols." He turned to his wife. "And all civilized people with the Nazis." He paused. "And it is happening again," he added softly.

His wife glanced about uncomfortably. "Jacob, don't be so melodramatic." It was only then that they each simultaneously recalled the presence of Adele.

"Hello," she twittered, cheerfully. "Don't mind me. I'm a stranger here myself," and received in return a relieved smile from Ruth.

"We really haven't had any time to become acquainted. Perhaps we can sit together."

"Yes," said Adele. "I see – "

"Ruth," said Jacob Rothenberg firmly, deliberately ignoring Adele, "I am not going to share a meal with George Sorenson or anyone else of that ilk."

"Jacob, I wasn't speaking of him. Ms. Jansen appears to be quite a charming – "

"Ms. Jansen may be all manner of things to all manner of people," her husband interrupted shortly, "but she keeps herself in very poor company. She chooses her friends unwisely. I don't have to approve of that and I don't. Come, Ruth." He moved off without waiting for his wife to answer.

Ruth looked at Adele, Adele at Ruth; both made the same helpless shrug at the same time – *Men! What can you do?* – and exchanged simultaneous smiles at the simultaneity of the gesture. A bond formed of a sort. Then Ruth Rothenberg followed her husband toward a distant table, leaving Adele alone, thinking.

*

A silver spoon struck a crystal goblet, repeatedly.

Franklin Fischer rose to speak.

What is it about him? Adele thought five minutes later. He was good. He said the right things, in the right order, and in the right way. He had what the military call command presence – the sort of personality who seems to obtain authority naturally and use it effectively and efficiently. She glanced around – the men were all nodding respectfully, the women with various degrees of open and subtle interest. She felt a ripple of it herself. Alpha male-type performances always appealed to her. But she had neither forgiven nor forgotten the scene at the board meeting. That interruption in front of the Rothenbergs had been more of the same – a petty, unnecessary humiliation. She stole a glance at George, seated to her right. All of his high spirits had fled. She found herself fiercely resenting the dampening of his mood. *The real alpha here*, she thought suddenly. It would have been useful for her to like Franklin Fischer, but she didn't think she was going to be able to manage that.

"I think most of you know this is in all probability – well, possibility – well, I hope – " (laughter) – "that this may be the last of our celebratory dinners." Mingled applause and good-natured boos. "You all know what I have been up to these last years; there's an excellent chance it will all be completed before the month is out." Long, sustained applause; the Project was evidently as well-known at the CFS offices as hers.

"None of you need worry about your future; you all know that CFS will endure, and in capable hands. That I am moving on to larger things does not mean I intend to abandon the most important work of my life. Ronald Howell – Ronnie, stand up –" the young fat man who'd escorted the model rose – "Ronnie's staying on; he's been doing most of the management these past eighteen months –" (applause again) – "and George – George?" George Sorenson stood up; Franklin Fischer gave him a long, slow look – "George will be around and available. He's one of those old and accomplished soldiers who'll be there until he simply fades away."

"Guess again," George muttered as he resumed his seat. The applause continued. She saw Jacob Rothenberg across the room, arms conspicuously folded. Adele's clap was as perfunctory as possible. No indication that George was his partner, no acknowledgment of his role in the Project, nothing of his plans to withdraw if and when. If any of that bothered George, he gave no indication. He was brooding about something else.

"And it is important work we do, ladies and gentlemen – important work. I refer not merely to the basic task with which we are charged, the care and management of the funds with which we are entrusted, so important to so many people. I refer to our larger work, even more important. Through our efforts, in combination with those of our rivals and colleagues, we provide a mechanism by means of which the diverse goods of the Earth can be assessed and evaluated in relation to each other. Do you wish to know how many bushels of Chinese rice you need accumulate to purchase a black ermine pelt imported from Russia? We can tell you. How many pounds of Maylasian rubber you need obtain to fetch an original Van Gogh? We can tell you that, too. In a world that is increasingly fractious, restive, and disorganized, in which both traditional and modern values become increasingly relative, we provide the truest measure, perhaps the only true measure."

He continued: "We do this with hard impartiality, on a level playing field. We are ruthless with those among us who attempt to distort the rules, to win the game by evading..."

He went on and on – and on, but Adele heard very little more. Her attention was now focused entirely to her right. George's dark mood was becoming darker every second. She was suddenly aware that how he felt was important to her.

In fact, extremely important to her.

*

"I'm glad to see you again," said Ruth Rothenberg, standing just inside the door to the powder room. "I don't usually feel compelled to apologize for Jacob, but I feel he overreacted tonight. I hope he didn't upset you too much."

"Not at all," Adele replied, "and I have to apologize myself." She smiled as the women stepped outside. "This meeting is no accident. I saw you get up and I came here. Why does your husband dislike George Sorenson so much? Can you tell me?"

"How much do you know about the man you're with?" asked Ruth carefully, appraising her.

"Not that much," Adele answered truthfully. "Only that he works with Franklin Fischer. And he's been kind to me," she added, feeling a sudden surge of loyalty. No reason to tell Ruth that this had begun as more of a business occasion than social.

"Then you may not know," said Ruth gently, "but George Sorenson isn't any ordinary businessman. He's the hatchet man for CFS. Wherever he's around something vicious is happening or about to happen. Jacob blames him more for what happened than he does Franklin Fischer."

"What was that?" Adele asked, disconcerted in spite of herself.

"Have you visited the building where Mr. Fischer has his business?"

"Yes."

"Until two years ago, that was my husband's building, his family's, for five generations. They've been on Wall Street that long. The building wasn't the most valuable thing Jacob owned, but it was the most important to him. The family's turned down all kinds of offers for it over the years. But two years ago he sold it and his firm, to Franklin Fischer."

"Why? What happened?"

"I'm not exactly sure," Ruth answered, "I'm not very good at business. From what I overheard, one of my husband's partners got what he thought was inside information. He took a large short position in a trucking stock. What he didn't know was that CFS was planning to put the company in play at the same time. The stock went way, way up, not down. My husband's partner was afraid to tell him; by the time he did, it was much, much too late. The only way the short sale could possibly be covered was to buy the shares from CFS or a holder CFS controlled. One of the concessions CFS demanded was the sale of the firm. It was that or close it down, throw everyone out of work. Jacob really didn't have any choice. He sold." She sighed. "Jacob is convinced George Sorenson was the architect of the whole scheme. He considers Franklin Fischer a very mediocre man. George is the one with the talent."

"Your husband could have filed suit," Adele said.

"And spend how many years and how many millions of dollars? And how much sympathy would a judge or jury have for a wealthy stock broker complaining about his own partner's greed and illegality?"

"Did CFS demand too low a price? Did he cheat your husband?" Adele asked, groping.

"Oh, no," Ruth said, gently again. "CFS doesn't work like that. The price was fair, even generous. Provided it was for something you wanted to sell in the first place." She took a quick nervous look over her shoulder. "I do have to be going. I'm sorry we couldn't have dinner together." She paused. "I regret my husband's rudeness to you. But I think I have to be candid. I don't disagree with his opinion that you've chosen your companions unwisely." She smiled. "Good evening. Good luck."

"Thank you," said Adele, as she left. "Good night." She turned around herself.

George Sorenson was watching her, had obviously been observing the whole scene for some time.

*

The atmosphere in the limousine going was entirely different than it had been coming. George stared out the passenger window, had nothing to say. Adele felt ridiculously, irrationally guilty.

"A penny for your thoughts," she said finally.

He regarded her. "What did the Rothenbergs say to you?" he asked after a while.

A long moment. "Nothing you would have wanted to hear," she answered at last. "They're not exactly members of your fan club."

"No," he said, and turned back to the window. "It was only business – hard business, but business. I needed an outfit with a rep in investment banking. For the Project. All legal, all above-board. If he can't take care of himself, he shouldn't blame other people." Adele said nothing. "I'd have liked to be friends with Jake Rothenberg," he added softly after another moment. "Class act."

"He respects you," Adele added helplessly. "Perhaps in time. . . " but George shook his head.

"What have other people said?" he asked. "To you. . . about me?"

"No one's said anything except Carolyn. Carolyn says Franklin supplies all the money and brains. She thinks you're Franklin Fischer's errand boy."

He nodded; a faint, distant smile. "Waddaya think?"

"I don't believe it," she said promptly. "I've seen the two of you together. I think he needs you a lot more than you need him."

A half-nod. "Carolyn's right about the money," he said softly. "As for the rest. . ." He turned to her. "Franklin's what you might call a financier," he said quietly. "I been carryin' him for twenty years." He turned his head to the window.

"I don't understand that," Adele asked. "Why do you go on with him?" Another long silence. "I wondered about that when you told me about it at lunch," she added.

"When I first met Franklin," he finally answered, without turning his head, "I was hard up for a break – totally hard up – and he had the bucks. The capital. So. He's the managing partner of CFS. He's the one who decides how much profit we distribute, how much we accumulate. He can even distribute to himself and not me." He smiled ruefully. "'In his unfettered discretion.' One of your people wrote it up ironclad. If I leave without his consent it all goes into a trust just as tight, and he's the trustee. I'm good at deals, but I made the worst one of my life that day. Everything I got is tied up. That's what I meant about my wife sees more." His tone had an edge to it; he gnawed his lip for a moment. "I love going to ask someone for my own money," he explained, and now the bitterness was open. "Thought there'd be a day, an out, sooner or later. . . but it didn't happen. Always in the middle of something, and the nut too big to walk away from, and getting bigger. No chance, until this media thing came along. Something he finally wanted as much as I want out."

Suddenly he did turn his head. "I'm not going to lay everything off on him," he said sharply. "I enjoyed the game – it feels good winning, and I didn't mind the blood. Not at all. Get back time. But lately. . ." He turned back to the window.

"I'm so tired of all this sh– nonsense," he said after a while, without turning his head. "All of it. That girl who was with Ronny? The model? Big trophy date, big deal. I been with her. He could do better buying one of those plastic inflatable girls on Forty-Second Street. The same result and a lot cheaper. You don't have to buy it diamonds."

Slowly he turned to face her, met her eyes. "And the special ones, like you." His voice was flat and dull. "I'm not getting anywhere with you, am I? You don't even like me." He began to turn away again.

Too much – much, much, much too much. He took her to nice lunches. He'd picked her up in this lovely limousine. Never mind what anyone else said, he'd been nothing but kind to her – and all she did in return was forget the dates and turn him down. Worse: What he said wasn't true, she *did* like him – quite a bit, she realized.

Without being fully conscious of what she was doing, Adele moved from her seat to his, quickly, athletically, was on his lap before he knew it, his head turned in surprise, her arms around his neck, and kissed him.

Steel struck flint.

*

She could not tear herself away.

Her thought, to the extent that there had been a thought, had been to kiss him quickly, a friendly kiss, move back to her own seat, smile and say, *I do like you*. But once started she could not stop. Almost at once it was miles beyond friendship, long, hard. . . passionate. Then he put his own arms around her, pulled her closer, may God have mercy on her, but she did, always would, respond to a man who knew what he wanted and went for it. He for sure was alpha, big-time alpha. She hadn't counted on that. Or any of it.

She hadn't anticipated that it would be heaven, absolute heaven, to be in his arms. When she opened her eyes, his face was before her. It was impossible not to kiss it; impossible to retreat. As far as the body was concerned, the libido, it was an all-systems-go blast-off. Somehow she reined herself in. She had to. The body was running way, way beyond the point where the rest of Adele was willing to go. She might like him, but she did not entirely trust him.

He looked down, still holding her, amazed and delighted. "You're no ang –" he gulped. "You should have come to that party dressed as a little tiger."

"Things aren't always –" *what they seem*, she'd intended to finish, but then he kissed her again and everything started all over again, wonderful, ridiculous tenth grade necking, two adults.

The last and largest of the surprises concerning George Sorenson, the one that explained all the others. But why should it have been a surprise? The chemistry had been there the whole time, she realized now, lurking underneath the surface of events. She'd felt the ripple the moment she laid eyes on him, at the Software Arts Expo. A total stranger had noticed. She'd felt it again when they were introduced, at the lunches, when they were dancing. But she'd met Tom the day after the Expo, and that event had overshadowed everything. Despite that, despite all the weight of reality, all the distractions, it had emerged, astonishing in its strength. She closed her eyes and opened her mouth; explored; let him explore; on and on and on. *Heaven*.

He shifted down in the seat, still holding her, while she ground herself into him, and flipped the panel of the inner window shut with his foot. The back cabin was now completely enclosed, dark and private. He shifted up in the seat and moved her towards the seat. He drew his hand up the s-curve between her hip and shoulder, then moved it slowly toward the center of her body. Sitting on his lap, she was fully aware of his state of arousal, of what was coming next.

She wrenched herself away. "No," she managed to gasp.

He could see she meant it. "Why?" he said, breathing hard himself.

"Because you've had too many women on that seat," she panted. "Because it shouldn't start like that between us." Which was true as far as it went.

"Doesn't matter how it starts," he panted, and pulled her back.

"No," she said, "I didn't mean to tease. I don't want it to start that way," and he realized she meant it. His grip relaxed. Still he held her lightly; she made no effort to leave his arms, it was too lovely; they looked into each other's eyes; irresistible; another long, lingering kiss.

Finally the car stopped. He let her pull back, but his arms were still around her. "We're here," he said simply. It occurred to Adele that she'd used the word "start"; that there was an implication in that. Should she withdraw it? She considered for only an instant. *No.*

"I do like you. I like you a lot," she said instead, truthfully, now superfluously.

"Evidently," George grinned, a changed man, a very, very happy man. "Can I come up?"

"No way." she grinned. "You know what will happen."

"Just to talk?"

"I don't trust you and I don't trust myself," Adele answered, still smiling, but becoming serious. "I do like you, George – but I don't let every man I like make love to me. Maybe everyone else does, but I don't. If we did that – now – it would be like the Macy's model. Or the inflato girl. You know that."

"That was a dumb thing to say. I take it back," said George, still with an idiot's grin.

"Too late," Adele smiled in turn, now gently disengaging herself and sliding towards the door, opening it.

"You know," he said, becoming serious in turn, taking her arm lightly, "I usually go away for the holidays. I own this place down in Zihuateneo – well, actually, I don't own it, foreigners can't own property in Mexico, it's a 99-year lease – but anyway, a condo, that's where I go. It's great to lie there on the beach and read about all the cold weather back here. And the Christmas stuff is a lot more authentic than what they do at Puerto Vallarta or Acapulco. I've gone there alone the last couple years. No one I really wanted to take. But it's no good like that."

"My holidays aren't nearly so interesting," she said gently, carefully, after a silence. "I go home to my dad's house. I visit with my brothers and their children. It must sound awfully dull, but I wouldn't trade it for anything. It's the only vacation I've taken the last two years."

"Ah, c'mon, Adele, don't be like that. You know what I mean," he said urgently, "I could postpone the trip if you like. Mid-January or later. I don't watch the pro football playoffs, anyway. It would still be great."

She regarded him. "Don't change any plans for me, George. What just happened. . . may have been just something that happened. I'm pretty serious about things like that. I can't promise you anything."

He tightened his grip ever so slightly. "But you will think about it? It is possible?"

She took his hand off her arm and opened the door. "I will think about it." She considered. "It's not impossible," she said carefully again. As far as she was willing to go this night. So many surprising reactions she had to assimilate.

"Can't I help you decide?" he implored, leaning towards her. "All kinds of shows in this city. All kinds of places. I'd love to take you out. Take you dancing. Money's not my problem," the Bronx accent now very natural, very pleasant on her ears.

Take you dancing. Her eyes half-closed. *That would be wonderful*, she thought wistfully. But out of the question for the moment. She was not going to start into any neurotic self-flagellation over what had happened in the limo. She had intended only a gesture of friendship. Spontaneity and the body, with its own reasons, had taken over. Such things happen. But to start deliberately a relationship which would of necessity have to begin at a high plateau of physical intensity. . . out of the question.

"I'd like that," she said, "but not until after NATPE. When we're done with the Project. After the 20th. It –" She stopped.

"What's the matter?" he asked. "You look like someone just stepped on your grave."

"Nothing," she smiled, composing herself. "I was remembering all the work I have to do before then." She opened the door and stepped out.

"O.K.," he shrugged. "Hell, I'm going to be tearing around like crazy until then anyway. But you can at least have lunch with me again," he went on. "You have to eat like everyone else. Friday? I'll be back in town. At my offices? Like before?"

She considered it, considered him. This had to be explored, followed up. From out of total nowhere, this man had made a major impression on her, at a time when she had thought such a thing was impossible. "All right," she smiled. "Friday."

He slipped to the edge of the seat, a bit behind her, put his hand under her chin as she turned, lifted her head, "Goodnight," kissed her again; and it happened again, long and lingering, thirty seconds, forty seconds, a minute, mouth to mouth, feet on the pavement, leaning through the window. She could not bring herself to pull away. It was simply too wonderful, despite the hello-young-lovers' grins she could feel from the chauffeur and passersby, despite a distinct undertow of guilt. Finally, somehow, she managed to break it off.

"My goodness," she breathed. "Goodnight, George," the door closed, and the limousine moved out into the traffic, a man in much improved spirits in the backseat.

Not bad.

*

She was alone in the elevator, drifting slowly upwards.

Much to think about. Surprised herself in the back of the limo. She cared for him more than she had realized. *Hatchet man*, maybe, that disturbed her, mostly on Lem's behalf, but he'd been nothing but good to her, so why shouldn't she like him? Zihuateneo? Possible, very possible, she'd been afraid to tell him exactly how possible. His face was suddenly before her. *George.* A tiger before the rest of the world; a very appealing combination of lamb and lion with her. Very, very appealing.

The elevator stopped at her floor. So why the guilt? For there was no question it was there; not the stupid, neurotic kind, a different type. The pleasure she'd enjoyed had a furtive aspect to it, the dangerous exhilaration a loyal wife must feel when she flirts with adultery. Except that Adele wasn't anyone's wife and she had no one to be loyal to.

Forgive me, Tom. I'm sorry, little one. I let it get away. Apologizing to two absent members of a fantasy family. Why was she reacting so inanely?

Why? Why do you think, stupid? Maybe because you spend your weekends driving out to talk to his old professors, and your daytimes waiting for his old girlfriends to call. She thought of George and the backseat. A good thing, a very interesting development. Maybe this whole thing with Tom was a bad idea. Maybe she should just give it up and accept what life was handing her.

No. The reaction was strong and instantaneous. What she'd started she'd finish. The clock on the microwave oven read 9:45 when she came through her door. George hadn't been kidding about the evening being an early one. The phone rang. She did not react for a moment. Then her heart jumped.

"Hello," she said.

"Hello," answered a woman's voice she'd never heard before. "Is this. . . is this Adele Jansen?"

"Yes," she breathed. "To whom am I speaking?" Her caller's voice had the oddest timbre – a strange register, as she would have expected of a person who has not heard herself speak in some time, but with an inner quietude, a poised dignity, that took Adele completely by surprise.

"My name is Peters. Millicent Peters. I received a message from you yesterday. I'd like to talk to you."

"I was hoping you'd call," Adele breathed again. Every thought of George Sorenson had disappeared for the nonce. "I want to talk to you, too," *stupid, obviously, you left the message.* "I – I – I – this sounds dumb, but I don't know what to call you. What you like to be called. I didn't ask your father."

"Milly," said the voice, with a short, low laugh. "Like all my friends used to. I'd like to think of you as one."

GHOST SHIP

"**Y**ou left the almost perfect message," Milly went on calmly. "I haven't phoned out to anyone in three years. I guess you got my number from my father. But how did you get his?"

Adele turned off the overhead room light, sat down at her desk, her gown still on. Adjusting rapidly, discarding all manner of preconceptions – what had she expected, anyway? A near hysteric? A person on the verge? Perhaps some wilting, hothouse flower trampled underfoot (poor Butterfly)? Certainly not this – a clear, composed contralto; great, quiet dignity; regality; a queen in exile. Whatever she had expected, it was certainly not this.

"I found out who Tom's academic adviser was, never mind how, Professor Goodson. He told me – a lot of things. He told me about you and Tom. He had your old home phone number. I called and your dad answered. He gave me this number."

"Did you tell him you were a friend of Tom's? Were you that honest with him?" Probing.

"No," said Adele, her read on the situation becoming firmer. Take no chances with this one. Don't even try. One false step and she will lay the receiver back down upon the hook and that, sister, will be that. "I told him I had this woman client who wanted to get even with him, that I was trying anything to find him. That maybe you could help."

"I see," said the voice calmly.

"I had to say something like that. Your father seems as angry at Tom as he ever was. And he blames him for all that's happened to you."

"Of course," said Milly. "I suppose he told you that I was a little princess? That I was a crown jewel and his other children are worthless? And that Tom ruined it all?"

"Yes," Adele agreed, after a moment, "something like that."

"I don't suppose," Milly went on, "he told you what a joke it all was. That somehow he'd turned me into an alabaster princess to make up for all the dirt he had in his own life. But he knew what kind of girl I really was – he knew it the whole time – it was an unholy alliance between us. And it cost me the love of my sisters and my baby brother. He rubbed their noses in what I was supposed to be every day of their lives. Not that I minded then. I accepted it as my due." She paused. "I'll tell you what kind of girl I really was, Ms. Jansen."

"Adele."

"Adele," she continued. "I learned early on that I could use men – that that was an easy way to get what I wanted – which is exactly what I did and how I lived. I had a million attention-getting devices and I used them all – how I dressed, how I talked, everything. I was a big theatrical phony. You wouldn't have cared for me for a second.

"One story. When I was a senior in high school, class standing was real important to me. I wanted to be salutatorian in the worst way. But I needed an A in physics and I couldn't get it into my head for the life of me. Well, I got my A, in the classroom after school one day, down on my knees, and I don't mean scrubbing floors. Don't shed any tears for me over what happened. I'm where I want to be. I'm where I belong. For now." Her voice was composed, gentle.

"Professor Goodson also felt bad for you, too, though," said Adele, reeling a bit. "He said he liked Tom, but there was a time when he could have strangled him because of what Tom did to you."

"You want me to talk about *him*," Milly said, after a moment, with the oddest accent on the pronoun. "I've never done that. I never intended to. My thoughts, memories – they're all locked up deep in my heart. They're all precious to me, the sad ones and the happy ones. And so personal. I've never thought I'd share them with anyone – I wondered if there was anyone who'd understand. And now you tell me you will. Why, Adele? Why should I? Why should I trust you?"

"Because of the message I left," Adele said slowly, speaking from the heart. "Because I think we have something in common. Because – because –" suddenly it gushed out – "because I already like you." She looked into her heart again, spoke: "Because what happened meant something. Because memories like that have to be shared. Or they decay. They lose their importance."

"Yes," Milly sighed. A long, long silence.

"Tom," Milly intervened suddenly, breaking the silence, in an induplicable tone of solemnity, relief, regret, and expectation – less the pronouncement than the invocation of a distant, mystical talisman, and Adele suddenly understood the odd accent – she'd been avoiding the name, the actual invocation, until she'd decided. "You want to talk about Tom."

She paused. "Perhaps it has to happen. Perhaps it's finally time." She paused again. "And I like you, too," she added. "That's important. I guess I've decided.

"Professor Goodson's very sweet," Milly continued, voice firming, committing herself, "but he doesn't know any better, either. Not that anyone on the outside could possibly have known. Tom didn't betray me, Adele. I betrayed him. It was the biggest mistake of my life. It was the most terrible thing I have ever done. I'll tell you everything I know, not that it's all that much. You may be disappointed. All I know is what seemed to happen. But nothing about Tom is what it seems to be. Or ever has been, or ever will be. I'm sure of that."

"Can you tell me what really happened?" Adele asked. "Would you?"

"What really happened," Milly echoed distantly. "If I know myself." Resonances in her voice of times long past, happenings on a distant, darkling shore. She began to speak even more firmly:

*

I had my life pretty well set up by the time I started at Binghamton. Everything was so simple. I was engaged – well, engaged to be engaged – to a young man named William Clarkson. Billy had these dreamboat California surfin' good looks. (*She laughed.*) I wish I could show you the picture they took of us at my senior prom. We were really quite the All-American couple. Anyway, he was three years ahead of me, in pre-med at Columbia. He'd even decided on his specialty – plastic surgery – and I was going to be the ideal doctor's wife. The perfect life for an alabaster princess. Or so I thought at the time.

Was that what I really wanted? Who was I, really? I know now I was never sure of the answer to those questions. They frightened me too much to ask them out loud. And the easy way seemed to make so much sense, to be such a straight path to follow. Billy got to share my bed while we were younger and I'd get to share his bankbook as time went on. A fair trade, a good bargain – too good a deal to turn down.

What nagging doubts, what moments of confusion I had I ignored. But then I had so little time for them. I had a blast at college. Billy would come down nearly every weekend – his folks got him this BMW for graduation – and take me off someplace, to the city, or skiing or something. The other girls in the dorm were green with envy, particularly the ones who had to fight for a date. That didn't bother me at all. In fact, it added to the pleasure. I was at the tippity-top of the pecking order, and I let everyone know it every chance I got. I knew a million ways to rub it in. Miss Sorority Queen, Binghamton style.

And if occasionally, I became restless – if every once in a while a second thought or three crept in – if I had some distant awareness that Billy was a first class creep and I was a grasping little bitch – it was easy enough to ignore all that. What small private dreams I had – so private – seemed teeny-tiny compared to all my concrete plans with Billy. I took the basic class in creative writing. Late at night, I wrote my private poetry. Sometimes I dreamt I could be a success at that. But it was all very personal, and I would have died if anyone even knew. I mean, *really!* Poetry at midnight; strictly for wallflowers.

Sometimes I thought I could be an actress. But that wasn't a dream I had to keep to myself. That fit right in with all the raw-taw social thing. I went out for the spring play in my first year, and I got a nice part. Then I went for it again when I was a sophomore and I got the lead. I had some private ambitions about that, too – how I would ever have worked it out married to a plastic surgeon and living in Westchester, I don't know. But I wasn't thinking about that sort of practicality then.

The spring play was *As You Like It*. Like I told you, I got the lead. Spring break at Columbia came a week or so after the auditions. Billy and one of his friends went down to one of the Florida resorts to blow off steam. I knew what that meant, but I pretended I didn't. Anyway, neither of us was particularly faithful to the other. (We really were an appalling pair.) So I was on my own for a while.

The first night of rehearsal was a Tuesday. It was only a read-through. Everyone came casual. It wasn't supposed to be anything special. But I got involved – I always did, that's why I thought I might have a future – and I finished on a full adrenaline high. It was only about 10:30, but I couldn't go home. I went over to the coffee house to get some coffee, or tea, or whatever. It was all very ordinary. It was a day like any other. The boy who played Orlando offered to see me home, but I wasn't having any of that. There was nothing he could do for me. The Union wasn't at all crowded. I was sitting there, at an empty table, going over my lines, when all at once there was someone in the light. I looked up and there was Tom.

*

"There was Tom," she repeated, "and everything began to change – from that very second."

"What was he like?" interrupted Adele. "Had you seen him before?"

"Oh, yes, yes," answered Milly, "everybody knew him. Not that I'd never really given him much thought. He was never really part of my world, if you know what I mean. He was only a junior, my first year, but he was already sort of a classroom legend. He was around the dorms a lot. You saw him with all sorts of girls, but even so he seemed distant and unapproachable. There were all kinds of kids, even faculty, who were in awe of him. Everyone had heard the story about him winning some playwriting contest when he was a freshman, then withdrawing the entry. That impressed me. I'd have loved to have the talent to do something like that. There were a few kids who laughed at him, of course, there always are, but not many. And there were stories – but I'll get into that later.

"It wasn't that he was difficult or unfriendly. When I was a freshman, word got around that if you were really in trouble with some subject, a foreign language or whatever, you could go to him and he'd help you, even do the assignment sometimes. If you could find him – and if you had the courage to ask. He was one of those people who're scary without trying, without wanting to be, because of who they are." Adele nodded as she listened.

"I'd only seen him once before that involved me in any way. It was that autumn, months before this. We played this weird kind of touch football at Binghamton, with six-person teams of three girls and three boys, and a girl always has to be quarterback. It's more fun than it sounds. I was quarterback on one of our dorm teams. I wasn't really that good. I think the boys looked forward to the touch part was the reason. At any rate, we were playing some league game and I suddenly looked up and there he was, standing to one side of the field, watching. I like to think now he was watching me, but I'm not sure my memory isn't playing tricks after what happened later. The horizon was behind him. I remember for sure thinking how impressive he was, still and magnificent. I suppose I was a little attracted to him before anything happened. But I wasn't planning to do anything about it."

Adele held the receiver. Private history, whispered mouth to ear, late at night. The only genuine kind.

*

But that night in April he stood in the light and I looked up. *I liked your story*, he said.

What do you mean? I answered, but I already knew.

Your story, he said. *The one in the -------.* That was our student literary magazine.

You see, I had been keeping a little secret that spring, one I was very proud of. I'd submitted a short story I'd written to the magazine and the editors had decided to publish it. I'd done it anonymously; it was fairly personal, humorous, a slice of life about me and my kid sister Martha Jean, Christmas shopping, how she couldn't make up her mind between two wallets. It happened back before my father began to poison everything. The story was much different than anything anyone would have believed of me. I'd made it anonymous because I was worried they'd reject it out of spite if they knew it was mine. I'd given lots of people plenty of reasons to be spiteful.

How did you know? I asked, and he only smiled that little no-smile of his. *May I sit down?* he said – he was still standing. Almost every other guy I'd ever known when he was coming on would have taken a seat for himself, but not Tom. It's funny for a man who's so good with women, but he's really shy. *Sure*, I said, and he sat down across from me.

How did you know I wrote that story? I asked again, and he told me. It seemed that Mr. Newcombe had been watching me much more closely than I had ever realized, that he knew a lot more about me than I would have ever dreamt. He'd seen me with my sister, and he'd overheard me use a couple of catchphrases from the story. He'd put two and two together. No one else bothered. I would have been worried if it were a different man, or if he'd told me in a different way, but I wasn't upset at all. I became more and more fascinated by him.

My script was open; I'd just read the speech of Rosalind's with the line, *one inch more is a whole South-sea of discovery.* Ever since then, that's been my favorite line. This night was the inch more. We began to talk, about the play – he has a genuine eidetic memory, you know; he didn't need to look at my script, not once – about Shakespeare, about poetry, then about everything – and everything began to change.

We sat there until 1:00, when the Union closed. Then we walked out onto one of the grassy fields. This was eight years ago. There was an unusually warm, early spring that year.

"I remember," said Adele, "it was my first year at Syracuse." Of course she remembered – a month after the catastrophe of Rush Week, with everyone else on campus gamboling about like frisky, nubile – very nubile – lambs, everyone, that is, except Adele Elizabeth Jansen, who declined all invitations, refused all offers, spent her Friday and Saturday nights in tight-lipped concentration in the dorm, playing bridge with women, every fiber in her body in smoldering rebellion. Meanwhile, several score miles south, Tom had been discovering the great love of his life.

"It was a wonderful spring. We -"

*

- strolled out onto the fields. Not hand in hand; in fact, none of it would have happened if he'd tried any of that before it was time. It was a spring that was a gift, a night that was a treasure, a magic carpet. Some little breeze had wiped all the haze away. The stars looked like torches, showing the way. We talked a little about that; he showed me how to pick out constellations besides Orion's Belt and the Big Dipper; there's *nothing* he doesn't know something about. But mostly we talked about magic forests, places where everything and everyone is transformed, the central metaphor in *As You Like It*. He found a knoll for me to sit on – he folded his coat and put it down so I wouldn't get wet – and we talked about Arden, the magic forest, how it was a matter of psychology, of human spirit, and not geography. That's hardly deep criticism of the play, but he kept working on it and turning it and twisting it, all sorts of variations. Tom can get so much out of so little! We talked and talked.

It got to be late. We both knew it was time to stop. I knew by then what had to happen. He took my hand and helped me up – that was the first time he touched me – and asked me if I'd come home with him. Of course there was no way I wasn't going. We went back to his place. He lived in this little apartment off campus and I stayed there the rest of the night.

That's how it began. We didn't say anything the next morning about it, but I was sure that he was going to meet me after class. Then about 11:00, I became really worried he wasn't. But there he was, on the steps at noon, after my last class, and we started up again as if we'd never stopped. I spent that next night with him, and all the days and nights after. By that time, I had gone into the middle of the forest, and nothing was ever going to be the same again. Ever.

He wasn't like anyone I had ever met or anyone else I was ever going to meet. He saw things, he could do things – so many open doors, so many new avenues, so many perspectives I'd sensed, but hadn't had the courage to explore. So many new insights about me. A whole new Milly Peters began to blossom around him, a girl I liked a lot more than the old one.

*

"He loved me," she said simply. "He loved me for qualities I didn't know I possessed until I met him. But he knew. Even before it started."

*

By the time a week went by, I was all but living with him. I moved a lot of my clothes over to his apartment, and I spent most of my time there. With any other man, that wouldn't have been possible, but the clothes Tom owned didn't fill two dresser drawers and a quarter of a closet. Billy was still in Florida, and he could stay there forever for all I cared. That was all over, though he didn't know it yet. It was while I was moving some ring binders aside to store some books of my own that I came across Tom's poetry. I was so surprised; he hadn't said anything about it, and yet it was so polished, so finely crafted! I didn't follow all of it, but it was obvious to me it belonged in print. It would have been obvious to anyone. I was puzzled why he'd never submitted any of it to anyone, not even the school magazine. But I wanted to make my own gift to him. I borrowed the volume and printed the poems out on a word processor. Then I collated them myself. It was another thing that surprised him. I'm very proud that I did that. Regardless of what happened later.

That was maybe the best day of all of them and they were all good. I can remember now how I felt when I first read what he'd written. It was bittersweet – I had to face up to the fact of exactly how far out of my league he was as a writer – but basically it was a wonderful discovery. You see, by then I was sure that Tom was some sort of genius, but I was afraid I was the only one who'd ever know. And then there I was suddenly, reading the proof positive, and the very first, I was certain of that. Everyone was going to find out what kind of guy my guy was.

I didn't know where all of it would lead, I hadn't the faintest idea. But I was determined to follow the path wherever it went. Not that there weren't problems; there were problems right from the start. But I wasn't going to give up on the new Milly and I certainly wasn't going to give up on Tom.

(She fell silent.)

*

"I have to ask," said Adele, finally. "What happened? If you can tell me. If it isn't too painful."

A long silence.

"It's very, *very* painful," Milly said. "I never thought I'd tell anyone about it before. I wonder," she said, her tone changing, sounding as if she were nineteen again, voice full of curiosity, "what you're really like. I wonder who you are. I never thought I'd tell anyone what I'm telling you. I wonder if we'd be friends if we knew each other well. I think so. I hope that would be true. But all I know about you is that Tom told you he loved you – and that you lied to my father." She laughed. "And very well, too."

"I wonder, too," Adele answered truthfully. "You're not at all what I expected." She paused. "I haven't lied to you," she added.

"I've got to get on with my story. I've got a dispensation for tonight, but I don't want to abuse it. I want to finish for you, and I want to find out about you. I said –"

*

– that there were problems from the start. I began to worry, almost as soon as I realized I was in love with him, that there was no way I could make him happy. That was a new kind of worry for me. Before all I'd ever thought

325

about was how the man could take care of me. But now I wanted him to feel as good about me as I did about him – and it was a big concern whether that would ever happen. He enjoyed being with me and I knew he cared about me. But I doubted he'd ever lighten up, brighten. I'm certain you know what I mean.

Little things bothered me. The apartment he lived in. . . so much happened the first night I didn't notice then, but later – it was so small! And it wasn't much different than a tool shed. He didn't have any decorations up, or personal things, or anything. No posters, no pennants, no pictures. Everything was functional. It bothered me. When I started moving myself in, I bought a few things to spruce it up. He liked music a lot, but he didn't even own a radio, let alone a stereo. It was embarrassing. Billy had just given me a boom box for my birthday, and my old portable was gathering dust in the dorm storage. I gave it to him–

(*"He still has it," Adele interjected.*)

He was touched to the core. He didn't make a big deal about it – he never makes a big deal out of anything – but I knew. I came close to crying. I wondered if anyone had ever given him anything. But I didn't know. He never said anything about himself. I told him everything, about me and my family. In fact, it was then, talking to him, I began to realize for the first time how wrong everything in my world was. But he never said a word about himself.

*

Oh, no, Adele thought. "He never said anything about where he came from? Who his family is?" she asked aloud, her heart sinking.

"Very little. Of course I wanted to know those things. It got to be exasperating, how evasive he'd be. The only time – one day we were in his apartment and I started to tickle him –"

Tickle Tom? The mind boggled.

"–he didn't laugh, of course, but finally he saw I was serious and he told me something. He's an orphan. He came from a foundling home in upstate New York. For some reason, it's very embarrassing to him. I couldn't make out the name. It sounded something like Arbor Rest. When I asked him if that was right, he said I had the wrong kind of crossing boughs. I knew he was playing some sort of game, but no matter how I pressed him after that, he wouldn't budge. Finally I dropped it. I figured I'd get back to it someday. But of course that never happened."

"Arborist?" Adele repeated, puzzled.

"That's what it sounded like. I'm not sure he was telling the truth."

*

What was scarier was a certain tension I could sense in him. Over the three weeks we were together, it got worse from day to day. It wasn't something you'd ever notice unless you were watching him as carefully as I was. His fingers would tremble a little, even the stubs on his left hand. He'd count them automatically, over and over and over. He thought he was being private, but I saw. He has this exercise routine, almost an hour every night. He takes himself to the breaking point. It was terrible to watch. It had nothing to do with building himself up.

Sometimes this horrible vacant look comes over his face – I couldn't stand that look – and it was there more often with each passing day. But the worst, the very worst, were the mornings. I couldn't bear to watch him when he first woke up. If I woke up before he did, I'd close my eyes and pretend to be asleep until that time had passed. It's as if he's lost his soul overnight and he has to find it all over again every morning.

I tried to find out what was the matter. He was my guy and I wanted to know. I'd ask him if anything was bothering him, if there was anything I could do. But he'd just shake his head, no, nothing, and change the subject. He had an oral examination coming up for a fellowship in German lit. I wondered if that was rattling him. It didn't make much sense he'd be nervous before any exam – no reason – but it was something to think.

It was reason enough for me to bide my time and hope I'd learn more as I went along. Partly it was hope about the test. But mostly, mostly I was afraid – afraid that he was telling me the entire, absolute truth, that there really wasn't anything I could do.

It got to be the night before the German exam. I ate on campus because of the rehearsal. Then I went over to my own dorm to check for messages. Tom had left me one – a short one, only that he loved me (he left it in code, citing one of the lines in the play), but that he couldn't see me that night. I was puzzled and a little concerned, but not over much. After all, he had the exam the next day and we'd spent nearly every free hour the last three weeks together. Also, Billy had been back from vacation two weeks. I'd held him off, but finally I'd made a date with him for dinner on Sunday night. I was going to give him the bad news, that it was over. So maybe a little breathing space was a good idea. I wasn't at all worried about Tom and me. I knew as surely as I had ever known anything in my life that what had happened between us was no crush.

*

Milly swallowed hard. "You're going to have to bear with me now," she said. "This next part is very, very difficult." Her voice was quavering slightly.

There was a lump in Adele's throat as well. She'd heard enough from Goodson to know what was coming. Listening to this was going to be horrible, completely horrible.

"Go on," she said.

*

But then he wasn't around Saturday or Sunday either. I became real upset then. He hadn't said anything about going out of town or leaving after the exam. I didn't know what to think. It didn't feel right to be in his apartment without him. So I stayed on campus. I did my class work, I memorized my lines, and I worried, more and more, the entire weekend.

Then came the dinner Sunday night with Billy.

I have to back up for a second. After the first few days, I hadn't been at all discrete with Tom. We went everywhere together; I even left his phone number and address for my overnight calls. Tom was my lover and I didn't care who knew it. I wanted everyone to know it. Besides, I wanted to fence him off a little bit. I knew he'd been with lots of other girls on campus. Since I'd made up my mind about Billy, it didn't seem to matter. It was all very open.

("Yes," said Adele, "Professor Goodson told me about you and Tom coming over to his home. He remembers it well.")

What? Oh, yes, the children's story. That was wonderful. I'm surprised he remembers it. He'd had a bit more to drink than he really should have. But Tom was always doing things like that. Anyway, I got dressed for what I thought was my last date with Billy: I really dolled myself up, I didn't want him to know that I was frantic with worry by that time. Where was Tom? I went down to see Billy, and I tried to be as cool as I could.

I expected him to be alone, but he wasn't. He was with this – well, whore, as it turned out. And he had pictures. Billy had been down to see me on campus often. A lot of people knew him. Some guy or some girl who disliked me – there was no way to find out exactly whom, there were so many who did – had tipped him off. Someone who didn't know Tom nearly as well as I did, but who knew one little thing more.

Billy had been diabolically clever. I'd never known him to be so clever before. He phoned some other people; somehow, he found someone who could take good pictures – then, when he was with me, he was perfect – every note exactly as it should be. He read me that night as if I were an open music score and he knew every note.

The pictures weren't particularly gross, just enough to prove to me what had happened. There was Tom passed out, and the women. . . then Billy paid the girl, very ostentatiously, very dramatically; and she told her story. She was vicious and condescending. Listening to her was like nails in my ears. She told me it went on all the time – that he partied all over the place. I—–

Somehow I knew she was telling the truth. My pride began to get involved. I hated to be sneered at by someone like that. Tom was still somewhere sleeping it off; there was no way to talk to him. Then she left and I was alone with Billy.

I was so hurt, so humiliated – but even then, Adele, even then, I knew that something more was going on than simple infidelity. That's what I've never told anyone before you. I didn't know why what was wrong was wrong – I've never found out – but I knew where the answer was. Even while I was still in shock.

*

"What?" said Adele.

"I said you left the almost perfect message," Milly answered, gently, but definitely putting her to the test. "But you left one thing out. Maybe the most important thing. If you know him that well."

"You're talking about the dream," Adele answered without any hesitation. "The recurrent nightmare."

"Yes," said Milly, "yes," almost hissing, a great distance in her voice. "You've seen it, then. Can you tell me what you saw? You're the first person I've talked to – and I've talked to so many – that knows about that. Please. Tell me."

Adele did.

*

You saw one of the milder ones.

It didn't happen the first night. It was so late by the time we got to his place, and everything that happened after we got there. But the next night! It was exactly as you described it, but it went on much longer, at least a half an hour, and he raved incomprehensibly. Don't feel bad you didn't do anything. That had to be the most frightening thing I've ever seen in my life. Later, the next few nights, I got brave enough to hold him in my arms, whisper to him; I'd like to think it helped, but I'm almost certain it didn't. I never wanted to love him more than those times, but I was powerless. Then it would be morning and he'd never discuss it, wouldn't say a word – except that he didn't know what he dreamed about. A door. . . nothing else.

The dreams got worse as time went on, longer and more intense. The worst one of all was the Thursday night before the exam. That was what had me so worried over the weekend. I didn't say that before because I was waiting to ask you. I was certain that some breaking point was coming. No one can go on like that indefinitely. I was scared for Tom, I wanted to be with him, to take care of him, and I didn't know where he was.

So I had a sense, while I was looking at the pictures, listening to the girl, that that was really what it was, the breaking point. But Billy was there, taunting me, gloating, feeding like a ghoul on all the negativity. We were all alone. He said he'd finally found out what I was, that I was no better than the woman he'd brought with him. Then he said if I didn't give Tom up he was going to tell everyone, expose the whole mess for what it was. Then he implied he was going to do that anyway, humiliate me in front of everyone.

I was shattered. I lost my balance completely. All I could think of was the humiliation, all the girls I'd laughed and sneered at who were going to be laughing and sneering at me. Billy – I knew he was a jerk, I'd planned to drop him, but that he might do it first – I could see all the good things I'd planned on disappearing. And Tom – I told you I had the beginning of an understanding, but there was still a lot of bewilderment. There I was looking at what seemed to be the crude, simple answer, meaning I'd been played. It hurt. It hurt like anything. If only I'd given myself time to think. . . if only I'd slowed down. . . but the new Milly Peters was so new. It had only been 22 days.

So I didn't think. I reacted exactly the way Billy thought I would. I did it the way the old Milly would have. I went for the gesture, the big, attention-getting gesture. I threw the pictures at him and I raced upstairs, crying my head off. People came out in the corridor to look. Then when I was in my room I thought of the most theatrical thing I could do, a way to make everyone feel sorry for me, to get even with both of them, Billy and Tom.

All that was the way the old Milly thought, what Billy had expected. But what I did he hadn't expected at all.

*

"I didn't really try to kill myself," said Milly. "Or even do myself real harm. I'd seen movies; I knew how it was done. You open your wrists and stick them in a bath so the blood won't coagulate. I never went near the bathtub. I knew Billy would follow me. I used this dinky two-edge disposable razor I used to shave my legs. I knew you could produce a lot of blood with little cuts on your wrists. A great effect, a big splash – and that's exactly what happened. By the time Billy got there, there was blood everywhere, I was still crying, everyone was shouting. Billy was the same kind of phony I was. He could see the cuts weren't that deep, but he made a big production out of binding my wrists, and holding me. Then the ambulance came and I was off to the infirmary. Before the doors closed, I could hear Billy telling everyone what had happened, what a bastard Tom was, how he'd pushed me to the brink. He didn't say anything about himself."

*

They kept me in the hospital for observation for the next few days. I reveled in it. Everyone treated me as if I were a little porcelain doll. My folks filled up the room with flowers. Billy stayed at Binghamton and visited me. I pretended he wasn't obnoxious.

Tom wanted to come, and the doctors had a big debate on whether that would be advisable. Finally, they let him. He brought along the binder I'd put together for him; I knew what he meant to do. But I came through for Billy and my family; I was really into the role, committed actress that I was. I threw an empty IV bottle at him and yelled all sorts of wild things at him. It was another wonderful scene. I was never in better form.

He endured it. That was the only time I ever saw him at all shaky. But you know how he sees through people. You can't lie to him, it's impossible. I'm certain he had a good idea of what had actually happened. But he didn't say anything about that. *I'm sorry, Milly*, was all he said, *I really thought it would be different. Don't blame yourself.*

I yelled at him to get out then. He looked at me – I will never forget that look; I'm going to have to live with that look until the day I die – then turned and left. I don't know what I would have done if I'd known then that that was the last thing he was ever going to say to me and the last time I was ever going to see him. I had some subconscious screwball idea that when he'd been punished enough we'd pick it up again.

That night Billy and a couple of his Binghamton friends jumped him near his apartment. Billy would never do that alone. He always has friends, he's that type. They beat him up where it wouldn't show; one of his ribs got broken. He came in for treatment and I guess he was there for a few hours. Maybe it was his being in the same building, or maybe it was that the time had come for me to come to my senses. For whatever reason, I had a long, restless night.

The first instant of the next morning, the second I opened my eyes, I realized what I'd done – I mean, what I'd *really* done. I didn't want the attention, I didn't want everyone's sympathy, I for sure didn't want Billy – what I wanted was Tom, and I didn't give a damn what he'd done or who thought what. I got out of my bed, I got dressed, I went downstairs, and out. I was running by the time I got to his apartment. I went upstairs. . .

He was gone. Everything was gone, except some clothes of mine that were still in the closet, the decorations, and the binder I'd made. The bed was bare except for the mattress pad. I knew then it was over, completely finished, that I was never going to go back to the forest with him again. I don't like weepy women–

("Neither do I," Adele interjected.)

I only wept when I could get something out of it. But I lay down on the mattress that day. I must have cried for at least two hours, just sobbing, all by myself. "Tom and Milly" was finished forever. It was all ruined and I'd done it. Everyone who was there at Binghamton then remembers me in the ambulance, and me throwing the bottle at Tom, the things I shouted at him. But no one knew about me all alone in that deserted apartment four days later. No one – you're the first person I've ever told. But what happened there was the truth, and the rest was the outward show. w

At any rate, I pulled myself together, went back to the hospital and checked myself out, then back to my dorm. Life seemed to get back to normal. People thought I'd drop out of the play, but no way. It had been too important a symbol for Tom and me. Besides, I'd only missed two rehearsals. I was hoping that he'd come to one of the performances, that I'd get a second chance.

But it didn't happen. He wasn't there. I gave this great performance – forgive me for bragging, believe me, it didn't mean a thing to me – this plucky blonde Rosalind with her wrists bandaged. I got wonderful ovations, even from the people who hated my guts – and all it cost me was the only man who'd ever really understood me and who cared for me more than all of them combined. A good trade, right? Something else I won't forget: standing in the middle of the stage with tears in my eyes (no one knew the real reason why), everyone clapping for me. I bowed, and smiled, and I wanted to die.

Billy came to the last performance. He'd brought an engagement ring with him. I think he expected me to fall into his arms and go back to bed with him. Instead, I told him we were through. He didn't believe me. He thought I still hadn't recovered completely.

I got through the rest of the school year – don't ask me how – and then I went home. Everyone treated with me kid gloves; I had a summer job at Billy's father's office, but my mom and dad wanted me to give it up and spend the summer recuperating. That was fine with me. There was a lot to think about. Which is what I did.

Billy and I were absolutely finished, but my dad would not accept the fact. He kept inviting Billy over – you know the line: *He's not coming to see you, honey, he's coming to see me* – and it got to be maddening. Because. . .

*

"Billy thought it was all about sex," Milly said, with exasperation in her voice. "That something had happened in bed with me and Tom that explained everything." She sighed. "This is so embarrassing, but it is part of it. I first had sex when I was thirteen. I didn't understand it and I didn't like it. For me, it was another method of getting what I wanted, one of the most effective. Later, it was a way of keeping Billy in line. But there was never anything in it for me.

"With Tom, it wasn't any different physically. I liked being with him and it pleased me to please him. He really likes sex. But for me it was the same old story, which is to say no story at all. I enjoyed what we did in bed, because of way he made love to me. But I'm not a very sexual woman – I look like I should be, but I'm not – and nothing really changed. Perhaps it would have if we'd gone on longer, but I doubt it. None of that stopped Billy from acting as if Tom had cast some spell on me physically. It drove me crazy. It wasn't true."

Another silvery laugh. "The only difference was that I knew Billy used me and I knew Tom loved me – and that was the only difference that mattered to me."

*

I came to two decisions that summer. One was that I wasn't going back to what I had been. The old Milly was dead. I finally accepted a date with Billy. He thought it was a new beginning, but it was actually the end of the end. I told him that it was over; this time there was something about the way I said it, the way I behaved, that convinced him I wasn't kidding. He started in on me again – how awful I was, what a fool I was being – but he stopped when he saw it wasn't working. It didn't make any difference to me anymore what he thought or said.

The second decision I implemented when I got back to school in the fall. I had to find out more about what had happened to me, why it had happened, everything. It couldn't have all been for nothing. It had to mean something. Which meant I had to find out more about Tom.

(*Adele stirred uneasily in her chair. This was getting very close to home.*)

I talked to everyone who knew anything – his professors, the girls he'd known before me, the ones he'd – partied – with, anyone who would talk to me.

It was surprising to find out how many people had been wondering about him. I learned a lot of things for the first time – about all his incompletes, about the undeclared major, about the alcohol programs he'd put himself in. Professor Goodson told me that he did get his degree, in a very unusual way. I was happy to learn about it, but it made me feel even guiltier. I was to blame for that.

And that's when I learned what I should have known before. He'd had dozens of girls by then – he's probably had hundreds of women by now – but I was the only one whom he'd ever taken home. I was the only one who knew how he lived. I was the only one he'd told he loved.

Until you. It's not a line with him, Adele. Whatever else, he doesn't lie – and when he does speak like that, he speaks from the heart.

*

"You and me, Adele," she said. "We're the only ones. If there were anyone else, I'm sure I'd know. The same way I heard from you. We're the only ones he's been truly intimate with. We're the only ones who've seen that dream." She paused. "That's the reason – I'm sure that's the reason – why he doesn't let anyone get close – why he takes women to bed, but doesn't sleep with them. You can say so much about parts of him – how perceptive he is, what he writes, his women – that you can forget all about the main thing. The main thing is that Tom is a very shy, unhappy man; and what he's shyest about is how really unhappy he is. I" – suddenly she gulped – "Give me a second. I got to myself."

(*Fine with Adele; it had gotten to her, too. She couldn't speak.*)

"Finally I heard about a place," Milly continued, recovering herself. "A house. Where he was very well known."

*

I got the name from a girl on campus. It was a cheap little rundown bungalow in a seedy part of town. There was nothing glamorous about it. The woman who ran it – a Mrs. Smith, a divorcee, maybe forty-five or so – had a list of names – working women, housewives, some of the coeds at Binghamton, anyone who wanted to pick up some extra money – whom she could contact if a man wanted to meet someone. She called what she was running a dating service. But she'd hold parties from time to time – she made a lot of money from parties – and she took in runaways. They were always welcome in her house. She made it sound like a work of charity. There was one watching television the morning I came no older than fifteen – still in her nightgown. I knew watching that she was a madam and a whore – no matter what she called herself.

My skin crawled when I went in. That Tom had ever been in a place like that! Everything looked sordid and tacky in the morning, whatever it might have seemed in the evening. But Mrs. Smith had seen parts of him that I hadn't. I had to talk to her. I had to know what he's like when he's like that.

*

"What is he like?" asked Adele. "Does his personality change?"

"Yes and no," said Milly. "He'd come there off and on. Never at any regular time. He was always at least half-drunk when he arrived, and he was always welcome. Everyone knew they were in for a good time. After a while, she didn't charge him anything, she made so much money off everyone else when he was around. But – but –

"She was a coarse, vulgar, useless woman. She was trying to belittle him, belittle me, all sorts of nasty little putdowns. But I heard the undertone in spite of that. She was in awe of him. I could tell from what she said and from what she didn't say. Whatever else Tom may be, he's never small – and he can make everyone around him around him feel big. The way she spoke, I caught the same sense of grandeur people felt on campus – only in this place it was the demonic type. It sounded as if he'd come to the edge of the world and sat looking off into the darkness beyond. That he didn't care anymore. Nothing meant anything. But he'd be aware of who was around him, starting things – he can still see through anyone, even then – and very funny, of course. He's always funny if you listen hard. But mean funny, not like he is sober."

There was a coldness in Milly's voice now, an iciness all the more disconcerting because the balance still remained. "So everyone has a great time. But of course, he keeps drinking and drinking – he's a binge drinker; once he starts, he doesn't stop until he's unconscious – and it takes a lot to get him to that. He gets – promiscuous; he'll have any woman who wants him. That's how they all have their petty revenge, all the little, sordid people. It must be great fun watching a brilliant man gradually become incoherent. Marionettes are what I thought of while she was talking – relieved and sad at the same time when it's over. Relieved, because the puppet master is finally done with them and they can finally have some peace. Sad because they won't dance again until he comes again."

Not bad, Adele thought. *She really could be a writer.* "You sound so angry."

"A lot had changed since April. I had a much better idea about victims and victimizers. That was my Tom she was talking about, yours, talking about him that way, using him that way! I hated her while I listened. I wanted to kill her." Milly paused. "She didn't know. I recognized the room from the photos," she added, in a voice that held more bitterness than Adele had ever heard in her life. "That was the place where Billy took the pictures. She was the woman who set Tom up. I hope there is a hell. I hope there's a hell just for her. Anyway," she went on, in a more normal tone, "when I'd heard enough to get the idea, I got up and left in mid-sentence, without a word. I could hear her laughing behind me, but it was a nervous laugh. Not that making her feel bad made me feel any better."

"I don't know why he hasn't caught some disease by now."

Milly laughed lightly. "I wondered the same thing. We're both naïve. He doesn't care when he's like that, but they do. They may be whores and johns, but they're not crazy. They don't do anything without a condom these days. Think about it: if you're expecting your turn with the life of the party, you for sure don't want him getting infected by someone else. They're all despicable, but they're no fools. The madam herself said it: 'It's only the amateurs that get burned.'"

"So you never did find out," Adele asked carefully. "Why, I mean."

"No. Except for the obvious guess. That he gets completely wasted because that's the only time he sleeps something like normal. I'm sure you've thought of that."

Adele kicked herself mentally several times. Indeed it was obvious, and she hadn't thought of it.

*

I learned more every day, but nothing helped. I got so few facts, but every intimation I got, everyone I talked to, it all went the same way. It's as if there's something elastic inside of him that stretches until it breaks. Or – another way I thought of it – a giant holding up a roof, doing it so well you take it for granted; he doesn't even let you see the effort. Perhaps he does it too well – because sooner or later, it becomes too heavy and, when it does fall, it caves in completely. I had to face the fact that I'd sensed that, even when Billy was showing me the photographs, that I'd known it didn't have anything to do with Tom and Milly, even while I was staging that whole ridiculous scene. I had to recognize the harm I'd done. I got more and more down on myself.

I was ashamed for other reasons. I talked to all sorts of girls. He'd caroused with plenty of girls on campus. Others he'd known casually when he was more – himself. Some he'd known well. Most of them knew me, remembered me. I'd cut them without mercy when I had the chance. With a lot

336

of them, now it was their turn. I could handle that. What got to me were the others. So many of them were the exact sort of girl I'd stepped on often when I was on top. Any of them could have let me have it – but most of them were kind to me, so much kinder than I would have been if the situation were reversed a year before. I felt ashamed.

I still had the black binder he'd left, the poems I collated. I sent them off to this New York publisher the librarian recommended, someone with a reputation for being interested in that sort of thing. That gave me some pleasure; I'm still glad I did that. I left a letter about it with the registrar and I even took out a little personal ad in the school paper so he'd know. I wanted him to know. . . and I guess I was still hoping. That gave everyone another big laugh. But laughter didn't matter too much to me anymore. By that time, I was beyond caring what anyone thought.

It went on. It didn't get better. I really hadn't been eating well since April. I wasn't sleeping well, either. Nothing really interested me; there was nothing I wanted to do. I was raised Catholic. I got up so early most mornings that I started going to early Mass. Not so much for the liturgy as for the dawn light, a quiet place to think, the peace. But it got to me. My father, Billy, Tom, everything new I wanted to be – the burden of it all, and no one to share. After a while I decided to come here – only for a little while. But I've stayed here ever since. I like it. It feels comfortable. And here's where you've found me.

*

She fell silent. Adele was silent, too; so much she'd heard, so much to digest. "What's it like?" she asked after a moment. "Is the rule very severe?"

"There's more vitality than you would suppose. A surprising amount of humor; I think that the harshness of the rule actually stimulates it. Not that I appreciated it when I first came. I was close to a nervous breakdown; I couldn't shake the guilt and I couldn't get my appetite back. Not for years. Tom must have sensed that. I think that's why he wrote the poem for me. It helped in so many ways – knowing that he wasn't angry with me, that he still cared for me after everything. And it's so beautiful."

The room where Adele sat was still. "It's the best thing he's ever done," Adele said sincerely. "Did you consider. . . I mean, after all, you still care –"

"Yes," Milly answered. "After I read it, I even had my bags packed. It's not a question of not caring. He's the first person I mention in my prayers in the morning and the last one at night. What stopped me was that I didn't think I could cope; I couldn't when I was nineteen, and I don't think I can now. That's what. Even so, I'd been wondering lately whether I should go to him. What was happening to him. Why he isn't publishing anymore. Whether anyone cared about him." She paused. "That's another reason I'm glad you called," she added.

Another silence. "I'm hoping you'll tell me now," Milly said, her voice brimming now with curiosity and eagerness, "about yourself. And Tom. How he is, when you saw him last. Everything."

"Of course," Adele answered. "I'm a lawyer. I live in Manhattan, and I'm an associate with a law firm named Hapgood, Thurlow, Anderson, & Davis. That's the firm that represents Jenet Furston, the publisher you sent Tom's poems to. About seven weeks ago. . ."

As good as her word, she did tell Milly everything. Except one thing.

*

". . . both knew there was no future, either long or short. So that was the last I saw of him," Adele finished, shifting her weight. *Sounds pretty cold, Delly,* Bri had said. It sounded colder and uglier to her every time she repeated it. Particularly this night.

"It's not that I didn't care for him," she went on defensively. "I've never met a man I wanted more. But what I saw. . . the things you've said. . . I could sense a cave opening up under my feet if it went on. . . I'm not a cold person, Milly," and now she could feel the ripple begin; willy-nilly she had conjured up the memories, guilt, longing, idiot – feeling so wonderfully small and fragile when he pressed her body against his, the gentleness of his touch when he comforted her in the museum. She stopped, unable to speak further. *Oh, Tom. Why couldn't it have been possible?*

"You couldn't be a cold person," Milly said simply. "You must be very special, or none of it would have happened. Besides," she added carefully, "I was only nineteen when all this happened. Perhaps if I'd been your age, with your experience, I'd have handled it the same way. Although I don't know I'd ever be that practical." Her voice changed suddenly. "Anyway, I really don't like talking about him all evening if he were a saint or demigod," sounding annoyed at herself. "He's not. He's an ordinary man in so many ways. He should get his face slapped for some of the things he does. He likes sex; he likes women; and he's very good at getting what he wants. If he wants you, he gets you."

"Well, I can hardly disagree with you about that," Adele answered. A moment's silence, and then she heard her own soft laughter echoed by the light, silvery ringing of Milly's own. Sisterhood for a moment, a rare thing in her life.

"Oh, dear, this really is too risqué," Milly said, "even with a dispensation." Then she became serious. "Most of the girls he was with knew what the limitations were – but there were a few who took it very seriously. . . who got really hurt. . . who hated him. But even the most hostile ones were curious about him. Wondered." She paused.

"He can do magic, you know," she added quietly, matter-of-factly. "It makes up for an awful lot," and Adele sucked in her breath, for Milly was no longer close to home. She was dead on the mark. "But I am puzzled about one thing. All this lasted only one day. You sound so together, so directed. Why are you going to all this trouble?"

Another silence.

"Something I didn't say," Adele finally answered. "He took care and so did I. But something went wrong. I'm pregnant." A sharp intake of breath on the other end of the line. "Don't misunderstand," Adele went on quickly, "I have an appointment on November 20th. I'm going to – terminate the pregnancy. I can imagine how you feel about that."

"Not what you think," Milly replied. "I'm my own person in all sorts of ways. It's a decision you have to make, I know that. You'll have my sympathy and my prayers no matter what you do. But," she continued wistfully, "I do know what my decision would be. There was a time when I prayed for that. Of course I had the patch so it wasn't possible. So perhaps I was just letting myself go."

"It's going to break my heart," Adele said in a low voice, "but I don't have any realistic alternative. At any rate, that's how all this began. I wanted to talk to Tom, tell him what had happened, hear what he had to say. It's way beyond that now. Everyone I've talked to, everything I've heard. . . is all so mysterious. The same as you, I have to find out why this has happened. I have to know what all of it means. I'm not going to rest until I do."

"It's getting very late," said Milly. "We're going to have to end this soon. I'm very glad I called."

"So am I," Adele answered warmly. "What's going to become of you, Milly? Are you going to stay in the convent forever?"

"No," she replied in the same firm tone of voice that she'd used earlier when discussing the madam, "I'd like to, but I can't. I have too much to offer now to stay in seclusion. If I were to do that, it would be as if the whole thing never happened, as if none of it meant anything – and that can't be true. I won't let it be true. I'm not going to stay in this little cell and leave the whole rest of the world to people like Billy and the old Milly. I can't."

Startled, Adele held the receiver away from her ear. A recent echo; so much like. . .what? Oh yes, what Jacob Rothenberg had said about Franklin Fischer and George a few hours earlier. Coincidence? She no longer believed in coincidence. "Whatever happened to Billy?"

"The last I heard was two years ago. He was just starting his residency – plastic surgery, as he'd planned. He was engaged then to a student nurse, another beauty queen. I wish her luck. It doesn't matter at all to me. I'm planning to leave here next March; I'm going to re-enrol at Binghamton. I won't need my family or anyone. There's an endowment here for novitiates like me, who've been here as long as I have; Mother Superior says they'll support me as far as I want to go."

The same silvery laugh. "I'm very popular here, you see. It's not at all like it was when I first went to college. It's as I said. Everything changed."

Her tone became urgent: "Adele – our time's almost up. There are two things: First, about Tom. I didn't find out that much; I really don't know anything. But I've thought about it over and over and over. This sounds so crazy, I'm shy to say it. But my hunch is he doesn't even know. Maybe it's something he deliberately doesn't know, but he doesn't know. I must have thought about the last thing he said to me ten thousand times. *I'm sorry, Milly, I thought it would be different.* I could swear he was telling me the truth. I don't think he knew why he did what he did or what caused it. How that would be I don't know. All this sounds nuts to me as I say it. But that's what I think."

You're right, thought Adele, *it does sound crazy*. But it made a peculiar sort of sense. *A blind elephant*, she had thought once.

"That great searchlight vision of his goes dark when he turns it on himself," she continued. "Or maybe he's afraid to turn it on himself. There's something in his life that scares him too much to look at it. He can do anything for anyone, but he can't do the least little thing for himself. That's what I believe. That's why I felt so guilty." Her tone changed.

"The second thing – the more important thing – be careful. If you're interested in Tom – if you're close to him in any sense – then the devil is near to you. I don't mean anything you'll read about it in the Bible, or a plot device in an airport paperback. I mean the *real* thing, something cold and negative and completely plausible, the way the world actually works. Not one you'll recognize easily; I didn't recognize the devil in Billy until it was way, way too late. Perhaps a very rational devil, very persuasive in the ordinary ways. But very close. Am I frightening you?"

"Yes," said Adele. The night seemed darker, the room smaller, the hour later.

"Good. I mean to. Tom's important, Adele. I don't know why. But he's important enough for the devil to hate. I know I sound crazy. But please – please take care of yourself. Be very careful. The devil is very close to you." She hesitated. "It would be wisest if you gave this up. Haven't others said that? They did to me."

"They have, but I can't do that," Adele answered, thinking, wondering what to think, wondering how to be careful. "But I'll remember what you said. Milly. . . is there anything at all I can do for you? Anything?" she added, standing, speaking quickly.

"Yes," Milly answered precisely, "there is. The next time you talk to that publisher client of yours, would you ask her to collect Tom's poems into one volume? We can only have ten books in our cells. Four of mine are his books. They're so small! Other sisters have these big thick novels. It isn't fair. I've complained that the rule should be based on width in inches, but no one's willing to do anything *that* radical." She laughed again; Adele laughed with her. "Now I have to say goodbye. Be very careful. Call me if you want to talk again, and I *will* call you back."

"Thank you," Adele answered, warmly, sincerely. Whatever else happened, wherever this led, at least, in the most unexpected, unlikely way, she'd made a friend. "Goodbye now. God bless you," and then the queen was gone, returned to her exile. A ghost ship, white damask sails trimmed with silk, vanished as mysteriously and elegantly as it had appeared.

*

Gown off. Quick shower. Too much to think about, much too much. Two hours earlier she'd been in George Sorenson's arms, holding him. Very nice, she liked George. Milly. Two small cuts on the wrist. A good effect, a good bargain. *The devil is very near you.* A cold, eerie feeling.

She lay down in her bed.

Who are you, Tom?

Sleep, difficult enough on ordinary nights, was going to be a virtual impossibility on this one. The sheer quantum of information, the size of its warp and woof – the startling and completely unexpected revelation of the degree of attraction for George Sorenson, the whispered voice of the cloistered nun – received on this, one of the most eventful nights of her life, was far too great to be knit readily into sleep. Events were finally beginning to move. That realization brought her no satisfaction. All that meant was that she had to move faster still herself, somehow outrun the dwindling sand in the hourglass.

Arbor Rest. Not that kind of crossing boughs. The one tangible clue – it skittered through all her restless thoughts. It was not until shortly after four in the morning, as Adele lay twisting in the turmoil of her insomniac bed, that one small, apparently inconsequential thread abruptly separated itself from the whole chaotic tangled mass – and she had the clue as to what to do next.

Bill Abercrombie was a superbly well-connected private detective. Who just happened to be a crossword puzzle enthusiast

AMBITIOUS YOUNG MAN

"You've been going out a lot, haven't you?" said Christina the next morning, as Adele picked up her messages.

"What?" Adele answered.

"It must be fun to burn the candle at both ends," the girl said enviously. Christina was seriously overweight and acned.

Adele shook her head. "I haven't been sleeping well." Christina smiled knowingly. "It's all this drizzle," Adele went on, mildly irritated. "It's getting to me." *My problems aren't that much different than yours*, she wanted to add, but didn't. It wasn't true.

Adele made a mental note to herself as she strode down the hall to her office. Normally, she used very little makeup, but obviously a bit more was required these days. The stress and fatigue were beginning to show.

*

In addition to the usual barrage of paper on the Project, a package from AI Squared had arrived overnight. Most of the material had been supplied by Peter Steinitz, the first distillation of his thoughts about crash mechanisms that might work for the AI Squared program. She went over it casually at first, and then became interested in spite of other cares. The wealth of ideas, alternatives, different routes, the fertility of their imaginations – and it was apparent from the letter Lem had included that the ultimate engineering decision would depend to a large extent on her own advice concerning the precise language of the warranty disclaimer. The tone of the cover letter was warm and familiar. She'd been accepted by the trio. She was going to be an intimate part of the history of this extraordinary company, an essential part of its story. She had arrived where she'd hoped to be seven weeks earlier.

A lot to do, a great responsibility. True, AI Squared was only in beta test – it would be years before the product shipped in volume. But Pete would need her advice as soon as possible to choose the design. No time like the present – and it would be a tonic to wade into a well-defined job, wrap her mind around a task in the here and now, after the surrealistic happenings of the night before. There was only one thing to do first. She phoned Walt Greenfield's office. He would not be available until 2:00 p.m. She was surprised to learn he wanted to see her – an interesting coincidence.

Then it was off to the library and a morning to be spent with one of the electronic legal databases. She picked up her briefcase.

The phone rang.

*

"Good morning, Adele," said Jenet Furston. "It's been some time since I've talked to you."

"Jenet – hello," answered Adele, pleased, but puzzled and impatient to be going. "What can I do for you?"

"This is more of a personal call, dear. Although I . . . I . . . I am curious if you ever finished that business you were going to handle for Tom."

"No. I finally put it on the backburner. I'll pick it up when and if he contacts me." Lying deliberately; mixed motives, partly pride, mostly affection, relieving Jenet from worry.

"Good. Good. I am relieved it's taken that turn. You know why. And how are things in other ways?" Adele could feel a curious hesitancy in her tone; she was deferring the reason for the call – unusual for Jenet.

"Very good, Jenet," she answered, still puzzled, biding her time. "I've been hoping that this firm could attract some high-tech clients in, that I'd get a chance to work on that sort of thing. We actually got one, and I made a good impression on the financier behind it who does a lot a work with Carolyn. I'll be doing some things there. And I'll be at NATPE."

"Good. Good. It's very interesting the first time you experience it. I'm sure being there will do your career some good."

"Why aren't you going, Jenet? It seems like an odd time for you to leave." Thinking of the conversation she'd overheard in Carolyn's office on a day that seemed to be from a million years ago. The day she met Tom.

"Oh," she laughed, "I'm old enough to do what I want these days. I don't really need either the experience or another deal. Besides, all the glitz. . . all the infernal deal making. . . reality shows. . . new ideas for VHS. I will have my production people there, my booth, and a hospitality suite. They don't say so in so many words, but they're all eager to prove they can succeed without me." Her voice lowered. "This was a very special time of year for my husband and me, and a very special place I'll be visiting. I do have business, but it's more than that. Much more."

"I see," said Adele, thoughtfully. Jenet sighed, then plunged in:

"Adele, I'm going to be on the Continent for the next three weeks.

When I return" – she hesitated – "I wonder if you would be my guest for dinner some evening at my town home. I can imagine how hectic your social life must be before Christmas. I was thinking between Christmas and New Year's."

"No," Adele replied. "I always go home to my dad's house then. But I'd love to have dinner with you, Jenet. Some weeknight before the holiday or after would be fine."

"'Dad's house,'" Jenet echoed distantly, mysteriously. "All right then. Do you have your calendar? Let's pick a date." Adele flipped open her PDA, and scanned the empty space. Her social life was not nearly as frantic as Jenet might imagine. The two women finally selected a Wednesday in the middle of the next month. "I'll look forward to that, Adele. To talking with you a bit more personally than we are able to do in this building. Goodbye, now."

"Jenet, before you go, there is one thing." She'd made Milly a promise. "While I was trying to communicate with Tom, I did talk to one person who thought it would be a great idea if you collected the four volumes he's written into one."

"Why?" said Jenet, surprised. "It would be a bit expensive for me for a book that's unlikely to do any better than the four do separately. And they're hardly pricey as it is; I price them to circulate, not for profit. I don't understand."

"This person is a novitiate in a convent," Adele explained. "And the rule of the order forbids more than ten books in the cell. She'd like to have all. . . of. . . Tom's. . . poetry. . . . . . collected. . . . . . . into. . . . . . one." Slowing down as she spoke, dawning realization that she'd said far, far too much. *Idiot, idiot, idiot.* Jenet was silent on the other end of the line.

"Oh, Adele," she said at last, with the saddest tone in her voice, "you weren't truthful with me earlier. You haven't at all finished with Tom – and you've gone far enough to have found out who the nun is in the poem. That's the person you meant, isn't it? You've talked to her." She sounded like an old, tired woman, the disappointments and frustrations of her own life evident.

"Yes," replied Adele. Denial was pointless.

"You weren't candid with me before either, were you?" she went on in a voice of wooden resignation. "You *did* become involved with him. I can feel it."

"Yes," Adele admitted again. "I said otherwise because I didn't want you to worry. I'm responsible for what happened, not you. Not," she added, rapidly improvising, "that that much happened. We spent an afternoon at the Metropolitan Museum. We talked. He's one of the most interesting people I've ever met. Later, I wanted to find out more about him. I never quit on anything once I start – and I haven't on this. That's really everything, Jenet. That's all. I don't want you to give this a second thought on your trip. It's not fair. Besides," she added again, "it'll all be over before we have our dinner. I'll tell you all about it then."

"You don't owe me any explanations, Adele," Jenet answered quietly. Failure – Jenet knew she was lying. "However," Jenet sighed, doing her best, "what's done is done. You're a competent young woman. I'm sure everything will be fine. I shouldn't have burdened you with my misgivings. They're probably only the morning dreams of an old woman. I'm sorry; I shouldn't have said anything. I'll –"

"You've nothing to be sorry for, Jenet," Adele cut in. "I –"

"*Please*, Adele!" Jenet retorted, in a voice of weary exasperation; then in an almost inaudible whisper, "don't even try." *I know you went to his bed, my dear.* "There's really nothing more to say. I'll leave word with my secretary to give you a ring if Tom calls in here. Goodbye now. I'm looking forward to our dinner."

"So am I. Bon voyage," Adele said as cheerfully as possible, but that wasn't going to work either, she could tell. She hung up the phone and sat, silent in her office, for a few long, long moments.

*

Her concentration should have been focused, seeking unique solutions to a unique problem, one of the rare tasks in law requiring some creativity. It should have been a riveting morning. Fun.

Instead, she found herself working with half a mind, drifting through the morning, most of her attention elsewhere. Her concentration was lagging. What Christina had said; no question – fatigue was starting to play a role.

She reread Lem's letter. More than cordial, actually; verging on the chatty, another little quote from Tom's work at the end. He was still hoping. That was apparent. A good guy, an important guy, a deserving guy – but it was George's arms she'd found herself in. Lem would have to understand that they were friends, but friends only, that it wasn't going to happen with him. George – the thought of him, the recollection of what had happened in the backseat of the limo, made her feel warm and sexy. That was something to look into seriously, when this was all over. She shook the thought out of her head and read over the menu for the search program.

Milly Peters – more information, more confusion. Had the old Milly really been the horror the new Milly described last night? Possibly. But the old Milly had ultimately been formidable enough to break free from her father and find an identity of her own. Tom wouldn't have found her interesting if she hadn't had that strength somewhere. Maybe she had been the arrogant, superficial fool she described, but she'd been no weakling.

She booted up the workstation automatically. It was the work of a moment, unconscious hands, to access the data on the Uniform Commercial Code, Article Two, the one that governed sale of goods and defined warranties of fitness and use. She hadn't looked at it since law school. A review of recent developments was the only sensible place to start on the AI Squared project.

Milly's life blown completely off course by Tom – but the relationship, eight years dead now, was still sufficiently important to her that she'd spent two hours telling a complete stranger everything she knew, much of which was personally embarrassing to her, this with a poise and self-possession that went all the way to the core as she did so. Amazing. No, clearly Milly was no weakling, then or now. A very impressive woman.

Adele shook her head at the screen, as page after page of text appeared, then disappeared. Too soon to store and print; for starters, she wanted a listing of cases about warrant disclaimers from the various states. The most recent UCC-2 stuff. Not everything; too much to print, too much to read. Synopses, say, of five, the most recent, from the highest appellate court of each. Her fingers flew over the keyboard again.

On the other hand. . .

Weakling or not, old Milly or new, he'd rolled through her life like a steamroller, hadn't he? By any rational standard, he'd destroyed her. The campus queen either tries to take her own life or stages a preposterous scene, take your pick (she believed Milly), but either way ends up closeting herself from the world in a small, stone room light years away from the place where she began. She thinks of herself as transformed. The result of a sojourn in a magic forest? Or an encounter with a monster sociopath? *He's important enough for the devil to hate.* Insight? Or religious paranoia? *Finds the best part of you and turns it into shit.* Georgia, the insufferable, unforgettable Georgia. *When you ask questions about Tom Newcombe, you don't get answers, you get more questions.* Jenet's warning from what seemed so long ago: *You could wander for years in those caves. You could lose your self entirely.* Maybe that was what had happened to Milly. She shifted uneasily in her seat.

Maybe that was what was happening to her.

"Oops," said a slightly older lawyer whose name she didn't know. "There it goes."

Startled, she looked at the screen – blank, now, except for a prompt for another request. Adele turned her head toward the speaker and grinned. "Wrong key," she chirped cheerfully. "But it's got an automatic retrieve routine." *It better* – forty five minutes at $17.00 a minute. . .

"I've lost so much stuff that way," the first commiserated. Adele nodded, smiling automatically, concentrating fully on the keyboard now, improvising rapidly – the program was so trivial she'd never really bothered to learn all its ins and outs. *It has to be this sort of path. This? No. Then try. . .*

"Got it," she beamed, as the screen refilled with data. *Whew.* "What?" said the other man. "I didn't know that."

"If you made as many goofs as I do, you would," Adele said. "You'd have to. Here. Let me have it print before I mess up again, then I'll show you the trick."

The laser printer began its familiar grind. A moment later, she demonstrated the retrieval path to a novice at least twenty years older than she. The image she'd had of Tom disappearing in those first, early days had been dead wrong. Not distant, silhouetted wings – instead, a man walking west towards the horizon at evening, the shadow growing larger and larger, hovering over everything, as dark as the secret behind his eyes, haunting her sleep, disrupting her dreams, distracting her work, now and then inflicting body and soul with hopeless longing, interfering with a new significant romantic interest. Maybe she should have listened to Jenet. Maybe what had happened to Milly was indeed exactly what was happening to her. *You wouldn't know how magic changes you, would you?*

Oh, well. Soon she'd be done. Soon everything would be over. November 20th. *I know what decision I'd make.* Everything over. Her eyes half closed. Her companion didn't notice.

"That's a neat trick," he said, approvingly.

"Yes," Adele answered.

*

At five minutes to two, she boarded the elevator and rode the two flights up to Walt Greenfield's office. The door opened; Josh Palmdale and Ralph Murdoch were waiting on the other side, talking. "Hi, guys," Adele smiled. Josh looked startled; Murdoch barely acknowledged her as he stepped by onto the elevator.

"–on tape made all the difference, as you know," Murdoch was saying as he stepped past. "First class work, Josh. You saved us all."

Startled now herself, she whirled around and stared. Murdoch kept talking garrulously, unaware. Josh's eye caught hers, white, rolling with uncustomary fear, as the door slid shut in front of him.

She strode down the hall and into Walt's office, more perplexed than anything else, definitely with one more subject on her mind than she'd had a minute before. Walt was standing away from his desk, staring out his window, lost in contemplation.

"Hello, Walt," she said to his back.

"Adele?" He turned, thoughts broken, deep waters rippled. "Oh, yeah. Right. I wanted to see you. But you wanted to see me. So shoot. Then I'll do my stuff." Not the Walt she'd come to know and appreciate. His voice was flat. His normal theatricality, the long running in-joke, was completely absent.

"I was coming up to ask you to phone Bill Abercrombie again for me. But I heard the most curious conversation on the way. Ralph Murdoch congratulating Josh on this taped confession he'd obtained."

"Yeah," Walt responded, moving back behind his desk, sitting heavily. "Yeah. I was wondering when you'd find out about that."

"What gives?" Adele asked simply.

"Your old pal Josh seizing an opportunity mainly," Walt answered, swiveling in his chair. "He had your letters redone for his signature before he returned the file to Ralph. He destroyed the originals. Clever boy."

"God!" Adele exclaimed, turning towards the window, arms folded. Law review all over again. *I'll never let what happened happen again*, she'd told Tom that day. Big talk. Now it had happened again. Josh the Moron. "Not that it matters that much to me. But God! How despicable."

"Fairly shrewd on his part, you have to admit." He leaned back in his chair and put his hands behind his head. "Don't worry about it personally, though. Word got back to Helen Wilder about what had happened. She was so incensed that she redid the originals for the file. I've done my own talking to the partners. The people who matter know what happened."

"And Ralph Murdoch?" she asked, turning back to face him. "What does he think?"

Walt shrugged. "Murdoch and his type are beyond persuasion. I don't know myself what he had in mind with that 'woman's touch' crap – probably that you'd go have tea with Henny and talk her out of it. Certainly not that you'd perform like a *lawyer*. That's a man's job. Look –" Walt got out of his chair and came around the desk – "there's less of that nonsense every day around here. But it'll never go away entirely. Ralph's a mediocrity himself. He knows it and he knows everybody else knows it. He probably got his start the same way Josh did. Competent women scare the hell out of him."

Her arms were folded. *Why bother? Why even try?* Sometimes it seemed hopeless.

"It's not going to affect you at all," Walt said, looking her directly in the face. "Your ticket's already punched. The only loser is the firm. Palmdale was going to be gone in another month. But with Ralph behind him, we're going to be stuck with him for at least another year. Plenty of time for him to kiss

Ralph's behind, and Lawton behinds, and see what happens. That's the American way." His tone had become very bitter.

"If it doesn't affect me or you, why are you so angry?" Adele asked.

"Because it's not fair. It isn't right," Walt answered, a bit surprised. "It offends me. I've got three daughters, Adele. Their futures matter more to me than any of this crap. I don't want to see them face this stuff." He inched a trifle closer, encroaching slightly into her zone. "You may rise above it – you're so damn smart, so damn pretty, and so damn nice--"

"Getting kind of close to the line, aren't you, Walt?" she said quietly. She'd never dreamt she'd have to deal with even a semi-pass from Walt Greenfield. He'd had quite a bit to drink at lunch, she realized then.

He reddened. "Yeah. Right. Sorry. Anyway, my girls might not – which reminds me." He moved back behind the desk and reached for his desk calendar. "I was wondering if you could come to dinner out at my home – this Sunday or the one after. I'd like you to meet my oldest daughter. I've talked a lot about you. She's reached an awkward age; she thinks it's got to be either tank-tops and boys or grades, if you know what I mean. Meeting you might help."

Adele laughed, flattered. "That is too bad. If she's a bright girl, she'll face all kinds of choices. But that isn't one of them. You can do both."

"That's what *I* say, but who am I? Dumb ol' Dad," he replied. "So – can you make it? This Sunday or next?"

"Sure," Adele answered, thinking of all her secrets. "But I'm not sure you want me for a role model, Walt. My personal life is pretty messy right at the moment."

"You mean the 'big deal' poet you left the office with a few weeks ago?" Walt said, grinning.

Her eyes widened. "Who told you that?"

"Who do you think? Young Mr. Palmdale, your ardent admirer. He's subtle about it, mind you; he's got pauses and raised eyebrows down to a fine art. But the gist of his version is that you and he had an understanding until this fellow came along, turned your head, and beat him out of his time. A modern American tragedy."

"Oh, *brother*," Adele replied, rolling her eyes up, shaking her head, and turning back towards the window. "Great. Just great. My exactly, exactly favorite kind of guy. He's never kissed, but he tells anyway."

Walt laughed again. "I thought that was the case. Another thing you shouldn't worry about. His story lacks – shall we say – credibility? Also according to Josh, the twenty-eighth floor support staff has more in common with a Turkish harem than the competent group of professionals the rest of us perceive. He hasn't learned yet that that sort of talk has become passé. At least with men my age." He straightened up. "So – which will it be – this Sunday or next?"

Adele thought for a moment. "This." The Sunday following, she'd either be in a clinic in the East 60s or back at her own apartment, alone, shattered. *Goodbye, little one.* Either way, she wouldn't be good dinner company.

"Don't look so delighted about it. It'll be a good dinner. No Borgias dwell in my house," Walt said, observing her a bit more closely.

"Sure," Adele smiled. "Now, will you call Bill for me?" Deliberately changing the subject.

Walt picked up the phone, and then put it down. "What the hay. I trust you. Here." He scribbled a number and handed it to her. "What you want Bill for. . . it's about that writer, isn't it?"

"Yes," she said after a moment, trusting him. "Our secret. Please don't ask more."

"Understood," he answered. "I wish I'd met him when he was here. He's the guy Helen Wilder worked late for, isn't he?" Adele nodded. "I'll tell you – snowing a judge or blowing a jury away – that's easy stuff, happens every day. But a man who can wow a word processor – *that's* doing something." He shook his head theatrically.

"Is that all?" Adele asked. "If we're done, I'll go back downstairs." And phone Bill Abercrombie.

"No, that isn't all," Walt said. "We haven't talked about the reason I wanted to see you." His mood blackened to the same dark hue it had been at when she entered the room. He got up and came over beside her, in front of the window, hands in pockets.

"There was another reason why Murdoch was overjoyed when you got that confession from Henny Lawton," he said quietly. "The big reason. He had one of his own. From James."

*

Adele felt as if she'd been hit in the stomach. "That can't be," she said reflexively. "There was nothing like that in the file."

"He'd purged the file. Before it got to me. Before I gave it to you. I told you Ralph and Josh are a lot alike. If you don't like what you see in a file, change it. Ralph knew what I'd think."

"But. . . but. . . the women – the adulteries –"

Walt shrugged. "He likes small, round fannies. He prefers the female kind" – he smiled mirthlessly – "most men do. But he can't keep his hands off the other kind, either, when they're available. Like his own son's."

She was still reeling. "But Walt – you mean, the other men that day – their sons – you mean, all of them are in some kind of perverse –"

"No, no, no, no," he answered. "That's where it gets rich. Henny's instincts were right, but her timing was all wrong. Nothing happened on that day. You proved that. But it happens a lot on all the other days." He laughed another mirthless laugh. "That poor kid. A molester for a father, a perjurer for a mother – what chance does he have? Of course," he added thoughtfully, "being worth 150 mil on the day you're born doubtless compensates to some extent."

"And Josh," she said, looking for some grain of sense in all this, "Josh? What does he say?"

"Oh, he's a wonder. He said worse things happen in football huddles. Big joke; Ralph Murdoch and Lawton laughed to beat the band. I didn't. I was trying to tell Jim Lawton something about the criminal laws of this state, that what he is doing, and will continue to do, is a felony, no matter how rich he is. Josh didn't help – to put it mildly. But he did make himself very popular."

Another silence. *Try to sort it out.*

"Tell me something," he suddenly said, throwing his arms around, "why do you want this? Can you tell me? Ten years ago, I was prosecuting guys like this. I put them in jail – or at least in a shrink's office. The money wasn't good, the hours were lousy, but I loved it! I wondered if I were making a difference; I wondered where it would all lead – but I never wondered whether it mattered. Never. Now I do, all the time."

"You're not responsible," she said, lying, thinking about the extent to which he was, the extent to which she was. *Try to sort it out.* "And – Walt" – timidly, but she had to say it – "I can tell you've had a little to drink. If I can, other people can, too."

He laughed. "'A little to drink'? I always have something to drink at lunch, Adele. These days. It started about five years ago. A glass of wine, then two. About a year ago, a bottle. Did you know it's in that size because it's supposed to be a single portion for a person at a meal? I thought I could handle it. Not bad for a Jew boy! Maybe I should've been born Irish." He laughed again. "Today, a bottle and two glasses. The new quota. Ten years ago, I never drank during working hours. Never." He sat down at his chair, swiveled.

"Why do you want this?" he asked, his hand in the air. "Can't you see? No, wait" – he held up his hand – "you have some cockamamie idea that if you do it all now, squirrel away your nuts for the winter, you can outrun the game, save a little time for yourself? Right?"

Adele took in his eyes for a moment, then nodded, slowly, affirmatively. "Something like that."

"Everyone thinks that – and everyone's wrong. Life doesn't work that way. You think of a rat race as a race between rats. But rats don't race each other. They run on wheels, on treadmills, against themselves. It's their own energy they run against. You never get ahead, Adele; the wheel's always faster than you are, no matter how fast you are. When it's finally run you off your legs, in goes the rest of you, snap, crackle, pop, into the furnace, nothing left. You never get ahead. That's the big lie."

"Why do you do it? Why don't you go back to the D.A.'s office?"

"Because," he said, "because my wife likes living in Darien; and she likes going to the Bahamas in the spring, and the lake in July. Plus that older girl of mine is going to get over tank-tops sooner or later; I want to send her to Radcliffe if she can make it. Another 45 big ones every year. 50 by the time my youngest is ready. The D. A. paid 75 grand when I left; it's about 90 now. This is a million-one every year, guaranteed. That's why.

"So I stay here, handling these impossible people, and reporting to that imbecile Murdoch. Ha! When I started here, I was a registered Republican. Ten years of this and I've become a fucking Communist. All power to all the people, baby! The Lawtons – three years ago, the Feds spent a fortune advertising on TV, if you're going to Europe, don't carry drugs. Remember?"

"Yes." Not that she could ever have afforded Europe, but she did remember.

"Every kid in the country must have seen it – every kid, that is, except Francie Lawton. That's Jim's sister. Wham! Busted in Rome, three ounces of nose candy in her duffel bag. I spend all summer cleaning up the mess the little peabrain'd gotten herself into. But the total bill came to 150 grand. Good work for the firm. This is the way we earn our bread," he half-sang, then snorted. "The Lawton's are hardly the worse. Ralph Murdoch's really assembled a collection. David Masterson, Victor Podgorny, Elwood –"

"Wait a minute," said Adele. "Victor Podgorny? You know him?"

"Sure. Who doesn't? Wall Street raider, takeover artist. Schmuck. Runs with Franklin Fischer and the CFS crowd. Victor's problem is that his girls keep getting younger as he gets older – and since he never liked 'em much older than twenty, it's become something of problem as the years roll by. Why?" he asked, suddenly concerned. "Do you know him?"

"He sits on the board of that little software company that retained us recently."

"Oh, yeah. Right. I meant to congratulate you about that. Podgorny's involved in that company?" he said thoughtfully. "That's strange. That's not his style. Victor likes big action, big moves – everything in play. Afterwards, a long soak in a big tub with some old wine and a young girl. I don't know why he'd get mixed up with a little outfit like that. He's no techie."

"Walt, what else do you know about Franklin Fischer and CFS?" Recollections of the board meeting. She was suddenly afraid – for Lem, for Pete, for herself.

"The Project, of course." He shrugged. "But you know more about that than I do. Why?"

"Because he's the chairman of the same board. He financed the company, in fact. It's called AI Squared, by the way."

"Now that *is* peculiar," said Walt, sobering as he thought. He glanced at the door, which remained closed, and lowered his voice. "I thought he was putting everything into the Project."

"What sort of person is he?"

Walt looked around reflexively. "The guy's a great client of this firm, but between you and me he scares the hell out of me. He's no one anybody wants to get on the wrong side of. He started out with a reinsurance firm, but then he went into managing portfolio money. He's never looked back. He hooked up with this market genius named Sorenson" – Walt looked up – "but you know him. You had lunch with him."

"All I know is he's kind to me, and he's Franklin Fischer's partner. I don't know anything else about him."

Walt raised his eyebrows. "He's a good contact for you. The two of them are two of the roughest customers on the Street. They haven't made any friends, not that that seems to bother them. Their results have always been sensational. The investors didn't give a damn about their methods; it was the bottom line that mattered. Jim Lawton has money with them; so does Ralph Murdoch and a lot of his clients. They're all investors in the Project. For a long time, it was strictly an in-house operation. But a couple of years ago CFS took over a small house with a little investment banking arm. They've done a few outside deals since then. This must be one of them."

"George Sorenson is also on the board, too," Adele said evenly.

Walt whistled. "All three of them – all involved in this? That has to be bad news for someone. What kind of company is it?"

"Nothing at all financially – not yet, anyway. But its founders have developed miracle software." She told Walt about the company, doing her best to convey the importance of what Lem and the others had achieved, not entirely successfully. Walt was not computer literate.

"I don't know," he said at last. "I suppose CFS and Podgorny can make venture capital investments like anyone else. But what with everything being poured into the Project. . . this company must be unique."

"It is," Adele said uncertainly, very doubtful that Franklin Fischer shared that perception. "Walt, what should I do?"

"What do you mean, 'What should you do?'" Walt asked, alarmed. "Why do you say that?"

"Because. . . because of all this mystery. All this strangeness," Adele answered, perplexed. "I mean, the guys who started this company – the president – asked me to look out for them. Maybe I should say something to him."

"Look, Adele," he responded, now clearly agitated, all the alcoholic courage gone, "don't go haywire. All this was what the reporters would say was off the record, O.K.? I give you credit for common sense. The Project was good for nearly thirty-five million dollars for this firm last year. It's going to be a two hundred-billion-dollar company when it's done, and we're going to have all its work. You can't go off half-cocked because of some combination of personalities. It may be only a coincidence. There's no smoking gun here. And these are the last guys in the world you want to get on the wrong side of without a reason. There's nothing to do. C'mon."

Everything he said made perfect sense. But he could not meet her eye.

"You have to learn to be a little more discrete. You shouldn't even have mentioned to me that Sorenson and Fischer are partners. I happen to know, but that's not supposed to get around. Fischer doesn't like it."

"All right," she said finally, signifying that she understood, not necessarily agreed. "But what about Bobby Lawton? You've got the smoking gun there."

"Yeah. Right," he agreed, then suddenly finger-pointing, "don't go off half-cocked on that one, either. Don't get yourself into trouble. I will do something about it, I promise. What, I don't know." He was doing a completely terrible Lionel Barrymore, but this time it wasn't funny.

*

Back in her office, it was a moment's work to dial Abercrombie; he wasn't in, but his secretary immediately reached him on a pager, and forwarded him.

"That was quick," she said.

"You interest me," Abercrombie said tersely.

"I have something else that might interest you," Adele answered, and filled him on the gist of the information she'd received from Milly. ArborRest, crossing boughs. Abercrombie grunted, an interested grunt, said he'd do what he could do, and rang off.

Silence now in her little corner of the world. Time to think. No reason not to. No way not to. The information gathering was over. Now she had to try to untangle it all.

What could I have done differently? Realistically, nothing. If monsters like Ralph Murdoch and Josh – Josh, that she had ever accepted – ever tolerated – didn't he realize, that the worst, the worst possible, was passivity in the face of – but what could she have *done?* That would have changed the outcome? Nothing. She'd only done her job; no reason to think twice.

All fine and good – *except if all that is true, why do I feel so guilty?* It had been her relentlessness that broke Henrietta Lawton down. Bobby Lawton. Poor Bobby Lawton. Last night, listening to Milly about her father, there'd been a flavor of incest in that, not articulated because both of them had understood it. But those attitudes had a distant kinship to normal sexuality. She could remember those times in her adolescence when her father involuntarily became aware of her as a sexual being – excruciatingly embarrassing for both of them. But natural. How could a boy Bobby's age possibly understand what was happening to him? Deal with it in any meaningful way?

What could I have done differently? Something.

Then, suddenly, the air was dark with menace, premonition. Bobby Lawton was an omen, a portent. The raven sat on her client chair, hoarsely croaking his name. The invisible gears of the distant machine had turned again. Then, with another sudden lurch, she experienced a moment of pure, undiluted vertigo – the floor was dissolving beneath her feet; the strength of the girders was gone, gone; the solidity of the steel was an airy, fantastic illusion. She had the sensation that she was falling, falling, spinning, through empty space, and with it, the uncanny feeling that this life she'd built for herself was melting. She realized she was hyperventilating.

Nonsense. Don't be silly. Calm down, get a hold of yourself. And face the real problem.

Bobby Lawton was in the past. That was the reality. More than that, it was Walt's problem much more than hers. There was nothing she could really do that would not rebound on him. She had lost a great deal of respect for him in the last quarter hour, but no affection. It was another problem, one in the present, that had to be addressed, the real cause of her upset. A problem that was entirely hers. She looked longingly at the phone.

All right, stupid, if that's what you think, pick up the phone. Do it. Lem had asked her specifically to look out for them. She put her hand on the receiver, lifted it, then put it down again. Pick up the phone, and say. . . what?

Hello, Lem. The guys on your board are pretty bad guys. Victor Podgorny is a Wall Street raider who likes girls who are too young; Franklin Fischer and George – (her inner voice caught for a second) – *Sorenson are super rough customers.* Would she really be telling him anything he didn't know? Anything he hadn't suspected from the start?

No. She took her hand off the receiver. There's no smoking gun here – in fact, nothing but smoke. Maybe Walt had it right. Maybe it was only a venture capital investment, as rare as that evidently was for them. The company certainly justified it; it might be long range, but the opportunity was extraordinary. She was not going to go upsetting applecarts at this point, not going to break rank without more. All the progress she'd made in two years could be erased in a moment.

And George.

She was under no illusions about him. *Rough customer*, that had come through loud and clear from the start – which had not stopped her from coming to his wonderful arms. She did not want to think that he would do Lem and the others harm. Was that wanting starting to cloud her judgment? Was the affection she'd developed for him undermining the loyalty she owed to them? How could she be sure it wasn't? Dear God; she put her head in her hands. Invisible gears, distant machines – actually, only another name for magic. Was it changing her? Had it transformed her already?

A shadow fell over her desk.

"Adele? Adele?" She looked up. Josh was standing in her doorway, drawn up to his full height, trying not to look nervous. "We have something to talk about."

Talk about? What? she thought wearily, then remembered. For a moment she was relieved, almost pleased. The Lawton situation bothered him; obviously Walt had misunderstood something. He went on. "It won't do you any good to take this any further. It would be my word against yours. Murdoch believes me. Besides –" his voice softened – "you didn't need the credit. The firm's accepted you. I had to do it. It was my only chance. I had to or I'd be out of here the next review." Now Adele did not know what he was talking about.

"It won't do either of us any good to stir up the mud." He noticed her perplexity. "About those letters," he explained.

Letters? For a moment she still didn't understand. . . then that nuance, that triviality was recalled. The boy, his complicity in that, meant nothing to him. The letters? He was too dense to realize that everyone who was involved already knew, that he was still there because it didn't matter. . . she became angry.

"I told you before you weren't welcome here without an invitation," she said icily. "I haven't invited you. Leave."

"You're not going to tell, are you?" he pleaded, retreating, the pompous facade slipping off. Not even using an adult word.

"That's something you'd better think about, Josh," she said, staring at him, "I'd worry a lot about that if I were you," knowing as she spoke she was taking out the anger and confusion she was feeling towards herself on him. Good grief, if he'd only asked her, she'd have probably shredded the originals herself. He slunk out of her office. She felt ashamed. Maybe for an encore she could take the elevator down to the street and kick a small dog.

"Please," he said, as the door closed behind him. She forgot about him immediately.

Another long look at the phone, thinking about Lem. *Knock it off, stupid, you know you're not going to make the call. Pull yourself together; get on with the day.* She sighed, ripped her attention away from the desk, picked up the printout from the morning, and began to read. The phone rang.

"Adele Jansen...Yes. Oh, hi, Bill."

"I'm pleased to report I've finally done something I can bill you for," although he sounded uncertain instead of pleased.

"You've found it, Bill?" she cried. "So quickly?!" Her mood altered at once.

"Yeah. Let me explain. It's not ArborRest. It's Arbalest. That's an old English word for crossbow. That's what your friend was saying about not that kind of crossing boughs. He was making a little joke."

"Bill, that's wonderful! What good news! I'm truly impressed."

"It's not completely good news." Now his tone was definitely subdued. "It's almost like a good news, bad news joke."

"Why?" she asked, beginning to become anxious. "What's wrong? What's the matter?"

He paused.

"It's not an orphanage or a foundling home. It's a private institution – north, near the Canadian and Vermont borders. It's notorious. The kids that stay there are the ones that no one can handle – either so psychotic they're unmanageable or violently, incorrigibly criminal. Ultra-dangerous, all of them. Bars on the windows, electronic locks, a ten-foot fence." He hesitated again.

"Like a prison for kids. That kind of place."

✳ ✳ ✳

WARRIOR AND MAIDEN

She reeled. The room was silent for a long moment.

"Adele, are you there?" Abercrombie asked.

"Yes. Yes," she said, thinking. Another long, quiet interval. "What sort of reputation does it have?" she asked at last. "Does it do good work?"

"It's notorious. It's where all the counties dump all their impossible kids," he said promptly. "I had a fairly good idea what the name actually meant from what you said. I called DSS in Albany and hit the jackpot. But I didn't have time to congratulate myself. You could feel the chill on the line the moment I mentioned the name Arbalest."

"Why?"

"I asked. According to the official, what goes on there is nothing less than institutionalized child abuse. The guy that runs it is a Dr. Philip Harlow, a board-certified psychiatrist. He's got a sidekick, a psychologist named Coppelman. They're into extremely aggressive behavior modification – physical and emotional assaults, sensory deprivation, psychotropic drugs, insulin shock, anything, everything."

"Why doesn't someone shut them down?" she asked, feeling sick.

"They've tried from time to time. But there are a few psychologists that believe in those methods. Every profession has its lunatic fringe. Harlow's licensed with all the degrees – in fact, a good pedigree. Mostly, no one gives a damn about the kids. They're the wastebasket kids from around the state, kids with real problems, kids that everyone wants to forget. There are about 300 of them there, 90 percent male. Most of them are at Arbalest because no other place will take them. It's in a fairly remote spot, it doesn't get inspected very often. They keep the grounds and the building spic and span, they have a few quack shrinks that support them, and they get away with it. That's how." A certain contempt had crept into his voice.

"It's the same thing as before," she said at last. "It's what you said. It doesn't add up. It's impossible to imagine him being uncontrollable or unmanageable. Even when he's drinking and – whoring"– she *hated* using that word –"it's all internalized. He never breaks loose. It doesn't make sense."

"Would you mind telling me who told you about Arbalest? Where you heard all this?" Adele did, a short, sanitized version of the night before.

He grunted. "What do you want me to do now? If anything?"

"There's no way to get his records?"

"Nope," he said positively. "I doubt they're even computerized. If they are, there's no chance they link up to any network. The state didn't have any number. And Harlow's real paranoid about investigators. There's no way I can sneak someone in to look at his file."

So the decision was that easy. She'd already made it. "Then I'm going there myself as soon as I can. I'll find out myself what happened."

"No. Don't even think it. That's an absolutely terrible idea," Abercrombie said instantly.

"It's the only way, Bill," she answered. She did not have to ask him the reasons for his opinion. She already knew.

"It's crazy," he went on. "Don't you realize the implications of what I was saying? Wasn't I clear? These guys are arrogant, amoral sadists. They're creeps. They're scared of investigators. They're going to assume any stranger is an investigator. The place is out in the middle of nowhere. You've got to know the first impression anyone has of you is not that you're the toughest person who ever came down the pike." He paused. "It's not until someone knows you better they find out different," he added quietly.

"Thanks," she said. "I did understand you, but I've got to go. I'll identify myself as a New York lawyer. They're not stupid. It's a state licensed facility. I'll be O.K."

"Smart people become stupid when they get scared," he replied, definitely agitated. "Later they realize what dumb moves they made, but then it's too late for everyone. Particularly the victim. Or maybe someone would think you could be intimidated into silence. Do you realize all the things that could happen to you there in an afternoon? How easy it would be to terrify you? Beat you where it doesn't show? Blow your mind permanently into the stratosphere with an overdose of Thorazine? For Chrissake, Adele! I'm not trying to scare you. I want you to change your mind."

"You're doing a very good job of scaring me," she said quietly, truthfully, "but you're not changing my mind."

"Then I'll do it," he said doggedly. "You don't have to worry about the money. I'll eat the fee."

"We both know why you didn't suggest that in the first place, Bill. You're a wonderful investigator, but you've got shamus written all over you. You won't find out anything. Whoever knows anything about this is much more likely to open up to me."

A long silence. "You're determined, then?" he asked at last.

"Yes."

"At least let me know when you're going, and how, and how long you expect to be there. Don't be afraid to say that there's someone who knows you're up there – don't worry that you're making a fool of yourself. I can't tell you the women I've known who ended up raped or murdered because they were reluctant to be impolite – and for Crissake don't be shy to call me if you do get in a jam. Promise me that anyway."

"Yes, I will, I promise," she said, genuinely touched by his attitude. "I'm sure I'll be all right."

"That's what they all say," he growled, and rang off.

A concrete task to complete was a good thing, a nice, mind-clearing anodyne. Checking her calendar was the work of a moment. Frustration. The earliest day she could possibly clear was Friday, and then only the afternoon. Two days lost. *Damn.*

Determinedly, she picked up the phone, pushed something back to Monday early, moved something else forward to Thursday. That done, she phoned Allegheny Airlines and made her plans.

"Bill," she said over the receiver a short time later, "I'm going to fly to Burlington at 3:00 Friday. I'll drive north that afternoon and stay overnight. I'll visit Arbalest the next day. Then I'll be on the 3:00 flight back to New York Saturday afternoon."

"There's nothing more to say then, is there?" he said quietly.

"No," she answered firmly, "except thank you. I know your advice is sensible. But I have to do this."

*

Now they all rolled through her mind every night, night after night. Milly. Bobby Lawton. The trauma waiting to collide with her life on November 20th, an iceberg moving silently on course through the waters. *The devil is very near you.* Jenet Furston and the mysterious matters she could only talk about at home. George Sorenson, a rough customer, and Lem Michaels, definitely not – the unusual direction her heart had taken. *Tells them a thing or two they didn't think anyone knew,* said Georgia Richmond. Adele tried her usual methods, blanking her mind, falling into a vortex of darkness, playing an endless game of hockey – but it had all gone beyond that, way beyond that, nothing worked. Sleep was endlessly difficult.

Above all, shadowing everyone, influencing everything: him – the quiet, gentle man who had concealed himself perfectly during the time they spent together. The questions she hadn't asked. The questions she should have asked.

Nothing happens by chance.

The play from Goodson arrived in the mail. She read it Tuesday night – very wry, very clever, though obviously the work of an eighteen-year old boy (who just happened to be a genius). It offered tantalizing hints, but no real insights. She took the frustration to bed with her.

Thus the nights rolled and boiled, Tuesday collapsed into Wednesday, and the workweek rolled towards its close. Calm, unbroken sleep seemed the forgotten dream of a vanished age. The weather reports said the rain would be intermittent, but it seemed to her that it was perpetual. She wondered sometimes how Bri was doing in Bogota. Fatigue was omnipresent now, an element of every waking minute. Six weeks ago everything in her life had seemed simple, easy. Now the abyss yawned at her from everywhere, gaping potholes in reality.

*

It seemed at one point as if Carolyn would go prattling on forever. On a different day, she could have tolerated, even sympathized with, that enthusiasm. But it was difficult this day for a person pretending to be herself, which is what Adele had become.

"NATPE begins on Monday. This is probably the most important week this firm has ever had," she said, eying the small group that she had assembled in the large conference room on the thirty-second floor. Sixteen people, the complete intellectual property division – four junior partners, and twelve associates; Adele was the youngest in the group. It was the superstar group in the firm, comprising less than 5 percent of the lawyers in the practice, but accounting for more than 30 percent of its gross revenues. Willis Rutter was also there, seconded over from the litigation division. He did not look happy.

"The rumors you've heard are correct. It looks like the first stage of the Project is finally – *finally* – going to be completed next week." A few scattered handclaps; Carolyn grinned theatrically and knocked on the wooden conference table. "That's the first thing. The entire system is going to be hungry for product. In particular, referring to the cable and satellite capacity, even with digital, quality is rather limited. But we are going to be HD capable with every program, with multiple levels of interactivity." A buzz went around the room; one low whistle. *That has to be because of Vinux*, Adele thought – whatever *that* is. She had cursorily searched the technical literature both hard copy and online in what little time she had, but found nothing. "I want you all scouting for product, all the time." Carolyn looked around the room.

"O.K., first: the hall is going to be crawling with the guys from Project targets all week long. They'll be everywhere. They're not going to be wearing neon signs or even badges. If you do find yourself talking to someone who's involved, and they find out who you are, stay cool. Stay calm. If they want chit-chat, chit-chat. If they have some simple question, answer it. If it gets more complex than that, smile and send them to someone on the list." Only eighteen names on that, and one of them Adele E. Jansen. Carolyn grinned suddenly. "As Walt Greenfield would put it: 'We're at the end of the drive. Don't want the cattle to stampede in sight of the slaughterhouse. And it only takes one'." She beamed around the room. "Pretty awful, huh?" A chuckle went around the room.

"Better'n Walt," someone said, and now everyone laughed, Adele included. Carolyn at least had sounded Texan; Walt couldn't even manage that. *She's really good at this*, Adele thought. At these times, she could visualize herself easily in that role. The legend in the firm was that Carolyn Hoffman had financed her legal education way back when she was a dancer, a Broadway gypsy. The darker side of the legend was that a lot of the dancing had been off-off-off Broadway. Carolyn waited until the laughter subsided.

"Second, I want to recruit as many new clients as possible, whether or not they're immediately useful to us. I have used up a great deal of my own good will with my clients getting them to agree to let us put ourselves in their booths. Also, with one exception, the CEOs of the outfits will be present and available to give us any reference we may need." Adele looked up. A small mystery solved; that's why she had pressed Jenet Furston so hard. "However, that's really a fail-safe. I am not expecting to do any hard deals on the floor. People," she said, turning towards all of them, "this next week is the reverse of our normal priorities. Billable time is definitely secondary. Visibility, popularity, a willingness to oblige – this is core practice development. I want everyone there to remember who we are. If – when – we pull this off, we can go from being one of the major players to absolute, positive number one." The attorneys glanced around at each other. Adele felt a pulse herself. It was exciting.

"Now, your assignments. I'm not going to be able to be hands-on very much; I will be on the floor, but I'll be all wrapped up with the Project. So coordinating is going to be Ed..." naming the most senior of the junior partners. Then she went around the room, specifying the task of each.

Adele shrank guiltily into the back of the room, trying for as long as possible to avoid Carolyn's eye. Lots of people snuck away on a Friday afternoon; it happened all the time – but she never had. Her billables were in line, everything was in order, but still. . . whatever her excursions in life, whatever her adventures, meticulous, scrupulous attention to the job, or her studies, the primary thing, had always been her fall back. In many ways, at age twenty-five she was not that far removed from the sixth-grader she'd once been who had driven all the other, older kids crazy with precise, meticulously done homework turned in day after day after day. Now, in a small but definite way, she was crossing over that line.

"Adele," Carolyn said finally. "You'll be with me with the Project people. With what little free time you do have, you'll be in the Furston booth. I've got you there because with Jenet gone it shouldn't be all that active. I don't really expect much from you except help with the Project. By the way, I'm sending you a revised schedule and the latest version of the contract. You should be thoroughly familiar with both by Monday." The room was deathly silent; not so much as a sigh or a sideward glance. What mutterings, what whisperings, that had occurred had all occurred in private. Adele felt defensive and resentful. *I didn't ask for this*, she wanted to say. She'd taken nothing away from any of them, but what good did knowing that do – for either them or her?

"One other thing: That software company that we brought in the other day. You're not going to have time for that board meeting. I've taken care of it. Greube's taken your report off the agenda. It'll have to wait till next time."

"I understand," Adele answered, trying in spite of all her weariness to remember that she should phone the three to explain. Carolyn nodded and turned.

"This is it, folks," she summarized, a bit nervously, aware of the lingering sullenness. "If we all hang together, we'll all be rich and famous together. One week." She smiled her starlet's smile; another round of anxious laughter.

"What about me?" asked Willis Rutter. "What do I do?"

"Oh," answered Carolyn, turning to him. "You'll be liaison to Ed and me, the Project list, do whatever needs to be done. Go between people."

"Carolyn," he answered, his voice going up in pitch, "all you need for that is a warm body. That's paralegal work."

"I'm not going to trust anything about this to support staff," Carolyn said evenly. "Too important. That's what I want you to do, Willis."

"But there's so much more I could do, Carolyn. I –"

"Ms. Hoffman to you, Mr. Rutter," she interrupted, her tone hard and cold. She took a step over to his chair. "I have given a great deal of thought to whom does what on this, Mr. Rutter. I know what I want you to do. Furthermore" – she stepped to confront him face to face – "if I see or hear – if I even *think* – that you are stepping beyond the bounds of the liaison function – that you are offering advice on your own, for example, or holding yourself out as an attorney with this firm – I will fire you on the spot. Then and there, on the floor. In full view of everyone. Noisily. And you can guess the kind of references you'll receive. Am I making myself clear?" The room had become deathly still.

"I am a member of this firm," he said, weakly.

"Since you brought the subject up," Carolyn answered, regarding him steadily, "I have to tell you that you're not going to be at the end of the year." Rutter turned pale; *poor Willis*, Adele thought. "I didn't mean to do it in front of everybody, but you left me no choice. That is the reason you are perfectly cast as a warm body. But there's six weeks of good pay and time to find yourself another position in this for you. Don't blow it. Do you understand?"

"Yes," he muttered, almost inaudibly.

"Yes, what?" she demanded.

"Yes, Car– Ms. Hoffman," he said, somewhat louder.

She wheeled around. "Does everyone understand me? This is one of the most important weeks in the history of this firm, in my own career. I don't want to crack the whip, but I will if I have to. No one" – she surveyed the room – "I mean no one – had better screw up. There will be consequences. Understand?" The we're-all-in-this-together ambiance had vanished. Her look went around the room again, then her briefcase was under her arm; head high, she swept through the door and back towards her own office.

"Bitch," someone finally said – Ed, her chief lieutenant, in fact – but only after she was well down the hall and then only in a very low voice. Someone else clapped Willis Rutter on the shoulder. Adele considered saying something to him, decided against; there was nothing she could say that he would not take the wrong way. The meeting broke up.

She stood up with her briefcase and umbrella. Her computer and most of her overnight things were in the briefcase; the rest was in a shoulder bag in her office. She had a lunch date with George. A little while later, she had a plane to catch.

*

Since Tuesday, when Walt described George Sorenson as a rough customer, she had been looking forward to this lunch with considerable trepidation. Now, to her complete surprise, as drizzle spotted the window of the taxicab, she found her mood changing entirely. She no longer felt tired. A tingly feeling of expectation spread out of her stomach and over her entire body. A slight stirring of guilt as well.

The taxicab rounded the corner. The brief ride was over – too brief, she was going to have to overtip. Right before she opened the back door, she remembered she'd forgotten something, reached behind her neck, undid a clasp.

She'd thought she'd have to ride the elevator up to his office or have the receptionist page him, but no, he was waiting for her in the lobby. He was so happy to see her! It was evident in his body language, in his beaming smile, in the long stride he took towards her. Her own heart was skipping, too. He looked wonderful. He squeezed her hand lightly; she returned it. It took an effort not to go straight into his arms. She could see he had to restrain himself as well.

She had not counted on this. Her body had surprised her again. They were going to pick up right where they left off on Monday night. What had happened in the back of that limo hadn't been a momentary lapse at all.

"You're not wearing your angel," he smiled.

"No," Adele answered, smiling herself. "You don't like it." Together they walked towards the elevator.

*

What on earth is it about this man? she thought about an hour later, the best hour she'd had since – since – well, since the last time she was with him – this despite the muted undertone of guilt that accompanied all the high spirits.

"The fish was delicious," she said.

"The filet must have come from a happy halibut. The sucker probably volunteered," and they both laughed. The type of bubbling high spirits where everything seems funny, and ordinary banter elevates itself to the level of wit.

"It obviously died a very happy fish," she answered.

"A contented fish. Like milk from contented cows. If you remember that." A shadow crossed his face. She smiled a small, intimate smile, a bit flirtatious, don't worry about it, and he brightened immediately.

She'd never dated an older man; in fact, she'd never even taken one seriously. George was 43 years old; her father was 67. He was closer to her age than to her father's, but not by all that much. *Hatchet man; rough customer* – she had intuited these things at the outset; now that intuition had been confirmed. He came from a completely different background. He didn't know anything about art or technology, or any of the things that interested her. His intelligence was the business shrewd type, an entirely different species than hers. They had absolutely nothing in common. Nothing.

Yet here she was, making stupid jokes of her own, laughing at his. Nothing disturbed the surging chemistry between them. The obvious pleasure he took in her company, the effect she thought she was having on him. His initial diffidence had completely disappeared. It had been replaced now by a composed, assured masculinity, with a slight tinge of schoolboy enthusiasm. There were very, very few women of any age who wouldn't have found him extremely attractive today.

"I missed you in St. Louis," he said. "There was a modernist exhibition

366

in the museum there. Hell, I haven't been in a museum in thirty years. But I went. Thought of you. If it'd been three weeks from now, if the damned Project were done, I'd have picked up the phone and asked you to fly down."

George Sorenson was no giant, no great-winged being. There was nothing at all magical about this. Good. She was sick of magic. She had had entirely enough of magic for a while, maybe for a lifetime. An entirely different image formed; a twig, stuck in the ground and forgotten; the discovery of a green leaf, then another, then another, against all probability. A small, improbable plant to wonder over, to nourish carefully. Perhaps all the more precious for that. *The flowers between the cracks*, she remembered vaguely, then remembered exactly where she'd heard that – *damn it!* – and somehow concealed her annoyance with herself.

"To meet you in St. Louis?" she prompted. He grinned and nodded. Privately, she wondered how she'd have reacted to the invite, if her situation had been different. . . her suspicion was that she would have been on the very first plane, with something sexy in her overnight bag.

"This really is a nice little dining room," she went on, looking around. "So light and airy. Even with the overcast."

"Good," he responded, "I'm glad you like it." He paused. "It's important to me that you like where you are when you're with me," he added quietly, which touched her to the core. Ordinary things sounded wonderful the way he said them.

"And say so. What you like and what you don't. You're different than anyone I've ever known," he went on. "It's tough for me to know what's going on in your head. You – ah – are not at all like the business types I hang around with."

Comparisons? Some were inevitable. Tom could have given lessons to any man she'd ever met. He'd wooed her in exactly the right way, top to bottom – first intriguing her curiosity, then dazzling her mind, finally winning her heart, after which she had neither the means nor the inclination to dispute his right to take possession of the rest. George? Here the body and its wisdom had led the way. The chemistry was actually better than with Tom. If it had been only that, she would have resisted it, but George, too, made all the right moves – different moves, but also right. The first was a giant; the second was an ordinary businessman, if immensely competent at his business. The ordinariness did not diminish him in her eyes. It was part of his charm – that, and his sudden, touching sweetness.

Suddenly she had to touch him; she reached across the table, laid her hand on his sleeve. "There's not that much to say," she said, gently. "There's nothing here that I don't like today." He took her hand lightly in his own, held it for a long moment.

"November 20th's next Saturday," he said quietly. "It'll all be over. Can we go out that evening? Or Sunday?"

Her smile froze on her face for an instant; behind the mask, her thoughts began to race wildly. *What to say? What to do?*

"Hello, George. . . Ms. Jansen," said Franklin Fischer, moving from behind her to one side of the table. George dropped her hand like a hot rock. "I'm sure you don't mind if I join you." Without waiting for a response, he pulled out a chair and signaled the waiter.

*

Both Adele and George straightened up in their chairs, shifted their weight. *Yes, we mind very much. Go away* – Adele despite the respite this afforded her.

"Bob," Franklin said to the young man who had materialized by the table, "I want a steak. Medium. Will you please tell the chef that medium means pink, not red? And hurry. I'm wanted downstairs. Ms. Jansen, please excuse us," he said, nodding perfunctorily towards her, dismissively, then turned his head.

"George, we have to talk. The Murrays are going to be here Monday." George flashed a glance of complete exasperation that could not have been improved by Oliver Hardy, then gave his attention to Franklin.

Idiot, idiot, idiot, she was thinking. *Moron! Why November 20th? Why didn't you say December 1st, or something?* Of course, at the time they'd been talking about some exploratory second meeting, dancing or something, so it seemed safe enough. How could she have possibly guessed that they'd have this wonderful lunch, that the potential of the relationship would become so much greater so quickly? That it would take on a definite sexual imminence? Well, she should have guessed somehow.

Great. Just great. Now what was she going to do? One thing for sure, she'd have to talk to Dr. Marshall about the practical aspect of all this. She half-cringed; fortunately, the two men were engaged with each other, and didn't notice. An absolutely mortifying phone call had become a necessary event in the near future. *Hello, Alice, this is Adele Jansen. You remember, your patient who got herself knocked up on the one-night stand? Well, I'm all set to hop in the sack with another guy and what I want to know, Alice, is, how long until* – dear God. She could depend on Alice to be polite, competent, overtly nonjudgmental. But dear God! She clenched her teeth.

Yet the potential existed. It was unrealistic to deny it, not to mention the implicit unfairness to George. He had wooed her with nothing but kindness

– in truth, the one of the two of them who had nurtured that little twig, produced the unexpected green. If it kept up like this, intimacy would be inevitable; she had given him no contrary signal. Could she imagine him making love to her? His body and hers, the full giving of self? *Oh, yes, yes, yes, easily* – the most natural thing in the world it seemed, right at this moment.

"Look. . . Franklin," said George, rubbing his hand through his hair, his composure gone, the irritation evident in his voice, "all this can wait until Monday, can't it?"

Somehow hold him off. All at once, she was overwhelmed with guilt. None of this was right, none of it. Here she was, sitting across the table from him, lying to him, planning how to keep him at bay until she could – dispose – *no, some other word* – she could not think of any – *I'm sorry, little one* – and – that again, the same old thing, always, it was always there – the great-winged shadow lay here as it lay everywhere else, falling between them even now. Her good mood had disappeared completely. She felt tired and old.

"All right," said Franklin amiably. "Monday it is. Early." The waiter put a steak down in front of him. He showed not the slightest sign of movement. George and Adele glanced at each other.

"Damn," Franklin Fischer sighed with exasperation. "Look at that. . . half raw." It looked pink enough to Adele. "Can't he get anything right? Bob!" The waiter started over, but he waved him away. "No, no, no, changed my mind, I don't have time to have it re-cooked." The waiter retreated; he looked up at George. "Would you *do* something about this, George? There's got to be someone in this city who can cook beef."

The overhang all this was creating in her life. If it were not for Tom, not for the pregnancy, she'd be exploring fully the possibilities with George Sorenson, cautiously, but with unreserved interest. What would she be feeling towards him right this moment if so much of her emotional vibrancy was not being drained by this useless quest? These long turbulent nights? It was painful to think of that – and also another source of guilt, because he certainly wasn't holding anything back. All her lies and secrets. Terrible.

Storm warning. If she didn't instantly get hold of herself. . . George would be sweetly protective, but she was not yet ready to expose that side of herself to him, not completely. Unthinkable in front of the other. Ever. She straightened up, composed herself, and looked across the table.

Franklin Fischer worked quickly on his meat. Once he looked up: "I do hope I'm not intruding," he said. *Bastard*, she thought. George was seething across the table.

"I didn't want to interrupt, and I haven't much time," he said, when he was finally finished. He glanced at George, then turned to Adele. "But I felt I owed it to myself to get to know you a bit better. George has been a changed man these last few weeks."

"Franklin –" George began warningly, but the other man continued, ignoring him:

"I always sensed my old friend had a bit of the romantic in him, but I never thought I'd see that side of him. He's typically been more practical than that."

"I wouldn't know anything at all about that," Adele said, giving George a quick smile. "I do know he's an awfully good lunch date."

"George is a very important man to me," he went on as if she had not spoken. "What affects him affects me. His decision to dissolve our partnership was immensely disappointing. Particularly when we stand on the verge of such a bold, new venture."

"That's nothing to do with her, Franklin. You know that," George said coldly. Franklin Fischer turned to him.

"I didn't mean to imply the contrary," he said. "Even so. . . I was hoping you'd reconsider." He turned his head to Adele. She stiffened. "In fact, I'd even wondered if *you* might persuade him to reconsider."

She shook her head, embarrassed and incredulous. "Mr. Fischer, I am afraid you've completely misunderstood my relationship with George. I..."

"I've heard him speak of you," Franklin Fischer interrupted. "You haven't." Across the table, George was a mask of pale rage.

"...don't have that kind of influence over him," she continued, ignoring him in turn. "And even if I did, I'd accept his decision about that sort of thing. The same way I'd expect him to accept mine."

"Franklin," George replied – she could tell he was barely controlling himself – "if you don't mind? I'd like to finish my lunch with my friend."

"Oh," Franklin answered, theatrically startled. "I'm sorry. Forgive me. I have spoken out of turn." He looked oddly at Adele again. "But this is a matter of great concern to me. I'm sure I'll have the opportunity to know you better. Perhaps we'll speak of it again." Then he pushed the chair abruptly to the table and exited rapidly through the front double door.

George Sorenson was a confusion of movement, agitated, furious, looking at her, then looking away. It moved her. She reached across the table. "Don't let it get to you, George," she said simply. "It didn't spoil anything."

He took her at her word, relaxed at once, took her hand.

*

They moved down the corridor. It was ten after one, time to get going to the airport. Suddenly he stopped, looked up and down the deserted hall, then took charge, put his hand on her back, began to move her gently but firmly towards the side of the hall. She noticed that a large potted plant, which looked as if it were standing against the wall, actually concealed a small alcove, with more than enough space for two people.

She let him guide her there. All the negativity rose to a crescendo, but her decision was not affected. No way he wasn't going to get his kiss, notwithstanding the turmoil, notwithstanding the presence of the shadow.

Which, as it had in the limo, turned out to be a lot more than a kiss. She was very close to the full take off point with him, would probably have been there if not for all the other factors. She opened her mouth, gnawed at his face, nipped his neck and earlobe, could not tear away, let his hands explore her back and backside, giving herself to him symbolically. His touch was wonderful – marvelous to be snug in his arms. She was sure she could trust him to ease up on his own before it got out of hand, and she was right.

"I can't believe this is happening," he finally managed to gasp. "I didn't think I could feel like this about anyone anymore. And that you're here. That I'm holding you. . . "

"George." She got out, deliberately putting her hands around his neck. He needed no second cue, stopped talking, and simply crushed her body against his. After a long moment he spoke.

"Can I see you on the 20th?" he asked.

She'd had time to collect her thoughts. "George, I goofed when I said that. I forgot. I'm having dinner with my field hockey club on Saturday night" – lying – "and I'm supposed to go out to the home of one of my partners on Sunday." Moving back the actual date of her dinner with Walt's family by one week. "So I can't."

"Oh," he said, deflated. "Well, the next weekend?"

"The next weekend's Thanksgiving. I'll be home with my dad." He looked extremely disappointed. She placed her hands lightly on his hips. "George, I'm not playing any games with you. Honest. I'm looking forward to going out with you. I didn't lie to you. I'm not seeing anyone now."

"I'm not the jealous type. Not even of the man who gave you the angel. But God! I want to see you myself. Be with you. Begin with you. Don't get on me for being impatient."

"Of course not. I want to be with you, too," she said truthfully. "You be a little patient with me."

"Well," he said determinedly, "couldn't I take you to dinner Tuesday night? Before Thanksgiving? The Project'll be wrapped up. The markets will be slow all week. It can't be that hectic at your place."

"All right," she answered, thinking rapidly, "but – George – I'll have to work the next day. Quite a lot if I want to go home. So –" she reddened slightly – "it would have to be dinner only. If you know what I mean." If he bought into that, including Thanksgiving it would be ten days at the earliest, Monday the 30th, before anything physical could happen, probably later than that as a practical matter. She hadn't talked to Dr. Marshall, but that had to be close to long enough. *God!* To be thinking like this! To be plotting like this! Another wave of shame engulfed her as she smiled at him. It had been a long time since she had a lower opinion of Adele Elizabeth Jansen.

"That's O.K.," he responded, pleased she'd had to make that kind of condition, unaware of the inner turmoil. "If – it – should happen between us, I wouldn't want it to be when we were rushed, like a work night. Monday would have been a mistake. I'd want it someplace where we had all the time in the world." He paused. "Have you thought at all about Zihuateneo?" he said finally, his hands neutrally on her waist. "Is it more possible?"

"Yes," she answered, "I have. It's becoming more possible all the time." She moved her own hands flat on his chest. Now was the time. "But George. . . George. . . if – if I did do that, if I let you make me – yours" – his grasp tightened slightly – "I couldn't stand it if I knew people were talking about you like Jacob Rothenberg did. Someone else – don't ask me to tell you who – said you were a super rough customer."

"What you heard is true," he said simply, calmly. "What I said in the car. Franklin and I been taking no prisoners for quite a while. There's no way I can change what's done."

"I know that," she said, looking up at him, eyes wide, deliberately doing girl – when the occasion required, she could do marvelous girl, mostly because it was 95 percent authentic – "but I couldn't stand it if it went on. It would break my heart."

"Well, that couldn't be allowed to happen," he said gently, looking down, ancient theme of warrior with maiden, then shifted his weight. "I've gotten so tired of all the shit myself," he said suddenly. "I was coming to the end of the line with it even before all this started. Franklin knows it. Finish the Project, a coupl'a other things, and that'll be that."

"George," she said, not moving, still looking up, meeting his eyes, as small, vulnerable, and compelling as she could possibly make herself, "promise me. . . please promise me. . . that AI Squared isn't one of them."

"Yes," he answered, after the briefest pause. "It's not one of them. A financing, pure and simple."

Her hands tightened against him. She was terrified. She wanted so much to believe him. But she did not. She remembered now that once before, the day the three had demonstrated the program, after the lunch she had been sure he was lying to her. "Please, George. . . please. . . swear to me you're telling the truth."

"I swear, Adele," he said, smiling, assured. "Trust me. All it is, is a company. Quite a company. I'm not lying to you." Another agony of doubt; another spike of fear; it was not enough; it was not sufficient; it did not ring true (not the way it did when he talked about the two of them); but it would have to do. It was all she was going to get.

He pulled her to him and kissed her again, lingering, wet, perhaps even more passionately than before, the passion somehow generated by the doubt. His hand moved up her body, cupped her left breast; she did not draw back. It wasn't a question of being shy or reluctant. She wanted him to know that; besides, his touch felt wonderful. As before, he stopped when it was time.

"I have to go now, George," she said, now pulling away. "I have a plane to catch."

He nodded. She'd told him about the trip at lunch, explained falsely that it was business. "I hate to let you go," he said as he gave way out of the alcove.

"But I have to," she said simply, as she stepped out. A last exchange of glances – she could feel the pull, to go back into his arms, kiss him again, knew he was feeling it, too, but this was public, and they both resisted – a tiny wave, then she walked towards the elevator. The weariness which she had brought with her to his offices began its return with each step she took.

*

The torrent of emotion reached a new crescendo as she walked towards the restroom on the first floor. Once inside, she glanced around almost surreptitiously, then reached into one of the small pouches in her purse. Quickly, she fished out the little gold angel and refastened the clasp behind her neck.

It didn't help at all, in fact, only added a new sense of betrayal to the mélange already there. But it was something she had to do. Whatever was in store for her and George Sorenson lay in the future. She could not, she would not, be worthy of that future until she had fully redeemed the past, reconciled all its mysteries.

✳ ✳ ✳

ROAD TRIP

A shadow fell over the entrance to the plush office.

"One more wiseass stunt like that," George Sorenson snarled, "and I pull the plug."

"But. . . George," Franklin Fischer answered, spreading out his arms, "all I meant to do was--"

"I said one more wiseass stunt, Franklin. You wanna keep talkin'? Find out right now whether I'm kiddin? Try me." A phrase that had become notorious on the Street. In George Sorenson's younger days, there had been a few who did try him. Without exception they remembered the experience with profound regret.

"George," Franklin Fischer answered, placating, "I'm sorry. I truly am. I misunderstood. And − George − I don't mean to offend − but this development has caught me by surprise. She seems no more than a girl. A slip of a girl. Carolyn informs me that young Steuer calls her Rebecca. As in Sunnybrook Farm. Carolyn herself wonders whether she is at all − ah -- experienced."

Memories − of a few moments in the backseat of a limo, more recent experiences in an alcove − flickered across his George Sorenson's face, replaced almost instantaneously by darker thoughts. Big green eyes. Promise me. . . you must promise me it doesn't have anything to do with AI Squared. Damn it. Shit.

"She's innocent. Not naïve. Big difference." He paused. "I don't know whether I'm pulling the plug anyway. I don't like this. I'm sick of it."

"I'm amazed," Franklin Fischer replied, genuinely. "When everything's nearly finished."

Sorenson shrugged. "I feel like I got another chance. Like I can do better."

So that's it, the other thought. Out loud he said, "You've had everything you needed or wanted. You've hardly had cause for complaint."

"For fifteen years, I've lived like a mill hand − work all week for someone else. Three squares a day and a whore on Saturday nights. I stood it because I got convinced I couldn't do any better. Now I think I can."

"George," Franklin Fischer said, a bit too sharply, "you're overreacting. Ms. Jansen is a trained attorney -- a Wall Street lawyer. By your own account she's a brilliant young woman. I'm sure she'll see the point in due time."

"Right," George answered glumly, with the barest hint of sarcasm, then went on with his own thoughts. "Maybe I should call it off. Maybe it'd be better to try out our *partnership contract. Find out if it is ironclad."*

"And suppose you discover it is ironclad, George? What would you do? Start all over again? At age 43? With all the friends you've made?" In an identical sarcastic tone. *"Perhaps Podgorny would back you. How drastic, George. How unnecessary."* The man doesn't even flinch, Fischer thought. He's serious. *"And what about Ms. Jansen? What could you do for her?"* he went on, fighting off a surge of panic. Good. It registered; George had thought of that, too. *"There must be an easier solution. Perhaps she should be invited completely into the inner circle right now."*

"Forget it," George said flatly, turning his head quickly towards the other. *"I don't want her near you. People around you turn into shit sooner or later. If I'd met her before, she wouldn't be a player now."*

Interesting, *thought the other. Aloud, he said, "I'll forget the implications of that, George. I recognize my own fault in this. You have a reason to be angry."* Suddenly he straightened up, galvanized; unthinkable, impossible to go forward without George Sorenson. *"George, I genuinely regret the misunderstanding at lunch. I didn't understand. But I am certain you are overreacting. We don't have a major impediment here – merely a point of negotiation. There must be a win-win solution here. Perhaps if Ms Jansen were included. . . ?"*

Good again. *George nodded his head imperceptibly. He'd been waiting for the cue. He leaned forward.*

"I been thinking. . . "

A few moments later, the negotiation completed, George Sorenson closed the office door behind him. Franklin Fischer waited until the sound of his footsteps faded. The notion of doing without George, the possibility that he would have to face all the new challenges without his chief problem solver. . . unthinkable, impossible. It always had been.

"Helot," he muttered softly. Then he picked up the phone.

*

"I hope he didn't bother you too much," said the young woman sitting to the left of Adele, next to the window.

"Why should he have bothered me?" she answered. "His ears were hurting. Of course he's going to cry." The plane was taxiing to a stop. "Besides, he's the only sincere one on the plane. If we'd all been doing what we felt, we'd all have been crying." *It's going to be a little choppy, folks. The weather over Burlington is unsettled. Be sure your seatbelts are fastened tightly.*

"Amen to that," muttered a male passenger as he squeezed by.

"You did wonders," said the young mother, gratefully.

"Oh, it was nothing," Adele answered, lifting the infant off her

375

shoulder and handing him back. "He probably stopped crying because his ears stopped hurting." *This can't be happe*–she'd begun to think when she first sat down, then sighed inwardly. No, of course it's happening, it had to happen, it was inevitable.

Plus it was a mercy in a way; it kept her mind off the phone call she'd made to Alice Marshall from the airport. The memory was going to make her wince for years to come – Alice's lucid professional explanations, the crisp advice, the judgment she had obviously formed but concealed so professionally. *Ten days is close, but may be a little early. Er. . . Adele, if your lifestyle is changing to this extent, don't you think you should go back on the pill? Or patch?*

"I doubt that. You've got a knack."

Adele smiled. "I was the youngest in my family. When I was a little girl, I was so envious of all my friends that had baby brothers or sisters. When we all got a little older, they'd had enough; they wanted nothing to do with kids and babies. But I did, because I'd never had the chance. So I did a lot of childcare when I was in high school. I still remember a few tricks."

"Thanks, again." Both women rose to leave. *Please, please, please, don't ask if. . .*

"Do you have any of your own?"

Adele walked out of the terminal, through the drizzle and the 5:00 darkness, towards the car rental lot. Forty-five minutes later she was at the edge of the parkway, looking into the darkness. The road went straight to the south. The turnoff to Arden Farms and Arbalest went east.

The temptation surprised her when it arose – unexpected, sudden and intense. *You don't have to do this.* She put her elbow on the window frame, her head in her hand. Abercrombie had frightened her. Home was only 150 miles away. The roads were smooth and easy. At this time of the year, the wind blew crisp and cold off the lake. Occasionally, there'd be a whiff of salt from the great seaway at St. Lawrence. She knew that smell from her dreams, the essential stuff of her childhood, cool and fresh. Dad had totally redecorated the house several times over the years, but her old room was still there – the guestroom nowadays. She could be there in three hours. Her father wouldn't ask why, only be delighted to see her. Make popcorn, talk late into the night, sleep in her own bed, wake up to coffee brewing and bacon sizzling – he'd try to spoil her the way he had all her life. So easy. So close. Home.

A horn honked behind her. Startled, she looked in the rear view mirror. Two cars had come up behind her while she was thinking. Her respite was over already. She sighed, sat up straight, and put the car in gear.

And turned left, going east through the incessant drizzle, over roads with which she was completely unfamiliar. She drove for about an hour and a half before stopping for the night at a chain motel. No way would she consider anything picturesque, not on a rainy night, not as a single woman, not for anything. Norman Bates.

*

She was back on the road at nine the next morning, only slightly refreshed after another long, fitful night of dreams and wonderings. In better times she would have slept like the dead after such a day.

The skies were grayer here than they had been in the City. The light, perpetual rain gradually changed to drizzle and then ceased altogether. The sky remained gray, the day dark. Few cars were on the road this morning. The landscape was rural, large farms and orchards, stretches of forest, dark and primitive, broken from time to time by small towns and villages. In better days she would have found the scenery reassuring, that such relatively unspoiled areas still remained so close to the great urban centers. Not this morning.

It was near 11:00. Ten miles, a small sign said – then, Arden Farms, five miles. Around a bend, through the thickest copse yet, up a rise – Arden Farms, pop. 3951, elev. 580 feet. She had arrived.

It was an extremely small town – a main street with a pharmacy, an old Paramount theater, a tiny hotel. The buildings looked to have been constructed in the late 40s and 50s, with little refurbishment. She pulled up to a service station, gassed up, and asked for directions to Arbalest.

It was about one mile further north – a right turn onto a two-lane road, a half-mile off the turnpike. Pine trees lined the way, which twisted and rose to a small plateau. Then one last turn, past a clearing, and at last it stood on a hill before her.

*

The first view came as a shock. The main building appeared to have a steeple. Then, as she approached, the ground rose, and perspectives became more accurate, Adele realized her initial impression was an optical illusion. The steeple was not on the institution itself, but on a church situated on a rise a few hundred yards behind. The steeple lowered black against clouds, gothically ominous.

She stopped the car outside the gate. A black and white sign about four feet long read "ARBALEST," in ornate, scripted letters, someone's modest attempt at calligraphy. Seen as it was, the main structure was an ordinary three-story building, painted a fresh, cream white. A wooden porch, divided by a short dirt walk to the entrance, ran the entire length of the front side. Two other buildings, only slightly smaller, clearly dormitories, stood behind the largest one on either side of it. The grounds were surrounded by a wrought-iron fence at least ten feet high, with spearheads at the top. A circular driveway surrounded a small oval lawn. Off to the north side was a square asphalt parking lot, not truly a part of the design plan, more in the nature of an afterthought. A chain steel fence enclosed the asphalt.

The entire scene was devoid of any sign of life. Real fear swelled inside her for a moment. *What am I doing here, anyway?* Firmly she suppressed it, put the car in gear, and rolled through the gate and into the driveway.

The impression changed radically as she drew nearer. The paint on the building was indeed fresh, but the wood paneling was scarred and cracked. Red patches of rust bespattered the black of the iron in the fence. What had appeared to be a green verdant lawn was patched irregularly and covered with crabgrass. Cracks were everywhere in the asphalt, with green shoots poking through. Its surface was rough and irregular, a brittle, glassy texture at the edges and near the worn areas, typical of ancient paving.

She guided the rental down the driveway and into the parking lot – entirely vacant this day – pulled up the brake, killed the engine, and stepped out. The air was chilly and pure. The hill sloped down towards a plain. Across a small dale on another rise was the church whose steeple had deceived her when she first drove up. A schoolyard and a playing field lay in front of it. She turned her head. It was a relief finally to see some activity on the Arbalest grounds, a dozen or so boys in their mid-teens kicking a soccer ball on a grassy swatch between the northern dorm and the main building.

Even so, she was becoming more and more apprehensive. *Get hold of yourself, idiot. Johnson and Jansen.* She picked up her briefcase – she was wearing one of her most formal business suits with a severe pleated skirt – and started back up the driveway towards the front door of the main building. Some of the boys turned their heads as she passed. The group was not exactly sullen, but extremely quiet, their play automatic and joyless. She walked up the short gravel path and into the entry hall.

Adele found herself in front of a reception area not unlike the one she remembered at the office at Roosevelt High. A counter four feet high with a Formica top stood directly behind the door. It ran about twelve feet in front, then cut at right angles to the wall, enclosing what was obviously the administrative area. Inside the enclosure were two wooden secretarial desks, several filing cabinets, old-fashioned dial phones, and three typewriter stands with IBM models upon them. Two gray-haired women sat behind the desks, sorting files. The office enclosure was off-center. A corridor to her right led to a series of offices. The only thing on the left was a single door, conspicuously locked, which had to lead to the dormitory area.

One of the ancient secretaries looked up. "May I help you?" she asked unsmilingly.

"Yes. I'm here to see Dr. Harlow."

"Do you have an appointment?"

The front room reeked of the stale breakfast food smell common to all institutions. The hospital in which her mother had spent the last two weeks of her life had smelled like that.

"No, but I'm sure he'll see me. It's very important. It's about a former inmate – that is, patient – of his."

The woman stiffened. "Doctor is a very busy man, Miss – Miss –"

"Jansen. Adele Jansen."

"Doctor doesn't see anyone without an appointment." She bent pointedly back towards her work.

"He'll see me," Adele said, smiling politely, but beginning to gather herself. The gloves were coming right off today. Her sense was that cuting it up wouldn't get her anywhere. "Call him for me, please."

"I thought I made myself clear," the woman answered, annoyed, looking up again. "The holidays are approaching. There is more restlessness, more difficulty, for us now than at any other time of year. Many of the patients who've been in other institutional settings anticipate they'll be going home. It's difficult for all of us, but particularly for Doctor."

"I've come a considerable distance, this is very important, and I know he'll see me," said Adele, her eyes narrowing, her voice hardening. "So please call him."

The secretary stood up. "Young woman, I am trying to explain to you. Doctor –"

"Don't call him 'Doctor,'" Adele snapped – it was working out the way she had anticipated; this was going to be hardball all the way – "he's 'the doctor' or 'Doctor Harlow.' There is more than one doctor in the world, you know. Now pick up the phone and call him. Now. Do it. He will see me."

"You impudent little snip," gasped the older woman, sucking in her breath, her expression the same mixture of astonishment and indignation as the old fart from Oneonta, a common reaction when people found out there was a little more to her than sugar and spice.

"And you are a surly, foolish bitch," Adele said as the other woman gasped again, "but it doesn't make any difference what either one of us is, because you are going to pick up that phone right now and get Dr. Harlow here or I am going to be back in a few days with subpoenas for all of you and depending on what I find back a few days later with the police," realizing as she improvised the threats that she meant every word of them – although how she was going to get subpoenas issued with no litigation pending was anybody's guess. But she'd find a way.

"You're an attorney?" the woman asked in a different tone of voice. "But you look so –"

"Yes," Adele snapped again, "from New York – and I have not come all this distance to have my time wasted by the likes of you. Pick up the phone" – pointing – "and call Dr. Harlow. Is he on the grounds or in town?"

"He's here," the woman muttered softly. She glared at Adele for a long moment, pursing her lips, shaking her head slowly, contemptuously. Adele fixed her eyes on her. The staring contest went on for several seconds – then, still shaking her head, the woman picked up the phone.

"What's the name of this patient who's so important to you?" she asked acidly.

"Newcombe. Thomas Bryant Newcombe."

The other gray-haired woman looked up sharply from her desk. The first one slowed her movement, collected herself – she thought she was inconspicuous, but she wasn't – then began to dial the phone. She put the receiver to her ear and turned her back on Adele. "Doctor? There's a young woman at the desk – a very rude, obnoxious" – she raised her voice to emphasize the adjectives – "young woman. She wants to see you about a former patient. What?. . . Who?. . . Yes. . . Yes. . . Well, she said..." Her voice became inaudible.

She put the receiver down and faced Adele again, still glaring. "Doctor will see you, but it may take some time. He's busy upstairs. But I must say, you are the most inso –"

"Thank you," Adele answered calmly. "I'll wait." An overstuffed chair sat in one corner, beside which was a small stand with some ancient periodicals. *Idiot*, she thought, should have anticipated this, should have brought some files to work on. All she had in the briefcase was a notepad, her laptop, and Carolyn's revised schedule, which she'd all but memorized. *Oh, well*, she sighed inwardly as she sat.

That smell. She'd been there twice in that last, awful fortnight. Actually, it hadn't been a hospital. It had been a hospice. She hadn't known the difference at the time.

Or known much of anything, when it came right down to it. It couldn't be happening, so it wasn't. Everything had gone so quickly, a matter of weeks from the night her father had taken her quietly aside after dinner, to the day Mom left for what Adele thought was the hospital. The wheelchair had been scary, but she put that out of her mind. The doctors at the hospital would give her a pill, or cut something out, and everything would be fine. She'd come back good as new, they'd be back in the attic (where the light was best) on Saturday afternoons, like always, as if her mother had never had cancer.

Moms don't die – especially not hers. Sometimes they get sick, sometimes they do go away for a while, but they don't die. Goldfish die. Besides, Mom phoned her every day at four, right after she got home from school. See, she hadn't even gone that far away; it couldn't be happening, so it wasn't. Twelve.

God, I hate that smell! She picked up a copy of TIME that turned out to be a year and a half old. Stupid – she didn't want to read this, she didn't want to have anything to do with this. All at once there was no way she could stay in that room for another instant.

"I'm going to step outside for a minute. I'll be on the driveway when *the* doctor calls."

"I won't be able to see you, Miss," the secretary said coldly.

"Yes, I know, but I'll be able to hear you," Adele answered sweetly. "And you will call me loudly enough, won't you? Wouldn't want to waste Doctor's time." She pushed open the door. "Some people," the receptionist said to her companion in an overloud voice. Adele felt the briefest temptation to turn and inform her that what she thought about Adele, or the doctor, or anything or anyone, didn't make the slightest difference to her. No. Pointless.

Fortunately, the rain had not resumed; it would have been embarrassing to walk straight back through the door. A north wind had come up. The air was noticeably colder than it had been thirty minutes earlier.

The worst memories of her childhood assailed her. On the day – the day – the call hadn't come at four o'clock. She'd even become angry – *angry*, idiot child that she'd been; she'd feel guilty about those few seconds of anger for the rest of her life – wondering how Mom could have forgotten. She went into the kitchen, made herself a peanut butter sandwich, and worried in spite of herself. About a half an hour later, she heard her father on the doorstep, slow, faltering steps.

Her parents had done a good job of keeping up the front. Between the care her father provided and the help of friends, her mother had been able to remain at home until the very end. She had taken to napping during the mornings to preserve the best of her dwindling strength for her daughter, her only child still living at home, her baby, her prize. The calls were placed at four o'clock during those last two weeks because it was the only time in the twenty-four-hour day she was not either woozy from morphine or in racking pain. She had fought for her life to her last labored breath, long after everyone who knew had begun to wish only for her peace. Adele did not know that, believed her father's consoling lie that it had been a peaceful death, would not be told the whole truth for nearly a decade, would be angry at first, then more grateful to him than she had ever been.

She walked down the driveway towards the rental car, deliberately trying to alter her mood, consciously bringing to mind happier things. Lunch yesterday with George had been wonderful. Being held by him had been wonderful. Wouldn't it be great if he were with her now? If he were right—

No, no, a different, more powerful memory was necessary. George was terrific, George might be her future, but right now she'd have to explain so much to him, tell him so much before he'd understand. No – not George, not now. Not enough time. Someone else.

You shouldn't have come, he'd say. *I would have told you that if you'd asked. All you're doing is making yourself unhappy. It isn't doing any good.*

I have to find out all about you. I have to do it as quickly as I can. I don't know why. Please don't be angry.

I'm not at all angry, but I'm not going to let you do this to yourself anymore. Come here, Adele, he'd say, his voice slightly firmer, and of course she would, she had to obey him when he spoke to her in that tone. He'd press her head against his shoulder, lift up her hair with the bad hand, she'd feel small and precious against his size, and somehow he has a blanket – of course he has a blanket, it was getting very cold, he'd wrap that around her. *I'm taking you away from here. This is not a good place for you. You should never have come here,* his voice very soft. Then they'd leave and it would all be over.

She shook her head, returned to the present; she was standing by the car, looking over the grounds of the school. Two boys were now on the grounds, shooting baskets against the wind, tiny black figures in the distance.

Suddenly she heard his voice again, this time not in fantasy, but in living memory. *I used to watch the kids blowing soap bubbles,* he'd said that day. She remembered the oddly passive construction of the sentence. Of course. *You stood right here, didn't you, Tom? Watching luckier children play games you couldn't play yourself. You stood here once, right where I'm standing now. I'm certain I'm right. Is this the place where you learned to watch so well? I know you were here. I know it.*

She turned and looked back at the main offices of Arbalest, a solid, white monolith. A bad place; an evil place; terrible things had happened to someone she loved in that building. Anger spread out of her abdomen and throughout her entire body. All fear disappeared. A quiet, seething fury took its place.

As she watched, as if on cue, the receptionist appeared on the porch.

"Miss! Miss! Doctor will see you now!" she called.

*

Philip Harlow was waiting for her inside, standing in front of the office enclosure, a thin, angular man of average height in his mid-fifties, wispy moustache and weakish chin. He wore a white doctor's smock, recently laundered, but frayed around the collar and sleeves. Curiosity was evident in his features, but a wary curiosity, not open. Rodentlike impressions flitted through her mind, a sense of animal cunning, rat, weasel.

"Hello," he said, with a guarded, uneasy smile, extending his hand, "my receptionist tells me you want to talk to me about a former patient. I'm a very busy man today, but I can spare you a moment or two."

"Certainly," said Adele, taking his hand. "This won't take long. I'd prefer to talk in your office."

"Are you from the State?" he asked.

"No," she answered (lying would be useless; he was certain to ask for identification). "But I want to discuss this in your office." *Where you can't gather strength from your toadies.*

"That won't be necessary," he said, smiling again. "Ms. Smithson told me the name of the person. Thomas Newcombe. I'm the founder of Arbalest; I've been here thirty-five years. I remember nearly all of my patients. I can assure you that no person by that name was ever admitted here."

You're lying, she thought. The smaller, silent woman looked up from her desk, met Adele's eyes meaningfully. "I'd like to talk in your office."

"But that won't be necessary. I said –"

"I'd like to speak in your office. I know that person was an inma –"

"Patient."

"–*inmate* here," she finished icily. Ms. Smithson pursed her lips again. "I'm sure I can refresh your recollection if you'll allow me. I'd like to speak in your office."

He looked warier, if possible, an instant of real fear, cornered, trapped. He sighed heavily. "All right. For a moment or two. The last door on the right. Ms. Smithson, hold any calls until this person and I are finished talking."

*

"Ms...."

"Jansen."

"Jansen, have a seat. There's a limit to how far obstreperousness can take you," he said, after they were in his office and the door was closed. "I'm

383

telling you the truth. There has never been anyone named Thomas Newcombe admitted here. Besides which," he added, "I did not care a bit for your characterizing my patients as 'inmates' before my staff. That was uncalled for."

"That's what everyone in social services in the state of New York thinks," Adele said, eying him directly. Backing down from this man would not help at all. "There's no harm in saying it out loud. What's uncalled for is you not telling me the truth. I know Mr. Newcombe was a – patient – here. I *know* it."

"How?" he blurted out. She said nothing, simply considered him, and let the word hang in the air. "I mean," he went on, finally understanding, "it isn't possible for you to know something that isn't true. There was no person named Thomas Newcombe ever admitted to Arbalest."

In his eyes, then, a sly, contemptuous ferality. He was keeping something from her deliberately, mocking her subtly. "That's not correct. You're not being honest with me. Dr. Harlow," she said coldly, "I'm going to find out about this, one way or another. I never quit on anything, I never lose, and I'm not going to go away. You'd be better off cooperating with me right now."

The room was silent for a moment.

"You're quite an audacious young woman," Harlow said softly, ominously. His hands were under the edge of the desk. "To come so far and talk so directly. This is a very small, isolated community, you know. We have little communication with the outside world. We –"

"Are you *threatening* me?" Adele snarled, rising from her seat. "You were *threatening* me!" Acting on the ancient casual advice of her mother, who had been raised on a farm back when their little town was still largely rural. *If you're ever in real trouble with a vicious animal, pumpkin, advance on it. Don't retreat. Retreating makes them confident.*

Harlow went white, held up his hands. "No, no, Ms. Jansen, I only meant –" Adele heard a step in the hall outside, reached for the handle of the door, threw it open. Another man in a white smock was standing there, one hand poised towards the doorknob, the other closed by his side. His mouth dropped open.

"Hello," Adele snarled again, "step inside." The man was too startled to do otherwise. "Tell me who you are and why Dr. Harlow called for you."

"This is Dr. Coppelman," Harlow interjected quickly. "Peter Coppelman. He's been my assistant for nearly 20 years. All I wanted to do was introduce you. Although," he added, quickly again, "I was concerned that Ms. Jansen was becoming hysterical."

She stepped quickly through the door. "You two! At the desks! Come here!" she called out calmly and clearly. The two came down the hall, the taller one still sullen.

"Do I appear to either of you to be hysterical?" she asked.

"Well," began the taller, eyes glinting, "if you ask me –"

"No," interrupted the shorter, mousy one, probably the first word she had spoken that day. "She's been forceful and direct, but she is in no way hysterical. Doctor Harlow," she went on, looking at the doctor directly, "it's nearly noon. My husband will be here to pick me up for lunch any second." There was another silence.

"What are you holding in your hand, doctor?" Adele asked evenly, looking at Coppelman.

"This?" he answered, holding up his hand. "This is a syringe. I was medicating some patients upstairs. It's empty."

Because you put the needle through the cloth of your trousers and emptied it down the back of your leg, she thought, nodding slowly, too angry and frustrated to be frightened. Then aloud, "All right. Now tell me the truth about Thomas Newcombe. Don't lie to me."

"I have told you the whole truth," Harlow said, "again and again," then turned to Coppelman. "You can see why I'd wonder if she was hysterical." As Coppelman nodded, he faced Adele. "There was never any person named Thomas Newcombe admitted here. Ever." He waved his hand. "You can inspect the files if you like."

She could sense it, she could feel it, she could see it in the reactions of all four – Harlow, Coppelman, the bitchy receptionist, smug in their knowledge – even the mousy one, though that one was silently imploring her to guess correctly. There was a clue hidden here, something very close, the same as in one of Bill Abercrombie's crosswords; if she found it, if she asked the exactly right question, the entire house of cards would tumble down, all the deceit and trumpery vanish. If.

"I'm going to find out," was the best she could do. Damn – the triumph was evident in their eyes, the smugness, the satisfaction. For this day, anyway, whatever secret it was, was safe.

"All right," said Harlow, secure in his world, "I've been patient enough long enough. I have something to say to you: Get out. I've been in this business for thirty-five years. Our staff here consists of Pete and me, a couple of nurses, every once in a while, an intern. The county doesn't even give me a full-time social worker anymore. The patients I take are the hardest cases in the state – three states. My methods are hard –"

"They have to be hard, everything else has failed," interjected Coppelman.

"–and they don't always succeed, but I'm proud of my results. I'm not ashamed of anything I've done. Dr. Coppelman and I don't have to take this crap from you or anyone like you. This is my place, my home. I am the master here. You're not welcome in it. Get out."

She started to say something, but he interrupted: "I said get out. Now, or I'll call the police."

She looked around at the four of them. It was over, no doubt about it. "All right." She picked up her briefcase, stepped between the two secretaries, and marched down the hall, veered sharply to the right, opened the latch to the administrative enclosure, and walked in.

"What are you doing?" asked Harlow.

"You said I could inspect your files. I'm taking you up on it," Adele answered, without looking back, pulling open the top drawer marked "A."

"But I was speaking rhetor–Ms. Jansen, I – Ms. Smithson," he finally said, choking with rage, "when this impossible young woman has finished examining our confidential files, escort her out. Don't let her remove or examine any of them unless she finds one concerning the mythical Mr. Newcombe. Good day," he finished, and left.

It took half an hour. The files contained nothing; she didn't really think they would.

"I'm finished," she said.

"Good," said Ms. Smithson. "Get on your way. You heard Doctor."

"In case one of the doctors changes his mind, here's my card," she said, scribbling her home number as well. It was a desperate try, but she had nothing else.

"I'll take that," said the mousy one. It occurred to Adele that the husband she said was coming for lunch had not yet arrived. Adele picked up her briefcase and unlatched the gate.

"Good day," said Ms. Smithson coldly. "You are the rudest young person I've met in a long time. These doctors you insulted so completely are caring, dedicated men. It's as Doctor Coppelman said: hard cases require hard medicine. Which –"

"–doesn't stop either one of them from loving it, does it?" Adele said wearily, as she pushed open the front door. It was all so obvious. How could Smithson live with herself? "Goodbye. I've had a wonderful time. Thank you for all the hospitality." The look of apoplectic fury on Ms. Smithson's face was scant consolation for the sense of complete, dead-end defeat she was feeling.

*

Twenty miles down the road she pulled over to the shoulder, trembling so violently she could not handle the wheel for a moment. The adrenaline surge which had carried her through at Arbalest was gone. The horrendous risk she'd taken! Abercrombie had been right! Those were frightened, dangerous people, the veneer of civilization obviously, dangerously thin – she shivered all over, nauseated, close to vomiting over the window.

And it had all been for nothing – *nothing!* She'd felt it in the room, almost a group taunting – something had been lying so close at hand, something she could almost feel. Yet she had not been able to put her hand on it, and now it was gone. Rage surged through her again, but then at once she was too tired for rage.

Her head rested against the wheel for a moment. She wondered at herself, marveled wearily at herself. This whole project had begun with Bri's common sense suggestion that she talk to Tom about what had happened. She had hardly begun before it became apparent that it wasn't worth it, that whatever was to be gained wasn't worth the cost. Yet she had persisted. Her self-understanding, her self-respect had become entangled, engaged. Now, sitting alone in a rented car on a deserted road in northeast New York, it had become painfully clear that those latter ends, too, did not justify these means, this cost. So. What? Quit? Back away?

No – the answer came surging out of her being – *no*. Not even slowdown. Find the way, follow the path to the end. She smiled at herself. *You really are a ninny.* If ever she reached the end of the road, if ever she did have that lunch or meeting or whatever with Tom (how distant, how naïve that plan seemed now!), nothing of what she'd learned would change anything. She would still do what she'd intended – bask in the glow of being with him, this time pick up the tab (a strange world, where you feel comfortable enough with a man to let him take you to bed, but not enough to split a check), and then close the door as firmly as before. She had made the sensible decision, the only decision, the morning after. So. . . why? Why persist?

No good answer – and yet she knew she was going to. In the short term, unraveling the puzzle had become the central goal of her life. The mysterious sense of urgency that had never quite left her had now become a roaring, howling wind, a force of nature – too strong to question, let alone resist. She had an inkling now she was never going to see Tom again, that the process of inquiry itself was widening the distance between them. But suspecting that was so, even knowing it was so, made no difference to what she was going to do. . . what for some reason she felt she had to do.

She thought of another fairy tale, the boy who didn't ask the question and had to wander for years and years and years. How long was she going to have to do this? How many doors were going to stay firmly, firmly shut, no matter how hard she pulled them? The thought was too burdensome and discouraging to think, at least right now. For now, she had to get to the airport, get on an airplane, go back to whence she'd come.

Then, when she wasn't so tired, consider what she was going to do next.

*

Adele walked through the door of her apartment at 9:30 that night completely exhausted, the plane at Burlington having been nearly two hours late. She'd had no lunch; dinner had been two hot dogs at the airport. She turned on the living room light automatically.

"Adele!" exclaimed Joan, somehow getting out from under a hirsute blob, sitting up on the couch and covering herself. "I thought you were away!"

"Oh," she said dully, "I'm sorry." One of Joan's two middle-aged lovers, the fat one, was hastily covering himself. "I'm going to my room," and switched off the light. She hoped they'd go elsewhere. The last thing she need this night was sound effects from the next room. The first thing was a bath, a long, long, hot bath, then crawl into her bed, sleep for about a century, and after that. . . think for a while.

The answering machine showed three messages. Two were Bill Abercrombie; one was from Carolyn, her voice full of impatience, ordering her to call at home first thing in the morning.

The phone rang at the same time as she unbuttoned the top button of her blouse. She picked up the receiver on the first ring. Even Joan and the gorilla didn't deserve two incidents of *coitus interruptus* within five minutes.

"Hello?"

"Adele? Adele Jansen?"

"Yes. Bill? Why are you calling me?"

He sounded embarrassed. "I've been calling every two hours since four." He paused. "Looking after you a little bit. If you didn't answer before noon tomorrow, I was going to the police," he said gruffly.

"Oh, Bill," she said, genuinely touched, "thank you. Thank you. And you were right to be worried. It's a truly awful place and truly awful people. But nothing happened. It was close, but nothing really happened."

"Are you all right? Did you learn anything?"

"Yes to the first, no to the second. But, Bill, what I mostly am is completely exhausted. Can I call you Monday and tell you all about it?"

"Of course," he said, gruffly again. "Sorry to bother you."

"No, no, no," she said, "I'm truly grateful. Good night now."

She put down the receiver, unbuttoned the next two buttons. The phone rang again; she heard a muffled exclamation from the next room, had to smile. Poor Joan. She picked up the phone; it had to be Bill with a second thought.

"Bill? I really can't talk to you –"

"This isn't Bill," said an unfamiliar woman's voice.

"Who is this?" Adele asked.

"We met today," she answered, with a certain lightness. "I'm Naomi Forster. I was the other one – the one that wasn't Ms. Smithson? You remember?"

"Yes," breathed Adele, suddenly no longer tired. "Thank you. Where did your husband have lunch, anyway?"

The other laughed. "I really don't know, I haven't asked him." Then, more seriously, "You made quite an impression this morning. Harlow and Coppelman spent the rest of the afternoon in Harlow's office. Rebecca Smithson's going to be talking about you for the next ten years. You're everything that's wrong with the younger generation."

"So I've been told," Adele answered. "I knew there was something more there. I was certain Harlow was lying to me."

"Oh, but that's why I'm calling," Mrs. Forster said, now deadly serious. "He wasn't lying. He was telling you the absolute, literal truth. But not the entire truth. It's completely right that there never was anyone admitted to Arbalest named Thomas Bryant Newcombe." She paused.

"But there was someone discharged by that name."

TALKING TO STRANGERS

Adele sucked in her breath. So *that* was it. The bastards.

"I thought there was something like that happening. But I couldn't think in time."

"You're hardly the first," she answered. "Harlow's had a lot of practice at that sort of thing."

"Can you tell me more?" Adele asked. "I'd appreciate it if you could tell me all you know."

"I intend to, but you're going to be disappointed," she replied. "I'm not a native of Arden Farms. My husband and I retired here thirteen years ago. He's done fine, but I got restless after a few years. I'd worked all my life; I couldn't stand it not doing anything. I looked around and I found this part-time job at Arbalest. I come in four days a week and do typing and filing." She paused. "I thought it was a good thing at the time, that I'd be contributing. I had no idea what went on there. No idea at all."

Adele nodded, listening, impatient to hear everything, impatient for her bath, but she had to let the other take her time. "It didn't take me long to find out. You hit it right on the head – he loves it. He loves the power and the viciousness. Coppelman's worse, if possible. Therapy's accidental."

"You don't seem like the type of person who'd stay on there."

"I'm not. At least, I hope I'm not. But" – she sighed – "this is a small community. Philip Harlow is very popular with most people here. Arden was his grandmother's maiden name, you know. The town's named after his family. Perhaps I'm a bit of a coward. What I hope is that I can do a bit of good from time to time, for people like you. And that someday, someday, if ever it does all come to a head – there'll be someone who knows."

"I'm glad you were there, anyway," Adele said. "What was in the syringe?"

"I'm not entirely sure – something that would have made you feel very good, but very groggy. Enough so that when you woke up in your car a few hours later you'd have got the message. Not so much that it would be easily traceable. He's done that with a few parents and relatives. They back off soon enough."

"How does he get away with it?" Adele asked, shaking her head.

"He'd say you had to be sedated. The local police wouldn't do anything. I know; it's happened. He's right that he gets the hardest cases. The ones that everyone else has given up on. Their relatives can be as difficult as they are. No one looks too hard at what Harlow does. It's not worth the trouble. Occasionally, some boy – they're nearly all boys – improves and he crows about it – oh, he gets away with it, Ms. Jansen, he gets away with it. Trust me. No one cares about these kids. It doesn't pay." Her voice was bitter. Adele said nothing, waited.

"In any case, I learned what was going on in the first few weeks. I wondered what I should do; I wondered what I could do. When we first moved to town, I made friends with some of the older women in town. We'd meet some mornings at this coffee shop after we'd done our shopping and sit around gibbety-gabbing. You know. One of them was Dora Johnson. I didn't know her too well – she kept to herself more than the rest of us – but I'd heard from someone that she used to be the county social worker at Arbalest. I called her up and went to lunch with her. I asked her what I should do."

She paused. "Dora told me there was nothing I could do. I was shocked. I couldn't believe it – I started to tell her what went on out there. She stopped me and said pretty much the same thing I've told you: that nobody gives a damn. Then she got the oddest, saddest look on her face. Said at least I should be glad I hadn't seen the worst, the very worst, a boy named Johnny Markland. I'd never seen her look like that about anything. Dora was a hard case."

"Johnny Markland? But I asked him about –" Adele interjected.

"I know who you asked him about. Let me finish. I'd been there long enough to know most of the files. I'd never heard of one by that name – and if it were that unusual, it would be marked, or very thick, or something. Dora – she still had that look – said that Johnny Markland was the name he came with, but he left with a different one. Thomas Newcombe. I asked her about it. I'd never heard of anything like that. I mean, they did bad, evil things, but nothing so strange – but she wouldn't say anything more. Said there were some things it was better not to know.

"I wasn't about to settle for that. I was curious. I looked and I found a file for Thomas Newcombe – Thomas Bryant Newcombe, the name you mentioned. But it was empty. Then I checked our patient logs. I found an entry for Thomas Newcombe, I can remember it exactly because it was so unusual: 'Thomas Newcombe, aka Jonathan Markland, discharged to the custody of J. Edelheit and Dora Johnson, under protest.' It was dated two or three years or so before I started – about fifteen or sixteen years ago. But that was all. I'd never seen any entry like it in the logs; I haven't seen another one in all the time I've been here since. The 'under protest' was in Harlow's own handwriting. Usually, he likes to keep his inmates – you had that right – as long as he can. When they are discharged, it's always to their family, or a closed mental institution, or back to the juvenile court that sent them. It's never like that."

"Who's J. Ed-el-heit? Can you spell the name it slowly?"

She did, then went on. "I wondered who it was, too. We also keep a log on entries and exits. I looked at that. J. Edelheit was one of our graduate assistants back then. But what was really peculiar was that the day Johnny – or Tom – was discharged was the last day that person came into the facility. But that was mid-April; usually, assistants stay through the school semester. And it was also the last day Dora Johnson came. Harlow told you another lie when he said he was without a social worker. The reason he doesn't have one is that he won't let the county send one. Not since Dora." She paused. "Something monumental must have happened that day."

"Do you know any more about J. Edelheit?"

"No. I tried to look at the personnel file, but it's logged out to Harlow personally. I don't even know if it was a man or a woman."

"How can I talk to Dora Johnson?"

"Dora passed on not long after I talked to her," Naomi said after a moment. "Not that it would have done you any good. She never said anything else. I tried to draw her out once or twice, but she wouldn't budge. I think she regretted what she did say."

"She said 'the worst.' Did she mean that it was the worst case or he was the worst boy?"

"I don't know, Ms. Jansen," the other answered quietly. "I've told you all I know. I wish I knew more myself."

The road had clearly come to an end. "Well, thank you," Adele said warmly. "Thank you for calling and thank you for everything. I hope I meet you again. I'm not always as rude and impossible as I must have seemed today."

"That's not at all how you seemed to me," the other answered. "You seemed like someone who was very, very worried. Also like someone who cares very much for someone else."

"Well," said Adele, blushing, after an awkward pause, "I don't know about that. But I am for sure very, very grateful to you."

"I hope I've helped," she said. "It makes me feel a little better about everything. I have to go now. Goodbye. Good luck."

*

Adele awoke the next morning less refreshed than she would have liked. The bath had been wonderfully relaxing, but she had much on her mind. She padded into the front room, determined to be as kind as possible to the couch lovers, only to discover via a note on the refrigerator that it wasn't necessary. Joan and friend were already up, already gone. Good. Great. Much to do today.

Another dreary, drizzly morning. The clock read 8:45 as she picked up the phone, punched in a number, and waited. "Hello, Irene? This is Adele. I'm afraid you're going to have to do without me today. I've got too much else to do."

The shriek from the other end could have been heard in the outer boroughs: "Adele!! You're kidding! How could you do this to me?! How could you do this to us?! Where am I going to find another right wing on this kind of notice?"

"I'm sorry, Irene, I really am, but I didn't know until only last night. Something's come up. Look outside; this is no day for field hockey anyway." She did her best to placate her friend and team captain, but only partially succeeded.

The next call she knew was going to be more satisfying.

"Hello, Bill? Bill Abercrombie? This is Adele Jansen. Good morning."

"What?" he said, groggily. "Who? Adele? What time is it? 8:55?! What the hell is it with you? Do you run on batteries or something?"

"I'm sorry, but something happened last night. I got a call from someone at Arbalest."

"Oh?" he answered, sounding considerably less groggy.

"Yes. It was one of the receptionists. She –"

"Adele, Adele," he interrupted patiently, "first tell me about the trip. Then tell me about the call." Of course he was right. She backtracked, filled him in quickly – "Report that," he said promptly when she told him about the syringe, "both to the locals and the state. One more item in the file. It all adds up" – then recited Naomi Forster's call. He was silent for a moment after she finished.

"I suppose I shouldn't be surprised," he said at last, "that the weirdest case of my career has become weirder. At least that explains why I couldn't find a birth certificate. I'll get that for you tomorrow, when the government offices open. Also, there's got to be some sort of commitment order or juvenile proceeding that put him there. I can have the court dockets searched, and I'll find that. But. . . but. . ." – the bewilderment was evident in his voice – "why he'd change his name. . . and informally. . . no court or anything. . . so young. . . no adoption or I would have found it the first time out. . . I don't understand it."

"Neither do I," she said. "Bill, I don't want to wait for tomorrow, I want to find J. Edelheit today. I want to talk to him or her as soon as I can. That's why I woke you up."

"Jeezus, Adele! This is my day off! You know, I was really worried about you and that harebrained trip," he said, more gently. Then, histrionically, "And this is the thanks I get? You want me to work Sunday??"

"*Please*, Bill – please? It won't take long. There's got to be a directory of clinical psychologists on some database you access. J. Edelheit is probably right there. The library doesn't open until noon and it'll be so much faster searching electronically. Please? Besides," she added, "you don't want to rot your brain watching football all day long."

"The hell I don't! That's *exactly* what I want to do, damn it! Turn down the sound, put on some Wagner, do the cross –"

"We'll be all finished by kick off," she pleaded. "I promise. It won't take that long, you know it won't. Just do this one thing for me, Bill – please? I have to get this done."

"I'm going to kill Greenfield the next time I see him," Abercrombie said, "for siccing you on me. But O.K., you win. I'll get on it. Do you mind," he asked rhetorically, "if I take a shower and have breakfast first?"

"Of course not," she answered, then paused. "But . . .keep it to twenty minutes?"

"*Jeezus*," he said. "You seemed so sweet."

*

Now the obligatory call to Carolyn. She sucked in her breath and punched the number, hoping.

"Hello?!?" came Carolyn's voice. "Just a minute." The sound of social clamor came over the line – "Put that down over there!" she heard Carolyn command someone in the background – then, "Who is this?"

"Adele."

"Where the hell were you Friday?" Carolyn demanded without further ado. "I looked all over for you. Just a second. I said over *there*!" she continued, talking away from the receiver. "This place is like Grand Central," she said again to Adele. "You'd think these people had never catered a brunch before. Where *were* you?"

Oh, no. She'd been caught. "Out. Family business. Family emergency. I sent a memo to your secretary," Adele lied, heart in mouth.

"Memo to my sec – oh, hello, Mr. – what was it – Williamson? Forgive me. I knew it was Williams or Williamson. After all, it's been six months. . . no, you're not early, the others are late." Carolyn laughed her gay Broadway laugh. "I'll be with you in a moment. I just have to finish this call. What do you mean, memo to my secretary?" she said into the receiver, voice low and ominous.

"There was no time to –"

"Adele," Carolyn went on in the same low tone, "I can't have this. Not from my own people. I made that clear. This is the Project. This is NATPE. The rewards come with responsibilities. After Friday, you can have the whole rest of your life for fami–ah, Mr. Williamson? There's Franklin now. Franklin, that's Robert Williamson – family emergencies. There is going to be no time for any personal life in the next five days. I hope you understand me. Now, there's been a change in plans. Three cable execs came in yesterday we didn't expect until Tuesday. They're at the Waldorf. George Sorenson got tickets for the new Lloyd–Weber thing, the preview matinée. George'll be your date. Meet –"

I can't, rose towards her lips, with the idea that she would twist and squirm and lie until she was free of it. Her stomach twisted into a cold, hard knot.

"What?" she heard Carolyn say to someone else, in her party voice. "You want – no matter, someone for sure will want the tickets. No problem at all. We're going to do a lot of business this week, but we're going to do a lot of fun, too. *Everybody's* going to leave happy. I promise!" More artificial laughter. "Adele, it's all off. But stay by the phone. . . and," she added in an even lower, harder tone, "I want to speak more to you about last Friday. Tomorrow sometime." The line went abruptly dead.

*

Whew. For a moment, Adele felt exhilaration over the narrowness of the escape. Almost immediately the feeling ebbed. For now, there was nothing to do but wait for Bill. She riffled desultorily through the Sunday Times as she ate – no time to read it thoroughly today. Her eye fell on a piece of puffery about the Lloyd–Weber show. *Damn.* From what she'd heard the production was bright and tuneful, visually spectacular – another record advance sale. If you didn't see it now, you couldn't until next August. It would have been lovely to go, in a big excited group. . . be with George. Instead, she was stuck here doing. . .

She watched the clock nervously. Twenty, twenty-five, thirty minutes went by. *Keep it to twenty minutes*, she'd said, but it had been a joke, she'd been trying to entertain him, not offend – surely he'd understood it? Thirty-five minutes. *C'mon, Bill, don't be like that.*

The phone finally rang.

*

"Took a while," he grunted shortly. "I knew there was some central directory, but I couldn't remember where. Then –"

"I would have thought it would be easy. I thought there'd be some national organization or society or something."

"You're good at this, but green," he answered. "Psychologists don't have to join a national association any more than lawyers do or doctors do. They're licensed state by state. Plus, your J. Edelheit may have become a licensed family counselor, or marriage counselor, or social counselor; you get the idea. Or might still be a psychological assistant. Or –"

"Psychological assistant?"

"What he or she was at Arbalest. You can't be licensed as a clinical psychologist without doing field work under somebody's supervision – 3,000 hours in California, for instance. Some people take years to get it all. She may be one of them."

"You really know a lot," she said, admiringly, still mildly worried she'd been too much of a snip an hour earlier.

He laughed a short, snorty laugh. "Most of which I learned in the last fifteen minutes. Like I said, I remembered someone had compiled a directory. It used to be a state by state thing, which would have been a nightmare, maybe an impossibility. But a few Congressmen got worried about bad therapists going from state to state and someone got a grant to put it all together. But I couldn't remember who. I had to check my own files – some project at University of Minnesota, it turned out. But then it got even easier; it turned up in my own backyard. The FBI bought it a couple of years ago, updates it every quarter. it's current through about August of this year. Records on everyone doing therapy in the United States – psychiatrists, psychologists, the works. I had it dumped onto my big machine a half an hour ago. I read the introduction before I phoned you."

"Bill, are we legal?" she asked timidly.

He laughed the same short laugh. "Would that stop you?"

"No," she answered truthfully, "but it would bother me," thinking of Goodwin.

"You can relax. Almost all of this stuff is public record. It links up to arrest records, which aren't, but we don't have to get into that. Yet. Adele," he went on seriously, "there are over 800,000 names in the file. If J. Edelheit has made any kind of career in counseling, he or she's in there someplace. But. . . if they gave it up. . . or went into business. . . "

"Then I'll have to think of something else," she said slowly. "I will."

"*That* I can believe."

"I'll cross that bridge when – if – I come to it. What are you doing now?"

"The FBI has it all broken down state by state. But I figured alphabetical would be better for your purposes. I'm having it resorted. Started twenty minutes ago, but it's a huge file. It's almost. . . there it is, timing's perfect. Done."

She felt a sudden hesitancy, almost fearful. "Well, I guess we better try the easiest thing first."

"Absolutely," he said, with doubt in his own voice. "Give you 8 to 5 it's not that simple. Nothing is, with your old pal."

"No takers," she answered.

"It's scanning," he said. "It's searching for the surname only. Here we are – Edelheit, Albert; Edelheit, David; Edelheit, Geoffrey; Edelheit, Patricia, Edelheit – *hell.* . . damn. Not that I didn't expect it. Sure of the spelling?"

"Yes," she said promptly. "She spelled it for me. Slowly. We can try other spellings later if it comes to that. I don't think that's the problem. The person could have been a young woman when she was there."

"Married," he grunted. "Name change. Goddamn patriarchy. What do you want to do now?"

"Does it have a separate field for first names? And for the places where people do this field work? You know, references?"

"Yes. Five fields for references."

"Then what I'd like you to do is relate Arbalest in the five fields, one after another, to the first names with the letter J. Harlow said he hadn't had all that many assistants." Call waiting began to beep in the receiver. "There can't be more than sixty or seventy; anyone named J. has got to be that person."

"No problem," he said. "Listen, why don't you take that call? This'll take twenty or thirty minutes. I'll call you back."

She depressed the receiver, picked it up when the phone rang.

"Hiya, neighbor," Walt Greenfield said, in an utterly unnatural accent. "How you gonna find your way to the homestead if you don't have directions?"

"Directions?" Adele asked, puzzled – then remembered. Still one more appointment she had completely forgotten. "Who's the voice?" she asked, changing the subject as rapidly as possible to cover the gaffe. "Buddy Ebsen?"

"Walter Brennan," he corrected. "I –"

"Daddy, that was terrible," a child's voice sounded in the background. "That didn't sound the least little bit like Walter Brennan."

"Critics," he said dismissively, in his natural voice. "Anyway, I looked for you Friday afternoon, but you weren't around. Carolyn tried to find you, too."

"Family business," she said evenly.

"I think the most practical thing is for you to take the train," he went on. "I've got the schedule here." He succinctly recited times and stations as she jotted. Not at all a good day to trust her memory – too many distractions. . . too much else on her mind. "See you at six," he said, and rang off.

She got up from her desk and looked out the window. The thrill of the chase had produced a small adrenaline surge, but now it was fading. She felt sluggish and weary. A great day for a nap, if it were not. . .

The phone rang.

"Bad news," Bill Abercrombie said gruffly. "Forty-three persons report clinical work at Arbalest, not counting Harlow and Coppelman. No one who's first name begins with a J. Only eleven women. By the way, none is more recent than eight years ago." After a moment, "At all possible you were being conned?"

She considered it momentarily. "No," she said firmly. "Naomi was on my side at the place. She wouldn't have made a call like that later to put me on." *Something monumental must have happened that day*, she'd said. "No," she reiterated, "what must have happened is that J. Whoever doesn't want anything to do with Arbalest. Doesn't even want to mention it in their resume."

"Could be," he admitted, "unless it's simply that she's – it has to be a woman – not in psychology anymore. What do you want me to do?" he asked simply. "I'll be here all day."

"Thanks, Bill," she said warmly. "Thanks. Let me think about it for a minute. I'll call you back."

*

What to *do?* She strolled back into the middle of the apartment, arms folded, trying to relax, trying to find some creativity. She knew so much now, it couldn't be. . .

Got it. Not a chance with high probability, but the best, in fact, the only. She paced quickly back into her own bedroom, sat down at her desk, reviewed the Binghamton transcript Bill had sent her, particularly the letter to the Admissions office from Professor Lambeth – yes, she'd remembered it correctly – then phoned Abercrombie. Not five minutes had passed.

"Hello, Adele," he said, picking up the phone without waiting for her to speak. "What do you want to do?"

"I want you to run every J who went to Binghamton as an undergrad, or a graduate student, or who did any assistantship work with a Professor James Lambeth of Binghamton – or uses him as a reference – between 19-- and 19--" (she named two years fifteen years apart) – "And then separate all the Johns, James's, and Jeffries – you know, as many men's names as you can think of. That's what I'd like."

"All right," he said, without saying more; they were now far beyond badinage. "I'll have to design a query. It'll take an hour or two at least, possibly longer. There've got to be thousands of 'J's, thousands of Binghamtons." She could hear his fingers clicking on the keyboard.

"O.K.," he said a minute later, "it's going to take a while. I'll call you when it's finished," and rang off.

She glanced at her desk clock. Only 10:15 – they'd made good time. But all that had left her with a boring morning. Waiting was the only thing to do in the interim; waiting and watching the drizzle. Had anyone ever really bet on raindrops running down a window? Right this second she could understand how.

The newspaper still lay largely unread, she had books to get through; she lacked the intellectual stamina for either. The alarming thought occurred to her again: that for the first time in her life she was approaching the limits of her strength. She put it to one side; she could not allow herself that worry.

The clock ticked. She pulled open the bottom right drawer, pulled out the two newest sketchbooks. She'd promised herself a sketch of Tom for some time, had chosen in fact the moment – the way he looked in front of the Rembrandt Aristotle – but then all at once she was sick of everything, weary of the process, fed up with all of it, surfeited with mystery and self-doubt and Thomas Bryant Newcombe. To hell with him. To bloody hell with all of it.

No. Not him. Absolutely not. Someone or something else. A pleasant thought occurred to her. Of course, long overdue. She opened the sketchbook.

The phone rang. "Bill?" she answered.

"No, not Bill," the caller said. "Only a guy on a bad day looking for some sunshine."

"George!" she said, picking up the phone and lying back on her bed. "I'm so glad you called. I was just thinking about you."

*

"I actually called with an invite. There's been a change in plans. Three of the cable execs got in a day early. We arranged to take 'em to the preview, but the guy from Dallas wants to see the game in the worst way. Don't ask me why. The Giants are minus 9. I rustled up four tickets; I get to go to the game with him and his wife, while Franklin and Carolyn go to the show with the others. I've got one extra ticket. I remembered what you said about work, but I thought I'd give it a shot. Tried you yesterday about the show, but you weren't home. Wanna come to the game? And who the hell is Bill?"

"I was gone. Family business. Bill's Bill Abercrombie, a computer guy running a program for me. A nice guy, but he must weigh 270 pounds and he

could be married or gay for all I know. It's not like that at all. As for the invite –
" she paused, chose her words carefully – "thanks, but no thanks. I'm truly
busy. I'd – I'd – *love* to be with you. At least if we'd gone to the show." She
deliberately lightened the tone: "As it worked out, I can think of a lot better
things to do on a Sunday afternoon than getting my hair wet, watching a lot of
young men ruin their knees and shorten their lives."

"So can I," he growled salaciously.

"*George!*" she said, almost giggling, moving the phone over, crossing
her knees, acting much younger than she was.

"So you're not much of a sports fan?"

"Not at all. It's only contact sports I dislike. I love basketball, and
baseball's enthralling, once you learn it. I have three older brothers, you know;
there were always sports around. I'm kind of a jock myself, if you must know."
Deliberately advancing the process of mutual recognition.

"Really!" he answered. "What sport? Basketball?"

"Nope. Field hockey. I started two years varsity at Syracuse, division I-
A. We made it to the Eastern Regional final my second year. My coach said I
might have made all-conference if I'd stayed with it, but I couldn't. What about
you?"

So it went for the next hour, intentionally opening the book of the past,
exploratory, flirtatious, lying on her back, phone cradled against her cheek like a
teenager, talking about everything, nothing, blood singing. It occurred to Adele
that the only good hours she'd had lately had been the ones with him.
Contemplating future possibilities with him relieved the pressures of the
moment. So did the deliberate revelation of the sorrows of the distant past. He
had to know about those to understand her, and his understanding was
becoming increasingly important to her.

"I'm sorry," George said gently. "I'm sorry I'll never get to meet her.
She must have been something special to produce someone like you." Then,
abruptly changing subjects before it became too serious: "I wish you were free. I
wish I were free. I wanna be with you, not these people."

"It would have been nice," she agreed. "Especially at the show." All at
once the circumstances piled up against her – her grim, dismal Saturday; the
afternoon that awaited her; the call to Carolyn – it would be wonderful to be
anyplace but here, particularly in the company of one George Sorenson.

"What's it like in Zihuataneo?" she blurted suddenly, before she
thought to stop herself.

A long moment went by. George took a deep breath. "Nice. The condo
I've got is on the top floor of twelve. I swear on a clear day you can see China
across the Gulf. I've rigged up a lot of audio and video equipment – wide-screen

TV, home theater, the works. These last few years – when I've been going alone – I've loaded up on all the movies I missed. A satellite dish, if anyone wanted to see anything else. The beach is coral white. Basically, it's a week of catching up, doing nothing."

"It sounds heavenly," she breathed. She stirred on the bed; suddenly she felt very hungry. Odd. So soon after breakfast.

"Daily maid service. I don't know if I'd keep it daily if you came. You thinking about it? What are you thinking?"

"You know I'm thinking about it," she said quietly. "And it gets more likely every time we talk. I'm not trying to tease you, George. I take these things very seriously; I take you very seriously. I don't know why you're being so patient with me," she said suddenly, "probably any unattached woman in this city would go in a minute with you if you asked her."

"I'm not going to take any unattached woman. I'm going to take you, Paloma –"

"Paloma?"

"Just slipped out. My private name for you. Spanish for `dove.' I'll drop it if you don't--"

"No, I like it. A lot."

"Anyway, it's you or no one. In fact," he added, very quietly, "if you decide no, I probably won't go myself. If you do go, I'm not going to take any movies. I'm gonna do a lotta thinking, a lotta planning." His voice took on a wistful tone: "About what I'm gonna do once I'm free of the hustle. All the shit. With Franklin and CFS two months behind and five thousand miles away." He became more decisive: "And I'm gonna spend the week saying a lot of things to you, doing a lot of things. It's been a long time since I've felt like this about anyone. Maybe never."

"George," she breathed, helpless, touched to her core by his simplicity and directness. The little plant, planted in such impromptu fashion, growing stronger, more beautiful, perhaps ready to become the star of the garden. Call waiting sounded on the receiver. Reality knocked at the door. Adele sat up on the bed, frustrated and impatient. She did not want to take the call. She wanted to keep talking with George. The signal beeped again and then again.

"That's Bill," she said at last. "I have to pick that up – and you're going to miss the kick off if you don't hurry. It's been wonderful talking to you." Too formal; she groped for words; she wanted to say something personal, meaningful. "George, I – I – I really would rather be with you. I mean it. Even at a football game. I'll miss you this afternoon. I'm going to be so glad in a week. When this is all over."

"Yeah," he said, obviously touched himself. "Yeah. When it's over.

NATPE. I wish – oh, the hell with it. See you at the show tomorrow – Paloma."

"Right," she said resignedly. "Goodbye," and depressed the receiver.

The phone rang in her hands.

*

"Abercrombie here," he said directly. "I've got it. A hundred and seventy-nine 'J's from Binghamton and Lambeth, spread all across the country. Addresses, phone numbers. Mostly in New York. Mostly women; I did what you asked. What now?"

"Send it," she said promptly, reaching for her briefcase, pulling out the laptop. Her temporary respite, the brief stay in the port safe from the storm – was over. "Let me boot up."

"O.K., I'm ready," she said a moment later. "After a few seconds, the screen blinked and signaled that the e-mail had been received. A list of that size comprised only a few thousand bytes. Adele reconnected the handset.

"You're going to call them all, aren't you?" he asked.

"Yes."

"Need any help?"

"No thanks, Bill," she said. "I'm not going to impose on your day any more than I have to. This, as they say, is woman's work. Go back to the crossword and the game and the Wagner. At least I kept my promise. We're done before kickoff." She realized she was becoming hungrier. An orange! God, she *had* to have an orange!

"Hell, I was only kidding about that," he said. "I'll help you out if you want."

"Thanks again, but I'll take care of it," she answered, politely, but becoming impatient – she had to get some food. "How much do I owe you? The federal run time must have cost something."

"Your money's no good with me," he growled. "Good luck. Tell me all about it later. Goodbye."

She hung up the phone with relief. Finally! Now to start. . . but first she *had* to have something to eat – an orange – the thought had become an obsession – no, not just one, *three* oranges, with juicy pulp, and she wouldn't ignore the rind, either, like most people. When she was nine, she'd helped her mother make an orange cake from scratch for Buck's 24th birthday, scraped the zest on a grater for the icing. She was going to do the same thing today, only add it to milk, a scoop of vanilla ice cream. She could taste it, feel it, smell it, touch it, the memory as vivid as the reality.

She had her coat on in an instant. It was only when her hand was on the doorknob, turning, that she realized exactly what it was she was experiencing. She sagged against the door frame

The little health food nut hadn't liked yesterdays' diet of hot dogs and stale potato chips any better than she had.

*

A half an hour later, she'd finished her oranges and her milkshake. The starting time had come – no more excuses – except that she didn't want to start. She wanted to sleep, or draw, or even watch the football game, anything but this. 179 calls – at an average of two minutes per call, *let's see.* . . 358 minutes. Six hours on the phone. Of course, the odds were – if the answer did indeed lie there - she wouldn't have to make all of them. . . there was probably some formula that predicted the number she'd likely have to make. Jack would probably know it. Tom would know for sure. Except that she didn't want to make even one. Mostly she wanted to nap, on this dreary day, underneath these leaden skies. For a moment, the thought of her bed was well-nigh irresistible.

Then there was the other problem. Sighing, she looked at the clock. 1:05. At 4:00, she was either going to have to get ready to catch the 5:05 to Walt's home or cancel. What pretext? She reviewed alternatives in her mind – decided on a sudden onset of stomach flu if it came to that. Adele shook her head at herself. She was for sure becoming too accomplished a liar. Too accomplished by half. Was there anyone she valued in the City whom she hadn't deceived? She thought. No, no one.

Maybe it wouldn't come to that. She pulled the chair closer to the stand and picked up the phone. Jessica Adams, Middlebury, Connecticut. The phone rang twice before someone answered. *I should have known,* she thought. *It had to be.*

Out loud she said, "Is your mommy home?"

*

Once into the grind it wasn't so bad – boring and monotonous, but ultimately endurable. Not efficient enough, though; only twenty-three calls complete in the first hour, not counting five "no answers." Behind her, the skies were grey and dreary. In front, bodies collided on the noiseless screen, there for distraction alone.

On and on it went. She did a little better the second hour, twenty-eight. It was a more time-consuming chore than she'd expected at first; something had to be said about what she was doing, without saying too much. These people were owed an explanation for even this small disruption of their lives.

At 3:26, she made the sixty-third call, to a phone number in Cleveland, indistinguishable in any discernible way from any of the others.

"Lawrence residence," answered a small child's voice.

"Is Dr. Lawrence available? Can I speak to her?"

"Dr. Lawrence? You must mean Mom."

"O.K.," she said, smiling. "Can I talk to your mom?"

"She's helpin' Dad watch Dallas get its butt kicked," the child responded. "I'll tell her someone's on the phone." She heard footsteps, then the receiver being grasped.

"This is Mrs. Lawrence," came a contralto voice. "You shouldn't ask for me by `Doctor.' My practice is very small. How may I help you?" Very controlled, very precise; there was a prim, white-starched quality about her voice.

"I'm trying to locate a J. Edelheit. I don't think – "

"That was my maiden name," she said slowly. "But why do you ask for me by that name? Why are you calling me? *Who* is this?"

The hairs on the back of Adele's neck stood up. "Did you do an assistantship at a place called Arbalest? In upstate New York?"

The feeling now was palpable; she could feel the chill across the line. "Who *is* this?" repeated the voice, in clipped, enunciated syllables.

"My name is Adele Jansen," she answered. "I'm a lawyer, calling from New York City. Please don't hang up. I'm not trying to pry. I'm trying to find out about something that happened there once. At Arbalest. Were you there?"

A long silence.

"That was sixteen years ago," Joanna Edelheit Lawrence said finally. "An episode I've put firmly behind me. Dr. Lambeth is deceased. No one knows. How did you ever–?"

"I have a list of all the 'J's who went to Binghamton and became psychologists. I was calling them all. You were the sixty-third."

"I see," Joanna Lawrence answered precisely, with a slight edge in her voice, then paused. "How did you get such a list? Isn't it illegal?"

"No," Adele replied, trying to not sound defensive, and succeeding. "It was compiled from public records. What I want to talk to you about," she said, pressing on, "is – "

"Oh, I *know* what it is that you're calling about," Joanna interrupted. "There's only one case – one child – that anyone would go to those lengths over. Only one that anyone would be interested in." She paused; a certain distance entered her voice. "After all this time."

"You're calling about Johnny Markland, aren't you?"

*

Adele sucked in her breath. "Yes."

"I knew it," she answered in the same distant way. "I always knew that someday I'd get a call like this." An entirely different voice than Professor Goodson's, definitely a completely different personality, but the echo from that earlier meeting was eerie, uncanny. Then, in brisk, professional tones, "So tell me. Who are you? What kind of trouble is he in?"

"He's not in any trouble," Adele answered, groping. "He's a writer. Not well-known, but well-respected. He writes his own poetry sometimes and he ghost writes for other people. But –"

"I don't know who you are," Dr. Lawrence broke in, the latent edge in her voice becoming openly hostile, "or what you mean, but that is one of the most completely tasteless jokes it's possible to make. I think it's better to end this right now."

"No, no, no, you *can't*. You *mustn't*," Adele replied, desperately. No time for anything but truth. "I wasn't joking. I was telling the truth, I swear. He's a writer and he writes these marvelous poems about numbers and philosophy and he isn't in any trouble. I'll send you the books if you don't believe me. I'm not calling for any reason that has to do with me being a lawyer. I'm calling because I care about him – very much – and I don't understand him at all. The more I learn, the less I understand. Please tell me what you know. *Please*."

The line was silent for a long moment. "I suppose it's not a question of belief or disbelief," she finally responded, in a far gentler tone. "Perhaps I shouldn't have put it that way. It's a question of commitments. I made several sixteen years ago, to a number of people – Johnny, among others. Or Tom – perhaps you know him by that name. The one to him was by far the most important. It's been a decade and a half. Perhaps it doesn't matter; others may have broken theirs, but I haven't broken mine. Then or now. I'm sorry."

"Please –" she began again, but Joanna Lawrence, nee Edelheit, interrupted.

"I can tell you are a persistent person," she said softly, "Ms. Jansen, but please don't try. I'm unpersuadable on this point. I put all of that firmly behind me years ago. I do not intend to return to it now. Don't embarrass us both," and Adele knew that avenue was useless.

"Can't you tell me anything?" she begged. "Can't you at least tell me who will talk to me?"

A sigh came over the line, then, after a moment, a low laugh. "You *are* persistent. I suppose I never made any promises about that. There was a county social worker named Dora Johnson, who--"

"Dora Johnson died some time ago."

"Oh. I'm sorry. Then try a woman named Gertha – Gertha Daniels. Actually, she's probably better to talk to than me in any case. She was there from the beginning. I only came in at the end." Adele repeated the name, checked the spelling. Unfortunately – the usual – Joanna Lawrence had no idea where Gertha Daniels was and had long since forgotten which county she had worked for.

"Thank you," Adele said gratefully when she'd finished. "I appreciate that you're honor bound. I'm thankful for what you have said." She hesitated. "Would you like to know what sort of person Tom – that is what he calls himself – is? I'll fill you in if you like."

"No," she answered promptly. "Absolutely not. I said I put it behind me. I didn't entirely succeed. I thought too much about that boy for too many years. No, thank you. I would be grateful if you'd send me his writing, though. I am curious about that. Very curious."

"Done," said Adele. An awkward silence filled the receiver.

"Ms. Jansen" – the voice hesitated – "please believe me about one thing. It's not my place to give you advice. . . but. . . there's no point in resurrecting any of this. What's been buried is best left buried. This has nothing to do with my own role. It is my professional opinion. Stirring it up won't change anything. It won't make any difference at all. Least of all to Johnny."

"He's become a very likable man, Dr. Lawrence," Adele answered, suddenly defensive; it occurred to her that, at a different time, in a different context, she would not particularly have cared for Joanna Lawrence nee Edelheit. "He's really very sweet."

"Oh, he was always lovable," she answered – and then it happened. She swallowed hard; there was a noticeable quaver, a break; suddenly the precise, scientific voice had lost its focus, its bearing. *The wind swirls around his heels*, thought Adele, remembering Goodson again. *Hurricanes. No one unbloodied.* And not Joanna Lawrence either, professional or not. "That was a part of the problem," Joanna continued, herself again. "I'd suppose – you'd know better – that a lot of people have come to care about him – and they all end up hurt in some way, don't they?" Adele was silent. "Being lovable doesn't make him any less a human time bomb, Ms. Jansen. I'm sorry" – her tone softened further – "I'm being so mysterious. It must be frustrating. But that boy was beyond love and beyond hope sixteen years ago. It's not possible that that much has changed."

"Do you think he's a sociopath?" Adele prompted quickly.

"I don't know what word –" she stopped abruptly. "You truly are persistent," Joanna Lawrence continued firmly. "I've already talked too much. That has to be all. Now I have to get back to my family. Good luck, Ms. Jansen. I hope you paid attention to what I said. Goodbye."

The line went dead. There was no point in attempting to renew the connection.

*

The clock read 3:50. She hung up the phone. She was satisfied in one sense that she'd gone a step further, but she was more bewildered and mystified than ever. She phoned Bill's office number, left a message – *I found J. Edelheit, Joanna Edelheit Lawrence. Please call me at the office at your earliest convenience.* It wouldn't be right to bother him at home. Nothing could realistically be done before morning. Besides, she'd bothered him enough for one day.

She changed, showered, made the train easily an hour later. Walt Greenfield's family proved to be as charming as he was. As she had hoped, Walt had only the mildest parental problems with his daughters. She became an instant comrade of the oldest one, Jennifer. Adele was the glamorous career woman of independent means, an object of extreme curiosity. She was able to show Jennifer some word-processing tricks on the laptop, enough to get her interested, maybe on the way. The only moment of friction occurred at dinner: *More salad, Adele? My goodness, Jennifer, I hope you learn to eat your vegetables the way Adele does. And it is so refreshing to meet someone from the firm who doesn't guzzle wine*, looking pointedly at her husband.

She left her problems back in the City, put on a good show. Smiling, charming, witty within decorous limits, pregnant out of wedlock, Adele Elizabeth Jansen did her level best to provide a suitable role model for Walter Greenfield's oldest daughter, Jennifer.

NATPE

*T*his, Adele thought, *is really something.* NATPE, the National Association of Television Programming Executives, its national convention. She'd heard and read about the great technology trade shows, CES and COMDEX, the glamor, the excitement, the hype, the spectacular display. But that was the work of ad men and publicity agents. What was unfolding around her this day was the work of pros. Money had been spent here, in great globs and clusters, and every penny showed.

A festival of sound, color, and light, extending for block after block, the world in miniature. The convention was staged in the same facility that had housed the Software Arts Expo only a few weeks before. But no sawdust was on the floor today. Now the hall was opened up to its full size, about twenty times the size it had been that night. The major production houses had arrived in force. One had erected a circus tent, complete with multi-coloured pennants at the pole tops that fluttered in a fan driven breeze. At another pavilion, a scaled-down aerodrome had been built, above which a small Fokker biplane circled a slowly moving model dirigible. She'd been curious enough to poke her head in there the first time she toured the floor, learned the exhibitor was promoting a miniseries remake of *Wings.* If even a fraction of the effects she saw on their large monitors – dogfights, plane crashes, the dirigible attack, superb computer graphics – translated to the small screen, they were going to enjoy a spectacular success.

Other booths attracted. But it was time to go to the rendezvous point. There the Project engulfed her. On and on the players came, in drips and drabs, groups of twos and threes, none larger than six. It was almost a receiving line; it reminded her of one of those eighteenth century English country estate parties that went on for days, with the guests feasting and dancing until they all collapsed with exhaustion. Adele stood among the other lawyers, the accountants, the counselors, mid- and high-level executives, the youngest and smallest by a large margin. *This is Adele Jansen. Hello, my name is Adele Jansen.* She still had no clear idea of her function. It was evident from the looks on some of the faces that they didn't either – but protocol demanded the introductions and Carolyn complied. Franklin Fischer greeted each new arrival, some with sturdy handshakes and a quick word, others with long, private conversations – men in overcoats, men with briefcases, all kinds, all types, from all parts of the country, nearly all men. Momentum gathered slowly, like driblets of water forming rivulets on a mountain overlooking the sea. The intensity accumulated all morning long. The dance had barely begun and already the tempo was incredibly rapid, the beat monstrously strong.

Finally, an intermission was called. At once she circled back to the Furston booth. Here, too, the excitement was palpable, the anticipation, the bustle, as executives, producers, advertising people, the merely curious, began to flood the hall. Adrenaline had carried her through the morning, even as the weariness, the anxiety, gnawed away. Her first NATPE; the Project – it all made a fabulous impression.

Even on someone whose thoughts were a million miles away.

*

She'd got to the office at 8:15 that morning to meet the early appointment she'd made to clear herself for the Arbalest trip. The AI Squared agenda was on her desk – six routine items, no big deal. By nine o'clock she was on the phone with Bill Abercrombie.

"Gertha Daniels, huh?" he grunted. "A social worker, but you don't know which county. That shouldn't be too hard. I'll get on it. I've already started a search for the birth certificate of Jonathan Markland. That's a snap. I should have something for you by midmorning."

"I'm going to be at the NATPE convention for most of the day, Bill," she answered. "I don't trust the battery on my cell. I'll call you with a number when I get there."

Then up to the thirty-second floor for a final pep talk from Carolyn to the troops – a quick glare from Carolyn, but otherwise nothing about Sunday – after which everyone departed for midtown and the convention site. She found the Furston booth easily enough – not nearly as opulent as many, but quietly tasteful – ascertained the phone bank numbers, called Abercrombie.

Now there was nothing to do but wait – that and keep her mind on the job, the reason she was here. Which was, after all, what she was being paid for.

*

"So you're the famous Adele Jansen," a smiling middle-aged man greeted her.

"Famous?" Adele repeated, smiling in turn.

"Jenet has talked about you from time to time," he replied, extending his hand. "I'm Bill Andrews. I'm the veep for television production for the Press. Welcome to our little booth. Make yourself at home, enjoy our hospitality. All I ask is that you keep out of harm's way when we're making a presentation. We are trying to sell some things, you know. Make a little boodle."

"I think I can manage," she said. "Scarcity is my middle name. I may get a phone call or two, but nothing that should tie you up. And if there's anything I can do for you –"

"Handshake deals happen here, usually. The paperwork comes later. I'll call you if anything comes up – or anyone wants to meet a pretty lawyer." He gestured. "Would you like to see what we're showing?"

"Sure."

He moved toward the door to what was obviously a screening room. "This is the first year Jenet hasn't gotten involved in production. We view that as a great opportunity. Don't get me wrong; my staff and I all love the old girl. But we do want to prove we can do it without her." Adele took a seat; Bill Andrews showed her capsule presentations of the twenty or so shows the Press had developed or was preparing to syndicate. She liked him, she was rooting for him – but the probable result, as far as she could see, was that he was going to prove the exact opposite of what he wanted.

"Very impressive," she said discreetly when it was over.

"I think we'll be O.K.," he said. "I –"

Someone tapped her on the shoulder. "Telephone," he said.

Don't get excited, moron. It could be anybody, anything – the office had the number, as well as Bill Abercrombie. Still, her heart was pounding as she moved to the phone bank. Six phones had been installed in the booth, each with a small kiosk of its own. Station managers who had to report back to a CEO or CFO expected privacy when they did so. Adele was grateful for a different reason.

"His full name is – or was – Jonathan David Markland," Abercrombie began immediately. "Born in Ithaca, New York. He's the only child of Anthony Sullivan Markland and Rachel Weinstein Markland." He grunted. "Half-Irish, half-Jewish. Perfect writer's pedigree. Your first source was a little off on his age. He only turned twenty-eight last months. His –"

"Are you sure this is the right Jonathan Markland?"

"Yes. I was getting to why. As soon as I found his birth certificate, I checked for theirs. I got those, too, that's why I'm so sure of their descent." He paused. "The birth certificates were linked to death certificates. They both died on the same day. Plane crash. When Johnny –"

"Call him Tom. I think of him as Tom."

"–Tom was twenty-one months old. I played a hunch. The guy is sufficiently unusual, the poetry and all; I figured maybe his folks were special, too. I checked the Times obits for the ten days or so after the date of death. We finally got some luck on this thing. They rated a half-column."

He went on: "His dad was going to Europe on a Fulbright. A mathematician – he evidently already had a reputation as a prodigy. Two doctoral degrees and he wasn't twenty-seven. Someone who knew him is quoted as saying the world had lost the next von Neumann. There's less about Rachel, but it says she was a graduate student of linguistics." He grunted. "Pattern's almost unreal. Says she'd done some translations and was working on a novel. They were over scouting housing – that's probably why Jona -Tom, wasn't with them. Plane crashed in Frankfurt, a commuter run between Frankfurt and Vienna." He paused. "These people have to be his parents."

She felt a lump in her throat, had to remind herself that all this happened a long time ago, that it was over. Everyone dies. "How did he get to Arbalest?"

"I don't know. From the sense of the obit, Tony Markland was an orphan when he died, only child, a late-born of another whiz kid. It does mention maternal grandparents, but both remarried, one living in California, the other in Idaho." He grunted again. "Looks like a pretty bitter divorce. That kind of geographical spread. The only local surviving relative is Rachel's sister, a Mrs. Mary Klein of -----, New York. It's likely she would have become his guardian. I've got contacts there. I'm checking on her whereabouts. I'm having them check the court dockets there and in Ithaca. I also asked them to check with the DSS in those places for Gertha Daniels. It's a good bet that one of those two counties is the one she worked in." He paused. "I told `em I wanted it ASAP. I knew you'd want me to."

"Right." Her eyes misted. "Thanks, Bill. Thank you. What would I do without you?"

"Something," he snorted. "I'm sure of that. I'll get back to you later in the day if I hear anything."

*

After the Project introductions, she wandered free down the aisles. Poor little Tom – how could a child that age possibly understand where his parents had gone, why they hadn't returned? She passed the Red Light district, so named because producers of porn and quasi-porn were displaying their wares there. Any number of well-endowed women in slinky dresses were around the booths, some signing autographs, attractive in a sleazy sort of way. What could he possibly have done to get himself sent to Arbalest? A writer's pedigree. Not a juvenile delinquent's.

She turned up an aisle. So tired, even with all the stimulation. At least it wouldn't be long now. All at once, the cold track had become red hot. But not much relief in that – that damned sense of urgency had increased exponentially with the heat. The faster events moved, the more it became necessary to outrun them.

"–not a bad promotional idea," she heard someone say at one of the smaller displays. "But do we lose the rights if we give the cartridge away free?" She moved closer.

"I don't know," another voice answered. "But I do know we're not going to get any players if they don't have the program." The booth was one of the smaller ones; this had to be some novel interactive game. She'd read about them.

"I know something about that," she twittered brightly. "I can help you." The two men turned.

"Don't interrupt," one said curtly, clearly the first speaker from the sound of his voice. "This is important."

"I had to," she smiled, ignoring his tone. "I'm an intellectual property lawyer with Hapgood, Thurlow. If you're talking about distributing software, you're talking about something I specialize in."

The second man grinned. "Better listen to her, Mr. Jackson. You're not getting any interest as it is." He turned and moved off.

The first man stared after him, and then turned to Adele. "Well, thanks. Thanks a lot. Thanks for fucking that sale up."

Adele moved past him, into the deserted booth. She stood in front of the console, seized the controls, played for thirty seconds or so – very, very interesting. The older man watched, stupefied. Then she looked back and up.

"I didn't fuck it up and you know it. He wasn't biting. If I have this right, the player at home needs a program to play with the player on TV. Only the players at home won't buy the program if it's not on TV, and the station managers won't put it on TV if there aren't any players at home. So no one's buying, which is a shame, because it's a good game, and people should get a chance to play it." She turned and faced him. "Have I got it right?" she said lightly.

He looked hard at her, then down at the card. "Mostly," he said, then looked up. "Add in an egomaniac programmer, a miser producer, and you've got it all." He looked hard again. "Who are you?"

"Adele Jansen," she said, extending her hand. He took it gingerly. "And I am who I say I am. There are all kinds of ways you can send out the package without throwing away all your rights. I'm not an engineer – I can't write the code myself – but I can point you in the right direction."

"And earn a fat fee for it, even if it's the wrong direction," he said, suspicious again. "I don't like lawyers."

Oaf, she thought. Aloud: "That's O.K., except that you happen to need one right now. I can do what I say I can. Did you read about the big Parallax case?" He nodded. "I did the work that broke it open."

He stared. "You??"

She nodded in turn. "Me. I'll tell you what; I'll prove it to you. I'll bring the brief in that did the job and go over it with you. If you believe me – and you will – all I ask in return is the chance to sit down with you and help with this problem." She held up her right hand. "Promise – there'll be no bill or fees until we've worked out a fee arrangement you're happy with. You really have a good game. People should get a chance to play it." Time to close. "Have we got a deal?"

He looked down at the card, then at her again, then shrugged. "All right. Like the man said, we're not getting any interest as it is."

"Good," she said, writing down the number of the booth. "I'll see you tomorrow or Thursday. Someone else from my firm may come with me, but no bill, like I promised." She stepped out of the booth. "Good luck until then."

An idea for an exit line occurred to her and she turned. "By the way, mister," she said, turning it on, with her most contrite schoolgirl look, "I'm truly sorry for fucking up your sale."

That did it. The pickleface actually cracked a smile. "Get lost," he said, shaking his head and grinning. "There oughta be a law against people like you. I'll see you later."

Doing the shtick had helped, relieved her anxiety, but only for a moment. As she started back up the aisle, her thoughts were already shifting towards Tom. Willis Rutter was coming in the opposite direction, moved towards her when he caught sight of her.

"Carolyn sent me to get you," he said tonelessly. "You're late for the big lunch with the big shots. On the Project."

Oh, shit. She'd forgotten. "Thanks," she said. "Willis, I wanted to tell you how sor –" but it was useless, he'd already turned his back. She found her way back to the Furston booth. She could see the remnants of the Project group disappearing through a farther exit. Carolyn was waiting there for her, with two men who were unfamiliar. Also with George.

Oops. She stepped behind a display, reached behind her neck, undid a clasp, took off the necklace, and dropped it into her purse. Then she proceeded up the aisle.

"Hi," Carolyn said cheerily. Introductions all around, hands shaken – George, smiling, took the opportunity to give her hand a small, private squeeze.

Her pulse picked up. The two men turned out to be the top executives of cable systems in Birmingham and the counties south of Dallas. "Sorry about the Cowboys," Adele said to the latter.

"Yeah," he answered. "You a fan?"

"No, she isn't," George answered, moving to her side, a bit proprietary. "An unfan, I think. But she's the type who keeps up with everything." He smiled at her again; she could not stop herself from beaming back at him; she hoped it was not all too obvious. Evidently not – the other three didn't seem to notice.

"Well, we're finally all here," Carolyn said brightly. "I could give you a lot of guesses about what Adele's specialty is, but since I doubt you'd ever get it, I'll tell you. Adele's our high-tech expert."

The two men turned and stared at her. "Really!" said the one from Birmingham.

"Um-hum. Second year associate, looks like a choir girl, but she's for real. One of our up-and-coming stars," Carolyn laughed, not meaning a word of it, building her up for the firm's sake.

"Do you know anything about megahertz?" Al from Birmingham asked.

"Sure," Adele answered, in character. "Of course, I've got a lot to learn about everything else, but the rest of our intellectual property department is so strong I can draw from them."

"My God," said the man from Dallas, "they get younger all the time." The three men moved off towards the exit. Carolyn lingered a few paces behind, signaled Adele to linger, too.

"Where were you?" she hissed. "I called. We waited ten minutes for you. More family business?"

Adele pulled out the card. "I had some free time. I was over at booth 171. There's a real interesting interactive game there. I overheard the guy talking about some problems I know we can help him solve. I've got an appointment to show him how later in the week. I didn't go that far."

Carolyn studied the card. "O.K.," she finally said, then looked up and sighed with exasperation. "O.K., I understand. It still won't do." She looked at Willis Rutter, standing behind Adele. "Willis, go back to the office. Talk to my secretary. Arrange for a pager for Adele." Willis glowered, then left. It occurred to Adele that Carolyn was already frazzled, nearly at rope's end, and it was barely past noon on Monday.

"Adele," Carolyn said softly, as foot traffic streamed by, "this is twice. It shouldn't have happened once. I have a ton of things to do this week. I feel like a sheepdog herding a pack of squirrels. Everyone goes in every direction. I can't police you, too. You are a member of the core team. This is your A, number-one priority. . . your only priority. Please keep that in mind." She paused. "I am not going to warn you again."

"I understand," Adele said wearily. Priorities. Abercrombie.

"Does the game have any chance?" asked Carolyn, glancing at the card, as they began to walk lowly up the aisle.

"I think so," Adele said guardedly. "I liked what I saw. I thought it would be useful to have someone else come over and play it. I may be too close."

Carolyn nodded. "Rutter will do fine for that. A perfect middlebrow review." She looked up. "They're at the door. We'd better catch up."

*

Lunch was at a restaurant three short blocks from the convention center the street, world famous, reserved in its entirety for the entire afternoon. Adele sat there smiling, dazed, close to exhaustion. Everything around her seemed to be unfolding in slow motion, as if in a dream. She had felt this way before occasionally, on days when she was extremely tired, as if she was looking up at the rest of the world from three feet underwater, as if normal reality went forward behind a pane of glass. Why hadn't Abercrombie called? Something inside her was begrudging now the passing of minutes, even the slippage of seconds. She realized she was dreading Bill's call as well as anticipating it.

A behavioral psychologist would have been fascinated by the way like found like in these gatherings. Through the welter of regional accents, styles of dress, personal character, somehow the CEOs had identified themselves. So too had the CFOs, the lower executives, the counselors, and the rest. Already a rough pecking order had been established. Everyone took their seats. George had seated himself at a different table, was engaged with several different individuals, probably the hardest cases. She moved by, trying not to distract him, but he had different plans. He deliberately broke off the dialog, waved and smiled. She could not help beaming back again. *Good luck.* She looked around for a place of her own.

The salad was delicious. The menu listed four entrees, each more interesting than the last. A bottle each of burgundy and chardonnay had been placed in the center of each table. But this was the type of lunch where people watched what others drank rather than drank themselves. Only the boldest or most addicted had anything. Adele found herself seated beside a man in his early thirties from the Southwest, an assistant manager. He had on cowboy boots and a string tie clasped with the letters OU in brass. His voice had a distinct twang. He seemed relieved that he was placed beside an innocuous girl, rather than any of the heavies in the room. She was relieved that nothing more would be required of her than in-one-ear, out-the-other listening.

At first, he brimmed with confidence. Big, exciting things were happening. Bit by bit, the picture changed. He'd obtained his job because of his reputation as a football player; he'd evidently been quite a linebacker at Oklahoma. But it was clear, even listening with one ear, that he perceived himself as underqualified. The changes the Project would bring terrified him.

"Don't you own any equity?" she asked.

"Nope." He grimaced. "My own blamed fault, too. They offered me some, but I thought it was a pissant deal. I didn't figure there'd be some gol' darn sci-fi software'd double or triple our capacity. And I didn't figure some dang fool Easterner" – he grinned – "would offer us four times what the system's worth. Nope," he shook his head, "all I got's my job."

Then, suddenly (it was, of course, inevitable that she would sit next to the one man in the room who...) his wallet was out, pictures of a pretty former cheerleader and three smiling school boys. ("Billy, the oldest's, gonna be a player. A helluva player.") She realized that he was not showing her the pictures to show them, but as a kind of prayer. *Who'd hurt kids like this? They might come after me, but they wouldn't hurt my kids. Would they?* She knew then she was listening to a very frightened man. He, too, was aware of engines operating in his life, but not the magic, invisible type. His were the very real, Shakespearean kind, engines of war, artillery, and thunder roaring just over the horizon. He and his type were cannon fodder to a deal like this, and he knew it. He had not the slightest notion he was speaking to one of the cannoneers.

Don't want a stampede on the way to the slaughterhouse, Carolyn had said. *Pack of squirrels.* The metaphors suddenly bothered her. *A business guy has to take care of himself*, George told her on the way to the dinner. She thought of the woman at Jake Rothenberg's old firm who was going to be terminated the moment the contractual obligation was fulfilled. There would be a human cost to this manipulation of capital. She looked around the room. The ambiance of fear pervaded it, too, along with excitement, greed, and a subtle, growing hysteria. Did Franklin Fischer sense that undercurrent, feed upon it? Did George? Was he counting on it? No matter where she went, no matter what she did, the screws got tighter every second. Why hadn't Abercrombie called?

"You know," Adele said gently, "you can have the arrangements reviewed by a lawyer of your own. That's completely appropriate in a deal of this type." Sensible, conventional advice to which no one could object. As far as she could go – her duty lay on the other side. Besides, the wheels were not going to slow down for either her or him.

"Well, thank you, ma'am," he smiled benignly, condescendingly, "I'll think about that," and she realized he was going to give her advice the same short shrift he would advice from any other young, diminutive woman. It was all too familiar to be any longer a cause for resentment. Neither that nor her sense that he'd never given two seconds' thought to the qualified person whose place he'd usurped unfairly prevented her from momentarily aching for him.

A silver spoon tapped a crystal goblet. Franklin Fischer rose to speak. This time he was short and to the point. All the various comments from all the lawyers had been read and assimilated. They were all supposed to be in by noon, but you can't hurry lawyers, we all know that. (Much laughter.) A revised, penultimate draft will be faxed ASAP, fair copies hand delivered before nine o'clock that night. Final, *final* comments, please, as soon as possible. (No laughter.) Final conference is set for 9:30 a.m., Wednesday, at the offices of Hapgood, Thurlow, large conference room, thirty-second floor. We'll be available for meetings afterward. I'm sure you all understand. (Mild applause.)

Then, with a flourish, he began introducing the executive team he had retained to commence operations with the new communication giant. Several names were well known, even to Adele. Low murmurs – then scattered applause – then heavy. She looked around; she sensed a credibility, a sense of belief, dawning even among the unbelievers. The Project, once a germ smaller than even a gleam in anyone's eye, was taking on flesh and blood, becoming a reality. Everyone there could see it – which was, of course, the whole point of this introductory luncheon.

Which was now over. The group was dispersing. The ex-linebacker thanked her politely for her company, grateful that he hadn't had to deal with anyone really important. Willis Rutter intruded between Carolyn and others. Irritated, she gestured towards Adele.

"Here's the pager," she said to Adele; then brightened and gestured at someone. Guests whirled by. "Willis," she said softly, "there was no reason to disturb me. Why didn't you take this straight to Adele?"

"But you said –" he began to smirk.

"What I'm saying now is that your six-weeks notice is down to five. Last day is now December 27th instead of January 4th." Willis Rutter stopped smirking. "If you want to be fired before Christmas, just keep trying. Now go find Anderson and stay with him until you're needed." Willis slunk away without another word or look.

"Carolyn," asked a middle-aged man from one side, "did you say eight o'clock?"

"Right," beamed Carolyn. "I drew a little map on the invite. I'll see you then."

"Carolyn," asked Adele, startled, because there'd been nothing like that on the schedule, "are you throwing some sort of reception? Am I supposed –"

"No, no, no, Rebecca," Carolyn snorted, and suddenly she looked a hundred years old. "It isn't on your agenda. It isn't your kind of party. You wouldn't be any use at all. Would she, George?", as she looked over Adele's shoulder. Adele wheeled and there he was, standing behind her.

"No need to talk like that," George growled softly.

"Oh, don't worry, George," Carolyn responded – it was obvious now she had enjoyed some wine – "I'm not going to spoil Adele's illusions. Or endanger your protégé's precious virtue in any other way. I'll leave that to you. For the ones who want bodies, I'll find much better ones than that." Adele flushed and stiffened.

"Cut it out," George answered.

"*You* cut it out, George. This isn't your show and you damn well know it. Get back in harness. We all have work to do. Adele, you've got a pager now. You've got no excuse. If you're paged, answer it." She checked her watch. "I've got to meet Franklin. I'll see you later." With that she swept away.

He took her elbow – hard, much too hard. "George, you're hurting me," she said. "Sorry," he answered, and softened his grip. Now they were through the door and alone in the corridor. What she could not tell him was how upsetting it had been to witness Carolyn deal with him so casually, to watch him helpless with rage, impuissant. He put his hands on her waist, started to pull her to him, but stopped, feeling the tension in her body. Too many questions had to be asked, answered. She forced herself out of her weariness.

"George," she said, "what's going on?"

"Nothing," he answered. "Believe me. Nothing. Everyone gettin' tense over a deal."

Now she allowed his arms around her. "George, believe me, I'm no virgin. I may look like a schoolgirl, but I have a past. I've never seen Carolyn behave like that. I know this is a big, important deal. I want to be a part of it – but I've thought from the start there was a lot you weren't telling me. How much of yourselves have all of you put into this? How important is it? Don't keep any secrets from me, George. Not now. You mustn't. Don't."

His hands remained where they were, trembling; he was seething, still embarrassed. "You have to trust me about this, Paloma. It has to do with plans that are years old, with me getting out of all this – with no one treating you or me like that," he added suddenly; he had sensed her fear, sensed the cause – "about you not getting hurt by any of it."

Chemistry began to take over; she felt herself weakening in spite of herself. "George –"

"Trust me, Paloma," he said again, urgently. "Believe me about this. You know how important you are to me. This is going to be the longest damn week. But then it'll all be over. I'll tell you everything then, I promise. When we go to dinner next week." He moved her closer; this time she did not resist. "Adele," he whispered, "you're a miracle to me. You're my goddam second chance. I –"

The door to the restaurant opened. The last guests flooded out; one of them shouted to him. She felt his frustration, felt her own; too bad, she knew what he had been about to say, music on her ears; for his part, he'd missed out on what would have been one of the sloppiest, wettest kisses of her whole career, all systems go.

She released herself. "I'd better go. I still work for Carolyn."

He glowered. "Don't worry about her."

*

She crossed the street to the convention hall, mind whirling underneath the drizzle. She felt the vertigo again. Everything was spinning rapidly, twisting out of control. Doubt, real fear – the rock, the anchor of her life, of her dreams for herself, was the solidity of her position at the firm. Now that, too, was shifting, twisting, moving out from under her. Could she ignore what had happened after lunch? Carolyn's crude sexual snipe? Rationalize it as nerves, wine, a reaction to the pressure? No. It was completely beyond the pale, intolerable. As a matter of principle, she had to do something, sooner or later. She was going to have to confront Carolyn, her mentor, her sponsor. Another piece of her life was slipping crazily out of joint, unmoored, floating away.

She moved down the corridor. The dance of incident had become frenzied – masked, sinister, whirling figures, features indistinguishable – too fast, much too fast. Confront Carolyn? Yes, but not this week, not with George and the Project and AI Squared and Tom and Bobby Lawton, and November 20th waiting like a knife at the end. Do it later rather than sooner – when the music was over, when the dance was done.

Faces were glum at the all-but-deserted Furston booth. She felt a twinge of sympathy. She was not the only one with problems. "Any messages for me?" she asked. Her thoughts began to move away from Carolyn, away from George, away from NATPE.

"No," the attendant said glumly. "Not much action of any kind."

"I'll be over at one of the production booths if anyone asks for me," Adele said softly. She couldn't think of anything consoling to say. She refastened the angel and left.

She threw herself into the balance of the afternoon – a good distraction, if nothing else. It started well and got better. She strolled up to the first interesting booth, smiled her shy smile, and asked if she could see the show.

The man smiled back at the young, cute curiosity seeker. In five minutes, he realized she was no ordinary curiosity seeker; in twenty, he was asking her pointed questions as to how fundamental game concepts could be protected when transported to different media. She answered as best she could, mentioned that some of the lawyers with whom she practiced knew a lot more – left with an appointment for a fixed time the next day.

Some places she played; at others, she simply listened, to interesting, overlong narrations about the origins of the program, the production difficulties, or whatnot. One more experienced than the others asked her a hugely technical question about graduated residuals scaled down over time – did she know the answer? No, she didn't, but she knew someone who did, one of her nicest partners, could they meet there tomorrow? They could indeed. All the while, at the back of her mind, she wondered if Abercrombie had learned anything, why he hadn't called.

By 4:30, she'd set up six client interviews, more than enough to fill her Tuesday morning, to placate Carolyn. It was time to go back to the booth.

She started back by a different route, was surprised to see George and Franklin standing with a group of Project executives. "I understand your point," one of the executives was saying. "But are you sure? They haven't licensed anyone yet."

"I'm sure," Franklin answered confidently. "I've bet the deal on it. I've bet my fortune on it. My estimates are correct."

The others nodded. She looked more closely at the exhibit, only one of several in the display, and then realized with a shock that this was it. The exhibitor was EBS. The banner above the booth read, in bold, multicolored letters:

VINUX
(Exclusive Property of EBS)
See it to believe it!!

So this was it; this was the "gol darn" sci-fi product, the technological linchpin of the whole deal. But she was more, not less, baffled. All along she had assumed that VINUX was something that Fischer Communications Company was going to have exclusively. But if it was an EBS product, it was going to be available to everybody. The Sherman and Clayton Antitrust Acts required that, as well as the common sense of EBS company policy. How could the Project pivot around its unique characteristics?

Franklin Fischer was still talking to the group when she exited. George caught sight of her, flashed a quick, silent smile; she felt a warmth that was by now familiar. Her thoughts fell into chaos again. Increasing warmth; increasing doubt; all part of the pattern. *Nothing happens by chance.* It was too late now to do anything but trust. How long had it been? Only a week since he picked her up for a dinner in a white stretch limousine. A middle-aged, twice divorced Bronx hustler turned financier, capturing the heart of an artist's daughter from the sticks? Can such things be? But it seemed more likely with every passing second. She fingered the necklace. History coiled around her like the serpents around Laocoön. Once she'd freed herself, she was going to find out for sure. So for now she'd better trust.

She smiled at him, made a tiny wave, moved off. She didn't want him close enough to see the angel. Hanging over everything, as always, the Shadow. The great wings – did he soar high overhead, watching all this? How small, how utterly insignificant all of these mad pirouettes must seem from the third floor of the Metropolitan Museum.

*

She had to pretend the atmosphere around the Furston booth wasn't as glum as it was. "How's it going?" she asked cheerfully, as if she didn't know.

Bill Andrews looked away from the meeting, managed a weak smile. "Oh, we'll do better tomorrow. You have a message. Someone named Abercrombie."

She nodded, turned, managed to control her pace as she moved to the booth. The number was unfamiliar.

"Hello," came his voice from what was obviously a cellular phone.

"This is Adele," she said.

"Right," he said. "Good news and bad. We couldn't locate Mary Klein. She and her husband moved away years ago. There's a docket – *Guardianship of Markland* – in –" he named the upstate county where Mary Klein had lived. "But it's empty. It was sealed and purged fifteen years ago. By order of the court."

"What date?" she asked quietly.

He named a day about two months after the day Tom had left Arbalest with Dora Johnson and Joanna Edelheit. Two months – in an age of crowded dockets, congested courts, about as fast as it could have possibly been done.

"I'd hardly call that good news, Bill," she said quietly. "That only leaves the social worker."

"But that's it. The good news is that I found Gertha Daniels. It's what I expected – she was a social worker in that county back then. For once, I got a straight trail. She works in Albany now, at a private children's shelter." He paused. "Not for too much longer," he said quietly. "They don't like her too much there. She's a big alkie. 6 DUIs in the last ten years. I've got her work and home number." He hesitated again. "I didn't call her. I figured you'd –"

"Yes. You're right," she said. "Thanks. Give me the numbers and the work and home address."

Her stomach had sunk to her shoes. She already knew what she had to do. Priorities. She had decided on hers yesterday. Great. Just great.

She left the booth and walked to the point where Carolyn had told them to rendezvous. The entire intellectual property team was gathered around Carolyn. She was still on the warpath, barely controlled: "It's good to hear of so many business cards passed out, but, frankly, people, I was hoping for a bit more. I was expecting a bit more." She noticed Adele approach. "How did you do?" she asked.

"Seven appointments," she said dully. "Six scheduled for tomorrow morning. The one I told you about at lunch for later in the week." She went over her notes. Willis Rutter was scowling from the depths of his soul. The other associates were writhing. Even the junior partners looked uncomfortable. Didn't any of them see how low her own mood was?

"Good," said Carolyn, turning around. "That proves it can be done. And she had to cope with the Project as well. Adele, why don't you explain how to everyone else?" She did: *get them talking about what they're doing and sooner or later they'll tell you something you can do.* She hated the role she was forced to play. The conscripted audience hated her playing it. All of her normal cheerfulness was gone. All of the sparkle had vanished. She dreaded to the marrow of her bones what the next morning would bring. No one noticed.

The meeting broke up. Some left for the office. Carolyn went to find Franklin Fischer. Adele circled back towards the EBS booth, hoping she could find someone to draw out for a crash course on VINUX. Tonight was the only time she had available for that.

Because the morning was not going to be available. The die was already cast. She had made up her mind. The urgent wind she had felt from the outset was now at gale force. She was going to go with the dictates of her inner sense. She was not going to lose any more time. Not one more minute. Not one more second.

And particularly not one more day.

✳ ✳ ✳

Joseph Wurtenbaugh

CUSTODIAN OF RECORDS

There's going to be hell to pay for this, Adele thought, as she pulled to the side of the road. She exited and walked towards the phone booth. It was 8:30 a.m., time for a phone call. She'd been driving for nearly two hours. Albany was still two hours away.

"This is Adele Jansen," she said, when Carolyn's secretary was finally on the line. "I'm sick. I won't be in today. Or at the show."

"Sick?!?" the secretary responded. "You can't be sick, Adele! You know what Carolyn told everyone. You –"

"I'm sick," she repeated firmly. "I can't work today."

"You don't sound sick," the woman answered.

"Well, I am. I won't be in today."

"Then you be the one to tell her. Good lord, do you know what she'd going to say when –"

"Goodbye," Adele said, and put the receiver firmly down on the hook. She knew all too well what Carolyn was going to say. A preview wasn't necessary.

*

She arrived in Albany two and a half hours later. According to the street map she'd picked up at the car rental, the children's home lay on the fringes of the Arbor Hill area, slightly to the north of the Hudson River. She crossed one of the bridges, turned, parked the car across the street, and sat there for a moment, studying the building.

It stood on the corner of two residential streets. The house was undoubtedly a converted residence or boarding house, perhaps even a small hotel once. The structure was ancient, but fresh paint was evident, predominantly white, but multi-hued around the entrance. The grounds were neat and trim. The overall affect was open and cheerful. A white sign, with the name of the Home in rainbow letters, had been hung with chains from the roof of the porch. It read:

THE DORA JOHNSON AFRICAN-AMERICAN
BATTERED CHILDREN'S HOME

It took her only a few seconds to recollect the name. Of course – the social worker who had left Arbalest with Tom and Joanna Edelheit. And now a different social worker had named a children's home several hundred miles away after her.

After a minute, she walked across the street and up the walk. The door opened into a large living room. A half-dozen black children of mixed ages and sexes were playing noisily around an old sofa. A young woman sat in their midst, trying simultaneously to read a story to two pre-schoolers sitting on her lap, and supervise the others. She was too distracted to notice Adele enter.

"Hello," said Adele. The young woman looked up. So did two of the other children. A small boy, no more than a year and half old, stared open-mouthed at her, with wide-eyed, artless curiosity. Evidently, white faces were not common here. She smiled more broadly, then stifled a gasp. The top half of his right ear was missing.

"Can I help you?" asked the supervisor politely, but not cordially.

"Yes, thank you. I'm here to see a woman named Gertha Daniels. My name is Adele Jansen. I don't have an appointment."

"She didn't come in today," the young woman answered. *That makes two of us,* Adele thought. The other turned to one of the older children. "Alexa, go fetch Mrs. Matthews. She's in the kitchen." The child ran through a door.

"We feed them in shifts," the woman explained. "You got here with the first lunch."

"It's a nice place," Adele answered, looking around. The room was spotless despite the activity, except for scattered toys and books. All of the children were eying her now. "Hello," she smiled again. "Hi," one of the older, braver ones finally replied, smiling shyly himself. Good, progress.

"Someone donated the house," the young woman said, warming up a bit. "But the rest is community. We're very proud of it." Adele nodded. An older woman came through the door with the child who had left. An assortment of wide-eyed children followed her. Adele was now surrounded by fifteen to twenty curious, staring children of all sizes and hues.

"I'm Beverly Matthews," she said, extending her hand. "How may I help you?" She seemed competent and professional.

"I'm Adele Jansen," said Adele, taking her hand. "I've come to see Gertha Daniels. I don't have an appointment."

"What about?" Her tone was slightly guarded. Adele noticed the younger woman also appraising her.

"Nothing that could affect anyone here. About a case she was involved in, fifteen years ago. When she was a social worker in ----- County." She paused. "I'm a lawyer in New York City, but this has nothing to do with that. This is personal. Very personal."

"What was the name of the case?" Beverly Matthews asked, relaxing a bit, but still guarded.

Why not? "A boy named Jonathan Markland," Adele said. Beverly Matthews nodded almost imperceptibly; Adele started. "You know him? You've heard the name?"

"Yes," said Beverly Matthews. "She mentioned him once – said he was a rich white kid who got her started on vodka." Her tone changed – crisp and factual: "Gertha didn't come in today, Miss Jansen. If it's for the usual reason, you'll find her at home, drunk or getting there. It's a shame. She and I founded this place. She's terrific when she's sober. She's getting less terrific all the time."

"I know the address," Adele said. "Can you give me directions?"

"Certainly," Mrs. Matthews said, and did. "Are you going there now?" Adele nodded. "It's further into the district. It's not. . . it'd be a really good idea to finish your business and be gone from there by dark. Understand?" Adele nodded again.

"Also," said the woman on the couch, "any kids around ask to watch your car, it's pretty smart to pay 'me."

"Thanks," Adele replied – not advice she really needed, but she was touched by the concern. She turned to leave and almost tripped over the small boy who'd been the first to approach. An old baby's trick, to move silently behind a preoccupied adult. Impulsively, she reached down, picked him up, kissed him on the top of his ear, and set him gently down on the couch beside the supervisor.

"Darling, all of them," Adele said.

"You take good care of yourself, hear?" the woman answered. Her smile had become genuinely warm.

*

An hour later, with lunch behind, Adele turned into the parking lot of the apartment complex where Gertha Daniels lived. The building was not quite dilapidated, but getting there rapidly, ruts in the asphalt, a general seediness in the air. She'd obtained a number of dollar bills from the luncheonette in case someone did ask to watch the car, but the lot was deserted. Good. (Probably.)

She verified the apartment number on the tenant's mailboxes. Fourth floor. The elevator was old and rusting, with a ragged, filthy carpet. The moment the door closed behind her, she was overwhelmed by the stench of cat urine. The four-flight journey took forever. When she stepped out of the compartment, the odor seemed to trail her down the hall. She came to the door of Gertha Daniels' apartment.

The doorbell didn't seem to work. She tried it again, heard nothing again, knocked once, then louder. Seconds went by. Was Gertha Daniels home? Maybe she'd gone into work during lunch. Maybe–

The door flew open. "I heard ya the firs' time," Gertha said angrily. "Waddaya want?"

She was five-eight or -nine, ebony hued, perhaps 175 pounds, slatternly, dressed in a dirty shift. She was wobbling drunk. Adele could smell her breath two feet away.

"Only to talk to you," Adele said. "About someone you knew once."

"Who?" she asked suspiciously.

"Jonathan Markland. A case you had when you were a social worker."

She stared for an instant, then half-closed her eyes and sagged against the door frame "Johnny," she said softly, almost mystically, then looked up. "So somebody's come. Someone's finally come about Johnny. Who are you?"

"Adele Jansen. I'm a lawyer in New York City. I –"

"Oh yeah, yeah, yeah, I shoulda known," Gertha interrupted, shaking her head, "another lawyer. Just what he needs. Just what I need. A little honky girl lawyer." She began to close the door. "Go away. I got nothing to say to you."

"No!" said Adele, stopping the door. For a second, the scene degenerated into a farcical wrestling match. "I didn't come to see you for anything about law. I came because I care about Tom. That's the name I know him by. I didn't learn the other name until I went to Arbalest."

Gertha stopped pushing the door. "Why'd you do that?" She closed her eyes momentarily. "What's happened now? What kind of trouble's he in?"

"No trouble," Adele said. "He lives in Manhattan. He's a writer, a poet. He writes wonderful poetry about math and philosophy. He makes his living ghost writing mysteries and screenplays." Gertha stared, complete bafflement in her expression. "He's not in any trouble," Adele repeated.

"That's not possible," Gertha said, more to herself than Adele. "That's not possible," she repeated. She looked up. "I wasn't always like this," she said. "I was real good at what I did once. You're tellin' me things that can't be."

"He's not a saint," Adele added quickly. "He goes on these gigantic benders of alcohol and sex. And he has nightmares, horrible dreams nearly every night. He's a very unhappy man."

Gertha looked up and over Adele, her expression a confusing mixture of pain, bewilderment, and amusement. "'Bad dreams.' Drinks too much." She looked down; tears had welled in her eyes. "Why am I talkin' to you? Why am I doin' this? I let that boy break my heart for too many years already." She ran her hand through her hair. "And you're lyin' to me, I know it. Go away. Leave me alone. There's nothin' you can do for Johnny – Tom – whoever. Nothin' anyone can do." Her tone was almost kindly; she renewed the pressure on the door.

"No," said Adele. "You can't. You mustn't. I've come too far." Desperately she rushed on: "I came because I care about Tom, Ms. Daniels. I came because I want to – I have to – find out about him. Everything I've told you is the truth. Let me open my briefcase: I'll prove it." The pressure stopped. Adele reached down and flipped the lid open.

"I brought along copies of his poems. Here they are. See? And his college records, too, if you want to see those." She looked Gertha directly in the eye. "Please don't send me away. It wouldn't be right. It wouldn't be fair. Talk to me. *Please*."

Gertha looked at her for a long moment. "Who are you?" She looked yet longer. "You know him, don't you?"

"Yes," said Adele without hesitating. "I met him at a reception at one of my clients. A day later he took me out to a museum. He really has become the most wonderful person, Ms. Daniels. I fell in love with him." She paused. "It didn't last. I broke it off. It wasn't that I didn't care; it was that I couldn't see how anything was possible with him." Gertha was still regarding her suspiciously. Adele gushed on, saying whatever it took, revealing everything: "And I'm pregnant with his baby. So I have to find out about him, Ms. Daniels. I have more right than anyone."

Gertha's look softened. "So that's it." She looked down at the books, then at Adele, thought for a moment – then sighed heavily. "All right, missy. Come in. I wanna find out a little about you, too." The door opened.

*

She led Adele into an alcoholic's apartment, cluttered, slovenly. Still holding the books, Gertha moved without stopping towards a table next to the kitchen. Adele stopped to look at a bookcase that stood on the other wall. The book covers were yellowed and wrinkled; the titles were an impressive mix of sociology, psychology, and serious fiction. Gertha Daniels had been a very serious reader. Once.

On the top was a series of framed photographs. An attractive black woman shone out of the first, trim, poised, confident, a brilliant smile, ready for the world. With a shock, Adele realized she was looking at Gertha as a young woman. The others were clearly family. The last in order showed Gertha, somewhat older, but still with the brilliant smile, holding a small, white boy, him holding a stuffed animal. She peered more closely. Could the boy possibly be. . . ?

Gertha stood up, stepped to the bookcase, and put the last frame firmly on the shelf, facedown. She returned to her chair, folded her arms; Adele faced her. "Tell me about yourself," she said. "Tell me how you found out about me."

Adele did, step by step. ". . . so I got your name from Joanna Edelheit. A friend of mine found out which county you used to work for; someone there knew that you worked in Albany. That was yesterday. I came here today," she concluded about forty-five minutes later.

Gertha shook her head, slowly turned the pages of one of the books. "I don't believe this," she said softly. "That it would turn out this way. Even for a little while. It isn't possible."

"What did you expect?" Adele asked.

"Bellevue. Prison," she answered calmly. "Lethal injection, even. Some sort of institution for sure. Unless suicide. The drunk tank, if he was lucky. Not this."

"Can you tell me why?" Adele asked. "What happened? Who is Tom, anyway?" Gertha said nothing, kept turning the pages. "There are no records," she went on. "Nothing in the big computer databases. Arbalest didn't have a file, not that anyone would have shown it to me. The court file doesn't exist anymore. No one seems to know anything. At least that they'll say."

Gertha snorted. "'Course there aren't any files. 'Course all of it's gone. That would suit a lot of people just fine." She looked up directly at Adele. "But it hasn't worked." She nodded to herself. "Hasn't worked at all." She looked straight up, straight at Adele, triumphant.

"Because I have 'em. I've got it all. I still have everything."

*

A chill ran down Adele's spine. Here? The answer lay here? In this rundown, mildewed apartment? The room became deathly, eerily still.

"You do?" she repeated stupidly.

"Yeah," Gertha nodded. "Everything." She looked away. "Shouldn't a done it. Wasn't healthy. Almost like a compulsion. But I've got it all. The whole story. I always hoped that someday. . . someone. . . " Her voice trailed off.

"May I see?" Adele asked, timidly, summoning up all her courage.

"I don't know," Gertha answered. She had sobered up considerably. "That's what I've been tryin' to decide. I don't know. I gotta think about what's good for Johnny and me – you too, missy. You think you want to know all of it, but you don't, not really. You got no idea what you're getting into. I was giving you good advice when I told you to go away. It'd still be best if you took it."

"But –" Adele began, then stopped when Gertha held up her hand.

"Don't talk more. You talk real well, but you've gone as far today as talk will take you." She looked down at the books. "I can't believe this. Not that I don't believe you – but – I was sure I'd hear more about Tom, but not like this. Not like this." She turned to Adele. "I'm going to leaf through this stuff, I'm going to sleep on it, and I'm going to think a lot about everything you said. Give me your card – – I'll call and tell you what I'm going to do."

Adele pulled out a card, wrote. Gertha stepped into the small kitchen. A half-gallon of vodka, open, three-quarters full, stood on the counter. She picked it up.

"Won't be needing any more of this," she remarked, moving towards the sink. "At least not tonight."

Adele handed her the card as she stepped back into the dining area. Gertha nodded. "I'd better walk you out. Sometimes the neighbor kids get a little frisky." She smiled suddenly, for the first time since she'd answered the door. Delightful: whatever else had happened to her, she still had her smile.

"I'd appreciate it if you'd make up your mind as soon as you can," Adele said, as they left the apartment. "If you decide to let me see it, I'll have UPS pick it up."

"You're in a real hurry, aren't you?" Gertha remarked, looking at her quizzically. "Don't take the elevator," she said as she turned towards the stairs. "Cats pee in it. What're you going to do about the baby?"

They walked a few more steps. "I have an appointment on Saturday," Adele said finally.

"Same thing happened to me once," Gertha said conversationally. "Seemed like the only thing to do at the time. Now I'm not so sure." They reached the ground floor and started over toward her car. Three teenagers on the sidewalk turned to watch them pass. No question she was relieved that Gertha was with her, as sad a commentary as that was.

She opened the door. "Well, thank you for your time," Adele said. "I know you're being conscientious. I'll accept whatever you decide."

"Bullshit," said Gertha, grinning from ear to ear. "If I don't give it all up, you'll be back up here after me with a buzz saw. I had you typed from the get-go." She became serious. "But I'm going to do what's right even so. There's reasons for that." She gestured towards the books, and then looked up suddenly, a new question in her eyes. "What does Johnny think about this stuff? Why does he write it? Does he say?"

Adele shrugged as she slid into the car. "That's one of the small mysteries," she said. "Everyone who's read him thinks what he writes is wonderful, but it doesn't seem to mean anything to him." She remembered something he'd said as she'd laid in his arms on a magic night. "He calls himself a hack. He says it's only doing numbers."

Gertha's eyes widened; then suddenly, bewilderingly, she was sobbing. "Oh, no, *NO!*" Adele was too startled to react. "It's the same! It's just the same!" She wiped her eyes with one hand and careened away from the car, off balance. In three steps, she was running.

"Gertha! *GERTHA!*" Adele called, stepping out of the car. But she did not turn, instead threw open the door to the stairway, and disappeared into the building. The sound of her footsteps resounding on the stairs was all that was left.

*

She pulled off into the parking lot of a roadside inn an hour and a half later, mind still brimming with thoughts. The craving for a salad, covered with tomato slices as thin and delicate as Damascus silk, had become overwhelming. *You little nut*, she thought fondly, the miasma of anxiety and weariness momentarily dispelled, *you're driving me crazy*.

Not for much longer, something infinitely cruel inside her snapped back. *Just four days*. She buried her face in her hands for a second. Her hands shook.

*

An exhausted Adele Jansen stepped out of the elevator on her own floor at 7:30 that evening. She'd run into traffic before she could drop off the car; then the train seemed to crawl into the City. She'd been up since 5:45. For the second time in four days, all she wanted to do was bathe and crawl into bed.

The door to her apartment was festooned with notes taped to the front. She peeled the first one off, then the second – Carolyn had sent four taxicabs for her. Once inside the apartment, she checked her answering machine. Eleven messages; she could guess whom they were from. The pager she'd left on her dresser had over thirty.

Not tonight, she thought dully, *tomorrow*, and moved toward the bathroom. The phone rang. It probably was – she really shouldn't – but it was so insistent. Wearily, she picked it up.

"Where *were* you?" Carolyn hissed.

*

The large conference room on the thirty-second floor was the ceremonial headquarters of the law firm of Hapgood, Thurlow, Anderson, & Davis. A forty-foot wall of plate glass faced the east. A magnificent expanse of city and sea was visible. Even on this kind of day, with gray, lowering clouds, the view was something memorable.

Adele had never seen the room so crowded. Well over a hundred people were jostling for space. The principals had chairs around the long conference table, Franklin and George at the head, Carolyn at Franklin's side, Harry Greube at hers. Three conference phone speakers had been placed in the middle of the table. Elsewhere, lawyers and accountants fought silent, intense wars for briefcase territory. Adele had situated herself on the east wall, as far away from Carolyn as she could be while still adjacent to the door. The atmosphere seethed with finality. This was it, the last day, the final hours – the expectant, gathered forces would be witness to either a triumph or a debacle; in either case, a spectacle.

(*. . . the single, most inexcusable act of irresponsibility that has occurred in my entire time with this firm. After all I've done for you! After all I've said about you! After all the warnings! Are you having a bad period?! Have you gone apeshit over some guy?! HAVE YOU LOST YOUR MIND?! HAVE. . .*)

Franklin Fischer stood up, took a deep breath. "We're ready to begin. Let's call the roll. Atlanta. . ."

"Check," came a squawk over the phone.

"Birmingham."

"Here," said Al.

"Boston." Another squawk from one of the conference speakers.

(*Where were you? Answer me! ANSWER ME!*

I can't. Personal business. I'm not saying more. She knew Carolyn too well to snivel and grovel; her mother's advice about dangerous animals. A long cold silence.

You've just chucked away two years, Carolyn said finally. *You know that, don't you? I'm going to have to rethink every opinion I ever had about you. I'm going to have to communicate that reconsideration to all of my partners. We are not going to have irresponsible people as partners in this firm, Miss Adele Elizabeth Jansen, no matter how brilliant they are – or may think they are.*

Shit, she suddenly exploded again, *I tried to keep some of your appointments myself. I made a complete ASS of myself.*)

"Tulsa. . ."

"Yo."

"Youngstown."

"Check."

"All right, everything is in place," Franklin Fischer concluded, the tension evident in his voice. "Let's get started. Harry?"

"Sure," said Harry Greube, standing up. "You've all got two copies of the last draft. One's redlined with all the changes; the other's fair – the one to be executed. Both went out FedEx to everybody yesterday. Everybody got it?" Nods around the room, a chorus of squawks from the speaker. "Good. You'll note there is very little redlined." His tone shifted in timbre, more authoritative: "I think we are awfully close to finality. I'm prepared to go over the whole document, but I do hope we can glide over Article VI. Most of the provisions in there are CCRs individual to each acquisition. Individual meetings are scheduled about those. So please, those of you from Anchorage, don't worry too much about whether the guys in Boston have protected themselves adequately or we'll be here forever." A ripple of laughter went around the room.

Adele riffled through the thick document on her lap, captioned "ACQUISITION AGREEMENT BETWEEN FISCHER COMMUNICATIONS ACQUISITION CORPORATION AND..." followed by twenty-nine names of corporations and businesses, all owners of media companies scattered around the United States. One hundred and twenty pages of impenetrable prose. She glanced down at the contract. She understood very little of it today, but she would, she would. She looked up, was unlucky enough to catch an icy stare from Carolyn.

(*Finally I rescheduled all of your appointments for Friday. You will keep each and every one, Adele. You will be at the Project meeting tomorrow – and – by the way – I've changed my mind – you will attend the AI Squared board meeting. No shirking of any responsibility. There won't be any family business, or personal business, or anything. Do you understand?*

Silence.

DO YOU UNDERSTAND?

Yes, Carolyn,* she said finally, hating herself, thinking of Walt Greenfield and the wine he drank.)

The discussion began in earnest. *Are you sure about the taxes?* Yes, very sure, all acquisitions are either share for share or share for assets, all the tests are met – 80 percent control, business purpose, continuity of interest, continuity of enterprise – you've had plenty of time to get your own tax opinions, we know they agree. (Heads nodded around the room; pens scratched.) *I've got dissenters* – fine, but we're not going to cram down more than 8 percent; you'll have to work it out yourself with the rest, there's only so many cash hits this deal will take. We committed to buy 25 businesses; if some of you can't go with us, we can live with that. *No, no, no, that's not what I meant at all. We're in.*

She had pulled out her laptop, was taking notes quietly, automatically, not fully aware of what her fingers were doing. It had been another long, bad night, rolling on her bed far into the morning, rehashing endlessly her meeting with Gertha Daniels, all the things she could have said differently, all the things she might have said better. Even so, a certain excitement began to lift her as the meeting progressed. The feeling of being present at the birth of something monumental was exhilarating.

"The fact that it's letter stock still bothers me," someone at the table said.

"We're committed to making a public market within twelve months," said Franklin Fischer.

"How can we be sure you'll follow through?"

"Look it, guys," George smiled amiably, "it's the only out for us, too. Only way we can get liquid. We're all in this together." And with that he began to take over...

"Registration rights?" one of the lawyers to her rear asked later.

"One more time, as the bride said to the groom," George Sorenson responded firmly. "No can do. Demands are out of the question; it's gotta be everyone or no one; since it can't be everyone, it's no one. You got piggybacks already in the contract, but I been honest with all of you: you're not gonna get underwriter's consent, float's gonna be too goddamn big. But the main thing is that nearly all of you can get out with Rule 144 in 90 days, 180 tops after the lockup ends. So you don't need –" He was implacable.

"The lockup's non-negotiable?" the same voice said. "Two and one half years?"

"The lockup's absolutely non-negotiable, friend," George answered, smiling, a rock. "I've set up market makers around the world. There's no way we can let anybody blow the market out on us. We'd all be up shit creek. Sorry, no can do." A murmur of agreement ran through the room.

He's terrific, Adele thought as she input. She felt a small erotic tingle welling up beneath the fatigue. *He's better than all of them.* Somehow he cut through the jungle of taxese, securities law, and the regulatory maze in a way that all the generalists could understand, without offending the specialists. He was out lawyering the lawyers, out accounting the accountants, marching relentlessly toward the goal. The warrior triumphs over all, then claims the maiden. If only . . .

She felt a presence at her shoulder.

"Phone call, Ms. Jansen," the secretary whispered. Adele had left word below that she was not to be interrupted – except for one person. Instantly, she left her seat, stepped over a briefcase, and moved to the door. She could feel

Carolyn's glare on her back.

*

"I made up my mind," said Gertha Daniels. "I read over all this junk. . . that Johnny would turn up this way. I still can't belie–anyway, I'm going to send you my stuff. Been keeping this shit for too long anyway. Keeping it for someone. If it's not you, I don't know."

"I'll contact UPS right now," Adele said. "Someone will be there within the hour."

"Why so fast?" Gertha asked, puzzled.

"I don't know. All I know is I want to see your file as soon as humanly possible." She hesitated. "And thank you. I want to talk more – soon. Right this second, there's a mee –"

"Don't thank me," Gertha cut in. "It was you mostly I was up all night thinking about. You don't want this, missy, you don't want anything to do with this. You got it all. Anyone can see that. If you're as smart as I think, you'll back off now. You don't want to mess with Johnny."

"Tom," she said. A pause. "I know what I'm doing," she added.

"Do you? I gave him that name," she answered softly. "Me. Names don't matter to what I'm saying. You don't want this. You say the word, I'll keep what I've got, it'll just be me and Johnny, and the others, one of these old days we'll all stand before the throne of God, and then it'll all come right."

My God, she thought. So unreal – four feet away, behind a door, voices were raised, sophisticated professionals argued about the disposition of billions of dollars, a major revolution in communications in the Western Hemisphere. Meanwhile, she was speaking to a childcare worker in Albany about a case that was fifteen years old. "Thank you," she said aloud, "but it's already gone too far. A long time ago. I have to know what's in your file. I have to know why all this has happened."

"Yeah," she answered, "yeah. That's what I thought. So it's you now. Good luck, missy, good luck." A child shrieked in the background. "God damn it, Alexa, keep your hands to yourself!" She addressed the phone again: "Send your messenger, but not til the end of the day today. It'll get there same time tomorrow. I have to write a lot of notes. I wrote a lot last night, I gotta write a lot more right now. Pickup's the Children's Center." She paused. "Sorry for bawling my head off. Kids give you any trouble?"

"No."

"Good." She went on: "Good luck, missy. Good luck. You'd better be made of iron," she finished softly. "You're going to wish you were."

*

She re-entered the conference room hazy and distracted – also, in some distant recess of her mind, frightened. For a moment, it was this meeting that seemed unreal, the three-piece suits, the intense talk, about people and events so far away, so very far.

But the meeting had a momentum, an urgency, of its own. She was disconcerted for an instant only. Then she was back in her seat, her laptop on her briefcase, her fingers on the keyboard. George was moving them all expertly, inexorably through the major issues; the direction of the meeting was evident. Noon came; sandwiches were brought in, soft drinks, milk, iced tea, and beer. (She smiled to herself. No one touched the beer. She was certain that, had so many others not been watching, it would have disappeared quickly.) George didn't touch anything.

Sometimes he used Wall Street jargon, sometimes street argot. Always he was up to date on every last financial detail; always, always, moving forward. Once only, he looked at her, flashed a quick, private smile, would have winked (she was certain) if he could have got away with it. Franklin Fischer was entirely silent. It had to be obvious to everyone who the muscle in CFS really was.

Around 2:00 some brave soul tentatively requested a recess. Instant unanimity coalesced around the table. Carolyn or someone pressed a button. The tea tray that was a tradition at Hapgood, Thurlow, Davis, & Anderson rolled into the conference room. Some partook. Others scattered towards urinals and fresh air. She drifted towards the cart, thinking of a diet cola, ending up with a canned iced tea. George was suddenly beside her, with his own iced tea.

"How're we doin'?" he asked.

"You're *wonderful*," she said.

"Surprised you, huh?" he grinned. He was tired, too, but not so much that he didn't enjoy that he was playing the hero in front of a woman he wanted. "Didn't think I had it in me?"

"I knew you'd be wonderful," she answered. "I didn't know you'd be *this* wonderful." Forty minutes had passed. People were returning, reassembling.

"Could be better," he whispered, turning to leave. "Could be in bed with you."

"*George!*" she said, doing girl again, pretending to be shocked.

The afternoon wore on. The important issues behind, the dialog descended to the trivial, managers speaking to hear themselves talk, attorneys wanting to leave at least one fingerprint on the deal to justify their fee. Boston did examine Anchorage's protections. *You're sure you can manage the utilities commission? Yes, positive.* Each person individually knew that everything that could be said had been said, but no one was willing to be the first to say so. Archetypal committee think.

"It all hangs on VINUX, though, don't it?" drawled a beefy man with a leathery face, sitting next to Jim from Dallas, the Cowboys fan from the day before. "That's where all the value added comes from. Only reason we're talking. Only reason you can afford the price. How you so sure EBS is going to sell it to you?" The room went silent.

"We're sure," George said evenly.

"Heard a lotta talk about chickens. Ain't seen any eggs," the other answered.

"Oh, God," the stranger sitting next to Adele whispered. "A deal breaker. There's a jerk like this in every crowd."

"There's a condition subsequent in the contracts," Harry Greube retorted a bit crossly. "You know that. If we don't acquire the systems or the rights within a calendar year, any one of you can rescind the deal. You're protected."

"Yeah, that's what it says, all right," he drawled. "But – how do we know you'll perform? How do we know where the FCC really stands? Suppose the patents don't issue? Suppose someone in Japan has already built a better mousetrap?" Adele looked up and around the room as she typed. The mood was deflating; for the first time all day, the deal faced a genuine threat. She looked at the Texan with genuine anger. He'd waited until the energy had subsided, timed the attack perfectly to coincide with the fatigue. A pure ego trip; his client wanted in, that had become obvious earlier. She glanced at George. Yes, it could fail, even now, the large event could pivot 180 degrees on this small incident.

She put her computer down; with what seemed like her last ounce of strength, she stood up. "Sir, I can answer some of your questions," she interrupted in a piping voice. Everyone turned.

"Stand up on the chair," the man to her left whispered. She nodded gratefully to him and took the advice.

"What you know?" the man with the leathery face asked.

"One or two things. The FCC's solidly behind Vinux. They think it's going to help them a lot with deregulated cable and satellite. It'll make universal HDTV possible even to small time operators. And DOD's behind it, too – they want it in place for communications redundancy. There was a big meeting at the EBS research facility in Rochester ten days ago, with everybody putting pressure on the copyright office to expedite this." Adele swayed slightly in the chair. She was running on her reserves now. Her eyes glittered with exhaustion, not intelligence. She hoped the makeup she'd used that morning masked the rings under her eyes.

A large murmur ran through the room. Some of the excitement of the morning returned. "How you know all this?" the leather face demanded.

"I went over to the EBS booth after hours the first day of the show. I talked to one of the engineers." She smiled. "Engineers are as gossipy as housewives. Plus he was a pretty excited young man."

"Un-hunh," said the other. "How'd you get him to talk to you, pretty lady?"

She let the question linger in the air for a long moment. Too late, he realized his mistake. "Excuse me. I didn't mean to imply –"

"I didn't let him buy me dinner, if that's what you mean," she interrupted softly, going for the kill.

"Hey," said someone. "Knock it off," said someone else. A low chorus of disapproval ran through the room. Not because of the sexism, Adele knew, but because others had recognized the nature of the thrust, were relieved it had been parried. In more than a few eyes she saw simple satisfaction; in others, those of the killers scattered around the table, recognition of one of their own, appreciation of a fine display of jugular instinct. The man with the leathery face reddened, and was silent.

"Who's she?" someone on the other side of the room asked.

"That's Adele Jansen," Carolyn beamed. "One of our most capable young associates here at Hapgood, Thurlow. For those of you who know the Parallax case, she did the work that broke it open."

"Their high-tech expert," Al from Birmingham interjected approvingly.

"Yes, that's true," Carolyn agreed, turning her broadest, toothiest smile at Adele. "But I have better news about that. As capable as Adele is, we have decided that it is unwise to depend on any one individual so entirely. As a partnership, we will be making strenuous efforts in the near future to bring someone in laterally in the high-tech field at the partnership level – to provide the services corporations such as this need." Adele felt as if she'd been punched in the solar plexus. All sense of triumph vanished.

"Hell, why not make her a partner now?" Al joked.

Carolyn shook her head smilingly. "That's not the way it works at law firms of this caliber, Al. It's not simply a question of talent. We know that Adele's brilliant, but all sorts of questions – such as loyalty, reliability, her commitment to the firm – remain to be answered." She turned to Adele again, smiling. "Partnership is at least five or six years away."

Another blow to the stomach.

*

Five minutes later, one of the speaker boxes squawked. "This is Park Forest, Illinois," the voice said. "I don't know about the rest of you, but I've got a company to run here. I've heard enough. Turn your clock off, Harry." A chuckle ran through the throng. "I'm going to sign the damn thing and get on with it. Congratulations, Franklin."

"Thanks," he said, beaming.

"There's a prepaid FedEx envelope in the package," Harry Greube added, also relieved.

"One thing, Bob, before you go," George said into the box. "You got a piece of pretty hot information there when we were talking about Vinux. You can't use it." He looked around the room. "That goes for everybody. The SEC is gonna be keeping a pretty close eye on all of us. I know it hurts, but you gotta lay off it. No one takes a position in EBS stock. It's in the contract, but I'll remind you anyway." His eyes swept the room again, met Adele's, broke away immediately, uncomfortable. Bewildered, she tried to catch his eye, but he would not meet her look. *Why?* she puzzled.

The meeting began to break up. A few of the cable executives signed on the spot. But most took the contracts with them for one last look. Personal meetings on the nuances of individual acquisitions would go on long into the night. Adele's day might be over, but George's day was only beginning. He shot her a frustrated smile. The warrior might know he had won the right, the maiden might know it, too, but the schedule precluded anything more. No explanations necessary, thank God.

Groups of twos and threes drifted out of the conference room. Adele accepted congratulations from a few passersby. Carolyn approached, turned. "I'm sure you understood my announcement. Actions have consequences," she said quietly, unsmilingly, then moved to where Franklin Fischer stood, and became the beaming hostess.

George was suddenly beside her, tired but happy. "Thanks," he said.

"George," she said, touching his arm, remembering how he'd looked away, "did I do something wrong? Are you angry at me?"

"Hell, no," he answered, surprised. "You came through." Before she could say anything else, with a light touch, he guided her to Franklin and Carolyn. Only a few of the participants remained.

"Told you," George said simply. "She saved our bacon there."

"C'mon," Carolyn answered, "it was only a tiny bump on the road."

"No," said Franklin, looking sharply at Carolyn, "George is correct. Thank you, Adele," he went on, nodding up and down, thinking to himself, and eying Adele. "George was right. You're very talented. A really valuable member of the team."

"Thanks," she said, uncertainly. She resisted the impulse to take George's arm for protection.

"When she is good, she is so good," Carolyn sighed. "The question is commitment." Franklin nodded absently, then looked up. Jim from Dallas and the leather-faced lawyer were heading towards the door.

"Just a moment," Franklin Fischer said evenly. Calmly, dispassionately, he moved in front of them. "Just a moment, Jim. There are two changes in your contract." He grabbed the fair copy out of Jim's hands, sat down at the table, wrote and initialed.

"There," he said. "The price isn't six dollars a share, it's four-fifty. That's the first. The second is, you sign this here and now, or you needn't bother returning here."

Both men began to sputter. "What do you mean?" asked the executive.

"I'll put it in a way you can understand," Franklin Fischer answered in a voice of low venom. "What are you worth?" he said in a soft, poisonously unctuous tone. "Enough to challenge me in my own meeting? Enough to derail all the energy, all the momentum I've put into this over the last five years? What are you *worth*?" he continued, his voice slightly louder, his tone slightly harsher, "enough to believe you could take me on in my house with no consequence? Enough to see your end of the deal collapse and endure all the misery I'm going to make for you down the line?"

The lawyer had gone dark red. He opened his mouth and–

"Don't," Franklin Fischer said. "One word from you, one miserable word from this ten-gallon shit-for-brains shyster, and I will tear up the contract in front of your eyes." The lawyer's mouth opened and closed – and finally closed. Fischer turned to the executive again, and leaned into his face.

"*WHAT ARE YOU WORTH*!!?" he thundered, and Adele recognized the phrase as his mantra, his battle cry. "Are you worth enough to actually stand up to me? Defy me!? *Embarrass* me? I don't think you are. In fact, I know you're not. You pathetic piece of useless protoplasm. In two weeks, you could be standing on the street corner selling pencils if I chose to put you there. I might choose anyway." He paused. The Texan blinked and swallowed. He did not say a word.

"So you can sign that contract in the next 30 seconds as it now stands and leave with what's left of your wretched self and your wretched system or you can march right out that door and take the consequences – and there will be consequences. So," almost pleasantly, "what are you worth, Jim? Think about it." He glanced at his watch. "You have ten seconds left."

A tide of raw territoriality surged through the room, the ambiance of the veldt. The Texans had invaded Fischer's turf, attacked his deal, insulted one of his women, and now they must be made to pay. For an instant, her intellect too dulled by fatigue to remind herself that this was not a veldt but a boardroom, Adele found herself swept up by instinct in that surge. Then her presence of mind returned. She glanced at Fischer to determine whether the display of anger had been theatrical or for real. She was startled to find her glance inadvertently meeting his own calm, studious appraisal of her. Embarrassed and uneasy, she broke off the eye contact at once and took a step nearer to George.

"Better sign, Jim," George said, who thankfully had not seen the exchange of glances. "Your little outfit was one of three we talked to in the Dallas region. We chose you more by drawing straws than any other reason. Either of the CEOs from the other two'll be on a plane in fifteen minutes if we call."

"God damn it, I was only doing my goddam job!" shouted the lawyer, with no trace whatsoever of a drawl or accent.

"You didn't have to talk to Ms. Jansen that way," George said flatly. "That wasn't part of your job." He turned. "Better sign, Jim."

Jim from Dallas turned furiously from one man to the other. "Five seconds," said Franklin Fischer. Jim reached for the pen, turned to the back of the contract, and scrawled his signature. "Damn you all!" he said.

"Jim, I –" the lawyer began.

"Shut up, Jack!" Jim said. "Shut up! Keep your big mouth shut!" The two men exited without another word. Adele, George, Carolyn, and Franklin Fischer were the only persons left in the room, which was littered now with soda cans and sandwich bags.

Carolyn and Franklin burst into laughter. George smiled a tired smile. Adele watched the other three, almost too tired to think, alien and distant. The show of tooth and claw, the triumphant gloating, robbed her of any satisfaction in her own performance. Several hundred miles to the north, an aging seeress had promised to unleash terrible secrets, and Adele had no doubt she would keep her word. She looked out the window, wondering about the dark sky outside, wondering about all the dark clouds that had gathered in her life, dreading what the next day would bring.

*

Adele prepared for bed at about 8:00. Sleep was becoming essential – and yet, even as she undressed, she knew it would be as difficult this night as it had been all the others. The certain knowledge that she was off the fast track, at least temporarily; the look George wouldn't return; above all, the file coming tomorrow from Gertha. *You don't want this, missy.* All the clouds.

On impulse, she picked up the phone. He might not be home; a highly eligible widower, he'd become quite a favorite with the local widows over the years. A number had come and gone in a decade and a half. According to Buck, there was a lot of harmless speculation as to whether anything serious was actually happening with whatever woman he was consoling at the moment. Adele formed no judgments; if ever a man was entitled. . .

As it happened, he answered the phone on the second ring. "Hello?"

"Hello, Daddy," she said

"Pumpkin! What a nice surprise. What's new in New York? Why do you call so close to the holiday?"

"Oh, a lot of reasons," she said. "Nothing important."

Because I'm scared, Daddy. Because I'm really scared. Because everything is way, way out of control. Because for the first time in my life I am reaching the limit of my strength. Because I don't know what tomorrow is going to bring, or how I'm going to cope with it, or anything. Because I am really, really scared.

Because for a while, just a little while, I want to be your little girl again

THREE BLIND MICE

A dark dawn. A dark day.

Storm clouds lowered over the city. The persistent drizzle had matured into light rain, becoming heavier with each passing moment. A storm was brewing. Gertha Daniels was with her from her first moment of consciousness. She finished breakfast at 8:15, glanced at her watch. 6:00 UPS pickup yesterday, expedited service. It would be on her desk by noon; 1:00 or 1:30 at the latest. The AI Squared board meeting would take up most of the morning. Good. It would help keep her mind off other things. Saturday, November 20th, was only two days away.

Adele glanced out the window at the dark, massed clouds. She had trod a dangerous path in a dangerous season. She had nearly reached its end. This is the day. All at once, she felt queasy, sickish. Her first taste of morning sickness? No, more than that. This was not a good day to be abroad, to voyage freely in the realms of men. George would be at the board meeting. Even the warm glow of that expectation was tinged with dread.

Better stay home today. Better stay in bed. Simultaneously with the thought, her head turned towards the wall clock in the kitchen. 8:40. She gulped down the last of her grapefruit juice, picked up her briefcase.

The time had come to leave. The time had come in general.

*

The rain had become heavy enough by 9:45 to make a taxicab mandatory. Carolyn and Harry Greube sat in the backseat, Adele to the right of the driver in front. A few words passed between Harry and Carolyn before it dawned on him that Adele and Carolyn hadn't acknowledged each other's existence, let alone spoken to each other. He looked from one to the other, then subsided into his own uneasy silence. The cab pulled up in front of the offices of Consolidated Financial Services.

Adele opened her umbrella and stepped out onto the curb. In an instant, Carolyn was standing beside her, waiting for Harry to come around the front of the cab. "Pouting won't help, Adele," Carolyn said in a low, toneless voice.

Neither will sniveling, she thought, but said nothing. The imbroglio with

Carolyn was one more item that was going to have to wait its turn. Besides, how bad could it be? She'd given the matter passing thought during the long night. She'd done her part and more yesterday. The Project was still online, and all the NATPE commitments would be met. How long could Carolyn possibly stay angry? This, too, shall pass. Gertha's file was probably on the truck by this time, unless the rain had slowed it.

The reception area was much less attractive in the diminished natural light. George stood there. She flushed with pleasure upon seeing him. He looked at Carolyn, then Harry – only then did he see her. He started, did a double take, then looked hard at Carolyn, who smiled and shrugged.

"Adele?" he said, bewildered.

"George? What's the matter?" she asked. Her anxiety increased several-fold.

"Nothing. . . I was expecting you'd be at NATPE. You surprised me," he said, smiling reassuringly, taking her hand and squeezing it lightly. Yet he, too, was tense. She could feel it in his hand, see it in his posture, in the quick nervous movements of his body. Why? His big day had been yesterday, and it had gone perfectly.

"Is everything all set?" he asked Harry Greube as they entered the elevator.

"Check," Harry said. Adele's head swiveled. He, too, had become very tense. She had felt uneasy since daybreak. The sense of brooding imminence increased.

"I want to touch base with Franklin," said Carolyn, when the elevator reached the fourth floor. "Come with me, Harry. George?"

"No," he said. "Not necessary. I'll keep Adele company." Carolyn and Harry walked quickly down the hall.

"George," she said, when they were alone in the corridor, "something is wrong today. I can feel it."

"Nothing," he answered. "It's nervous time now. The contract's are all out. Nothing to do but wait. Maybe answer a few more dumb questions." His eyes flitted around the hall, seeking everything but hers. "Let's go down to the conference room and get ready."

A door opened in front of them just beyond the alcove with the rubber plant. "Oh, hi," the young woman who emerged said to Adele.

"Hello?" replied Adele uncertainly.

"There's no reason you should remember," the other answered cheerfully, over her shoulder, as she passed. "You helped me get my briefcase shut a few weeks ago. Remember?" She went on down the hall.

"Yes," said Adele, her heart leaping, wheeling to face George – the first break in the unrelievedly somber mood of this morning. "I thought you were going to fire her."

"Oh," he answered, deadpan, "I had to rethink that. Jane's a pretty sharp gal. It'd have been a shame to lose her. No reason everybody here has to run on the treadmill. Nine to five will do for some."

"Oh, George," she said helplessly. *You did that for me*; besides, she wanted to find something reassuring. His hands came to her waist; he looked over her shoulder; she looked down the corridor; empty. It seemed safe to risk a quick kiss which, like all the others, lingered on, this time beyond safety. *I think it's about time you called your travel agent*, was what she intended to say when they pulled apart.

"Ahem," said Lem Michaels, clearing his throat, behind George. Peter Steinitz stood next to him.

*

George and Adele separated instantly.

"Well, you guys seem to be getting along," Peter remarked quizzically.

"I guess you're not going with Tom Newcombe anymore," Lem added, his disappointment visible in his expression. She did her best to meet his look, not entirely successfully.

"Adele makes her own decisions," George retorted stiffly. "It's not your business." Adele turned sharply at him. He had spoken much more harshly, was glaring much more icily than necessary. What Lem had said was perfectly natural. George was fully aware of the white lie she'd told Lem.

He glanced at his watch. "We got no time for this," he went on. "It's two minutes after ten. The meeting's waiting." Without waiting for an answer, he turned and walked towards the boardroom. The others followed. Adele could feel Lem's eyes on her, sense his thoughts, reappraising her, wondering at himself, bewilderment, hurt feelings. Never mind George; she was determined to say something to him after the meeting. *These things happen, Lem. I didn't know back then.*

The others were seated when they entered the room – Franklin Fischer at the head of the long table, Victor Podgorny to one side, George taking his seat at the other. Carolyn and Harry Greube were further down the table. Printed agendas had been placed in front of their designated chairs. Lem, Peter, and Adele sat down.

"Call the meeting to order," said Franklin Fischer peremptorily, coldly. "The agenda, as you can see, has been revised. The first six items are the same. It's the seventh I want to take up first."

Revised? Seventh?? The one she'd seen on Monday only had six.

"The matter of your resignations. From this board. From my company. Now. Today."

*

She could not believe her ears. Lem's mouth dropped open; Peter Steinitz stared at the head of the table.

"What did you say?"

"I *said*, in plain English, I want your resignations. I want you out of my company. Today," repeated Franklin Fischer.

She looked around the room. Harry, Carolyn, Victor Podgorny, all calm, nonchalant – they'd all known. And George? Her heart stood still. George, too; he looked fixedly ahead from Franklin Fischer's left, refusing to meet her eye. *Oh, no.*

"But – what? I don't understand. You're kidding," said Lem dazedly.

"I'm not kidding, Lem," Franklin retorted softly. "Vic, George and I have given this matter a lot of thought. We want you three gentlemen – Mr. Chiang goes too – out of management. We can't afford to take a chance on you."

"Amen," added Victor Podgorny.

"You can't do this," Lem said.

"Guess again, fella," Podgorny rejoined flatly. "We're the majority of the board. We got the majority of the shares. And we've seen enough of you. You're out." Fischer smiled slightly.

"But. . . why?" asked Peter Steinitz, bewilderedly.

Franklin Fischer stood up and moved around the table. "I'll tell you why. Too much immaturity. Too much bad temper" – he looked directly at Steinitz – ". . .flagrant breaches of fiduciary duty."

"Fiduciary duty?" Lem repeated stupidly.

"Yes. The responsibility you have as an officer and director to the shareholders. The responsibility I have as chairman of the board. About which you seem to have no understanding."

"What the hell are you talking about?" Befuddlement was giving way to rage.

"Massive overstatements of the potential of the program, to this board and others. We can all get sued for pronouncements of that nature. And giving serious consideration to building in a design flaw – mind you, that was good, creative legal work" – he looked at Adele; she was becoming horribly certain that this was a script, that that last part was in at the insistence of George – "but you, as president, should never have proceeded on it without more investigation. We were all *shocked* when counsel more – experienced – than Ms. Jansen explained to us how serious the consequences could be." He returned to his seat and sat down heavily.

"And that tantrum you threw at the first board meeting didn't help a bit," Victor Podgorny added.

"I'm afraid you're through, Lem," Franklin Fischer said levelly. "All of you. I'm not going to take the risk of you any longer. The board has already decided to remove you as officers. I want you off the board. I want you out altogether. You had your chance."

Lem opened his mouth, but Peter Steinitz, who'd been holding his head in his hands, put his hand on Lem's arm. "Don't. Don't even try. It's a fix. Don't you see?"

A long deadly silence settled in the room. Lem Michaels looked slowly around the room, paused at Adele – what complete contempt was in his eyes! – took in the others. She tried frantically to think of something, anything, to say, realized she was too confused and ignorant herself to intervene. Her head turned to the head of the table, hoping – praying – that George would do something, that he wasn't part of this. But he was still avoiding her, his eyes down and fixed on the agenda. *George*, she thought, *oh, no, no, no, George.*

"Pete's right," Lem Michaels said at last. "This is a set-up. We didn't do anything you didn't know about or encourage. You had this in mind from day one."

Theatrical shock played over Franklin Fischer's features. "Lem –"

"You're not going to get away with it," Lem continued. "We can get lawyers, too." He looked again at Adele. "Honest lawyers. We haven't done anything that justifies this. I know it."

"That would be a most imprudent course of action to take, Mr. Michaels," said Harry Greube, clearing his throat. "The shareholder's contract you signed – freely and voluntarily – is most explicit about what the consequences of that would be. As it stands now, the stock you, Mr. Steinitz, and Mr. Chen own in AI Squared is yours to keep. Worth several hundred thousand each, I understand. But in the event of a litigation or lawsuit undertaken in bad faith – any action that causes detriment to the company – the board has the right, indeed the obligation, to repurchase your holding at the original issue price – about one-quarter of a cent per share. The clause specifically mentions protests against board action taken on the advice of counsel as being in bad faith." He paused. "Mr. Sorenson sought our written opinion about this situation a week ago. We were reluctantly forced to agree that your irresponsibility as officers required your removal by this board. Given the rendering of that opinion, you would be taking a colossal risk if you contested this decision."

"Your law firm," Victor Podgorny commented. "You chose 'em."

"Now I've got it," Lem said. He looked at Adele again, a look of complete, unmitigated contempt.

"In other words," Peter Steinitz said heavily, after another long silence, "if we even try to protest this idiocy, we get cut off without a dime and you keep our work. But if we leave peaceably, we get a nice little bribe for our cooperation."

"That is not exactly the way I would have put it," answered Harry, "but that is the practical reality, yes."

Peter Steinitz put his head heavily into his hands again. "You've got to admit it's been well done, Lem. It's been very, very well done."

Lem looked down the table, directly at Franklin Fischer.

"Thief," he said flatly.

*

"Lem," Franklin Fischer said incredulously. "Really. Thief?" He rose from his chair and moved slowly down to where Lem was sitting. "I think you have to be a bit more honest with yourself.

"I'm not enjoying this scene. Do you think I like this one bit more than you do? But I have to be realistic, and you must be as well. You must be aware – you, more than anyone – of how utterly misfit you are for the business world. You have intelligence. You have talent; I'm certain you are going to have a tremendous academic career. But a businessman? A leader? Other talents are required for that. No one is adept at everything. You must know that you are not cut out for that role. You are an ivory tower type, Lem. Accept it. From the standpoint of one who knows, there was no practicality in anything you planned. Your equity is safe. Your effort will be rewarded. Take the money and go back to your retreat. That's where you belong."

"What we planned was eminently practical," Lem said quietly. "I consider all of us very practical people. I wonder if you really digested the business plan."

"I read it thoroughly, Lem," Franklin Fischer answered, with sad amusement. Adele remembered his copy, still on the conference table. "It was funny; it was pathetic; it was schoolboy fantasy. You're a mature man – in most ways. If I was abrupt earlier, I apologize. But you must know I'm correct."

"I think we did just fine in the real world, Mr. Fischer," Lem responded, his ears turning pink. "We sold your deal for you."

"YOU sold?!?" Podgorny broke in. "You sold?! The hell you did!

Salesmen and whores sold the deal, Mr. Michaels. Same as always. All you were was a big joke. Bucky Beaver, the industrial tycoon. 'I'd like to show you this, I'd like you to see that.' Coming on to cocktail waitresses like a boy scout. It was the big laugh on the road. You trying to score and striking out everywhere." He unwrapped a cigar. "You didn't win the game, pal. You never found out what it was."

Lem bit his lip. George turned his head sharply to Podgorny. He knew this was too much. But he said nothing, nor would he meet her eye. He wasn't going to help. Franklin Fischer spoke:

"Vic, that was vulgar and unnecessary." He turned to Lem. "But I think there was a kernel of truth there, Lem," he continued in a kind, avuncular manner. "Something you should pay attention to. My impression is that this is an established pattern with you, Lem. To be quite candid, I don't think you relate well to people – men or women. Part of the reason may be your disfigurement, but partly these are simply skills you lack. Not that you don't have other talents. More valuable talents. But that management skill is precisely the skill that a growth company like AI Squared will require." He shook his head sadly. "We're not thieves, Lem. Our responsibility is to take the company in a direction that's best for all its shareholders. Yourselves included. That's what we intend to do. And this square hole requires a square peg – which you are so obviously not. I don't mean to be unpleasant about it, but our decisions are final. And correct."

Say something, Lem, Adele implored silently. He had to do it himself; intervention by her, or anyone – it was too late for George – would only make it worse.

Lem remained silent. Franklin Fischer sat down heavily in his chair and turned to Peter Steinitz.

"As for you, my hot-tempered friend –" he began.

"Screw you, Fischer," Peter interjected. "Go fuck yourself in the ass. New York faggot gonif."

Franklin Fischer stood again and walked to the other end of the room. "Carolyn," he said without turning back. "Tell them. Tell them I'm a patient man, but there are limits to my patience. Ask them what they're worth, if they're worth enough to display this kind of juvenile contempt. Tell them the amount of stock they've got is pocket change to me. Tell them if they're not out of here in thirty seconds I may change my mind. I may just buy them back for peanuts and let them sue. Tell them what legal fees will run them. Ask them what they're worth."

"School's out, little boys," Carolyn said, smiling, with quiet sarcasm. "It's grown-up time. You'd better go." The room fell silent.

Lem sat motionless. "I let you down, Pete," he said after a time. Adele was close enough to see tears in his eyes.

Peter stood up. "Time to go, big guy," he answered. "We're not doing ourselves any good here. We'll leave, we'll think, we'll talk." He lifted Lem up bodily by his arm. The agenda (revised) and the other papers went back in the briefcases. The door closed behind them.

Carolyn let out a low, satisfied chuckle. Harry Greube smiled shyly, a smile of victory. George kept his eyes locked on the table.

"Good riddance," Victor Podgorny said firmly.

*

The tension in the room evaporated. "Well done, Harry," Carolyn smiled. "Well done, everybody." George refused to lift his head.

"What's going on?" Adele cried, leaping to her feet. "What have you done? *Why?!?*"

No one answered. "What do you mean, breach of fiduciary duty?" she continued, advancing on Harry. "They don't have real operations yet! What I suggested was completely experimental. It's still a development stage company. They couldn't breach their fiduciary duty if they tried! What were you talking about?"

Harry shot a quick, eloquent glance at Carolyn. *Didn't she know?* Carolyn shook her head, an almost imperceptible negative nod. *Enough.* She remembered now the one missing file.

"Peter Steinitz was right, wasn't he?" she said, taking them all in a look. "It's a fix. You planned this from the beginning." No one answered – a series of furtive, guilty looks and movements.

Then, all at once, without any warning, without any chance to prepare herself, the storm was upon her. What Lem must be feeling! How cruelly he'd been used, all his legitimate ambitions thrown back into his face as taunts! What he must think of all of them, of her! She stood now before the pack the one way she had never wanted to be seen, the squishy, soft girl fully visible, biting at her lip, tears welling in her eyes, breath becoming short, her heart so very visible, so very vulnerable, on her sleeve.

"Poor little Rebecca," said Carolyn, her voice an odd combination of contempt and sympathy. "It always hurts when you get your cherry popped. Or haven't you found that out yet? You know, I've wondered."

Podgorny laughed.

"Hey!" said George, finally looking up. "Knock it off. Leave her alone."

She could not bear to face them any longer. Mustering as much dignity as she had left – next to none – she turned and walked briskly out of the room, down the hall.

*

She was in luck. They were standing before the elevator, waiting.

"–got at least to get our own lawyer," Pete was saying. "We have to get a second opinion about where we stand." Lem remained silent.

"If there's anything I can do," said Adele, hoping the two wouldn't notice the quaver in her voice.

Pete brightened. Lem straightened up.

"Yes," said Lem. "There's something you can do. You can get lost. You can leave me alone. Haven't you done enough already?" Surprised, Pete turned to him. "You weren't there, Pete," Lem continued. "It was when you and Chen went down to the trading room. I talked to her about all the stuff that bothered us. I asked if we could trust her. I made it personal, a point of personal honor. She said we could, that everything was all right. I believed her. Later, after the first board meeting, I believed her again. You're the worst, Adele," he added, turning to her, his voice flat and dull. "The very worst of all. I was on guard with the others, but you took me good. You were perfect. What a number you did in the restaurant. Congratulations."

"I didn't know anything at all about this," she managed to sputter.

"You're lying," Lem said evenly.

"No, she isn't," Pete interposed.

"You don't know," Lem retorted.

"Yes, I do," Pete answered. "Look at her."

"Can you honestly tell me you had no idea that something like this was coming down?" Lem said, looking harder at her. She met his gaze. "Can you say that?"

"No," she said at last, gathering herself, "I can't. I had suspicions, I had doubts, I had my own questions – even before I met you. But I didn't have anything concrete. I was afraid if I said anything I'd increase the paranoia. That it would make things worse."

"Also upset your boyfriend," Lem said in the same dead tone of finality. *No*, she thought frantically, *he wasn't anything to me then. I was so proud to be a part of what you were doing. I didn't want to risk doing anything that might upset it. That has to be what it was.* But she wasn't sure.

"You could have told us what you thought – let me know your suspicions – let us make up our own minds about it. That's really all I asked you to do that day. You said you would, but you didn't." *He's right*, she thought. "And we're not paranoid, Adele. It wasn't paranoia. They really were out to get us." He smiled a feeble, bitter smile.

"How you must have laughed at me. How you all must have laughed. What a big joke." He suddenly pushed his front teeth out, ridiculously exaggerating his overbite. "All my life. 'It's God's will, Lem,' my dad said. 'Four eyes.' 'Beaver tooth.' Nerd. Always. What a fool I was even to think. . . I thought I was handling it right, but they run a pretty woman lawyer on me and I fall hook, line, and sinker. Sorenson must have seen what a horny bastard I was on the road." He turned to Peter Steinitz. "Fischer was right about the pattern, Pete. And he was right about the rest. I was the one who egged you guys on; I thought, if we could pull this off, everything would be different. At least for me. I was kidding myself. I should have known. We'd all be better off if we'd stayed at Ithaca. Chiang was right."

That's not true, she thought, with a lump in her throat. *You're worth a hundred of everyone in that room put together.*

Including George.

Including me.

"Ten minutes more of this," said Pete, "and you'll be already to enrol in Self-Pitiers Anonymous. C'mon – we gotta find a lawyer and figure out a way to get back in the game." Lem nodded without looking at him. Pete turned to her. "You think of anything, let us know?" Adele nodded. "You got fucked, too, I can tell. I remember how you liked the program. Lem'll come around."

"No," he answered dully. "She's one of them. She's the worst."

"Franklin Fischer had no right to talk to you like that," Adele finally managed to choke out.

"Why not?" Lem asked distantly. "He was correct. Statements with a positive truth value always have utility." The elevator door opened. "Hey, and don't you kid *yourself*. Fischer's not the main man. It was George Sorenson who set this up."

"Sorenson," Peter Steinitz nodded affirmatively. "He's the brains in the outfit. Anyone can see that. Fischer's just a thief."

Lem and Peter stepped into the elevator. He turned.

"Your lover," he said bitterly, as the door closed. Adele stood silent for a moment, then moved automatically, unthinkingly down the hall.

But I only – she began. *Shut up, stupid,* something inside her answered ruthlessly, *he's right. Cut the wounded nobility crap. You saw it as your golden career opportunity; that's why you kept your mouth shut. And later? You knew he wasn't being straight. You didn't press him because you were falling in love with him. Lem was right about that, too.*

If I'd given them two percent of the attention I gave to Tom. . .

Without noticing, she came to the boardroom door and pushed it open. Franklin Fischer, Carolyn, Harry Greube, and Victor Podgorny – the four of them had gone. George Sorenson stood alone on the other side of the room.

He looked frightened; she could say that much for him. Outside, behind him, the sky had become even darker.

*

"You lied to me," she said incredulously. "You held me in your arms, you looked me in the eye, you kissed me, and you *lied* to me."

"Yes," he answered, then went on, very, very quietly: "You weren't supposed to see this."

"Why?" she asked, in the same bewildered tone. "Why?"

"For you. For me. Because the plan was too far down the road," he answered. "Because I had no choice. If I'd told you the truth, I'd have had to get you completely involved. Or you'd have screwed it up. It wouldn't work either way."

"I don't understand," she said, shaking her head, still dazed. "The AI program is worthless without Lem and the others. Without them, it's experimental junk."

He shrugged. "It's not worthless. In fact, it's the key, the mainspring of all the rest. In the shape it is right now." His tone became crisper and further. "Monday we're going to merge AI Squared with a little computer company called Astraper. Do you know it?"

"Yes," she said. "It competes with EBS in a lot of computer markets. Not very well."

"Right," he nodded. "What you probably didn't know is that it's controlled by Victor Podgorny. After the merger's done, right afterwards –" he sucked in his breath – "we're going to put EBS into play."

"Into play? You mean, an acquisition? A hostile takeover bid? *EBS?*"

"Yeah," he nodded.

"But that's impossible," she said, bewildered again. "The number of shares – I mean – what's the word?"

"Float."

"The float must be in the billions. The tens of billions."

"Right." He nodded. "It is impossible. But it is possible to scare the hell out of them. The stock's scattered all over the map, no major owners; there aren't any strong managers, either. The go-getters left long ago. There's going to be a lot of publicity about the magic new program Astraper is going to put resident on all its machines. It makes one hell of a demo, you know that yourself.

452

It's going to scare the hell out of EBS management. All there is over there are lawyers and candy ass MBAs. Ivy League chicken shit. They'll break and run. They always do. Sharks can't swallow whales, Adele. But whales flee from sharks just the same."

She nodded. He continued: "Plus I got a line in to some of those middle managers. I've wired that to the extent I can. So EBS'll come around. Especially when the terms are as reasonable as I'm going to make them. All I want is one little thing – not money, not a division, not even a product – just an exclusive license for one product, only one, at a fair and reasonable price, for a five-year period."

She saw it all now. "Rights to VINUX," she said woodenly. "That's how you're going to get it for the Project. Greenmailing EBS." He nodded solemnly.

"So you used me," she went on. "Lem was right. You used me to charm him into bringing AI Squared to Hapgood. So you could get that phony opinion from Greube. That was what was happening that day I went through the memo. You were sizing me up to see how I'd appeal to him."

He nodded again. "I didn't know you then."

"It's brilliant," she said hollowly. "You're very good at this, George. I didn't realize. You planned everything."

He shook his head negatively. "No. Not everything. What's happened between me and you wasn't anything I planned. I didn't figure that you'd become more important to me than anything else in the world."

"Perhaps that was a reason for calling it all off," she said.

He shook his head. "You were a big reason for going forward."

She half-closed her eyes. "Please – *please* – don't tell me that this – this – awful scene – this morning had anything to do with me."

He hesitated. "Do you want me to lie to you again?"

"No," she responded after a moment.

"It had everything to do with you," he said. "Finishing the deal is the only way I get free of all this. It's the only way I can be the kind of man you want me to be – the kind people don't talk about. It's the only way I can do the things I want to do for you. It's the only way I could get you some of what you need."

"What do you mean?" she asked, her eyes widening. "Do you mean–?"

"Yeah," he nodded. "I worked it out with Fischer. We optioned a big block of stock in Astraper for you five days ago. In your name." He picked up a three-page document. "Not enough to make you rich – not these days – but enough to give you a stake. When the stock moves, it's going to have a minimum mid-seven figure value." He shrugged. "Soft, eleven or twelve mil. Probable, eight. Five's as hard as rock. Cinch."

"Why?" she asked, aghast. Lem Michaels – the program – destroyed for her??

"So you'll be all right. So whatever happens between us, I won't have to know that you're somewhere being ground down, the way everyone else is. So you'll have a chance."

No! something inside of her began to scream, *not like this! Not vampire style, the blood price paid by someone else!* He paused, smiled a tight, nervous little smile. "I didn't want to play Joe Hero in front of you. I don't like that. I didn't want you to know. Not until later. So it wouldn't make any difference. The goddamn deal's going to be a money machine for everybody. Your share's not a big deal."

"Victor Podgorny?" she asked out loud.

He half-smiled. "Victor thinks the takeover plan is the whole plan. He's a fool. When we fold the tent, he's going to the cleaners. Don't worry about him. He deserves it. He's a pig."

"And Lem? And Pete? Chiang?" Her eyes welled with tears.

"They're going to do very well," he said uneasily. "End up very rich young guys. About the same as you. Astraper is going to go on a long ride before the balloon bursts. Trust me, I'll get 'em out in time."

"How can you ask me to trust you? How can you even use that word right now?"

"Because the time for lying is behind, Adele," he answered. "You know I'm being level with you now." He changed his tone. "I love you, Paloma. You know that. All this had to be. You gotta know that, too."

The other day when he spoke it, the word had had its own music. Today it clanked in her ear like a penny rattling in a beggar's tin cup.

"And the program? The AI program? What happens to it?"

He shrugged. "An idea. You can't destroy an idea. If it's strong enough, it'll resurface."

*

He doesn't know, does he? she thought, her heart breaking. *How could anyone so smart, so good at plans, have miscalculated so badly?*

This is the worst. Worse than the anguish she'd felt on Lem's behalf, his dreams in shreds, worse than her own humiliation, worse than all the rage and anger. She'd come to cherish that little plant, the stick in the ground, blossoming so unexpectedly, looked forward to nurturing and tending it, to its growth. But on this morning the seedling had been ripped savagely out of the earth in which it nursed. Now it lay on barren soil, leaves scattered, roots drying in the sun.

You don't know yet, do you, George?

*

"I'd better go," she said, looking away from him, stepping towards her seat and her briefcase.

"I was hoping you'd stay for lunch. Maybe we could start to get this over with?" he said. She shook her head without looking up. "Adele?" he asked, becoming more anxious. "Paloma?

"Look, it had to happen. There was nothing I could do. It had gone too far. It's the way the world is," he said, becoming more and more tense. "Lem and Pete. It's inevitable. They're sheep in a land of wolves. They don't know how to look out for themselves. If it hadn't been us, it would have been someone else. No way to stop it. I was taking care of you, of us. I can do that. I didn't mean to hurt you. Look at me, please? Adele, look at me!"

She looked up, said nothing. He was beginning to comprehend, to feel the chasm that had opened between them.

"Look!" he suddenly exploded. "Do you think I like–?" He threw up his hands. "I been watching these Punch and Judy shows for twenty years. Assholes and jerk-offs like Franklin and Podgorny, guys who have to have blood as well as money. Do you think I didn't know he was twisting the knife? 'Cutting the helots down to size,' Franklin calls it, and I know he means me, too, you don't have to tell me. You, too, if he got the chance. Damn it, I'm so tired of this shit!" She locked the briefcase without looking up, afraid of looking up. Now he comprehended fully what had happened. "You weren't supposed to see this," he said in complete, desperate frustration.

"Why?" she asked tonelessly, straightening up and meeting his eye. "So you could lie to me? So you could take me to Zihuateneo and we'd both pretend it never happened?" A long silence.

"Yes," he said, finally, meeting her eyes, not without nobility, even now. "No. I don't know. I don't know what I was gonna say. I only know I didn't want you to see this."

"I think it's better that I did," she said softly.

"Damn it, why won't you understand?!" he exploded. "Jeez. Gimme a break! Why don't you get it? How far do you think you're going to get without any capital, without a stake? How long do you think you'll keep on being you? Working for Carolyn? Don't you know what's going to happen to you? Don't you realize – couldn't you see –" he picked up the discarded AI Squared business plan and shook it at her – "this wasn't the beginning of your big success?

Getting mixed up with this? This was the beginning of the end for you. I couldn't let that happen. I had to let it go and hope I could square it later with you. I was taking a chance I'd screw up everything. Don't you understand?"

A distant memory of her meditation in Carolyn's office the day Jenet first mentioned Thomas Newcombe echoed then in her consciousness, the faraway worry that this hard world would mold her to its own image in spite of herself. All the compromises she'd made over AI Squared came back to her. George had worried about it, too, and had been willing to risk everything to prevent it. The nobility she'd always suspected in him, now emergent, fully visible. . . and all it did was make everything harder.

"How can you be so goddamned innocent?!" He ran his fingers through his hair. "Why do you get to me the way you do!?" There was nothing more to say. His tone changed, became almost pleading: "Say something, please? Please?" he begged. She looked up, shrugged a helpless shrug, and picked up her briefcase.

His tone softened further. He picked up the option. "Doesn't this mean anything to you?"

She felt a strange sensation on her face, hot and wet. Tears trickled down her cheeks, for the first time in a long, long time. "I know what it means, George. It's an awful lot of money." So much money that she was not going to think more of it, leave while the raw image of Lem was still with her, before the thought of what the money would buy, what it could insure, clawed its way into her thought processes. She turned and went through the door and down the corridor, moving briskly, then more briskly. She did not want him to catch up with her.

"Adele!" he called, as she neared the elevator.

"Adele!" he called again, now with a note of panic in his voice.

*

There it was.

Funny, she'd woken that morning consumed by it, dreading it – then forgotten all about it as she roamed the rainy streets around noon, under her umbrella, appetiteless, fleeing the look in Lem's face, mourning the loss of George. Nothing had altered the chemistry. He had never been more appealing, large-souled, and protective. She longed to accept the comfort he had to offer. But to forgive him she first had to forgive herself, and that wasn't possible. A chasm had opened between them.

She remembered Gertha only as she returned to her office, hoped for a moment – but there it was. The messenger had made good time. It was an ordinary boxed file, not much different in color than the ones in Adele's office, except discolored and splotchy, probably from one or more alcoholic accidents.

Send it back, something inside her said. *Don't go near it.* Should be at NATPE anyway. *No.* This is the day. *Nothing happens by chance.* First, the enormity of the morning; now, the afternoon. Logical. Besides, Carolyn and Franklin Fischer would still be out gloating somewhere. No one would miss her for an hour or two. That might be all it would take.

She did not want to risk interruption. She thought for a moment, then picked up the file and moved down to Greg Steuer's old office, Glee Club headquarters, temporarily vacant. The door closed softly behind her. She left the light off. The fluorescent illumination from the hall would do well enough.

She undid the cord around the file.

*

The contents consisted of one large, thick manila folder, to which a small photograph envelope was attached. *Go in order.*

Three photographs were contained in the small envelope. Three people were in the first – man, woman, and child, attractive, naturally posed. The baby leaned out of the frame, hand extended toward the camera, with a marvelous half-moon grin, ready for anything. She studied it more closely; with a small shock, she realized she was looking at a picture of Tom as an infant.

She examined the picture in detail. These people were Anthony Markland, Rachel Weinstein, and their son. Rachel had a brightness of her own, similar to her son's, obviously photogenic, almost leaping off the page. Husband and wife were about the same height; hers was a large-boned beauty, a big woman. Tom had inherited his frame and the general outlines of his features from his mother. His eyes were his father's.

The second was a Polaroid, Tom sitting on Gertha's lap, holding a large, white stuffed bear. She'd been right at Gertha's apartment; the picture Gertha had turned down had been an enlargement of this. She felt a small thrill of triumph, then remembered this was hardly the day to be congratulating herself on her deductive powers. Tom smiled in this one, too, but the smile had become tentative, uncertain. Innocence had been lost.

The first photograph had born no legend, but something was written on the back of this, in faded pencil. *This is the day Johnny goes to court!*

The third photograph puzzled her the most. Two people, man and woman, a somewhat stiffly constructed portrait, that seemed to bear no relationship to the other two. She turned it over; nothing on the back. She looked hard, harder. Got it. The woman had to be Mary Klein, Rachel

Weinstein's sister, but a faded, bleached out version thereof, with none of Rachel's vitality. The man was probably her husband.

She replaced the pictures carefully, taking one last look at the baby picture. *You must have been a beautiful baby.* He had been – marvelous, open. Something appalling had happened. The answer lay in the large manila folder she was holding. She felt a twinge of pure fear.

Nonsense, she told herself. This is the day. She positioned the manila folder in front of her, straightened up in her chair, and opened it.

Joseph Wurtenbaugh

TALES OF CHILDHOOD

H er head fell out of her hands, almost hit the desk.
Fool. Idiot. Idiot. Moron. Nincompoop. So obvious. So incredibly obvious.

That was no birthmark. He hadn't had any accident to his left hand. It had been systematically – what did the report say, so clinically? *Either struck repeated blows with a small hammer or – or – a vise?* Mangled slowly, slowly, over time. One finger at a time.

And the birthmark, the birthmark – she'd wondered at its size that night. *Scar tissue consistent with intense, repeated scaldings.*

She stared at the first pages of the file, hoping she could disbelieve, knowing she could not.

He'd been. . .

*

The horror of the police and medical examiner reports was intensified, not diminished, by the cold professional language. A first grade teacher at the elementary school that one Mary Beth Klein attended overheard the child laughing, telling her friends about Johnny, the boy at her house who was always bad, who lived in a closet. A few days later, she overheard one of Mary Beth's friends repeating the same thing. The stories sounded sufficiently disturbing and authentic to prompt her to call the police.

An Officer Dickson stopped by on routine patrol. Finding the Klein residence deserted, he pushed open the door and looked around. Through an open door, he noticed a closet door with a chain lock on it. Curious, he took off the lock and opened the door. In the closet he found a half-dressed male child, later identified as Jonathan Markland, aged four years and three months. Three fingers on his left hand had been mutilated; huge areas of discolored scar tissue were observed on his back. The closet contained no clothes, only a workbench with a vise and small hammer. A teakettle sat upon it. Dickson also observed what he thought were bloodstains on the light wood floor.

Dickson wrapped the silent child in a blanket and went for the phone. Mary Klein arrived home at that moment. Indignant, she demanded the return of the boy, insisting that the police officer had no business in her home, no right to take him, demanding that he leave and leave Johnny behind him. Sullivan informed her that it was too late, that he had already phoned Child Protective Services, and that she was under arrest for felony child endangerment, assault with intent to inflict severe bodily injury, mayhem, and attempted murder.

The child was taken to the children's shelter, where he was released to the custody of a social worker named Gertha Daniels. According to the fragmented statement he gave, he had spent most of the last twenty-seven months in the closet. On those rare occasions when he was out, or company came to the house, he had remained silent about the abuse. From what the social worker could piece together, the Kleins had evidently told him his mother and father would one day return to him if he did, that he was in the closet because he'd done something bad to make them go away.

Mary Klein was taken to the woman's detention center, where she was Mirandized and questioned. She informed her interrogators that the child had suffered his injuries by accident, that he had been locked in the closet on the afternoon for his own safety during her temporary absence. She repeatedly threatened the investigating officers with civil lawsuits.

Her husband, Herbert Klein, was arrested at his home upon his return in the evening from his dental offices, and transported to the police station. He was observed to be visibly pale and upset when he arrived at the station. During interrogation, after receiving Miranda warnings, he at first denied any wrongdoing; then broke down in tears, and informed the officers that everything that had happened was his wife's fault, that he had had nothing to do with anything, that he should not be blamed. Questioning ceased at that point because of the arrival of Vincent Driscoll, retained counsel for the Kleins.

The medical report confirmed that the discolorations were due to scarring caused by repeated exposures to heat, probably in the form of scalding water. Based on x-rays taken immediately after the arrest, the examiner opined that the initial maiming of the left hand had begun approximately two years earlier. (Adele calculated about ninety days after the plane crash.) He took due note of the instrumentalities in the closet, was unable to state whether the hammer or the vise had been the implement used. But he was certain it was one or the other.

*

Gertha had written her first note. It read:

If you're like me when I was your age, you're probably asking 'why?' I've been twenty-five years in this business and I don't know. In some of the police reports I didn't keep, there was evidence that Johnny's daddy had left a fair amount of money. They wanted to get their hands on it; that came out later. But if Johnny died it would all have gone to his dad's people. So Johnny had to stay alive.

But why they couldn't just steal from him? Why she had to lock him in a closet? Why she had to do the other things? I don't know. My best guess is those pictures I put at the start of this. I think Mary Klein felt her sister got all the breaks from God – she was prettier, she was smarter – Mary was the reasonable facsimile her whole life. That's why I put her picture in my file; that's my best guess. I think she hated her sister from before she could remember. Then, when Johnny came to live with them, she saw it happening again, the same dazzle, that she didn't have, that her kids didn't have – and she couldn't stand it. That's what I think. No one will ever know.

What I am certain of is that Mary Klein was psychotic about Johnny – all you had to do was meet her once to know that – and Herbert was a namby-pamby, anything-you-say-boss coward. And we all knew, right from the start, all of us, that they were good for it. Roy Dickson said he knew the second she came in the house.

I thought at the time that would be enough.

*

She read on, numb. Xeroxed copies of three letters on official stationery followed.

Ronert Tieger, Director
Child Protective Services
— — — — — — County, New York
January 15, 19-- *(twenty-three years earlier)*

Gertha Daniels, M.S.S.
Dear Gertha,

Sue Reed has mentioned to me that you are signing out the Markland boy to yourself for overnights on a regular basis. Any special reason?

Very truly yours
Ron

–

January 17, 19--
Dear Ron,

Don't sweat it. It's not a biggie. When he first came in, he was as traumatized as any kid I've ever seen. Sue agreed. Children's' shelter services didn't seem adequate. So I've been taking him home with me. Nothing goes on, but a lot of rocking and hugging and talking. (No Black Power, if that was what you were worried about. He's a little young for politics.) Also, I bought him a big white teddy bear and mutilated its left hand. It's his favorite thing. We do a lot of talking about that bear, about how it hurt its hand and what it's going to say in court about it someday. (Can you get the county to pay me back? Can ya? Can ya? Please, massa?) I promise you the bear's going to tell the truth.

Anyway, Johnny's doing great. He's quite an amazingly resilient little fellow. If you have to worry about anybody, worry about me. I'm falling in love with him.

All Power to the People,

Gertha

–

Susan Reed
Director, Children's Shelter
April 15, 19– –

Dear Gertha,

I thought I'd drop you a note about your little protégé. Johnny's progress is sensational! That rocking chair of yours must have some magic in it. When he first came here, he was so withdrawn; now, when we do our singing, he sits in the middle and sings out as loudly as the rest. He's become a sort of mascot to the older girls, the cutest little cuddlebug.

I can't be entirely sure, but I'm beginning to suspect that your Johnny is an exceptionally gifted young man. He sits in with the first graders now – there isn't much else to do here mornings – and Becky Mathis swears he understands everything. Sarah Harrison – one of the Harrison twins, the molest case – has taken to reading him stories. Sarah says he gives her some of the words, although that young lady is hardly known for her truthfulness. It's too early to say, but I think you might have caught yourself quite a catch.

When I think how he looked his first night here! Every time I see that poor little hand I want to kill someone!!

Anyway, congratulations! Well done!! Sure hope the trial goes well!!!

Love,

Sue

–

Susan Reed had drawn a little face in the "o" of the word "love."

Adele folded the letters in half, moving on. Underneath them was the title page of the transcript of a judicial hearing.

People of the State of New York,

```
Plaintiff
v.
Herbert Klein and Mary Klein
Defendants
```

```
October 18, 19--
```

The transcript was 286 pages long; she thumbed through it rapidly. Young Tom had been on the witness stand for nearly three-fourths of the time. It made sense to go through that carefully, skim the rest. She turned quickly towards the place where his testimony began, overshot it by a few pages. She began to look for the right place, when her eye fell on a passage Gertha had highlighted:

```
Q. You said you were told your mommy would come back if you were
good and said nothing, is that right?
A. Yes.
Q. But your mommy hasn't come back, has she?
A. No.
Q. And that's because you were bad, wasn't it? Because you got into
trouble and you told lies?
```

Her blood turned to ice. Her breath stopped. She could not believe her eyes. She reread the passage twice. She turned the page. It went on. And on.

And on.

-

He had not confined himself to a single question, a single page, or even a single hour. He had made this the persistent, hammering theme of a brutal inquiry that lasted more than a day. *You were a bad boy, Johnny. You're lying, aren't you? You wouldn't have been punished if you weren't bad. Your mother wouldn't have left if you'd been good.* Few of the questions had any relation at all to the criminal case. It was not a cross examination intended to elucidate truth; it was a cross examination intended to destroy.

```
Q. If you were good, your mommy would be back, wouldn't she?
A. Yes.
Q. But she isn't back - and that's because you weren't good, isn't
it?
A. I was good.
```

Once or twice he'd tried to fight back:

```
Q. She might have come back if you hadn't lied, mightn't she?
A. I didn't lie. Maybe she will come back.
```

-

How could he? How could anyone? Adele thought dazedly. She read and reread, not quite able to believe what she was reading. The scene etched itself in her consciousness – the child barely tall enough to see over the witness stand, the judge towering over him, the attorney five times his weight, the defendants glaring sullenly at him – a little boy confronting the inexplicable hatred of adults. Without any help. Without any caring. *How could it be? Where was everybody?* How could the reporter, the clerk, the others – how could all of them have just sat there?

I'll bet, she thought, half-aloud, gulping for air, almost sobbing, *I'll bet they didn't even let him keep the bear.* She paged quickly through the transcript to the place where the cross-examination began.

Mr. Driscoll: Before I begin my examination, your Honor, I would request the court order that the stuffed toy the witness is holding be removed from young master Markland's lap.

Mr. Simpson: I would object for the record, your Honor. The witness will not be five years old until next Thursday. I am informed by the social worker that the toy is important to his testimony.

Mr. Driscoll: This witness is no more entitled to the use of a prop than any other complaining witness in a criminal prosecution. Young master Markland may be only five, but he is old enough to lie, to betray. He is old enough to be taken into the home of Dr. and Mrs. Klein out of kindness, out of love, and to repay their favors, the hospitality of their home, by embroiling two of the most respected citizens in this community in an outrageous slander. I ask that the teddy bear be removed.
The Court: The bailiff will remove the stuffed bear.

The weariness that had besieged Adele temporarily disappeared, as she read on and on. No one had intervened. No one had done anything. *Put it down*, something inside her said, *close the damn thing.* But she could not. Compulsively, she read on. *Get a hold of yourself*, another voice cautioned. All this happened twenty-three years ago. There's nothing anyone can do now. But a storm of violent emotion, a combination of outraged justice and vengeful fury, was mounting inside her. *This is my Tom I'm talking about, yours, using him like that.*

Nothing had gone right.

The Court: I will tell you, Mr. Simpson, I have developed the gravest doubts about the credibility of young master Markland. That there has been coaching - considerable coaching of this witness - is apparent to this court, I have raised three children and I have

six grandchildren. None of them ever spoke like that when they were
five. He sounds like he's ten. If it were real.

I can believe none of your children talked like that, she thought viciously,
you miserable, contemptible old fart.

Yet despite all the innuendo, all the sarcasm, all the expression of
doubt, all the remorseless, unending psychological sadism, the reality of the
case had come through.

Q. What did you do all that time you said you stayed in the closet?
A. I told myself stories. And my numbers. Daddy said always do your
numbers. I did my numbers.
Q. Numbers?
A. Daddy said to always do my numbers.
Q. How did you do numbers in a closet?
A. On my fingers. In my mind.
Q. Really. What a bright boy you must be. What did you learn?
A. Sevenses are different than tenses.
Q. Really. We'll all have to remember that. Write that down, Madam
Reporter, a seven is different than a ten. Did you learn that even
bright boys have to be punished when they're bad? When they lie?
  ‒

He meant base seven and base ten, asshole, she thought savagely. *He knew
more about math when he was four than you ‒ than you ‒* she leaned back from the
desk, shivering, as wave after wave of pure, undifferentiated fury swept through
her frame. She settled herself down and went on reading.

The hearing had gone rapidly after Driscoll had finished with young
Tom. The prosecutor had called other witnesses to the stand.

The teacher who had overheard May Beth Klein giggling over the plight
of the boy in the closet? Objection, hearsay; only imminent complaints of the
victim himself or admissions of the defendants are admissible. *Sustained.*

The observations of Officer Dickson of bloodstains in the closet where
the boy had been locked? Objection, product of an illegal entry; Officer Dickson
should not have entered the Klein home without a warrant. *Sustained.*

The testimony of the doctors who had x-rayed the hand and observed
the scar tissue, as to the period over which the fractures and lesions had
occurred? Objection, inadequate preliminary foundation; the medical theory on
which such opinions are based is new and untested. *Sustained.*

The Klein's had taken the stand at the hearing, rather unorthodox
procedure in a felony defense as Adele understood it. But it worked for them.
Mary Klein insisted adamantly upon her innocence. What sort of child was
Jonathan? *Jonathan was an unruly, undisciplined child from the moment I took custody*

of him. My sister had spoiled him. How did he get the scar tissue on his back? *He spilt boiling water on himself. He had been reprimanded for reaching on the stove before. It didn't work.* How was his hand injured? *Herbert likes to work with wood. He has power tools in the basement. Jonathan turned on the lathe and badly injured himself. He'd been disciplined about that before, too.* Why aren't there any hospital or medical records? *Herbert is a trained health professional. He had all he needed to repair the damage at home – an anaesthetic, Xylocaine...*

(Gertha had added an asterisk there. The footnote at the bottom of the page read:

The receipts for the Xylocaine were all for delivery to his office. The Kleins had two children under twelve. No one in their right mind would keep that stuff at home. Plus Johnny wasn't unruly at all. He was one of the sweetest kids we ever had in the shelter. You can tell the bad ones; most of 'em kick up their heels from day one. Mary Klein was lying through her teeth. Everyone in the court knew it. The judge knew it.)

...splints, antiseptic. There was no need to go to the hospital. Is there anything more you wish to say? *Yes. To believe this is true, you have to believe that my husband and I are monsters. We're not. What is true is that little boy over there is a vicious, spoiled, lying brat. He's getting even with us for the very moderate discipline he refused to accept. I only wish my sister were alive to see what she's wrought.*

Herbert Klein also took the stand. His testimony was more subdued, but also unequivocal. His demeanor when he arrived at the police station? He'd been devastated by the accusation; also, Officer Driscoll's bearing and attitude in the police car had unnerved him. The statements he'd made about it being his wife's fault? All he meant was that it was her fault for accepting Johnny into their home.

Mr. Driscoll: Defense rests. Submitted.
Mr. Simpson: Nothing more for the State. Submitted.
The Court: Thank you. I think I've made my concerns about this case apparent throughout this proceeding. I have the gravest possible doubts about the veracity of the complaining witness. The court must note the utter absence of any corroborating evidence of his accusation. It is entirely possible, even probable, that the injuries occurred in the manner Mrs. Klein indicated. The record does not support a holding.

—

The Kleins were most honorably discharged.

Adele sat back in her chair, reeling. It couldn't be. It could not be. Such things don't happen. The inexplicable hostility of the court to a pre-schooler; the perfunctory way in which the state's attorney walked through his case. Didn't anybody–

Suddenly Peter Steinitz's voice from the morning echoed through her brain.

It was a fix. Don't you see?

Perhaps not money. Perhaps – worse – simply that a member of the club had been accused by an outsider. But for whatever reason, the pack had gathered together to protect one of its own.

Gertha had written another note. It read:

I took him back to my apartment after it was over, for one night before he had to go back to the Shelter. He didn't talk at all to me, didn't say anything. We were back to square one. In one day, the bastards had undone everything it took me eight months to accomplish.

He went back to the Shelter the next day. But he wasn't any cuddle bug anymore; the liveliness was gone. He spent all his time with the Harrison twin, reading stories.

And he never sang again.

Adele noticed there was something wrong with her left hand.

*

She'd been turning the pages with her right. As she had, her left hand had been digging into the desktop, as if some part of her subconscious being had thought, in some *Twilight Zonish* kind of way, to pull the top off of time, seize these demons in the midst of their monstrosity, and put an end to it. The wood filings underneath her nails had ultimately distracted her. She looked down; unconsciously, she'd dug three furrows into the desk, half an inch deep. The gashes showed a newly wounded pink. She wondered for a second who they'd blame, Greg Steuer or someone else. She'd broken a nail.

For the first time in her life, Adele experienced genuine, murderous rage. It burned through her entire soul, blistered her heart. *Did they know what they'd done? Did any of them? Did that monster lawyer?* How did things go at the office, honey? A real good day, sweetheart. Terrorized a kid.

–

Gertha's note continued:

That night was the first night in my life I bought liquor to get to sleep – a half-pint of vodka. I was shattered. I thought I'd done my best, but all I'd done was set Johnny up.

Still, I planned to make it up. I figured what I did once I could do again.

It didn't work out that way.

Two letters followed.

–

Ronert Tieger
Director, Children's Protective Services
October 29, 19--

Susan Reed
Director, Children's Shelter

Dear Susan:

It has been forcibly brought to my attention that certain social workers have been taking children resident in the shelter on overnight stays. This practice must stop. In particular, interactions between staff workers and children who are to be witnesses in ongoing litigation must cease. Above all, there is to be no further contact between Gertha Daniels and the Markland boy.

Sincerely,

Ron

—

Gertha Daniels, Social Worker
Department of Social Services

The Honorable Thomas Spencer
Judge, Supreme Court of New York
November 3, 19--
In re: Wardship of Markland

Your Honor,

Word has reached me through DSS that this court is seriously considering returning Jonathan Markland to the Klein household. If the court does that, they are going to kill him or injure him so badly there will be no recovery. If that happens, I can guarantee you everyone is going to hear about it – everyone. Don't think you'll be able to cover it up, because you won't.

Don't do it.

Sincerely,
Gertha Daniels, M.S.W.

—

A police report, dated November 9, 19--, followed. Roy Dickson in the company of Gertha Daniels had reinterviewed the little boy in the Children's Shelter. He now disclaimed all memory of what had happened to him; he couldn't say; he wouldn't say; he didn't remember – above all, more than anything, he did not want to go back to court. Refiling of the charges before a different judge or in a new venue was out of the question. Driscoll had won completely.

(The day of the autumnal equinox; the day she met Tom. The party had swirled around them. Jenet had stood back as she introduced Adele to the tall, quiet man. *I admire your courage,* he'd said. *I'm scared to death of courts and law myself.*)

Dickson did not remain coolly professional throughout this report, as he had in the first. It concluded:

Despite the travesty that occurred at the first hearing and the present state of mind of the victim, this officer would make the strongest possible recommendation that the case be refiled and prosecuted to the full limits of law. This officer will never forget the discovery of the crime scene. The evil which occurred here must not be ignored.

The case was not refiled.

—

In re Wardship of Jonathan M.
November 16, 19–

The judge was the same as the one who'd sat at the preliminary hearing. It had to be unusual for a judge of the Supreme Court to designate himself as a sitting magistrate in a prelim, even in a small county, but Adele was bitter now, not surprised. She opened the cover and read.

The Court: Case of Markland. It was my original thought to terminate this wardship and return this child to a family which constitutes his only living family, and which can deal with his problems effectively. However, certain insinuations have been made and bruited about and—

Mr. Driscoll: Irresponsible insinuations, your Honor. Sorry to interrupt.

The Court: I agree, Mr. Driscoll, very irresponsible. The person who has made them will be dealt with. However, be that as it may, the accusations have been made — and as this is an active child who may do further injury to himself, I do not believe a return to his home would be prudent. I communicated these thoughts to you several days ago, Mr. Driscoll. Have your clients made any investigation of the placement alternatives available?

Mr. Driscoll: My clients have strong opinions on the subject, your Honor. They view young master Markland as uncontrollable; they could not take responsibility for the results in any normal family in which he was placed. Consequently, they have examined the feasibility of institutional placements. Although it will cause some drain on their personal finances, there is an institution in northeast New York. . .

—

Gertha wrote:

Back then, no one knew too much about Arbalest. But I did know it was intended for seriously delinquent and disturbed teenage boys. They had no one there under the age of twelve. I knew that the guy who ran it was heavily into extremely aggressive behavioral modification techniques. But I also knew he was a licensed psychiatrist and he had to be at least semi-professional. He had to know that the program he ran was no place for a five-year old.

What I should have done is gone to some other judge, or the papers, or something. But I knew I was on thin ice, and I wanted to keep my job. I wanted to do just enough to take care of business, and no more. You see, I had big plans for myself. I didn't want to blow it. So instead of making a fuss, I went down to the Children's Shelter and packed up for him on the day before he was going to leave. The next day I put his little suitcase with his little clothes inside, and I put his bear in his lap. That bear was more important to him than anything by that time. He waved a little wave and smiled, and I hoped again. Maybe it could still be all right. I wondered how long it would be – a week? ten days? – before they sent him back. They had to know how ridiculous it all was.

They kept him for the next seven and one-half years.

-

Dr. Paul Harlow, Director
Arbalest Children's Center
December 6, 19--

The Honorable Thomas Spencer
Judge, Supreme Court of New York
In re: Jonathan Markland

Dear Judge Spencer,

Pursuant to your order of November 16, 19--, we have completed an extensive evaluation of this referral. Our review included extensive interviews with Jonathan, analysis of the police report and reporter's transcript of the preliminary hearing, a long interview with the stepmother, Mrs. Herbert Klein, and consideration of your own comments on this situation.

Based on all the above, I am happy to report that we believe that Johnny can be benefited by placement at Arbalest. The unruliness of his reported behavior, the sophistication of his deceptive pattern, and his obstinacy in clinging to his account of his injuries – all seem to indicate that our therapeutic approach would be appropriate to this situation. He is clearly a manipulative youngster in need of a structured environment.

I have already discussed the financial arrangements with Dr. and Mrs. Klein.

Thank you for this referral.

Very truly yours,
Paul Harlow, M. D.

—

Memorandum
To: S. N. Deems, Staff member
From: P. Harlow, M. D.
Subject: Markland, Jonathan
Date: 12/23/--

To confirm in writing what I've told you repeatedly, despite the appearances Jonathan Markland has a confirmed character disorder, Oppositional Defiant Disorder (severe), DSM 313.81. All the investigators agreed that his injuries were self-inflicted, the result of repeated disobedience of parental commands. All agree that he has invented grandiose lies to justify himself. I have had the benefit of reviewing reports which I did not choose to include in the file. It is typical of this conduct disorder that it does not manifest itself as clearly in a clinical setting as it does among adults with whom the child is familiar. Your sympathy for this young man is completely misplaced.

If we are to have any success at all with this impudent young man, we must be consistently stern with this young person in the same manner as our other patients. No visitors. No Christmas privileges.

Above all, that ridiculous white bear he carries everywhere with him must be destroyed at once.

If you wish to resign before complying with these instructions, that is your decision. I might remind you that I have considerably more experience with antisocial children than you do, and that jobs of the type you hold are extraordinarily scarce in this part of New York. Of course, I could not give you a positive reference under those circumstances.

—

Gertha Daniels, Social Worker
-----, New York
January 22, 19--

Dear Gertha,

I want to reiterate how much I enjoyed your visit last Friday. The pleasure of making a new friend was some compensation for the sleepless weekend your file caused me.

I'm delaying telling you what I'm writing about, because I can hardly bear to write these words. I went out to see the Markland child first thing Monday morning. What a beautiful child! You are entirely correct that the pattern of abuse is obvious from the most cursory inspection. Only a judge could wonder about it! Johnny seemed reasonably well-nourished, if a little thin. He is very, very subdued – I am quite concerned about him. He spoke only monosyllables, except for one complete sentence, when he asked me about the bear you gave him.

Outside in the hall, the staff worker, a young woman named Deems, almost burst into tears. I hate to write this myself, Gertha, but the bear was destroyed a few weeks after he got there, on Harlow's orders. Also, Johnny didn't have Christmas or any of the other privileges that most of the other boys receive. Fortunately, he is too young and has been too deprived to realize the implications of the latter. The only thing he mentioned was the bear.

I have saved the worst until the last. I confronted Philip Harlow about all this. I was in a rage. Harlow told me that he fully intends to keep young Johnny for as long as necessary to 'treat' him. When I sputtered, he calmly reminded me of the judge's opinions, the stepmother's, and his own medical and psychiatric degrees – as if all that absolved him of not seeing what's there in front of his own two eyes! He fully intends to comply with the law, to have the regular tutor instruct him specially, etc, etc. But he will remain at Arbalest. Harlow absolutely will not permit you to visit him.

I don't know if you know this, but a lot of us locally have begun to suspect that Philip Harlow is a child hater; that the interest in hard cases is only a rationalization for doing what he wants to do anyway. As far as I'm concerned, I had all the proof I need today.

It broke my heart to say goodbye to Johnny, but I had to. I don't know what to do next, Gertha. If you have any ideas, please write or call as soon as you can.

Love,
Dora

-

Gertha Daniels, Social Worker
-----, New York
February 2, 19--

Dear Gertha,

This is a very painful letter for me to write. I have followed up on both of your suggestions. As to the first, the Legal Aid office here is very small and very understaffed. The young man I talked to was barely sympathetic; I suspect his primary objective was not to endanger his own career. In any case, he told me that the case, even if it were to be reopened, would have to be reopened in - ---- County, absent an extraordinary showing. He doubts a habeas corpus petition would be granted in this county. Most of all, Johnny would have to testify again, in front of the same lawyer, with the same judge somewhere in the courtroom. We both know that that's impossible.

Your other idea – to take it to the press. I have given that a great deal of thought. I have talked it over for a long time with my husband, who, believe me, is on our side in this. He has known Philip Harlow all his life and despises him.

Gertha, to put it bluntly, I can't make a cause celebre out of this. I was born in this town; so was Sam; I intend to live and die here. We have three children. The Harlows are a very powerful family here; Harlow built his so-called facility on what used to be his grandfather's orchard. I can't take them on. Even if I could get the local paper interested in this, how big a splash would it make? What would it really change?

What I've decided to do instead is build up a dossier, to build a stronger case. I spoke to Susan Deems, the staff worker. She's going to get me copies of everything that goes into the file about Johnny. Hopefully – before too much longer – I'll have enough so that no one can muddy the waters. I'm enclosing two things for you right now, a letter Harlow wrote to the judge in December and his instructions about the bear.

Don't call or write to me to tell me I'm a coward, because I know I am. But I have my own responsibilities to my own loved ones. I know you understand even if you don't agree.

I'm not going to write any more now. I'm going to do a little drinking and a little crying, and then go to bed. Please forgive me.

Love,
Dora

*

The emotional turmoil fell out of Adele's consciousness into her abdomen. A churning, unsettled nausea developed. She felt as if she were going to be sick.

She heard a commotion outside in the hall. The door to her regular office was wrenched open. "Adele?" she heard Willis Rutter ask.

She slid down in the chair of the dark office and listened.

"Where's Adele Jansen?" she overhead Willis Rutter asking Josh Palmdale.

"I don't know," Josh answered. "Isn't she in her office? Why?"

"Hoffman's fallen out of her tree. There's a mess of those TV execs who want to sign off on the Project. Some big shot should be there, only he isn't because he's looking for Jansen. Hoffman wants to murder her." He chuckled.

"Looks like all her chickens have finally come home to roost." He walked straight by the dark office in which she sat.

You got that right, Willis, she thought wearily. *Every last one of them*. Then she turned the next page and continued reading. She noticed her right hand was trembling.

*

The next section of Gertha's file consisted of nothing but the clinical notes Harlow had written over the next two and one-half years. Adele's rage, which had subsided to a dull ache, a turning of her stomach, slowly began to reignite. The pretense that there was any therapeutic purpose whatsoever in any of it faded and died. The mask slipped halfway, then fell off altogether. Philip Harlow was determined to break the child's will, for no better or more noble reason than it opposed his own – or perhaps because he hated and envied even the little glow that was left to Tom. Privileges were revoked, discipline ordered. On several occasions, the log noted the administration of corporal punishment. At one point, he was confined to his room for nearly six weeks. Harlow's idea of treating a child who'd been found locked in a closet was to lock him in another one. There was no indication that he ever had any visitors.

Through a red haze, Adele saw Harlow's ratty little face, heard his thin voice – *This is my place; I am the master here* – and beneath all the jargon, all the clichés, she sensed the point – an exercise in authority for authority's sake. But it was apparent, even through the haze of the psychiatric diction, that none of what he tried worked – or rather, worked in reverse. The boy did not break. The boy began not to respond. Harlow himself had to include several guarded, elliptical references to increasing withdrawal, increasing unwillingness to communicate.

Stop it, she told herself, but it was no use. Her heart was pounding with fury again; her stomach tightened more. The first part of the file was about Johnny Markland; now she began to sense the creation of the personality she knew as Thomas Newcombe, forged day by day in this monstrous smithy. The child standing by the iron gate, watching ordinary children at ordinary play; the student ten years later who would write a play entitled "Predestination"; the man who twenty years later would put the single word "WHY?" above his desk, for a silly, irresponsible moron to wonder about before he made marvelous love to her.

Correspondence between Gertha and Dora Johnson had continued, all focused on the question of how much was enough. Gertha had also included clippings about the others involved as well. Her own dismissal from the civil

474

service of – – – – County occurred about a year after Tom had been committed to Arbalest. The curt letter, signed by Ronert Tieger, cited her flagrant disregard for established policies and procedures of the Department of Social Services, in particular unwarranted intervention in active litigation.

A Xeroxed newspaper clipping was enclosed. The headline read "POLICE OFFICER DISMISSED FROM FORCE." The text began:

Roy Dickson, a police officer who had been awarded two citations for valor in the field, was today dismissed...

The story explained that Dickson had on several occasions been unnecessarily rough in his treatment of suspects and arrestees in his custody. Gertha had marked the last paragraph of the story with a yellow marker.

When asked to explain how such a distinguished officer could fall into such disgrace, Lieutenant Walsh stated that somewhere along the line Dickson had lost faith in the system. Dickson himself refused to comment, responding to the same question with an obscene gesture with the thumb and little finger of his left hand.

Two years and nine months after he first arrived at Arbalest, shortly before Tom's eighth birthday, Harlow added a long report to the log. Adele skimmed it rapidly.

–

Memorandum
To: File
From: P. Harlow
Subject: Markland, Jonathan – Revised Diagnoses

Refer to previous notes on this patient. Extensive observations of this patient lead me to revise my original diagnosis. Jonathan's withdrawn and uncommunicative state has been observed over time to be typical of his personality rather than aberrant. Constant, obsessive playing with the stumps on his left hand. This, and other factors noted elsewhere cause me to revise the diagnosis as follows:

Axis I: Organic Personality Disorder (in partial remission at the time of the first diagnoses) DSM 310.10

Axis II: Oppositional Defiant Disorder (severe), DSM 313.81. (Principal Diagnosis)

Note the inclusion of DSM 313.81. I remain convinced of the basic correctness of my original evaluation. Although there is evidence of mental disturbance, Jonathan is fundamentally a stubborn, intractable child who regards therapeutic intervention as a test of wills. I do not intend to lose the contest.

–

A full panel of phenothiazines was prescribed. Adele felt her nausea becoming worse; she'd thought she'd touched bottom, realized now she hadn't begun to realize the worst.

The phenothiazines didn't work. The boy threw them all up. She remembered reading somewhere that that in itself was a contra-indicator of mental illness. It didn't matter at all to Harlow. He moved on to a series of insulin shock treatments. No result. She turned the page.

Treatment Order
Patient: Markland, Jonathan, DOB 10/25/--
Treatment: Patient to receive twice weekly for six weeks, electro sh--

*

It was no longer a question of maybe feeling sick. She *was* sick.

The wastebasket was empty except for the lining. She made it just in time. Her stomach heaved and heaved again. Hydrochloric acid rolled up into her sinus cavities, along with bits and pieces of her breakfast, and dinner from the night before. Her stomach was now entirely empty, but there was one – then another – last excruciating spasm. The taste of stomach acid and snot rolled into the back of her mouth. For a moment she worried about the baby, then realized how absurd that was.

The wastebasket had to be emptied. She rolled the lining together at the top, her hands shaking, stood up and stepped away from the desk – and slipped and fell heavily on her knees.

Fool. Idiot, she thought. *Small motor coordination's always been better than large. If your hands are trembling, it stands to reason your legs are unsteady.* She rose carefully to her feet, controlled herself, picked up the lining, and slipped down the hall.

Thank God. The corridor was deserted. She dropped the thing in the trash receptacle in the lavatory, then checked herself in the mirror. What a mess. Her purse was back in the dark office. She cleaned herself as best she could with soap and paper towels, blew her nose. *If George could see me now*, she thought, then suddenly missed him so acutely she was on the verge of tears. She'd give anything if she could be in his arms somewhere this moment, dancing marvelously and making the lightest, most meaningless small talk.

*

Gertha Daniels, Social Worker
Department of Social Services

Albany, New York
January 9, ----

Dear Gertha,

Let me give you the full report. I agreed with you, I was certain I had him. The record of abuse had become so patently, obviously clear! To anyone!!

I've thought a lot about what went wrong at State. I didn't say it very well on the phone. What it amounts to is this. It's gone on so long that bad's become good. What I mean is that when I told them about all that has happened, no one really believes me. They're all bureaucrats – who wants to rock the boat? They can't – or won't – believe the system has failed this catastrophically. If a child that young has been at Arbalest that long, there has to be a reason, they think. (I don't know whether I ever told you, but the average stay at Arbalest is only seven months.) And the cruelty that's happened seems to confirm the opinion. If a licensed psychiatrist is doing things like that to a boy of his age, then he must be a real hard case. And I don't have a degree, as you know. I have no credentials to put against his, and that obviously means everything to these people.

I went out to Legal Aid and then to our District Attorney's office. Nothing; everything's happening under legal process of the court. I persuaded the new Legal Aid attorney (a nice young man) to prepare a writ of habeas corpus, but he has little hope.

I saved the worst for last. I visited Johnny again. He's not doing well, Gertha – regressing very badly, in a way that must be apparent to everyone but Harlow. He was diapered. He doesn't talk to anyone – ever. All he does is thumb through his books; sometimes he holds them upside down. Susan Deems swears he's reading them like that, but her attitude about this child borders on the hysterical.

You needn't have apologized to me about the way you shouted. You were right to. You were right and I was wrong three years ago; I should have made my stink then. I don't know what to do now.

Love,

Dora

–

The next sections of the file related to finance. Page after page of Arbalest ledger entries from month after month after year. Gertha had carefully highlighted the journal entry for "Markland, Jonathan" each month. It took for a moment for Adele to get the point. The fee paid each month, though increasing over time, was always precisely 50 percent more than the standard fee paid by the others. It was not hard to guess why. The ledgers were followed by page after page of photocopies of cancelled checks, all signed by Mary or

Herbert Klein, and all written on "The Jonathan Markland Trust." *Oh, no,* she thought, *oh, no,* but Gertha's note confirmed the worst:

In case you're wondering, it was Johnny's own money that paid for all this hospitality. Driscoll's speech in court about financial drain was a crock, like everything else he said.

—

Dr. Peter Coppelman, Ph. D.
Rochester, New York
April 9, 19- -
Dear Dr. Coppelman,

I am pleased to offer you the position of associate director of the Arbalest Children's Center at a starting salary of $55,000 per annum, beginning May 1st. As you know, I have interviewed numerous candidates for this position over the years without finding anyone satisfactory. It is a pleasure at last to discover a professional whose insights and philosophy with respect to these unfortunate situations are so compatible with my own. I feel that the combination of our two disciplines will enable us to enrich considerably the treatment and therapeutic alternatives available at Arbalest.

Please give this offer your most careful consideration.

Kindest regards,

Paul

—

Memorandum
To: File
From: Dr. Peter Coppelman, Ph. D.
Subject: Markland, Jonathan - Revised Diagnosis
Date: May 18, 19- -

At the request of Dr. Harlow, I have performed my own evaluation of this patient. Normal psychological testing proved to be impossible. The boy refuses to respond to normal questioning or communicate in any manner. He does not participate in games. Physical appearance is unkempt and disheveled. He defecates and urinates in his clothing on occasion. Other than this, he adheres scrupulously to house rules, apparently in the hope that his defiant attitude will be overlooked. Dr. Harlow has noted elsewhere in this file his stubborn resistance to all forms of intervention.

He sits in the tutorial classes with the older boys with the appearance of rapt attention – a pathetic spectacle. The balance of his time is spent poring over books (some of which he holds upside down, nearly all of which are far above any reading level he could possibly have attained), or by himself on the grounds of the institution.

Based on all of the above, my tentative evaluation is:

Axis I: Organic Personality Disorder (in partial remission at the time of the first diagnoses) DSM 310.10

Axis II: Oppositional Defiant Disorder (severe), DSM 313.81. (Principal Diagnosis)

Autistic Disorder, childhood onset (severe), DSM 299.00

Axis III: n/a

Axis IV: n/a

Axis V: Current GAF: 40

Highest GAF in the last year: 50

Although I hesitate to make any recommendation where so brilliant a therapist as Philip Harlow has experienced nothing but frustration, I think a course of aggressive behavior modification, something akin to that tried successfully with other autistic children. You understand that aggressive physical interaction would be required.

—

At the bottom of the memo, Harlow had appended a note that had obviously not been intended to be retained in the file: *Go ahead. Nothing I've tried with the little bastard has worked.*

Tom was nine and a half years old at the time.

There followed another note obviously not meant for posterity.

—

September 29, 19--

Pete,

Some bad news. Dora Johnson, who has made herself a nuisance about Markland for as long as I can remember, caught sight of the boy the other day and took him into the hospital. Evidently there's some new law that requires any potential child abuse be reported to the cops. The upshot is that I got a visit this morning from Chief Wiley. I was able to square it – he's known my family forever, and I explained to him the nature of the therapy. The way Markland looks on the grounds was the clincher, so he went away satisfied.

But I'm afraid we're going to have to call off the therapy. I'm as disappointed as you are; I think your diagnosis of autism was brilliant, and I think you were right on the verge of a breakthrough. I know you're going to be a terrific addition to our staff. But we can't risk an accident. If it's any consolation, that kid has driven me crazy since I met him. One of these days between the two of us, we'll find a way to get through to him. For sure, I'm not going to let the little creep get away with it.

One last thing. I've been looking through this file. It's gotten very cumbersome. We have state inspectors coming in two weeks. I really don't think it's fair to burden them with all these false starts and speculations. I'd like you to purge the following documents...

–

As best she could, Adele tried to track them in her mind. As nearly as she could see, Harlow had ordered Coppelman to destroy all the records of Tom's first three years at Arbalest, including the diagnosis of schizophrenia, the drugs, and the electroshock treatments. Anyone glancing at the file would assume the placement was relatively recent – Tom was reaching an age where the referral made more sense – and Coppelman's diagnosis was evidently partially confirmed by his physical appearance. Adele knew nothing about the ethics of psychology, but purging the file had to be completely unethical, if not outright illegal.

–

Gertha Daniels, Social Worker
Albany, New York
February 18, 19--

Dear Gertha,

This will confirm our plans for the 20th. I can't tell you how I'm looking forward to seeing you. I don't think there'll be any problem at all with Johnny being there.

I do want you to prepare yourself for a shock. I've tried to describe to you what's been going on; I'm sure you've formed images in your mind. Unless you've been very, very imaginative, I think you're going to find the reality is much, much worse.

Love,

Dora

–

If you thought you heard me bawl the other day, Gertha's note read, *you should have seen me that January 20th, when I saw what they'd done to my boy. It had been five years since I'd seen him. I don't think he'd had a real haircut since I got him one. Put a bowl on his head and snipped. His clothes were someone's oversized hand-me downs, and soiled with his own dirt; he didn't always make it to the bathroom. (He hadn't had any problem like that when he was with me.) He had a rope for a belt. He looked like a ten-year old version of someone you'd see on the closed ward at State. Almost every night he had terrible nightmares. He woke everybody up.*

He wouldn't say a word to anyone, just looked and listened. He didn't recognize me; he didn't answer when I spoke to him. Even so, I could tell he wasn't autistic or any of that other nonsense. You could see it in his face, in his eyes. He knew everything that was going on around him. What it was that he'd learned from the bastards that it was better not to say anything. Harlow and Coppelman hadn't got anything right. Even that holding books upside down; I noticed he always opened them at the front and went back to the place he'd stopped. Maybe he was deliberately conning them. I didn't think so at the time, but now I'm not so sure.

Dora had told me what had happened over the phone. Basically, Harlow and Coppelman had given up. Johnny wasn't any fun anymore. He didn't react no matter what they did. They began ignoring him; moved on to fresher meat. Dora began taking him home on weekends, then during the week; Harlow didn't give a damn, just so he got paid every month. The first time he came home with her, her husband – Sam Johnson was a living doll – took one look at him and went straight to the police. But it was the same thing – no one gave a damn. The Arden family dominated that town. Dora was hoping he'd improve before I saw him. But after she'd had him home a few visits, and nothing changed, she called me.

After I got done crying, she had to stop me from driving into town, buying a gun, and doing business right then and there. I've always been hotheaded. But I settled down. I picked up Johnny and his book; it was like picking up a big rag doll, he didn't help, didn't hinder; and took him into the room I was staying in. I sat him down in the rocking chair, I turned the book right side up; and I started to read to him, and talk to him, the same way as five years before. I wasn't even back where I'd started; I was much, much further back.

I started coming up every weekend. I bought him some clothes. I'd take him on little trips, or to the movies, or something. Always I'd talk to him as if he were any other little boy, as if he were answering me back, 'Johnny' this and 'Johnny' that. Nothing. I might as well have been talking to a wall. Nights I'd sit with the Johnson family, watching TV or playing some board game, holding him. He was interested and curious, I could tell, but he never tried to play and he never said a word. Only watched.

I made a little progress; the toilet thing, for one; and he responded a little bit physically, hugged me back, that kind of thing. But not nearly enough to please myself. Johnny had become the best little inmate they had at Arbalest; he knew the house rules better than they did. He'd learned he could lie low if he stuck to them. But I figured it was only a matter of time before Coppelman or Harlow came up with another bright idea. And it was tough on the Johnson family, even though they all liked Johnny a lot. It wasn't easy having a strange black woman there every weekend. Those nightmares – the only thing Harlow did was make him sleep off by himself, so he wouldn't bother anybody, but the Johnson house wasn't that big. But mostly I was scared that what they'd done to him was permanent, that it wasn't ever going to be better. He was getting close to eleven. Time was running out. I got more and more scared.

Finally, one night we were sitting, Dora's daughters were playing Clue, and I was doing my 'Johnny' this and 'Johnny' that number, when it hit me that he wasn't ever going to answer to that name, that there'd been too much pain, too much misery, that had happened to Johnny Markland. Johnny Markland had died when that bear died. Forget the books; maybe what was needed was a little home cooking. I took him into the other room.

"You're not Johnny anymore," I said. "Johnny went to heaven with his bear." I'd been afraid to say anything about that bear, but now it seemed right. He looked up at me. "You're a different boy with a different name. Your name is −"

So that's how he got the name he uses now. I named him for the son I wanted, the one I'm never going to have. 'Thomas' was my father's name, 'Bryant' was my mom's maiden name, and 'Newcombe' was my grandmother's. It pleases me now he writes his books with the names I gave him.

I went back out and got all the Johnsons together and told them about the new name. Sam and Dora got the picture right away; Sam made a big occasion out of it, went and opened a bottle of champagne and toasted the new name very seriously. The girls thought it was kind of neat; Dolores, the oldest, lit a candle. It all got to be weirdly right. I asked Dora and everybody to call him 'Tom' from then on and they all did.

I decided something else that night − that it was time for me to back off. I was too much involved with the old Johnny. If he had any chance at all it was to get away from all that, and I was a big part of it. It broke my heart to give up my boy, but it had to be. Dora promised she'd keep it going for me, and bring me all the news.

He just watched all this, same as he always did, like a little baby owl. Nothing changed at first. There was no miracle. But gradually things got better.

−

Gertha Daniels, Social Worker
Albany, New York
June 1, 19-- (fifteen months later)

Dear Gertha,

I'll do my best to summarize what I said on the phone. He'd been interacting more and more with Denise, playing games. Denise has been very good at ignoring the fact that he doesn't talk, as well as the fact that Tom (you see, I wrote that naturally. We've all come to think of him as that) nearly always wins. At any rate, they were sitting at the kitchen table while I got what passes for dinner around here on.

Denise said something like, "That was a good move, Tom."

And he looked over at me and said, as if it were nothing, "Is that my name?" He spoke. He finally SPOKE!! Denise almost fell out of her chair, and I − I had to stop myself from making a big scene. Sam was happier when he heard about it than I'd seen him in years.

He didn't say much more that night − only a few monosyllables. But it's started! It's finally started!! You must be so proud!!!

Love,

Dora

–

Memorandum
To: File
From: Paul Harlow, Director
Subject: Markland, Jonathan
Date: July 2, 19--

Spoke to Mrs. Rodriguez <u>re</u> the reports of Ernesto Hernandez that he speaks to the Markland boy in Spanish. Counseled her to cease spreading rumors if she wishes to remain employed here. Communicated Dr. Coppelman's tentative opinion that the child is hopelessly retarded.

–

Gertha Daniels, Social Worker
Albany, New York
September 6, 19--
Dear Gertha,

Sam and the girls are out to a Labor Day picnic. I've stayed behind to summarize all that has happened. Tom's reading in the other room.

(1) Tom is at our house nearly every day now. He sleeps up at Arbalest, but I pick him up after the morning classes right after lunch, and deliver him back after dinner. Weekends he's here. Sam has always been very proud of his daughters, but I know he appreciates having another male in the house. And I'm falling in love with him, as you have. It's working out.

(2) He is still very guarded. He talks in our home, but not much, and almost never outside it. That's good for the obvious reason. This is a very small town.

(3) Gertha, I can't tell about his memory. I really can't. He never talks about anything that happened to 'Johnny' – but I have the distinct impression that he remembers a lot more than he says. It's like he refuses to remember. I don't know enough to say more.

(4) All we Johnsons are convinced that your old friend at the Children's Shelter was right. Tom is an <u>exceptionally</u> bright boy. Susan taught him a little algebra out of her ninth-grade textbook; he's gone through two-thirds of the course work on his own in the last two months. He evidently picked up more in those tutorials than those beasts gave him credit for. And he is both fluent and literate in Spanish. He got that from the maids and the Hispanic inmates. There's no question in my mind that he could do seventh grade coursework –

483

that's amazing when you think of it – but I don't dare enrol him in school. Anyway, he might even be better off sitting in with the high school kids at Arbalest. He doesn't have to be told to keep his mouth shut. It comes to him instinctively.

(5) That's the end of the good news. Now for the bad. His nightmares aren't getting any better; in fact, I think they are becoming worse – and he is the saddest, quietest little boy you ever met, at an age when most other boys are outgoing to the point of obnoxiousness. Denise keeps trying to bring him out of it, but I'm not sure he's capable of that. I'm becoming worried that we've seen all the adjustment he's capable of making – not that what's happened isn't astonishing enough.

(6) Something that will please you. <u>He is not going back there</u> – I mean, when word of all this finally gets back to Harlow. <u>He is not going back.</u> Sam and I had a long, long talk about it all. When I look at Tom, and talk to him, all I can think of is my cowardice five years ago. I'm not going to do that again.

Finally, Gertha, while I'm not being a coward anymore, I have to say one other thing, even at the risk of endangering a friendship which has come to mean a great deal to me and my family. You're a much, <u>much</u> better social worker than I ever will be, so I know you already know. Your drinking has gone way, <u>way</u> beyond simple tippling. You either already are an alcoholic or you're shortly going to become one. It is time you addressed this problem; perhaps you have been waiting for me or someone else to speak. I would hate to think of the Markland case doing any more damage than it already has.

Love,

Dora

–

Some news clippings followed. "PROMINENT JUDGE RETIRES EARLY," read the first. Four months later, a clipping announced the appointment of a prominent local trial attorney to Spencer's seat. She didn't have to read the name. Vincent Driscoll. Of course.

–

Date: March 14, 19- -
Paul,

This is not for the file, but Rebecca Smithson reported something remarkable to me a few days ago. She'd become suspicious about Johnson's interest in the Markland boy, the number of times she'd taken him home. Ms. Smithson's a bit of snoop, you know; in any case, she checked around; her niece told her that a few of the kids in town are saying that he's started answering to a different name, that he's developed an entirely new identity – and also that he's some sort of oddball genius.

It all sounded incredible, but what the hell. I figured I'd check it out; I wasn't doing anything Saturday anyway. So I followed them. Damned if there doesn't appear to be something to it. He talks to her! I couldn't quite overhear the name she used, but it wasn't Johnny. I watched them at lunch from behind a newspaper (me and James Bond). He was poring over this high school geometry book. I guess that's where the genius rumors come from. It's as pathetic as the old upside-down stuff; he turns the pages too rapidly to be truly reading.

But do you know what this implies? What the possibilities are? Does he really have a different persona? Perhaps multiple personalities, DSM 300.14? I want you to cancel all these visits so we can keep him here and get to work on him. If we've done this much, it's got to be possible to bring him all the way back.

Pete

P.S. I always thought the little bastard was holding back on us.

—

Memorandum
From: Dr. Paul Harlow, Director
To: Joanna Edelheit, Graduate Assistant
Subject: Markland, Jonathan
Date: April 3, 19--

Joanna,

The attached file represents an interesting project for you in your third week here. The patient in question is one of our more intractable cases, a young boy suffering from childhood autism, plus a number of character disorders. In addition, Dr. Coppelman has concluded he is hopelessly retarded. There is probably an organic basis for all this. When he arrived here eighteen months ago, I doubted we could make any progress at all. However, really inventive intervention by Peter produced a dramatic remission. Young Jonathan snapped out of it, although he apparently answers to a different name than his own. Progress was so good that I began permitting out of placement visits to our social worker, Dora Johnson.

This proved to be a mistake. When Dr. Coppelman notified me that further intervention was necessary, with a consequent restriction on visitation, someone leaked the internal memorandum to Johnson. She has adamantly refused to surrender the child. Indeed, she is threatening a rather messy litigation if he is not discharged to her custody immediately. She and I have been back and forth over the phone about this. Finally, when I described your resume, she reluctantly agreed to make the boy available for an interview. This misguided woman had mistaken what can only be a temporary respite in the

485

progress of the disease for a permanent solution. It is important for this sad little child's own good that he return here for further treatment.

The file is attached. As you can see, our approach to Jonathan has been in accordance with the highest clinical standards, in spite of anything Mrs. Johnson might say to the contrary. She has always been a person of doubtful veracity. Please discuss any questions, problems, or doubts you may have with me; I will be able to fill you in. I emphasize again the importance of this child's return. Dora Johnson has no clinical training of any kind. She has only a local high school education, and is in no way equipped to evaluate a case of that type. I have no doubt your analysis of this situation will conform to Dr. Coppelman's and my own. Johnson's phone number and address are attached. The interview will of necessity have to be off site.

—

Memorandum
To: file
From: Joanna Edelheit, candidate Ph. D.
Subject: Markland, Jonathan
Dated: April 9th, 19--

Pursuant to Dr. Harlow's memorandum of April 3d, I met the patient in the company of his companion, Mrs. Dora Johnson, at (*the address had been obliterated*). The boy is an apparently well-developed twelve-year-old adolescent, of above normal height, weight appropriate to height. Responds appropriately to normal questioning, except that (a) he is unusually guarded – had to be reassured by Mrs. Johnson before answering – and (b) does not answer to his given name but instead to Tom. Reasonably oriented as to time, place, etc. Note: no sign of organic personality etiology – discuss with Dr. Harlow. Also, "Tom" is clearly not retarded.

Administered Rorschach, TAT, and Stanford-Binet. Responses to Rorschach difficult to interpret – highly imaginative, indications of severe stress (discuss with Coppelman and Lambeth). TAT within normal limits, though indications of enormous latent rage. Testing error of some sort occurred with the Stanford-Binet.

While Tom took the Stanford, I allowed Mrs. Johnson to review the file. Mrs. Johnson immediately stated that the file was fictitious, that numerous documents had been purged, that the history of Markland at Arbalest is far longer than indicated, that in fact he has been resident since he was five. Though I found that difficult to believe, I agreed to meet tomorrow with a social worker Mrs. Johnson says has possession of accurate records; also to retest Markland with WISC and Kaufman and obtain a sensible estimate of actual intelligence.

—

Memorandum
To: Drs. Harlow and Coppelman
From: Joanna Edelheit, candidate Ph. D.
Subject: Markland, Jonathan, aka Thomas Bryant Newcombe
Date: April 11, 19--

(1) As you requested, I will confirm in writing that Jonathan Markland has been moved, and that I have not disclosed his whereabouts to you. I take full responsibility for my actions.

(2) The raw scores you requested are attached. Dr. Coppelman may not wish to acknowledge it, but this boy tests out over 190 every time, no matter what test is administered, no matter what the circumstances. I confirmed the results informally. He is both fluent and literate in Spanish. I had him translate an article in the Sun and I watched him converse about its contents with a Puerto Rican waitress at the cafe where I administered the tests. He has at least a twelfth-grade knowledge of geometry and algebra. I could not test him adequately. My own grasp of the relevant mathematics is not as good as his.

One final confirmation; he is precociously perceptive for a boy his age. Out of nowhere, he asked me if I'd had a quarrel with my fiancé. I had, and naturally asked him how he knew. He'd noticed the whiteness on my ring finger. He added that it had to be a fiancé, that wives don't take off wedding rings no matter how serious the quarrel.

My conclusions as to his mental abilities are based on these factors, and not any of the emotional reactions you falsely ascribed to me. My professional objectivity is a point of pride with me, and has been noted by others.

(3) I will also confirm I have no intention of returning either Markland or the file to your custody. You will have to trust me that it exists, and that it is absolutely convincing. If you follow through, if either I or Dora Johnson are subjected to prosecution, the contents will be made public – including the orders for insulin shock and electroshock treatment for a seven-year old child, signed in your own hand. I have also retained a copy of the memorandum you sent to me in which you indicated Markland had been placed with you only a year before.

(4) I have considered carefully the advice you gave me yesterday. Your advice is more accurately characterized as threats. Nonetheless, I am going to do what I know to be right, regardless of what you do to me, regardless of any reprisals. This is going to stop. Now. Today. This instant. Whatever I have to do. Please believe me about this.

(5) Though I do have strong feelings about this situation, my decisions have been based strictly on what I believe to be my duty here. I am not a hysterical young woman, as much as you might wish to think so. Also, as you requested, I have reconsidered the comparison to Mengele. I have decided I was unfair – to Mengele. At least he did what he did in the name of an ideology, however demented. Your motives do not extend beyond greed and sadism. I have no intention of apologizing to either of you.

(6) I intend to remove all mention of Arbalest from my c.v. Please do me the same courtesy.

–

Good for you, Joanna, she thought wearily. So well done. So much better than some other people. Joanna Edelheit was not quite as unemotional as she'd thought. Part of the typescript was smeared; she'd clearly wept over it. The discharge order, signed under protest, was next. Then followed another letter:

–

Herbert R. Klein, D.D.S.
–––––––––, New York
April 29, 19––
Dear Paul,

I'm going to put this in writing so there's no misunderstanding and we won't have to repeat our conversation on the phone. No one's questioning you, or your medical judgment, or accusing you of anything. But we are going to go along with this. You have to understand what we're up against. These people are serious. We tried to tell Edelheit the trouble she could get into, but she doesn't give a damn. And it isn't only her judgment against yours. She went over the file with a professor of hers, Lambeth, some pointy-head at Binghamton. He came up with her when we met. If we don't cave in, they're going to start a crusade about this thing. They say the only thing stopping them is that they say they don't want the kid's life turned into any more of a circus than it already is.

Let's not argue about who told who what, or what shouldn't have been in writing and is, or any of that crap. Let's agree we have different recollections, let's agree to disagree, and leave it at that. (And please don't explain you talked to my wife. It's not the same thing. We all know she's always had a screw loose about that kid.) We've all had a great ten years; let's leave it at that. Vince Driscoll says he's going to sign the order and that's that. He says that all he did was his job for his client and he's damned if he's going to be pilloried for that. He's also going to order the court file purged.

I don't mean to imply that any of us did anything wrong. None of us did anything that everyone doesn't do. But you know how the newspapers are these days. Every little thing becomes a scandal. Judge Spencer and I go back a long way. Nothing's ever happened, but you know how it would look. (I don't think it came up on the phone, but that Edelheit bitch asked the judge that question at the meeting. They weren't exactly poker faces. Lambeth asked about who paid you. They already know more than is good.)

So that's the way it is. I know this has taken a lot of your time, so I'm enclosing a check for your trouble. I am sure it's enough.

Doctor, if you do try and fight this, I have to tell you – I'll have to swear I didn't know anything about this. Vince is adamant he never got any reports. He'll open his file to prove it if he has to. Tom Spencer says annual reviews are a formality and everyone knows it. And I don't really think you want Mary to testify. It won't do anybody any good.

Let's just get beyond this.

All the best,

Herbert Klein

-

So that's the great Dr. Klein, she thought contemptuously. *It's people like you. Or maybe people like me.* She read the letter again. *We all know she's always had a screw loose about that kid.* They'd known, all of them. Every day of every year.

The formal court order was the next in order; Adele was close to the end of the file. Tom's commitment to Arbalest was ended. The case was transferred to Dora Johnson's county. What was left of his trust – several tens of thousands of dollars, enough to support him through college, and nothing more, was turned over to Dora Johnson and the public guardian there. Nothing, not a hint, not an implication, that anything was out of order, that books existed that had to be balanced; no recognition that they had all been collaborators in a monstrous evil; simply the typical reaction of vermin to the threat of light. After seven and one-half years – ten since the child had been locked in a closet – it was over.

Except for the dreams, a voice reminded her. *Except for the dreams.*

Adele turned the page. It contained a Xeroxed clipping of a profile from the society section of the local newspaper. "Prominent Dentist to Move" - there, staring out from the page, were Herbert and Mary Klein, the husband standing behind a sofa upon which his wife and three children (two girls, one boy) were seated. The setting was the opulent living room of a spacious home. The news item chronicled the success of the beloved Herbert Klein, his tenderness to his pediatric patients, his importance to the community.

He will be missed, the article concluded.

-

Of course, Gertha wrote, *I was glad to see him out. But it didn't make me feel all that much better. Dora neither. It had always been easy. All it was, was a demented woman and her weak-kneed husband – one solid push, not even that hard, and they'd have all fallen over like the Queen of Heart's soldiers. Only no one did. It wasn't that Joanna was any different from the rest of us – she had her degrees, but I have mine. It was that she really meant it. She didn't give a damn what happened to her. She was going to stop it. I had to think of how worried I'd been about my job, my career, and all.*

We all knew that it had come much, much too late. None of that stopped me drinking.

There were only a few pages left.

Joanna Edelheit
New York, N. Y.
September 12, 19-- (five months later)

Dear Gertha and Dora,

Enclosed is a little something for your file – Harlow's revenge, which I rather expected. It doesn't faze me in the least. Michael and I had been having mild disagreements as to where we should live after the marriage. What this means is that he wins. Good-bye to New York. I'm sure I'll like Shaker Heights.

All of you have been much too effusive about my role in all this. By the time I came on the scene, the record you two had assembled and lived with was so overwhelming that the choices were clear. Unlike Dora, I never had to worry about family and community. You both give me too much credit. It was really a simple matter of what's right.

Which leads me reluctantly to the point. I am closing the door firmly on all of it – Martha Klein, Harlow, especially Johnny. The fact is that all our rage and frustration against this injustice won't change anything. The die is cast. It is a virtual certainty he's going to end up institutionalized. There is no point in lavishing emotional energy and thought on this any longer. It's useless. I'm really addressing this to you, Gertha.

I'll admit it's easier said than done. I've thought about him often; I've even dreamt about him. (He was a haunting twelve-year-old. I do not even want to think what he'll be like when he's twenty.) But we all know there is no way he can cope in any long-term sense with the violence, with the lost identity, with all of it. He is doomed, and dangerous, and that's all there is to it. I don't mean to be cold, but I see no realistic hope of any kind here. It's better to close the door.

This is my last letter. Not that I won't be thinking of you; not that I will ever forget my two comrades-in-arms; but the time has come to move on.

God bless both of you.

Sincerely,

490

Joanna

–

Another letter was attached, addressed to the State Board of Psychology of New York. Wearily, Adele read it, with another small, sickening lurch. *Concerning Joanna Edelheit, a diplomate of SUNY (Binghamton). Regret to inform. . . an unstable young woman. . . became emotionally involved in the treatment of a patient. . . violation of the confidentiality of our files. . . sufficient interference to require premature discharge. . . Please keep this report in confidence. I am not certain of the young woman's reaction. Very truly yours, Paul Harlow, M. D.*

There was only one letter left.

–

Gertha Daniels
Albany, New York
November 18, 19-- *(three years later)*
Dear Gertha,

This is going to be among the last of our many letters, Gertha. Outside of my family, you're the first to know. I've received some very bad news from the clinic. The lumpectomy the surgeon thought was sufficient wasn't. The cancer has evidently metastasized to my pancreas. It is evidently only a matter of months. It is time to get everything in order.

Let me bring you up to date on Tom. (You named him well; he's really much more a "Tom" than a "Johnny.") It's apparent now he's reached his full height. Every night he does the exercises Sam taught him; they don't help with the sleep problem, but he's filled out nicely. He has really become quite a handsome young man! One of the coaches at the last school tried to get him to come out for football or basketball, but of course he has no interest in organized sports (or organized anything, for that matter).

Also, intellectually, he continues to astound everyone, despite all the different high schools. At our last meeting, Dr. Lambeth told me he is a genuine autodidact, thereby enriching my vocabulary. (It means someone who is self-taught – you see, you can still learn something even when you're dying!) The last time he was with us, he charmed the socks off Linda, making up stories for her, his own variations on her favorites. He really has a gift! Lately, he's become very interested in some obscure Protestant theology. No one quite knows what to make of him.

But the rest of it continues unchanged. I have had to switch foster homes again. Paperwork on Tom seems to take up half my day. As always, it's not that they didn't like him. It is the sleeping pattern. The nightmares get more and more entrenched each passing day; no one can hope any longer for improvement. He has no intimate friends. He has become a quiet brooding boy whom most of the other teenagers find a bit intimidating (except for some of the girls, of course, who become a bit fluttery). Nothing seems to bring him any joy.

The alcohol abuse continues the same. (I could kill the kid that introduced him to beer!) Counselling doesn't do any good. I've made him make me promises and I know he means to keep them. But. . . Dr. Lambeth (the same time he introduced me to the word "autodidact") said we could forget all the Fancy Dan psychology; he says what happens is that Tom can't stand the pressure any longer and breaks down. He is very pessimistic that counselling will ever be effective. I'm afraid I agree.

I suppose I owe you the whole truth. It wasn't only the nightmares this last time. The foster-father found him in a disgraceful condition with a divorcee (thirty-five!) who lives next door. The woman claimed that he'd initiated it – which, unfortunately, I believe. With a different boy, it might be humorous, but with this one. . .

I am thinking of my own reckoning up these days. It's odd; I think I've lived a good life. My girls have made me proud of them. I've been a good wife to my husband, and I did some good in my community. But I know what I'm going to have to account for when I meet my Creator – the one time in my life when I lacked courage. Sam tries to console me, reminds me of what I've done, what I've accomplished; but every once in a while, when I am with Tom, I will see that bewildered little boy peep out that I met ten years ago – and I know – I know – that's what I have to answer for. And I don't have any answers.

I know you've been angry with me, Gertha, but nonetheless you have become my best friend in the world. We have been through so much! If you are not at my funeral, I promise I'll come back and haunt you! Please respect a dying woman's last wish. Stop drinking. Don't let this thing destroy you.

Love,
Dora

–

She'd reached the end of the file. Gertha's last note read:

The doctors had been telling kind lies to Dora; she didn't have months. She died eight days after she wrote the letter. Never told her how I felt. Years later, I named the Center after her, but it was too late then – like everything else I did. Of course I went to the funeral. Couldn't take a chance on being haunted. But I didn't do the other thing. I couldn't.

I should tell you something about myself. I got into social work because I wanted to work in the inner city. I took the job in ----- County because it was the only one available. I figured I'd get a little experience and come back to Bedford-Stuyvesant. I never imagined I'd get wiped out by a white kid – a rich white kid, at that. But children belong to the people who love them; it's got nothing to do with race, or legal custody, or parents, none of that shit. I didn't know that then. So I let them take my boy and I left him to live with monsters. It was all I thought about for ten years and it destroyed my life.

But I see it a little differently since you came. These are rich, beautiful poems. What it means to me is, he got over after all, despite everything, despite what we all thought. Maybe he's not that far off from where he was meant to be. I never would have believed it. None of us would. We didn't think he had any chance at all.

That's why I decided to give this up to you. It's been too long anyway; Dora and Joanna were right about that. I feel like someone in a horror movie where they can only get rid of a curse if they give it to someone else. It's all yours now, Missy. You call me if you need anything, if I can do anything at all. But it's yours. Good luck.

As for me, this is the first four days in a row I've gone without vodka in twenty years. Your doing, Missy, and thanks. If there's hope for Johnny Markland, there's hope for everyone.

Slowly Adele closed the file. She had come to the end.

*

She could hear the rain pounding into the windows on the offices across the corridor. The wind must have come up. She sat in the darkened office for what seemed like a long time, numb, dazed, fighting for comprehension, groping for meaning.

They'd all gotten away with it, hadn't they? That was her first thought. Every last one of them. Herbert Klein had retired, fled at the slightest risk of discovery. Wherever he was now, he was undoubtedly as beloved there as he had been in the first little town. Mary Klein was probably pouring tea this very moment for a group of society matrons, none of whom had any idea she was a psychotic child abuser. Thomas Spencer, the judge, had retired honorably on his pension. Driscoll (damn him! *damn* him!) had become a judge. Harlow and Coppelman still ran their chamber of horrors in a far corner of the Earth. All of them had prospered.

And their victim? Condemned to wander through life without joy, without purpose, damned even in his sleep, the prisoner of a past he could not reconcile, futureless, an enigma to everyone, including himself. *Oh yes,* he'd said as he stood before the Van Eyck, *I forgot that one. Destiny. . . predestination. Not like that, of course.* What was done could not be undone.

She found herself back in her own office, holding the file. She had no recollection of walking down the corridor. The portrait of her mother gazed down upon her, an artist in search of a subject. Joanna, Gertha, Dora – all of them had expected he'd wind up as a criminal or in an insane asylum. Made sense. But it hadn't happened, had it? The water that had been heated with such intensity for ten years had frozen instead of boiled. *Anything is possible.* He wasn't in an institution. Somehow he'd evolved instead into a tall, quiet man who escorted foolish, silly young nincompoop morons around museums and kept his own secrets. And dreamt.

That wasn't what the destiny which shapes means to ends had intended. The billiard balls had been aligned correctly, the cue ball had been perfectly struck – but instead of the ball sinking forever into the pocket, it had spun up off the table entirely at a mad, incomprehensible angle, into another plane entirely. A different man, a different being. . . one so easy to love.

She sat at her desk, still groping for rationality. Lem, Bobby Lawton, her thoughts the morning she spoke to Carolyn, after she learned she was on the Project. Threes – she'd been on the right track. There had been a clue. What had come had indeed come in threes. But she hadn't been counting the right things.

Everything has to be different, she thought suddenly. Everything. It all has to be different. That's what this means. It can't mean anything else.

Think, damn it, she told herself. Reality? The reality was she was off-center, had been for some time, had been denying it. Now she had lost her equilibrium altogether. State the obvious: it was necessary, essential, that she talk to someone about this, that she unburden herself. Her family was out of the question. Bri was too far away. George? Suddenly she longed for him again. But no. Not about this, not about the man who gave her the angel. Numbly, automatically, she paged through her address book on her PDA. Someone.

She stopped at the Ps. *Petrosian, Armen.* Of course; the family psychologist; the afternoon she met Tom; in fact, it fit the pattern. The equinox. She picked up the phone with deliberate haste, cutting off thinking time.

"Hello?" She was in luck: he was in, and not with a patient. She composed herself.

"Hello, doctor" – she gulped, realizing only after she'd spoken that she did not have full control of her voice – "you probably don't remember me. My name is Adele Jansen. We met at the reception for your book. I was the little snip who got into an argument with you." She covered the receiver, gulped again.

He laughed pleasantly. "I don't have any memory of that. Why have you called?"

She took a deep breath. "I want to talk to you about something – someone – as soon as I can" – (it was going) – "a friend – I have a" – (going) – "fi – fi – fi – file" – (Gone. No use.)

"Are you all right?" he asked, concerned.

"N-n-n-n-nu-nuh-no," she finally managed to choke out, half-sobbing. "I – want – to – send – you – some – information," articulating each syllable carefully. "I'm – hop-ing – you – can – ex-plain – some-thing – to – me," ending with another half sob.

"Of course," he said after a short silence. "Normally, I see no patients on Thursday. My evening is free." He paused. "But I will see you."

They agreed to meet at 9:30. It took a half an hour to write her own notes to complement Gertha's. She put the file carefully together. The three photographs fell out. She put the two pictures of Tom back hastily; she could not bear to look at them. For a long time, she stared at the picture of Herbert and Mary Klein.

The monster in the cave. Georgia Richmond had guessed right. One did exist. She looked at the photograph. "Banal" was too grandiloquent a word. Ordinary, so impossibly ordinary. Carolyn would approve. Mary Klein had done what was necessary.

"She's waiting for you, you know," she said at last, voice shaking. "Your sister. Somewhere she's waiting. She hasn't left yet, and she won't. Not until she's finished with you. Someday. . . somehow –"

Stop it. She was going crazy. She didn't believe in that kind of afterlife. What had happened had happened. It was beyond change. Justice was something that related to here, now, a means of adjusting real things between real people. *Stop it.* With a forcible effort of will, she launched herself out of her chair, down to reception, and dispatched the file by messenger.

She returned to her office still numb. Everything had to be different, but the big changes would have to wait for a little while. In the short term, she knew exactly what she was going to do. She cleared off her desktop. Was there anything left to do? Automatically, out of force of habit, she reviewed her agenda.

Suddenly she sat bolt upright in her judicial chair.

*

It shouldn't be impulsive. But it wasn't, really, was it? She'd been wrestling with it for six weeks now. The little one had intruded into everything. . . Tom's baby, and there was a glow with that thought. . . she checked herself, looked deeply into her own heart. Was she really. . . ?

Yes. No doubt. O.K. if that's the case, then *do it. Am Anfang war die Tat.* Do the deed. Don't talk, don't think. Do. She picked up the phone – hesitated one last time – then firmly, crisply punched in the number.

"Hello, can I speak to Dr. Marshall. . . Hello, Alice? Cancel for me for Saturday. I've changed my mind. I'm going to have my baby. . . I know what I said last week, but this is final. . . Yes. Cancel it. I mean it. I guess I should see you about prenatal. What? Oh, believe me, I've been eating well," having to stifle laughter, because it might become hysteria too fast, too easily.

She hung up the phone. The universe reeled; the consequences of this last, irrevocable decision were unfathomable. Worlds were dying, worlds were being born. Good. Good. A beginning; everything would be different. A brief candle warmth lit her being for a moment – *A good day for you, little one, at least* – but for a moment only, lost in the vastness of the darkness, the utterness of the desolation.

She checked her agenda again. Now there was indeed nothing left.

*

She killed the lights in her office, sat back in her chair, and rolled up the left sleeve of her blouse. No sense in ruining a good blouse. It wasn't the blouse's fault. Nothing was anybody's fault. Simply a matter of ordinary and necessary. She put her head in the crook of her elbow. It had been a long time. For a while, nothing happened. She rolled her thoughts over – that look on Lem's face, Bobby Lawton. . . George – *I love you, George,* she thought – then deliberately brought out the worst – compared the forlorn, beleaguered man she had encountered with the smiling, open baby, the child who deserved, all that was with all that should have been. *We're not in real time any more, Adele,* he'd been able to say. *You know all about real time, don't you, little boy. It's something that happens to you in a closet.*

There we go. The beginning of a let down. *You can do it, stupid.* The phone rang; she ignored it. Other memories pinching in. The best, the worst. *I love you, Adele. . .*

"I love you, too, Tom," she declared aloud. Finally, it was happening. Now comes the torrent. Arm on desk, face in elbow, alone in her office, Adele cried, not the decorous weeping of a mature woman, but the loud, racking sobs of a child, cried in a way she had not cried in thirteen years, not since the day her mother died.

Joseph Wurtenbaugh

ANOTHER DREAMSCAPE

dele rang the doorbell of Professor Armen Petrosian's apartment at exactly 9:30 that evening. The door opened at once. "Ms. Jansen? Come in, come in," the small man said gently. His mittel-European accent was less pronounced than she remembered.

"Thank you for seeing me on such short notice," Adele said automatically. She looked around, at an orderly, well-furnished suite of rooms. The apartment building was located in the upper Village, not far from NYU. It was a good bet that the professor had some relationship with the University.

"I see patients in my sitting room," he said. "Of course you are not a patient, but even so. . . it seems appropriate." She followed him into the room, and took a seat in a large, overstuffed chair. The room was dim. The only light was from a small table lamp. Gertha's file was in the center of the desk. She looked away from it, around the room, at his degrees.

"I had completely forgotten whatever incident occurred at the reception," Petrosian remarked softly, smiling. "I had much, much, too much wine that day. Everything was somewhat blurry. What I remembered of you was the charming note I received a few days later, apologizing for conduct that I could not myself recall. Very amusing." Adele somehow managed a smile.

"Are you a psychologist or a psychiatrist?" she asked.

"Both," he answered promptly, "but I practice psychology. Human behavior can be studied and modified. Human thought as physiology is destined to remain the province of witch doctors for the next several centuries." He looked at her more closely. "Have you eaten?"

"Yes," she replied. Adele had forced herself to choke down a salad and a piece of white fish at a restaurant; she was eating for two now. She'd spent the balance of the hours at the movies, watching a film about which she could not recall the slightest detail.

He tapped the file gently. "You knew nothing of these events, I presume, until you read this material." She nodded. "And you have come to me hoping that I can provide some sort of explanation of this personality."

She nodded affirmatively again. "Yes."

He shrugged, a Slavic gesture of helplessness. "I assume you are not interested in more of this DSM nonsense." She shuddered and shook her head.

"If it pleased you, I could give you one that seems to have been overlooked, DSM 300.22, Agoraphobia, with limited symptom attacks, well-compensated. Your friend seems to prefer closed spaces to open. Anonymity is comfortable, safe to him. Exposure, publicity, recognition appear to make him restless. What others think are good days are very bad for him. And if you wanted to hear the DSM numbers for semi-amnesic conditions, parasomnial disorders, and the like, I would be happy to furnish those. But I doubt very much you have sought this consultation for any such purpose." She shook her head again. Again, she was close to tears. "You are seeking explanations."

She nodded. "Yes."

He sighed, gestured towards the chair. "Every week, thirty or more mature adults sit in the chair in which you are sitting. They discuss problems with which they are unable to cope. They drink too much and can't stop. They use dangerous drugs. They become romantically involved with the wrong people, or the right people who are unavailable. They are too active sexually or not active enough. I do what I can. I share what little wisdom I have, I listen and react. But to explain to them why they do what they do? No. An hour a week is not enough; perhaps in several years, nonstop. But for such investigations there is insufficient time, either mine or theirs."

He leaned forward in his chair and put his hand on the file. "Now you send me a description of a human being with this unique history and you request my opinion. My dear young lady, I could examine this individual for a hundred thousand years and not be able to ascertain the inner workings of his personality. The professionals who reacted to your account of his present day existence with incredulity, who exclaimed that what you related was not possible – they are all commendably competent. I share their assessment. The case you have presented me cannot have arisen according to any conventional understanding. The WISC score at age 12 and one half – incomprehensible, unbelievable. I should disregard it – I am no friend to intelligence testing in any case – had it not been authenticated by subsequent performance." He sat back in his chair.

"Your own surmises are very much the same as I would make, as anyone would make. The recurrent nightmare has some relation to the fear and anger that is habitually suppressed. So do the periodic descents into excesses of alcohol and random sexualizing. That this has some relation to the transferred identity is also obvious. Beyond this, all is as mysterious to me as it is to you. This may surprise you, but I do not think that psychological intervention is desirable here."

"You do surprise me," she answered truthfully.

"How do I say?" he said, throwing up a hand. "Because these

adjustments are so fragile. So delicate." He thought for a moment, then swiveled in his chair. "Few things in the old Soviet Union were comparable to anything in the United States, but there is one thing that is clearly superior. I mean the circuses. When I was a boy, my parents took me with them once to Moscow for a party meeting, this before they became disillusioned. We went to the circus. One animal act I saw I have never forgotten. A brown bear rode a bicycle across a rope; as it did, it balanced a pole on its shoulders. At the top of the pole was a teacup, with a raw egg inside of it." He paused. "Your – Johnny? Tom? –"

"Tom. One of the letters is right. He's much more a 'Tom' than a 'Johnny.'"

"–Tom performs the same balancing trick every day of his life. The persona he presents to the world is as delicately balanced, as close to destruction, as the egg in the teacup. An enormous strain, an enormous tension, lies concealed beneath the surface." He paused. "How he does it – how any of this can be – all this is a mystery. It will always remain a mystery."

"He doesn't seem fragile," she responded uncertainly. "In fact, he's a very strong personality."

"Oh, but the bear *is* strong!" Petrosian exclaimed. "It has to be strong to be on the rope at all, to keep the pole aloft in the first place. But there are limits to its strength. Sooner or later the rope runs out. Sooner or later it is not possible to turn the pedals quickly enough. Sooner or later its strength fails. Then – inevitably – it falls, no matter how strong it is."

"Yes, but – but –" and then the enormity was upon her again, she was weeping uncontrollably. Petrosian had anticipated her. His handkerchief was in her hand almost before she had begun. When that failed to stem the waterfall, he moved to her chair and pressed her head firmly, paternally, against his shoulder. "Now, now."

"I'm so sorry," she said at last. "I'm never like this. I'm always so collected. It's only that he's so sweet, so nice. That something like this – it's so unfair – it's so –" and she was off again. He simply held her again, for a long, damp minute or so.

"Such a baby," she finally was able to gasp, as she disengaged herself. She noticed tears in his eyes as he sat back down at his desk and looked away from her.

"I remember a few years ago," he said slowly, "I read in the newspapers of events for which I had longed all my life. I received calls from Armenia. I rejoiced for the family, the friends, even the enemies I left behind, for the deliverance that had finally arrived. At one point in my life, I would have thought that those days would have been times of complete happiness, of absolute jubilation. But even then, I doubted, I worried. Perhaps it was better when the powerful among nations were arrayed against each other. Perhaps we will all come to regret the day of unity. Perhaps the time will come when we will look back with nostalgia on these days of political conflicts, for the distraction they provided."

He swiveled in his chair. "The old battles aren't over, Ms. Jansen. They're never going to be. There is only one war: the powerful against the powerless. Always and everywhere, no matter what mask it wears at a given time and place. Often oppressors wear the garb of law. Perhaps that is even their preferred disguise." His voice was full of compassion. "How terrible to find out that truth in this way. How terrible for you."

"Isn't there anything that can be done for him?" she asked, voice trembling.

"Not in my opinion," he said softly. "What he has achieved as it is is a miracle of a sort. You must realize," he went on, "what you see before you this day, what you focus upon, this day is the image of an abused, terrified child. But Mr. Newcombe is a child no longer. He is a grown man now of twenty-eight years, and awesome gifts. He finishes other people's mystery novels for them, better than they can themselves. He writes poetry that renders into concrete imagery rarefied and esoteric concepts of mathematical theory. At the age of nineteen he writes an apparently comic play with a theological discussion concealed so expertly that only a scholar in the field can discern it. Incredible!" he remarked, almost to himself. "Only seven years after. . ." He shook his head and resumed:

"If he is not acquainted with his past now, you must realize that it is not because he lacks the resources or ability to explore it. He is not truly amnesiac. He does not explore it because he chooses not to. There is a strong volitional element in this. Consciously, unconsciously – a mixture of both – he holds these memories at bay. Ignorance for him is literally bliss. And who could disagree?" He shook his head. "No. There is no therapeutic procedure that would not destabilize him radically. Thomas Newcombe has reached stasis, as unsatisfactory as that may be in many respects."

"Then. . . nothing?" she repeated. *Stupid*, she thought, *you knew that*.

He spread his hands helplessly.

"Thank you, doctor," she gulped, reaching for the file. "Thank you. How much do I owe you?"

"Not much in money. I'll send you a bill," he said, regarding her. "But I would like you to repay the favor I've done you. I would ask you to satisfy my curiosity about something."

"Oh?" said Adele. "What?"

"What you have learned about yourself from all this." She looked startled. "It is apparent that this file has been kept by someone else for many years. You must have undertaken considerable efforts to obtain it. The contents came as a shock of horrific proportions; that also is apparent. Forgive me for saying so, but it is also obvious that you are emotionally involved with Mr. Newcombe. Surely the combination of all these circumstances has produced some insight into yourself."

"No," she said, starting to wrap the file.

"Ms. Jansen," he said, gently. "Something."

"Maybe one thing," she said shakily, putting the file back on his desk. "Not very important. Something that I'm going to have to think about. Nothing that would interest you."

"I have taken some time for you," he said, even more gently. "Please."

"Nothing important. Nothing I could make you understand."

"What is it?" he nudged. "Indulge my whim."

"Only – only –" she was on the verge again, held back – "that something someone said to me this morning is true."

"Which would be?"

"That I'm the worst. That of all of them, I'm the very, very worst."

*

"I had thought something of the kind," he murmured. "Perhaps you will tell me the reason for such an extraordinarily harsh self-condemnation."

"Because I *know* better," she said emphatically. "I knew better all along. The others, all the sickening rationalizations – that's me, I did the same thing. But I did it because I wanted to. I remember admitting to myself on the subway I was a coward. I knew even then admitting it didn't justify it. All of us, except Milly." Petrosian looked up; she had not used that name in her note. Adele rambled on, speaking more quickly: "She didn't know nearly as much as I did, but at least she tried. I didn't even try; it's not only Tom, it's Bobby Lawton and Lem, all of it, AI Squared, I didn't ask the questions because I didn't want to hear the answers, I didn't do it because I wanted it to be easy. I –"

She was verging again. Petrosian put his hand across the desk, on her shoulder, and steadied her. Adele fell silent, grateful for the intervention.

"Perhaps it would help if I told you of my own thoughts," he said quietly. "I have always had a high regard for heroes. The great explorers, the great warriors, the great intellects were the idols of my youth. It is a strange world we inhabit these days in that respect. Athletes who do their deeds between painted lines are described as 'courageous.' Businessmen who succeed in carefully circumscribed arenas are deemed 'visionaries.'" He smiled and shook his head. "How easy it has all become.

"The man you love –" she flushed, but said nothing – "is undoubtedly perceived as a strange, peculiar man by most of the people with whom he associates. He acts in ways he cannot explain. He becomes involved in situations which are demeaning, incomprehensible, and which shame him. But, I tell you, if ever I came face to face with this person –"

"You've seen him," she interjected.

"I have?" he asked, surprised.

"Yes. He was at the same reception that I met you."

He opened the file, reviewed her notes, pinched his nose, and strained. "It is all so blurry. I do recall distantly a tall man, who seemed surprisingly familiar with –"

"That was Tom," she said flatly. "You've met him."

"Yes?" he said, musing, then continued: "Women sit in your chair, who have succeeded in breaking off their latest love affair, and call themselves survivors. Young men, proud that some irregularity in the Dow Jones did not eliminate the last penny of their capital, describe themselves the same way." He paused. "Even in my own country, persons who were spared for no other reason than the executioner randomly chose a different victim boast of their longevity." He tapped the file. "But you have come face to face with the genuine article – a true Survivor. He has endured and persevered in the face of cruelties and obstacles that would have destroyed lesser human beings a dozen times over. I admire this man. I am very much looking forward to becoming acquainted with his poetry."

"Yes," she answered after a moment, "it pleases me very much to hear you say that." This was helping. Her composure was beginning to return.

"But," he went on, his tone changed, "but this admiration of mine has its limits. It is not an attitude that could be implemented in any meaningful way on a day-to-day basis. I would shake Mr. Newcombe's hand, my respect would show in my eyes. But interaction? Involvement?" He shook his head. "No. The pattern of his life is fixed. No meaningful alteration is possible. Your practical decisions were correct. They were realistic, not cowardly. You are hardly the worst. You would have been playing foolish games with your own life to have gone further with this man."

"And if we all do that," she asked after a moment, "if all the sensible people behave sensibly, where does that leave him? What happens to him?"

"You know the answer to that yourself," he replied softly, not afraid to meet her eye. "No one can live with these tensions at his core indefinitely. Sooner or later the bear will fall and not remount the rope. The task is so difficult, and he always falls in the end. Do you think I am not aware of what it is I have implied? Awareness of that sort is what drives conscientious social workers to drink, and mediocre psychologists to take pen to hand."

"And love? Caring?" she asked stupidly. "That wouldn't make a difference?"

"There is no one who does not benefit from love," he answered. "But a fundamental difference. . .?" He let the answer drift. "Young women of the last century had that illusion sometimes, that a roué or drunkard could be reformed by the power of their love. But the inevitable outcome was that they themselves were drawn into the maelstrom." Adele thought of Milly. "Best to love at a distance. Best to care from a place of safety." He paused. "Please remember it is you for whom I am concerned. Your friend is not present with us."

"Then they've won completely, haven't they?" she said dully. "They won before he ever had a chance. Then Joanna and the others are right. There's no hope."

Now he could not meet her look. She wanted to be angry with him, but could not; she could see the pain in his own face. Instead, a heavy, leaden despair filled her being. "Thank you, doctor," she said, rising. "I've taken too much of your time. It's time for me to go. You've been enormously helpful, but I think I have to get through the rest of this by myself."

"You are welcome to stay longer," he replied. "It is apparent that you are still a bit shaky. I am an M.D. Would you like me to prescribe a sedative?"

"No," she answered instantly. "I won't. I can't." Petrosian appeared perplexed. He deserved an explanation. "I'm going to have a baby."

He was taken aback for a moment. "His?" he asked, tapping the file. She nodded. "Are you sure? Such a momentous decision to make in the aftermath of –"

"Thank you," she said. "I'm sure. It's the right thing. It's what I wanted to do all along." She shouldered her purse. "Good night, Dr. Petrosian. Thank you again for everything."

"Wait a moment," he said, picking up the file. "You have forgotten something. Here. Take it with you." His hand and voice trembled as he handed it to her; in that tremble they became friends for life.

"Feel free to call again," he called lightly after her as she showed herself out. "If you have need."

*

She would not sleep this night, she knew. For long hours she didn't even try. The late movie blared from the television unwatched, unheard.

Scattered images wandered before her eyes – white bears and locked doors, the panic in George's face; scraps of phrases sounded in her ears. *If you weren't a bad boy, your mother would come back. Face facts, Mr. Michaels; you've failed again.* Her soul had been rent wide open this day. Hot acid had been poured into the gashes.

At 3:30 a.m., she tried to sleep, more out of an awareness that she should sleep than any conscious feeling of need. She lay down on her bed. After a minute, she got up and got dressed to go out. This afternoon she'd thought it was hard to travel back in time, but it wasn't at all, it was easy! But somehow she'd got all gnarled up in streamers.

Adele shook herself free. She was coming out of the haunted house at Carolyn's Halloween party. Good – then none of it has happened yet! *It was all a dream, I don't have to live it.* Someone asked her to dance. George? No, Lem; how lucky for him Carolyn invited him. *Of course I'll dance with you,* she answered. *I'm a wonderful dancer. I'm so glad you got your teeth fixed,* because he had, he looked wonderful, and he danced divinely, except that she wasn't dancing with him, she was dancing with Franklin Fischer. How had that happened? *This is my show,* he whispered. She didn't want to dance with him. *Tell him to go away,* Milly said, but Adele couldn't, because she'd lost her voice.

I was only doing my job, said an overweight, middle-aged man she'd never met, but knew was Vincent Driscoll. *I vass only followink ordairs,* everyone echoed back. He was led off to be hung with the other dummies and everyone laughed, because he should have known that it was the same thing without being hung – everyone laughed but Adele, because she knew now this wasn't a dream, but a nightmare.

But for a while it was all right. Gertha, the young Gertha, was dancing with Sam Johnson. Mr. Johnson? I never met you, but I admire you so much. *Thank you; I came here specially to meet you.* Walt Greenfield was dancing with Rebecca Smithson. Adele could hear his John Wayne, terrible as always. Georgia Richmond was with Paul Harlow. She saw it now – all the dancers, all the music, all part of a pattern, they were all there. Of course! It was all part of the same code. So simple – why hadn't she thought of it? Run the AI Program; it'll tell you everything in less than twenty questions. Where was her laptop? How could she have forgotten it? She took it everywhere.

Suddenly Gertha, the old Gertha, the alcoholic hag, was beside her, holding the computer. *Here it is,* she said. *Thank you,* Adele said gratefully. But it was dead! Completely dead! *Of course,* said Gertha, *you forgot to recharge it. But what do I do now?* Adele asked. *Go away,* Gertha said. *Leave me alone. Ideas belong to the people who love them. You have to dance till he's done playin' with you. You know who.*

She was back on the dance floor with Franklin Fischer. He held her much too tightly. The music was too fast. She didn't want to dance with him, she wanted to dance with George. Where was George? Oh, there he was. He pulled a string crazily, and she was frightened, but it wasn't the real George, only the puppet George; someone had pulled his string. The Hanged Man swung around, but not on a gibbet. It swung from a vise holding its left hand to a beam. And it wasn't a dummy, it was Lem, and he hadn't had his teeth fixed after all; his buck toothed grin leered obscenely at her. She tried to turn away, but couldn't. Then the corpse winked at her as she watched. She wanted to scream, but couldn't do that, either.

Brown, twisting, sinuous bodies, writhing all around her; the room was small, overcrowded; she knew where she was now, became more frightened. On a large throne sat a tall quiet man, watching, watching, but she did not dare look him in the face. Across the room she saw a small dummy with a small white bottom. *Bobby Lawton,* she thought insanely, *what horrible taste!* All of a sudden, the bottom twitched. She looked around. Oh, no! How could she not have seen it sooner! What she'd thought were dummies hung around the floor weren't dummies at all. They were all living, bleeding–

*

She awoke sweating, in a full adrenaline panic. Her night clock showed 3:38; she had only been asleep eight minutes; the entire nightmare couldn't have lasted more than a few seconds. *This must be what it's like,* she thought. *Every night.*

She went back to the living room, turned on the light, sat down on the couch; events pounded through her mind. She'd made the biggest mistake it is possible to make. A mortal man had presented her with magic, forged in the fires of his own soul, and she had refused the gift. *We're not in real time anymore, Adele.* At once her face was in her hands and it was upon her again, sobbing, completely beyond control. She tried the normal self-flagellation – *get hold of yourself, st-*. . . but it didn't work; she wasn't up for it; there was too much reality to it.

Dawn found her still seated on the couch of the living room, waiting for the day, her hands on her abdomen. She had not attempted sleep again. She'd tried to console herself with the dream books, but they seemed so far off, so childish. She had no ideas for sketches that she'd ever want to see again. The television was still on, still unwatched. The rim of the sun peeped slowly over the world's edge.

This is the day everything ends, she thought. *This is it.*

She hugged herself. *At least you're safe, little one.* Scattered thoughts of the baby had been the only consolation during the night. There had been no more tears; what good were tears? Slowly, awkwardly, the cool, calm girl was regaining control. The milk had been spilt twenty-five years ago. One of the two things of which she had become intuitively certain during the long hours was that she was never again in her life going to see Thomas Bryant Newcombe. The same as Milly, she'd had her one chance and she'd failed. One was all you get; never again. Tom would never know that she was the mother of his first (? – she hoped) child.

She rose, and staggered towards the bathroom. What she saw in the mirror revolted her. *And people used to call you a pretty girl*, she thought, then managed a wan smile. A lot of makeup would be necessary today; she had to do something about the circles under her eyes, the paleness in her cheeks. She had appointments to keep this morning. She had a banquet to attend this evening. Not for worlds would she have missed any of it.

For the long, dismal day, the endless searching night, had brought her to a second intuitive certainty – the invisible machinery whose gears she had sensed working on the day she joined the Project had not finished its cycle. It had begun to whir on the day she met Tom; it would not be still until the NATPE dinner was over, the Project complete. *Nothing happens by chance*; today, somehow, she was certain she was going to discover what all of it meant, what the pattern really indicated.

By 8:30, she had succeeded in creating a satisfactory illusion of wellbeing. *Not bad*, she thought, looking into the mirror. The time had come to leave. She looked around her apartment as if she were a stranger.

Because everything had to be different. Maybe everything already was.

For this is the day everything ends.

Joseph Wurtenbaugh

THE DEVIL HIMSELF

T he drizzle had become smuggier the whole day long. The forecasters all said a storm was coming, but so far it was the same, unseasonable southern rain that had lingered long into November – too warm to be natural.

The vase clock read 5:15. Adele stood behind the locked door of her office, changing into her second piece of evening wear, the one George hadn't seen, a full-fledged evening gown. It was the first time she'd been back there since morning. The hours since dawn had mushed together, an impressionistic montage of color and brightness, hectic people, transmuted shapes and figures. The last day of NATPE had produced an atmosphere of understated frenzy.

Grimly, she had marched through her appointments, a tiny ball of purposefulness becoming harder and harder within her. Outwardly, she flashed an automatic smile, chirped, and semi-flirted. Inwardly, numb, encased in ice, she wondered – *Can they all be so blind? Can't any see they're dealing with a zombie?* Six appointments – two were polite: *You made some very interesting points, but we're satisfied with our present counsel, thank you, Ms. Jansen.* Three others indifferently invited her to call and say more. The best were the people who had been concerned about residuals. All she had to do there was introduce Ed Anderson, a superstar in his own right, and sit back. When the two of them left, they were almost certain the producer would become a Hapgood client.

All of a sudden, in the middle of the afternoon, the exhibition floor was alive with festive, middle-aged executives, an eerie, unnerving reminiscence of her nightmare. Carolyn was beside her, beaming a large, theatrical smile. "Number twenty-five signed on about a half an hour ago," she said. "We're there. We've made it." George was nowhere in sight. The celebration moved on. Carolyn lagged behind. The smile disappeared abruptly.

"I still expect you at the banquet tonight," she said coldly. "Too many people have mentioned your performance yesterday. Meet at the CFS offices at seven. As for the rest, I'll deal with you Monday. In my office. Ten sharp." Then she whirled and caught up with the others.

Adele smiled wanly. Big joke. *There isn't going to be a Monday, Carolyn. At least not one in any time continuum that you or I could imagine. This is the day everything ends.*

The great convention was winding down. Now the aisles were less crowded, mostly curious exhibitors who hadn't had time all week to see the sights. Now, too, small private parties were breaking out, some toasting success, others anesthetizing failure. Champagne had been broken out at the Furston booth. After a moment, she realized the occasion was not a celebration, but a wake.

"I guess we'll have to take it back to the old girl," Bill Andrews said, with barely concealed bitterness. "I was hoping. . ." The week had been a bust. The others berated, complained, laughed, and drank more. Death's door hilarity. Adele did her best to commiserate. *Don't they know? The unreality of all of it? None of it matters. It's all gone in a puff of wind.* All around, the displays, the show, everything, was ending.

Now it was 5:45, back in her office, and she was dressed. The gown was the slinkiest thing she owned, white and off one shoulder, something that would have come as a considerable shock to the Glee Club, something that George would have. . . if only. . . No. For a moment, the entire weight of the last seven weeks leaned against her.

So tired.

But now the time had come to leave. For the first time since the whole improbable saga began, she had a sense that she had caught up with, outpaced in fact, events. Now they gathered behind and above her, gaining weight, building momentum. The time would soon be at hand.

*

The offices of CFS were deserted. All the lights on the first floor were on. Surprised, she walked past the empty reception desk into the trading room in which she had once been terrified. No one was present, but an explanation was. A large banner was hung across the center of the room, over Franklin Fischer's desk: "25 AND COUNTING". Plastic cups, an occasional beer can, empty wine bottles, half-eaten pieces of white cake with raspberry filling, littered the cubicles. Obviously, the party that had swept by at the convention had ended here. She peeked around the doors, into the adjoining offices. No one.

The silence was eerie. A bit apprehensively, Adele walked back out to the elevator. Both were on the ground floor, doors open. She rode up to the fourth. No one was there, either. The lights were out, except for a dim glow at the end of the corridor. She moved cautiously down the hall towards that. As she neared the other end of the corridor, she heard voices. Carolyn and Franklin were still talking in his office in normal tones, occasional laughter. She absolutely did not want to join them. She decided to wait in the boardroom down the hall.

She opened the door and stepped in.

George Sorenson was sitting at the head of the table, in the darkness, his head in his hands. He looked up when he heard her.

*

"Adele!" he said, brightening momentarily, moving to her, putting his hands on her waist. She bit her lip, shook her head sideways, took his wrists, and gently, but emphatically, removed his arms. He was not the first man to discover that she was much stronger than she looked – all the years of field hockey, all the slap shots.

"Oh," he said, understanding. He peered more closely. "The angel," he said dully.

"Yes," she answered after a moment. "It's a little casual for the occasion, but it's what I'm going to wear."

"I looked for you yesterday," he went on. "I wanted to talk more."

"I wasn't avoiding you," she said, truthfully, after another long moment. "There was something I had to do." He stood facing her in the darkness, searching for words, as awkward and tentative as the day he had first come to lunch.

"What do you want from me, Adele?" he said suddenly, spreading his hands out, in his flat, unadorned Bronx voice. "Tell me something I don't know; I blew it, O.K.? I goofed it up. The guys and the thing were what it was all about with you. You're the death before dishonor type. I should have figured it out. I'm sorry." His hands spread wider.

"But. . . but. . . I was trying, Paloma. For you. For us. I don't know you all that well yet – only well enough to love you. You have to guess a little bit at the start with anyone, like flying on instruments. I took my best shot – for you." He looked at her more carefully. "That so terrible? You hate me for that?"

Hate him?? As she stood two feet away from him, she felt the chemistry as strongly as ever. Her heart was beating, her pulse was racing. He was wonderfully attractive to her, silhouetted against the window – and not a bad man, either, not at all. What had happened was as much her fault as his. If only she'd been clear that what she wanted was not a girl's request, but a woman's demand – he was clever; he might have found a way. But now she felt the chasm as well as the chemistry, the gulf that stood between them. He, and all that he was, was inextricably bound up with the "everything" that had to be different.

"You can't not believe in second chances," he went on, bewildered. "I couldn't have fallen for you so hard so fast if you didn't. What do you want, Adele? What do I have to do? There has to be a way to get back here."

Not believe in second chances? There were universes, entire worlds, where George Sorenson had all the chances he needed, an infinity of them, if that's what was required.

But right now this one wasn't one of them.

"Do you want me to get down on my knees? Do you want me to beg? I'll do anything you say."

"I don't hate you, George," Adele answered at last, measuring her words, "and it's not you who needs forgiveness. It's mostly me. Things I've done, things I haven't done."

"That's not possible," he replied instantly. "You couldn't have done anything I couldn't forgive you for. It can't lie there."

What to say?? What to do?? *Give him the one thing you've never given him,* a voice inside her ordered. *The truth, for a change.*

"There's a lot about me, who I am, what I've been doing, that you don't know," she began, summoning herself up. "A lot I should have told you at the beginning. In the first place, the whole time I've known you I've been pre –"

The door opened. "Pardon us for interrupting," said Franklin Fischer, suavely. Carolyn stood beside him, with a peculiar look, as if she were enjoying the same grim private joke. "It's time we were preparing for the banquet. It's time we firmed up our arrangements."

*

"Listening in again, Franklin?" George said coldly.

"Quite illuminating, George," Franklin Fischer said. "'Do you want me to get down on my knees?' `I'll do anything you say.'" He shook his head sadly. "How are the mighty fallen. To hear you abasing yourself in that manner. To a wisp of a girl. I never would have believed it."

"I got my priorities set, Franklin," George replied, looking at him. "You got your company. I want my friend back. I know what she's worth. I'm not embarrassed to beg her if I have to. Mostly, I don't think it's any of your business anymore."

"You see?" Franklin Fischer continued, as if George had said nothing, turning to Carolyn. "It is as I said." He turned back to George. "To think of one of the lions of Wall Street humbled in this manner. You've lost touch with reality, my friend. You've taken leave of your senses and your common sense. This is the arena you belong in, George; this is your natural milieu. This is a great day; this is a day of destiny; but it is only the start. Only the beginning. I don't want to lose you, George. I don't think I can afford to lose you." He shifted his glance to Adele.

"She's only another woman, George," he added softly. "She's the same as all the rest. It has been very difficult these last weeks to watch you as you lost your head over her."

"I don't like the way this is goin'," George responded, still cold. He turned to Carolyn. "You bring the dissolution?" Carolyn nodded. "Good. We sign it, we go to the party – you become a big communications guy, you go on with your mission, I try to get back to where I was with Adele." He glanced at her, then looked back. "Whether I can do that is what scares me. Otherwise everything's jake. Everybody's happy." He looked again at Carolyn. "So where is it?"

"Here it is, George," Carolyn said calmly. She'd been holding a file. She opened it and laid a document on the table, surprisingly thin. "Exactly as agreed."

The lawyer in Adele was astounded. Only two pages? George caught her eye, and answered her unspoken question.

"Short and sweet," he said. "The simpler, the better."

"The only thing is, George, I'm not sure I'm going to sign it," Franklin Fischer said pleasantly.

Adele thought George would panic. She had underestimated him. All he did was raise an eyebrow and turn to Carolyn.

"There are reasons enough, George," Carolyn said calmly. "The deal required you do everything you could in good faith to complete it. Yesterday, when we were rounding up the last signatures, you weren't there." She smiled knowingly. "Your own words. Think of all the money, all the time, all the –"

"Cut the lawyer crap," George interjected, smiling coldly. "Save it for the schmucks. You think I'd leave this to the courts?" He eyed Franklin Fischer. "You think I didn't figure on this? I've never seen you keep to a deal when you can welsh on one. You think I can't undo this still?" His smile was broader. "You think I'm kiddin'? Try me. Sign the goddamn thing; you can complete your mission, I'll try and get my friend to like me again. We'll both be happy."

"Jeezus, George," Carolyn said, shaking her head. "You sound like a schoolboy."

George ignored her, focused on Franklin Fischer.

"This time I may try you," Fischer answered steadily. "The situation has changed since last Friday. I have twenty-seven names on a dotted line now; all I needed was twenty-five. And all the EBS machinery is in place."

"Tell me something I don't know," George replied, still unfazed. "I keep my end of bargains, Franklin. Everything's set up and it'll run like a watch.

Unless someone fucks it up. Why you think I insisted on the cash out right now? You got a clear open field – unless I decide to make a couple phone calls. A few people at EBS I haven't told you about." His smile broadened. "You thought I plain forgot about an escrow? Schmuck. Would've screwed up the capital requirements. Not possible." He paused. "But I'm done carryin' you, friend. Someone else is gonna have to. Sign the thing."

"I see." Franklin Fischer was also unfazed. "I knew there would be something. But I don't know how I'll manage without you, George. I always assumed somehow somewhere along the line you'd change your mind. And I think I would have been correct, if it hadn't been for. . ." He looked at Adele, then back at George. He spread his hands.

"I don't want war with you, George. You're an astute lieutenant. It's foolish for the two of us to quarrel. I didn't come to offer war. I had something else entirely in mind. I'll sign the dissolution agreement. All I want – the only thing I want – is your consent to redo our arrangements this evening. I'd like you to take Carolyn to the dinner. I'd like the pleasure of escorting Ms. Jansen. That she'll go with me and – come with me to our little soirée afterwards."

"You're crazy," George answered. "You're completely nuts."

"Not at all, my friend, not at all," Franklin Fischer rejoined softly. "You're not yourself, George. You're not seeing reality clearly. You think so much is possible for you that is not – and –" he gestured towards Adele – "all the daydreaming has to do with her. It's all tied up with her. I had thought at one time she might be part of the solution. But she's obviously the fundamental problem." He paused. "Losing you, George, would be bad enough. But to lose you to an illusion? Your false notions about yourself are all bound up with your false perceptions of her. 'I know her worth,' you said. Do you? She's the same as the rest of us, George – the same goals, the same ambitions. If she hasn't come to terms with herself yet, it's because she hasn't had the need. When push comes to shove, she'll make the same compromises." He turned and eyed Adele calmly. "Perhaps she's begun already," he added softly.

"And, ultimately, to get what she wants she will do what she has to – the same as anyone else. Don't you see? There is no new, improved George Sorenson, waiting to emerge from the cocoon. It is no more possible for you to walk away from this life than it is for you to flap your arms and fly to the moon. This life you created is you; try to abandon it and you will destroy yourself. The same thing will be true of Adele ultimately. The same thing is true of all of us." He looked at her again.

"A climber – the only slight distinction is that she's been naïve enough, and lucky enough, to think she could avoid paying the price. Carolyn has warned us both about that all along. Now I can see how right she was it is. But put her face to face with the inevitable cost, and she will pay it. I'm convinced of that. I'm going to prove that to you – tonight, at the dinner, and afterward. More melodramatically than I would have liked, but there is no other way. Then this will all be behind and we'll be partners as we always have been. There are going to be so many new adventures, so many new fron –"

"You are nuts," George said, now aroused. "I got into trouble with her trying to keep her away from you guys. You think I'm going to stand for that?"

"Then it will be war," Franklin answered without hesitation. Adele could see he meant it. "Such a foolish, unnecessary war. . . and you without the resources to fight it properly. George, how can you be so concerned about Adele joining us at the party? What possible difference can it make? This is what I mean by taking leave of your senses. She'll be wiser for the experience and so will you. So much wiser."

"No," George replied. "I don't want her anywhere near you. Not for a minute; not even for a second." He hesitated. "People who get mixed up with you have a way of staying mixed up. If it's war you want, it's war you've got. I can take care of myself." He shook his head. "You really want to try me?"

"Amazing," Franklin Fischer said, shaking his head in turn and picking up the dissolution agreement. "With everything at stake, you are arguing with me about an evening with a woman. Amazing. I stand by my point. I want to bring you back to your senses. I can see no other means." He paused and smiled.

"Besides, you and your – friend – are a thing of the past. Don't you know? You shattered it completely Thursday morning." He smiled more broadly. "I had the idea she should come to the board meeting. Her own misconceptions about you seem to have been the inspiration for yours about her. I felt she should see you as you really are, before she became too deeply enamored. Carolyn agreed."

"Well, well, well," George answered. "So it was you. What a shrewdie you turned out to be. I've never known you to be such a shrewdie before." He hesitated, then continued. "But it's still no dice. I'll take my chances with you, and I'll take my chances I can put it back with her. She doesn't hate me –"

"We know," Carolyn interposed, shaking her head again. "We heard."

"I'll take my chances," he went on, ignoring her. "I got all tangled up in the money thing twenty years ago. Not twice." He smiled. "Besides. . . war? Easy talk, Franklin. The time will come. You'll need me. You'll back off sooner or later."

"'Those whom the gods destroy, they first make mad,'" he answered softly, sarcastically. "You fool." The he turned to Adele. "Perhaps you have more sense, Ms. Jansen. Perhaps –"

"I'll go with you to the dinner, Mr. Fischer," she replied.

*

Because of a word Franklin Fischer had used without thinking – freedom.

Because of what Gertha had written: *I left him to live with monsters. I thought of nothing else and it destroyed my life.* She was not going to leave George Sorenson entangled with monsters.

Because there is only one way to do it – Joanna's way. *It stops now. Today. This instant.*

Because in truth and in fact this was her fight.

Because this was where it had been heading all along.

*

"Adele!" George exclaimed, startled, appalled. Carolyn smiled knowingly.

"I'll go to the banquet with you," Adele continued. "I may or may not be leaving with you."

Franklin Fischer contemplated her for a moment, then smiled broadly. "Excellent. That will be sufficient – for now. We can discuss our plans for the balance of the evening while we're there. I'm sure you'll be reasonable – eventually. Everything will fall into place."

Adele nodded. "Good. Then sign the dissolution," she said tonelessly, without taking her eyes off him. Franklin Fischer did not move. "Or I'm not going with you," she added, bluffing a little; she didn't know what she'd do if he wouldn't.

"Adele. . . Paloma," George broke in, as agitated as she'd ever seen him, "don't do this. I don't want you anywhere near this guy." He turned to Franklin. "All right. . . O.K. . . you win." He gestured towards the document on the table. "You can tear up the goddamned thing. I'll stay. We'll go on with CFS like we did."

Franklin Fischer smiled. "This is my day, George. My destiny. You were a fool to think you could overcome that. Still. . ." He eyed George with a cold contempt and held up the document. "All this, balanced against an evening with a woman. . . and you strike the balance the other way." He shook his head decisively. "No. The moonshine is what concerns me, George. What use to me are you if you remain caught up in it?" He turned back to Adele. "A generous offer, but I believe I will escort Ms. Jansen nonetheless."

"Then sign the dissolution," Adele said, hoping that the day would come quickly when she could tell George that when he played Joe Hero, he did it very, very well. Franklin Fischer looked at Carolyn.

"It won't do them any good until it's delivered," Carolyn said, shrugging. "Sign it, but keep it with you. . . until you think it's the right time to deliver it," she went on calmly.

Fischer nodded silently, and then stepped to the table. With a quick, deft movement he uncapped a fountain pen, turned to the last page, and signed. For a moment he held it protectively.

"Witness it, Carolyn," Adele ordered peremptorily. The smile left Carolyn's face. "How dare you talk – " she began.

"I said witness it," Adele interrupted.

"Do it, Carolyn," Franklin Fischer said smugly. "It won't make any difference." He slid the document and the pen to Carolyn's side of the table. Still scowling, she lifted the page and signed her own name underneath Franklin Fischer's. "Satisfied?" she said querulously, looking at Adele.

Adele nodded slightly. "I'll go to the dinner with you now, Mr. Fischer."

"Then I think our arrangements for this evening are settled," Franklin Fischer replied easily, confidently. "George, if you would be so good as to escort Ms. Hoffman? The limousines are waiting at the back entrance. I'd like some private words with Ms. Jansen."

"Franklin, if you. . . if you so much as – " George Sorenson was choking with fury. *Don't worry, George*, she would have liked to say, but it was not possible.

"You'll do what?" Franklin said easily. "Hate me? You've hated me for eighteen years, George. It hasn't made any difference. The limousines are idling. You two really must be on your way."

"Just a moment," said Carolyn, approaching and eying Adele professionally. "Gown's all right. . . what kind of coat are you wearing?"

"My wool coat." The only one she owned.

"As I thought," Carolyn sighed. "Not nearly dressy enough. It's likely we're all going to be photographed. I brought along one of my furs for you."

"I'm not wearing a fur, Carolyn," Adele said.

"Adele, I – "

"I've never worn a fur in my life and I'm not starting tonight."

"Adele's coat will suffice, Carolyn," Franklin Fischer intoned.

Carolyn shrugged helplessly, peered more closely. "That necklace is pathetic. I'll loan you something more appropriate."

Adele shook her head again. "No."

Carolyn lost patience. "This is not a social event, Ms. Jansen. This is part of your professional responsibility. You can't go to an event like this wearing something like that."

"Yes, I can," Adele said doggedly, "because I'm going to. I'm not taking off my angel. For you or anyone."

Carolyn became angrier. "You are the most stubborn –"

"Carolyn," Franklin Fischer said wearily, "you must be leaving. Her jewelry seems to me to be adequate. Unusual, but adequate. After all, she's not going to be the focus of anyone's attention."

Carolyn eyed her one more time, then nodded. "All right." She stepped to the door. "When Franklin first suggested this – change – to me," she said softly, to Adele, "I didn't agree. Not until Tuesday – and the board meeting yesterday. Then it made sense. You can't remain as innocent as you are, Rebecca. It's too dangerous. To yourself and others." She glanced at George. "I wish it could be different, but it can't. Franklin's right. As usual." She shifted her fur around her shoulders. For a moment, she seemed closer to sixty than forty. Adele could smell vodka on her breath, wondered for a moment what the evening held in store for her.

"Enough," Franklin Fischer said easily.

George's eyes had narrowed to slits. "You go on ahead. I gotta go back to my place. I'll meet you there." Carolyn shrugged. "Certainly." She moved out the door. George turned around, took Adele in, then glared again at Franklin Fischer, who ignored him. Then he, too, was gone, moving briskly down the hall.

Adele stood alone in the darkened boardroom with Franklin Fischer. A long moment passed. Then he stood, spread his arms, and smiled a smile of boyish charm.

"You must think I have horns and a tail," he said.

*

She did not reply.

"I can hardly say I blame you. The scenes you've witnessed in the last two days – it wouldn't be natural if you didn't blame me. Do you think I enjoyed them?" he said disarmingly. "I didn't. I don't like pain. I'm not evil, Adele – not a bit. All this was bound to happen. There was an inevitability to it. And hasn't it all worked out for the best? Young Michaels was no businessman. We could all see that. You could, too. The moment when he had to face that fact was as a painful one for him – for me as well. But –" he paused – "but –

"He will go back to the academe – where he belongs, Adele, where he belongs. He will succeed there. He will do brilliant things – and he will be a rich young man as well. I truly believe a time will come when he will view Thursday,

November 18th, as one of the best days of his life."

Adele said nothing

"And George?" he continued, then glanced for a moment at the release. His expression was sad, almost regretful. "Before yesterday, did you have any idea of the quality of man with whom you'd become involved? George is a Wall Street legend, Adele – the hardest, shrewdest, most practical man I've ever encountered. I knew he'd have something in reserve tonight because he always does. He's a creature perfectly adapted to this environment. He thrives here. The real George Sorenson would never have missed the signings yesterday – or become enmeshed in this preposterous dialog tonight. Of course you know the reason why. He thinks of me as his dark angel. He's associated all sorts of fantastical notions about himself with you. I know it's not your fault, but that is the reality. I wish there had been some other, less drastic method to bring him back to his senses. But I could think of none.

""Do you know the details of our arrangement? You should. Years ago, when he first approached me, he agreed that the management of our capital would remain under my exclusive control, until one of us dissolved the partnership. It was my capital, after all. I never abused the privilege, I was never unfair. Of course I knew a day would come – but *now*?? When we have climbed the mountain, with the world at our feet? The power, the prestige, the wealth – it makes everything we have done to date seem trifling, pin money, pocket change. George knows this better than I do, he knows most things better than I. And he would turn his back on all his for . . . what? An illusion, a mirage. This is not the George Sorenson I have known. This makes no sense.

"Now – tonight – he would revise his plans again. For you – or more, accurately, the mirage you've come to embody. It's almost the punch line to a bad joke." He glanced sorrowfully at the document again.

Then he looked up at Adele and sighed heavily. "He can't avoid his destiny. The dreams he dreams of a newer, better George Sorenson are patent delusions. All this is – let us not mince words – is an ordinary midlife crisis, nothing more. The type that occurs in every life. I owe it to our partnership – to our friendship – yes, despite what you heard – not to let him lose himself like that."

He gestured around the room. "There has been an inevitability in all of it, Adele. A reason for it. Fischer Communications Company is going to become the most powerful media company in the world – the cutting edge for change. It's going to expose the helots, the vermin, the useless, for what they are. Not right away, of course. Herculean work remains to be done before it becomes the refined instrument I need. A colossal amount of dead wood has to be eliminated. I'll need all the assistance I can get. I can't lose George." He paused. "Nor you," he added.

"Because there was also an inevitability about us. About you and me. This moment had to come. George can't avoid his destiny – and neither can you."

He moved closer to her, almost looming. "I can see the future, Adele. I don't flinch from it; I embrace it. That's the secret of my power, over George, over all of you. You're a part of that future. Accept it. Acknowledge it." He moved closer. "You're more talented than I am. So is George, much more. So, for that matter, is Carolyn. Actually, there are only two things I'm good at. One is knowing what I want. The other is getting it." The room was lit only by the eerie glow of the lights across the street; it seemed as if that was the last light left in the universe. He was morbidly fascinating in the semi-dark.

"This is what you have aspired to all along, Adele. This is what you've worked for, what you've dreamt about. You're no different than any of us." He smiled again. "You've made your compromises, you're prepared to make others. You wouldn't be standing here, in this room, if you hadn't. This is only one more, Adele. Trivial in itself. More important than the others only because of what's at stake."

He switched gears: "Everything you've done, all that you've accomplished, has led to this night. Surely you didn't think you'd do what you've done and escape unscathed? This is the only possible end to that journey. You knew what was involved from the beginning, and yet you went on. You knew there'd be consequences." She looked up at him, startled. He was apparently talking about the new company – and yet, for one spit second, she could have sworn that he was talking about . . .

"No one forced you to join the Project," he continued, "you did it freely. It's not possible to walk in, accept the benefit of the bargain, and then walk out again on your own terms." He smiled gently, companionably, somehow with a note of confiding wisdom, and rolled his eyes over her.

"That truly is quite an attractive gown," he said softly. "I have no quarrel with George's taste. Only his priorities." Something glimmered in her face; he noticed.

"Don't become angry. I'm simply stating a fact. Men are fascinated by power. Women are fascinated by powerful men – so I have found. You're one of them, Adele. You're drawn to powerful men, Adele. I could see it in your eyes yesterday. I can see it in your bearing tonight. Acquiescence – surrender – is your natural end – a denouement you find natural, even exciting, and not at all diminishing. Surrender for a woman is not defeat." He spread his hands. "I know this is crude, clumsy – I am sorry for that. I wish it had not been so abrupt. We should have more time. I wish events had not conspired against us."

He paused. "But does that change anything? There is more at issue here than George and the partnership. There is something inevitable for you here, something inescapable. I felt that yesterday. You did as well. You glimpsed your own destiny yesterday – and I know you can see the pattern clearly tonight. If so, if there is more. . . there is no shame in accepting one's fate, Adele. None at all in coming to terms with the inevitable. Particularly for a woman."

Physically, he was not an unattractive man. He was close enough now to whisper to her: "I always succeed, Adele. What is inevitable is irresistible. Most women know that. I think you know that better than most. In fact, I know you feel a little excitement in that very thought." He paused; his tone softened: "And it is for the best, for your best. I will be very, very good to you, I promise. I'm quite familiar with the care and keeping of beautiful women. In fact, I'm something of a connoisseur."

His tone changed abruptly again: "But that is the only inevitable aspect of any of this. Carolyn's anger with you? Her plans to bring in a high-tech partner vertically? I can stop that. You can be a partner at Hapgood before another six months have elapsed. I can do that, too – and you will only be receiving what you know you've earned. You know that. No one doubts your ability. Companies? I can bring you a hundred companies like AI Squared. George? George will have his money – his services are all I want – and he'll have you back." He smiled. "We are all adults. He said he could forgive you anything. He will. You know that. You know all these things."

Fischer spread his hands. "You feel guilty about any of these events? You can redeem all of them – your entire bad conscience. It's not too late. You can restore everything. All you have to do is what comes most naturally, and that is acceptance of what has to be."

He could do what he said, she knew that. An ambiance of irresistible force permeated the room, the world. By any objective standard, he was right. Levers had fallen into place for him all week long, all night long – in spite of all George's planning, in spite of all his care. Levers had fallen for him all his life. They always would.

He dropped his eyes again. "Anything is possible for you, Adele. Merely do what I ask for this evening. Do as I ask. Come with me to the party– and everything you want will be yours. Don't resist; resistance is useless. Don't surrender to me. Surrender to your own dreams. Surrender to what you've always wanted. Surrender to your own self."

Even closer now, edging into the zone of her space. His face was only inches from hers. Softly, gently he put his hand on her bare shoulder.

So this is the one, she thought wearily. *The ultimate predator.* It figured: of course, he would be found here, right in the center of events, and it was a good line, a great line, in fact. But she heard the last of it with only one ear. From the deep recesses of her mind, the old memories were returning, the ones she never revisited of her own free will. The Friday evening of the Spring Rush. . .

*

"What's going on?" seventeen-year-old Adele Jansen asked, looking up at the man she adored. Roger the Rush Chairman was straightening his collar with his back to her. He always put his clothes back on before she did. She knew already that this was not the typical Friday night fraternity party. The punch was much stronger; beneath the raucousness throughout the house, she sensed a hint of something ominous in the atmosphere. "What's happening?" she asked again.

"Big night, little girl," he answered finally, with a lazy smile, turning toward her. "All the important rushes are here. Guys we have to get." He sat down on the edge of the bed; she had not yet begun to dress. "Everyone's pitching in." He paused. "I'd kind of like you to help."

"Help?" Adele said. "How?"

His smile broadened. "No big deal, girl. Nothing that doesn't happen all the time. Do a little favor." He leaned over and kissed her lightly. "Some friends of mine. That's all."

Her stomach twisted over and over. For an instant, she did not believe what she'd heard; then she understood, with a familiar palpitating excitement.

It had begun nine months before. She'd been invited to a get-acquainted party at one of the fraternities – no big deal, every female freshman with even a semblance of attractiveness was also invited. The weather was good and classes hadn't started yet. She stood on the grass in the back yard, drinking the third and fourth, later the fifth, beers of her entire life. An upperclassman asked her to dance. The first was fast, the second slow; they didn't really dance; swayed together. His body felt good against hers. He asked her up to his room. *Why not?* She was a big college girl now.

They lay on his bed. She got hot quickly, as she always did, but everything was under control. She allowed him to undress her partially. A fever began to heat her blood. Then he was going further than she liked. *No*, she said. What exactly he responded next, she could not remember – something like, *you're a girl, you're going to be made, girls are made to be made.* In any case, it was not the precise formulation that did it – it was the growling, primitive male sexuality that accompanied it – demanding, dangerous. . . macho. . . thrilling.

No one had ever come on to her like that. She'd grown up in a small town, where everyone knew her. She was totally unprepared for the full-fledged hormonal blast that roared through her, an all but uncontrollable response. The remainder of her clothes disappeared almost instantaneously. A few seconds later, with a minimum of pain, her virginity (which had been reserved for Bri) was lost to a complete stranger. One delirious shock of pleasure followed another – then suddenly she knew she was one of the lucky ones. She was going to find out everything the first time out. The bodies moved, her blood roared, and then came a moment of such blinding, absolute ecstasy that she cried out in spite of herself. She had sensed that this sort of reward lay at the end of the road, but nothing had prepared her for its intensity.

Still in shock, she let her – seducer? – lead her downstairs, exhibiting his triumph. Quietly he slapped the hand of a friend. "First virgin of the new year," he crowed quietly. "And absolute dynamite." She had an impression he'd won a bet or pool. She would have expected she'd be appalled, but not so. It seemed natural; if she felt so much like a conquest, why shouldn't he behave like a conqueror? He hadn't even done the responsible thing, had inseminated her without taking any care. It was only his good luck she was on the pill. A coarse, insensitive lout – yet she had discovered a universe she hadn't known existed underneath his body.

With that she was off, on a sexual odyssey that lasted most of her freshman year. She'd gone from virgin to sexual addict in a matter of seconds. Scholastically, college held no terrors, despite an immense course load. She had been superbly prepared, and most of the units were survey classes, more tedious than challenging. Even the advanced placements were unthreatening. The pattern was set in the first few weeks. The weekends would become imminent; the invitations to the party would come – needless to say, she had become a very, *very* popular girl overnight – and she would go. Never the same boy twice; never overnight; nothing remotely close to a relationship. Intimacy held no interest for her. Concubinage was what intoxicated her.

So it had gone, week by week, growing entanglement, growing sense of descent, until a night in mid-November, when the shape of the inevitable last act began to take form. Roger was a senior, enrolled in a survey art history class. He paid no attention to her – no one in the class did – until the week after the first written report was due, after which the instructor directed too many questions at her for her to remain inconspicuous. She felt his eyes on her after that and recognized his interest, a small movement in the larger frame of events.

Then, on that night, he was in front of her. A slight, somewhat smug smile – *You're that freshman Adele. Would you like to dance?* Her pulsed raced; excitement built; it had begun. He pressed her against him, awkward but wonderful, and she could feel his own blood heat. He took her upstairs. Only afterwards did she learn his name. She had paid no attention to it in class.

She began to dress to leave. *Where do you think you're going, little girl?* he asked, supine, with the same smug smile. *Home,* she answered a bit nervously. *Back to the dorm, I mean. I can't sleep here. The bed's too small.* A polite fiction she had used more than once. In point of fact, she did not know what the beds were like to sleep in. He smiled again. *No, you're not,* he said, patting the mattress. *Not until I say you can. You belong to me now. Come here.* With that, the fruit, ripening those first weeks, matured and burst. She stopped buttoning her blouse and returned to his bed, more excited than ever, knowing as she did that she was crossing over a line that she should never have crossed over.

His directness enthralled her. She went back to his frat house the next night because he told her to, and spent the night with him – also spent the following Sunday afternoon. Then he did let her go back to her dorm. Monday, coming back from the library, she ran into him. *Where are you going?* he said. *Back to my dorm,* she answered. *No, you're not,* he'd smiled in the same way, *I thought I told you. . .* and she'd gone with him, exulting, horrified, wondering about herself, and spent another afternoon and night in his room. Sexually, she reached a pinnacle. Her essential physicality, conjoined with a novel sense of complete surrender, combined with a growing fearfulness that masqueraded as nervous exhilaration, resulted in exquisite, overpowering experiences. At that time, she attributed them to the forcefulness of his masculinity and his prowess in bed.

On it went. She was in love, she thought, or in awe, or in something. Nothing she did seemed to make any impression on him. His mastery over her became more complete with each passing moment. As it did, she discovered virtues – worldliness, sophistication – in an abundance she'd never known in any other human being. Her brightest wit, her best jokes, fazed him not at all. *Little girl,* he addressed her, never by name, and she accepted the diminutive as her due. He was amused, not delighted, by the intensity of her sexual reactions, which, like everything else she did, became a subject of subtle ridicule. Her pride became involved. She was determined to win him over, make an impression, but nothing seemed to work. Somehow the more she tried, the more unattainable he became. He was too far above her for anything to work.

Even then, only 17 and lost in sexual addiction, Adele was too bright not to have doubts, misgivings. But to question Roger's mastery was also to question the reality of the New Adele, the sophisticated worldly woman she had suddenly become. She balked only at the recreational drugs he and his friends used so casually, and he was wise enough not to insist. But that would come in time, they both knew.

Finally, the Friday night of Spring Rush arrived.

There were three friends of Roger's who needed favors that night. Her exhilaration reached a peak. Her blood was racing faster, but now, too, for the first time in a long time, she heard the voice of her real self. *This isn't playing at whoredom. This is the real thing. Don't do this.* But she had long since fallen out of the habit of saying no to herself. The perversity itself clamored on insistently. *This is it. This is the ultimate.* A whirlwind of confusion stormed through her being; she was simultaneously appalled, and delighted in being appalled.

The first of Roger's friends was named Alan Something, a pale, somewhat blobbish boy with glasses. It didn't seem to matter to him that the bed was unmade, that she was still sticky with Roger's sweat and semen. He did not introduce himself. He undressed wordlessly, with a nod and indifferent smile. He pulled a torn T-shirt over his head. His shoes fell heavily on the floor.

As he did, the excitement, all the frantic exhilaration, disappeared as suddenly and directly as if someone had switched off a light, replaced in an instant by a staggering sense of grim, squalid reality. She became aware only of the disorder of the room, the grime and subtle filth. Did Roger ever clean it? *This can't be happening*, she thought. She eyed the stranger. *I don't even like him.* Now, finally, she began to think of somehow getting out of this. *No*, intervened the voice of better reason suddenly, coldly, the voice of the woman she would soon become, *no. You led yourself here. Better to see it through. Better to find out, learn the lesson. Besides, you always finish what you start, don't you?*

Now, still wordlessly, he was upon her, attempting to arouse her in the way he probably thought James Bond did it. His touch made her skin crawl. Her body, with all its marvelous responses, even now did not fail her completely. She felt a debased, weary pleasure. But this night she could not lose herself in sensation. She had the feeling of standing outside herself, a disassociated, neutral observer, numb, as if someone had injected a powerful quantity of Novocain deep in her soul. Images assailed her. Not a year before she had given the valedictory address for her class to the entire town, charmed them all in the manner she had mastered. Not nine months before she had come to school with the world at her feet. Now she lay with a grunting boor who hadn't the courtesy to ask her name. . . and it occurred to her that he, not she, was right, that her name didn't matter in this filthy room, nor the fact that she could probably outsmart him in ways he didn't even know existed, nor that her mother had been a great artist. Nothing mattered except his need and the satisfaction of it.

This is wrong. This is all wrong. That thought pounded through her skull. This wasn't the ultimate at all. It was not the culmination of the naïve, exuberant sexuality with which it had all begun, but a grisly, ugly parody of that, a threat to everything she wanted for herself. Somehow the role of primitive female, only one of many she could play, had come to usurp all the others. She felt the first stirrings of panic. Her companion mistook it for passion and came to completion.

"I've been wanting to get into you for six weeks," he grunted as he dressed. Then the most instantly forgettable human being she ever met in her life departed. *At least I've touched bottom*, she thought.

Adele was in error. Touching bottom actually occurred with the second. His name was David, a football player, red-shirting, but a future superstar (so Roger said), as if any of that made any difference to her. He had a shy, backward charm. In different circumstances, she might have liked him. They went to Roger's room and undressed. The bed was still unmade, still warm, sheets stained and damp; the traces of the first two men were still on her body. Within ten seconds, while David was trying to adjust a condom, he'd splattered all over her. He dissolved in misery; held her, kissed her, apologized for ejaculating. It happened to him all the time, it had nothing to do with her, please don't say anything to anyone, maybe he shouldn't even try. Future All-American or not, he lay back on the pillow in despair.

No way she was going to leave anyone in that state, even on what she now knew to be the worst night of her life. She kissed him lightly on his chin, on his chest, above his navel, below his navel; without making any big deal about it, went to work. She'd learned more than a few tricks in the last eight months. After what seemed like forever, she drew a response. He reached down and pulled her up, rolled her over, and succeeded, probably for the first time in his life.

Afterward, he tried to say something tender, something loving. He tried to make love. Everything was wrong; everything was in reverse. She realized that beneath the numb vagueness she was angry, angry with herself, angry with all of them, angrier than she had ever been in her life. *That's enough*, said the inner voice. *Go home. Get out of here. Quickly.* "I'm going to go home now," she said, interrupting him. He realized then that nothing he said was going to make any difference.

"I'm sorry," he said finally. "I'm truly sorry."

It's all right, was what she meant to say. "You should be," is what came out. She dressed quickly and noticed the look on his face. "It's all right," she managed to choke out.

There was a third waiting. Roger was with him, expectant. She noticed a certain wariness in Roger's face. "I don't want to do this anymore," she said, apologetically. Disappointment appeared on the third boy's face. Roger appraised him, appraised her. . . then smiled at her lightly. "You've had a long night, little girl. Maybe you'd better go home," and kissed her lightly on the forehead.

A tremendous, overwhelming sense of gratitude surged over her. He *did* care! He *did* understand! Perhaps she had misjudged him. Perhaps there was hope after all. She smiled weakly herself, kissed him lightly, and let herself out the back of the darkened house. It was about 1:30.

The grass was soft under her feet. The moon was new, but the stars were bright. *I could not have done that,* the girl – still seven months short of her eighteenth birthday – told herself. *That couldn't have happened.* But it had.

She approached the dorm entrance, went up to her floor, showered and went to bed. Sleep came fitfully. At four o'clock she rose and showered again. *I could not have done that.* But she had. She slept a little better, rose at 7:30, showered and went down to breakfast, only to find she wasn't hungry. She went back upstairs, showered and went off to the library. She was afraid the phone would ring, afraid it would be Roger, afraid of herself, afraid of everything. She found she could not concentrate. She returned to the dorm, showered and went to lunch, where she found herself still without an appetite. The stained, unmade bed – she could not get it out of her mind. Yesterday everything she'd done had seemed adventurous and daring, the first chapters of freedom and adulthood; today it all appeared sordid and shameful.

Memories of the night before flooded her consciousness. The kiss on the forehead. *You've had enough, little girl.* How could someone who cared for her have done this to her? Suddenly the curtain was ripped off completely; the grinning skull appeared, and with it she heard for the first time in her life the authentic voice of the grown-up Adele. *Because he doesn't care for you,* it said. *Because he hates you. You're someone and he's no one, he knows it, and he can't stand it.* She recognized truth. Roger *hated* her – and she'd been pitifully, stupidly, grotesquely grateful – grateful! – *GRATEFUL!* – for that tiny crumb of common courtesy. For that pathetic kiss on the forehead! *GRATEFUL!!That he hadn't forced her to do the third one! GRATEFUL!! For a pimp's kiss!!* Rage swept over her. She found her teeth gritted and her hands clenched in complete, visceral fury. Grate– she was too angry to enunciate the word fully, even mentally. (For the rest of her life, whenever the memory assailed her, she would choke on that word, a psychological stammer.)

Even this was not the worst. The worst was, despite the insight, despite the anger, despite the newly acquired wisdom, something inside of her wanted to crawl back. Wave after wave of pure panic swept over her. *What's wrong with me? What am I becoming? What have I become?* The enjoyment of being enjoyed, the delight not merely in giving pleasure, but being it, had seemed natural, quintessentially feminine, the archetypal female mode. How could it have led her to this place? Created this threat to her very self? *I will not allow this to be,* she decided suddenly, a resolve emanating out of the core of her being. With that thought, her girlhood finally died. Her innocence, which had lingered on long after her virginity, vanished with it; and the woman who would be casually described as a control freak two years later came into being.

She wrote a light, graceful note to Bri, declining a Spring Break invitation. With heart in mouth, she phoned the frat, felt a mixture of disappointment and relief that Roger wasn't available, left a message that she would not be over that night. Adele was now alone in her room; everyone else was out celebrating the spring. She tried to read, but couldn't. She took a shower, retired, and went promptly to restless sleep.

At 7:26 p.m. on Saturday night.

For the next few days, Adele lived like a cave dweller, leaving her room only for class and meals, afraid to answer the telephone, afraid of a chance meeting, afraid of her own self. When the break came, she returned home, tight-lipped and stony faced. She helped prepare Easter dinner. She smiled and played with Buck's children. The balance of the week she spent in her room, door closed, pleading the press of studies and a mild cold. Privately, her father worried and wondered what had happened to the vibrant, open girl who had left home eight months before. She smiled reassuringly at him when she closed the door to her room behind her on Sunday to return to school. But something had turned to steel. Her plans were made. Adele the Freshman was gone forever. She girded herself for a confrontation.

Which never occurred.

There was no confrontation. There was nothing to confront. There never had been. That was possibly the most frightening discovery of all. Viewed with clear eyes, the haze gone, she saw Roger as he was: a nothing, a dweeb, a pathetic hanger-on, both socially and academically. (Why else would he have been in a freshman survey course?) His would-be sophistication was nothing more than a loser's permanent sneer. His smugness evaporated like morning dew at the change in her. He made one more attempt at the erstwhile pseudo mastery. When that failed, a series of whining, begging phone calls followed, each more irritating than the last. Finally, he gave up and drifted off to who-knows-where. She never found out, because it wasn't important enough to her to do so.

The conclusion was inescapable. If it hadn't been Roger, it would have been someone else, because it hadn't been Roger at all. . . not the first night, nor the in-between nights, nor the last, darkest night. All along it had been Adele Jansen. The genie that appeared when she surrendered her only, only self to a man, capable of wondrous things in the dark, when unstoppered and roaming free in the daylight, became a demon that could scatter the cornerstones of her life around like so many children's building blocks. Never again – she drew the lesson – *never!* With that, she resumed her life. The foundations on which it had been built in the first seventeen years were too strong to be dislodged by one misadventure. Roger fell back into the distance.

But never again did she go to a fraternity party. Never again did she do anything casually romantic. But neither did she ever stop living on the edge, afraid in the pit of her stomach that she hadn't learned anything – that despite all her reassurances to herself, she wasn't capable of learning anything. The Neanderthal Adele had never left, would never leave, was never far off. The boy who had claimed her virginity had been only a boy. Roger was a worthless mediocrity. Even so, she'd come close to losing her self completely in sensual music she herself had composed, succumbing to a sexual illusion. How long would it have gone on if Roger hadn't been fool enough to dramatize the power over her she had bestowed upon him? Suppose he'd been smooth, and sophisticated?

Now, standing here, tonight, with Franklin Fischer's manipulative touch on her bare shoulder, weary, burdened with deadening fatigue, she was face to face now with the Ultimate Predator, by any definition she cared to name – because he had the insight, he had the charm, he had the alpha male behavior down pat. There was a certain charm in this, a certain attractiveness, a certain familiar sick appeal. No doubt.

Except that it wasn't working.

Because too much had changed. Because she had, after all, learned something. Because now all this seemed about as sexy as getting hit in the face with a brick.

*

"No," Adele said, removing his hand, not nearly as gently as she'd removed George's.

"No?" he repeated blankly, not comprehending.

"'No,' Mr. Fischer," she replied. "It's a simple word. Only two letters. Even little children understand it."

"Perhaps you misunderstood," he said. "You –"

"I understood perfectly," she interrupted. "No. No to everything. I didn't buy into anything you said." No trace of cream puff now. Franklin Fischer was biting straight into the granite.

"You are drawn to powerful men," he said. "Don't deny that."

"I don't," she said, meeting his eye. "I find George immensely attractive for that reason." He opened his mouth to say something, then realized the more subtle point, and closed it again. A trace of exasperation showed.

"Adele," he said, sitting down, a strained, darkening patience in his voice, "I thought you were sensible. Didn't you understand? Don't you realize that in disregarding what I've said you devalue yourself? What are you worth? Apart from your usefulness, nothing. There's nothing special about you – or me, or anyone. Don't deceive yourself." He considered his words.

"There is no higher purpose. You're made of shit and sweat. We all are. The difference is what we make of ourselves. If George turns his back on his life, his rightful place, he turns his back on himself. He diminishes to nothing. Deny yourself your destiny, the inevitability of this night, and you eliminate all your achievements at the same time. Then what are you? Another helot. You owe it to yourself to side with me."

"*No*, Mr. Fischer," she repeated. "I said it. I meant it – and I haven't really achieved that much. Nothing that's important to me anymore. At least not the way you mean."

"Another helot," he repeated, "if stripped of the sum of your contributions. If you don't surrender to the moment, you lose your own measure. If you abandon that, you abandon your right to judge. That's George's error; don't adopt it. Without that you sink to the same –" he smiled a twisted smile and pointed a finger – "you're no different than any common whore. You get fucked in the same place where you were born, between your urethra and your anus – between piss and shit, Adele - your asshole and your peehole, do you understand? – piss, pussy and shit. That's all life is, without mature judgment. That's what you descend to, if you abandon your own sense of your worthiness. Piss, pussy and shit. That's all. Is that really all you want for yourself?" He had hoped to shock her.

She smiled instead, a sudden, private smile. "What's so funny?" he asked, amazed.

Her smile was steady, her voice even: "Nothing, really. I was just thinking of all the men I've known who'd hand your head to you for the way you just talked to me."

"Who? What?" he said, uncertainly. She had thrown him completely off-balance for a moment. "Who do you mean? Relatives? Your lovers?"

"I've only had one lover," she answered.

"Carolyn wondered if that many," he murmured, recovering some composure.

"And he wouldn't do anything like that," she continued, ignoring him. "He wouldn't lay a hand on you. He doesn't believe in violence. He'd do something much, much worse. I don't know exactly."

"How lucky for me, then," he said, his composure fully returned, "that he's not here. None of those men are here, Adele. I'm the only one. That's the point. That's what destiny is."

She nodded again. "Then I guess I have to take care of myself, don't I? The answer's still no, Mr. –"

"Franklin," smiling broadly.

"Mr. Fischer. I'm going with you to the dinner. Nothing more."

He sighed heavily, shook his head, and half closed his eyes. "You obstinate, foolish young woman. You *are* the source of George's problems. I have no doubt whatsoever. What gives you the right to ignore common sense? No one has that right. Who do you think you are? Royalty? A princess?"

She eyed him, unsmiling. After a moment, she nodded. "You've got it right. That's exactly what I am."

He shook his head from side to side. "You're behind the times, Ms. Jansen. No privileges accompany that status anymore. Princesses get fucked the same as the others. As I told you."

She thought, then nodded solemnly. "You're right again, Mr. Fischer. There aren't any privileges at all anymore. We do get fucked – over and over." Her use of the word startled him. "As badly as anyone else." She paused. "But the obligations are still the same," she added quietly. "That hasn't changed. I didn't know that until yesterday."

"This isn't getting us anywhere," Franklin Fischer said. "It's time to go." He shook his head again. "I'd hoped to enlist you in a war, Adele – the newest and most important. Between the useful and the useless. I –"

"There's only one war, Mr. Fischer," she interrupted, "and that isn't it." She moved on calmly, not bothering to explain. "And I know you've miscalculated. George Sorenson isn't coming back to you no matter what happens. What happened wasn't any ordinary midlife crisis."

He shrugged. "We'll see. I disagree with you." He rose from his chair to his full height. "But I'll cope in that event. I've always coped. There have been many adventures in this life of mine, long before the Project. I hardly told you anything. You have no idea who I am or of the obstacles I have surmounted already. I'm a survivor, Adele. I've always been very proud of that."

She gave no reply. But at the word 'survivor' the broadest smile yet spread across her face, tinged with open, unconcealed contempt. For a moment rage bristled in his own face. For a moment, she thought he might strike her.

*

"I don't think I should forget this," he said, checking himself. He picked up the dissolution agreement, folded it in half, and placed it carefully inside his coat, in the breast pocket. "It would be a shame if it got lost overnight. . . if anyone left the dinner early and retrieved it. Carolyn's advice was sound. I'll hold it. . . until the morning."

He went on: "There's a lot of time between now and then, even for a princess. To think about what all this means; to consider what this represents; to compare the years and years and years it took to achieve this with the few moments I'm asking. To reflect on reality and inevitability. To realize your quarrel is with destiny, not me."

He contemplated her. "You have very polished repartee, Adele. I should have realized. You *are* more talented than I am. But I told you I'm used to that. I've heard enough. You can't stop yourself thinking; you can't help being a realist; and you're very, very fond of George. The night is still very young, Adele – and what must be for you still must be. Ultimately you will be mine because only that makes sense. I repeat my promise. I will be very, very good to you when that time comes. Our misunderstanding here is a small thing." He glanced at his watch. "It's time we were leaving."

He stepped to the door and held it open for her. After a moment, she moved under his arm into the corridor. Together they walked down the dark hall, towards the elevator and the waiting limousine.

A GOOD JOKE

T he mist did not have the same effect on visibility at street level as it had one floor up. The street lights, the office lights, the headlights – all lit up the route as if it the moon were full. The limousine was the same one that George had used on their date. She sat in the same place, across the cabin from Franklin Fischer. He smiled and slid the chauffeur's panel shut.

The hotel was only a few blocks north and west of the CFS offices, but it was apparent that the journey would take some time. Every limousine in the world seemed to be on the streets of Manhattan tonight, headed towards the banquet.

"Impressive, isn't it?" Franklin Fischer remarked. She nodded – no sense in denying the obvious. "You belong in this world, Adele, with these people." He smiled more broadly. "You're talented, of course, and attractive enough. But everyone at this level is talented and attractive. They still must come to terms with reality. This is what you've worked for, Adele. This has been your goal. There truly is no other choice. Am I saying anything you don't already know? I doubt it."

She did not answer. The dissolution agreement was still in the breast pocket of his coat.

They inched forward in the traffic, surrounded on all sides by wealth, by power. Adele looked into the compartment of the limousine beside them. A gorgeous woman, diamond tiara, a huge sapphire and diamond necklace, over an ample white bosom – a strapless white evening gown, largely silk. She could not see the woman's escort. The woman smiled and nodded. Somehow Adele smiled back.

"All I've talked to you is common sense," Franklin Fischer said softly. "Rationality. Realism. Commitment is required in this as in anything." He saw someone in another adjoining car, touched his hand to his forehead, and waved. "What are we talking of? An evening,a moment – perhaps a dalliance, if you choose. Nothing of importance. Perhaps in the last century. Not in this. A token, an emblem – nothing significant."

Funny. For eight years she'd worried about the squishy soft sentimental girl, feared the strength of impulses that might prove ungovernable. But except for the period when she'd gone careening backward after the unexpected discovery of sex, the squishy soft sentimentalist was never wrong. Her instincts never betrayed her; they had warned her about Bobby Lawton, about Lem, had urged her to close the door behind her and stay. *Oh Tom, Tom. . .*

Funny. The danger had always lain on the other side. She hadn't seen it. The cool, calm girl was the one who got herself into trouble – and she'd never realized it. She had ignored or rationalized all the warnings. *The devil is very, very close to you*, Milly had said. She had wondered if that were religious paranoia.

"I can see searchlights ahead," he remarked, looking over her shoulder through the front window. "We're finally making progress."

"Searchlights?"

"Yes," he said. "More than a dozen of them, positioned around the convention center. The lights meet at vertices nearly fifteen thousand feet up. A truly creative effect. Someone told me it's called a 'cathedral of light.'"

Adele smiled wanly. He frowned, perplexed, not understanding. The effect doubtless had been creative the first time it was done, by Speer for Hitler at the great Nuremberg rallies of 1933. Since then, the effect had been re-created countless times. Did anyone know how truly tasteless it was? Would any of them care if they did?

"We're getting quite close," he said, then looked down at her. "This is my world, Adele. This is my day. I am not going to fail, here, now. You're not going to deny me. I mean you no harm. Quite the contrary – you will find yourself here." He tapped his coat. "You have to make the commitment. You can't quarrel with your own ambition, your own destiny."

The coat was still securely buttoned. The car was drawing ever closer to its destination. *Think, Adele.* She had to think of something, do something. But it was now – she calculated – thirty-six hours since she'd slept, and then not well. So tired; too tired to think.

His hand was still tapping his own chest. Could she. . .? Think the unthinkable. . . only one night – what could happen? No question of dishonor in this day and age. . . everything George had worked for. . . Do it? Close her eyes, pretend she's someone else? She'd done that once before.

"What exactly do you want of me?" The words slipped out before she could stop them, exhaustion the cause. She could have bitten her tongue.

He smiled very, very broadly – "Inevitable, Adele," he breathed softly – then waited a moment. "We'll be going to a party at Carolyn's townhouse. Some of the principals agree with me that the completion of the Project requires a celebration a bit more lively than champagne and white cake. Their wives left this morning."

Right, she thought wearily. *Carolyn's party – of course. But not just a party. The father of lies.* "The answer's still no, Mr. Fischer."

He continued grinning, ignored her. "Of course it is, Adele. Of course. For now." Then he looked up. "We're here." A doorman holding an umbrella approached her door.

No, she thought, and wrapped that word tightly around something deep in her being. "No" it was, and "no" – somehow – it had to remain.

Except that she had to think of something for George – and she didn't know what, and she didn't know what she even had left to think with.

*

Four massive searchlights stood in a small arc on the other side of the circular drive-in. Adele looked up at the beams cutting through the night like laser swords. The wind blew dew and fog through the beams, wisps of water and fog raveling and unraveling surrealistically hundreds of feet overhead. Enough illumination fell on the cobbled walk outside the hotel entrance to light up the multi-colored stones like children's tiles. A few wet, matted leaves lay scattered on the sidewalk. Other doormen were holding umbrellas, leading beautifully dressed guests to the large glass doors. The scene had an eerie, insane resemblance to an Impressionistic painting of Paris in the autumn.

Inside the door, in the lobby, was pandemonium. Flash photographers were everywhere, bulbs popping randomly, couples stopping to smile, and then hurrying on. Arc lights and video cameras were scattered all over the floor. Some television journalists were still doing interviews, others completing voiceovers. People scurried between them, moving in all directions – men in evening dress with boutonnières, glittering women, hair piled high, bare, exquisite shoulders of all colors – milky cream, dusky brown, palest yellow, café-au-lait, ebony black – dazzling wraps and jewelry. The huge banquet was hardly the only activity in the hotel tonight. The hospitality suites were still going full blast. Private parties were spilling over into one another, becoming semiprivate and public.

She handed her cloth coat to the doorman. Franklin Fischer gave him his topcoat, tipped him, and pocketed the claim checks. He moved easily through the chaotic frenzy on all sides of him. Someone stopped to congratulate him, shake his hand; then another, then another, then he was surrounded. The word was out. He smiled warmly and naturally, moved on. Adele trailed a few feet behind him, having shaken off his touch the moment they were through the door, ignored the hand he had extended to lead her. She took in the entire spectacle, trying to find her bearings, to get her feet underneath her. Carolyn had been right. She was significantly underdressed – the least of her problems this night.

"George," Franklin Fischer called out lightly. There they were, George and Carolyn, stiff, hostile figures, standing in front of the entrance to the Mediterranean Room, the same hall to which George had brought her twelve days earlier, again opened up to its full massive proportions.

"You guys made any plans?" he asked without further preliminaries. His face was a mask, his eyes dark linear voids, his mouth contorted. He was facing his own ultimate crisis this night, she realized. "I believe Adele's considering her options," Franklin Fischer answered quietly. His coat remained firmly buttoned.

"Same deal, Franklin," George said. "Tear the damn thing up. We go on like before. I'll see she gets home O.K." A part of Adele desperately hoped Fischer would accept, that he'd do what George asked, that she could then step over to George and accept his protection – later find a private place and talk to him a long, long time, tell him about a secret she'd kept, a man she was always going to love, a decision she'd made, and find out if he really could forgive her anything. Maybe everything could be different for him, too. Maybe the chasm wasn't as wide as she'd thought.

"I don't think that's feasible, George," Franklin Fischer replied, still pleasant. "Adele and I've had the opportunity to discuss this situation at length. I'm fairly confident of the option she'll choose." Oddly, she was also glad to hear that. There would be no compromise. Before George could say anything, someone else stopped to congratulate Franklin Fischer. More handshaking, shoulder-clapping, small talk; she drifted away from the group, to the verge of the entrance, and looked in.

Hundreds of tables with sparkling white tablecloths dotted the hall. At the front was a raised dais for the speakers. Waiters in immaculately starched uniforms, station captains in cutaways, hurried about the vast space. Adele glanced down at the table nearest her: ten settings, eight pieces of silverware each; three wine glasses and a water glass. The wine was already on the table, red, white, and champagne. The salads were also set out, each with a patterned garnish of lobster, crab, and shrimp; several thousand portions, done by hand.

"I'm going to be sitting up there fairly soon," said Franklin Fischer, pointing towards the dais. "Magnificent, isn't it? You deserve to be in settings like this. You belong in them." He put his hand on her bare shoulder again; she moved a step away; he smiled broadly. "There's an open bar at the back of the hall," he remarked. "Would either of you ladies like something to drink?"

"No," said Adele.

"None for me," Carolyn answered. She turned to George. "There's going to be a party later at my place . . .as you know," she said softly.

Adele watched him stiffen and become even grimmer. Her first resolution firmed; no way she was going to leave him among these monsters. Once again, almost against her will, she considered the unthinkable. *You can't stop yourself thinking*, he'd said. Damn him, he was right. A party, he had said. Only a moment. . . only an evening. . .

Only an evening? It's not only an evening and you know it, Jansen. He means to destroy you tonight – the same way he's destroyed Carolyn – and destroy George by destroying you. But the baby. . . the baby will need money. *The baby will need a mother who still owns her own soul.*

She had to be a survivor herself tonight; she had to do it alone; and somehow she had to make good for George. *How?* People were beginning to file in, to take their places; someone waved to Franklin Fischer from a short distance away. "The tables I've reserved are over there," he said, then dropped his voice. "Don't you see it's useless? Don't you see it's inevitable?"

The sheer weight of the world! The sense of power, of opulence, all of it concentrated in this one room! The powerful, reveling in their collective strength – so weighty, so invincible. All at once resistance seemed hopeless, impossible for one puny girl.

"Resistance is useless. They've all made their compromises," Fischer said in her ear, as if reading her thoughts. "Every last one of them – or they wouldn't be here. You're no different. You're too bright not to understand that. This is what you want. This is what you've aimed for. There is no resisting the logic of your life." He looked around. "It's about time we took our seats."

"No," answered Adele. "Not now. Not yet." Each step further she went was one step she had to go back.

"All right," said Franklin Fischer indifferently. "A moment or too longer." Out of the corner of one eye, Adele could see Carolyn grinning, misery looking forward to company.

On and on they came, the great and near great from all the cities of the world. Men resplendent in their tuxedos, the women in their brilliant gowns – entertainers and politicians, executives and novelists, courtesans and statesmen – at home, comfortable, hobnobbing and chatting, each luxuriating in the shared presence of all the others. Voices sounded, silverware clattered, chairs scraped, corks popped. How do you contend with that? How can you possibly hope to win?

"It's time we took our seats, Adele," Franklin Fischer intoned firmly. She looked around; there was no way to delay further. She felt his hand on her shoulder again, moving her forward. *What really is the use?* she thought, forgetting the hand for a moment too long before she stepped away. *No*, she answered herself back through her fatigue. Somehow, *no.*

"Hello, Adele," came a different voice from behind her, very softly, yet cutting through the clatter, like a song she'd heard once, long, long ago, in a dream. The hair rose on the back of her neck. A chill ran down her spine. "It's good to see you again."

This, too? Now? So much for her morning intuition. But she realized in the same instant that that had been reverse intuition, a predictor of its opposite, because this particular event truly was inevitable, it could not have been otherwise. An acute *deja vu* sense, that she had lived through all this before, many times before. Her visual memory was far more acute than her aural; she remembered the softness of the voice, but she'd forgotten entirely the lilt, the basic musicality.

Deliberately she put her hands on her elbows, took an instant to compose herself. Slowly, she turned about face. All this took no more than a sixteenth of a second, but it seemed an eternity. She planted her feet, tilted her head, and looked straight up.

"Hello, Tom," she said.

*

He was holding a manila envelope in his left hand. A shorter man, much more nattily dressed than he, flanked him on the right.

She was surprised at first: he looked the same. But why not? Only seven weeks had passed. Underneath an old topcoat, he was wearing the same mildly frayed sports jacket he'd had on the first time she saw him. It had to be what he always wore to major occasions. His hair was slightly matted by wetness. He must have walked at least a short distance through the weather. Otherwise nothing was different.

His expression had a certain wistful longing when first she turned; that changed almost immediately. His eyes widened perceptibly, the Thomas B. Newcombe equivalent of a different person staggering backward. A brief quizzical look at her – *What the hell's going on here?* – then a series of quick, darting glances from one to the other – George, Carolyn, Franklin Fischer, herself – taking it all in. Two or three seconds passed – a long moment in real time – she realized suddenly he'd frozen all of them, like deer in headlights. She had never met anyone else in her life who could do that. *No longer a child; a grown man with awesome powers*, Petrosian had said. She glanced at Franklin Fischer. All at once, he seemed ridiculously small.

"Don't," Tom said softly, looking over her head. She turned, realized he was talking to George Sorenson, who started and stared back at him. Then he turned again to Adele.

"Are you all right?" he asked.

"Yes," she said, truthfully, surprising herself. Something had begun to build within her from the moment she heard his voice.

"You're sure?"

"Of course she's sure," came Franklin Fischer unevenly, his poise shaken for the first time. "I'm escorting her. Young man, who are you?"

Tom ignored him. "You sure?"

"I'm sure, Tom," she said, meaning it.

"Young man," said Franklin Fischer said simultaneously, "who are you? You have no business intruding here."

Now Tom raised his eyes and met Fischer's. In all the times Adele had envisioned him since they parted, she'd never once imagined him angry. But of course he became angry, like anyone else, and its form was exactly as she should have guessed. His expression hardly changed, but his eyes! His eyes could have frozen the continent of Africa. She stole a glance at Fischer – a small but perceptible (and very welcome) shock. Franklin Fischer was afraid of him.

Then a look of complete, dismissive indifference came over his face – *You are too trivial to matter.* Franklin Fischer flushed with anger – after all, this was *his* day, *his* destiny. George Sorenson slowly, softly began to chuckle.

"Tom," interjected the short natty man, tugging on Tom's sleeve nervously, "c'mon, Tom. We're late." One of his so-called friends – she found herself agreeing with Georgia Richmond for the first and undoubtedly the last time in her life: "Creep" was indeed the perfect word.

"In a sec, Danny," Tom replied, still glowering in his own way. He regarded Adele one more time; she shook her head imperceptibly, *No, I'm all right*; then slowly, he allowed his friend to drag him away. George was laughing still louder. Franklin Fischer's ears were bright red.

"Young man!" he said, starting after them, raising his voice. "Who are you?" Tom turned his back, ignoring Fischer, infuriating him.

"Answer my questions! Who are you?! What do you do?? What right do you have to be here? What are you *worth*!?" he went on, becoming angrier, louder still, unaware of his voice ringing down the lobby. Onlookers began to gather, curious. A ring formed around the two men. Two of the television cameramen moved closer, sensing developing action.

"You heard me! Don't you dare turn your back on me!" Fischer continued, seizing as he spoke the left sleeve of Tom's coat.

"WHAT ARE YOU WORTH!?!" Franklin Fischer roared. "Worth enough –"

Tom wheeled around then. Now all the anger, the fury, all the fires that burned within him were suddenly visible, pouring out of him, naked, open, huge, terrifying. All of it was about to come bursting forth, all the revenge to which he was entitled, unleashed on one man, one human being, at one point in time.

"TOM!" Adele shouted, afraid for him, not Fischer, "DON'T!" He looked over at her – met her eye – then, to her immense relief, was back under control. Instead, he shook his arm free in one motion; the two men's eyes met.

"What are you worth?" Franklin Fischer repeated, reflexively, feebly, stupidly – timidly. His arrogant confidence had vanished completely. In its place was a pure, elemental fear - a mortal dread, extending to the depths of his soul, and immediately visible to everyone. Franklin Fischer was afraid. The commanding man of the world had been replaced in a nanosecond by a cowardly, ridiculous blowhard. The transformation was irresistibly comic. Tom paused for dramatic effect.

"Counting numbers," he then said, infinite contempt in his voice, a look of pitying, dismissive disgust on his face. "Trivial. Child's play." Franklin Fischer opened and closed his mouth, puzzled, uncomprehending, and buffoonishly stupid. Tom let Danny drag him to the edge of the spectators that ringed them.

"Twerp," he added in a tone of utter judgmental finality, with another shake of his head. Then he and his friend disappeared into the crowd.

Laughter roared up from the spectators. Franklin Fischer found himself alone in the middle of the floor, ringed by a laughing, jeering throng. (*This couldn't be happening! Not on his day! Not with his destiny!*) Adele found herself laughing with the rest – the transforming fear, the stupid question, the answer that made the question sound as stupid as it was, the perfect congruity of the final epithet, above all, the sudden, complete reduction of overbearing bully to pompous, craven fool. She saw Carolyn laughing in spite of herself; George roaring, too.

Better. Franklin Fischer lived almost all his years in luck. But all the bad luck of his entire life coalesced into those five seconds. The two television newsmen, positioned by chance, could hardly have been better stationed if one had been directed by Fellini, the other by Spielberg. Each had captured every last nuance of the encounter, from the initial roaring advance to the final "twerp," all of the absurdity, all of the comedy. Both men knew instantly they had priceless footage. It was film that was destined to be seen over and over and over in the years to come.

Fischer knew what had happened. He more than anyone sensed the humiliation of the utter turnabout. He whirled about face, as if trying to confront the source of the hilarity. But the laugher was everywhere. Without thinking, he whirled around again. His ears became redder and his glare fiercer, like an overwrought cartoon character seeking an outlet. The laughter grew; the cameras kept turning. Adele realized she'd been right back at the CFS offices;

her lover had indeed done something much, much worse. After a few seconds, Franklin Fischer finally became aware he wasn't doing himself any good. He pushed his way through the ring of spectators and returned to the other three. Everyone began to disperse.

"I'm going to find that man," he seethed, the patrician attitude vanished completely. "I'm going to destroy that man. Who was he?" he said, confronting Adele.

"That's the man who gave her the angel, Franklin," George said flatly. He had stopped laughing before any of the others.

"Yes," Adele agreed, looking out at the crowd.

"We have to go in, Franklin," Carolyn said timidly, trying to pretend she hadn't been laughing herself. Adele continued scanning. Tom had that trick of disappearing when he wanted to; she was certain he was still around somewhere.

She found him at last, standing off to one side, looking back at her, his companion pulling at him – clearly still concerned, wondering whether he should intervene further. She shook her head imperceptibly from side by side – *No, it's all right* – one last questioning look, and then he allowed himself to be dragged away by Danny. *There were giants in those days* – the thought came unbidden to her mind.

"The dinner's about to start," Carolyn pleaded.

*

They moved towards their table, one of fifteen that CFS had bought. Someone in the next aisle gestured at Franklin Fischer, said something, and laughed. Fischer turned, glowering, realized it was useless. Carolyn tried to calm him, but he went on and on, with wild imprecations, threats, vows of revenge. All the aristocratic veneer was gone. Some of the media executives seated at the tables stood and began to applaud. He ignored them.

"If you think it's bad now, Franklin," George said, pleasantly, "wait until you see the tape."

"*Tape?* What tape?!?" he exclaimed.

"The news tape. Two TV guys got everything," George informed him pleasantly.

"News people!!" he almost shouted. "What – how – why didn't you –"

"Eh, you been such a shrewdie all night long, I figured let you handle it," George explained, pleasantly again. Franklin Fischer was almost spitting with rage.

Adele trailed them, marveling.

He was back. He was finally back – and somehow in a moment everything had shifted, righted itself. Penelope could stop unweaving her shroud. Robin of Locksley could come out of Sherwood Forest. High overhead, the six swans (in the least well-known of the great stories in the Grimm Brothers' collection) had returned to save their sister. The tumult in Adele's blood erased all the exhaustion. *Anything is possible*, he'd said, which by implication means nothing is inevitable. Franklin Fischer was raving a pace or two in front of her. She regarded him with amazement – how could she have ever for one second have taken that useless, blathering mediocrity seriously? It could only have been the weariness. Laughter had completely broken the spell. *All it takes is one solid push, not even that hard.* Now *think!* and thoughts now came quickly, easily.

Carolyn had finally coaxed Franklin Fischer into enough awareness of his surroundings to acknowledge the applause. As they reached their seats, however, he'd completely forgotten the altered arrangements. Automatically, he seated Carolyn, then took the seat to her immediate left. Only two remained; George pulled out her chair, then sat down to her left.

Only Adele did not sit down. Instead she bent over Franklin Fischer. "Mr. Fischer, that was *awful*," she said anxiously. "Of all things, on such an important day for you. You look so red and hot. This hall's so crowded. Here. Let me," unbuttoning the top button of his suit.

"Why, thank you," Franklin Fischer replied, distracted. "No!" Carolyn said urgently, realizing, but it was too late. The dissolution agreement stood high out of his pocket; with one swift, deft movement of her artist-athlete hands, she had it. Fischer made a feeble, half-hearted wave at it. Almost simultaneously the salad fork was in Adele's other hand, ringing against the crystal water glass. Others in the tables nearby heard the cue, joined in.

"Miss," said the master of the ceremonies, a stand-up comic turned sitcom star, leaning down from the dais, only fifteen feet away, "miss, we're about to start."

"Adele," Carolyn hissed, "stop that at once! There's a major function afterward. I've planned for –"

"Oh, this will only take a *second*," Adele beamed, ignoring Carolyn, focusing on the dais, cocking her head and putting all the cute she could muster into the look. Before he could react, she had mounted a chair. The tapping became a crescendo. The emcee took her in, considered, then shrugged and smiled himself. "O.K. But do it quick."

"Ladies and gentlemen," she went on, in her best Roosevelt debating style, improvising rapidly, "I don't know how many of you know it, but this, the first day of a glorious new adventure for you and for the American communications industry, is the last day for one of the pioneer firms in financial planning and portfolio management, Consolidated Financial Services. Tonight, the two partners come to an amiable parting of the ways. I have been asked to present the dissolution agreement to a man I have come to admire and respect enormously – George Sorenson – by the way, the real architect of Fischer Communications Company. And may I introduce the new head of that company, Franklin Fischer. Would you both please stand?" With an enormous flourish, she presented the agreement to George, who held it tightly.

"Let's have a big round of applause for Franklin Fischer," the emcee said through the mike, perceiving instantly where the bread was buttered. Applause began, scattered at first, and then swelling towards a new crescendo. News of the monster deal had traveled rapidly over the convention. Who knew what lay ahead? Better to celebrate it now and see what happened. Slowly the entire hall rose and cheered. George, Adele, and Franklin Fischer turned and acknowledged it. Flashbulbs popped; more tape ran. Out of the corner of her eye, like a brace of quail breaking cover, Adele saw reporters leave their seats and move hurriedly to the phones. She turned face to face with Fischer. Only the hatred in his eyes above the photographic smile gave him away, and only to her.

"Smile, Mr. Fischer," she whispered beneath her own smile. "Everyone's watching. Remember the cameras."

"You're through," he whispered back, through gleaming white teeth. "I hope you know how completely through you are. Here. Everywhere."

"Counting numbers," she replied, turning again, with a half bow, "twerp," the first of many, many. He stiffened, but kept up the company front.

Finally, the applause subsided. All three sat down. Franklin Fischer immediately turned his back on Adele and took up with Carolyn. The lights dimmed. The emcee told a few brisk jokes, and then the waiters began the dinner service. The major program would occur after everyone was fed.

The event would probably be superb. Too bad she was never going to see it.

It had been easy, so easy. The Franklin Fischers are always easy. If she hadn't found one way, she would have found another. Now came the hard part, the super hard part. She met George's eye – and realized at once that perhaps the hardest of the hard tasks was the first one.

"I know what you're going to do," he said quietly. "You'd best get moving."

She shook her head helplessly. "George, I – I don't know what to say. I did what I could." Two waiters put the entrees down in front of them – filet mignon with mushroom cap and fresh Béarnaise sauce. That even now, knowing where the real inevitability lay, it was a wrench to leave him. . . she did not say. She could not.

"Mistake, you know. You should stay here. With me. You and I are a natural, Paloma. You know that, you can feel it in my arms. That's quite a guy, but he's a problem guy – and you're mine, not his. You should stay." Dull, aching pain was in his tone. "But you're not going to, are you?"

I wish there were two of me, she thought. Then, all at once, her heart gave up all its secrets: if she had never met Tom, she would have gone to Zihuateneo with this improbable man; married him; borne him children, made him a home, made him happy; enriched him with purpose, benefited from his experience; succeeded on her own terms at Hapgood, Thurlow or the equivalent; together done great things. Transformed all the dreams nestled in the treasure drawer into reality – had it all. It was easy, it was at her fingertips, it had been all along – but now none of that was going to happen. If she had never met Tom, if there were no Tom.

If.

She hesitated a last moment, grieving privately over things that would never be. "No," she said softly, pushing her chair back into the dark aisle. "I know you're right, but no."

"You can't forgive me?"

"I've forgiven you already," she answered immediately. "I could forgive you anything. I love you, George. But I have to leave."

"If that's it," he said, his eyes upon her, "best get going then." A short, quivery half smile passed between them – and then she was away. She caught sight of Carolyn's ferocious glare out of the corner of her eye.

"Be going myself," she heard George say behind her, in an entirely different tone. "Gotta sign something, get it notarized, and some copies made. I'll work out a sale program next coupla' days. First cash accounts I'm going to close are the dailies at Manny-Hanny, Monday sharp. You want your checks certified?" She did not hear Fischer's reply.

Her exit from the hall was momentarily blocked by a throng of latecomers coming through the entrance. She ducked and weaved, finally made her way through the door. A few of them glared after her, annoyed at losing even a few seconds' celebration to anyone so aberrant as to leave the feast when it had barely begun. None of them gave it more than an instant's thought.

She was, after all, only one more small, pretty girl in a city that abounds with them.

*

In the short term, Adele knew exactly where she was going. She threaded her way to the registration desk. Where was the Furston Press hospitality suite? On the eighth floor – two adjoining suites, in fact, with an inner partition removed.

A few moments later she was there. Her expectations were met exactly – large dark room, densely crowded, bar tables everywhere, an open bar, ample hot and cold hors-d'oeuvres – not quite as opulent as the dinner taking place below, but Jenet had laid out a good table. Her appetite had returned in full. Suddenly she was ravenously hungry. Time was precious, but she had to eat. She scooped some of the hot, some of the cold foodstuffs onto a small plate, found some space, and wolfed it down as decorously as she could. Then she stood, worried that even that small lapse of time had been too much delay.

But they had to be there. It only made sense. She circled between larger people, searching, her eyes becoming accustomed to the darkness, her glances darting around the room.

Found him. Her heart skipped a beat. He was sitting with two other men, three other women, at the far corner of the room. She recognized two of the women from the red light part of the convention. Five of the six players laughed and conversed; the sixth, Tom, sat with his back to the wall, his coat over him, arms out of the sleeves, watching, half-smiling, half lidded. The others were animated. She started; his eyes, his being were completely dead – Dracula about to enter the castle of death.

She borrowed a trick from his repertoire, simply stood and watched for long moments. He did little, but he dominated them all. Danny talked with quick jittery gestures. Every few moments, he'd looked to the corner for approval, reassurance. Once Tom nodded ever so slightly. The other man behaved the same. The woman sitting next to him said something; all at once Tom leaned forward, said no more than two or three words. The two women shrieked with laughter; before they'd finished, he'd returned to the position of repose. The woman to his immediate left obviously found him fascinating. He was generating enormous amounts of electricity, but no warmth. The woman was one of the unfortunates who don't understand the difference.

He had an ordinary tumbler in front of him, filled to the top with an amber liquid. Could it be. . . she'd never seen hard liquor served like that. As she watched, he reached for it casually, raised it, and returned it gracefully to the table half full. With that, she stepped forward. It was time.

She stood silent in front of the table, until they all looked up at her. Tom of course had noticed her first. They waited; she sensed Danny was amused. *Please, God, you haven't really been very helpful this whole time. Please, please, please, this one time, just this one time, the voice, the throaty, impressive contralto. Please. Just this once.*

"Tom," she said, as firmly as she could, "put your coat on. I'm taking you home," in what came out as the worst twitterchirp of her entire life.

For a second or two, no one said anything. Then Danny laughed and turned to the others. "Tweetiebird," he said to the table. One of the floozies laughed. Another few seconds. Nothing happened; what was he going. . .?

Then slowly Tom put his arms through the sleeves of his topcoat, picked up the manila envelope he'd been carrying in the lobby, and rose to his feet. "You got it wrong, Danny," he said softly, to his friend. "That's one of the great women in the world. One of the inheritors. When she calls you, you have to go." Danny swiveled around to look at her, an entirely different expression on his face. Adele tried not to look smug and failed utterly. Tom brushed by him; she realized then there had never been any question about his decision. He'd delayed a moment to watch the others react – one of his thousand little tricks.

"Tom!" Danny said urgently. "Hey, c'mon, fella! A party's not a party without you." *I'll bet*, she thought. Already the attitude of the three women at the table was different, as if a bubble had popped. They were exchanging puzzled looks, wondering how they'd possibly ended up here, when so many rich, lonely media executives in need of consolation were still on the premises. With the departure of the magician, the magic left as well.

"Ah, it'll be all right," he answered gently, putting his hand on the other's shoulder. "You'll do O.K. I wasn't going to finish this one out anyway." He moved behind Adele, who could not resist a short glare at Danny and a small triumphant smile at the rest.

"What now?" Tom asked. Not touching her.

"Let's go find a taxi," she said, herself not daring to take his hand.

"All right," he responded, then turned to the table. "Bye all," he said. There was a sullen, disorganized response from the table. The two of them moved through the crowd.

"Are you all right?" she asked.

"Yes," he answered promptly. "That drink was the first. What about you? Don't you need a coat?"

She remembered then the claim check, still in Franklin Fischer's pocket. "The ticket's with someone else," she said carefully.

"Um-hum," he said, understanding immediately, darkening, eyes narrowing, all but glowering. Astonishing; most un-Tom-like. Something he'd said came back to her: *When your higher brain functions that well, why should it surprise you that your lower brain does, too?* Well, his higher brain also functioned superbly, and he, too, had a lower one, the male kind, which had obviously not appreciated for a second the spectacle of another male encroaching on his territory. Interesting. Useful.

"Do you want to borrow mine?" he continued.

She thought of how incongruous they already looked, he in his shabby, presentable outfit, she in a dazzling white, off-shoulder evening dress; of how completely absurd she'd feel in a man's topcoat that came all the way down to her ankles. "No," she said. "I'm warm enough." She looked about. "The taxi stand's this way."

Seldom was a going-forth so completely different than the coming-hither – no stretch limousines here, no glitter. The only point in common was a portion of the ring of giant searchlights, still prowling their way through the dark heavens.

They stood, side by side, close, but not touching, not saying anything, waiting their turn for a cab. What had to happen was not going to be easy, but it couldn't possibly be as difficult as what had come before. She was certain the quiet giant on her right already knew exactly what she had in mind. She was equally certain that he had his own ideas, much different than hers. Tough, but not as hard as what had come before.

Her own resolution was becoming firmer. She knew now for certain that the destinies of the three persons she valued most in the universe – the little being sleeping inside her, the Adele-who-could-be, and the bewildered genius standing at her side – were in some incomprehensible way linked together, as incredible as that had seemed at one time.

Which you would have known a long time ago if you weren't such a complete, useless, feeble-minded moron.

A STILL HUSH

The doormen at this entrance had the umbrellas furled. Adele could see the moon, veiled by opaque clouds. "Has the rain come?" she asked.

"Just drizzle," the uniformed man replied. "Norther's coming." He paused, curious about the oddly matched couple. "It will be nice to get some real weather for a change." Tom said nothing. The doorman lifted his whistle to his lips. "Got something for you."

The taxi moved to the front. Out jumped a sandy-haired Middle-Eastern man in his mid-twenties. "You two?" Adele nodded, *yes*. He looked her over, particularly the immaculate white evening dress, then grinned. "Don't sweat it, lady. Cleanest backseat in the city." Adele smiled appreciatively at him. A nice young man. A good omen.

The doorman helped her into the back; Tom entered unobtrusively on the other side. The driver leaned back – "Where to?" – quietly, Tom told him. "I think it'll be better for you if I go over west, then turn," the driver said. "Crosstown's still a mess. The big party you been at." Tom nodded again, and they were off, in silence, even the cabbie. Somehow he had caught a cue from Tom.

The cab traveled west. She'd made the same mistake twice, once thirteen years before when she'd drawn the wrong conclusions from her mother's life; the second, seven weeks ago. Few people get the first chance. Almost no one gets a second. By some miracle of life, she had been granted a third. *Don't blow it, stupid*, she thought. *Don't let it get away.*

He looked out the window, silent but not taciturn, fully aware of her in that way he had, even though facing away. Petrosian's words flashed through her mind – an egg in a teacup, balanced by a tightrope walker. A delicate balance here – never mind the force he could bring to bear at a given time – one that, whatever happened, must not be upset. She thought of all the secrets of his she was going to have to keep from him, all the motives that must remain hidden – all the reasons, even for love, that could never be spoken aloud.

She felt no sexual pulse in the car – ironic, inasmuch as they were parents, but good, because it would be distracting. There was no doubt in her mind he already knew the tenor of the thoughts she had. Adele shivered slightly in the car. *This*, she thought, reversing herself, *is not going to be easy.*

"Where have you been, Tom?" she asked quietly, beginning.

"Around," he shrugged. He tapped the envelope. "Working. My own stuff this time."

"*Oh!*" she cried softly, genuinely pleased. "Jenet will be delighted!"

"Yes," he said shortly. "I didn't come back to my own place until two days ago. I picked up my mail at the Press today. That's where people usually write me." He turned to her. "There were two letters there that surprised me. One was from my old faculty adviser at Binghamton. The other was from a friend of mine who lives in a convent in Vermont. They both wanted me to know that they'd talked to you." He paused, then went on: "Both of them liked you quite a bit. Both of them commended you to me. Milly was particularly effusive. But they both thought I should know you'd talked to them."

He continued: "I've never told anyone in the City where I went to school – and I didn't think anyone who knew me could find out where Milly Peters was."

"How did you?" she asked.

"She wrote me right before she took the veil," he answered in his deep, soft voice, "apologizing for some things that weren't her fault." A flash of real pain flickered through his eyes. "She said she was O.K., but I didn't believe her. I published something for her. It wasn't nearly enough. She deserved a lot more." The cab became silent for a moment. "You've taken quite a bit of trouble over me, Adele. I don't think those are the only persons you talked to. I think you talked to quite a few people. I think you've found out things about me I never wanted anyone to know. That I don't want to know myself."

"Are you angry with me?" she asked, reeling. Suppose it went on like this? Suppose he wanted to know all she knew?

"A little at first," he answered, shrugging. "But basically, it doesn't make any difference anymore. You can do what you like. What I mostly am is curious. Why?" He turned and looked her directly in the eye.

"You're pregnant, aren't you?"

*

(In the front of the cab, the driver's mouth dropped open.)

"No," she lied, without batting an eye or moving a muscle, grateful she'd observed him those few moments at the table. She'd been expecting this, the direct question, sooner or later, and had prepared for it. The literal lie was the virtual truth. She'd already made her mind up about the baby. Why she was here, what she intended, had nothing to do with that.

He held her eyes for a long moment; his glance went over her body;

547

then he broke it off and turned back to the window. She half-closed her eyes and let her breath silently out. "All right, then," he said, facing away. "Why? What do you want of me, Adele?"

"I love you," she said gently; what was the use of subtlety? "So I'm going to stay with you and be with you." He nodded, up and down, not in assent, an I-thought-as-much nod. The cab reached First Avenue, and turned south.

(The driver was listening intently. This was already one of the Top 10 Fares of All Time and climbing rapidly in the standings.)

"Wide river," Tom remarked softly, looking out. "All the great cities in the world arose beside rivers. I've read that everywhere the rich live in the heights, the poor on the flatlands. A universal principle about cities. About people."

"I've read that, too," she said carefully. "But where people do live isn't the same as where they should live."

"Some rivers are too wide," he answered. "Some distances are too great. Wishing very, very seldom makes anything so. A lot of things that could be, aren't."

"Some because they aren't meant to be, and others because they are, but people are afraid of them, of how quickly they happen and how enormous they are." She hesitated. "I'm not afraid anymore, Tom," she added quietly.

"Some things aren't possible," he said softly, sounding rocklike. "Take it all for all, the answer can be that simple. When we get to where I live, I'm going to put you back in the cab and you're going to go back to where you belong. To what you deserve."

"Where I *belong*?" she half-laughed. "Are you serious? Do you know how many bridges I burned tonight? Do you know who that was you had that little set-to with?"

"I suppose," he shrugged, "some media tycoon. The way everyone was kowtowing." He faced her, half-smiled. "I do know what's going on. I don't live in a closet" – somehow she prevented herself from starting – "You can never be completely rid of that type," he said. "You can never really get ahead of them." He paused. "But you can make jokes," he added softly. Then he turned towards her.

"I didn't care for him. He didn't want you for any of the reasons you're important. He wanted to collect you." He eyed her directly. "You shouldn't have gone to that dinner. You should be home, fast asleep. You're completely exhausted. When's the last time you had a decent night's rest?"

When have you? she thought. "It's been a long week," she said carefully. "But if you know who that man was, then you know," she went on, hoping she was making progress, "I burned all my bridges."

"All but one," he answered softly. "The most important one. Don't try to con me, Adele. The man standing behind you is in love with you. He was going to deal with the guy if I didn't. I was worried it would get out of hand. A rich man, too; I bet a nice guy; for sure, he had no use for that bimbo he was stuck with. If you walked back into that place, he'd fall down on his knees and bless the day." He paused. "That's the kind of person you should be with. Someone who cares about you, someone who can do something for you – someone you can do something for yourself. Not me. Not anyone like me."

Damn him and that great searchlight vision! She was getting nowhere. "That wasn't meant to be, and this is," she pressed doggedly on. "That man himself knew it," she lied.

"A good guy, like I said," he replied evenly. "'Meant to be'? There is no such thing." The cab turned west on the cross street to his apartment; another turn, and they were there, in front of the small plaza that stood in front of the apartment building in which he lived. The engine died; he looked at her.

And she had thought for even a moment this would be the *easy* part? *Fool. Moron.* Franklin Fischers were a dime a dozen; this man was a titan, a one-in-a-century, who knew what you were going to say before you said it, what you were thinking before you knew yourself – and who was, in his quiet way, as determined as she. *How much do I have to do?* she wondered to the heavens. *How much is required of me?*

"If I thought you didn't love me," she said, going forward despite all, "I'd let you send me back. But you said it, you meant it, and it's still true. You owe me at least talk, Tom. You have to do that much."

"Love's not the issue. It's never been." He took her in for another second, then turned to the driver. "Can you wait for a few minutes?"

"Sure." (Could he wait? *Could he wait??* Try and stop him! This was now the All-Time Number 1 and getting better by the second.)

Adele smiled gratefully and began to slide towards the door. Then Tom said the most frightening thing he could possibly have said to her:

"Besides," he said, "there's something I want to talk to you about." She looked perplexed. "The door, Adele."

"What?" she said, her blood freezing.

"The door," he repeated patiently. "The door in the dream. You know what that dream's all about. Somehow you've found out. You know why it is I dream the way I do. I'd like to find out more about that."

*

The street had become moonbright. The pavement glistened underfoot.

The wind had died to nothing. The cabbie, not wanting to miss anything, leaned against the driver's door. Tom took her elbow and moved her gently, fifty feet down the block, within eyesight, but out of earshot, underneath the awning of a closed haberdashery. He stood four feet away, four light-years away, and waited. Adele had thought maniacally during the few seconds that had passed, but there was only one possible alternative.

"I never found out," she said, looking at him directly. The egg in the teacup; whatever happened, the balance mustn't be disturbed. "There are things about you no one knows. I learned enough to know we belong together. I didn't have to learn anything to know I loved you."

"Thank you," he answered quietly, and did not return to the subject. *A strong volitional element*, Petrosian had said. He was right. Tom really didn't want to know. Thank God.

"Doesn't loving you mean anything to you?" she asked. "Isn't it at all important?"

"It's very, very important," he answered, gently again. "But what it means is that whatever it is you found out about me got you all tangled up with yourself. You have tremendous natural warmth, Adele. Anyone can see that. I value your sympathy, your kindness. It means a lot to me." He paused. "But you can't change your life on that basis."

She smiled. "'Natural warmth'? The people at my office call me an ice maiden," and instantly could have kicked herself. *Go back two squares, moron* – as if the opinion of anyone else would matter to a man with his spectacular insight. Stupid.

He shrugged dismissively, as expected. "Be that as it may."

"Nothing I found out changed anything," she went on, seeking to distract. "I came to love you when we were at the museum, the same way I do now," and realized, as she spoke, she was speaking truth.

"And the 'you,' Adele? The person? Who is that? What is that?" He spoke with more intensity than she had ever heard him before. "I don't know. Who I am. . . what I am. . . I don't know. Do you? I never met my mother. I don't know my father's name. I have no family, I have no past" – he stopped and looked hard at her; he *knew* she knew; you can't lie to Thomas Newcombe–

"I have no friends worth knowing. I don't own anything, any property. I have no money to speak of. I'm not going anyplace. I don't have any place in this world. I don't fit in anywhere." His voice was as quiet and modulated as always, without any self-pity or complaint, a simple recital of fact. "I have nothing to offer you remotely worthy of your value. I never will have. Not even myself – I don't even have that." He straightened up slightly. "I can't do anything for you. Not the smallest start on what you deserve."

He stood alone and magnificent in the moonlight. "I'm not a lucky man, Adele," he added quietly.

Then his tone changed: "And that's not the worst."

"I know about that, too," she interposed softly.

He held up his hand, halting her, and shook his head. "Tell me something I don't know," he said, a bit impatiently. "You've talked to Milly and John Goodson –" he peered at her more closely – "yes, of course, and Georgia. That would have to be. A better person than she thinks she is, if she'd only give herself a chance." He went on. "I know you think you know. But you don't. The people who do aren't talking. I've come through scenes where I'm lucky to be alive afterward. I've got things on my conscience that shame me to think of them. There are people who wish I had never been born, and maybe they're right. I'm not going to explain, or describe, or say anything more. Explanations always become justifications, no matter how you try to limit them. What it comes down to is, things that shouldn't happen do, over and over – no matter what I say, or the resolutions I make, or who's around me. I don't know why, but 'why' doesn't matter."

He was talking about misery, his own misery; from the tone of his voice, he might as easily have been discussing the weather in China. Where was the howl of pain? Where was the cry of rage? How was it possible? How did he *do* it?

He rose ever so slightly to his full height. "I'm damned, Adele – damned. I have been all my life. I was damned before I was born. I don't mean to sound dramatic; I mean to state a fact. I don't believe in the ins and outs of the idiot theology, but the underlying mystery is real. I don't know why or when, or what the reason is, but I know it's true. Nothing I do makes any difference. Nothing ever changes. One day is the same as the next. I can't change anything." He paused; his tone became firm again. "But no one else is going to get sucked into this maelstrom – never again. Especially not someone like you. I do have control over that; that I can do something about. Whatever this means, whyever it's happened, wherever I'm going, I'm going there alone. And that's how it is, and how it will be, and how it has to be. You have to leave. I'm sorry."

She contemplated him for a moment. He was magnificent. He owed the world exactly nothing. It had stolen his parents, savaged his innocence, deprived him of every quality of mercy, purloined his memory, assailed him with ridicule and hatred, ultimately deprived him even of the consolation of sleep. Everyone who knew anything expected him either to implode into insanity or explode into criminality. Neither had happened. Instead, he paid the price in shame and privacy and the deep recesses of the night. What miraculous inner gyroscope kept him on his course? It defied all reason. Yet he kept on. Something there was, composed entirely of gravity and darkness, that craved his soul; he would not give it up; and it would go on taking its revenge upon him, forever.

Damned? _Damned??_ *In your innocence you are sanctifying grace itself. Don't you know? You hold continents in your right hand; you dispose of oceans with your left. But you don't* know *that, do you?* Then, all at once, the strongest intuitive certainty of her life, from the tip of her hair to the soles of her feet, from the marrow of her bones to the fringe of her epidermis, at the core of her being – that that was what it had all been about, the plane crash, the monster aunt, the complete breakdown of all the mechanisms of civilization. *So that you wouldn't know.*

Nothing happens by chance.

"What do you remember?" she asked, stalling for time.

He shrugged. "Before Binghamton? A lot of foster homes and schools; decent people getting hurt; nothing working out. Before that? An institution. A bad place. Before that? Nothing that I want to remember. That's when the door closed. Scraps and shreds. Faces, voices in the darkness. A toy." He stopped and a faraway look came into his eyes. "A ratty old stuffed bear," he said softly, almost to himself. "And that's all. Nothing else."

Magnificent, yes, but also bewildered and helpless and always would be – easy to forget that, but she could not allow herself to do so. All the beautiful words she could never say to him; all the lovely things about himself he must never know.

"Does any of that matter?" she asked. "What's important is that I'm here, that you're here. You couldn't have given up completely. You wouldn't have invited me out if you had. You wouldn't have offered me love."

"Concupiscence," he answered promptly. "Lust. You're a very desirable woman, Adele. And the interlude's screwed up some things for you, hasn't it? Things have gone wrong; I can tell. One more thing I have to answer for."

"That isn't true," Adele replied. "It wasn't only sex. You were trying with me. You told me you loved me. You meant it."

He hesitated, groping for an answer. "How do you know?" he said awkwardly. "Women have never been a problem for me. You were only one more. Better than most."

She was momentarily taken aback, ridiculously hurt; then caught herself and began to smile quietly. "You know I've talked to Milly Peters and you think I'd believe that?" He reddened. Good; at last a break, however small. At long last the wizard had missed a step, however slight the stumble. "You can't lie to me any more than I can lie to you. I *know* how you feel about me. You've thought about me every day since we were together. You want me back in your arms as badly as I want to be there."

"About every five minutes," he admitted quietly after a few seconds. "All right, I shouldn't have tried that. But I said before it's not a question of not caring about you. You know that."

"We love each other, Tom," she said. "That has to count for something."

"Something, yes, but not enough. Once I believed that was enough," he answered. "Once I thought love would make all the difference. It didn't. Nothing does. People got hurt. You should have seen what Milly was. Now she's shut herself up in a convent."

"And prays for you and thinks about you and regrets nothing except what she did," Adele replied instantly; then, more softly, "you're a very easy person to love, Tom."

"Thank you again," he said gently. "But that makes me more, not less, responsible for you being here. For you. You have to leave me be, Adele."

"No," she answered, in an accent as flat and unambiguous as she'd used with Franklin Fischer an hour or so before. "Never. You're going to have to send me away, Tom. I'm not going to leave you again." He looked at her more closely, curious, having caught something. Better; a slight tendril of hope. "I liked Milly a lot, but I'm older and I think I'm stronger. I've found out where I belong, where I should be; I think I knew it all along. That's all. It's enough. I don't know where you're going any more than you do. All I know is I'll be with you there."

"'Whither thou goest, there go I'?" he said, shaking his head.

"Something like that," she nodded, after a moment. "Maybe exactly like that."

"Pretty old-fashioned, Ms. Jansen." He sighed and put his hands in his pockets. "I have a responsibility to you. You have a responsibility to yourself. I won't let you limit yourself. A person like you shouldn't accept any limitations at all."

"'Old-fashioned'? Do you think words like that bother me?" she asked softly. "I'm not giving up on anything that I can be or do. There are all kinds of things I'm going to do. Don't you understand? Being with you doesn't eliminate possibilities; it opens them up." She looked up. "I belonged to you before I was created, before the world was created. Knowing that doesn't limit me. It enables me, it frees me."

"Which is only another way of saying we're very, very powerfully attracted to one another," he said. "I know that; I won't argue about it. It's a fact. But getting mixed up in a pattern that's fixed, that doesn't change? There's no liberation in that. To say otherwise is to surrender to a fever of the blood. A rationalization."

"There's not that much difference between rationalizations and rationales," she answered, quoting him to himself, then went on: "Do you think I could live well – do you think I could even live with myself – if I left you thinking that? Knowing that you'd given up hope? Do you know what Milly would say if she could hear you? Jenet? Do you think I would ever quit on you on that note? Love may not save, but hope does. You can't give up hope, Tom. Not if you care about any of us. You can't stop trying."

"That only works in Disney movies, Adele," he answered. "This is reality. Trying doesn't change anything."

"But that's it," she insisted doggedly. "That's exactly what I mean. Hoping *is* trying – that's all it is – and it may not change anything, it probably won't, but doing it makes all the difference anyway. That's why it saves. That's how it saves. That's the paradox."

He opened his mouth to say something, then stopped. "You know," he said reflectively, "that's not bad. I can use that."

"Tom?" she said very, very softly. Still another small break; perhaps, just perhaps – she could hope herself – she was making progress.

There was a long, long silence. "You're asking so much," he replied, the tone of his voice changing ever so slightly. "I'd have to change everything. It would be like coming back from the dead. I've made up my mind about a lot of things."

"Please unmake it," she said instantly. "Please. For me. For us. It's simple. Take what's yours. All you have to do is believe."

He appraised her for a long, long moment. "Believe that I've gone to the ball and come away with the princess? That it could actually be?" She scarcely dared to breathe. His tone was questioning; he was actually weighing the possibility, considering the alternatives.

"Believe it," she said even more softly. "It's happened. Anything is possible. I shouldn't have to tell you that; I learned it from you." She paused meaningfully. "I love you," she said, in the softest, lowest tone she had. "I'm never going to love anyone else like I love you." Maybe – it was barely possible –

He contemplated her for another long, long moment – those extraordinary thought processes at which she'd marveled at the museum. She held her breath again.

*

"No," he said, after a long moment, in a voice that broke her heart, a weary resignation, somehow imbued with all the need, all the longing. "You're a priceless, priceless person. Even the slight chance that all this is theater of the blood is too great. Sooner or later, everyone who gets close to me gets hurt. You're one of the most valuable people in the world, Adele. You should be with a man who recognizes that, who can do something about it." He paused. "I can't tell you how much I wish I were that man." A long silence. "But I'm not," he said, in a low voice, tone of finality, pronouncing absolute, irrevocable judgment upon himself. The same stoic acceptance she had seen the morning after, in her own office, when Josh confronted him, magnified a thousand times. The look Milly would never forget – and now it was etched in Adele's memory as well. She had to look away; she could not bear the pain in his eyes. "I have to do this alone. This moment will pass. Time'll go on. You'll come to where you should be."

She could not believe her ears; she'd been so close! "What!" she cried, her anger and frustration audible, "'We'll always have Paris?' Fuck that shit!" hoping for shock effect. But it didn't work. The only response was his half smile. He saw right through her immediately.

"I don't think there's anything more to say," he answered, very gently. "I think the time has come for you to go," he continued, gentle again, advancing towards her.

"No," she said, stepping backward. If she allowed him to touch her, he would lead her resistless back to the cab. "You put the value on me. Why can't you accept my valuation of you?"

"The whole world will resound with what I say," he responded. "No one echoes you." And he took another step.

"Can't you at least let me spend the night? Please won't you make love to me? Can't it wait until morning?" The first time in her life she had made an overt sexual proposal to a man.

He stopped, considering; his eyes flickered over her, a carnal sizing up this time. For a second she hoped – he was a strongly sexed male, and the gown, thank God, showed off everything he could look forward to. Give her a chance and she'd show him a night he wouldn't forget if he lived to be 500. Anything could happen. But then he shook his head; he'd seen through her again. "It would only be more difficult tomorrow. Adele," he went on firmly, "it's time for you to go."

"I *love* you," she said desperately, because she couldn't think of anything else to say, knowing as she spoke it wouldn't work – too obvious, too girly-girl, too traditionally female.

He stopped again; the same unbearable look of outsider's longing swept over his face. "Yes. I love you, too. But so? So what? What then? What would we *do*?" he asked. "How would we act? How would we live? The feeling is nothing. Its expression is less than nothing. The doing's everything. And there's nothing to do." Her own reflections on the subway the morning after, echoed maddeningly back at her – and now he was in front of her. The time had come.

Tears she made no attempt to check flooded her eyes and rolled down her cheeks. "It isn't fair!" she pleaded. "You said you loved me! I believed you! I believe you now! You meant it! It's true! That means you'll be there for me if I want you! And I *do* want you! That means *I* have the right to decide, not you! It's not fair! It's my right to decide, not yours! You can't break your promise to me!"

But she could see the implacable determination in his eyes, along with the resignation, the pain. Nothing she had said had altered his decision. Nothing she could say would. She almost gnashed her teeth; he was going to do what he would do on the basis of his version of the exact reasons she'd left the morning after. She had seen through their shallowness. Why couldn't he?

She looked away, disbelieving. She'd *lost*. For the first time in her life, in the most important thing she'd ever done, she'd *lost*. She'd come all this distance and she'd lost. That no one had ever beaten Thomas Newcombe; that all the forces of the world had not been able to overcome him, even when he was small and vulnerable – that knowledge was scant consolation. Dazedly, automatically, she began to consider the aftermath – write to him to tell him about his baby, consider some way to do something for him from a distance (Milly's situation), the new job she was going to have to find, George. . . George? Why not? Her true love had given her to him, hadn't he?

But for now it was over. She looked up, resigned, ready to go, ready to let him lead her back to the taxi.

He was no longer in front of her. He had stepped back into the sidewalk. He was looking around and up.

*

The moon was high and full. Droplets of water glowed on the street, shining on the metal grillwork of the store entrances. By some acoustic miracle, all of the noise of the City had died away; the air had become completely silent. The taxi driver was immobile and watchful. Nothing anywhere on the street moved. A hush had fallen over all creation, as if the whole world were watching a man and a woman converse on a sidewalk, breathless about the outcome.

She caught his awareness instantly. "It's happened again, hasn't it?" she said, stepping out onto the walk and looking up and around herself. "We're not in real time anymore."

"No," he answered shortly, still taking in the night.

"We did do magic that day, didn't we?" she said wistfully,

remembering, wanting him more than she had ever wanted anyone or anything.

"Yes," he answered again, then looked at her; she was about ten feet away from him. "More than you know," which baffled her, but there was no time to ask. He turned his gaze north, to where the giant searchlights blazed into the heavens. From far, far away came the sound of a police siren, in some eerie, uncanny manner an element of the silence rather than its disturber.

"Who was it wrote 'unreal city'?" she asked, following his gaze – normally something she'd know instantly, but she was too tired and depressed to make the effort.

"Eliot," he answered promptly, not looking back. "In a very bad poem."

They watched the searchlights for a moment longer. Adele felt a small stirring of wind – as if time were wind, as if all the tall buildings were leaves of grass stirring on the Kansas plain. The cyclone would come. The Project, NATPE, the raucous feast in the Mediterranean Room – all of it seemed so trivial and petty. City of ghosts, land of shadows; all at once the man standing beside her seemed the only substantial being left in the world – and shortly he, too, would be gone. She looked at Tom.

"It will all pass away, won't it?" she asked tonelessly. "All the pomp, all the circumstance, everything. None of it's built to last. One day there'll be nothing left – except the powerful rhymes and the square root of the number two. And that's what you see, and how you live."

He shrugged, times past and times to come somehow passing before his eyes. "Not at all a new thought, Adele. Hardly profound. Everybody used to know that." He paused. "Perhaps it's possible to build too well," he added softly.

"And you're going to send me back into it," she said, in a voice like lead. "You're going to make me live there without you."

He shook his head slightly, side to side. "Oh, no," he sighed. "You're not going anywhere you don't want to go."

*

"What?" she said, not entirely believing she'd heard what she heard. A tiny flame lit in her being.

"You're not going anywhere you don't want to go," he repeated. He turned to face her.

"You win," he said simply. "The last thing you said is right. It is your decision, not mine. I did make you a promise of a type. I'd been thinking about that even before you spoke."

She half-closed her eyes. "Tom, please don't tell me all this was some sort of test."

"I don't know. I really don't. I hope not," he said. "It's only that for me – having you – isn't only the stuff of dreams. It's the stuff of daydreams. The epitome of the unexamined life – the paradigm – is to believe everything you want to believe for no better reason than you want to believe it. That this could be – that this might be actual – it wouldn't be right for me to accept it without confronting it. It wouldn't be right."

He faced her squarely, then sighed. "I better tell you the truth. I much more than care about you, Adele; there's never been anyone like you for me. Not even Milly. Even though you and I had so little time." The tone of his voice had hardly changed – perhaps a bit softer, perhaps a bit more musical – but now he was doing magic. "These last weeks, you're all I've thought about, you're all I've dreamt about. You're what – never mind." He cocked his head and looked down at her.

"I remember the first time I saw you," he went on, with the wonderful lilt. "You should have seen yourself. You'd got into an argument with the short psychologist. He was four sheets to the wind and you were as much right as wrong. But you were mad at yourself for losing your temper. You were so determined to do the right thing. You kept circling around the group trying to get a word in edgewise, trying to straighten up something that didn't matter at all. I knew exactly the sort of person you are right then – and I wanted you more than anything. Even then." His tone was avuncular, almost paternal.

"I love you, sure. Of course. But who wouldn't? Somehow you've rolled it all together: you're tough-minded and feminine, both at once – and sweet – sexy in the bargain. There must be five million women in the City and if you –"

"Tom," she interrupted, now feeling very warm, very good, "no multidimensional Cartesian coordinates. Not tonight. Don't embarrass me."

He colored slightly again, and now she felt warmer still. The wizard was voluntarily laying down all his arms. "I can guess what it's like to live your life," he said reflectively. "To be in your head. You get up in the morning, you go to work. You want so much, you feel you deserve so much – and with reason – but you worry. Time passes. Things develop slowly, so slowly. You have your successes, but the City is crawling with success and you wonder if yours are all bubble triumphs. You wonder if you're right about what you think, if you're right about yourself, if you're really making progress, if anything will ever happen. But happen it will, Adele – everything you want. The world at your feet, and happy for the favor. I'll lend you my eyes if you want them."

Suddenly the half smile. "It's happening already, I bet – prospects beckoning where you never expected, interest in you from out of nowhere, adventure around every corner." She thought of George, of the Project.

"Everything's going to fall into place for you. I know I did that little shtick for you tonight, with the look and the cameramen, but you would have got through the nonsense without me. You didn't need me." (She wasn't so sure.)

"I get to most things faster than other people," he continued. "So maybe I've seen what you are a little earlier than the others. But the rest'll follow. I can see it as I stand here as clearly as if it were happening now. You're going to get what you want. You're going to have everything you ever dreamt about. Love? No problem. Anyone would love you. In that respect, I'm only one among many, many. You're going to have whomever you want." Suddenly he shook his head. "*Yes*, I was disappointed when you left. *Yes*, I wanted you to stay. But I didn't blame you. I wasn't angry. You did the right thing, the sensible thing." That word again. Someday she'd tell him how much she'd come to loathe it.

"I'm not going to say 'no' to you" – suddenly, the half-smile – "does anyone? I won't make a loser out of you. You're right, the choice is yours. But is this what you really want? Is it what you really deserve? My sense is you're a pretty competitive person. You win – if you want to – but ask yourself if this game is truly worth the winning. Don't do it just to do it."

He squared himself up, spread his hands, and let out his breath. "I'll do what you want, Adele. I'll be yours if that's what you truly want. But I think it's better if you get in the taxi and go back. You can be anyone. You can have anything. You shouldn't settle for me."

*

She felt an enormous serenity, a music. Still – *be careful* – the master magician hadn't really surrendered, only told her he would grant her wish. "What I want?" she said softly. "That's small stuff. Who I am is why I'm here. Part of what I am is being yours. It's not only love, Tom; it's you. It's everything." She hesitated, then spoke very carefully: "It is my decision – and I'm calling you. To let me be with you, for you to stay with me, for us to take care of each other. I know what's at stake. So" – she suddenly smiled – "yes, I know what I'm doing, and, no, I'm not crazy."

"That's the second time. Quoting me back to myself isn't fair."

"This is much more important than fair. Besides, that sort of fairness is a masculine concept. You have to abide by it. I don't. I'm not male."

"Definitely not." He half-smiled and looked at her, shaking his head. Another siren sounded in the distance. Time went by. He turned towards it, the searchlights, the city, looked back at her – then extended his hand towards the north, palm up. *The City, the world.*

She shook her own head in return. "No," she said aloud. "Price is too high."

His expression was one of gentle concern. *Do you really know what you're doing?* He appraised her again, then slowly extended his arm north again, palm down. For a big man, his gestures were remarkably subtle; palm up, he had offered her the world; now he was comparing her favorably with the entire rest of the universe. Not bad. Again, she shook her head from side to side, not saying anything this time. *I belong here.*

He looked back at the taxi driver, shrugged a "whatcha-gonna-do" shrug. The driver, who had heard little, but seen much, was grinning ear to ear. Tom looked back at Adele. "I don't deserve you," he said helplessly, almost pleading.

Her turn to grin ear to ear; time to risk a joke: "You're absolutely right," she answered gently. "You don't. But you have me anyway," and all he could do was half-smile himself and shake his head.

Thoughts raced through her mind. Seven weeks before, winged magic had flashed across her life. Willy-nilly, she had been forced to find wings herself and fly off, in pursuit of a wizard, over pathless distances. Along the way, she'd been cursed by witches and befriended by knights. She'd met priests and scholars, warlocks and jesters. She'd spoken to a queen in exile and come to love a man who should be king – a man whom she had repaid in part and someday must repay in full. She'd discovered a dark tower and journeyed to it. She'd entered it alone and come out again, unscathed. At long last she'd come face to face with the Devil himself – and she'd got through that, too, with a little help from her friends. It could be – it might just be – that she was the genuine article herself. A Survivor.

And now it was almost over.

She looked at Tom and waited. Perhaps they'd do it differently in the third millennium – perhaps a different woman would do it differently now – simply shake hands and make a deal – but she was who she was, Adele Elizabeth Jansen, old-fashioned, and she infinitely preferred being chosen to choosing (of course, also old-fashioned, only when only one choice was realistically possible). The final symbolic gesture she left to him, to claim her for his own, to take her to himself.

Time lingered on. She was no longer troubled. He was doing the same thing he did when he made love, letting the moment ripen before he plucked it, the time build. Reminding her of himself, familiar male idiocy, as if she needed reminding: Did he think she of all people would ever forget his stature? Fool, but then they all are. She shivered slightly in the dark. She hadn't noticed the cold before, but now she missed her coat.

The time had come. Slowly, carefully he took off his top coat. "Well," he said, "I guess that's it, I guess. There's nothing more to say. O.K.," he said, more forcefully, definitely crossing the line, "I'm not a guy who's going to stand around thinking while" – his voice caught ever so slightly – "his girl freezes to death. You'd better come here, angel; I'll get you warm; then we'll go upstairs" – his voice caught even more slightly – "to where I live."

It's over, she thought wearily, dazed herself, with a dawning realization. *This is it. This is where I make my stand. Here. With this man.* The great storms still raged far out at sea, but now the waters lapped calm and even about the prow, the wharf beckoned, the journey had ended. A fragmentary memory, the freighter she'd seen from Carolyn's window, the morning she first heard his name, limping in from the sea, its voyage finished. That the monster would take its revenge on her – that she had placed herself in the line of fire – of these things she had not the slightest doubt. *He must be very important for the devil to hate him so much.* But those were worries for another day. The worries of this one were behind.

"Come here, angel," he repeated.

She held her head high and moved toward him.

*

She took two steps toward him; she never took the third. He caught her with his left hand, her favorite, and brought her to him with the force of a screen door slammed in a hurricane. His right arm came around; she was enveloped at once against his body, pressed herself against him, wonderful. He lifted her hair and stroked her back and arms. She managed to join her own hands behind his back, hugged him in turn as hard as she could. He brought the coat over her; at once she was warm when she'd been cold. She had the sense that she had been traveling for a long, long time, much longer than seven weeks, and was finally home.

"I only wanted to see you again," he said, speaking as if he were assimilating a fact beyond belief. "That's all. The only reason I went – to see you – once. But to have you. . . to be holding you again. . . to be actually holding you. . . " If Adele had heard him, she would have been pleased – the only time in all the time they had together when she would have observed him completely nonplussed, absolutely stunned, in shock.

But she did not hear him. Canopied beneath the coat, warm in his arms, head pressed flat against his chest, eyes closed, she was swearing the fiercest and most terrible vow she would ever make on this earth.

Joseph Wurtenbaugh

SACRAMENTAL RITES

He recovered his composure after a few seconds. He reached under his coat, put his hand under her chin, very gently lifted her head, and kissed her softly, ceremonially. She closed her eyes only for an instant. She wanted to see his face, memorize the moment. He looked at her, caressed her face, and then kissed her again, much harder, a lover's kiss. Now she did close her eyes and open her mouth, let him explore and penetrate symbolically, wonderful.

He broke it off. "I'd better take care of the taxi," he said, "or we'll go broke right off the bat." The "we'll" thrilled her. The driver, by the look of him, had no interest at all in collecting the fare. "It's O.K., buddy," she heard him say.

"You have to get along with the company," she heard Tom reply.

"Yeah. . . right," the driver sighed. "I'll check the meter." He looked into the cab. "Well, I'll be damned," she heard him say, bewildered. "I could have sworn. . . well, anyway, that's what it says." Tom looked at the meter, paid him something. The cabbie accepted it reluctantly, then looked over at Adele. She knew she looked ridiculous – in an evening dress and a man's topcoat, five sizes too large for her – but she didn't feel ridiculous.

"Goodbye, lady!" he called as he entered the cab. "Good luck!" Adele gave him a tiny finger wave. Tom reached into the backseat and picked up the manila envelope he'd been carrying all evening. The driver stepped into the front – he didn't really want to leave, but the show was over, and the world was waiting – and then he was gone, a happy man simply by virtue of having been a witness. They were alone on the street. Tom returned to her.

"Nice guy," he remarked.

"Yes," she said. Words seemed inadequate. She could feel her mood changing entirely. The dam had broken: all the frustration, the fear, all the suppressed fury, all the pain, the guilt at the lies, all the restraints, the relief, the triumph, all of it bursting forth, lower brain rejoicing, transmuting into a lightness of the heart, a giddiness of the head. All at once she felt wonderful. What was called for was a celebration and she knew at once exactly – *exactly* – the kind of celebration she wanted to have.

"We'd better go inside," he said. "Wind's coming up." *It's over*, she thought again, and again, and exaltation rushed to her head like champagne.

Hormones began to roar into her bloodstream. She was suddenly wildly, joyously, triumphantly aware of his body. In the rush of events the knowledge that he was, among other things, a virile, attractive man had been pushed completely to one side. But now memories were swarming through her consciousness – the touch of his hand; the feel of his mouth; the complete, undiluted male pleasure he found in a woman's body.

She nodded. He took her hand; hand in hand, they started up the street. "Why are you are wearing that?" he asked conversationally, gesturing at the pendant with the angel.

"Why, Tom!" she exclaimed, amazed. "Don't you know? You gave it to me."

"Yeah," he said as they neared his building, "but as a keepsake. I never thought you'd put it on. It's horrible."

*

They stepped through the front door. A firestorm was brewing in her blood. She squeezed his hand, partly to squeeze it, mostly to keep her own hand busy.

They walked through the small, dark lobby, past the mailboxes. He pressed the button for the elevator, then pulled her to him again. She almost exploded right then. She had to restrain herself not to unbutton his shirt, or brazenly put her hands on his belt buckle. He kissed her again, harder still. She opened her mouth and gnawed at him, while he explored where he wanted, hands all over her. The penetration was much more than symbolic this time, but still not even close to the filling-up she required. Adele came to a decision; the news about the baby could wait until morning. She wanted her lover as vibrant and uninhibited as he could possibly be this night.

She could feel a buoyancy in him as well beneath the normal quietude, a delight in life, however temporary. She could sense the same awareness of her physicality as she had of his, and the same problem with his hands. The tension, the strain in his body surprised her. He hadn't been nearly as eager the first night they were together. Could it be that. . .? "Tom," she whispered, "how long–?"

"I haven't been with anyone since I was with you," he confirmed. She stepped back, startled. "I told you: I couldn't get you out of my mind. I couldn't think about anyone else."

An impulse of wild, happy joy; another quantum leap in her blood temperature. *This might work; it might actually work.* "But for a mature man," she said, with deliberately girlish naïveté, the celebration beginning, "that must be awfully frustrating."

He smiled his half smile. "How would you know?"

"I can guess."

The bell rang above the elevator door, signaling the arrival of the car. Tom and Adele stepped apart somewhat guiltily. The door opened; a middle-aged couple emerged, smiled a greeting and left. Tom escorted her in; the door closed, and he pulled her to him again.

"I was on a work binge," he explained, tapping the manila envelope against her back. "Fourteen-, eighteen-hour days; one thirty-six hour stretch. I didn't have time to think about it."

"But seven weeks!" The elevator began to move.

"At the time, it seemed pretty easy," he said. "Right this second, yes, it does seem like a very, very long time." His hand moved rhythmically up her rib cage, from hip to shoulder, and down again. She could tell he was holding himself back from cupping her breast. Foolish man – that's exactly where that hand belonged.

She deliberately pressed against him. "It sounds awful!" she said, with feigned, wide-eyed innocence, moving her hands on his chest. "Look at you, you poor baby! You're so tense you're quivering! You're even sweating! It's probably not even healthy!" She put her hands within his shoulders, pressed her torso against his chest, opened her green eyes wide, and looked directly into his. "Tell me, tell me, is there *anything* – anything at all – I can do to help?" The elevator passed the second floor.

"Yes," he said, vastly amused, fully aware she was doing a shtick, but responding anyway. "You can have mercy. Until we get upstairs."

But she continued looking up at him, her eyes wide and imploring. She was completely on fire now. *Why wait until then? Why not do me here? Now? What are you waiting for? Are you chicken? You're not a wimp, are you?* Their eyes met. The elevator passed the third floor.

All at once, then, his right hand shot out like a jackhammer. The brake jammed on with an enormous metallic screech. The elevator stopped dead. "As you wish, angel," he said softly, his eyes flashing. "Ask, and you shall receive. Dress stays on, underthings off – now."

"Tom," she said, more excited than ever, but a bit timid now in the face of what she'd wrought – "Tom, can't this wait until we get to your apartment?"

He laid his hand against her cheek. "We made all the big decisions downstairs. Outside, out there in the big world, you can do anything you want. I'll be there. But this is the small world, this is only you and me, this is me making love to you. I told you once you don't have a vote here, you don't tonight, and you're never going to. Underthings off, angel."

Her ears were roaring. He needn't have repeated himself; she'd already begun wrestling the undergarments off, amazed at herself. Arguing with her lover after he'd taken charge, not responding instantly – where was the fun in that?

But her blood was much too wild tonight to be quieted by simple acquiescence. She stopped what she was doing and looked up at him – tall and wonderful and hers. This should not be that easy for him. If he wanted to take her, he was going to have to subdue her first.

Without any warning at all, she flung herself at him.

*

Fifteen feet above and four feet over, on the fourth floor, two couples approached the elevator door. A party down the hall was breaking up. One of the men pressed the button, then looked up at the floor indicator.

"Damn," he said to his wife, "it's stuck."

*

"Enough," Tom said, pulling her hands gently to her side.

"I'm sorry," she breathed. "I'm sure I can sew it up."

"In four places?" he said calmly, but his own breath was becoming shorter. "It's an old shirt anyway. And Adele. . . about my hair," he went on, "I don't mind having it pulled. I do mind having it pulled out."

"Sorry," she said again, breathing. "I can't help it," and then tore into him again, undoubtedly getting into more trouble with him, but she was looking for that sort of trouble right now. He did not stop her, instead gnawed back at her with his own passion. A few seconds of raw animal splendor ensued, until he took charge again, this time for good.

"No more female nonsense," he growled. "Get that stuff off. Do as you're told," and now the time for argument was definitely over. She slid her panties down her thighs and stepped out of them.

"I don't have anything with me, but I haven't been with anyone since," he said. "I told you the truth. Are you all right?"

"Yes," she said carefully. "I can't get pregnant tonight."

"All right," he said, putting his hands under her bottom and hoisting her off her feet, "undo me." She complied, her hands trembling on his belt buckle. "This isn't nearly as easy as they make it look in the movies," he went on. It didn't look at all easy in the movies she'd seen. In fact, she'd wondered if it were possible. "You have to do some work; I have all I can do just to hold you up. Ready. . .?"

They moved together – she helped – she became more doubtful it could be done – then – *Wonderful! Heaven!* She closed her eyes and moaned his name softly.

"You feel terrific, angel," he sighed in her ear, "just right. Now pleasure yourself. Enjoy me."

That was an easy direction to follow.

*

"They really should have two elevators in a building this size," a woman remarked crossly. There were now eight people waiting for the car.

"It's an older building. . . probably the code's changed."

"Do you want to walk?" a man asked his wife.

"No," she answered, thinking of four flights of stairs in the semi-dark in heels. "Let's wait a while longer."

*

This is great, Adele thought, eyes closed, chin resting on his shoulder – the freedom of movement, the novelty. Small movements produced enormous rushes of sensation. The way the two of them must have appeared also gave her pleasure – any adult would have realized what they were doing, but his topcoat completely covered her. His trousers still hung around his upper thighs. The only part of either body exposed was the calves of her legs, protruding just slightly underneath the bottom of the coat behind her. For whatever reason, the image pleased her.

Prolonging the experience would have been very nice, but this was a semi-public place. She began to move towards the finish, which was coming soon, and which was going to be fantastic.

"Adele," he whispered suddenly in a neutral tone.

"*What!?*" she said, exasperated.

"Sorry to interrupt, but you've hooked both your legs behind my knees. If you keep it up, you're going to trip me –"

"Oh," she breathed, "sorry," and conscientiously moved her feet outside his calves.

"–which would not be good for any of the three of us."

She closed her eyes and resumed. After a second, she almost fell off his shoulder. Her eyelids flew up like a doll's. "What! The three –" Then, slowly,

slowly she closed her eyes again. "How, Tom?" she said, teeth clenched. "*How!?* Just tell me how. I thought I did it so well."

"You did," he answered, "but when I turned away in the cab I still had you in the rear-view mirror. You closed your eyes and let out your breath, and I knew." He paused. "Sometimes the first question is only the setup," he added, giving away one of his own secrets.

She let out a long breath. "In the words of the immortal Moe," she said, "remind me to kill you later." Then suddenly she was really angry. "And now I've lost it! It's all gone and I was so close! Tom, so help me!"

"You can't get back there?"

"No," she said bitterly.

He slid his hand up the back of her thighs. "Not even if I did *this*. . . or this?"

"Tom," she gasped, in an entirely different tone.

"Or *that*. . . or this?"

"*Tom*," she all but moaned, "please. . . no."

"What's the matter?" he said, suddenly concerned. "This shouldn't hurt. I'm not pressing that hard."

"It's not that," she said timidly, then hesitated. "It's *embarrassing* to like that so much. "

"Oh dear," he replied, without the slightest discernible trace of sympathy in his voice. "You mean *this* embarrasses you. . . or *that*. . .?"

Tom, she tried to say, but it came out a semi-moan. The rhythm was not her own anymore. One wave, then another, then another, each pulse harder, more intense, driving her relentlessly up towards something fantastic. She gulped for breath and the intake came out as another, louder moan. God, his hands, his large unforgiving hands! His revenge, of course, for her earlier temerity. . . wonderful, wonderful revenge. Now he was driving her implacably, remorselessly up, and now she was on the verge, helpless, and a last surge was upon her, too big for reality. The shards of the world shattered. Her hands clutched the coat frantically, convulsively. "Put your head against my chest, angel," he said as calmly as he could. "As I recall, we're reaching a point where you become a pretty noisy individual."

*

"Did you hear something?" someone on the fourth floor asked. "I hope no one's trapped in there."

"It would be awful if you were claustrophobic," someone else said.

"Obviously," said a third sarcastically. There were now ten people in front of the door.

*

In a series of small delicious shudders, her body finally relaxed. It had been wonderful, wonderful. All the tension was released. She felt like a bowl of limp spaghetti. Their bodies were still together; he was still tense, eager, undischarged. Time now for him to please himself, produce another small bubble of pleasure for her.

"That's one," he said instead. "Now we go for two."

"Oh, Tom, *I can't*," she answered. "I don't think there's a working hormone left in my body."

"Really?" he replied. "Not even if I did *this*. . . or *that*?" shifting his hands and repositioning her simultaneously.

All the strands of limp spaghetti instantly became piano wire. Not only was it going to happen again, it had to.

*

The host of the party came down the hall. "What's the problem?" he asked. Four of his other guests followed.

"Elevator's stuck."

"Really?" he said, surprised. "That's never happened before. Should I call the manager?"

"I think someone may be trapped in there," said the woman who thought she'd heard a sound.

*

The movements were still small, the sensuality large, but the atmosphere had changed – no longer lighthearted, healthy animal fun, but the most serious kind of lovemaking possible, the most intense of her life. He was doing the work now, familiar movement, ancient sexual themes. She was constitutionally incapable of silence – but she'd laid her head above his shoulder, mouth against his ear, and her mouthings, whispers, sighs, were intended for him alone, goading him. *Do you know what it is you're doing to me?* But of course he did, he wasn't deaf, and she could feel his response, in his hands, in his mouth, in the driving urgency of his body.

Old, familiar themes – the sense of being taken, that her lover had full possession of her only, only self. Only this was not an illusion, this was really happening, and it was going to be permanent. What he was taking she had freely chosen to give, but even so. . . the surging blood, the overwhelming male territoriality, the knowledge that there wasn't one particle of her being that would not bear his imprint forever afterwards, produced an instinctive, momentary panic. For an instant, she wanted to stop, break rhythm, somehow back off and keep something for herself – this was all so ultimately, ultimately final. But – no – no holding back – in fact – the opposite. . .

Somehow, she found a crease in his body and wedged herself even more tightly, his arms pulled her even closer. Somehow, as impossible as it seemed, the intensity became greater. *Do it,* she may have said or may have breathed or may only have thought. *Do it. Take me. Take all of me. Take what belongs to you. Make me yours.*

The tension crescendoed towards the peak. His hands were everywhere. His own finish was going to trigger hers, she was certain of it, this one more marvelous than the last. His muscles stiffened; he was almost there; then, all at once, he did lose his balance, staggered one step to his left, tried to recover, then crashed heavily into the side of the cabin. It seemed as if the entire universe shook, but it didn't, it was only the elevator cabin. He bridged the weight with his left arm; she was completely unharmed. She had tightened her legs around him; their bodies were still together.

"It killed me to write that first note," he gasped, bracing himself against the side, voice husky, speaking more from the heart than she ever heard him before or after. "It was going to kill me again to put you in the taxi. I'm not giving you up again, angel. Not to anyone. Not for anything. I won't. I can't. You're mine. No one else's. You belong to me."

"Yours. . . yours," she managed to croak; she felt his body break, felt a wild engendering shudder, familiar pulse, felt herself break with him, a monumental coming together, tension surge and snap, a final consummation, no retreat possible; heard herself crying out, too late remembered she had forgotten to bury her head in his coat.

*

"I am certain someone is trapped down there," the woman said. "This time I know I heard something."

"So did I," someone agreed.

"We'd better get the manager," the host said.

"There was movement in the shaft," a man remarked. "Perhaps it's becoming unstuck."

*

The problem with impromptu sex, Adele thought, *is that it's impromptu.* What she would have liked to do is go somewhere and glow for a week. What she had to do was get them moving. It didn't help that Tom, typical male, seemed more inclined to sleep than anything else.

"Tom. . . help me," she said. "Put the pantyhose in your pocket. Where's my underwear?"

"You're going to put it on?" he asked, handing the garment to her.

"It's ruin the panties or ruin the dress," she answered, acting as she spoke. "I'm a mess. I've got to get cleaned up. You're a very virile man." She shook her head. "Seven weeks."

"Ready?" he asked after a moment.

"Yes." His arm slammed forward and the brake released; the elevator groaned and started up. He reached over and touched her hand. She smiled feebly. "I hope there's no one on the landing."

"Probably not," he answered. "This is a quiet building. It's late."

The door opened. Together, they stepped out and confronted the nineteen persons who had assembled in front of it.

*

Adele remembered at once that a woman had one more prerogative in these situations than did a man, a cowardly, ignoble one, one which she had always despised and held in contempt. Now she understood at once its wisdom. She immediately whirled around and buried herself in Tom's coat. Let him handle it. If he wanted to go around ravishing innocent women in elevators without the slightest provocation, he could deal with the consequences himself. She wasn't raising her head until all these strangers were all gone. His arm came up around her protectively.

"What happened?" asked one of the men.

"We thought the cable was going to snap," Tom lied calmly. "I put on the brake until we were sure." With her head turned, Adele watched ten or so people step into the compartment, the door close. *Please, God, please give all the men the usual male nose; give all the women head colds*. The cabin was full of musky animal smells, not unpleasant, but anyone with the slightest sense of smell would know instantly what had taken place.

"We thought it was stuck," someone said.

"That was afterwards," Tom answered. "First we thought something was wrong with the cable. There was a bump."

"That was after the elevator stopped," someone else said.

"That was the second bump," Tom replied. "Didn't you feel the first bump?" She peeked around; Tom continued to create fiction. Thank heaven the topcoat was covering the dress; his sports jacket covered the tears in his shirt. One of the men at the rear listening to the lies, more sophisticated than the rest, shook his head and rolled his eyes heavenward. Adele turned her head back, her face crimson.

"Do you think it's safe?" a woman asked.

"Oh, yes," Tom said. "There's no question I overreacted. I'm sure it's all right." He lowered his voice, and gave her back the mildest of squeezes. "My wife doesn't like closed spaces. I tend to be more protective of her than I should be."

The hairs on the back of her neck stood up. He never used words casually, would especially not use that one loosely. Not now. She rolled her head up his chest. He said something to the others, then glanced down at her, met her eyes. *I meant it.* He'd meant her to hear.

Was this the way it was done? Was it really so easy, so informal? In any case, her turn. There was no time to think and really nothing to think about. She wasn't backing down. She pulled her head up, turned and faced them, smiled, reached behind her, and took his hand – the bad left one – good; excellent; perfect. "I'm the one who should apologize. I'm really such a baby. My" – she turned her head to Tom, met his eyes in turn, squeezed his hand lightly, then looked back at the others – "my husband takes much better care of me than he really should. I'm sorry I made such a fuss."

The tension in the group began to dissipate. People seemed to warm to them; smiles and acknowledgments; the elevator arrived again and another few people boarded. *We must look a natural couple*, she thought. No one seemed to notice that their dress didn't match at all. The host said goodnight and went back down the hall – a good thing he didn't know Tom. Now there were only three left waiting to depart, a middle-aged married couple and the sophisticated man.

"Such nice young people," the woman remarked pleasantly. "How long have you been married?"

"Actually, this evening," Tom answered. *Actually, about two minutes ago,* Adele thought.

"Oh!" the woman beamed. "How wonderful! Congratulations! Good luck!" Her husband smiled and nodded. The elevator returned and they got onboard. The sophisticated man stepped to the door, then turned to Tom.

"How was it?" he asked quietly.

"Fantastic," Tom answered instantly, in the same quiet tone. "She gives great elevator." Adele went beet red again. The man nodded, then did a double take and grinned – the joke had been so flat, so deadpan that he initially did not recognize it as such.

Everyone had left. Two ways to marry someone, Adele reflected. You can do it as publicly as possible, standing up in a cathedral in front of all your friends – or you can do it as privately as possible, standing up in an elevator between the third and fourth floors of an old apartment building. She knew now she was never going to find out how the public method felt. But based on what she did know, she voted for private.

*

They walked down the hall and reached the door. She watched him unlock it. As the sexual energy faded, so did the giddiness, the exhilaration, the high spirits. The erotic energy spent in the elevator had been the last energy she had. She felt bone weary, drained, more tired than she had ever been in her life.

The interior of the apartment was so familiar she almost cried. She was back to the place she should never have left. It was not quite as neat as when he'd first brought her there, but still neat enough. Her guess is that it was never really untidy. "I have to use the bathroom," she said; he nodded; and she left. She did her best to stem the flood, but it was hopeless. She considered a shower. She didn't have the strength.

Tom was quietly stripping the bed when she returned. "I think you could do with a change of sheets," he said quietly, without looking back. Then he straightened up and looked at her. "You're too tired to move." He took two strides over to her. She realized he was right. "You need to rinse off. You'll never sleep comfortably that way."

She shook her head negatively – not meaning that she disagreed, meaning that she couldn't.

"Here," he said gently, lifting her up. "Tom. . ." she protested feebly, but he carried her easily back into the bathroom.

"Where's the catch on this thing?" He meant the dress.

"At the top. Then another one to the left." It was an effort to speak.

"Got it. O.K., can you lift your arms?" She found it took an act of will. He took her elbow and raised it. He undressed her calmly and efficiently, in the manner of a male nurse, without any trace of romance. The dress came off. She'd treasure a swatch of the cloth as a souvenir, but she'd never wear it again. It was soaked with sweat and both their body fluids. She'd made a mistake in the elevator. She should have saved the panties.

"I'm not so good with bras," he said apologetically.

"Do your best," she said wearily. Right now, reaching behind her back seemed as difficult as swimming to Japan.

"O.K.," he said finally. Off it came. "Now help me just a little bit. . . hands up. . . that's good." She was bare. He held her with one arm, with the other opened the shower and tested the water. "That'll do nicely. . . O.K. now step up. . . too hard? . . .here, let me." He lifted her knee up lightly, moved her over the wall of the tub. She was behind the water; he was holding her up with one hand. "O.K., step in. . . watch out for your hair, turn your head. . .feels good, doesn't it?" It felt wonderful. "I'm going to wash you now." He must have been the only bachelor in New York who owned washcloths. His hands moved swiftly, nonerotically, over her body, marvelously soothing. He handed her the cloth. "You'd better finish yourself," he said shyly, and she felt a flicker of amusement – after all that had happened, that he'd feel shy about touching her any place. She used the cloth without being precisely aware of what she was doing. The simple act of remaining vertical took an effort.

"Finished? O.K., over the rim again. . . need help? Here we go. . ." He put his hand under her knees and moved her out. He was getting his shirt wet. She wanted to say something, didn't have the strength. "Here's the towel. . ." It was wonderfully clean and fluffy. Her surprise showed in her face. Single men didn't live like this.

"When I'm home, I wash the linen three times a week," he explained, reading her. "I have to; you know why. It's no big deal to do the towels, too." He dried her off, his hands large and wonderful.

"What had you decided about the baby?" he asked conversationally.

"To give birth," she answered. "No matter what you'd decided. Not at first – at first – never mind. Our baby – who the father was, was very, very important to me the whole time." She paused. "Tom, I've never been in that situation before," she added quietly, meaning to ask him a question.

"I don't have any other children, Adele," he answered quietly, understanding. "I haven't impregnated anyone. Most of the time, I've been careful; a few times, I've been lucky." She felt enormous relief.

"Why didn't you say anything?" she asked.

"It was clear the way you handled it, it wasn't the reason you'd come."

Suddenly there was so much she wanted to say to him – not about himself, but about Bobby Lawton, and George, and Lem, the wonderful computer program, Carolyn and Franklin Fischer, all the things she'd learned about the fragility of the world, Petrosian and the one, eternal war, all of it. She started to talk. She was too tired to be rational. To her horror, she heard herself babbling aloud, a nonsensical mishmash, acting out involuntarily the one movie cliché she hated the most, the one where the heroine is too frightened to inform the hero coherently about the danger he faces. Worse. She found herself sobbing again. This would never do – all right, maybe she hadn't been teary enough before, but this Weeping Wanda stuff had to stop. Enough was enough.

He kissed away her tears, then laid a finger above her lips. "You're trying to tell me you've been having adventures," he whispered. "I already knew that. We'll talk another time. You're too tired even to be yourself. Don't worry," he said, very softly, very tenderly, "I'm never mistaking you for a weak person," and she remembered all over again why she loved him, why she should never have left.

He picked her up and carried her out into the other room, over to the dresser. "I'm sorry, the pyjama top is clean, but it's not fresh. It'll have to do." She nodded. She raised her arms and he pulled it over her head; in a moment, she was dressed and ready for bed. She liked the clean but slightly used pyjama top better than the fresh one. It had a nice Tom smell to it. "Over here, then. . ." he picked her up effortlessly and set her down on his reading chair. "Watch while I finish the bed," he said. "Here. Take this until I need it." He picked up a blanket, put it over her, and tucked the edge underneath her chin. It was wool, and scratchy, but warm and perfect. "Just rest. This will only take a second. It won't bother me at all if you fall asleep."

She watched, but did not sleep. He was too good at making beds. That should have been a clue. She looked around the apartment. It had more furnishings these days, but still was fundamentally a tool shed. Milly had it right. That was going to have to change. She watched him move around the bed, methodically, efficiently.

Despite her exhaustion, she felt a great peace, a contentment. She had not been born for an easy path, for a convenient life. It had been a mistake ever to think so. This had to be one of the happiest days of his life; probably the best; but his demeanor was the same as the day she first met him. The darkness behind his eyes was unchanged as he creased the fold on the top sheet. Nothing that had happened had caused him to erupt into real joy. Demons still gnawed underneath. She was not going to have one easy day, not one period of real peace. Peace of mind was not part of the bargain. How had it happened? Against all the odds? Her hands came automatically to her abdomen.

Was it you, little one? Was it you all the time? "We didn't make our baby when the condom broke," she said suddenly. "It was the third time." She had reached a point of weariness at which it was impossible to think sequentially. Her mind bounced randomly from thought to thought, like a ping pong ball in a room of angles.

"You couldn't possibly know that," he answered softly, not looking up from his work.

"I *know*," she replied decisively, and he remained silent, having the good sense not to argue with a crazy person. He finished with the top blanket, then turned to her. "I'm going to change now. Then I'll put you to bed." She managed a nod. He got out his own night things, disappeared into the bathroom.

Two hours ago, he had nonchalantly humiliated a multibillionaire. Now he did servant's work with the same facility, the same incisiveness, without any hesitation, comparison, or self-consciousness. Did he perceive the anomaly? Of course. Did it matter to him? Almost certainly not. An ordinary man in so many ways – a little taller than most, much better at making beds, and now hers, as she was his.

She thought back over the night. All at once, something he'd said struck her. *That little shtick I did with the look and the cameramen.* The <u>look</u>??? She had thought at the time he meant to do Franklin Fischer violence. Suddenly she was not so sure. Had he planned it all from the start, maybe not the final denouement, but the general idea. . . lured Fischer out and destroyed him with laughter? She thought about it: possible, entirely possible. Poor, stupid Franklin. Good advice about the giants of the world: they come along rarely. Often they are completely disguised. Sometimes they themselves don't know who they are. But if you do encounter one, be very, very careful. Get in the way, and he or she will crush you without breaking stride, without looking back, without thinking twice.

And she had earned the protection of one of them. That couldn't possibly be bad. Couldn't possibly. She heard the hiss of the shower.

Who are you, Tom?

The failure to ask that question – she had traveled halfway around reality to redeem it. Her entire universe had been rearranged. But the riddle remained unsolved. With all the wisdom she had gathered, she was no closer to the center. A question unanswered and unanswerable, least of all by the man himself. As Jenet had predicted. . . as had Goodson, in different words. *Fundamental mysteries*, Tom'd described that day at the museum. Did he know he himself was one of them?

Tom was back now, dressed for bed. He moved over to her. "Time to sleep, angel," he said softly, reached down and picked her and the blanket up as if they were weightless. He carried them over to the bed; holding her in one arm, he pulled back the cover and sheet. "In you go."

Wonderful! Cool and crisp. Perfect. He spread the blanket out, pulled it under the mattress. A splatter of rain hit the window.

""The storm's here," he remarked. "About time." *We did that*, she thought insanely. Then another random thought struck her. An important thought: Franklin Fischer and his version of realism.

"Tom – something I want to ask – the devil in Faust – Mephistopheles – how does he describe himself – the famous phrase–?"

He looked at her, puzzled. "*`Ich bin der Geist der stehts verneint`*? `I am the spirit that always says no`?"

The way he really is, Milly had told her. "That's right," she said. "That's exactly right. I'm glad you didn't listen," she went on, extending her hand, without moving otherwise. "I'm so glad." He squeezed her hand gently, perhaps a bit baffled, but largely understanding. Then he reached for the lamp.

Now the lights were out and he was beside her, on his back. He shifted her onto his chest; easily, naturally she found her one special place on his shoulder. How had she ever left this place! She must have been mad! She nestled against him; he pulled her in. Perfect. Sleep was now dropping rapidly, a dark heavy curtain, but she willed herself awake for another few seconds. She was certain he would not miss his exit line.

From out of the darkness it came: "I love you, angel."

She had noticed the pet name the first time he used it, but said nothing. She had no objection to it at all, other than it still had to be earned.

She snuggled closer; the contrast between the warmth of his body and the chill of the sheets was marvelous. "I love you, too, Tom."

And now the wheel had finally turned completely around, all the way back to where it had been – and was ready to turn again. She wondered if she'd have even one night's reprieve. But for now, she was done. Darkness descended instantaneously.

She slept.

And for this night, for this one night, at least, found peace.

END, PART II

REVELATIONS AND RECRIMINATIONS

She groped towards consciousness, the way a bottom fish might swim towards light. She was almost there. The water was breaking. Her eyelids were fluttering. Suddenly she heard a deep voice: *You're only waking up now because you're used to waking up. Go back to sleep. You haven't slept nearly long enough. Go back to sleep.*

She was close enough to consciousness to wonder momentarily where she was, who was speaking to her. Then. . . *oh, it's Tom*, she thought dreamily, *then it's all right*; she was on his shoulder; a moment of awareness – *go back to sleep*, he repeated – and then she went back down, drew herself into him – slept and slept and slept.

*

Now she had to tear herself away from all the lovely morning dreams and wake. She lingered in delicious semi-sleep for a few moments longer. Somehow, she could feel that the rain had turned icy cold overnight, pounding outside, real weather for a change. The blanket was warm on one side, Tom on the other, with his marvellous shoulder. Now she felt his hand, stroking her body gently. Heaven – who would ever wake up from this if she had a choice? But she had no choice, because she was already awake.

Her eyes fluttered open. She found herself looking across the pillow at Tom. Her head was still on his arm. He was wide awake.

"Hello," she said, yawning, stretching, coming to life. "Tom? How long have you been awake? What time is it?"

"Ten-fifteen," he answered. "About two and one half hours."

"Just looking at me?" she asked.

"Just looking at you," he replied softly.

"Tom," she started to say, but before she could do anything, she felt herself moving up on top of his chest, lifted effortlessly with one arm. *God, he was strong!* Now she was astraddle his body, her eyes on his.

He did nothing more than contemplate her for long, long moments.

The expression on his face – a combination of gratitude, respect, admiration, and love – was something she would treasure for the rest of her life. Perhaps that alone was worth everything.

"So I wasn't dreaming," he said softly, caressing her face lightly.

"No," she answered back in the same tone, touching him in the same way.

His look lingered for another instant, then he broke it off, with his half smile. "Well?" he asked.

"Well?" she asked in return.

"Well," he said, "I think we should get publicly married. Soon. We owe it to our child."

"Yes," she agreed, understanding exactly what he meant by the word 'publicly.' "I'll find out how soon today, when I go into the office. I know we need a blood test. Perhaps next Friday, after Thanksgiving." He nodded. She went on, more quietly: "The holiday'll give my family a chance to meet you. It'll be enough of a shock as it is." He nodded again. "I'm sure they'll like you," she added, and wondered even as she spoke if she were correct.

He shifted his weight underneath her. "We should get started on the day," he said. "I'll make you breakfast."

"Just like that?" she said, disappointed.

"Just like that," he answered, understanding her. "I'm worried about the baby."

"You know that's not a problem at this stage," she said.

His eyes twinkled. "You can't reason with cocks, Adele. They have no brains. Only reactions."

"So I've been told," she sighed.

Oh, well.

They breakfasted a short while later, clean and refreshed, the euphoric glow still about them. The talk was of mundane plans, day-to-day life. By tacit agreement, the turbulent events of the night before were not post-mortemed. Perhaps they never would be. His apartment was small, but they'd have to stay here through next Sunday; her roommate couldn't move before then. There were some things she had to do in the office today. Dinner out tonight? Fine. He would get his blood done by the insurance doctor, no sweat; she'd have Alice Marshall do hers on Monday. One of her partners used to be a district attorney. He knew lots of judges; he could recommend somebody. Friday would be a good day, the semi-holiday after Thanksgiving, nothing much happening in the courts. Perhaps this one time her family members, the ones available, would do better to come to the City for the holiday. Somehow this morning Adele could ignore the vague air of unreality about it all.

"I have to tell you," he said finally, very uncomfortably, "something else went on since I've seen you."

"What?" she asked.

"The work I've been doing," he answered. "It involves you." Now definitely shy, very hesitant, he moved to the computer desk. He picked up the manila envelope he'd been carrying the night before and opened it. "Here." he said, and took his seat on the computer chair.

She looked at the manuscript:

THE METROPOLITAN SONNETS
by T. B. Newcombe
Respectfully dedicated to
Ms. Adele Elizabeth Jansen

She looked up, directly into his eyes, uncomprehending for a moment. He shrugged – *open it* – and looked away, diffident, definitely ill at ease. She did, scanned quickly the first page, then the next. Each contained three fourteen-line poems, sonnets. The subject was immediately obvious; she looked up at him, startled, then read the first and second poems carefully. Music – pure music – the music he could make out of the English language!

"It's our day at the Met," she said, amazed. "You made a sonnet sequence out of it."

"Yes," he nodded.

"But. . . but. . . how?" she asked, dazed, but wondering – why should this upset him? She riffled through the manuscript – scanning quickly, nine chapters, over twenty sonnets in each, slightly over 200 poems. "How could you possibly do all this in only two months?"

"Oh, no way," he answered instantly, "no way. In a sense, I've been working on this all my life. Everything I had in my notebook – scraps, fragments, notions, the accumulation of – I don't know, five, ten years, some even longer – a lot of themes to which I've given a lot of thought – it all came together. In addition to your other qualities, you make a great central metaphor."

She read the first one carefully – a marvelously chimed piece of verse, with a rhythm, a sense of pace, internal rhymes that were instantly memorable – he had begun the narrative at the time they entered the museum. The second recited the prosaic event of ticket taking, which he had somehow imbued with a mythological presence, in the most subtle counterpoint to the playfulness of the rhyme scheme, solemn and rollicking fun both at once.

"I'm overwhelmed," she said truthfully, becoming more bewildered –

perplexed at herself, since she would have expected to feel nothing but excitement at this – and yet she did feel something more, something else entirely.

"Prose comes easy," Tom went on quietly, quickly, uncharacteristically. "Poetry is very, very difficult. If I get eight good lines a day, it's an awfully good day. That's why this goes back so far. They're modified Pushkin sonnets, suitable for long narratives. But the rhyme scheme's too easy; I had to make it a little harder on myself. So the `d' rhyme in the last becomes the `a' rhyme in the next. Plus I imposed a few other conditions that you have to read carefully to discover. In general, the more constraints, the better." He paused. "The tension between the expansiveness of the thought and the severity of the architecture is what gives a line its strength. The more tightly compressed the spring, the greater its power."

She nodded. Those words were words she would come to know by heart. Even in the later years, when she had resigned herself to living in the midst of a permanent media feeding frenzy, Adele always made herself accessible to responsible critics and scholars. The statements he had just uttered she would have occasion to repeat again and again and again. In what years they had together, this was the only occasion he ever described his methods. Many of the questioners could not conceal their exasperation that she had not asked about 'the few other conditions' that 'you have to read carefully to discover' when she had the opportunity. She always apologized as charmingly as she could for the oversight. What she never told any of them was that the drift of the conversation had nothing to do with aesthetics, that he had said what he did when he did to distract, not enlighten.

But she was not distracted this morning. "You wrote these for me when you never expected to see me again," she said slowly, thinking rapidly. "I mean, that's wonderful, but. . ."

"That made no difference," he replied instantly. "You would still have been you. The day would still have happened."

Why wasn't that thrillingly romantic? The prosaic truth was. . . it plain wasn't – dark and ominous instead. "But how were you going to get them to me?" she asked aloud.

"You were going to mail them," she went on, answering her own question, "there wouldn't be any other way." She looked at the manuscript. "There's no letter here. There's no way you wouldn't have included a letter," she said positively.

He shrugged again, now clearly discomfited. She looked at the wastebasket. "Is it in there? Did you destroy it while I was sleeping?"

"Yes," he admitted. "The letter's out of date now."

She glanced at it – shredded paper, torn to bits – then looked him in the face, still wondering out loud: "But then why didn't you simply crumple it? You didn't do that. You tore it into shreds small enough that I couldn't possibly read it."

His hand came up half-heartedly, as if he could wave it all away. "It's way, way out of date."

She glanced at the manuscript, then stepped to the wastebasket and picked up a scrap. "It looks like the same font." Adele faced the computer. "I bet the file's still on disk," she said, then looked back at him. "I'd like to read the letter, Tom," she went on quietly, with a sick feeling of dread mounting in the pit of her stomach.

Several seconds elapsed. "I'd really appreciate it if you wouldn't, angel," he said quietly. "It doesn't say anything worth reading."

"Anything you write is worth reading," she answered. "Please boot it up, Tom. Tom? I know the program – it has an automatic save feature – and I'll find the file myself, unless you encrypted it, which I doubt very much you did. And if I had to, I'd put the paper shreds back together."

He appraised her again, and then sat down heavily at the keyboard. The machine beeped into life; when she moved behind him, the screen was filled with text. It read:

Ms. Adele Elizabeth Jansen
Hapgood, Thurlow, Anderson, & Davis
New York, New York

Dear Ms. Jansen,

You will recognize the subject of these sonnets at once; I hope the poems meet with your approval. The effort that has gone into their creation has been amply repaid by the pleasure the contemplation of our hours together has given me, a prospect almost as pleasant as were the hours themselves.

I have no interest in the copyright to this work; you may take my signature below as an assignment of all right, interest, benefit and so forth in this work to you, Adele Elizabeth Jansen – this last perhaps not in the manner of your own glib legalese, but I'm sure sufficient.

Again, thank you for the gift of your time.
Sincerely,
Thomas Bryant Newcombe

Adele scanned it quickly. For a moment, she was reassured, but for a moment only. "You managed to delete something," she said. "There's an ellipsis. You know this program better than I thought. That's not the whole letter. You'd never start a letter to me like that. You eliminated the first paragraph."

"Angel –" he said, shaking his head, beginning to rise. Standing behind him, she put her hands lightly on his shoulders; he sat back heavily. "My darling," she said gently, "I know what it says. All I'm curious about is how you said it."

Because she did know.

*

I have my own reasons for getting done with this, he'd said on the first morning in her office. But he had no other plans.

Jenet doesn't have to worry. . . at least not about that, he'd said at the same time. But what was it Jenet should worry about?

It's got to stop. . . and it will, he'd said at the restaurant after they'd been to the Met. But Petrosian said he'd reached stasis, that no meaningful change was realistically possible.

Whatever you may hear of me later, he'd written in his note the morning after. She'd thought at the time his meaning was general. It wasn't; it had been specific. She knew that now.

Sooner or later the bear will refuse to remount, Petrosian had said. *The trick is so difficult and he always falls.* Which could be sooner as easily as later.

I wasn't going to see this one through to the end, Danny, he'd said as he left the table the night before. Why not?

It doesn't make any difference anymore, he said in the backseat of the taxi. But why shouldn't it?

It would be like coming back from the dead, he'd said to her last night, as he stood alone in the darkness.

So she knew.

*

Tom shifted his weight, gave her a dismal, trapped look, then hit two keys. The screen changed. The letter in full read:

Ms. Adele Elizabeth Jansen
Hapgood, Thurlow, Anderson, & Davis
New York, New York

Dear Ms. Jansen

By the time you receive the package in which this letter is enclosed, I will be dead. The decisions I have made in that regard were made long, long before our brief encounter and were irrevocable in every respect. Our meeting, however, caused me to delay their implementation a matter of some weeks until I could complete the attached verses in a form suitable for dedication to you.

You will recognize the subject of these sonnets at once; I hope the poems meet with your approval. The effort that has gone into their creation has been amply repaid by the pleasure the contemplation of our hours together has given me, a prospect almost as pleasant as were the hours themselves.

Again, thank you for the gift of your time.
Sincerely,
Thomas Bryant Newcombe

*

Even so, even having deduced correctly, reading the elegant formal prose, her blood ran cold. She felt a rush to tears. But she was more herself now, and so remained dry-eyed. "Tom," she gulped, "is this anything I have to worry about?"

"No," he said promptly, decisively. "I said, out of date. Everything changed last night. I wouldn't do that to you. I won't make a loser out of you." He swiveled the chair slowly around and pulled her onto his knees. "I made promises to you – that I'd go on, that I'd do my best for you. I won't break them. You're too important." *Completely consistent,* she thought. *His own life doesn't mean two pins to him, but hurting me. . .* and then she was close to tears, and a bit beyond, despite the restoration of strength.

"I meant what I wrote about the copyright," he remarked, clicking off the computer. The screen went blank. He removed the manuscript gently from her hands, turned back to the title page, and began to scribble.

"How?" she asked as he wrote.

"Poison," he answered without looking up. "An overdose of soporifics." He finished writing and looked up. "To sleep soundly for once," he said, softly, almost to himself, and now it took a real effort to hold onto herself.

"Did you do anything about it?"

"Yes," he said. "Barbiturates. They're in the medicine cabinet." He tapped the manuscript. "I finished this Monday. It was something I had to do for you. Then. . ." He shrugged. "You have to understand. Nothing ever changed, nothing was ever any better. What was the point? Why go on with it?" The bear had indeed grown weary, sooner even than Petrosian had realized. "Thursday night was going to be the night."

"Why did you wait?" she asked shakily.

A long pause. "I had to see you again," he said. "I had to – only see you. Once. You weren't at your office. That's why I went to the convention. That's the only reason. Not what Danny thought." He shook his head. "I'm not usually that soft on myself." He touched her lightly. "Don't worry, angel. I'm not going to do anything like that."

"You'd better not," she said, more shaky. "You're right about what it would do to me. You'd more than just hurt me, to know I'd failed like that. You'd – you'd –" then stopped, realizing it had been a mistake to begin talking, that she was losing it. Tom had become aware first, stood, and moved her firmly into his arms and against him while she recovered herself. The he sat back down in the chair with Adele again on his knee.

"I was afraid that would upset you," he said. "Believe me, it's all behind. I'll do my best for you, angel, whatever that is. I said I'd try and I will. I keep my promises. I may be a lot of things, but I'm no coward."

"You're right twice," she said, touching him, eyes moist. "You're no coward. And you are many, many things." She looked at the manuscript on the computer table, the blank screen, and shuddered involuntarily. The horrific thought occurred to her , that a universe might well have come into being in which she had received the letter and the manuscript in the manner first intended, on the Monday she returned from Alice's recommended clinic – raw, bleeding, empty.

But as dreadful as the discovery had been, one consolation came with it: at last, at last, at last, she had discovered the source of the mysterious sense of urgency that had plagued her all this time. She had found out what it was she had been racing against the last seven weeks. Somehow her subconscious had caught the cue. She had won the race without ever knowing what her opponent was.

She shuddered again. It had been so close, so horribly, horribly close.

*

It was comfy and cozy on his knee, natural to her; she shifted up into his lap. A light kiss led to a heavier one, then somehow they were back on the bed. "Are your reactions back?" she asked hopefully, because now a distraction was necessary, a gesture essential.

"No," he said. "I'm still on strike." She noticed his clothes were still on. He kissed her under her neck, then above her breasts, then just below. "But there are other methods." He kissed her just above her navel, then below. Adele realized she was about to receive the first intimate kiss of her life. Although more fortunate than many women, there had been occasions when she'd craved that service. But she'd always been too shy to ask and she'd never been with a volunteer. "Tom?" she questioned, tremendously excited, definitely distracted, but unsure. "I don't know about this."

He looked up at her, eyes sparkling. "Oh, you have led a sheltered life," he said, and got on with it.

*

A short while later, after she'd peeled herself off the ceiling and dressed again, Adele studied herself in the bathroom mirror. "What do you think?" she asked Tom.

She was dressed now in a pair of his trousers, cinched as tightly as they could be, pant legs rolled up, and one of his shirts, nearly half of it tucked in. The whole look was pathetic, but she had to wear *something* to get back to her apartment, and the once unblemished evening dress was out of the question.

He spread his arms and raised an eyebrow. "I don't see what else you can do," he said finally, diplomatically. "But you do look a bit – er – unusual."

She looked critically for a moment longer, then sighed. "What I look like is someone's little sister. I should be used to that, but I'm not. Oh, well." She rolled up the evening dress and picked up the manuscript. "What do you want me to do with this?"

He shrugged. "Whatever you like. They're yours. Shred them if you like."

"Don't be ridiculous," she smiled, deciding to make two copies at the office this day, one to run up to Jenet, one for her to read – although the thought of the reading brought with it a curious reluctance. She knew too much about how they had been created, what they had been meant to be, to be able to enjoy them fully. Still. . . Jenet. A plan had already occurred to her. "I'll only be a few hours." Suddenly she was anxious. "What are you going to do? Are you planning to write?"

"I didn't have any plans," he said quietly, chillingly. "I'm all written out for now. I'll probably go back to war with Gödel. . . listen to the Met, they're doing *Parsifal* today. I'll be O.K." His half-smile appeared. "I'll be here, angel. Don't worry."

But she did worry as she left, and knew that that worry was going to be a permanent part of her life from then on.

*

What with the weather, getting through the traffic, changing clothes (at last, thank God!), packing up minimal needs for the week ahead, cutting a four-inch patch out of the evening dress for the treasure drawer, she did not arrive at her office until after 2:30. After that, Adele moved quickly. She had work to do, and time was short.

Her first stop was at Harry Greube's office on the thirtieth floor. Luck was with her. No one was around and all the corporate books were in apple-pie, alphabetical order. She needed only a moment to find the AI books, and search out what she had hoped was there. The next stop was at one of the deserted word processing consoles.

Mr. Lemuel Michaels
President, Artificial Intelligence, Inc.
--------, New Jersey
November 20th, 19--

Dear Lem,

There were irregularities in the board meeting on Thursday of which I think you should be aware. Section 2 of Article II of the corporate bylaws requires three days' notice of the agenda. You didn't get any notice at all, and you didn't waive notice. The vote of the Board was therefore illegal. Your resignations aren't valid.

All of what happened was tied into a master plan to put together the media company you've no doubt read about by this time. The plan is in a very sensitive stage and even the threat of a lawsuit will give you some leverage. Pete was right; you should retain a lawyer and get back in the game. You should at least try to get the rights to develop the algorithm in a different code. I'm sure they'll give that up.

Lem, I want you to know that I didn't know what was going to happen at that meeting. But I don't blame you at all for the way you reacted. I did have an idea that something was wrong and that's what you'd asked me about. I blame only myself. But please don't believe I have written this letter for any other reason except to make it up to you, as best I can. It's not Humpty-Dumpty; it can be put together again.

Finally, trust George Sorenson, especially if he tells you to sell your stock. I know he didn't do right by you, but he never intended to take your money. He also will try to make it up to you; I know it. He is not a bad man.

Very truly yours,
Adele E. Jansen

She read it over, ignoring the lump she felt in her throat at the bare mention of George. The letter seemed incomplete; she wanted to do something else for Lem, to convince him she was speaking truth; in a moment she knew what. She opened the desk and pulled out a leaf of blank bond paper. Quickly she sketched Lem as she'd seen him in her dream, with his teeth straightened. After a few moments, she studied her work. Not bad; *my goodness, he could be a good-looking man!* But never hers; the click simply wasn't there, teeth or no teeth; she felt much relief in that knowledge. She looked at the sketch for another moment, then wrote in script:

This is how I always saw you. This is how you could look.

Adele

This was not entirely true, but she wanted to encourage him. In another moment the letter was addressed, metered, and posted. Then it was down to the twenty-eighth floor, and other business. She passed the massive copy machines Hapgood used for discovery compliance and the like. *Yes*, she thought absently, *make two copies of Tom's manuscript.* But her thoughts rolled on, focused on the other major unresolved problem, Bobby Lawton. One error – AI Squared – had been rectified, as best she was able, given that time lost can never be fully regained.

But Bobby Lawton was a harder nut. On the one hand, the Joanna way was the only way – *it stops now. Today.* But on the other, there was Walt, and his family, and all the eggs that would be broken there. Should she blow right by him anyway? Or was she going to begin a new life with another compromise? Long moments of agonizing thought. Bobby Lawton. . . but, still, Walt, his lovely children. . . her own sense of moral purpose did not necessarily justify doing harm to them. Life isn't that easy. Despite that one bad afternoon, she did not believe he was as lost to the reality of the matter as she had been. In fact, the abundance of wine that day was a sort of proof – and he had said he'd do something. More thought.

Lost in the contemplation of alternatives, she drifted towards the elevator. She found a manila envelope, stuffed the manuscript inside, wrote a hasty note to Jenet, and rode up. By the time the elevator reached the Furston floor, she had made her mind up. *Two weeks – and if Walt doesn't do something, I will.* Reluctantly – but it made sense, it seemed to fit – she nodded to herself. Bobby would be with his mother over the holiday anyway. *Two weeks* – and hope Walt acts first. Warn him anyway. She considered it once more in front of the big door, nodded again. Automatically, absently, she dropped the envelope through the mail slot. . . and only then, as it slid to the bottom, did she recollect that she had not in fact made the copies below, but only reminded herself to do so, that it was the original, destined for the treasure drawer, that she had just delivered to Jenet's office.

Adele felt a moment of intense irritation. Absent-mindedness was for other people. Adele Elizabeth Jansen was not absent-minded. She stuck her hand back down the mail slot, chancing it that no overly inquisitive security guard would be wandering by. But no such luck; it had slid out of reach. *Damn.* Well, the matter would keep until Monday. . . and with that thought, felt a curious mixture of relief and regret. Perhaps it hadn't been absentmindedness at all. For the first, but hardly the last time, she confronted the basic ambivalence she felt about the poems. Perhaps, in her heart of hearts, she was genuinely reluctant. . . that *horrible* letter. . . she mused on that matter for a moment, then straightened up. It would keep to Monday, and there was still plenty to do today.

Back in her own office, she made the entry about Bobby Lawton in her computer calendar. Now an interlude before the next thing, collecting her thoughts, reflecting. . . the minutes dragged on. . . she realized then she was procrastinating. *What are you waiting for? Do it.* Adele picked up the phone, summoned all her nerve, half closed her eyes, then willed herself to punch in the number.

"Hello?"

"Hello, Daddy," she answered.

"Pumpkin! Two calls in a week? When you're coming home so soon? You called at a good time. Ohio State just finished beating Michigan and the West Coast game hasn't started yet. So shoot, what's the news?"

She took a deep breath. "Well, Daddy, I'm pregnant, I lost my job yesterday, and I'm getting married Friday to a man you've never met."

Her father laughed pleasantly. "Big joke, Adele. What's really the news?"

*

After forty-five minutes of disbelief (*You're kidding. . . oh my God, you're not kidding!*), plans, altered plans, and mildly understated hysteria, the call was over. Adele put down the receiver and looked over her office. . . her VDT. . . her worktable, dominated by the overflowing files on the Project. . . all at once, the reality, the tangibility, of the surroundings, it overwhelmed her. The old Adele was suddenly in charge, and the old Adele was in the grip of a complete visceral, panic.

This was her life, *this* was what she had planned on. In the name of heaven, what in the *hell* had she done to herself in the last seven weeks? Was she *crazy*? Had she taken leave of her senses? How was she going to live? How were she and Tom going to survive, put food on the table? What were they going to do for money? Security?

Seven weeks ago – for heavens' sake, *three* weeks ago – she'd been anointed, a soon-to-be partner, fastest track of all time, seven figures a year guaranteed and going up year by year, each year, every year. Good God, what had she *done*? Abandoned all of it to link up with a man who was only half a man? Thrown everything away in a single day? It wasn't too late; she'd done well on Wednesday; she could still crawl back, there'd be a penalty to pay, of course; Carolyn and Franklin and–

No. She straightened up and took control of herself. Her panic subsided. Money? Tom could earn money. Jenet herself could give him all the work he wanted. Tom could make money – and she would find a job, too, whatever Franklin Fischer may have said.

But what of the rest? How was she ever going to construct a normal environment for a child and cope with Tom's problems simultaneously? Was any kind of sensible solution possible? Her heart sank again, not in panic now, but from a numbing realization of the sheer scale of the problems she'd taken upon herself. With a wrench, she realized that intra-family adoption was still an alternative she was going to have to consider, that rearing her own child might be a luxury she could not afford.

Enough – problems for another day. On to the next chore. Adele moved out of her office and down to storage, picked up two packing cartons and the day-old editions of the newspapers, returned to her office. She stood up on her client chair. Very carefully, she took down the portrait of her mother, folded the newspaper around it, then placed it carefully in the bottom of the carton. Then she stood up to take down her bar certificate.

"That's the smartest thing you've done in a couple of weeks," Carolyn said coldly, at the entrance to her office.

*

Adele wheeled around. Carolyn was accompanied by a junior associate with a gurney. "Paul," she said, pointing her finger at the files on the Project organized neatly on Adele's worktable, "pick that stuff up and take it up to my office." The associate, a tall, slender, blondish young man whom Adele hadn't met, whisked out from behind the gurney, moved quickly to the table, and began to stack the files. Like Harry Greube two days earlier, he could hardly wait to finish and get away.

"Up to my office," Carolyn repeated when he was finished, utterly unnecessarily. Paul was already moving down the corridor with long strides, as rapidly as he could move, pushing the gurney ahead of him. Carolyn and Adele were alone together.

"That was quite a show you put on last night," Carolyn said, after a moment. "Everyone was wowed. People kept shaking Franklin's hand all night long. Of course, it completely undercut the press conference, the announcement I'd been planning – for over two years now – but it wasn't bad. Not as bad as the questions Franklin had to answer about that incident in the lobby. Or watching it on the news later." She picked up the oval vase with the clock and examined it carefully. "This has to be the ugliest vase I've ever seen," she remarked. "Completely inappropriate for a law office." Adele was silent.

"I misjudged you," Carolyn continued, replacing the vase. "I recognized the potential. I knew you had a lot to learn. But I thought you'd stay the course. I trusted that you knew where your prospects lay. Even people without potential know that." She looked up. "I was an idiot. This whole week it seemed like if you could do something to frustrate me, to frustrate the Project, you did it. Your 'personal business,' your sudden illness. . . vanishing after the board meeting. . . and then your little impromptu announcement. With all the people who were depending on it, with all the effort that had gone into it – all of which you knew. You knew perfectly well what you were doing. You," she intoned solemnly, "Adele Jansen, are the most self-centered, irresponsible person with whom I have ever been associated."

Adele looked at her for a moment, then turned her back, stepped back on the chair, and took down her diploma from law school. "Aren't you going to say anything?" Carolyn demanded.

"No," Adele replied, folding a newspaper carefully around the frame.

"But at least I think I know the reason," Carolyn continued, with the slightest edge in her voice. "That man in the lobby – the one who made that preposterous scene. *He* was your personal business – and *he* was the reason why you suddenly got sick. I ran into Bill Andrews later; he was laughing; he told me who he was. Thomas Newcombe. Jenet's project. The man you left work with a few months ago. The man you left with last night." She shook her head disgustedly. "And then it began to make made sense. So Adele fell in love. . . la-de-da. . . maybe even discovered sex. . . tra-la-la. . . and of course everything had to be second to that." A quiet fury now in her voice: "Didn't it occur to you that's what they say about all of us? That our brains are between our legs? Didn't it bother you that you were proving all the chauvinists *right*? Do you know – are you aware of – all the years I've had to live with – to contend with –" Abruptly she folded her arms and contained herself.

"But what I'll never understand," she continued softly, incredulously, "is how you could toy with George Sorenson the whole time. Didn't you care at all? How could you look yourself in the mirror? Franklin had great plans for George. There were going to be wonderful opportunities. And CFS – George would have been a fool to leave. Franklin was sure he'd come to his senses.

"But now – but now," – she threw her hands up in the air – "it's going to be dissolved. You saw to that. People are going to lose their jobs, Adele. The sell-off may even impact the market. I don't know what your petty calculations were. I never guessed you were that calculating. But it's obvious you are." Adele turned away abruptly; she did not want Carolyn to see – to scoff at – her heart, naked and vulnerable. *George* – she was with Tom, she had to be with him, but that did not stop her from wanting. . . *Idiot*, she told herself, *such a baby*. Silently she turned and removed her framed diploma from the wall.

"You're not going to say anything," Carolyn's voice sounded again behind her.

Words tripped to her tongue. *You laughed too, Carolyn. And you knew – the whole time – what Franklin Fischer had in mind, for me, for George, for you. And now you are denying what you know to be the truth.* But what was the use? This was Carolyn's arena, her reality – no intruders welcome. Words were not adequate, at least not the ones she knew. Maybe Tom could do it. *Counting numbers*, she smiled suddenly, and enjoyed the joke again. No irrationals need apply in Franklin's universe, but they're just as real, there are more of them, and they're more important.

"Perhaps you're right to be quiet." Carolyn said, with feigned reflectiveness. "As I said, it's really my fault. It's always the quiet ones who lose their heads when they get a taste." Then she went on more briskly, "I want you to know if it were a perfect world you would be out of here. Now. Today."

"That suits me" Adele said. "I don't want to be here one more second."

"Oh, no, Adele," Carolyn answered. "Life's not that easy. You made too big an impression to just disappear. People are going to be asking about you. You'll stay, Adele, until the Project is completely closed. You may be finished in the big time, but you can still dream your wretched little dreams in the sticks. If you want to ever work anywhere at all, if you don't want me to make my own Project to see to your complete and utter misery, you'll stay."

Adele thought rapidly. The threats Carolyn was making were no different than the ones that Franklin had made the night before. Neither set frightened her. But she had her own reasons for staying on, not the least of which was a pause for breath. "All right," she said, "consider this my two-weeks' notice."

"Three weeks" said Carolyn, after a moment. "Three weeks from yesterday. Thanksgiving's a stub week." Adele considered, then nodded almost imperceptibly.

Carolyn smiled sourly. "It's going to be a long three weeks, Adele. Very dull. Very lonely. Do you know the word 'Coventry'? Better look it up. You'll be available in case we have to trot you out for any of the sellers. But other than that, you're going to be surprised at how little our clients care who does their work for them. And if you think you're going to get any kind of reference from here from anyone. . . think again. Franklin told me what he told you; let me repeat it: you're through, completely finished. Here and everywhere that matters. My partners and I don't give recommendations to cunts. Three weeks from now, you're on your own." She looked around the room. "Funny thing – you weren't going to be in this office very much longer in any case. You were going to be moving up. I guess it's out instead."

She reached into her purse. "Franklin asked me to give you something." She threw up a handful of confetti. Scraps of paper littered the desk; Adele could see enough to know that it was the stock option George had obtained for her, torn into microbits. "Oh, and I almost forgot. Here's the ticket for your coat. I don't know whether or not you ever will wear a fur. But I'm quite sure you'll never be able to afford one." Carolyn shouldered the purse. "Goodbye, Adele." She turned to go, moving stiffly and awkwardly.

"How was the party, Carolyn?" Adele asked quietly. Because she knew, had known the night before – that the final night of hospitality had been a bacchanal, that promises had been made to complete the Project that weren't written in any of the contracts, that those promises had been kept last night in any number of sad, foolish, sordid scenes – that the Project had in truth been completed in the Van Eyck hell, among any number of meaningless orgasms and sticky, weary overused flesh. She half-closed her eyes; she might very easily have ended up there as well. It had been close for her, too, as close as it had been for Tom.

Carolyn stiffened. "I did what I had to," she muttered, without turning back. "More than you can say. Three weeks," she said more loudly. Then she marched down the hall, head erect.

*

Adele finished packing her belongings. *Believing exactly what you want to believe; the paradigm of the unexamined life.* Carolyn and Josh, Josh and Vincent Driscoll, all of them, all alike, armored in smugness, the hypocrites in heaven – so many of them. She did not feel fury, or depression, only a certain indefinable sadness tinged with relief. She walked down a corridor as deserted as it had been on that horrible, horrible Thursday two days before.

Then, finally, the time had come to go home to what was home now, home to her husband. The euphoria of the night and morning was rapidly giving way to anxiety. The road ahead seemed so impossibly steep and rocky. *Home to her husband* – a nice phrase, she liked rolling it around in her mind – but would he actually be home when she got there?

In a moment, she was out of the building, into the street, moving with quiet determination. The worry was inevitable, the anxiety was an element of everything she had chosen, and there really wasn't much more to say, was there?

Joseph Wurtenbaugh

CHIPS FALLING

What happens the day after you've made the great romantic gesture? Adele had always wondered. When the bride flees from the altar and boards a bus with the man who refused to forever hold his peace, when does she get off? How does she get back into normal clothes? What do the two of them do the morning after? Adele had always wondered. When the business executive throws the immoral job in the boss's face, what does he do for next month's rent? Food still has to be put on the table, the kids still need shoes – what happens? How does he manage? The last thing Adele Jansen would ever have expected in her orderly, well-planned life was that she would be able to speak from experience about any such event.

Yet anyone who wanted to find out what it was like to marry on the impetus of wisdom garnered in a moment, or to abandon a job instantaneously upon the recognition of a moral imperative, could feel free to ring up Adele Elizabeth Jansen and find out.

Because, as it had turned out, she'd managed to do *both* simultaneously.

*

A nervous dinner out Saturday, marred by the interruptions of strangers recognizing Tom and congratulating him on the marvelous putdown, now on all the news shows. A long dull Sunday shut in by the rain. The discovery of at least a minor incompatibility – he did almost everything to background music; she couldn't tolerate it. Rather than say anything – it was, after all, his apartment (she was still thinking like that) – she endured it. The thought crossed her mind to ask him to reprint the poems, but she realized in the same instant she did *not* want to read them – not right then, anyway, not until the jumble inside her soul had sorted itself out. For his part, Tom's sensitivity to her moods seemed to have vanished entirely. He was lost in his own thoughts. An attempt at lovemaking in the evening, more out of a sense of mutual obligation than any real desire, was a complete fiasco – he only semi-potent, she not really interested – nothing meshing, nothing in sync. *This*, she thought, *must be the way it always is for women who don't like it.*

"Tom," she asked suddenly at one point during the long Sunday afternoon, "do you dance?"

He shook his head. "No," he said softly. "I'm a rotten dancer."

"So am I," she said, wistfully, too wistfully, after a moment; he looked at her for a second too long. Certain trains of thought led nowhere – better to shake them off. But that was not possible, on this interminable, boring afternoon, with that infernal, never ending music. In desperation she tried to draw, to do some preliminary sketches for the album she'd started. But the moment the blank page was before her, depictions of George – as he'd looked in the boardroom the night before, at the NATPE dinner, as he'd been at the Halloween party three weeks before – assailed her, saturated her consciousness, crowded out everything else. Since it was unthinkable to execute any of them, she doodled aimlessly, watching the rain drip and listening to the infernal music and the ticking of the clock.

She found only two good omens in all the morass of confusion and doubt. One was that his shoulder remained broad and warm, his protective arm around her strong and tender. The other was that his sleep on Saturday night remained unbroken. She began to wonder if Petrosian and her own instincts were wrong, if some improvement were possible.

That illusion was rudely shattered at 2:00 a.m. Monday morning. Now she could tell Milly, if and when they ever met, that she, too, had seen a bad one.

*

She was awake the moment she felt the first stirrings; she knew exactly where she was and what had happened. His lips began to move silently as before; his body to shake. His eyes did not fly open tonight (thank God!); instead, his head jerked crazily from side to side, again with a likeness to broken clockwork. Adele tried not to be afraid, did not entirely succeed; his bad hand twisted the corner of the pillow into a knot, his legs kicked again and again. The possessor of the man's body was now a lost little boy, come back now in the dead of night to search for his place among the living. For a moment, she was terrified.

Calmness, moron, said the cool, calm girl, now definitely the servant of the squishy soft other, *you can do this.* It was going to take an effort of will; but Milly had done it. She would do no less. Now he twisted towards her, now there was an opening, now she forced herself to slip between his arms and had hers around his head and shoulders, pulled herself to him. Instantly, he began to quiet. For one of the last times in her life, she felt real shame. There was nothing to be afraid of here; there never had been. The persona she held in her arms was an abused, bewildered child, as helpless as a kitten.

"It's all right, baby," she said, "it's all right. Nothing's going to hurt you anymore. It's all over. The door's not going to open, baby; it's not going to open." He showed no reaction, but she went on anyway; this was part of her life's work now, not merely one night. Finally he settled back into real sleep, without calling her name. *Good.* She glanced at the clock again; only 2:10; it had seemed much longer. She held him for another few long moments; very quietly, so as not to wake him; then she wept, for him and for everything.

But the deep sleep that had been so restorative the past two nights was not to be hers on this one. *What have I gotten myself into?* She awoke groggy and unrested, to another uneasy morning.

*

Carolyn had wasted no time over the weekend. On Monday, when she entered her office, Adele found on her desk a neatly prepared list, reassigning every matter for which she had any responsibility to someone else. The principal beneficiary seemed to be Willis Rutter. All morning long, baffled associates and junior partners went in and out of her office. Most behaved as if she had suddenly taken ill with a highly contagious virus, untouchabilititis, and that it would be a good idea to get in and get out of her presence as quickly as possible. Willis Rutter had to remain longer. Basic itemization of the transferred files took considerable time.

"I have some ideas about this case I'd like to go over with you, Willis," she remarked at last. "I hadn't written them up yet."

"*Really*, Adele," Willis replied in a smug voice, "I'm quite capable of reaching my own conclusions. I don't need your help." With that, he picked up the reassigned files and left. For Willis Rutter, Adele realized then, this turn of events was proof that a just and generous God in fact existed. He thought something had changed. He had no knowledge of Carolyn's plan to hire in an expert in such matters, no sense that this windfall had come to him because he was a useful stopgap, who would not pose a territorial problem because he wouldn't be around to establish any. Would Willis believe her if she told him that? She shook her head helplessly.

Midmorning, she found time to phone Walt Greenfield. "Hello, Walt," she said when he answered. "I –"

"Adele!" he said urgently, with no attempt at a funny voice. "What the hell is going on!? The wildest rumors are flying around up here, that you and Carolyn –"

"They're all true, Walt," she said. "We had a big disagreement. I'll be leaving Hapgood two weeks from Friday."

"Jesus Christ!" he replied, genuinely shocked. "I don't understand – I mean, what could possibly have gone that badly wrong? This is absurd! Carolyn Hoffman doesn't have the right to act that unilaterally! I'm going to get a meeting together of –"

"Walt," she said gently, genuinely touched, "I'm leaving. I want to. It's my decision as well as hers. It's done. Thanks, but no thanks. That's not why I called. I'm getting married on Friday," she went on briskly, "I want you to recommend a judge."

"What?" he answered weakly, after a long moment, in a voice that sounded uncannily like her father's.

Adele almost laughed aloud: all unknowing, Walter Greenfield, the Man of a Thousand Voices, had just performed the first decent imitation of his life.

*

Walt called a judge; the judge's clerk called back; all was arranged in half an hour. She put on her coat to leave; a bad day, she thought, when the most exciting thing you have to look forward to is having blood drawn.

Cynthia, at the reception desk, looked up as she passed. "Adele," she asked, agitated, "is it true? Are you leaving?"

"It's true, Cynthia," she answered quietly, noticing the girl's stricken look. "I'm leaving. I'm going to miss you. I'm going to miss all of you," being polite, then realizing as she spoke that she meant it, that leaving would indeed be painful, very, very painful. Nonetheless, she felt a bit smug about the stir she'd caused.

By the afternoon, however, the offices were astir with a totally different excitement. All of the securities lawyers, even the most junior associates, were suddenly involved in meetings. Anyone with any talent for anything was drafted or on call. Staff was being taken aside in private groups and sternly instructed about the illegality of insider trading. The first draft of a tender offer was being circulated to every lawyer in the firm, any comment welcome. The whole firm was afoot, on the war path – with one exception.

She had to admit to herself, then, how important royal status had been to her – the esteem in which she had been held, the admiration, even the envy. All gone now, gone so quickly; she walked alone along the corridor, idle – she *hated* being idle – a big meeting was going on in the conference room on the twenty-eighth floor. The temptation to poke her head in and say, cheerfully, *Is there anything I can do?* was well-nigh irresistible. But somehow she did resist.

The offices palpitated with excitement. Adele was not included. The only saving grace was that the firm could care less if she spent the afternoon reading poetry. She took the short elevator ride up to the Press. . . only to discover that Jenet had contacted her office for messages that morning, found out about the new manuscript, and ordered it sent immediately to her in Trieste. Tom's book was probably halfway across the Atlantic by then. Shrugging her shoulders, Adele went back down to her office, to a task list with no items on it. She was not going to give way to the temptation to leave. That was exactly what Carolyn wanted. Straightening herself up, she went up to the library, where she read advance sheets, ignoring the panting lawyers who raced in and out of the stacks on the other side, until a reasonable time had come to depart.

Whereupon she went home, where she and Tom puzzled over one another for another long, exasperating evening.

Tuesday, if possible, was longer and duller than the day before. She got a stack of resumes and job letters out. Since she maintained her address book electronically, since she knew how to do a merge mail, that task took no longer than forty minutes. Joan finally called in response to the messages Adele had left, and Adele gave her the big news. The young women had long ago agreed that if either became seriously involved, the other would leave. Joan, who had both plenty of money and plenty of other places to sleep, congratulated Adele in squealing tones and agreed to vacate the place a week from Sunday.

It was 10:15. She had literally nothing left to do. For a few irrational moments, she even missed Josh and the other nuisances. She checked her calendar over and over again, but there was nothing. Meanwhile, the excitement around her was reaching a fever pitch. People hurried up and down the halls. Preliminary proofs from the printers seemed to be everywhere. One of the Glee Club members ostentatiously covered his copy up as she wandered by. She had become taboo. She did not enjoy the experience.

At the end of another endless day, she wandered home. She remained essentially confident of the decisions she had made. It was right to slough the old life off like a snake sloughs off its old skin. Still, if that were so, why did the new one itch so much?

*

When she entered the small apartment that evening, fatigued with boredom, she found him in the kitchen, cooking.

"Nice," she said. "What is it?"

"A lemon butter sauce," he said. "Bought the book at the store. I'm going to broil a piece of halibut in a second. A nice green salad and some peas. Pregnant woman's dinner."

Already she felt better. "You don't have to cook for me, Tom," she said.

He added parsley and looked up. "I'd do anything for you, angel," he said quietly and she knew right then – *right* then – that the malaise that had hung over them the last few days was lifting, that he'd worked through whatever it was he had to work through. The man she loved had reappeared again. She moved to the reading chair and sat down – on something. She pulled it out from underneath.

"What are these?" she asked.

"Earphones," he answered. "I was rehashing Sunday afternoon. You don't like opera, do you?"

"I hate opera," she answered promptly. "And I hate background music. I should have said something."

"I should have known," he replied, readying the halibut for the broiler. "You're a visual person. I'm aural. We're completely incompatible. There's no way we could ever get along," and something flashed in his face.

"Evidently," Adele answered, with a grin of her own. She noticed something on the computer desk.

"What's this?" she asked again.

"Evening newspaper," he responded.

"What's that for?" she said.

"You'll see," he answered, eyes sparkling, and began to serve the salad.

Can I trust my judgment? she thought an hour later. *Is he really this good?* He had sat down in the reading chair, and presented her with the newspaper. She perched on the arm of the chair, her residual uncertainty evident in the tension in her body. He asked her to select a human interest story from the back section. She'd chosen an account of an unusual child stealing, involving a phony appointment at a doctor's office – then a topic. A political story, minorities in Eastern Europe, had been her choice. Then he'd begun, sketching in wide terms at first, then greater and greater detail, none of the particulars overlooked. On and on he went, a secret treaty signed by the leader of the Ukrainian partisan army, the UPA, during World War II, the stolen child his only grandchild, the mother's bewilderment, then her involvement, the characters growing into life and dimension moment by moment, nuance by nuance. The wine had affected James Goodson's memory. The improvisation was not seamless; Tom had to backtrack quite a few times, redo details – but it was still amazing overall.

"So now Alice has the gun on Smyslov and Minasian both." Now she was in his lap, her head on his shoulder, completely enchanted. "She remembers what it was like to be in his arms; she can't believe he's the beast Smyslov says he is. Smyslov tells her not to be a fool, reminds her that Minasian himself admitted he was KGB. The sun is setting over Moscow. It gleams on the brass carillon she can see in the distance, on the rim of Smyslov's glasses, on Minasian's gold tooth, the one that upset her so much when they first met. So.

What does Alice do?"

"Kills Smyslov, of course," Adele answered firmly. "It has to be Smyslov. That explains why he wasn't killed in the ambush." She realized he'd set that up long before. Still she held back, not quite able to trust herself, to believe – because she wanted to believe so much, that all this was real, that his gift truly was this enormous. "So she shoots him. If she could step on his face before he dies, she'd do that too." She blushed slightly. He'd got her all wound up in spite of herself.

"Aren't you the bloodthirsty one?" Tom said, stroking her slightly. "But you're right, of course." He began to wind it up now. He had not permitted her to listen passively; her suggestions had been requested, accepted, added to the flow, easily, gracefully. Adele forced herself to withhold judgment, not to marvel. It could be all it was that she'd become his biggest fan – of necessity. Perhaps the complex story sounded so amazingly finished because she wanted it to sound that way.

"The door opens and she's face to face with the Premier. Smiling, he ushers her into the office next door, where she sees –"

"Her son," Adele interjected, felt him nod. "Thank goodness. When I read junk fiction, I like happy endings."

"Of course," Tom said. "Minasian explains he's been undercover with the outlaw Ukranians all along. He couldn't have told her earlier. It would have sounded like another part of the legend. The boy was smuggled out of the car before the explosion. He explains that if Bogatichurck had left too, Smyslov would have known something had gone wrong. So the old man insisted on staying, sacrificing himself." To her embarrassment, she felt a lump in her throat, had to check tears. *All it is is a story, stupid.* "That was the way he wanted it. Alice reminds herself that's how he won all the medals. And the curtain comes down."

"Aren't Alice and Minasian going to be together?" Adele asked timidly, after a moment.

"I think not. That's a little too much. There are happy endings and sappy endings. Save it for a sequel," he answered. He folded the newspaper. "That's your new style story, angel. The new villains are going to be dissident leaders of minorities and retrograde Stalinists. Muslims bent on revenge, of course. You're going to see saintly Russian Premiers and heroic KGB for the next thirty years. Remember, you heard it here first." He yawned. "At least it beats nonagenarian Nazis. Or cloned, or cryogenically preserved. And they can always go back to Irishmen or Palestinians if all else fails." His tone held the barest hint of sarcasm.

So ordinary – really nothing more than an evening spent with a special,

special man; she'd had a few of those. But somehow most of the bruises, the wounds to her ego, the buffets she'd taken all day long, had been salved. She sat up from the chair. "That was really very good," she said shyly. "Aren't you going to do something with it?"

"Oh, no," he said promptly, putting down the paper. "Why? A story like a zillion others. Just to amuse you. Only a way of killing time. Just doing numbers."

Adele went five feet straight up into the air. If there were any such track event as the sitting high jump, she must have surely set the world record. "Tom," she said, not bothering to fully recover, eyes closed and arms around him, "I hate that expression. That is the worst expression in the world. Please don't ever, *ever* say that again."

"All right," he said softly, sounding less perplexed than she would have liked.

I can do something here, she thought later, as she prepared for bed. *I can make this work.* An immense relief accompanied the thought. Now she returned to the bedroom, hoping to be vouchsafed the final omen; and then his hands were upon her, confident, assertive, eager, gentle all at once. She sighed again with relief. This was the touch she recognized, his true touch, familiar and new both at once. He was obviously over his inhibitions. Now he'd loosened something and her nightdress was slipping to the floor. Something natural and good was certain to happen; and it did.

*

Adele bounded out of bed the next morning, bursting with energy. *If you're going to wife the guy, stupid*, she thought, *you wife the guy.* Somehow, overnight, she'd climbed her own mountain. She shook her head in disbelief – three days squandered sitting around. Instantly she knew she was not going into the office this day; she wasn't even going to call in; no one would miss her. She was going to be married in only two days, she had a dinner to do in one, and there were a million other things to do.

First, to a clothing store, where she discovered the sign that advertised one day's alterations was not wholly truth in advertising. It took every bit of charm, flattery, and coquettishness she could muster ("You wouldn't make my groom stand beside me in a shabby old sports coat, would you? Would you?" "Miss, tomorrow's *Thanksgiving*." "But today isn't.") to prevail. Tom looked on, responding on cue, occasionally cuing her, playing the part of a fellow victim, a man indifferent to clothes – in this case, type casting. The two of them could be, she realized, entertaining – the protestations became theatrical, the denouement inevitable – you know you're winning when everyone's having a good time. When they finally left, it was agreed that the dark blue suit would be ready on Friday at eleven, the other later the next week.

Then to a discount jeweler for rings – Tom took the largest size they had – then the food market. A sense of fun going up and down the aisles, an exuberance, a return of the playfulness that had so surprised her when they first met. For this day, at least, the tall, weary man was enjoying himself in his own quiet way, she was her old chirpy Adele – and this day would do until the next one came along.

"My old high school boyfriend used to call this my 'whirling dervish' mood," she said lightly. "He said he always kept out of my way then." She snapped her fingers. "That's one more. I've got to send him a cable."

Brian Johnson, Esq.
United States Embassy
Bogota, Columbia

> *DEAR BRI,*
> *CONGRATS TO ME –*

*

Two card tables placed together, a tablecloth covering both. Becky brought plates, silverware, and three cooked dishes; Jack and her father brought themselves. Her announcement had come too late for Buck, now in his fortieth year and finally approaching financial solvency, his fourth video rental store taking up all his time. He and the kids sent their love and congratulations. Michael, the grizzled blue collar philosopher (only 33) sent his as well. He was up in Montreal doing the kind of masonry that only he could do. Her father told her that the news that his baby sister had decided to marry had triggered some long overdue seriousness about the woman he'd been seeing for nearly half a decade.

Then the food was nearly ready. Her mood had been nervous, apprehensive. What would they think? What would he think? She was inordinately proud of the men in her family, all of them living their well-directed lives, Jack despite his tragedy; each in his own way gifted, bent on small, day-to-day achievements of which the public took scant notice. The brick-and-mortar people of reality, the men who rebuild the world every morning.

So now two of those men sat at the improvised table, not exactly hostile, but bewildered, troubled, full of questions – communicating an uneasiness that compounded her own. She bit her lip; it was so important to her that they like him. . .

Tom had had another horrible night the night before; but today he was not merely good, he was not merely superb, he was perfect – reserved, but not diffident, quiet but not taciturn, with the mildest hint of appropriate possessiveness as regards her. Becky, the easiest, became entranced quickly; her father sat back, his anxieties reduced, if not entirely relieved; Jack, the most difficult, bleary-eyed and reserved, gradually drawn out in spite of himself. Adele kept silent – she wanted them to meet him and was glad they liked him. However, there was a trace element of performance in his manner that troubled her – and too much bewilderment, too much perplexity, too much suddenness for her family to be reconciled in just one day.

"I'm trying to understand this, pumpkin," her father said, when they were alone for a moment. "Maybe if I weren't an absolute moron I'd know, but as it is, I don't understand. "

"I'm sorry, Daddy," she said. "It couldn't have been any other way. I thought about all of it for the longest time. I thought about all my options. It wasn't at all a snap decision. But when I finally made it, it had to be sudden."

"Can you tell me more?" her father asked, genuine frustration in his voice.

"I can't," she said, "only that it all worked out the way it should have. And that I didn't do anything to embarrass you. Or us," and now it was upon her; her eyes had flooded and she had had to choke out the last word. For this man, as for Tom, the aspect of the cool, calm girl never obscured his view of the squishy, soft one. "Daddy, I didn't do anything dishonorable."

"Hey, now *wait* a minute," her father said, putting down the towel and taking her in a firm paternal embrace, "I didn't mean anything at all like that." He hugged her tighter. "It's not possible for you to do anything to embarrass me. You've made me proud of you every day of your life. My always brilliant, sometimes unfathomable daughter," patting her head. *Oh, Daddy,* she thought, eyes half-closed in shame at different thoughts, older memories, *if only you knew.* "Even if you have seldom been less fathomable."

Adele was relieved beyond any measure she had anticipated to receive his blessing. But as always at these moments, one person had not been mentioned, one name not invoked, the blessing she craved more than any other. Her father never did, never had, tried to speak for her – not from the very first day of his widowerhood. The debt that his extraordinary daughter owed to the legacy of her extraordinary mother was one that only she could define, only she could discharge.

"A couple of other things," he went on quickly, before it became too emotional, and that's when she learned that they'd all taken rooms in the city; that he planned to give her away, if possible, even if before a judge; that regardless of the confusion and perplexity her decision had engendered, her family intended to stand by her completely. Good; wonderful; if the day was going to be nothing like anything she'd planned in her wedding dream book, at least it would be special in its own way.

Adele put her arms around her father and hugged him tightly. He smoothed her hair, patted her shoulder, and tried to ignore his own doubts. If only he knew what the future held for her – hell, if only he knew what the present held for her. He shook his head.

If only he had some idea – speak truth: *any* idea – of why she had done what she had done.

*

Bogota, Columbia, one day later

The snores of the marquise woke him up. His head felt like one of the soccer balls the street children kicked over the cobbled streets. How she was going to feel when she was finally roused was unimaginable. She was the pint-size type, but she'd drunk half again as much as he. For a moment, he could not remember where he was; then the name of the hotel came to him. He fished the cable out that had started – or rather, finished – it all.

CONGRATS TO ME STOP CALL ME MOM STOP GUY DECIDED TO DO THE RIGHT THING STOP TOM AND I TO BE MARRIED FRIDAY 11/26 STOP PLEASE SEND EXPENSIVE GIFT STOP LOVE YOU ALWAYS STOP JOHNSON AND JANSEN

LOVE DELLY

The call that had begun it all had come ten days before, three days before he was to meet Linda at the airport. "Personal call, Mr. Johnson. Long distance. From America." Resisting the temptation to remind the receptionist that Bogota was also America, he picked up the phone.

"Hello, Brian?" came the politician's voice, clear despite the distance.

"Hi – er – Judge," he answered. His father-in-law was actually not a judge any longer, in fact, a New Hampshire assemblyman, but his friends still called him that. Brian could not bring himself to call him "Pop" or "Dad."

They chatted about meaningless things – the weather here, the weather there – for a moment or two. "I'm looking forward to seeing Linda tomorrow," he said finally.

"That's the principal reason I called, Brian," his father-in-law said, after a significant pause. "Linda won't be coming then."

"Why not?" he asked urgently, still innocent. "Is there something wrong? Is the pregnancy O.K.?"

"That's part of it," said his mother-in-law, listening silently to the phone call on an extension. "She's not pregnant anymore."

"What?" he breathed. "Did something –"

"No," said her father. "It was her own choice."

"We had a lot of time to discuss this," continued her mother. "It was obvious to all of us that Linda is much too young – too unready – to assume the responsibilities of parenthood. We decided it was better for all concerned that the pregnancy be terminated."

"She – you – did this without even talking to me? Without saying anything?" He was choking with rage.

"You're a bit too persuasive, Brian. We felt this was a situation in which the advice of her family was the more important – that a dissenting voice would only add to the confusion." Her mother's tone stiffened: "She is wondering – has been wondering for some time – whether the entire marriage was not a mistake. But perhaps she can state her own mind best."

"Brian –" he heard his wife's voice, filled with the pettiness of her parents, "Brian, don't blame my parents. I came to these decisions on my own."

"I'll blame who I want to blame," Brian said.

"Now, Brian," said his father-in-law, on the other line, with a victor's magnanimity "don't be like that. There's no need for bitterness. There'll be plenty of other opportunities for you and Linda."

"For me, yes," he said evenly. "Not for her. The only man you'll ever allow near her is with her now. So why don't you just take her to bed right now, judge, and get on with it."

He hung up the phone in the midst of their startled gasps, pleased with himself, but for a moment only. The only offense he'd committed against the doting Amblers was wresting their child away from them. Poor Linda – she had yielded to the temptation to retreat into their house now and she was never going to come out again. What a pathetic trio – and yet so unlike him to rub their noses in it – Brian Johnson, who could normally make the harshest condemnation sound like a love letter. He put his face in his hands, thinking of his lost child, lost love, lost life. Suddenly, much to his surprise, tears were streaming between his fingers.

The next few days were the dreariest of his life. He didn't like losing any more than Delly did, even when the game was rigged. He'd loved Linda, no matter what she thought. Somehow he got through his rounds, somehow he kept the front up. Johnson and Jansen. It wasn't until a week had passed that it hit him, all at once, at 10:05 in the morning, as he sat at his desk.

He was free – *free!* The weight of the old life had vanished in the twinkling of an eye and he could feel new strength, confidence. Why had he ever been reluctant? What an idiot! The 20th had passed; Delly and the – procedure. He had in his desk a long, long handwritten letter, of condolence, reassurance, composed before the call from Linda, for no other reason than that he'd been worried about her. There was a limit to what anyone should endure alone, even Delly – especially Delly, and especially that – and, unless she'd talked to the guy, that's the way she was doing it. Alone.

Now he'd deliver it personally – take her in his arms, smooth her hair, comfort her, say what he should have said a long, long time ago. *What happened doesn't matter. Come with me. It's a big world out there, Delly. Plenty of room for you. Global thermonuclear law, the coming thing, your kind of game. Lots to do. Make lots of babies along the way. Come with me. I love you, I never stopped loving you, I'm always going to love you.*

He was lost in eagerness, in daydreams, when the phone rang. "Cable for you, Mr. Johnson." He heard the first line – *congrats to me* – and went into immediate shock.

The Marquise d'Alejandro was the young wife of an elderly proconsul, the marriage a notorious misalliance. Blessed with spectacular good looks, she fought the curse of perpetual boredom with sex, cocaine, and alcohol. From the moment Brian arrived on station, she had set her eye on him. Her interest was so obvious it had caused a fair amount of good natured kidding, semi-serious complaints about the frustration caused by the sudden unavailability of her favors to others.

He rarely drank at diplomatic parties, but tonight he had more than one cocktail before the dinner, wine with it. The Marquise was also present. She excused herself at one point to powder her nose. It occurred to him that she was almost exactly Delly's height, though the resemblance ended there – large brown eyes, raven black hair, voluptuous Hispanic figure that would one day soon run to fat, but in prime condition now. *Why not?* he thought drunkenly, excused himself. He stopped her outside the chamber door; she was surprised and pleased. The work of a moment to whisper something in her ear, stroke her hair, make a suggestion; the assignation was agreed in ten seconds. He did not really remember how they got into the taxi, only that she chose the hotel because she was familiar with it.

"Bull!" she laughed a short time later. "Stallion!" Unfamiliar praise; the not-thinking-of-onions problem was not his problem tonight. For all her sexual sophistication, the Marquise was too naïve to realize that she was experiencing a deed of anger, not love, an act of drunken desperation. Later there was more wine and more sex, too much of both.

Now he looked at her unclothed, snoring body and wondered how soon he could decently get away – wondered what he could possibly say to the Ambassador to explain their mutual departure. (Her husband was indifferent to his wife's infidelities, but passionate about propriety.) He reread the cable in the equatorial sunlight. A fly buzzed lazily around the room. He had always been late with Delly, late for everything. In a psychology class, he had learned that that trait in itself was a kind of diffidence, a type of neurotic testing. Perhaps he'd always been overawed by her. Now he was ultimately late. She was gone now, gone for good.

The dust in the streaming sunlight hurt his eyes. Suddenly he realized that he had years and years and years to wander, and that he had gotten off to a very poor start.

*

Trieste, Italy – same day, evening

"*Grazie*," said the old woman, closing the manuscript and turning her head as the waiter put the cappuccino down. He smiled, nodded, and retreated. The cafe was now nearly deserted; there were only two customers left, closing time was near. Yet she gave no indication that she intended to leave. Instead, she sipped the coffee slowly, lost in her thought.

The waiter had been curious about her all evening. He knew at once she was not looking for romance, as are so many unattached American women. Also, the absence of an escort did not seem to faze her. She'd spent most of the evening reading the manuscript, skipping here, stopping there, apparently at random. He could see over her shoulder that it was smudgy; clearly she'd read it before. At first her mood had been gay, open, her excitement obvious. As the evening wore on and on, she became more subdued, thoughtful. He wondered what she was thinking about. . . .*blown to smithereens*, the old woman was in fact thinking. *Everything changed, everything different. What am I going to say to her now? What can I do that makes any difference?* Suddenly she remembered the hour. Shaking the reverie out of her head, she smiled and signaled the waiter. He started forward. Time for one final sigh.

It's always been this way, Jenny, she reminded herself sternly as she rose. *You should be used to it. Don't become maudlin. It's always been this way.* Even so, she paused at the door frame, lost in thought, shaking her head slightly.

All the promises I made to Emily Jansen . . . how am I ever going to keep them?

*

"Here we are," said Adele's father unnecessarily, as the cab pulled up in front of the courthouse. "You look radiant, pumpkin." He helped her out of the car. Becky was already out, on the other side, smiling. There was no train to encumber her. She was dressed in her one remaining evening dress, the one she'd worn to the CFS dinner, peach colored and high-collared, barely appropriate for this occasion. This real, matter-of-fact day contained not one element of the grandiosity about which she'd fantasized in her sketchbooks. But she had a bride's excitement nonetheless. *Nothing is going to take this away from me,* Adele thought. *Nothing.*

Not even the early editions of the afternoon newspapers, headlines in nine-point type blazing forth the news of events normally reserved for the financial pages, about the astonishing tender offer made by a small company named Astraper for all the outstanding shares of Electronic Business Systems.

EXILE

T his was a good idea," Joan burbled excitedly. "This is going to be fun."
She twisted a bright red ribbon around the wreath for the door of the
common room. "I wish we'd done it sooner, before you turned into an
old married lady."

"Never got around to it, I guess," Adele answered, applying scissors
expertly to a different decoration, one for the corridor outside.

"Well, at least we're doing it now," Joan replied. "One day more and it
would have been too late for me. What a good idea!"

"Can I help?" Tom asked, drifting up from behind.

"Yes, my love," Adele answered, without looking up. "You can find
some quiet place to read and keep out of harm's way. Also, out of the way of the
caterers. Go." He drifted away again.

"What a hunk," Joan whispered as he left.

"What?!" Adele answered, "I wouldn't have thought he was your type,"
then reproved herself. *Dummy.* She had yet to meet the man who wasn't Joan's
type.

"Are you serious?" Joan replied. "So big and quiet and scary. I get
goose bumps every time he speaks. Tell me," she asked, dropping her voice even
lower, "what's he like in bed?" Joan's kind of question.

Adele smiled enigmatically, raised one eyebrow, reached for another
decoration, and said nothing. Her kind of answer.

The day after the wedding, she'd phoned Joan about the prospect of a
reception/Christmas/farewell party. Joan agreed instantly, somewhat surprised
since Adele had never shown much interest in staging a party before.

"A week from Sunday, then," Adele said. "I'll take care of the
invitations on my machine. When can I get your list?"

"I won't be home for a few days. Take it off my phone list," Joan
answered. "You know where. Open bar?" she continued, "or hold it to white
wine and eggnog?"

"*Absolutely* open bar," Adele answered evenly. "I want to be sure that
anyone who wants a drink gets a drink. I wouldn't have it any other way. There
may be some very heavy drinkers coming. We mustn't disappoint them."

By six o'clock, the common room was ready – serving dishes out, glasses stacked, decorations up. The room glistened with anticipation; Adele was satisfied. The party was not to start until 7:00 – the inevitable concession to football telecasts. She would have preferred Saturday night to Sunday, but the room had not been available. One of the caterers came up to her.

"Madam," he said, in a thick Puerto Rican accent, "everything is ready. May we turn on the television? For a rest?"

"Of course," Adele answered. The Hispanic moved to the large television placed in one corner of the room and turned it on. The screen brightened. Completely taken aback, Adele sucked in her breath. There, dominating the center, suavely answering questions on one of the people-in-the-news programs, sat Franklin Fischer. For a moment, Adele was perplexed; Victor Podgorny was still the front man on the acquisition. The interest of Consolidated Financial Services and Fischer Acquisitions Corporation was one of the most closely guarded secrets in the office. What was Franklin Fischer doing on television?

"Please leave the channel there," she said.

". . .good a sense of humor as anyone," Franklin Fischer was saying somewhat formally. "And the video is funny; there's no question about that. But I do feel the joke has gone a bit too far in this instance. The incident was not what it appears to be. The time has come to set the record straight." She realized now she was watching a popular celebrity gossip program, one on which trivial incidents were occasionally subjected to intense scrutiny.

"Which is?" asked a smirking young female media journalist.

Franklin Fischer sighed a theatrical sigh. "The young man in question is named Newcombe. He's a freelance writer and a poet – or so he calls himself. You know the type. Most of the people who know him consider him a ne'er-do-well. I was in the company of my fiancée, Carolyn Hoffman, the well-known attorney, but another young woman, who had rejected his advances, was also with us. Mr. Newcombe misinterpreted the situation. He became angry. In my opinion, he was extremely intoxicated. He said unrepeatable things to Carolyn. I had to do something. That's how it all began."

Why bother with the big lies, Adele thought, *when the little ones work so well?* Twist the knob a quarter turn. That's all it takes.

"Why did you say, 'What are you worth?'" asked another young journalist.

"It was meant to be sarcastic. I was reacting to the imputation he'd placed on Carolyn."

"He doesn't seem intoxicated," said the first one.

"Not at all," added another panelist. "You're the one who seems out of control. And you can see Ms. Hoffman laughing herself at the corner of the ABC tape. She doesn't seem insulted."

"I am fully aware that the circumstances became inadvertently ridiculous," Franklin Fischer replied stiffly, "even to Carolyn. And I will concede I was furious. Still –"

"Perhaps we should see the tape again," said the host. "Mr. Fischer, *you* asked to appear," he added softly, noticing the expression on Fischer's face.

*

With the announcement of the hostile raid on EBS, the frenzy in the offices of Hapgood, Thurlow had mounted to new heights. The initial incredulity of EBS management quickly gave way to anger and fear; the giant had the resources to mobilize its own professional forces even over the long Thanksgiving weekend. By Monday morning, when Adele returned to work, a three-day newlywed, defence and counterattack were in full swing.

A battlefield mentality had set in. Rumors swept with the speed of tornadoes through the four office floors. . . EBS has filed suit in eleven states, also seeking a federal injunction. . . a regulation on the London USM – *Oh, God!* – but they're not on the Unregulated Securities Market, they're on the regular exchange – *whew*! A nuance in Louisiana law (that state always a problem, because of its unique law derived from the Napoleonic Code) is a real problem. . . on all these issues, memoranda had been prepared, months, even years, in advance, usually by associates who had little idea for what purpose they'd ultimately be used, all related to a master plan set forth in detail in the one file Adele had not seen. But now each had to be rechecked and re-evaluated, with no time to do the task leisurely.

Adele went quietly through her own agenda amid all the noise and confusion. Hers and Joan's party was only six days away. The invitations went out to Joan's invitees, at least those for whom Adele had addresses, and her own list on Monday. But she wasn't finished. She wanted as many guests as possible. She asked Cynthia to mention the occasion to anyone who asked about her; she also put up little signs on the Hapgood bulletin boards. Later in the week, she saw Willis Rutter sniggering at one. Finally, she went up to the Furston Press. Jenet was not due back in the country for a week.

"I'll tell anyone who asks," Jenet's assistant said. "By the way, Jenet said to say hello."

"Oh?" Adele asked.

"Yes. She contacted me yesterday. About Mr. Newc –" the girl beamed at her – "about your husband's manuscript. She was pretty excited. I think she was more excited by that than she was disappointed by NATPE."

"Really?" said Adele, pleased. "I'm glad she likes it." She paused. "Of course, I'd still like the original back."

"Jenet didn't want to be disturbed. She wants to remain *incommunicado*. But if you really insist –"

"No, no," Adele answered. If Jenet wanted to keep the original manuscript longer, fine. And the more excited, the better. The solution to some practical problems was dependent on that.

*

The offices of Hapgood, Thurlow became more and more a war zone. Heroes were born, reputations were lost. Victor Podgorny was constantly present, even sleeping overnight on the couch in Richard Collishaw's office. After two unfortunate incidents, the word spread like wildfire among female personnel that it was a wise idea to stand at least an arm's length away from him.

Greg Steuer moved among them, one of many foot soldiers from CFS, greeting people he'd left only a few weeks earlier that he hadn't expected to see in years. He concealed his anxieties as best he could. The dissolution of CFS, announced a week earlier, had come as a colossal shock to him. He had known nothing of its imminence at the time he accepted the job offer made by Franklin Fischer. Now he was frightened. To change jobs twice within a matter of weeks would leave a scar on his resume that would be all but unexplainable. The news of Adele Jansen's downfall, which at a different time would have been a cause for enormous private rejoicing, seemed trivial in comparison. What he was asked to do, he did quickly and without complaint, and hoped against hope that there would be a place for him when all was settled.

(He did not know – would never know – that the decision about him had been made several weeks earlier, in fact, at the time of his hiring – that the termination notice, not yet dated, had already been written. *He'll do for a warm body*, Carolyn had said to Franklin Fischer over the coffee they habitually took at 11:00 on Saturday morning, *nothing more*.)

Josh Palmdale unexpectedly came into his own. His major gift in life had always been presentability. When the media began to besiege the Hapgood offices, he was the one whom they seized upon as spokesman for the firm and for Astraper. (Older, wiser, more sensible heads had no wish to be identified with the adventure until the outcome was clearer.) He was the one who reported on the progress of the Louisiana case, the initial strategy, the final success, speaking as clearly and confidently about a litigation he did not understand as if he himself were conducting it. He came to epitomize the modern young Turk on the move, in stark contrast to the old, staid representatives of EBS. Josh's father began videotaping the evening news broadcasts.

Adele's skeleton-at-the-feast sense, acute the week before, faded as the week wore on. Outside her door, history scurried down the corridor; inside, slowly, methodically, like an Incan highway builder, she continued with the selection and placement of the small stones of her new life. Occasionally she worried about Walt Greenfield, about a reminder she'd written to herself eight days before. She was touched when Armen Petrosian, concerned over *her* silence, telephoned her. She told him her news and invited him to the reception. She puzzled over the cable she received from Bri, congratulatory yet oddly formal, and worried mildly about that as well.

One other thing above all others preyed on her mind. She had heard nothing from George Sorenson since the NATPE party. She ached to talk to him; she was afraid to talk to him. Two possible scenarios – gratitude, a sense of freedom upon liberation from CFS. The other. . .

At about 11:00 Thursday morning, she steeled her determination and picked up the phone.

"I'd like to speak to George Sorenson."

"Mr. Sorenson is no longer associated with this firm," the answer came back crisply. "We are not authorized to accept any messages on his behalf."

"Oh, but it wasn't him I wanted to talk to," Adele responded smoothly. "It was his personal assistant." The voice began a litanous response; she interrupted: "Could you please connect me?" After a bit of cajoling, the call was transferred.

"Hello? Are you Mr. Sorenson's assistant? I'd like to know how to reach him. His phone's not listed."

"I'm not authorized to give that number out, or take any messages for Mr. Sorenson. My instructions are quite clear."

"I have to talk to him," Adele answered smoothly. *Take a chance*; the decency, the honor she'd sensed in him, must have been apparent to this person. They couldn't all be like Franklin over there. "He might have mentioned a woman he was seeing in the weeks before he left. I'm that person. I had lunch with him twice over at CFS."

"Just a moment," the voice answered in a lower tone. An instant of silence; Adele had a sense of someone looking around to be certain she was alone. The voice dropped to a whisper. "His number is. . ."

She focused her will again, punched in the number. The phone rang. The receiver engaged. "Hello, George?" she chirped as brightly as she could. "George? Are you there?" The line remained silent.

"Hello, par – pa – par – Pa-lo-ma?" finally came the response, in a clearly intoxicated, almost inaudible croak that was a pale shadow of the voice she remembered. Adele glanced at the vase clock: only 11:10. The worst case scenario had materialized. A small worry matured into a large one.

*

The tape played to the final epithet: "twerp"; everyone in the common room laughed (Joan stole another glance at Tom, now absorbed in the silverware); the screen was blank for a moment, then Franklin Fischer's face appeared again, grim and drawn. The Hispanic caterer approached Tom.

"You do not laugh at your own joke, sir?" he asked, curious.

"*No, lo encuentro chistoso*," Tom answered, in perfect Spanish. He moved over deliberately.

"*Porque?*" asked the other, slightly surprised by his fluency.

"*El hombre, al que interrogan, es un hombre poderoso y vengativo. Su negocio es el mismo que el de ellos. Observa cuidadosamente. Te das cuenta? Aun hoy, el planea su venganza. Se arrepentiran pronto de esta noche. Demasiado pronto.*" The smaller man turned and stared at the television, reacted, then looked hard at Tom. He took the silverware away from Tom. "*No, senor, gracias. Por favor,*" the caterer said. Tom shrugged and moved off.

"What did he say?" Adele asked the caterer.

"He said that the man they question is a powerful, vindictive man. His business is the same as theirs; he will not forgive them lightly. He said to look carefully and watch how even now he plans his revenge. I looked, through his eyes, and I saw."

"Gracias," Adele said softly. The caterer shook his head, and continued wrapping silverware, incidentally about a hundred times faster than Tom.

Bill Abercrombie was the first of the guests to arrive, at 6:45, grumbling. The television was immediately switched to the Jets game on the coast. Adele's plans began to go awry when the first big wave of guests arrived, shortly after seven. Among them was Joan's couch mate of two weeks previous, the gorilla. Joan greeted him with open face, frozen smile, at the door of the common room.

"Adele!" she hissed urgently, after he'd passed. "Where did you get his name?"

"Why, from your address book, of course," Adele said, bewildered. "The one in the drawer on the phone stand."

"Not the one in the drawer under the kitchen phone?" Joan went on.

"No," Adele answered. "The one in the phone stand. I didn't know you had another one."

"Oh God! Oh my *God!*" Joan bounded down the hall to the closet like a frightened deer. In a moment her coat was on. "I just remembered a movie I want to see! Goodbye, Adele! Have fun!"

And so Adele was left alone as the only hostess. Standing by the door in the hall, she greeted her guests and Joan's for the balance of the evening. The pace of arrivals picked up. She did her best with a number of persons she didn't recognize, friends and acquaintances of Joan's, a few who seemed to know Tom.

Then an entirely different group confronted her – glittery, bright; sharp, staccato laughter; an air of cynical amusement. Poised and gracious, Adele made them welcome. Danny, the man who had been with Tom at NATPE, was among their number. As the others entered, he motioned her aside.

"Er – Adele," he said awkwardly. She nodded, smiled a bright, glittery smile. "Listen ah – what I said that night – ah – you know –"

"Tweetiebird," Adele filled in, smiling, nodding slightly.

"Yeah. Right. I wanna say – I didn't mean –"

"That's all right," Adele said brightly, "it was nothing. I've forgotten it already," lying outrageously; she hadn't forgotten and she hadn't the slightest plan to do any forgiving. *You little creep.* "Why don't you join the party?"

Danny grinned, nodded, and – without offering any congratulations on her marriage (in fact, none of them had) – moved over to the bar, where the others had already congregated. Bill Abercrombie was among them, enjoying himself, drink in hand.

*

"My wife sends her love. So does my daughter. Pretty quick notice or they'd be here," Walt Greenfield, the only member of the firm to stop by, said at 9:05. "I get this by phone, by the way. Haven't seen either of them in a week. Trapped in the office. Believe me, it's a relief to get away," he continued. "The whole goddam place has gone berserk."

"What's the latest?" Adele asked.

"The word is out on the Street that they're gonna try to Pacman us. An EBS tender offer comes out tomorrow; it's already at press. The plot thickens," he said in what she assumed was a Boris Karloff, execrable as always. She nodded; she had been smiling and hostessing for two hours now. Shop talk was a blessing. "It's gonna be a real nuthouse tomorrow." He stood up.

"Well," he said, "where's the winner? The man I came to see? Palmdale's would-be rival?" Adele pointed, and watched Walt leave, a spasm of fear going through her. Tomorrow was the first working day after the two weeks she'd given herself on the Lawton matter. He'd said nothing about that; if nothing else happened, tomorrow she was going to phone either the deputy district attorney or Henrietta Lawton (the Canon of Ethics be damned) after which all hell would most assuredly break loose. She shivered. She did not even pretend to herself – she would much rather it did not.

Across the room, Walt Greenfield was introducing himself to Tom. She regarded him again. *C'mon, Walt,* she prayed. Adele had no more interest in facing a disciplinary committee than anyone else.

A movement at the door, some late arrivals, broke her mood. She was almost to the door before she recognized her new guests. Pure delight surged through her.

"What the hell's the matter?" asked Peter Steinitz. "We're not crashing, are we?"

"I phoned to make an appointment with you," said Lem, "but you were out. The receptionist told us about the party and said anyone was invited. Ah. . . here we are. I hope it's all right."

"Of course," said Adele unnecessarily. Anyone with eyes could have seen the spring-like joy in her face. "It's wonderful you came. But I'm completely surprised. I sort of thought I was *persona non grata* with you guys."

"*Ahem,*" interjected Pete, looking sharply at Lem.

"Let me tell you what happened," Lem went on hurriedly, pointedly ignoring him. Lem had remained in brooding despair after they left that Thursday; Chiang didn't know enough about American institutions to participate. On his own, Pete had sought out legal counsel, but got nowhere. No one wanted to take on the Hapgood, Thurlow juggernaut. *Quit while you're ahead* was the unequivocal advice, thrice repeated. Her letter, upon arriving the Monday before, had the effect of a bomb, detonating on impact. Pete had carried the day, insisting they take her at her word and see George Sorenson before they saw anyone else. When they phoned the CFS offices, it turned out he'd left word that he'd see them at home if they called. His personal assistant saw to it that they got the message.

"We met Friday in his apartment – this fabulous place on Fifth Avenue. He made it so easy," Lem said. "Read your letter and asked us what we wanted. I told him the rights to the algorithm and he wrote out a release then and there. We talked about how much we needed to recode, to start over, and he said he'd take care of it. Do it himself, if he had to. He also said to short our Astraper stock no later than Tuesday; that'd get us some capital. So here we are," he went on brightly. "So –"

"*Ahem,*" Peter interjected again, looking even more sharply at Lem. "Before we go any further, someone has something to say to you."

"The reason I called was –"

"*Ahem*," said Peter, still more forcefully, looking innocently up at Lem, "someone has something to say to you." There was the briefest pause. "That is, if he still wants to be president of this organization." A significant silence.

"All right, all right," Lem sighed at last. "I'm sorry. I owe you an apology. I really blew my stack at you that day. I said a lot of things that were off the wall. I shouldn't have."

"It's all right," Adele said, this time truthfully. "I didn't do my best for you, and I should have. I had it coming." She bit her lip. "How was George?" she asked as brightly as she could, pulse quickening, heart in mouth.

"Not so good," Pete said quietly after a moment. "He looked pretty down. What happened at the board meeting came up – no way to avoid it – and he said not to be too hard on him, that it had cost him the most." She had to turn away from them, then, a lump in her throat, mist in her eyes, not wanting Lem in particular to see.

"We're starting over," Lem said firmly, switching subjects, perhaps having noticed. "In every way. I don't know if it's a good sign when you start over by having teeth pulled, but –"

"Oh, Lem!" she cried. "You're going to do it!"

"Yeah, I'm going to do it," Lem said, smiling. "Saw the orthodontist last week. Four molars come out Wednesday. And then our first organization meeting for the new corporation one day later, on Thursday. Then the dentist puts in the device Friday. A big week." An expectant hush fell over the group; all three were looking at her.

"Yes?" Adele asked, not comprehending.

"Well, can you make it?" Lem said patiently.

"What!" she exclaimed. "After all that happened – you want me to be involved with you, one of your lawyers? Give me a break!"

The men exchanged the glances of adults who'd been listening to the ravings of an idiot child. "Of course," said Chiang. "Who else?" said Peter. "Don't be so slow," said Lem. "And not one of the lawyers – the lawyer."

"Two's a crowd – if they're lawyers," Peter added firmly. "After Greube."

"People," Adele said, "I'm out of a job. I don't know where I'm going to be – and I don't know anything except the basics about corporations, or securities, leases, and commercial stuff. C'mon."

"You can learn, can't you?" Pete asked.

"Look – Adele – we're not doing you any favors, at least financially. It isn't going to be easy," Lem continued. "We're not going to let this become a get-rich-quick scheme, like before. The development's going to be long and slow. We're not going out again until we're ready. It'll be a long, long time before we're back to where we were." He sighed. "And it could be you're wrong – that it is Humpty-Dumpty, and we can't put it together again."

Peter closed his eyes. "When people contact Astraper and find out what a kludge it actually is."

Adele cringed herself. All week long, there'd been orchestrated publicity about the miracle product that Astraper intended to add to the EBS product line. A videotape of one of the demonstrations done at a dog-and-pony show during the AI Squared public offering had been shown on two of the network news shows two nights earlier. The public was coming to believe; it added to the excitement; George had calculated perfectly. The proxy statement for the tender contained all the appropriate caveats and warnings, but no one read that.

"So maybe we can't do it," Lem finished. "Perhaps it is broken too badly to mend." He shook his head. "But we're not giving up. Franklin Fischer was right about one thing: We did sell out. We're not going to do that again. We can't promise that you'll get rich quickly – or that you'll get rich at all. We can pay reasonable fees, we can give you a mess of cheap stock, and that's about it." He paused. "It's going to be a long, slow road. What we're going to do is too big to be otherwise. We'll want to see it get good, solid roots everywhere before we surrender control of even a part of it to anybody."

"I don't know whether you're talking about software or crabgrass," Peter cracked, with the mixture of admiration and cynicism Adele had come to realize characterized his attitude towards his friend. Chiang smiled.

"No promises," Lem concluded. "But we want you with us. We want you to be a part of the story."

All three regarded her. The Lem who was speaking was the Lem she'd met on the first day she saw them, the confident, practical visionary. "I've learned a few things myself," she said carefully. "Perhaps the same thing. I've come to prefer long roads much more than short. Plus I owe you. So," she smiled, "count me in. I'll be there. Thursday. I was born on a Thursday. And I'll try not to screw up."

"There's only one condition," Peter said solemnly, paused, then grinned. "You've got to give me a sketch like you did Lem. I want to see myself tall and slender, thanks." Everyone laughed. Adele smiled and nodded. "And signed," Peter added, suddenly serious, with a significant look. All at once she realized how grateful he was, how important that drawing had actually been to Lem. "All right," she agreed.

"Done," Peter said emphatically. "Listen, fellas, let's meet the great man, get our signatures" – he held up his hand; she realized with pleasure that they had brought Tom's books for autographs – "and leave our lawyer to her celebration. Huh? Waddaya say?" He turned to Adele. "Where is he?"

"Over there," she said, managing a smile. "The tall, good-looking one."

Peter looked over, looked again, and did a double take. "*Him*? That's *him*?? The guy that put down Fischer? Lem," he said, "look. It turns out Tom Newcombe is your hero." Lem looked himself and did his own double take. "He must have watched that news footage three hundred times," Pete continued. Lem blushed slightly and glared back comically: "Enough, big-mouth."

They did not stay long. Lem was the first of the group out. "It's getting pretty noisy in there," he remarked. The others lagged behind. "Look, while we have a second," he whispered, "what the hell happened? The last time I saw you George and you were – well, you know – and then a week later you're married to Tom. What happened? Can I ask?"

"Yes," said Adele, smiling, "you can ask," and said nothing more.

After a moment, Lem smiled in turn and shook his head. "God," he said, "you do keep your secrets." Pete and Chiang were beside him now. "Some barrel of laughs," Pete said, semi-accusatory.

"You wouldn't have believed me," Adele answered unapologetically. "You had to find out for yourself." Hurried goodbyes, and a promise to be there Thursday morning. She watched them leave; for this alone, the evening had been worth it.

*

The food was gone. The decorations drooped. Now it was very late. Even the bartender was weary. Except for people such as Adele Elizabeth Jansen Newcombe and other walking dead, the next day was an ordinary working day. Joan's two married lovers and her fiancé were engaged in an extremely animated conversation by the television; Adele had a pretty good idea about what. Joan was going to have an interesting day tomorrow. Except for them and a boisterous group by the bar, the party had largely broken up.

Walt Greenfield was among the last to leave; the hotel room in which he would be sleeping, a safe walk away, was short on amenities. "Goodnight," Adele said.

"Goodnight yourself," he answered somberly. "And congratulations. Sort of. You didn't say he was the putdown artist." He shook his head. "Boy. Boy-oh-boy. Jesus. Carolyn's already made it clear that anyone who even thinks `counting numbers' near her or any of her stooges can start looking elsewhere." He became more serious still. "Carolyn's coming out of this whole thing very big,

Adele. As big as the City. I don't know where you're going to be able to catch on. Hell, I may have to catch on somewhere myself – a lot of us. She's going to be the power in the firm now, not Collishaw. Everything's going to be different. I don't mind telling you: I'm scared."

She shrugged helplessly. "I don't know what to say, Walt." He eyed her carefully, then spoke again:

"There's something else I wanted to talk to you about," he said.

"What? More about Astraper?"

"Oh no. God, no," he said. "Not that. I took the opportunity, what with Ralph and Josh running around, to have lunch with Jim Lawton over at his club. Just me and him. We talked about a lot of things, but mostly about how he's not having any unsupervised visits with that kid and how he's going to get counseling." He smiled. "He asked if he was on court probation and I told him, no, he was on Greenfield probation, which is a hell of a lot tougher. You know," he went on, "I think he was actually relieved. I think he was grateful for the direction. For the common sense. What? Is something the matter?"

Adele had half-closed her eyes. *Thank God*, she thought. *Thank God*. Finally called one right.

"I am so glad to hear that," she said aloud. "You should be proud of yourself, Walt."

"Yeah, right. Except that I shoulda done it the first time. Anyway, you're going to have a real rough time, kid," he continued. Her relief concerning Lawton began to fade. "Carolyn has a thing about you. It's goddam frightening to hear her. I'll do what I can. So will a lot of people; but. . ." he waved his hands helplessly. She understood him at once. There are a zillion lawyers in the City; essentially, it's a fungible skill; why should anyone take on someone with a powerful enemy?

She nodded; he saw a shadow pass across her face. "Well, you may be right," Adele answered. "I'll think about it." She glanced to her right, through the doorway. "I've got to get back to my guests. Goodnight, Walt. I'm so glad you came;" with a little squeeze of his hand, she vanished back into the throng. Her light, completely misleading charm was as effective as ever.

He watched for a moment as she said something to Bill Abercrombie, then moved gracefully over to her husband. All at once, Walt Greenfield was looking at her now as if he were seeing her for the first time. So small! So young! He thought of his own daughter; he remembered the crude, cruel account Carolyn had given of her emotional reactions at the AI board meeting, the derisive yes-man laughter on the thirty-second floor. Suddenly he was terribly, terribly angry. *So help me*, he thought, *the next time* – then stopped, realizing the absurdity of the thought. *Next time*. There wasn't going to be a next time.

Certainly not for Adele. Maybe not for Walt Greenfield either. He left frustrated on behalf of both of them.

* * *

DOMESTIC LIFE

Tuesday morning, as Adele was coming back from the library, notes in hand concerning corporate start-ups – piece o' cake – her luck ran out. The elevator down contained Carolyn, Harry Greube, a few other partners, the core of the general staff on the EBS merger, Josh Palmdale among them, now a valued member of the team.

"–going nowhere," someone exclaimed happily, not immediately noticing a Jonah had stepped onboard. "All the blocs of Astraper are tied up tight. Whoever set this up –" the speaker became aware an Unclean One was among the Elect and stopped abruptly.

"Victor Podgorny planned it all brilliantly," Carolyn said, filling the void. Adele's head swiveled around reflexively. She met Carolyn's eye directly, her glare unmistakable. In spite of herself, Carolyn averted her eyes.

"I'm truly sorry you resigned when you did, Adele," she responded, defensive in spite of herself, trying to recover. "We never did have that talk after NATPE. One thing –"

Something snapped. "One thing we would have talked about for sure, Carolyn," Adele said, biting off each word, "is what you said after the lunch on the first day of NATPE. You made a complete ass of yourself. It was inexcusable." Carolyn's mouth dropped open; she did not know, would never know, how much she reminded Adele of an old fool from Oneonta she'd known once.

"How dare you –" she began. The elevator stopped at the twenty-eighth floor. Adele exited, turned, and held the door.

"And while we're on the same subject," she interrupted, "I never was a virgin, Carolyn. What I actually am," she continued, jiggling slightly, "is a retired slut." She let the door go; it closed quickly in all their startled faces, a magnificent tableau. She walked down the hall toward her office, cheerful for a moment – that would give them at least five minutes' worth of gossip on something besides EBS – but becoming more depressed second by second.

They had all gotten away with it before – and they were all getting away with it again. Nothing ever changes.

Adele put her notes down on her desk and shook her head free of thought. *Enough.* She shouldered her purse; she had no more time for this. She had a truly important lunch scheduled.

*

In one of those coincidences that happen with some regularity in real life, the place he'd picked was the same one where she'd last seen Bri. But unlike her former boyfriend, George was on time. He looked terrible, his face puffy and pale. Even so, it was thrilling – scarily thrilling – to see him. The chemistry between them was no respecter of wedding vows.

"Hi," said Adele, smiling awkwardly, with her tiny wave. *Really, stupid* – she had rehearsed more opening lines than de Bergerac had nose insults, from the lightest of the light to the heaviest of the heavy – and now, in his presence, the best she could do was "Hi." *Really.* "How are you feeling?"

"Dumb," George answered flatly. "Sorry about the other day. Didn't expect the call." He eyed her. "You're looking great yourself. How's it with you?"

"Really good," she said, "until the other day." He colored. She experienced the same clumsiness she'd known at that first lunch – only now it was her problem, not his. The head waiter seated them. "Lem and the others came Sunday night," she gushed on, nervously. "They said some nice things about you. I'm glad that's mended."

"They remember to short their stock?"

"I'm certain they have. Lem said something about it. I'll check and be sure when I get back."

"Franklin's going entirely by my book. Balloon'll pop Wednesday or Thursday, Friday latest. If they go today, they won't skim all the cream, but they'll do fine. Look, I'm sorry," he went on in the same breath, opening up, "didn't want to have you see me in that state."

"It's not a problem," Adele answered. "George? What's been happening? Can you tell me? If you want to?"

"Not much," he said. "Nothing, really." Adele remained silent, regarding him, tacitly insisting on more.

"I felt pretty good on the night," he said finally. "I had the release. O.K., I'd lost you, but you were O.K. I felt good about that – that you –"

"I don't want you to talk about that," she interrupted. "I want to hear about you."

Now he gulped air. "O.K. So I thought I'd do all right. Closed all the money accounts that Monday. Worked out a buy/sell program for myself. Everything was set. Right? So. . ." His expression became bleak. "So. . . what? Everything was over. I didn't want to go back to the Street. I'm so tired of all that shit. So what? I went over to the museums – spent some time at the Met, then at MOMA. Big mistake. Found myself missing somebody." He looked up at her. "Pulled out my little black book," he said, his eyes not turning away. "Bigger, blacker mistake. Whores and semi-whores. Inflato girls. I'm through playing with dolls. It made everything worse." His expression became darker. "The holiday came. Thought I'd take a chance – maybe I'd learned something – phoned my ex – no dice. The door there's shut for good. No solicitors."

Bitch, Adele thought.

"So," he sighed, gulped again, and went on, "I guess there's no way not to say. It got to me. All this money and no place to go. No one, nothing – and a lot I had to do for it. . . Franklin. . . I got too used to him." He shook his head. "He wasn't the kind of kid who'd pull the wings off of flies. He's the kind who'd pay the other kids a nickel for each wingless fly they brought him." He paused. "And I've turned him loose," he added. "And that got to me."

Adele was silent, thinking thoughts too much like his to be usefully spoken aloud.

"And. . . yeah. . . you. . . " he said softly, looking at his hands, after a long moment. "That night I thought I'd be Joe Sportsmanship and I tried. I did try. I got no kick at all against the other fella. Good guy. But after the holiday, I began missing you, Paloma. I –" He looked up.

"It's all right," she answered. "I still like it."

"I feel like a jerk," he went on. "I don't wanna bring you into this. We didn't make each other any promises. You don't owe me anything. But I got to missing you – fierce – the phone ringing, and hoping it would be you. . . looking forward to seeing you. . . thinking about Zihuateneo. And where was I ever gonna find anyone like that? So I don't know. The past seemed as blank as a sheet and the future the same. I'm not much of a boozer. But it got to me."

"George, I don't know what to say," she said truthfully, uncertain how to respond.

"No reason you have to say anything," he shrugged. "I gotta get used to it. What happened between us was an illusion, like Franklin said. Midlife crisis. It didn't –"

"It was *not* an illusion," Adele answered emphatically, the right course becoming obvious as she remembered the last time she'd seen him. "It was much more than that. And I do owe you something, George. I've never told you the whole truth. Not once. And you deserve that. You deserved it all along."

He looked up, interested.

She told him everything then, all the secrets she had kept, holding back only the ones she'd learned about Tom, which were of no importance to him.

*

"In June," Adele answered. "Nine months from September." She paused. "So I was never free with you. Not for a second." She weighed her words carefully. "But I fell in love with you anyway, at a time when I didn't think that could happen with anybody," she continued. "Everything that happened between us was absolutely real, George. Everything."

George Sorenson had been taking it all in, nodding and thinking. The ambiance in the room had changed; the mood was familiar. Now he settled back. "So that's the story, huh? One day late and I lose the girl?"

"Yes," she said carefully, now a bit nervous, hoping she'd done the right thing. "That's the story. I hope it helps. The truth, I mean."

"Yeah," he answered thoughtfully. "It does." He looked at her thoughtfully. "You know I meant what I said that night. A baby wouldn't have made any difference to me. I'd have respected you for that. Hell, there wouldn't even have been anything to forgive."

"I know now," she replied. "I suspected then. There was too much going on that night to think." She paused, remembering something. "There also wasn't enough time to tell you what a hero you became to me then. And always will be."

"Cut it out," he answered softly, cooling slightly. "But I'm glad you told me the rest. What are you going to do now? I know you're out of work. Pregnant. I liked – what's his name?"

"Tom."

"–Tom, but he didn't exactly seem like a money guy." Adele shook her head. "Which reminds me. I got a wedding present for you." He reached into his coat and pulled out a white envelope, passed it over to her. She opened the envelope, smiled at the card, and peeked long enough at the check – certified, of course – to notice the six zeros.

"What is this?" she asked. "The hard number?"

"Nope," he answered promptly. "Value as of ten this morning. We're way above the hard number." He eyed her directly. "You earned the shares, Paloma. Franklin had no right."

"I can't accept this, George," Adele answered, handing him back the check. "Here."

"Why?" he asked, puzzled, hurt. "Pocket change, compared to the rest."

"That's not the point," she replied. "I don't want anything to do with Franklin or the Project – not ever. . . and I can't take money from you, George, you more than anyone." He still looked bewildered; she shifted her weight on the chair and leaned forward. "I didn't make it clear, I guess. What happened between us was real. What I felt for you then; what I feel for you now. Nothing's different. The last thing I thought when I left the table at NATPE is that I wished there were two of me. If I were a different person than who I am," she went on, dead serious, "I'd be his wife and your mistress. I'd have you both." She smiled. "I can't take your money, George."

He was startled for a moment, then began to grin himself. "I'm the lover, huh?"

"Always," Adele said promptly. "You get to me just being you. He has to put some effort into it," and that really lit him up.

"So no money," she went on, smiling, relieved to see him pleased with himself. "But I am going to keep the card. It's very funny. And we could use a microwave. The one we have is ancient."

"Right," he said, shaking his head, a slight smile. "A microwave. Real tough order, but I'll see what I can do. Well. I'm glad you came. I wondered before, but it's better." He shook his head, serious now himself. "What am I going to do? Where am I ever going to find anyone else like you?" His tone was reflective now, but still with the slight edge of despair.

"What are you going to do in the short term?" she asked apprehensively.

"Leave town. Nothing left here." He regarded her. "Not to Zihuateneo. I'm not going back. Already got the place on the market. No, I thought I'd drive for a while, see the country. Think. Get away."

"In a big Mercedes? Or a little red sports car?"

"Naw," he answered with a slight forced smile. "In. . ." he named a popular medium-priced sedan – "Best value for the money. That's what I live by."

Adele started to reply, then stopped. An idea had struck her. She reached again into her purse, for her calendar and address book. "I met a girl," she remarked, writing, "I liked a lot while I was trying to find Tom. I think you might like her, too. She lives in Vermont if you go up that way. Here."

(And if she had ever had any doubt about the depth of her feeling for George Sorenson, it ended right then. Stab after stab of raw cutting jealousy tore away at her as she wrote. This note was the outward sign, the final seal, of the fact that she was not his, and he would never be hers. Something naked and primitive within her fought back in furious rebellion at that finality. The animal Adele could have cared less that the civilized Adele had chosen differently, or that only one choice was possible. That primal female wanted George and would always want George.)

He looked at the writing, glanced up at her, his surprise evident, then began to laugh, harder and harder. Diners from adjacent tables looked around discreetly. "Jeez, Adele! After all we've said to each other! After everything that's happened! The best you can do is set me up with a *NUN*?"

"A novice, really," said Adele, a bit defensively. "She'll be leaving the convent soon. She's a wonderful person." She forbore to tell him – more accurately, that naked primitive thing choked on the words – that Millicent Peters was considered to be an exceptionally beautiful young woman. But she did have to add one thing more: "You should know she also knows Tom. She was his college girlfriend. It was a very serious affair."

"Hell," he said, still chuckling, "that doesn't matter. The way it's worked out, that's almost the Good Housekeeping Seal of Approval. A nun," he continued, still amused, putting the number and address in his coat pocket. Adele stood up.

"I'd better be going," she said.

"Right," he said, and stood up himself. At once the mood became sad and serious. There was a finality to this leave-taking. Never again would she be able to be with him like this. Even the might-have-been, the what-if, was disappearing today. For a moment, she fervently hoped he'd move her to one of those private nooks he seemed to have mapped out all over the City and take her into his arms. She yearned to give him the kiss he hadn't received after the NATPE lunch. No way; she didn't dare. If she went to his embrace, it was entirely possible she would go to his bed, baby or not, marriage or not, become a newlywed adulteress. He walked behind her and pushed open the door. For a moment, she hoped and feared what he might or might not do. For an instant, it was entirely up to him.

George moved her into the middle of the lobby and took her hand. He knew. He'd felt the tug as well. Their eyes met. "Good short-term buy," he murmured. "Lousy long-term hold." She nodded her gratitude and disappointment.

"Adele," George said quietly, as they reached the door, "does your – does Tom – ever say anything about me?"

"Yes," she smiled, a bit guarded. "He figured out that you're a good dancer."

"I meant earlier," George replied. "I meant on the NATPE night."

The truth, she thought. "He liked you. He could tell you and me – cared about each other. One of the reasons he got involved with Franklin was he was afraid of what you'd do if he didn't."

"Observant S.O.B.," George said. They were at the door. "You didn't ask me how I knew Franklin thought you and me was an illusion. Franklin didn't say that to my face." He paused. "I sent Carolyn on alone after we left the boardroom that night. I listened to what Franklin had to say to you; he'd left the intercom on, the jerk, he's lousy with details. I heard it all." Now he did touch her, drew his hand down her sleeve very lightly, non-erotically.

"When you told him about all the men that would take his head off for what he'd said, I wonder if you included me."

"Yes," she answered, the only possible answer, not sure if it were true or not. On the night, it had been more something to say than anything she'd given serious thought.

He lifted his hand and turned away. "Promise me if you do get in a bind – a real bind – about money, I'll hear from you. Don't be an idiot." She nodded.

"You see, I owe Tom even if I don't owe you. He was right what he told you: I didn't go straight to NATPE when I left. I went home" – he looked her directly in the face – "to get my gun. Sullivan Act. I've got a permit." She froze.

"If you'd decided to leave with Franklin," he said quietly, "the moment you got up out of your chair. . . that second. . . I was going to kill him." The silence lingered for a moment longer. He had spoken matter-of-factly, without drama, stating a fact.

The tension became too great. "I have to go," she said. "Right," he answered almost simultaneously. Adele stepped into the doorway and gave her tiny wave; it was time to leave. She delayed to the point of awkwardness. She didn't want to go. As she finally took her leave, he was rereading the contact info.

"A nun," he said out loud, smiling to himself, then laughed again. A passer-by turned to wonder at him.

*

Now the final chapters were being written. The nervous, frenetic exhilaration of the first few days of the campaign had hardened into a bright, steady euphoria, the crackling energy transformed into a shining, invincible sword – or, more accurately, harpoon. The whale was in full flight. It was evident, obvious, in the headlines, in the text, in what was in the lines of the Teleprompters and what was between them – in the bland, hollow denials of EBS management. The entire nation watched, fascinated by the growing sense that another Goliath was falling to another David. The skyrocketing price of Astraper common stock was trumpeted on all the front pages. Victor Podgorny seemed to be everywhere, smug and arrogant, his cigar puffing in Churchillian style. Franklin Fischer was invisible. The role of CFS in everything, the relation it bore to a different company born with much fanfare at NATPE three weeks earlier – all of this remained unknown.

Increasingly certain now of victory, Richard Collishaw and the other heavyweights were the ones who appeared on the news bytes. Josh had departed from the scene, gone, but not forgotten, and well-satisfied. He had seized his chance; he had made his mark. The corridors of Hapgood, Thurlow had become corridors of power. Confidence glowed from the woodwork, permeated the air. In some strange way, the excitement of the entire country was focalized here, in these offices, visible in the quickened pace, the heightened sense of purpose, amid everyone in the firm. What happened here had become important, newsworthy.

Alone in her darkened office, Adele Jansen Newcombe continued doggedly along her own path. Coventry, Carolyn had promised, and Carolyn was as good as her word. She had become invisible, a non-person. Richard Collishaw gave her only the barest, most imperceptible nod the few times they passed in the hall. Once she encountered Victor Podgorny; a genial, patronizing contempt showed in his eyes, in tandem with a distant, morbid sexuality. *In a while, perhaps you'll do* – she could feel his thought – clearly a man who liked his women weak, and perceived her as weakened. She passed him by without a second glance, privately savoring at least one aspect of the denouement George had described to her, relishing the thought that she could have warned him. The other instant celebrities ignored her altogether. Walt Greenfield popped his head in her door, sat down and gossiped for an hour, then took her to lunch. She was touched. But the hint of defiance in his attitude, the realization that his was a small, genuine act of courage, was as depressing as it was moving.

The enthusiasm that affected everyone? It was too omnipresent not to affect her – and she was too self-aware not to admit to a feeling of being left out, a feeling that did indeed hurt. But the fever was not contagious. The conviction she'd had since the NATPE evening, that a monstrous evil was taking shape, coming into being, grew and strengthened. George had said the same thing at lunch. She felt it around her, the subtle viciousness she'd sensed the week before intensifying in direct proportion to the increased pace. Lawyers hurried by her – going where? The paralegals and word processors produced draft after draft – for what? Did any of them know what this was really all about? So far there had been no indication that anyone at Hapgood (besides the core group) knew what the true purpose of all the commotion was. Would it make any difference to any of them if they did know?

As she walked back from her lunch with Walt Greenfield, it occurred to Adele that at least one more question remained to be answered if she were to understand all that had happened.

It was time to find out something about Franklin Fischer.

*

An inquiry that proved much, much easier to resolve than the first. She sat at one of the data terminals and considered what she'd learned from the databases she'd explored, tried to digest it all. The answer to the minor question had proven to be simple. Who exactly was Franklin Fischer?

Nobody. No one.

A nondescript biography. Educated at one of the traditional Eastern seaboard private colleges she would have suspected, without any special honors or distinctions. Married and divorced, without children. No special civic contributions; no demonstrable interest in charity or the arts; no sponsorship of any particular cause; no major accomplishments. No publications, only a few pieces of puff publicity. In hard fact, until he'd met George Sorenson and begun CFS, the only significant thing he'd ever done in his life had been to be born the son of a multimillionaire.

She smiled, almost laughed, to herself at that. *The old-fashioned way.* She should have guessed. And then all at once Adele stopped laughing. The chill was fierce, palpable, direct. She sat back. For how many years had the spider sat patiently, waiting for its malice to curdle into venom! For how long had it hated all the usurpers, the latecomers, fearing their energy, their capability! The strength and size of the web! The havoc it had wreaked on George, on Carolyn. . . and the pleasure, the gloating she had sensed in that darkened boardroom in its subtle, ultimate revenge. Would she, too, have been caught if it weren't for. . . ?

Adele stood up abruptly and left the library. A monster had been set loose, she was certain of it, and she was one of those who had unleashed it. She turned the corner hurriedly – and, as it seemed it had to be, almost ran into them – Carolyn, Harry Greube, Richard Collishaw, one or two other lawyers. . . and Franklin Fischer, briefcases in hand, top and overcoats buttoned.

Adele drew herself up. Carolyn stepped deliberately by, pointedly ignoring her; Greube and the others followed her lead. Franklin Fischer paused for a moment, eyed her, then moved on with the slightest hint of a smirk. *I said 'through'. Do you know now what I meant?* She watched them march irregularly down the hall, proud and purposeful. Victor Podgorny was not in the group; if they were going to the meeting she thought they were, he didn't even know the meeting had been set. Served him right, of course, but that didn't mean it didn't count as one more trophy for the great Mr. Fischer.

Adele went directly back down to the twenty-eighth floor, thinking about Franklin Fischer and his massive new communications company. The chill in her office was no less than that in the library.

Enough, she thought. There was nothing she could do about it that day.

Then her thoughts ran to the home to which she would be retracing her steps only an hour or so later, where there were no clear answers and never would be – only steadily deepening mysteries and increasingly enveloping warmth.

*

Some things familiar. Some things strange.

At the beginning, Adele had had some hope that a day would come when she would be used to it – when the interruption of sleep would seem the most natural and inevitable thing in the world – *didn't everyone?* – when the dark, brooding silences, that horrible vacant look, would seem every day, unremarkable occurrences. At the metabolic level, that had indeed occurred. Her body had accepted completely the bifurcation of the night; she woke instantly on the first stirring, slept again instantly when the disturbance had run its course, woke refreshed.

But the other adjustments? At the personal level? No. Never. After three weeks, she knew she would never be reconciled to it. *How did I miss all this? How could I not have seen?* she thought repeatedly; the cracks and fissures in his being were so obvious now, so transparent. Of course, he had been wooing then. Now, inevitably, the guard came down and he appeared as he was. *How could I have been so blind?*

Don't hate, she told herself on some of the darker nights. Gradually she realized that the tension was permanent, now one of the basic structures of her life. Hatred was useless. Revenge was impossible. All that had been done, had been done decades before. If she gave way to hatred, they were both done for. Yet sometimes in the blackness of morning, despite all her warnings, rage did overcome her, complete fury at the old villains and the new, Franklin Fischer and Josh Palmdale, Carolyn Hoffman, thieves, whores, and grasping mediocrities, seethed until she calmed herself. *Useless because it's wrong; wrong because it's useless; go back to sleep.* And so she did, or at least tried to do.

Her friends started dropping by once she and Tom had reoccupied her old apartment, partly concern, partly curiosity. He charmed them all, quietly and effectively. Yet again there was that slight trace of performance. She wondered if he were ever entirely natural with anyone. At the darkest moments, she wondered if he had ever been entirely natural with her.

What's he really like? her more perceptive friends called back to ask. Adele did her best for them, all the while wondering herself: *I wish I knew, Irene.* In the same way as with her family, she was reminded again and again of how little she understood, how difficult it was to make anyone else understand, how isolated in the most fundamental sense the life she had chosen (or which had chosen her) actually was. And sometimes – also in spite of herself – she became afraid.

Not that there were not compensations; there were definitely compensations.

Because he could do magic. Milly had been right about that as well.

*

Adele had long since crossed the threshold of belief. There had only been a half-dozen occasions – he was wise enough not to abuse the gift by overusing it – but no doubt lingered any longer in her mind. She was married to one of the greatest performance artists in the world, perhaps who had ever lived – the heir to the ancient traditions of the strolling minstrel, bards speaking in low voices before a fire. All he need do was walk onto a stage holding a newspaper and fifteen minutes later he would have been the stuff of legend.

Adele found herself almost embarrassed at how much she enjoyed these times. Each time he began, the cool, calm girl promised herself that this time she would remain objective and clear sighted. So far, her failure rate was one hundred percent. He got her every time. The gift for nuance was too great, his instinct for the corroborative detail too good. She found it easy to lose herself in the spell – easy, too, to blind herself for a time to the monstrous price that had been paid for it.

But he did not only create fiction for her on these small, marvellous evenings.

They'd come back to his small apartment after the wedding and a long festive lunch with her family. She was surprised and pleased to find herself as disoriented and breathless as any other bride, the day a kaleidoscopic blur, as different as it had been from anything she had ever imagined. Linda had given her a white silk nightgown to wear on the night, floor length and virginal, absurdly inappropriate for a woman in her condition. She'd put it on with enormous pleasure, come out of the bathroom wondering how long she'd have it on – she hoped for some considerable period of time. She was in too serious a mood for simple animal fun.

Tom was in the reading chair. She sat down with and upon him. "Are we going to do another novel?" she asked, rather hoping he'd been thinking about the sequel to the story he'd created three nights earlier.

"I don't think so," he answered quietly. "Let's have some reality tonight. I need to know some things. I want you to tell me everything that happened to you between the time I left you and the time I saw you next."

There was a great deal she had intended to keep to herself. But gently, naturally, easily, inevitably, he drew her out. *You can't keep secrets from him, it's impossible*, and in short order she realized it was hopeless even to try. She told him all about AI Squared, her long drawn-out reflections over the baby, her meetings with John Goodson and Milly – stopping only where it had been implicitly agreed she must stop – the Project, and Carolyn. She felt him stiffen beneath her when she related her encounter with Franklin Fischer. She told him everything.

Except one thing.

"And that's when I found you in the hospitality suite," Adele concluded. "And you know the rest." She lifted her head and looked at him. His eyes were twinkling with amusement. The semi-smile played on his face. "What's so funny?" she asked, perplexed.

"Only wondering when you're going to trust me well enough to tell me more about the man standing behind you at NATPE," he said, very, very gently. Adele blushed beet red. "About all I know now is that he's an excellent dancer." She might have told him right then, but his hands were upon her and the time had obviously come for the nightgown to be lost – which it was.

In the same slow, easy way, he drew her out on other matters – Jack's perplexity over her pregnancy, the reasons for it, her hidden thought that it might be wiser to let Jack and Linda adopt. *What do you want to do, Tom?* she asked afterward, late one night. He took the question seriously, then met her eye. *I'll try*, he said quietly, *the same as for you*, and that settled that. She grieved for Jack, but he'd have to find a different way.

So strange – to have a talent of this incomparability a constant presence in her life. So familiar – he liked pleasing her, enjoyed showing off, as most men do in front of their women. Ordinary moments enriched, commonplace events suddenly enlarged – an everyday magic that she was beginning to suspect was for all practical purposes inexhaustible. Compensation enough, perhaps, in that alone – many of her friends would have thought so.

On a Wednesday morning two days before her last day at the firm, as she was dressing for the forced idleness that passed these days for work, the thought struck her forcibly that she was falling more and more deeply in love with him with each passing day.

Which was not necessarily a good thing.

*

If only she hadn't had to confront the money worry during these turbulent days!

"Don't worry about money, angel," Tom said, reading her mind, as he turned back to his idling. "It always takes care of itself."

Easy for you to say, she thought later at her office, and then felt immensely guilty. Still, how were they going to put bread on the table? Jenet's assistant had called to arrange an appointment about the manuscript Adele had delivered. There was tension in her voice; Jenet had distributed copies of the *Sonnets* to her staff, each page separately numbered and each copy logged, and wanted to wait until she had received all their reactions. In the normal course of business, Friday would be the earliest possible day, but if anyone else, *anyone*, had seen that manuscript, Jenet would drop everything and meet immediately. Adele answered that Friday would be fine. Very sweet, Jenet's enthusiasm, but in plain fact Tom's first four books hadn't made back the advances. She could not – did not – expect the business woman in Jenet to give way to the literary enthusiast. So how?

In the evenings, she gave herself freely to the magic he did. But her frustration the mornings after nearly boiled over. She was sure there had been people in the Viennese audiences that listened to Mozart improvise who obsessed in exactly the same way about the ephemerality of what they heard – and those were people whose well-being did not depend on its preservation! If only he would give himself over for a few hours to memorializing what he so casually did and discarded! The financial anxieties that plagued her would vanish in an instant. But the master magician seemed entirely content to perform, as before, for an audience of one. She longed to say something, anything, even to beg. But there were rules about such matters – or so Adele thought. His gift was his gift, to use as he chose.

So she gritted her teeth and hoped – or more accurately, prayed – that if they really got into a major league pickle, he'd do something besides simply entertain her.

He gave no sign that he even recognized the need, let alone heard the prayer.

*

The frenzied excitement of the EBS tender had become a normal element of the ambiance of the Hapgood corridors, so much so that old habits began to re-emerge. The Glee Club, reconstituted, was back in session. Adele found herself an object of gossip once more, though hardly the same kind as of old. *You can buy ideas*, she overheard Josh Palmdale pontificating. *That's what Podgorny says. It's stamina that matters. She didn't have it. I met the guy once. Damaged goods, if ever there was.* She moved away. *They're all alike,* she heard him add. *Brains between her legs.*

So what was she supposed to do? Flee? Retreat? Soon, now, the most polished media professionals would be with him, smoothing out the wrinkles in Franklin Fischer's demented megalomania, sugar coating the poison. He'd never load people into boxcars himself – only provide the reasons, the rationalizations, and the rationales. *The type who pays for wingless flies*, George said. Her hands clenched on her desk. Retreat? Flee? Impossible.

And even apart from that. . . let the tale end the way the Glee Club wanted it told? Let her version of the Same Old Story become the Carolyn and Josh Palmdale version – the Woman Who Gave Up Everything for Love?

Yecch. Double Yecch. No; *never* – and yet. . . what to do?

Everything has to be different, she had promised herself on the blackest day of her life. Despite all the uncertainties of her new life, despite the revised frustrations, she took comfort in the fact that she had succeeded at exactly that, at making everything different. How they were going to survive, by what means they'd get by, she had no idea. But somehow the worries did not undermine her basic confidence that they would – somehow. *I'm not afraid anymore*, she'd said in the back of the cab that night, and she knew now she'd spoken truth. She was never going to be afraid again – not like that. A good place to end up.

Happy? Not exactly. Contented? Definitely not. But living now with a growing but inarticulable sense that she was where she belonged, that she had chosen her stand wisely. This was the place where she had always been destined to carve out her own middle ground, between the leering hypocrites above and the yawning hell below.

Ten weeks earlier the professional route had seemed safe and easy, the personal goals stark, open questions. Now all was reversed. She had chosen the right man, as difficult as it had been and as improbable as the man had seemed at one time. Now it was the outer world over which she seethed and fumed. *I can't stay here*, Milly had said. *I know too much*. Milly had been right about that, too – and neither could Adele retreat to a kitchen in some suburb and forget all the ugliness which she had assisted in creating. No way. Day and night, she wrestled with that problem.

For the present, there was consolation enough in bright, impossible magic, in an unrepentant male sexual territoriality, in the wide, strong left shoulder, in the protective arm ending with the sad, damaged left hand that encircled her nightly – above all, the wondrously reassuring certainty that, in his untheatrical, unimposing way, he had become her husband in fact as well as name. Drifting into unconsciousness, sometimes for a moment it seemed possible to forget the future, to let it come however it would.

Possible, too, to ignore – because it had to be ignored, because the key was to focus on the day, on the here-and-now – another reality. The sunburst of energy that the NATPE night had generated was fading. His pattern of sleep disruption was becoming more and more pronounced; his vacant pauses longer and darker. Day by day, the darkness within was engulfing him. Old patterns, entrenched patterns were reasserting themselves. Perhaps they had become fiercer, more formidable than ever. The lost, bewildered boy who was father to this man – beyond touching, beyond cure – had witnessed everything he loved destroyed for no other or better reason than that he had loved it. Perhaps now in the dead of night guilt ravaged him on her behalf as well, that he had allowed her into her life, that in so doing he had endangered her.

The worst night of all was the Thursday before her last day at Hapgood.

PRESIDENT OF THE SORORITY

S ister Mary Dolores
Convent of the Sacred Heart
-------, Vermont
December 12, 19--

Dear Milly,

I am writing this letter somewhat belatedly. I hope you'll forgive me. It took me a lot of time to find words to say to you. Tom and I were married on the evening of November 19th by our public pledge to one another. A week later we had a formal ceremony before Judge Pulaski of the New York Supreme Court. We have been living in the apartment where you phoned me since last Sunday.

The words I had most trouble finding are how to thank you for all the wisdom you imparted to me that night. I did ask more questions about Tom. I found out more. I received answers, or so the world would call them. I finally discovered that there are no final explanations, that the core is an ultimate mystery. Knowing that does stop me from loving Tom, or him from loving me. That will do. It is enough.

Everything you said to me that night was true. But the most significant of all was that 'Tom is important'. You were right, Milly; he is important; he would be, even if he never wrote another line of verse or told another story. He's important because he proves by his own existence something that he is fond of saying in good moments and bad, that anything is possible, that there are depths in human existence beyond understanding, that it isn't all a matter of counting numbers and conditioned reflexes. It is very important to everyone that he not fail.

I will always regard you as one of my closest friends, even if we never should meet face to face. But I can't believe that won't happen. (There's so much I have to tell you!) I don't know where we will end up living, but we will always be reachable through my father (at --------------) or at any of four 'Annals of Cinema' video stores owned by my brother James Richard (my family calls him Buck) in the same area.

Good luck with your new life. Write as soon as you can. God bless you.

Love,

Adele

P.S. I almost forgot. I gave your name and address to a man named George Sorenson. He may already have been in contact with you. He is a wonderful man, someone who would have been much more than a good friend of mine if I hadn't been so completely involved with Tom. I'm sure you'll have something to say to each other.

It's all part of the same story. I simply have to see you. You're the only person who would even begin to understand. Adele

*

Adele sealed the letter in her office. This was the last day, the very last two hours, of her time with the prestigious law firm of Hapgood, Thurlow, Davis, & Anderson – now the foremost in the City. Goodbye to the look-and-feel memo. Goodbye to the Glee Club and "Ice Maiden". Would anyone remember her two weeks from now? Probably not. Carolyn had been right. None of the clients, not even those with which she thought she had an understanding, had been at all perturbed by her departure. She had received a few desultory calls, a mixture of curiosity and condolence, and that was all.

Enough, she told herself. At least her last day had not been without incident. The office had crackled with renewed tension in the morning; then, early in the afternoon, scurrying movement, pounding feet. A few minutes later, Josh Palmdale had rushed down the hall and into his office. Adele did not have to leave her own office to know what had happened. The Astraper balloon had obviously popped, as planned.

Now it was time to leave the office for the last time, first to her appointment with Jenet, then home to Tom. She checked her briefcase to be sure she had the letter and the last of her personal items, then exited the scene of her triumphs and tragedy without a backward glance.

The corridor was empty. The door to Josh's office was ajar; from the hall she could hear him on the phone, despair in his voice: "I didn't know, Dad. . . no, it's final. . . I couldn't; it all happened so fast. . . were we able to get anything back?. . . I didn't know. . . " She stopped; he looked up, a look of utter anguish on his face – then, embarrassed by the unexpected intimacy, she moved away quickly.

Oh, no, Josh, she thought. She knew at once what had happened. The powers-that-be had not entrusted Josh with the full scope of the plan. Thinking he knew it all, he'd obviously failed to take the advice about inside trading that all the secretaries had received – and so he and his family, pathetic little fish, had swum into the same net George had so coldly spread for Podgorny. With EBS having bought Franklin Fischer and the bankers' group off with the grant of rights of Vinux to Fischer Communications, the hostile takeover was canceled and the stock of Astraper had dropped like a stone.

Adele tried to forget that look. She reminded herself that he was a pompous, hypocritical liar and thief (and now inside trader). She tried to gloat, then sighed. In spite of herself, she was deeply moved, sorry for the creep. The natural warmth with which she'd been blessed and cursed was an integral part of her nature. She was never going to escape it.

She departed from the law firm of Hapgood, Thurlow, Anderson, & Davis exactly the way she'd arrived twenty-eight months before. No one took any special notice. No one paid any attention at all.

*

The only other occupant of the elevator cabin was Bill Andrews, the executive for the Furston Press who'd been in charge of the NATPE exhibit. He reacted to her in a way that she could not read – almost startled when she stepped aboard, then greeting her with a lopsided, uncomfortable grin. "Well, *hello*," he said, in a peculiar tone.

"Hello, Bill," she answered mildly, a bit puzzled. "How is everything? How's Jenet?" The elevator began its ascent.

"The old girl's fine," Bill replied in a light voice. "Never seen her better."

"Good," Adele said conversationally. "All recovered from NATPE, then?"

"Well, *yes*," he responded, in another peculiar voice, as if there was something she should know that she didn't. She looked at him more closely. She had the distinct but baffling impression she was being regarded as a Very Important Person. A second later the doors of the cabin opened at the main office floor of the Furston Press.

Bill Andrews gave her a small, clumsy wave and moved down the left hall. Adele heard his voice in the first office as she walked to the reception desk. "Hello," she said pleasantly to the young woman behind the desk, "I'm here to see Jenet Furston."

"Your name?" the girl asked.

"Newcombe," Adele answered. "Adele Jansen Newcombe." (She'd wrestled with the name issue for a few days – *goddam patriarchy* – finally given up. The prosaic fact was, she liked the sound of it. Tom had shrugged when she told him of her decision, pointed out that the six syllables had a nice iambic rhythm.)

The receptionist's head turned as if on a swivel and her mouth all but dropped open. "Yes, of course," she said, and touched the button to buzz Jenet.

Totally confused now, Adele looked away and down the hall. The occupant of the office at which Bill Andrews had stopped – male and middle-aged – had poked his head out and around the corner to stare at her. She inadvertently caught his eye. He blushed in embarrassment and ducked back into his office.

Adele sat down on one of the plush sofas and tried to interest herself in a magazine. What in the world was going on here? She could swear the receptionist was watching her surreptitiously, all the while pretending she was not. Had they all taken leave of their senses? Hadn't any of them ever seen a young woman lawyer before?

*

Jenet came radiantly through the door. "Adele!" she said, beaming, extending her hands in greeting. Italy had obviously agreed with her. She looked twenty years younger than she had a month before.

"Jenet," Adele said wonderingly. "You look wonderful."

Jenet laughed, a light, delighted, oddly off-balance laugh. "Do I? Thank you, dear. Let's go back to my office. We have much to discuss."

Adele was no longer in doubt, she was certain: the whole place was alive with a certain kind of electricity, an excitement – something of the sort that had overtaken Hapgood, Thurlow two weeks earlier, but without the undertone of frenzy. A great many people lingering in the corridors, or at the door of the offices. But Adele had the uncanny sense – no, but it had to be paranoia – still she had the sense – that they were all eying – well, *her*. She tried to shake it off – *Oh, do be sensible* – but could not. Too many veiled looks, too many whispers, almost a palpable buzz.

"My assistant told me you married Tom," Jenet said as they walked, with the same hint of frazzled giddiness.

"Yes. About three weeks ago," Adele answered, bracing herself for the reaction.

"Congratulations," Jenet responded instead. Additional amazement. "I must send you a gift." All at once, Adele saw a sign, posted above one of the doors, printed out on a laser printer in large type: "DISCUSSION OF THE 'SONNETS' IS STRICTLY PROHIBITED IN THESE OFFICES." She looked; the same sign was posted over other doors.

It couldn't be. . . they weren't referring to. . .? But if not, what, then. . .? Something very warm began to glow within her.

"Here we are," said Jenet, in the same high, happy tone, as she ushered Adele into her office. All at once, the warm air chilled. Carolyn Hoffman looked calmly up at her from a seat in front of Jenet's desk. *Only you?* her expression seemed to say. *No big deal.*

*

Adele turned away. Who needed this? But nothing seemed to faze Jenet, who stepped briskly to a cabinet on the far end of the room. "Tea, Adele? Or coffee?" she asked in the same bright voice. "It's a bit early for champagne, but perhaps the occasion calls for it," and laughed again the same light laugh.

"No, thank you, Jenet," Adele said; she remained standing until she had some clue as to what this all meant. "What occasion do you mean?" she asked Jenet, as she returned to her desk.

Jenet was momentarily taken aback. "Of course," she said thoughtfully, more soberly, recovering herself, "you wouldn't know. You're too close. What the occasion is – what I'm talking about – what's happened – is this," she went on, picking up a manuscript from her desk.

"That? Tom's book? *The Metropolitan Sonnets?*" Adele went on, bewildered, as she took her seat.

"Yes, *that*," Carolyn interjected with calm sarcasm. "Poetry. An ordinary book of verse is what's caused all this. Jenet, with all the important things that are happening, if I had known that the only reason you called for me was something this routine – "

Jenet looked at Carolyn, then, in the same sober, thoughtful way: "You wouldn't know, either," she remarked softly. Then she held up the manuscript. "This isn't routine, Carolyn – and this is no ordinary book of verse. This," she went on quietly, holding the manuscript up, "this is the last, crowning masterwork of the second millennium."

*

With an assertion of will, Adele stopped herself from sitting bolt up. She was not certain that she'd correctly heard what she thought she'd heard.

"Don't exaggerate, Jenet," Carolyn said, with a trace of impatience, and flashed an irritated glance at Adele, as if somehow this was all her fault.

"Exaggerate?" Jenet answered, even more softly. "No, Carolyn, no. I think not. I was over in Trieste and I thought I'd check in for news. I was worried NATPE hadn't gone well; I thought I'd say a kind word to Bill and the others. My assistant told me Thomas Newcombe had submitted a new manuscript, that apparently it was dedicated to Adele. I became very curious. Anything Tom writes is of interest to me. But also. . . I hoped that it would relieve certain – ah – personal concerns I had about Adele. About Tom.

"I thought it would be a book like the other four. Brilliant, but destined for obscurity." Jenet suddenly smiled. "Someone once said that publishing poetry and waiting for the response was like throwing rose petals into the Grand Canyon and waiting for the echo. Based on my experience, I'd say that person made it sound too easy. I was under no illusions, Carolyn." She became dead serious again. "I don't think I'd read half a chapter before I knew what it was I was holding." She looked at the manuscript and shook her head. "The book I've been waiting forty years for. A book that proves that so many things I worried had become impossible can still be done." She half-closed her eyes. "And I'm the one who's going to publish it."

"Jenet. Jenet," Carolyn sighed sympathetically. "I understand how this could happen. How much you want this. But I don't think it would be fair of me – it wouldn't be right –" she sighed again – "the world has changed, Jenet. This is a media society. Images, not ideas. You know that. You've profited by it, in spite of yourself. You have to be realistic. You have to face the cold truth. The book you long for – the one you think you have – is unwritable. No one cares anymore." She smiled gently. "Publish it by all means, if you must. But please don't make a fool of yourself over it. Jenet. Please. For your own sake."

Jenet smiled wanly. "If there is one thing I know, it is the popular taste. God help me, there have been times in my life when I thought I was cursed with the knowledge. This is a world that is exploding with poetry and rhyme. I have no taste for rap music, but of course I have to be aware of it – and I know how vigorous and exciting and immediate it can be. I had speculated there might be a masterwork waiting to emerge from all that restless energy – and now I know that one has. A colossal masterpiece." She turned to her window. "I think our disagreement is not so much what I don't know, dear," her tone stiffening slightly, "as what you may have forgotten."

"You are giving way to your own wishful thinking," Carolyn said.

"People are going to buy this book, Carolyn," Jenet went on, almost as if Carolyn hadn't spoken. "People are going to buy it – ordinary people" – then she smiled again, the same light, slightly off-kilter laugh – "I wondered about myself, too, you see. I trust my taste, but in something like this! I felt like Jonathan in the Temple. So I had copies made, with numbered pages, and I had it circulated. Not only to my friends. Around here, everywhere. Do you know the impact these poems have had in these offices? In only two weeks? Some of the younger ones – people interested in nothing but photo-ops; likable people, whom I valued, but despaired of; people out there who thought the world was created by Apple and Sony– are talking of nothing else. People who take cable television seriously." Jenet was now as giddy as a schoolgirl, joy rising to the surface like the bubbles in champagne.

"Someone hears something in the verse – someone sees something else – I feel eyes popping open around me. It's contagious. Because you don't get to read a work that reinvents the world every day. It only happens about every thousand years or so. They can all feel it. Profound but accessible, quotable – it's only two weeks and I am hearing some phrases all over this office – the sheer brilliance." She was serious, so serious that it was almost alarming. "The sheer, total brilliance," she repeated quietly.

Jenet turned to Adele, ignoring Carolyn momentarily – and a wave of conflicting emotions poured through her face. "And you, Adele. . . what you must have thought when you first read these poems." She became wistful. "I'd love to know what was inside your consciousness then. To have known what went through your mind." She paused.

"When you first read this."

*

But I didn't read. . . I haven't read. . . the words almost escaped. Her mind was reeling, a delirium of her own. Jenet's happiness was catching. "I don't think it's right for me to say," she managed instead.

"Of course," Jenet nodded sympathetically.

"Jenet, you are being ridiculous," Carolyn said calmly, though beneath the calm something was happening.

"The manuscript was circulated to all my editors," Jenet replied as if she hadn't heard. "Jan Heim is in charge of our Scientific and Technical Division. He showed the fifth chapter to two authors, of a book about computer logic. They were enthralled; they asked permission – I gave it – they circulated the fifth chapter alone around the company they work for." She picked up a different file on her desk. "I have sixteen inquiries, Carolyn – sixteen! – about date and availability. From one company, from the circulation of one chapter – in five working days. Paul Robertson – one of my assistant producers – he turns out to be a Dante enthusiast – I never knew. He says that Tom stands in the same relation to men like Gödel and Turing that Dante did to Aquinas." Jenet eyed Carolyn directly. "It isn't only my little troop here. It isn't something that could remain in this room, even if I wanted it to."

"This is not an ordinary book of verse, Carolyn," she finished quietly. She spread her hands over the manuscript. "Other things – other miracles – you can sense that, even if you can't quite state it – the whole of it correlates – cross-correlates; it's so dense with literary and scientific references an army of scholars couldn't unearth them all. Though they'll try!" She laughed gaily. "There are layered meanings – you can tell that even at a first reading. Jan is convinced that there's a detailed numerological scheme beneath it all. He's trying to puzzle it all out. For example, why nine chapters? Why twenty-three sonnets in each?"

(*Nine twenty-three*, thought Adele. *September 23rd. The day we went to the Met. He'd think of something like that.*)

"The energy that he's poured into it," Jenet continued. "It's galvanizing, exhilarating. It leaps off the page. As if writing this book were his last act on Earth, his will and testament."

(*Careful*, she thought, maintaining a poker face. *Too close. Much too close.*)

"Plus the lovely Joycean notion, that all this richness is always present, that it exists in all human encounters. Sell?" Jenet looked up, amused, as if she had just heard something very foolish. "Sell, Carolyn? It's going to sell very well indeed. For the next five or six centuries."

*

The lovely Joycean notion. . . Adele had not thought much about that day – The Day – in the last turbulent weeks. It had been overshadowed by other events – and also the private mortification of the knowledge of all she hadn't grasped, had ignored, had turned her back upon. But now the memories were returning.

"For example, the second chapter," Jenet went on. "The uses of time. I don't think there's a single concept, a single approach, that he hasn't – "

Yes, of course, right at the beginning. The casting of the spell. Then the long silences, the mysterious thoughts. Was he starting even then? He must have been. In the background she could hear Jenet going on, sensed Carolyn writhing.

"Nothing like it since Pope – or perhaps Lucretius. . . the notion of being and becoming in the third. . . the metaphor of the portrait. . . exquisite development. . . natural segue to the farewell to the Sun God in the fourth. . . all the more compelling for its wistfulness. . . the fifth, Jan's chapter, the structures of pure thought, a visit to an ice palace. . . the commonplace mysteries in the sixth, God present in the most everyday phenomena. . . perhaps it is itself the religious text it prophecies. . . "

They had spoken of such things. They had even spoken of them in the same order. It hadn't been accidental. It couldn't have been. He must have begun even then. Before he'd ever touched her meaningfully. She knew now, she did not have to listen to Jenet to know. . . and yet she continued to listen, marveling.

"The seventh, when Adele, having heard it all, wiser than the poet, chooses her own path, the path of ordinary humanity and simple kindness. . .

'One of the angels that no one paints.' The eighth, the descending generations, mother to daughter –" Jenet suddenly caught herself, gave Adele an odd, perplexing glance, and stopped short.

"Jenet, please!" Carolyn said, reddening further. "How can this – such things don't happen – the larger public –"

"The larger public might surprise you, Carolyn," Jenet answered, her own tone stiffening. She turned to Adele. "What you must have thought," she repeated softly. "To read it for the first time. To find yourself at the center of it all."

She could say nothing. Luckily, Jenet did not expect her to.

Jenet went on. "First the warm companion; then the cynical realist; then an acolyte, an apprentice at your mother's feet –" Jenet shifted in her seat, uncomfortable again – "finally the apotheosis of Woman, all women." She shook her head. "You breathe through every line of the verse. Sometimes I thought I could hear your voice as I read. There is a sense in which this whole wonderful exercise is simply a portrait of you."

(*You make a wonderful central metaphor*, he'd said. He'd meant it.)

"If he had glorified you in the way of the Metaphysical poets, or the Italians, it would be comic in this day and age, perhaps even offensive. But it's not like that at all." Jenet gave her the most peculiar look. "The Adele I've known – the qualities I've enjoyed and admired – the young woman I'm sure I know – and yet – and yet – exalted somehow, elevated –"

(*The vertical*, she thought. *That stupid idea. He never gave up on it. It's all a big tease. No matter what else besides. He's playing with me. Still.*)

"–companion, guide, then lover –"

(*Lover. Of course. That, too.* An uneasy thought crossed her mind. *I hope he didn't ... he wouldn't have...*)

"Not at all a goddess –" she smiled – "but at the end perhaps a bit of an angel. Marvelous." She leafed through the manuscript, then looked again at Adele. "All of reality refracted through a man, a woman – through you – transformed – do you understand what it is I'm saying, Adele?" Jenet finished softly, looking at her in a way she would not forget until the day she died.

"I think so," Adele answered awkwardly. "You're trying to tell me my husband has made me famous."

An expression Adele had never seen before on anyone came over Jenet's face – an expression of mingled joy, tenderness, ancient wisdom and. . . pity. "Oh, no, my dear, no. Not that. Nothing so trivial as celebrity. Nothing that unimportant." She paused, and her look somehow deepened.

"What I'm trying to tell you, Adele, is that your husband has made you immortal," she said softly.

*

The clock seemed to stop; her blood ran cold; she could not believe her ears.

"You're being preposterous, Jenet," Carolyn said coldly, and now it was coming out of the closet, the first taste of something Adele would have to endure for the rest of her life. "Stop it. You're speaking nonsense." She straightened up, assumed with obvious effort a poise of professional equanimity, beamed her most beaming smile. "Jenet, I know how much you've wanted to leave some lasting impression in the world of letters," she said in an understanding voice. "I can imagine how easily you could fall prey to your own hopes. But this is only a book of poetry. No one except people like you will ever read it. And not that many of them. As for the great unwashed –"

"It's going to be enormously influential," Jenet interjected calmly. "The word of mouth will spread the same way it did in my office. Even if it were only a *succes d'estime*, it would still permeate."

"Jenet –" Carolyn was now obviously becoming furious – "I'd hate to see you hurt yourself with a futile self-delusion. And. . . " She turned to Adele and the professional pose cracked entirely – "Adele Jansen? That this would happen to ADELE JANSEN?"

Jenet was unfazed now, ignored her. "Even if there were nothing in the first eight chapters, Carolyn, it would become a classic for the ninth. No one has ever written the language of love like this. I can say that without qualification. Physical without being direct, erotic without being obvious. Mind meets mind, body meets body. The way everyone always hopes a sexual relationship will be, but so seldom is. And at the same time summarizing, clarifying. . . " – she threw up her hands – "all that has gone before. . . as if all that were always, as if all things were, always present in the interaction between a man and a woman." She shook her head. "A miracle. The last and culminating miracle in an entire book of miracles."

She smiled suddenly. "And humorous, as well. Really, Adele," she said, lightly, turning, "Titian pink???"

(*What?! No!!! Oh no! Worst case!! Please, God, please, Tom.* Famous or not, immortal or not, she did not want the entire rest of posterity to know what color her nipples had been on a particular night in September of 1989.)

"He seems to be referring to your lips, although there will be those who will suspect a more indelicate meaning."

(*Thank you, God. Thank you, Tom.*)

Carolyn started to say something, but Jenet got there first. "I told you he was an extremely gifted man," she said mildly. "My frustration was that he didn't seem to care if anyone knew it. For whatever reason –" she shot a swift glance at Adele – "he very much wanted people to read this. He saw to it that they will.

"What did you think?" Jenet went on, now facing Adele, "when you first opened the cover? I wonder. Will you ever say? Did you realize even then – at the first – that you'd joined a very special sorority – Beatrice, the Dark Lady, Petrarch's Laura – only a very few others?" She smiled. "Perhaps you even become the president. There's a sense of co-authorship here, a sense of union; you're not merely the passive receptacle of another's art. You're a part of it all. The others must stand on their pedestals. The Adele in the Metropolitan Sonnets is so real. So vibrant.

"What people are going to think of you. The questions they're going to ask." Jenet tapped the manuscript and shook her head. "Is all this really possible? Could all of this come out of a single meeting, a single afternoon, a single incident between two people? It hardly seems possible." She looked up. "What really happened, Adele? What lies behind this? What is the whole story? Will you ever speak?"

*

(*Speak?* she thought – and say what? That the work had been intended as a farewell gift from a suicide? Tell of her own shameful role in the whole improbable story? Reveal even a portion of what she'd learned from Gertha Daniels? Or the "oh gee" fact that he'd done this at a time when he thought he'd never see her again? Above all, imply any of what she'd come to believe was the ultimate truth about him and his work – that the core reality lay in the phrase "doing numbers" – that to Tom its creation was nothing more than a way of killing time, the way other persons play solitaire or do crossword puzzles – multiplied a thousand thousand times – a means of maintaining distance between persona and self, the mature genius indeed the child of the little boy locked in the closet, both of them grasping at the remnants of sanity by resolving puzzles of their own invention? No way. Out of the question.

No. *Never.* Silence.)

"No," Adele said, shaking her head. "You have to read my husband's poem. It's all there. I have nothing to add. I never will."

"Good," Jenet said softly. "Excellent."

"That's because there is no story," Carolyn snorted. "There is nothing to say. This whole thing is a crock."

Jenet swiveled around as if she had only now heard Carolyn. "Carolyn, why are you so bitter? What's the reason for all this hostility?"

"Because all of this is an illusion. Because you're talking nonsense." She leaned forward. "Perhaps you don't know that this writer you're talking about is the same impudent young man who insulted my fiancé."

Jenet looked at her oddly, genuinely baffled. "The 'counting numbers' tape? Of course, I've seen it; it's hilarious. Carolyn –" she spread her hands slightly, perplexed – "what does it matter what a poet of this caliber says to a businessman? A day will come – not so long from now – when Mr. Fischer will feel honored by that incident."

Carolyn's mouth literally dropped open; she groped, not merely for words, but for concept, for understanding. For the first time, at the visceral level, in the core of her abdomen, Adele understood – believed. The world had indeed been turned upside down. The last were now first. She could hear it in the authenticity in Jenet's voice; she could see it in Carolyn's expression, the same understanding thundering into her consciousness at the same moment. What Jenet was saying was true. This was really happening.

Jenet had focused on Carolyn again. Unobtrusively, Adele closed her eyes.

*

That this was the happiest single moment she was ever going to experience on this Earth, she knew for certain – happiness that ten people hardly ever experience in their combined lifetimes. It had arisen quickly; it would flee with the same suddenness; she meant to savor it all, now, as completely as she could.

And then came another certainty – it was never meant to be, this book. It had come into being despite all the gravity, all the darkness, all the Projects, all the Franklin Fischers, despite the determined will of a great infernal creature that always says no. *But we did it anyway*, she thought, then corrected herself. *No . . .him. He did it. He's the poet*, she thought. *And me? I – I . . .* she thought with a giddy, dazzled wonder, *I am the poet's inspiration*, and it seemed her entire soul was suffused with sunshine.

"I really don't understand, Carolyn," Jenet said.

"And there's *her*," Carolyn said, her voice rising, pointing across the seat. "*Her!!* What you're talking about Adele is nonsense. Even if you were right, she wouldn't deserve it. It wouldn't be right, it wouldn't be just." Now it was all coming to the surface. "It would be a travesty. It would be absurd. ADELE JANSEN??? Beatrice? The woman in the Shakespearean sonnets? Be serious, Jenet! Be serious! Look at her!"

"I have looked at her," Jenet answered coldly. "I still don't understand what you mean."

"I mean she wouldn't deserve it," Carolyn repeated. "Even if you were right. She's nothing; she's a *nobody*. 'The apotheosis of all women?' Women like Adele Jansen are an embarrassment to women. I gave her every opportunity at the firm – she had all the chances anyone could ask for – and she blew it. She refused to accept the responsibilities that go with that, the commitment!"

"I heard there was a falling out," Jenet said mildly. She turned her head. "Adele, what happened? Do you have anything to say?"

"No," said Adele firmly. "I left because I had to leave. That's all there was."

"You lying little bitch," Carolyn rejoined. "How dare you!"

"Carolyn," Jenet said sharply, "enough."

"You don't understand *anything*, Jenet," Carolyn snapped. "Nothing. She doesn't deserve it. She's like all the others: she quit when the going got really tough. And now you say she's going to become some sort of icon for the whole world? That's stupid! It's absurd! Have it your way. Even if you're right, all she is or ever was is a pretty girl who walked around a museum one afternoon with a genius. That's the whole of it!"

"No," Jenet said instantly, "that's not all." She turned to Adele. "I can tell. Adele has made her decision. Silence. It's one I respect – in fact, of which I approve. But the story she isn't telling is quite a story. I'm sure of it."

"Oh, grow *up*, Jenet! Your instincts again? Get in touch with reality! Perhaps it is wonderful poetry. But there's no story. Why should you make such a big thing about Adele? Why canonize her?" She all but ground her teeth. "You're letting her get away with it – don't you see? Don't you see how foolish it is? It's going the wrong way – for everybody!"

"I don't think Adele is diminished in any way by what's happened," Jenet responded, steel in her voice. "And I hope the day never comes when a woman is in any way embarrassed by being the inspiration of poetry. That's not a world I'd care to live in."

"It's the world you *do* live in, Jenet," Carolyn said flatly. "It's the world that exists. It's the reality. I've tried to warn you often enough. I hope this time you listen."

Jenet stiffened, looked from woman to woman. "Thank you for that, Carolyn," she said quietly. "You've made a decision I was contemplating much, much easier. Adele," she went on, "what are your plans? What are you going to do?"

Adele shrugged. "I've been looking for work. I don't know where I'll find it." Jenet did not notice the quick smirk that passed over Carolyn's face.

"Also, I'm going –" Adele stopped abruptly. She did not want to say anything about the baby. Not in front of Carolyn.

Jenet looked steadily at her. "You haven't really comprehended it yet, have you, dear?" she said softly, thoughtfully. "Any more than she. Money. . . " She reached for her desk, picked up a document. "One of my editors – one whose last day of employment at this firm was this day – leaked portions of the manuscript to a friend of his. The result was an offer from the Hallmark people. They are willing to pay five hundred thousand dollars right now for the rights into perpetuity to the eighth and ninth chapters for their greeting cards. Mother's Day in the one case, I suppose, Valentine's in the other." Carolyn's flush disappeared. She went pale. So did Adele. "I was not pleased by his initiative," Jenet went on, ignoring both of them. "This is too important a book to be distributed casually in that manner. And it was done in defiance of my explicit instructions. So he must find a position elsewhere." She looked up. "Not that you should accept such an offer – that would be dreadfully premature – but that you have some realization of the tangible value of the copyright you own."

She turned to Carolyn. "Perhaps I should have begun with this trivia. Perhaps you would have understood immediately then. I'm sorry. It seemed to me the least significant thing."

She sighed and smiled ruefully. "For my own part, I was planning to negotiate with you, Adele. I had intended to start at seven hundred fifty thousand dollars and haggle with you in the normal manner. But after all that's been said" – she glanced sharply at Carolyn – "but after all that's been said this afternoon I believe I'll give you my final number right at the outset – three million – including credit for the unpaid portion of the earlier advances, of course. You must be honorable in these matters, Adele; you'll recoup them soon enough; those books are going to sell, too."

She smiled again at Adele – for this time Adele had not been able to keep herself from gasping – fondly and somehow sadly. "Money isn't going to be your problem, dear," she said. "Does that make any difference to you? To your plans?"

The numbers that Jenet had casually revealed would have staggered Adele ten minutes before, but oddly they had no effect now. She thought of Milly and Rothenberg, Franklin Fischer and Lem Michaels – of all she'd learned, of the one and only war, of what had become important to her.

"Yes and no," she said decisively. "That's wonderfully generous of you, Jenet. But I'm still going to find a job. A place. Here – in the City. If I can."

"Good," Jenet said softly, sounding almost relived. "Very good. Because wherever you go – wherever that place is – the Furston Press account is going with you."

*

"You can't be serious," Carolyn said, real horror in her voice.

"We paid a bit more than four million dollars in legal fees last year," Jenet went on, ignoring her. "Perhaps that's even enough to start your own firm."

"Jenet!" Carolyn sputtered. "You can't mean what you're saying! All Adele's ever done is intellectual property – you have FCC problems, labor, contract disputes – my God, Jenet, you file tax returns in sixty-one countries! She can't possibly –"

"You can find people to help you with those sorts of problems. Can't you? Associates or other partners?" Jenet asked.

Adele thought. She thought of a junior partner who did horrible impersonations; she thought of a few others; she thought of all she wanted to do, to accomplish, on her own. "Yes," she said slowly. "I can manage that."

"Good," Jenet responded. "I'd strongly encourage you to go in that direction. I think you would have a very, very awkward time in any firm that isn't your own. With all that's about to happen."

"There's more, Jenet," Carolyn said desperately. "We've just completed the largest communications deal in history. It would be so embarrassing to me to have you leave me at this" – she checked herself – "there are going to be all kinds of opportunities. . . everything you always wanted to do. . . everything –"

"I heard, Carolyn," Jenet answered. "Bill told me about it; evidently, it was all anyone talked about at NATPE. Congratulations are in order, I suppose. So. . . congratulations. . . and I suppose a prudent person would leap at the chance. . . but – Carolyn" – she shrugged helplessly – "I don't think so. There's something about it – the usual thing – I can't quite put my finger on – but I want nothing to do with it. Most of all," she rushed on unexpectedly, "I blame that – deal – for what's happened to you. You've changed, somehow, during the time you've been working on this Project of yours. You've become hard and violent. We've always had our differences, but I remember when you were sympathetic, even kindly, towards my foibles. You're not at all that person anymore. I find it uncomfortable to be with you. I'm sorry, dear," she concluded, "but my decision is final. It is one I've been contemplating for some time."

Something passed through Carolyn's eyes in the nanosecond that followed – something that might have been fear, or regret, or a wistful longing for roads not taken. But then her face was hard and bitter again. She looked around the room; then, briskly, picked up her briefcase, and stood up.

"All right," she said. "I've seen enough. I know what's going to happen.

The legend machine is going to go right into operation. In fact, it's in operation now. All of you – all the professors, all the literastes, all you pretentious people – are going to dance your dances around her, and make your pretty speeches, and make a big giant person out of this mouse, this nobody." She paused. "But before I go, let me at least give you a small bit of truth. I want to remember at least I tried. Do you want to know all that happened between Thomas Newcombe and Adele Jansen? Do you want to know all she's done to earn this recognition you're about to heap upon her?"

Carolyn stared into Jenet's face, put her hands on the front of the desk, and leaned forward into her.

*

"*Nothing* happened," she said, shaking her head. "Nothing. I know. I was there. She came to the office every day. She billed her time. She worked on the cases I gave her and she went home again at night. She called in sick during one of the days at NATPE because she wanted a day off, and she got into trouble with me. And Jenet – you should also know that the poet's inspiration had a little flirtation with my fiancé's partner. She toyed with him and hurt him very badly, and caused a lot of bad feeling between them." Carolyn straightened up. "In fact, this explains something I'd wondered about." She turned to Adele, pausing for dramatic effect. "Simply a question of a better offer. Nothing more." She turned back to Jenet.

"And that's all, Jenet. That's *ALL*."

She stepped back from the desk. "Adele Jansen didn't do one thing that was difficult. Not one. She didn't do one thing that was heroic. There was nothing inspirational or courageous about any of this. There wasn't one day she spent that wasn't ordinary. And you and your kind are going to immortalize her – I believe you about that, I am a witness to its beginnings. Well, she doesn't deserve it, Jenet. She didn't do anything. I am a witness to that, too. *God!*"

The phone rang insistently before Jenet or Adele could say anything. Jenet picked it up on the second ring, looking annoyed. "Hello?" she said, listened, then, more exasperated, covered the receiver. "I have to talk to this person. His problems aren't nearly as important as this, but they are important to him. His biggest problem," she went on, looking at Adele, "is that your husband isn't going to be finishing anymore books for him. That has become unthinkable." She uncovered the receiver and began to speak. Adele arose, moved over to the doorway where Carolyn still lingered.

"Perhaps you didn't know," Carolyn said quietly, deliberately. "The Project's finished. EBS surrendered today. We're going to get Vinux. We'll be in operation within four months."

"I guessed from the way everyone was running around," Adele answered calmly, in the same quiet tone. "I'm so happy for George. He must be proud that his plans worked out."

"George won't know until he reads about it in the papers tomorrow," Carolyn responded, sotto voce. "He's gone on a driving trip. Up north, I think. But it was never him, Adele. He always lacked stamina. This was Franklin all the way. You never figured that out." She paused. "It would be very wise of you if you ducked back into some vine-covered cottage and let Jenet do her thing. You never belonged here. You must know that now. Don't stay in the City, Adele. It won't work out."

Adele shook her head. "No way. Not a chance. I'm not leaving. I know too much; I've found out too much. I'm not going to leave the world for vermin like you to crawl around in." Carolyn stiffened. Adele eyed her directly, said nothing more.

"I'm glad you put it that way," Carolyn answered, not averting her eyes. "I really am. Because I'm not going to let you get away with it, Adele Jansen. Jenet and the other biddies can try all the mythmaking they want. Franklin and I are going to burst them all. I'm going to find out all about Mr. Thomas Bryant Newcombe, and all about you, and I'm going to expose all the fraud and hypocrisy. You're not going to get away with any of it."

She reached for the door. "You and I aren't finished, Adele," she hissed as she turned the knob, looking back. "You and I are only beginning."

One last look of pure, icy hatred. Then the door was shut and Carolyn Sims Hoffman was gone, down the darkened hall. Gone, but not forgotten – Adele had a sudden, intuitive certainty that everything that had already happened was nothing more than a preface, that the larger battle had only begun. The twist on her life's journey, that had begun on a day like any other when, on a whim, she took someone's battered left hand and walked out of her office – one, two, three, straight into eternity – was not ended. Never would be.

"I overheard." Jenet had replaced the receiver. She stood and moved around her desk. Her body was framed by the window behind her. Night had fallen. December lights twinkled all over the city and on the black sea below. Suddenly she seemed ancient and weary, a thousand years old. "Perhaps it's for the best, Adele. Perhaps. . . to experience this so early. . . " She folded her arms.

"What do you mean?" Adele asked.

"When I first read the poems," Jenet continued, "at first – I was so happy for you. To be enshrined in that manner! How many people – how many women have dreamt of that – and it had happened to you! To the one person I would have wished. But then I began to think, to wonder what it will be like – to be the flesh-and-blood human being associated with the Adele of the Sonnets. To have to confront that being for the rest of your life. And the book does have a religious aspect – to be caught up in that as well. The people who are going to be awed by you without having met you – the ones who will hate you – the others, the majority, wondering exactly who you are, what you are. If it were something as ordinary as fame, I could help you. I know something about that. . . but I can't really do anything. . . I don't have Tom's gift. . . " She faltered, then resumed.

"I don't know what any of this means. Not really. I was happy at first for you. Then I wondered if this wasn't what I'd been afraid of for you all along. I didn't know what to think. I still don't." The room became still again.

"Jenet," Adele said suddenly, "if I may – ask – why? I mean, I know you like me; Jenet, I like you – but you act as if there's something more, that I'm special to you –"

Oh, yes. Very special.

"–in some way. And I don't understand. Was that what you meant to tell me Wednesday?" Adele went on, a bit hesitantly.

*

Yes. That and much more.

That I knew your mother – Emily. That though I did not know her long, I knew her well. She was the best friend of my life. That I met her during the worst of all summers. . . the one after I learned I had made myself barren. I'd heard of her; we chanced to meet; it pleased me to commission my portrait – and so she painted a picture of me, as a mother, holding a child – for I insisted on that. She left the title deliberately obscure - `Woman with Child' - so that the model for the child could not be easily identified as her marvelous eighteen-month-old daughter.

You, pumpkin.

"A penny for your thoughts, Jenet," Adele said, wondering, for the older woman was lost in thought.

How I learned gradually that she was not the person her little town perceived. That she was a very, very frustrated woman torn constantly between her devotion to her family and awareness of the enormity of the talent she was wasting. That she had declined a Fulbright, married too early, afraid her wonderful young man would not wait for her, and realized too late that he surely would have. That we wept together over lost lives. That she was not what she seemed.

"Jenet?" Adele prodded. "Jenet?"

Or tell you of the phone call I received two days before she died. In so much pain she could hardly speak. Of how she entrusted you to me. She'll need a woman,

655

Jenny. You. I've always thought of you as her godmother. *I hadn't known she was dying. I hadn't even known she was ill.*

"I'd be defrauding you dear," Jenet said. "As you once said. Nothing important."

Of how I have watched you from a distance for thirteen years. I had thought to intervene often enough. . . but you always succeeded without me. So I kept my peace. I know too well the folly of making a rough path too easy.

"Nothing important, Adele," Jenet repeated. "I had hoped to become better acquainted with you. That's all. I'm very fond of you, you know."

On Wednesday night I'd looked forward to telling you everything. Of how long and silently I've loved you. That what's mine is yours.

"Are you sure?" Adele asked, with the slightest trace of suspicion.

But now? Everything changed, in the twinkling of an eye. The entire universe rearranged. . . where you're going. . . what's going to become of you. . . I have no idea. Silence, then. Your mother's blessing has always been your North Star, your compass point. I know that more than anyone.

"Quite sure," Jenet answered quietly. "I hope I can still expect you then."

And you will need that star more than ever now. The way ahead is going to twist and turn unimaginably. The North Star is more important than ever before. Certainly more than the awareness of an old woman's devotion. And therefor I think I shall keep my secret as well as you keep yours. For now; perhaps for always. I will not tell you how proud your mother would be if she could see the person you are. . . the woman you've become. I think the best thing I can do for you is let you wonder about that a little while longer.

And I will hope that you'll forgive me someday. . . when. . . if. . . ever.

Oh, Jenny, Jenny – once again the one thing you want most escapes you.

But then that's always been the way, hasn't it? I suppose I should be used to it.

"Yes," Adele responded. "I'll be there."

And the one secret I will always keep for you, my dear one. You did a beautiful job – you completely deceived Carolyn – but I've lived a bit longer. You didn't fool me. You haven't read those poems. You had no idea there was this sort of reward in store for you when you walked away from everything. Whatever the reason, whatever the cause, that had nothing to do with it.

What really happened, Adele? What's the secret? I guess I must remain as baffled as everyone else.

*

She isn't saying everything, Adele thought, but was instantly distracted.

Goodson was right. Swirling, recurrent tumult was inevitable around Tom. Thoughts whirled wildly through her mind, all too big, too quick to grasp. How she would approach Walt Greenfield about a new firm, the implications of Carolyn's threat. . . and the poems, the Sonnets, her irrational sense that all the rest related to that transforming force. Too much to grasp, too much to assimilate – it would have to wait.

"Here are the contracts," Jenet went on, reaching again to her desk, becoming businesslike. "You'll find everything in standard form. It calls for the payment of the advance next month, January –" Adele looked perplexed – "that's for tax reasons." She handed Adele the manila envelope as she opened her office door. "You're going to have to start thinking about such things," Jenet smiled.

"I'd like the manuscript back," Adele said. "The original. I kept my own copies, of course, but. . . " Jenet nodded, unlocked the safe drawer in her desk, and removed the one on top.

"Here it is," she said. They moved down the hall.

"You editors are very loyal, Jenet," Adele remarked. "So many people here and it's near six."

"They've stayed to see you, dear," Jenet answered gently, and Adele felt the same chill she'd felt in Jenet's office at the word "immortal." "You are an object of great curiosity here." She shook her head. "As you soon will be everywhere. Enjoy what little remains of your anonymity, Adele. You have about four months of privacy left. I'm planning to delay publication that long – until the ground is thoroughly prepared, with publicity and pre-reviews and everything – that's the reason I was upset that the manuscript had been leaked to Hallmark. But when it does come out, it's going to be a monumental explosion." A wistfulness crept in her voice.

They were almost to the door of the reception area. "You haven't mentioned Tom's reaction to all of this," Jenet said casually. "This has to be one of the best days of his life."

Best days of his life. Tom. Adele felt her blood turn to ice. Her heart stopped beating. She stopped dead in the corridor.

*

For him the best days are the worst days, Petrosian had said. *Mildly agoraphobic. . . prefers anonymity and closed space* – but Petrosian was wise, not infallible, and that time he had been wrong, dead wrong. Tom wasn't mildly agoraphobic. He was a full-fledged agoraphobe, and he could no more live with the exposure this publication would bring than a fish could live in acid water. He knew that. He had never intended to see this day. He had planned –

Her blood froze. *Oh, no no no no no NO no no.*

"I have to go home," Adele said, moving quickly, panic in her voice. "I have to leave right now."

"Why?" Jenet asked, shaken by her agitation.

"Because something's the matter with Tom," Adele said, quickening her pace still more. "I'm sure of it. Don't ask me to explain."

"No," Jenet answered, moving with her, bewildered but accepting. "Let me help." The receptionist had her back to them.

". . . younger than I thought she'd be – and a little shorter. But I knew right away who she was. The instant she walked in. There's a magnificence about her, a grandeur. I sensed it right away. Even before she said her name, I knew. . . no, he wasn't with her. . . " With a shock, Adele realized the young woman was talking about her. *Magnificence? Grandeur?* Was this the way strangers were going to react to her from now on? She wasn't at all sure she liked it. . . no. . . in fact she was quite sure she *didn't* like it. *'Poet's inspiration'?* Poet's inspiration be damned. It was already old news.

"Linda, if I may interrupt," Jenet said in a formal voice. Startled, the girl hung up at once. "If you would be so good as to summon a cab for Mrs. Newcombe."

"Yes, ma'am," Linda replied, avoiding Jenet's look.

"I have to go, Jenet," Adele said. "I'll call." She stepped quickly to the elevator, pressed the call button, pressed it again, and then stupidly again and again. Behind her Linda finished the call and replaced the phone.

"To whom were you talking, Linda?" Jenet said, in a voice of pure ice. "Let me tell you: You were talking to someone to whom you've shown the Sonnets manuscript. I believe my instructions on that point were quite clear. I have very firm plans as to how that book is to be promoted, and they do not include any premature leaks. These internships are highly sought after, and I cannot tolerate any –"

The elevator arrived. Adele stayed her anxiety, held the door, and turned. "Jenet!" she semi-shouted. "Please? Don't. Not today. Please?"

Jenet looked at her for a moment, then turned back to the frightened girl. "Well, well, well – s story for your grandchildren. Your position rescued by the intervention of Adele Jansen Newcombe herself. But you may take this as your final warning, dear. If I so much –"

The door closed and the cabin began its descent.

*

The city was swarming with holiday shoppers and Friday night diners. The streets were a mess. "Can you please go faster?" Adele begged the driver. "This is very important."

"I'm doin' the best I can," the driver muttered, inching his way, managing to cut into the center lane.

Calm down, stupid, she told herself. As a practical matter, there was no way they could go any faster. Nonetheless, her pulse raced, her breath came short – in spite of all she'd told herself, she was frantic. *Come on!*

Adele forced herself to sit back into the backseat. Deliberately, she opened the manuscript. There were two chapters which she had to read right then – first, the eighth. Acolyte? At her mother's feet? And that peculiar look of Jenet's. . . she had to read that one.

She read – and felt her heart stop beating for the second time in thirty minutes. How had he known? *How??* She hadn't said that much that day, no more than a few dozen words – and yet every tone, all the emotional accents – perfect, in brilliant, musical verse, warmth all but bursting out of them. How had he known? A time warp, a fly on the wall, in that long-ago attic, on those Saturday afternoons only she remembered, the art shows? *Momma, too,* she thought, also immortalized, because there would be questions about that, too, and those were questions she would answer – with pleasure, with gusto.

Then she paged on to the next chapter, the last. Yes. As she suspected. The work that she alone had heard, that she had thought had vanished forever on the night of its creation – now here, visible, refined and perfected, exhibited to the world. She read the first sonnet, then part of the second, then closed the manuscript. It was enough. Jenet was right. This was priceless stuff.

"Faster, *please*," she implored. The driver shot her an irritated glance. *Nothing happens by chance. He's not too far off from where he should have been.* Was the creation of this book the reason for all the horror? Had he been formed for this purpose? Had the hand of God been present in it from the beginning? No. If that were true – if it was even possible it was true – she wanted nothing to do with it. If God was like that – if there were even the possibility God was like that – she'd rather go to hell.

They were getting close – a block and a half away. Where had all these cars come from? She could do better on foot. "Stop the car, please," she said. "I'm getting out here." The cab pulled to a gap between two parked cars. She opened the door and leaped out.

Hurriedly, she riffled through her purse. The only bill she had that was large enough was much too large, a twenty. *What possible difference does it make?* she thought suddenly.

"Here," she said.

"Lady," the driver began, "this –"

"Keep it!" Adele yelled as she moved away. In one stride, she was trotting; in two, she was in full flight. She kicked off her shoes – good news for any bag ladies, if such there were in the east sixties, who wore a four double c – then she was racing down the sidewalk, dodging other pedestrians, bumps, irritated looks – not much different than a breakaway in her old field hockey days. The light turned for her on cue and she sprinted across 6--th street, dashed up the sidewalk, and shot down the block towards her own building. She shifted the manila envelope to her left hand, seized the door frame with her right, pivoted, and sped into the lobby.

Two couples, one of which she recognized, were waiting for the elevator. Adele elbowed them aside. Groceries spilled; wine fell on the tiled floor, fortunately didn't break. She pounded the call button again and again and again while the others stared.

She jumped into the cabin when the door opened, hit the disk for her floor, and the door closed. "I'm sorry," she said to the astonished group as the door began to close. "I really am."

She stomped her feet as the elevator rose. It took long, too long, way too long, to reach her level. But finally, finally, finally she was there. She swept down the corridor, fished for her keys frantically in her purse; fumbling, clumsy, at last she had the key out, into the lock.

The door swung open and she poured into the room.

"Tom?" she called out.

✳ ✳ ✳

Joseph Wurtenbaugh

THURSDAY'S CHILD

I f it was any consolation – it wasn't – she wasn't minutes too late. She was hours too late. The apartment was black and cold, devoid of life.

"Tom?" she called again, more quietly, moving swiftly through the living room, the bedrooms, her heart now leaden, sinking into her stomach. Finally she was in the kitchen. A note was on the refrigerator. It read:

Angel,

I can't be myself anymore. Leave me be for a little while. Let me put it back together. It's all too much. I can't stay here right now. I don't want you to see me like this. I love you. Let me alone for a while. I'll be back. I won't break my promise.

Love,
T.

P. S. Unless I'm very much mistaken, you found out this afternoon why you needn't have worried about money.

*

She read the note twice – gulped – then read it again. The postscript – *you found out this afternoon.* The key, of course. The door, the door in the dream – now she understood its horror completely. The terror did not lie in what had happened behind it, but what lay outside – the fear simply that it would open, as all doors do, and he would stand exposed, in all his matchless beauty. For the child had learned this, if nothing else: exposure was perilous, mortally dangerous, unendurably frightening.

So he was gone. The inevitable exposure, an agoraphobe's nightmare, was the final, backbreaking straw. But at least it was not the worst. *I made you a promise.* She felt a shuddering sense of relief and relaxation. Wearily, she moved into her old bedroom, opened the treasure drawer, and put the note carefully in. Everything he wrote was important. Even this. *The best day and the worst day. So fair and foul.* She turned on the light above the desk. Her hand shook as she did.

We did do magic that day, she'd said. *More than you know*, he'd answered, and she hadn't understood him. For a moment she trembled between tears and laughter; all at once, inexplicably, it came down on the side of laughter. She sat heavily on the couch; she roared, she shrieked. Was it going to go on this way for the rest of her life? Was she always going to finish one step behind? It was too much. It was too *much*. In the moments of the brightest public triumph would there always be this dark, private agony? Probably. . . certainly! Of course – what else!? For a few moments her laughter rang in the silent apartment, until she was out of breath.

The single desk light shadowed the room. Adele placed the original, already well traveled manuscript in the treasure drawer – *The Metropolitan Sonnets*, with Tom's scribbled dedication. Perhaps it would have been better if it had gone straight in there, if it had never traveled an inch. A better day would have come. She studied it for a moment, then picked it up. All at once, she knew that she was looking at the only visible acknowledgment he would ever make that he was the author of those poems. She would have to move it to her safe deposit box on Monday (the one that housed Gertha's file and the other odds-and-ends she had collected during her journey). Odd – from the beginning she'd felt two ways about the book, love offering or not. Maybe in her heart of hearts she had always sensed how dangerous it truly was. She looked at the manuscript now with a kind of dread. Reading the poems had become a grim, thankless chore – still, one she would perform. She owed it to Tom; she owed it to their child; she owed it to Rachel Feinstein and Anthony Markland. No one else.

She contemplated the title page, the dedication, for a last moment. *Beatrice? Laura? The Dark Lady? Can such things be?* And yet she felt at the core of her being that Jenet was right. So be it. If she had joined the sorority, if she might in fact be the president, then she above all had to abide by its rules. Old rules, really not very good ones, but too well established to be amended now. If the men had written the poetry, the women had kept their secrets. With that thought, the resolution she had tentatively made in Jenet's office, the tactic she had adopted instinctively these past few weeks, hardened into concrete. Silence. All she knew about Thomas Bryant Newcombe – everything that had happened, the whole extraordinary story – all of it was going with her to her grave. Not a word; let the world wonder – it didn't deserve any better.

Beatrice? The lamp lit her face like candlelight in church. Actually, truth be told, she much preferred it Carolyn's way: *just a pretty girl who spent an afternoon in a museum with a genius.* She touched the manuscript very softly and shook her head.

"But we weren't in real time that day, Carolyn," she said very, very quietly. "You wouldn't understand that. You don't know any other kind. I do. I think I always did – even when everything was at its worst. And that was the difference."

Adele put the manuscript on the right side of her desk where she would not overlook it Monday. Laughter had disappeared; a rush to tears, then. She stood up, began to move towards the ph–

And now it came down upon her with crushing force. Tom wasn't there; this place was dark and lonely, desolate without his presence, without his being. She wasn't going to hear his voice, sit with him. She wasn't going to be repossessed tonight, with that exactly correct combination of force and gentleness, or rest later on her special place on his shoulder. She and their unborn child were going to sleep alone for this night, and for how many more to come? God! She had missed him so acutely when she had barely known him. Now. . . she sat down heavily. . . *oh, God!*––

All at once, then, she understood. This was it, the monster's revenge – to want the one thing she couldn't have, Tom, her lover, her husband, whole and healthy, the man who had won her, whom she'd won in turn, his flesh and blood presence, all the effects of fallible life, all the precious time possible together; to be aware that the time that was rightfully hers was being squandered among his enemies; to know that it had been stolen from her, from him, by thieves who had vanished years before into history, by events that could not be altered; to spend the rest of her life scratching, raging against the impervious shield of past time; to experience this dead, heartsick agony of loss over and over and over and over again. She thought of the receptionist, that ridiculous look of awe and respect, so distant from any of the real truth.

She buried her face in her hands. On a night of true magic, when anything was possible, she'd been afraid. She'd wished for the moment instead of the man – *Please don't let this end; let it last forever; please* – and her wish had been granted. . . and in the same breath, she had cursed herself. What a fool to think that the curse would ever be entirely expiated! What a dummy to think that magic ever fully completes its process! Now she found herself frozen in that moment, the proverbial fly in amber, forced to confront the irony of the world's celebration of it – and the man? So much more important and valuable than the moment – that much further removed. She felt a quick surge to tears.

No. Somehow Adele steadied herself. Tears would be unworthy of her. She thought again of her mother. Whatever her mother would have said, she would not have approved of tears. Besides. . . *I'll be back*, he'd written. . . damaged, weakened, yes but not destroyed – at some essential level he was indestructible. A Survivor. . . as was she. All at once she was prouder of him, of herself, than she had ever been – than she could possibly have been of anything he'd ever written or ever could write, of any conceivable enshrinement of herself. She would find her own consolation there – in the private knowledge of that triumph of the spirit. Nowhere else.

The time had come to remind herself of something – a pledge. She opened the center drawer of the desk and took out a small envelope. Everything else important was in the safety-deposit box. This alone she had kept, hiding it, in the midst of ordinary ragtag junk. Besides, even if he did find it – extremely unlikely; he never rummaged through her things – even more unlikely he'd know what it was. Slowly, carefully she opened the envelope. The photograph, Anthony Markland, his wife, Rachel, and the marvelous, open baby beckoning toward the camera. She looked hard at the picture for a long moment; then repeated aloud the terrible vow she'd made three weeks earlier, pressed close against Tom's chest.

"I am going to retrieve that smile, my love," she said softly. "I am going to hear you laugh out loud once before I die. I swear to God. I swear it on everything that's holy. I swear on my mother's grave."

Adele touched her forefinger to her lips, then pressed it lightly against the baby's face. No one who might have seen her then would have thought of her as cute. No one ever would again. Somewhere, somehow, in the last ten weeks, a terrible, terrible beauty had been born. Carefully, she replaced the photograph in the envelope, muddled it up in the ordinary bric-a-brac, then stood up.

"The name's changed," she spoke aloud to the empty room, a bit throatily, "Adele Jansen Newcombe. Nothing else. I don't quit – never – and I'm not going to lose. This is one you're not going to get." Nothing changed. The stillness in the air remained the same, neither eerie nor ominous, nothing except the normal quietude of a December evening. Still, she felt better, let the moment linger on.

The world's great age was beginning anew. Everything that had been done would have to be redone, over and over and over. It was not lost on her that in Petrosian's one and only war – the only thing in the large world in which she any longer had any interest– a weapon of immense power had just been thrust in her hands. One which she intended to wield wisely. The cost? How much it cost, how much she wished that things could be otherwise – that was her burden. That would remain her secret.

Enough, moron, she thought suddenly. *You gonna talk to yourself all night?* The time for tears and laughter was over. Time does not stand still. . . *at least not when he's not* – she fought back tears again. Time to begin. Time to get going.

And above all, not to give up hope, no matter what happened. She reached for the wall switch. Adele had expected this day; she had planned for it. She had not staged that reception and spent all Joan's money on liquor for those imbeciles for nothing. The drink that Bill Abercrombie had held at that party had contained nothing but ginger ale. What she'd wanted were names, resources, leads – never again was Tom going to disappear on her without a trace. Never. And she'd known she'd need help; there were limits to what even she could do. Soon – too soon – the idea of waddling up and down the eastern seaboard in search of her husband would be unthinkable.

She pressed the switch; light flooded the room. Adele gulped as she picked up the phone. The plan – this first time – was simply to locate his whereabouts, watch him as this – interlude – ran its course, intervene only if necessary. She gulped again – such an easy plan to formulate, so hard, so painful to implement! *Ignore the heartache, dummy, part of the deal, you knew that.* She picked up the phone, pressed in Abercrombie's number.

But God, how she missed him!

Where on this small planet the small hell to which he'd been consigned actually was, made little difference to her now. What he did there made even less. With whom he did it made least of all. Her own loneliness was only pain, to be endured. But, as her own soul depended upon it, as his might as well, she was determined that he would not dream alone.

END

From the Author:

Thank you for reading *'Thursday's Child'*. I hope you enjoyed it.

My true name is Frank Dudley Berry, Jr. My author's site at Amazon is linked here. Writing is an avocation. I don't begin anything unless I have an idea that interests me, and an entertaining way of expressing it. *Thursday's Child* is the only romance I am ever going to write. I had a number of ambitions in writing this book – to present a warm, compelling, exceptionally strong heroine, in the way I have come to know and admire feminine strength; to create a tense, convincing, but absolutely non-violent melodrama; to make a statement about the sacramental power of art; and, above all, to combine a narrative that provides all the satisfactions of an 'ordinary' romance with a novel of ideas. (Adele never stops thinking and evaluating everything she encounters.) The ultimate judgment of the extent to which these ambitions have been realized of course lies with the reader.

I have written a number of other works that might interest readers who liked *Thursday's Child.*

'The Old Soul' is a blend of science fiction, scientific observation, and speculation, based a unique view of reincarnation and the phenomenon of déjà vu. It was an Editor's Choice Kindle Select novella in 2012

'Warm Moonlight' is another novella, presenting a warm and touching resolution of an intergenerational conflict. Amazon had it translated into German to add to its German catalogue.

'Newton in the New Age' is a broad, farcical domestic comedy, not as celebrated as the first two, but of equal merit. All three novellas are available as Kindle Selects at Amazon, and priced accordingly.

Finally, I have recently published a novel, 'A Prophet Without Honor', Written in epistolary style and populated with interesting, fully-realized characters, it's a multi-generational narrative and a seamless blend of authentic fact and sound speculation. The plot focuses on the one great, unrealized opportunity of the twentieth century – but it also has more than its fair share of romance.

I hope you'll take a look at these pieces. I think you'll like them.

- Frank Dudley Berry, Jr
(Joseph Wurtenbaugh)

Joseph Wurtenbaugh

CPSIA information can be obtained
at www.ICGtesting.com
Printed in the USA
LVHW010233260420
654436LV00004B/1173